DARK RIDER

LOUIS ZARA

Dark

A NOVEL BASED
ON THE LIFE OF
STEPHEN CRANE

Rider

CLEVELAND AND NEW YORK

THE WORLD PUBLISHING COMPANY

PUBLISHED BY The World Publishing Company

2231 WEST 110TH STREET, CLEVELAND 2, OHIO

PUBLISHED SIMULTANEOUSLY IN CANADA BY

NELSON, FOSTER & SCOTT LTD.

Library of Congress Catalog Card Number: 61-11099

FIRST EDITION

11-4-63 Publisher's Central Bureau) Kellogg Foundation # 1.25 g.

For

MARLENE

ACKNOWLEDGMENTS

SIXTY-ONE YEARS after the death of Stephen Crane much about his brief, meteoric career remains publicly undocumented; a definitive biography is still needed. Fortunately, I was able to call upon certain Crane scholars, admirers, relatives, and friends, including the last of those who knew him boy and young man. Although I was frankly engaged in a novelization, some guided, some inspired, some graciously made available caches of valuable unpublished materials, and a few, entering upon the spirit of the literary chase, accompanied me part way over trails grown cold these six decades.

Of this number, I am privileged to acknowledge my debt to the following:

Elbert Hubbard II, David B. Eisenberg, Henry McBride, Charles Collins, G. Archer Crane, Mr. and Mrs. Paul Dix Anthony, Dr. Charles R. Smyth, Vincent Starrett, Dr. F. K. von Siebold, Frederick B. Smillie, Charles Honce, Roberta B. Sutton, Lester G. Wells, Anson C. Crane, Miriam V. Studley, Howard K. Crane, Gruff Barker, Marcus A. McCorison, Rev. Jacques Widdicomb, Paul Revere Reynolds, Jr., M. Dorothy Woodruff, Dr. M. Halsey Thomas, Aura E. Severinghaus, Daniel G. Hoffman, Peter Beilenson, Mrs. Wilbur F. Crane, Jr., Rev. Eric Kullberg, D. Nelson Raynor, and Jacob Blanck; also, The Library of Congress, The National Archives, Syracuse University, New York Public Library, Methodist Library of New York, New York Academy of Medicine, Brooklyn Public Library, Columbia University, Univer-

9

sity of Virginia, Dartmouth College, Philadelphia Free Library, and Chicago Public Library.

I make acknowledgment also to the basic study of Stephen Crane by the late Thomas Beer, to the excellent biography by John Berryman, and to the persistent and valuable re-examinations of Robert Wooster Stallman.

Five others were especially helpful: a great bibliophile, Clifton Waller Barrett; a gallant lady, Edith F. Crane; a generous colleague, Ames W. Williams; my wise and patient editor, William Targ, who originally suggested the book and, with amazing forbearance, lived it with me for three difficult years; and Marlene Zara, whose brilliant analyses of Stephen Crane and his writings shed new light on the dark side of the moon.

Louis Zara

New York City, March, 1961

Contents

Contents

I. Lake of Fire

*S*TEVIE was no bigger than a smelt, blond, blue-eyed, and fair-skinned, and of no use at camp meetings. Every day, except on the Sabbath, he was allowed to take sandpail and shovel and play at the seashore, within sight of the hotels with their scaly turrets and the thin lightning rods that ascended heavenward like cruel hatpins.

He was not to stray. Stevie, never go near the water; Stevie, never get sand on your clothes! However, before the soft wonder of green sea and turquoise sky, the child defiantly kicked off his shoes and rolled down his stockings. He scampered toward the hard new beach where the sand was fresh and sugar-smooth, and the ocean frothed and spilled. In the sea, burning eels writhed, were kindled and were quenched, and kindled again.

Barefoot, he trudged cheerfully far, far out until the gray and white sea gulls confronted him. On wetly cool soles, it was pleasant to wriggle his toes as he paraded around and around over sand raisined with crumbs of shells, shards of razor clams, bull's-eyes, and black scallops. Far behind him, the wide world crouched in the gingerbread houses and the great Auditorium with its tall doors open and the faint choruses of "Hallelujah!" or "Beautiful, beautiful Zion!" He hummed softly "Lallelujah!"

At Ocean Grove stood God's great house, like the Temple of Solomon built entirely without nails. In the late August heat, the faithful by the thousands and tens of thousands had streamed from canvas tents and simple cottages, from clapboard hotels and ram-

15

shackle boarding houses. Stevie had seen them pouring down the tree-lined avenues toward the Pilgrim's Pathway. He had heard them lifting their voices in holy song, crying "Hallelujah!" over the blare of cornet and trombone, as they converged upon the golden Auditorium.

Under the peaked roof, the multitudes hushed for the Call to Repentance. Hundreds, thousands, leaped to their feet, moaned and crowded toward the Mourner's Bench, while the Spirit, unrelenting, swept rank and rank after them. Saints and sinners joined in the fine old hymns that unite Christians on the brink of Redemption.

When hearts had calmed, and the glistering eyes had fixed upon the gaunt, gray preacher—that was his Papa with the uplifted forefinger—the sacred Word of God would be cited and praised anew, and the faithful would mass for the great March around Jerusalem. Then could attentive ears hear the cold breakers muttering their rebellious fugue to the glory of the Creator.

Stevie heard it as the wind shifted and the gulls, unfolding their wings, flapped lazily and went seaward. Sandpipers skittered away. A dark trawler swam up.

Casually, he dug and dug deep into the silvergray sand. With his rompered bottom he tamped a mound hard. Enthroning himself, he rested dimpled chin on dimpled hands and exulted in the thunderous waves.

The sea had mustered a shaking fury. The waters had become oily green, the combers sporting white ribbons. The horizon had misted, the sky was clabbered.

The capricious sun peered at the boy on the beach through a milky clot. He licked the salt from his lips.

In the distance, out of the green sea, rose foam-lipped white horses, four abreast over the crest of the waves; on their gleaming backs sat four black riders with glittering eyes. They shouted and brandished silver swords.

He shot to his feet, but they had already vanished. Only the rolling surf, a noisy tern, and soapsuds at the lip of the shore.

The shovel bit his ankle; he kicked it. They never stayed; they always disappeared. He had tried to catch them before and never could. When he looked, they were gone.

If he were not watching, they might come again. Slyly, he cupped his palms on his sandy knees. The sea approached, sniffed, and drew back. Rising and falling in his stomach, it was a moss-green sea. Overhead, the sky curved like his mother's arms. The waves swelled and came forward hoydenishly, like children out of school shouting and waving white fists. A greenhead fly buzzed his ear, and he chased it.

Suddenly a frothing breaker was chasing him. He grabbed his pail and shovel and beat it up the beach. Looking back, he saw the surf slapping viciously at his sand castle, which obligingly dissolved.

He gravely dug a shallow trench, scooped sand over his feet and shins and thighs, and patted it smooth. Gingerly, he leaned all the way back: the sky was blue, like Papa's eyes, like his own. Aggie's eyes were black, so were Mama's. He swept more sand over his belly and more over his chest. Up to his neck he was like a turtle. He jerked his head in and out: turtle, turtle! His arms were windmill-free. He was lying in a cradle, but he could hear the sea. He heard the sands shifting; the sands were crying. The sun, searing his eyelids, made him sleepy. No clouds. The wind had wiped an old rag across the sky and left it streaked. The sun was a yellow hole; when he stared, it stared right back.

Scorching in the sun, hazy dream figures crowded around him, echoing Papa's voice, Mama's voice, and Aggie's. He could hear them and see them: soft eyes and long hair, flashing teeth and lips that laughed or threatened, shapeless figures that loomed and hovered.

He scrambled to his feet and shook like a puppy, sand clumping from his thighs. His cheeks burned; that was how he knew. Artfully, he turned. Great, foam-lipped white horses were returning four abreast over the waves. On their broad backs sat four hooded riders, their eyes glittering and long cloaks flowing, brandishing silver swords in the sunlight. He gaped at the flaring nostrils, at the frothing mouths and the flashing hooves. A vein distended in a ferocious muzzle, the swollen roundness of a great belly, the lifted tails——

A dark rider turned in the saddle.

Child and rider met in an electric exchange of glances. The scowl on the little round face melted at the clicking jolt of recognition. He wanted to call out, but the stern gaze froze him. Rider and companions vanished again.

Stevie's arm remained lifted, the words choked in his throat. He had seen—what, whom, had he seen? Beads of perspiration broke through his scalp; a globule clung to his eyebrow. Where was the rider, where were the others? He struggled to recapture that shivering moment.

It hadn't been a dream. As he had been caught looking, something cold and terrible had trickled down his spine. Fearfully, he spun landward. Would they come after him? They would swoop down with their swords and slash off his head! Tears blistered in his eyes, as he braced himself for the blow.

For a moment, he stood transfixed. Nothing. The beach was almost deserted, only a bearded caretaker toting a burlap sack. On the rise, beyond the sparse grasses, ladies' garments whipped impudently on the clotheslines. Farther back, the hotels, broad as charwomen; distantly, groves of trees; beyond Asbury Park and its bathhouses and refreshment stands, more hotels, the Coleman and the Ocean with their colored flags. Mothers in flapping skirts carried parcels; the wind greedily assailed their thighs. From the telegraph poles, music lines without notes ran into the air and disappeared.

Had they gone? Slowly—— Gone. Gulls and terns skirmished over the jetty, and fell like arrowheads from the sky. Dragonflies swept by, riding piggyback. Behind him, the sea hissed and a thousand shells waited, shells that had sometime been alive. He had once carried home a big horse-conch. "Ugh, Stevie!" Aggie had offered to throw it out. "Someone's living in there!" He had peeked inside. Sure enough, someone black and sticky was.

He hugged the broad breast of the beach and listened to the whispering sands; the ocean thrummed like a monster's heart. Before his eyes colors, ruby and indigo, swirled and boiled to form the torn mouth of a gaping cave. Someone kissed his forehead.

"Aggie?" With a shriek, he pushed the sand away and scampered erect. He was wet and bedraggled.

Secretly, the desperate waves, like old snakes on their bellies, had glided in and slipped under him.

"Stevie, you're a mess!" His rompers were soaked. Grains of sand slid from his hands. "Will you get it!" Now the waves were retreating, but he was drenched to his ankles in the spittled water.

He was reeling as new breakers rolled in, louder and higher. Lights flashed, and they came stealthily once again, the four foam-lipped white horses with their dark, hooded riders, cloaks waving and the curved swords sparkling. He heard the neighing, and tramped forward.

Then the sea engulfed them. They were turning, plunging in a trough parallel to the shore, their hooves rising, striking, bellies washing in the surf.

He heard clang and clang of spear on shield, and dashed on. He would see their faces. Insolently, a wavelet tugged at his leg. The sands moved; the entire beach advanced. He went down, clutching. He came up, blowing and coughing and rubbing his chest.

He splashed on. *There!* No, there! They were gone. The riders, fixed deeply in the hollows of his eyes, had been playing hide-and-go-seek in the charging seas. His teeth chattered.

He went down again. His eyes shot open so wide that the waves spilled from the sky. A crash lifted him, swung him up, flung him out. A torrent engulfed him; he was rolled over and over and hurled toward the shore. He swallowed sea water, retched until his eardrums hurt, and, in a rage that mingled panic and anger, stood screeching on the soggy beach.

His shin had been scraped raw. He proudly studied the wound and pinched it until the blood oozed.

"Stevie! Stevie!"

Vaguely, he heard Aggie calling. She had been at the meeting.

18

"Stevie, this instant!"

He limped. "Yo, Aggie, I'm coming."

His sister trudged across the sand, her long skirts trailing, the black parasol shielding her bonnet and shoulders. At the sight of the dark horror in her eyes, he hobbled faster, turning to shake his fist at the sea.

"I'm wounded, Aggie, wounded!" Like the soldiers in the War, about whom George and Will argued. He jabbered his story. "Black riders . . . they came . . . and horses! Shining swords. . . . One looked at me!"

"Heavens and mercy! Whatever are you talking about?"

"Swords!" He pranced up and down. He wished he could remember the face he had seen.

"Never mind!" she scolded. "You mischief, I saw you. Shoes and stockings off like a heathen boy!" She seized his hand. "Weren't you told to stay on the plank-walk? What will Mama say? You're burned to a crisp."

"They had swords!" he babbled. "They had swords!"

She stared at the seething waters and tugged kindly at him. "Oh, Stevie!" Her cool fingers went to the hot brow and touched the flaming neck. "Broiled! And it's ninety in the shade. You'll be sick!"

"Horses!"

"Wait till I tell——"

He clung to her skirts and the strong limbs beneath. She clamped him against her bosom, one hand at the parasol, the other under his bottom to clutch the shoes and the lone stocking she had found. He rode contentedly, smelling her chestnut hair, peeking into her ear, repeating, "My, my!" roguishly. The beach bobbed up, bobbed down. His knees were comfortably moored to her moving breast.

In the middle of the night, he awakened screaming. They had appeared again. They had plunged into the room, riding out of the sea, and had filled every corner with the surf and a bluish light. The hooves dashed high on his bed; one silver shoe scraped his cheek.

Aggie turned up the lamp. In the flickering yellow light, she tried to still his cries. They were there, the four black riders and the terrible white steeds. "Hush, Stevie, hush!"

His face was blazing, his mouth stung. A glowing iron ring bound his scalp. "Mama!" He wanted his Mama.

"Hush, Stevie, hush!" Aggie crooned. "It's the middle of the night!" He was never, never, to leave his room and wander through the house to frighten his parents out of their wits. He had done that before; that was why he was in Aggie's care.

"Stevie, you're a big boy!"

He sobbed brokenheartedly.

Eighteen-year-old Aggie clutched him to her heart. "Hush, little

Stevie, hush!" She persuaded him to lie beside her. His forehead and temples throbbing fiercely, he sobbed at her shoulder.

Night after night, long after his skin was peeling, his nose a raw button, the black riders returned. He shrieked, "Mama!" When tired Aggie did not stir, he crawled over the edge of the bed and shuffled barefoot into the dark hall.

The door he sought was closed. He cupped the white knob. All around him, the surf was alive and boiling, the horses rearing, towering, hooves threatening. He cooled his forehead against the jamb, and pleaded, "Mama! Mama!" He dared not shriek or kick, and anger Papa.

He gave up bitterly. All doors were open, except hers. The dark walls leaned out obliquely; the baseboards tripped him. "Mama!"

At last, the riders vanished. His brothers were snoring. By the glimmer of light she had left on for a "moon," he crept back to Aggie's room and fell into her sleep-moist arms.

CHAPTER 2

As the weeks passed, the black riders faded altogether, and if he dreamed it was of other figures, distorted and soul-shaking, which the sunlight mercifully banished each morning.

One night he awakened violently. His Mama had groaned. He listened sharply, his whole body rigid. Her bed had creaked, and creaked again.

There were brass beds in four rooms, and the muslin-curtained tester in the fifth. He knew each by its creak or bounce or thrust. The ropes were giving on the tester-bed.

"Sh!" Aggie restrained him. In the pale yellow lamplight Stevie's shadow was a crooked goblin on the wall.

"Mama!"

"Where are you going?"

He cocked his ears. A scuffling! "Mama——" His cry ended in a whimper.

Aggie slipped her arm about his neck. The cold fingers—Aggie's fingers were always cold!—caressed his cheek. "Go back to sleep!"

"I heard!" As Mama groaned again, he jabbed his knee into the girl's groin.

"Stevie!" She pushed him away.

A strange sensation prickled his skin. What were they doing? He wanted to press his face into the pillow and sob and kick. Anger at the dimly-comprehended hardened the muscles of his throat and jammed a merciless rod into his abdomen.

"You're digging into me!" She forced his fingers open.

He sat up agitatedly. He had heard it again. "Mama!" He must get to her.

Bump-bump! Bump-bump! Aggie's heart was thumping through her nightgown.

He heard a low, pleased laugh and became enraged. Why was Mama laughing in the middle of the night?

"Stevie, be still and go back to sleep!" With a flounce of the blankets, she gave him her back.

"Ag, tucker me in!"

She would not reply.

He nestled against her roundness, dropping his hand to her hip. Aggie's shoulder blades were sharp, the bones in her spine a row of little spools. Bump-bump! Her heart was beating very fast.

"Aggie!" he pleaded. He pressed his lips into the fine chestnut hair; she smelled of special soap.

Soon the darkness became taffy on his eyelids. The tester-bed was silent.

In the morning, he watched Mama anxiously. She appeared cheerful, not upset at all. She was wearing a blue-striped gown with a high collar, and was making a merry clatter at the stove. "Mama!"

She murmured, "Yes, Stevie?" and pushed the skillets and poured out yellow batter that sizzled. He sniffed butter browning, and stood on tiptoe to watch the cakes frying. "Mama!"

He saw the frock coat advancing. Papa's upper lip was freshly shaven, his beard neatly trimmed.

At the table the parents' glances met serenely. Stevie regarded them with a twinge of envy. He stabbed his spoon into his porridge, and grumpily let it topple to the side of the bowl. What had they been doing in the dark?

After breakfast, he slipped upstairs to their room. The door that was shut against him every night stood wide open during the day. From the threshold, he eyed the rumpled bedding suspiciously. At the foot of the big dark bed stood the walnut spool-cradle in which he, and his brothers and sisters before him, even the dead ones, had been rocked through infancy. The funny stuffed doll with the long dress, which he used to call "Henry," had taken his place in the cradle; it had never grown up.

In Aggie's room he deployed his brass soldier buttons on the floor, lined them up in rows, called commands, and marched them, "Hup, hup, hup!" A shoemaker's bobbin was his cannon, "Boom!" If only he had Henry for his army; but he dared not invade the parents' room. He aimed his finger at the largest button and grated, "Fire, Henry, dammit!"

When he had tired of the battle, he chugged through the rooms like a steam engine, "Choo-choo!" He hid in the closets; he crouched under the coats and dresses, and inhaled the fragrance of moth balls. He crawled far under Aggie's bed; Injuns were on the warpath.

Voices from the parlor brought him to the top of the staircase. Papa and Mama were going away. Once more, a pang of jealousy. But they were taking him along.

"Stephen!"

As Papa came up for him, the boy saw, in the center of his father's crown, a bald spot as large as a cartwheel dollar. His Papa was old.

Smugly, Stevie sat between them, swinging his feet in the black shoes with the red tassels, as the buggy lurched through the crowded streets. They moved past vans and carts, down avenues where great houses supported lawns and gardens, and small dogs barked desperately through iron fences. They traveled past lumberyards, coalyards, the gas works, and across the railroad tracks. They trotted smoothly in the shadow of a long, red freight train. For a long time they followed a swollen hayrick.

They came to a halt at a great stableyard where, against the wall, stood victorias, cabs, dearborns, and hansoms, each with shafts lifted as though it had surrendered. In a boarded enclosure, a piebald mare was nuzzling her foal.

A short, red-bearded man in a dark flannel shirt and braces, and faded trousers, advanced from the stable, his head aflame in the sunlight.

"Mr. Plimsoll!"

The man grinned broadly. As he came on, his belly pushed out the leather apron. Before and behind, he seemed equally round.

"Reverend Crane!" His shoes were nasty from the stalls.

"We'll be moving again, Plimsoll. We'll want you and one of your vans."

"Preachers allus movin'," Plimsoll said, and led the horse and buggy into the yard. Yellow oat-grains clung to his apron, a single straw to his temple. A red bandana handkerchief was about to fall from his pocket.

"So you brought the young 'un." He snatched Stevie from the seat. "Goin' to help move, boy?" He gave him three swings and perched him on the bales of hay near the fence. "Don't go nowhere now."

He led the minister and his wife along the wall toward the gilt sign, "Office." Considerately, he pointed a safe path for the woman. "Animals," he explained gravely.

A Negro hostler, in a dirty gray bowler and corduroy breeches, with one good brace and a length of yellow rope for the other shoulder, came from the stable, leading a large white horse with a peaked straw hat over her ears.

Stevie gawked. She was an old animal, with a shaggy mane and thick twitching shoulders. Her eye was wild; the ancient, feathered legs were studded with chestnuts. Her back swooped low like the curve on a roller coaster.

"Wan' a ride, boy?"

He shook his head dubiously. He had never been on the back of a horse. Katie, who pulled the family buggy, was either in harness or in her stall, feeding from the box after a long trip with Papa.

"Come fo' a free ride, boy!"

The hostler opened his arms. Fearlessly, Stevie dropped into them. The man smelled of horses and old clothes.

"Push de laigs open!"

For a moment, Stevie perched uncertainly. He uttered a shriek as the animal began to move; he was being carried away.

"Now, boy——"

As the man offered to take Stevie down, Mrs. Crane strode across the yard. "Jim," she called sternly, "let him stay up there, and ride around. I don't want him to be afraid of anything!"

Jim grunted, "Yes, Ma'am."

"Lead that horse!"

The child was in a red fury. Jaws agape and knees clamped to the beast, he beat his fists against his chest, and howled.

His mother's hands were clasped grimly. "Go ahead, Jim, all around the yard."

"Mama!"

"Jim!"

"Yes, Ma'am."

"Mama!"

He had never seen her so furious. "I won't have a son of mine be afraid!" She was shouting.

"I'll fall down!" he threatened.

She came forward, blazing anger. "Don't you dare!"

"Mama!"

"Giddap!" she called.

The horse moved faster. Stevie choked his sobs and clung in terror as they went round again.

"Once more!" she commanded.

Mr. Plimsoll appeared with Papa.

The minister's brow clouded. "Who seated that boy——"

"I did!" she replied with a tremor in her voice.

In the face of his father's disapproval, Stevie was suddenly no longer afraid. "Giddap, Bossy!" he shouted.

Plimsoll roared, "Bossy? Bossy is a cow!"

Jim doubled over.

"He'll have a good seat!" Plimsoll gasped. "Look at him, Reverend!"

Reverend Crane, swiftly adjudging the scene, checked his displeasure. "Excellent!" he said coolly.

"You may take him down now, Jim," said Mrs. Crane.

"Giddap, giddap!" Stevie shouted and waved his arms. Briskly, they jogged around once more, Jim trotting after him.

"Enough!" Papa called peremptorily. "Obey your mother!"

Dismounted, Stevie ignored his parents and trudged happily beside Jim into the stable. He looked on while the mare chomped on a measure of oats. He stared at the equine teeth and stuck out his own.

He wandered from stall to stall. Long heads hung over the boards; wondering eyes observed him, solid hooves clopped. In this world of strength and rich, hot smells, he sat proudly on a three-legged stool and watched Jim's brown fingers mending a harness strap.

He was glad that he was no longer afraid of horses. Perhaps when he grew up, he might become a horse himself.

CHAPTER 3

The entire family had assembled to help with the moving. Even Nellie and Townley, the married children, had come home. Voices were raised as they swarmed through the parsonage; no one hushed them. In their shirtsleeves, George and Townley tugged and carried, lifted lamps and tables, and rolled up rugs on long bamboo poles.

In the attic, Will and Ted were testing rickety chairs and setting aside old garments for the poor. Stephen heard them tooting "Hail, Columbia!"

"My fife!" murmured Mrs. Crane. She had played it as a child. She glanced nervously at her husband.

Will shouted that he had found the albums that she treasured. Townley called out that the family pictures depicted their subjects "at the moment of being stabbed!" Papa glared and strode to the parlor.

When they brought down the wicker trunks and the packing cases, Nellie took possession of the albums. She glanced at the photographs of her brothers and shrieked with laughter. Ted and Burt quietly ducked into the other rooms.

Fannie, Townley's wife, a little reed of a woman with reddish hair and a listless gaze, thoughtfully leafed the pages. "Where are *you*, Townley?"

" 'Where are you, Townley?' " Ludie mocked.

The largest trunk was Papa's trunk, a brass-bound affair that Reverend Crane had purchased at the factory where he had labored three years to put himself through the College of New Jersey.

Mama held up a white gown. "I wore this in New York the day we were married," she said wistfully. "Your father was twenty-nine, and already President of Pennington Seminary."

Burt, and Van Nortwick, Nellie's silent, boyish husband, were working in the cellar. As lightning flashed and thunder rumbled across the sky, they dashed up to clear the yard and to drag back the domestic apparatus which they had, imprudently, deposited near the tool shed.

Since the lace curtains had been taken down a week ago, the parsonage had been denuded to the eyes of passers-by, a condition that particularly irked Nellie. She enjoyed washing, starching, and stretching curtains on the cruel pin-frames; careful Nellie never pricked her fingers.

Mama called on Burt to scour the ice-chest and to sweep the cold-room on the back porch. She was vexed to see Fannie weeping over the photographs of the Crane children who had died.

Nellie merrily chattered on about the fine things in the Nortwick household. Aggie, attending to the cups and saucers, tried to catch her eye. Poor Fannie was sobbing.

Barrels and boxes stood everywhere on the bare floors. Pictures had left light rectangles on the wallpaper, dark pockmarks where the nails had been driven.

Stevie, with a runny cold and an earache, had been lying on the divan. He had worked the cotton pellets from his ears. Mama, taller than the younger women, was suddenly addressing them in that low tone that meant "secrets." He climbed down, and wandered over to stand between their skirts.

"The pitcher has arrived!" Nellie sniffed. He knew the rest: "Little pitchers have big ears!"

His two sisters, Nellie and Aggie, were grown women; Aggie was seven years the younger. Nellie was tall and gaunt but with happiness and pride shining from every gesture. Aggie was short and sad. They were different in every way.

Aggie's hair was chestnut, brushed back, braided and wound in a coronet. Her high forehead shone; the jet black eyes glittered in the pale face. On Sundays, she wore a black ribbon, with the ties resting on her collar. On weekdays, her costume was a plain dark gown in which she floated through the house like a wraith.

Nellie wore her rich auburn hair drawn to a bun on the back of her neck. She had Mama's strong Roman nose, and Papa's large, expressive blue eyes. She had been very tall when she had arrived in the red velvet hat trimmed with gay feathers, of which Papa disapproved, and trailing ribbons. In a simple dress, and low shoes, she was still taller than Aggie.

She spoke out rapidly on any matter, gesticulating even when she addressed Papa. Her smile revealed long white teeth.

Aggie, who could be lively enough with her brothers, was reserved with Papa and Mama. Generally, she listened with eyes downcast. When Papa raised his voice, she shuddered.

Mama measured her words as if she were dripping honey from a spoon. Not Nellie; George said that she let no one get a word in "except with a shoehorn." The stylish bonnet she had brought for Aggie, the younger girl had fingered mistrustfully. "Try it!" Aggie had refused; Papa might frown.

"If you mean to please Papa all your life, you'll never get married. He'll send them away, every one, as he did Philip Harrow. I would have walked out of the house before——"

"Nellie! He'll hear you!" She blushed to have her affairs discussed in Fannie's presence.

Stevie remembered Philip Harrow riding to the house on a brown saddle horse. Where had he disappeared to?

"You have said enough," Mama declared sharply. "Everything your father does is for Aggie's own good."

Nellie contritely slipped an arm about her sister's waist. Aggie, who was not very strong, suffered fainting spells, and headaches that rivaled even Papa's. "That will all change," Mama often assured her, "after you're married." Stevie asked, "Why?" Mama said, "Never mind!"

Aggie, too, was a neat one, forever picking lint from her skirt and from the upholstery, lint that no one else could see. Like Nellie, she could devote herself to the cleaning of windows already so bright and clear that hapless robins and warblers thudded against them.

"If you would send Agnes Elizabeth to me instead of to Hacketts-town Seminary," Nellie buzzed, "I would see to it that she met decent young men——"

"Agnes must go to school!"

Here, Nellie aimed an imperious finger, and Stevie had to retreat. Once more, he sprawled on the divan, groaning as his ear throbbed.

Reverend Crane, fatigued after officiating at two funerals in a single day, was slowly packing his books.

"Father!" Aggie held out an apron to slip under his armpits and tie at the back. He yielded good-naturedly.

Though she feared his slightest frown, his younger daughter attended him extravagantly. She fetched his slippers, she took his coat, she brushed his clothes and hung them to air. She filed his sermons, laid out his books, and addressed him as if Destiny had appointed her his handmaiden.

With a grim air, he took from their places of honor on the mantelpiece, next to the striking clock with the bronze filigrees and the agate pillars, the slender volumes that bore, on each leather backbone, the name CRANE in shiny gold letters. He tenderly wiped the books one by one. Occasionally, he leafed through and nodded, or pursed his lips.

These alone, of all the volumes in the house, were forbidden to idle hands. In rare moments of leisure, Mama borrowed a copy, but she replaced it promptly lest the empty space between the volumes, like a missing tooth, annoy Papa.

In the spring, when Stevie had discovered the magic of words and begun to spell them off grain sacks, flour barrels, boxes of dried fruit, and merchants' signs, Mama had taken his hand and introduced him to Papa's books. *Holiness The Birthright of God's Children*, she pointed to one title. *Methodism and Its Methods* was another. *The Right Way* was a third. What is imprinted earliest on a young mind will surely be the last forgotten.

"Your Papa wrote every one!"

There was also *An Essay on Dancing* which, she assured parish callers, was an essay *against* dancing. Another, *The Arts of Intoxication*, was a treatise "exposing the arts of intoxication *and their evils!*" There were more, small books and solemn, the fruits of thirty years in the ministry.

Papa carefully lowered the volumes into a special book-chest. He gathered also those tomes that were stamped PECK. *Rule of Faith, Christian Perfection,* and *History of the Wyoming Valley* were by Grandpa George. *The Central Idea of Christianity,* and *What Must I Do To Be Saved?* were by Mama's uncle, Bishop Peck. Papa clicked the two catches and snapped the brass lock.

He took down the framed diplomas, from the College of New Jersey, which was now called Princeton, and from Dickinson College, dusted them and slipped them into flannelette bags.

"Mind the books, Stephen!" He went off to assemble the spare copies, which he kept on the top shelf of the storage closet. Aggie would pack the works of John Wesley, the Shakespeare, the Bunyan, the Josephus, the Milton, and the others, including the new set of Herbert Spencer.

"What are you doing, Stephen?" Mama, dustcap over her hair, nudged him. "Inhale the camphor, Stephen!" He was sliding back and forth on the book-chest.

He seized the camphor bag from his neck and took a long, loud sniff. "I'm watching books!" His voice was as scratchy as a crow's.

"One day when you are grown, these books may guide you through life." In a whisper, "Your Papa is a good and righteous man."

He listened, open-mouthed. "Righteous" had a rich sound. Aggie had read to him about Noah and the Ark. Noah, a righteous man, had built the Ark while waiting for the Flood.

Ted was removing the nickel-plated head from the cold parlor stove. He had pulled off the cast-iron doors with the mica windows. The grates must be taken out and the legs unbolted. Stevie thrust his head inside. "Woo!" Like a cave or the mouth of a monster, a cave with teeth. Ted yanked him out.

Will trundled in the extra leaves for the big, round table. By squeezing the chairs in side by side, the entire family could be seated. Stevie's high stool was pushed slightly behind Mama's chair.

Reverend Crane entered. "God bless all here!"

Truly there was strength of a kind at this board, he thought. His big-shouldered sons had not directed their energies in pursuit of God's work, as he had so ardently wished; however, they were God-fearing men. William would study the law, Wilbur would go into medicine; one could not predict what Townley might do. They were not to be blamed, for theirs had been a discontinuous education, a year in school here and a year in school there as he had moved from one charge to another. He forgave George and Ted, he forgave them all. . . . His pride, which he sought every day to deny, would not allow him to confess that he was disappointed. God's will.

Nellie was chattering again. Papa's stolid glance reminded her that in this household there was silence at meals.

Stevie, trapping a slippery chicken wing in his fist, observed Papa eating delicately. When Papa had one of his severe headaches and sat ghostly in the dark of the parlor, he commanded Mama to proceed without him. Then the drumstick would be offered to Stevie. Sweeter meat the child had never tasted than his Papa's portion.

Especially on Saturday morning at breakfast, when Papa consumed his one egg of the week, and tapped the shell as gently as if he expected an answering tap from inside. With his spoon, Papa cut off the top and bit into it thoughtfully. Then, dipping into the golden yolk, he offered the first melting taste to his youngest child.

"My father died when I was eleven," he once declared, as if to explain his tenderness. "When I was thirteen my mother passed on in Holy Triumph. I was laboring with these hands when I was only twelve. Hard years!"

Stevie peered at his father's hands. They were small and shapely, not like the huge, red hands, with the pointed knuckles, of Great-uncle Andrew or Great-uncle William. Even Grandpa George had bigger fists than Papa. Grandpa George and the great-uncles had worked in their father's smithy, shoeing horses and building wagons, before they had become preachers.

While they were eating the roast chicken, the browned loin of pork, the hot biscuits, the mashed potatoes, and the other vegetables that Nellie and Aggie had prepared, a warm, family spirit prevailed. Lightning flashed, thunder rumbled, and gusts of rain drummed at the windowpanes.

"Van," George prodded, "does little Nell still play the banjo?"

Van glanced uneasily at his father-in-law and did not reply.

Nellie, signaling to her mother, began to hum, " 'Tis the old-time religion, the old-time religion!"

Townley nodded at Fannie; he was proud of his wife's voice. Listless Fannie merely gazed into space.

Ted eyed his father diffidently but joined in "Old-time Religion!" Then Will with his clear tenor, and, finally, her dark eyes shining, even Mama hummed, " 'Tis the old-time religion!"

Gravely, as if he feared to unbend, Reverend Crane wet his lips and, leading with one hand, called, "Children, everyone!"

Around the table, the revival hymn rose vigorously. Thunder rolled again. Water coursed into the rainbarrel under the back porch.

"Satan, Satan!" Stevie demanded. He clanked his spoon on his plate. "Mama, 'Satan shout'!"

Reverend Crane disapproved of the older, fiercer hymns that reached back to the undisciplined days of frontier religion. But at the plea in Mama's dark eyes, he yielded.

Townley led vociferously in the first verse:

> "This day my soul was caught on fire.
> Hallelujah!
> I feel that Heaven is coming nigher.
> O Glory Hallelujah!"

"Everyone!" he cried.
The little house lifted.

> "Shout, shout, we're gaining ground.
> Hallelujah!
> We'll shout old Satan's kingdom down.
> Hallelujah!"

In the midst of the good feeling, Reverend Crane, with a glance at Townley's flushed face, declared grimly, "My sons would rather sing hymns around my table than pray to the Lord in his Temple!"

Silence fell upon the table.

"I have spoken the truth!" he maintained, his blue eyes hard as sapphires. "Shall we compromise with the truth to save tender feelings?"

He addressed Townley: "Doubtless the information was not intended for my ears. But when I heard that you had attended a theater performance in Newark, and had taken your young wife with you, I wondered what lessons, drilled into you at your father's knee, you had retained."

Fannie clapped her hands to her face.

"Have you forgotten my views, and the views of your Church, on this subject? Or have you deliberately chosen to ignore them? A minister's son! The theater will never be reformed. The truly refined despise it, the wise and good abhor it. For the theater must, by its very nature, be indecent or die. There is not a city on the face of the globe where the theater can thrive unless it goes down into the depths of infamy and becomes the panderer of all vice and shame. Why then do you choose to disgrace me? Is this exemplary Christian conduct? Speak! Defend your actions if you can!"

Townley's features were waxen.

Reverend Crane folded his hands. "Let us pray for our children, for our erring brother and our misled daughter." He shut his eyes and moved his lips. Mama and Aggie prayed silently with him. The others sat uncomfortably.

Fannie uttered a sob.

"Come, children," Mrs. Crane arose. "We sit in idleness. The wagon will be here at six o'clock in the morning. There is still work to be done."

Aggie nodded to Papa and all heads lowered. He gazed not at his family, but at some distant object: "We have the Lord to thank for this food. He provides us with shelter, He sustains our bodies and nourishes our souls. Shall we not continue to praise Him forever and aye?" Sometimes he added an exhortation against the pleasures of the flesh, against sloth, gluttony, foolish recreation, and kindred errors. Today, he repeated only, "God bless all here!"

Stevie repeated, "God bless!"

It was bright morning, and the rain had ended. The sun was flooding the uncurtained windows. Mr. Plimsoll was backing his team to the curb. Neighbors were drifting by for a last friendly word.

Reverend Crane nervously put on a collar; Aggie produced his frock coat. Mama undid her dustcap and apron. Together, they stood on the verandah and shook hands with the erstwhile members of their flock. "God bless you! God bless you and keep you!"

Plimsoll and Jim, the hostler, and George, Van, Ted, Burt, Will, and Townley tramped past with the household goods.

As the house emptied, Stevie dashed from Nellie's side. Mama had disappeared! She was not on the first floor. He climbed the bare staircase. She was standing bemused before the ugly, bare walls in the forbidden bedroom. The paws of the tester-bed had left hard, round prints on the floor; the room was a cave from which the bears had fled.

He followed at her skirts as she made the last rounds. Beneath their feet, boards creaked. The doors were taller, the window frames towered; vagrant echoes mocked them, ran ahead and tagged after.

Stevie marveled that everything from the big house should have been swallowed inside the van. Their whole life and all its past had been reduced to little pieces. The heads and ends of the brass beds stood side by side, big brothers near little brothers. The dining-room table had been placed topside down, with its legs in the air; a bureau, also upside down, but minus its mirror, stood upon it, with a rag rug, that Mama and Aggie had made out of scraps, stuck between them. The copper wash boiler, wrapped in an old quilt, had landed in the walnut spool-cradle. Even the chamber pots were there, and

Jim the hostler had hung a horseshoe of Stevie's on a nail on the wall.
"My soldiers!"

Aggie had remembered. The buttons and the bobbins had been placed in a soapbox in the buggy, in case the child languished for amusement on the long ride to the new home.

CHAPTER 4

Not at the next charge, but at the parish after, the congregation owned no parsonage, so the minister's family was housed in an ancient, three-story frame dwelling near the church. A previous resident had attacked the clapboards with orange paint and, in an hour of blind whimsy, had added a black trim. Fortunately, a girdle of sycamores and maples partially cloaked the frightfulness. From the path that wandered to the unpaved street, the house loomed, in Townley's wry phrase, "like a crouching tiger."

Stevie, peering up the lane, discovered the face on the tiger, shining eyes in the upper windows when the sun sparkled, eyebrows in the peaks of the front gables. The fierce eyes followed him.

He was free to play inside the whitewashed picket fence, or on the border of the vegetable patch that Mama had started in the back yard and Aggie and Ludie tended after school. However, he was lonely. Townley was working for the Newark *Advertiser*. Will was boarding at Hackettstown Seminary. George, Nellie, Ted and Burt had disappeared. Even Mama was frequently away, meeting with ladies who talked of "temperance" and "missionaries." He roved the empty house and addressed the silent furnishings. He must not venture within thirty feet of Papa, who was always studying, or writing a sermon or a new book.

He was also forbidden to enter the stable to talk to Katie. He must not climb the black-faced, red-coated jockey that stood at the gutter to receive the reins of any carriage that came to their door. He must not scamper up and down the stairs. He must not open the icebox to see if the ice had melted. He must not clamber on the chairs and jump to the floor. He must not hide in the vacant rooms on the third floor. He must not squeak the pump handle and flood the kitchen sink. He must not, *positively* must not, invade the cellar and move the fruit jars as if they were soldiers. He must not——

In the stable, he often consulted Katie, who nodded politely. Her lips and nostrils were black leather, her ears like velvet. She switched her tail and stomped her feet. Even when she slept, she wore those iron shoes.

Crouching in the attic, where strange sounds boiled like the sea, and pressing his nose to the misted window, he gazed longingly at the river far below. The water was as peaceful as a dish of custard. A few craft drifted; an occasional breeze riffled cat's-paws on the surface. He wondered if Ted and Will would ever keep their promise to teach him to swim "nainked."

The Crane household moved again, to Paterson, to Bloomington. New streets appeared, new houses, new people, even new horses and dogs. Stevie had to learn a speech: "My name is Stephen Crane. My father is Reverend Jonathan Townley Crane." He could pick out every letter in his name from the masthead of *The Christian Advocate* and *The Heathen Woman's Friend,* except the letter p, which was not to be found in either.

When Grandpa George Peck died, Mama and Papa went off to bury him in the cemetery at the Old Forty-Fort church. When they returned, Mama was as pale as a church candle. Papa explained that Grandpa George had been a great man. He had never graduated from any school, yet such was his genius that he had taught himself Greek and Hebrew, and had become Principal of Cazenovia Seminary, and had helped to found Wyoming Seminary. He had been editor of *The Quarterly Review* and of *The Christian Advocate.* He had met President Jackson and had known President Lincoln.

"A man could be proud," Papa declared, "very proud."

Stevie was proudest of the drum they had brought him, a very ancient and darkened drum upon which Grandpa George had pounded as a boy. Every afternoon, he practiced in the stable while Katie stomped restlessly.

Ludie demanded a turn. Stevie refused.

Whereupon Ludie thrust him aside and jumped upon the drum with both feet. There was a roll like the hammering of hooves on the stable floor, and, with a sharp crack, the old skin burst.

"Dam-ol' Ludie!" Stevie fell savagely upon him. "Dam-ol' Ludie!" Enraged, he kicked and scratched till Ludie leaped from the broken drum and fled.

The frustrated victor stared into the jagged hole. There was nothing inside. He pulled at the stiff, torn lip of the skin. A drum was empty! He had imagined that it must contain wondrous echoes, or a mechanism to produce thunders. Nothing!

Ludie sheepishly returned.

"Drum-buster Ludie!"

The other pointed out that if Stevie turned the drum upside down he could still pound out a noise.

Stevie glared at him scornfully. "Drum-buster Ludie!"

Will, who was no longer at Wesleyan University but at New York University, examined the wreckage and promised to buy a new one. Whenever he made a promise, he promptly disappeared for months.

Stevie's brothers and sisters constantly vanished and reappeared. Burt had been entered at Hackettstown Seminary, the school for which Papa had helped to raise the building funds. Unfortunately, Ludie was not old enough to disappear. Stevie coveted Mama's fife, which Ludie had taken for his own.

He missed Aggie, although he no longer needed an older sister to wash or dress him, or to peer into his ears and inspect his neck. But no one else was so tenderly concerned for him.

When she reappeared between semesters, the sun became brighter. At night, he tried to stay awake until, after her studies, she came to tuck him in.

It was a game with them. She made the ritual motions of tucking the blanket in at his feet and at his shoulders and sides.

"Tucker me good, Aggie. I'm not tuckered in yet."

For him she saved all the stamps that reached the household. Formerly, all postage stamps had belonged to Townley; now they were Stevie's. Stamps reminded him of George, who worked in the post office in Jersey City.

Appointed to fetch the mail from the postman's hand, Stevie called out the names from the envelopes as he handed them to Mama. "Mrs. Doctor Crane!" She had been president of the Newark branch of the Women's Foreign Missionary Society, and corresponding secretary of the New York branch. Words were little meteors that whizzed past; he tried to reach out and catch them.

"I can read everything," he reported to Aggie, "only I can't understand it."

He had been declared ready for school when he fell ill again. He lay in bed day after day, with red pimply rashes on his face and on his chest and hands, and ran high fevers. Mama anxiously spent hours in his room. Papa came in to say special prayers.

"I could not endure it again!" she repeated over and over. "Lord, I lost two with the scarlet fever."

Aggie recalled that once long ago, five years before Stevie had been born, a poor woman who had been turned out of her boarding-place with three children ill of scarlet fever, had come to their door. There was snow on the ground and a bitter frost. Mama had taken them in. The strange children had recovered, but three Crane children had contracted the disease. Little Almira Blanche, a year and two months old, and Elizabeth Townley, barely five, had died.

"I won't die!"

"Of course not, dear one," Aggie shuddered. "You'll live to be older than the uncles."

At his bedside, she read to him so dramatically that the convalescent exulted. The meanings eluded him but, as her voice rose and fell, the emotions she experienced were communicated. He listened attentively.

"Ag, does it have a name?"

"*The Mill On The Floss.*" She displayed the gilt-stamped title on the blue covers. "By George Eliot. It's not really for a seven-year-old."

"What's 'floss'?"

"The name of the river where they lived. Like Raritan or Hackensack." Her eyes were as black as cherries.

"Ag, who is Tom?"

"Tom is the brother in the story."

"Who's Maggie?"

"Maggie is Tom's sister. Tom and Maggie are brother and sister. They love each other very much."

He gravely wagged his head as she perused the next scenes to herself.

"Read me, Ag, read me!"

She skimmed pages. "This is not for little children."

When she had resumed reading aloud, he interrupted, "Who's Stephen?"

She flushed. "Stephen loves Maggie."

He said shrewdly, "Stephen loves Aggie!" They were both imprisoned in that fat book.

She squeezed his hand. "I mean in the story, dear."

"More, more! Read me!" He tugged at her.

"It's a *novel!* Papa would be terribly angry." She seemed to cringe. "You must never tell Papa!"

Maggie's betrayal had depressed her. She wished that she had not been so foolish as to read to him from a strange book. "No more!" she said firmly.

She concealed the thick volume next to her memory book in the bottom drawer of her bureau. She copied one of Maggie's reflections that seemed to speak directly of her own dilemma: "'I couldn't live in peace if I put a willful sin between myself and God.'"

On another evening, she succumbed to his pleadings and bowdlerized a summary of the chapters she had skipped. She resumed with the flood on the Floss River. Maggie had taken the boat and gone to the rescue of her brother Tom. Stevie listened intently.

Maggie had saved Tom, but the Floss was rising rapidly. Brother and sister saw that they would soon be lost in the merciless waters. They embraced and went bravely to their deaths together.

Aggie suppressed a sob.

"Where's Stephen?"

She replied hoarsely, "He's not there!"

"Yes, he is!" he retorted. "He wouldn't forget her, Ag. He'll come, you'll see!"

"No, he won't." She would not tell him that the Stephen in the story had defected. Barely whispering, she ended the tale. Her face was pale, her eyes shining with sadness. So life ended; so women

34

suffered and were betrayed. On the single gravestone of brother and sister had been inscribed, "In their death they were not divided."

"Who?"

"Tom and Maggie, the brother and sister."

"But Stevie——"

"He wasn't there. He didn't come. He deserted her and never returned."

He was incredulous. "He let her die?"

"Yes." She could hardly speak. "He abandoned her."

The boy flung his arms about his sister. "Aggie, don't cry. I wouldn't desert you. I would come back. I'd save you!"

Through her tears, she protested, "It's only a story. It's not real, Stevie."

"Then why are you crying?" he pouted. She was a girl; that was why. "I'll never leave you."

Something burst inside the girl. She snatched at her book and fled the room.

He was angry and glum. He disliked the ending of *The Mill On The Floss*. However, the Stephen was real; *he* was Stephen and he was real. He was unhappy for her. Poor Aggie. Poor Maggie!

He found the book in her reticule. He wanted to see his name in print: "Stephen."

"What book is that?" his father's voice demanded. Stephen shivered and surrendered it.

Papa shook the volume in the girl's face. She trembled as if the joints in her shoulders and wrists had become unhinged.

"I am ashamed of my own child. You disobey not me, your parent, who may, in your estimation, merit this disobedience, but the rigid iron rule we have preached for twenty years: Total abstinence from novel-reading now and forever! You know that the Church warns its communicants to abstain from 'reading books which do not tend to the knowledge or the love of God'!"

She whimpered, "I'm sorry, father."

"In my own household, the only daughter left in our midst, the comfort of our old age, as it were, ignores and defies me! How often have you heard me preach it, Agnes? When the novel usurps the place of the Bible; when secret prayer is hurried over, or wholly neglected, because of a burning desire to know what comes next in the story; when meditation on divine things is forgotten in endless daydreams of love and worldly splendor; or worse still, when real life is thrown into the shade by the unreal, and made to appear mean and insipid; when the action of conscience and sober realism is swept aside by the wild delirium of mental intoxication, what result can we look for save apostasy and final ruin?"

Aggie was sobbing.

"Dear girl," he went on sorrowfully, "God help you."

She jumped. He had, disdainfully, let the heavy volume fall into her lap.

"I can do no more." His spectacles glittered. "No more. Shame!"

"Father!" she cried after him. "Father, don't abandon me!"

Stevie dashed to her side. "Aggie, Aggie, don't cry!"

She embraced him and clung to him, but continued to weep. "Stevie, Stevie, how could you——" Of course, he was a child and could not understand.

"Read me, Ag!" he went on stubbornly.

She burst into fresh hysterical weeping.

CHAPTER 5

Two black horses, with white stars on their foreheads, blinders and gleaming brass frontlets and trappings, pulled up with a large blue van. A tall, skinny man, in a bowler hat and tight yellow pants, leaped to the ground.

Mama was at the screen-door. "The dealer has come."

Reverend Crane fixed his broad-brimmed black hat, and came out. Sternly, "You are Mr. Cogan?"

The caller swept off his bowler. His narrow head was bald and freckled. "Reverend Crane——"

"We'll go to the stable!"

They walked down the narrow path beside the house. Mama let the screen-door close sharply. Stephen, retrieving his top, swooped past her, slid across the back porch, and sat on the bottom step.

Papa led Katie out. The mare stood sadly while the skinny man walked around her. He ran a hard palm across her flank, and about her ribcage. He picked up a hoof and studied pastern and shoe. He lifted Katie's tail, and the mare shuddered.

"She's no spring chicken, Reverend."

"She's a fine mare, Cogan. She's gentle and strong. She's pulled me many a mile on God's work."

Katie lowered her head as Papa stroked her muzzle.

Stevie scooted across the yard and hung over the back fence.

Cogan scratched the tip of his nose. Seizing the bridle, he pushed back Katie's upper lip. The horse rolled her eyes and tried to toss her head.

Stevie cocked his head. The skinny man was counting her teeth!

Reverend Crane glanced uneasily at his son. He signed to the dealer to follow him to the stable again.

"I'll give you——"

They stood in the doorway, outlined in a shaft of light from the back window. The dealer hooked a thumb into his braces. "What do you say, Reverend?"

"Cogan, how can I be sure that she will be treated kindly?"

"Can't go with her whoever takes her! I'll do my best."

"Very well, Cogan!" Papa said huskily. "Very well."

"I don't rightly need that buggy of yours, neither. Just to sweeten the pot, I'll give you a price. Cogan's an honest dealer."

Stevie gasped. "Papa!"

"Go into the house, boy!"

"Papa!"

"Go!"

The van swung about and crunched in the cinders. The skinny man pulled a lever and the back came down into a sloping ramp. He took out his clasp-purse and counted bills.

Papa threw his arm about Katie's neck. He was not talking to the mare, yet she appeared to be listening, for she bobbed her head.

Cogan caught the bridle and ran Katie up the ramp—*clop! clop!*— and into the van. He came down and yanked on the lever. Only half of the rear end arose. Katie thrust her head out, and whinnied.

Stevie stormed into the house. "Mama! Mama! They're stealing Katie!"

"Be quiet! He is not stealing. Papa is selling her."

"Selling? You can't sell a horse!"

"We can't take her with us. Not where we're going, eighty, ninety miles away."

So they were moving *again!* This time, far, far away, perhaps to the other side of the earth.

He dashed to the stable. Who would eat all the feed? A sack of oats, with the top rolled down like a boy's stocking, sat near the pump.

On the shelf, beside the coal oil, stood the carriage lamps and the red lantern. Katie's harness, her collar, her red blanket, and her sleighbells had been forgotten. He stroked the blanket. She would shiver on the cold days; she was an old horse.

He stepped into her stall. He stuck the toe of his shoe into a crack, climbed up, and leaned over. His arms were too short for a horse's forelegs. He bared his teeth and chewed, and felt unutterably lonely. The feed was so gritty that he spat it out. He guessed he probably would never be a horse after all.

The railroad station was of red brick, twice as wide as a church, and almost as high. Inside the waiting room, dozens of people milled about with baggage and bundles, and small children. A burly man in an official cap and sleeve-garters was writing on a blackboard. He strode off, swinging a red lantern.

Aggie threw herself into Mama's arms. Mama lifted Aggie's veil and kissed her cheek. "Write every week, Agnes Elizabeth. I shall be worrying."

Papa's face was struggling as he planted a kiss on Aggie's forehead.

Ludie burst into tears and ran from the depot. His sister sped after him, but she returned alone.

Stevie, having clambered up on a bench, was as tall as she. Aggie gazed at him through brimming eyes. "Stevie!"

"Where are you going, Aggie?" he quaked. Her bosom was firm in her dress-up suit. "Aggie!"

"I'm going to board at Hackettstown Seminary."

"You're going away!"

"Yes, Stevie. You be a good boy!"

"Don't go, Aggie, don't go!" He clutched at her.

"Heavens and mercy! I won't be far, I'll come to see you every holiday."

"Aggie!" he muttered helplessly.

He accepted his Papa's cold hand; he had nowhere else to turn. Standing between Papa and Mama, he perceived that Aggie was already a stranger. In her traveling suit, with the new hat and the little veil that made her face mysterious, and the tips of black shoes peeping from beneath her hem, she was a pretty young lady going off into a world where trains thundered away on different tracks and never came back. She was abandoning him.

As they boarded the train, vapor swirled and sounds boiled noisily. Ludie, pretending that he had not been crying, swaggered ahead, tapping the green upholstery. He reached two facing seats at the end of the car, and flapped his arms. "Taken!" he cried hoarsely. "Taken!"

Below their window, Aggie looked like a visiting aunt, with her parcels and her leather bag. Mama uttered last-minute cautions which the girl could not hear.

"Yawl-a-boh!" the conductor shouted. "Yawl-a-boh!"

As the car wrenched itself free, Stevie toppled backward. The engine hooted. A bell clanged. The locomotive exhaled a blast of steam and caused Aggie to disappear. The coach jerked, and they were on the high road, with trees and houses falling away.

The conductor called, "All tickets, please!" He studied the long strips and punched them, pocketed some, returned others. He paused respectfully over the passes that Papa reached up. "Thank you, Reverend." How did he know?

Through the window, yellow and orange lights flickered. For long distances, they traveled in total darkness that was punctuated only when a flaming tail of hot ashes swept back from the firebox.

Ludie arose and picked at his clothes.

"Take Stephen!"

He refused the small boy's outstretched hand. The jerking train swerved Stevie across the aisle and dumped him into the lap of a little girl wearing a red tam-o'-shanter. She stuck out her tongue, on the tip of which was a tiny red candy heart. Stevie wrinkled his nose at her, and she promptly turned her bottom in his direction. He was shocked.

When they returned, Ludie dashed for the window seat. Stevie begged to sit beside Mama; as usual, Ludie won out.

For a long time, Stevie stared at Papa and the stern upper lip, the silken beard, the wrinkled lines in the pale forehead. His father was an old man.

"We did not make the trip to the cemetery," Mama said regretfully.

Papa shrugged. "With Katie gone——"

"We should have driven to Evergreen before the horse was sold. Who knows when we may return? I have five children lying there in their graves."

As she turned her cheek to his shoulder, Papa covered her hand.

"A man cannot know," she whispered, "but a mother should. The infant was three months old and three days, too young to be taken anywhere. Later, I wanted only to board the train to get her to her own little bed." A sob escaped her. "Suddenly, she was still and cold. And I sat by such a window the long way home with my child dead in my arms."

"Sh!"

Stevie regarded them sleepily. The train was speeding. From the other seats bobbed a sea of indistinct faces. His stomach felt uneasy.

"For me," Papa was saying, "the new place will be a sanctuary; not a crossroad, but a sanctuary."

"Please God that they appreciate a true minister of God."

Stevie moaned. As he half raised his eyes, Papa's blue stare seemed to fix upon him balefully. He threw his head back, and breathed deeply.

He was riding swiftly on Katie's broad back, clutching at her mane. Faster, faster! The wind was cool on his lips. They were galloping down a narrow road, the surf roaring on either side. Katie's smooth hide jounced at his crotch, and he went up and came down. The sharp breeze chilled his teeth and turned them to bright gold. He leaned forward and brought his legs back; he seemed to be floating on the bare saddle of the horse. "Giddap! Giddap!"

Suddenly, the ocean was gone, and they were on a highway. He exulted: he was running away with Katie! They reached a fork which, like the print of a gull's foot, slit the road into three parts.

A shadow fell across him. Katie reared. A tall, bearded stranger was blocking their way. Stevie clung, and jerked to the left. The mare would have dashed on, but the man, with a contemptuous laugh, again loomed in her way. Stevie slapped at Katie and sought to veer off to the right. With a sneer, the man spread his legs and, a third time, confronted them.

Once more, Katie reared, and whinnied in fear. For a moment, boy and mount hung in midair. Stevie twisted and, frantically, commanded the mare to leap straight ahead. But the stranger was nimbler still. With a bold arm, he dared once more to obstruct them. Katie reared a third time, then, trembling, descended.

The stranger leered. Seizing the bridle, he tugged with all his might and forced Katie to her knees. It was absurd. Stevie could feel himself toppling. He saw the ground coming up—and the stranger's head. With incredible ferocity, he brought his fists together and struck. The blow encountered silky hair and hard bone. The man uttered a weird cry, spun about, and collapsed in the sand.

Katie scrambled to her feet, Stevie agilely retaining his seat. Again Katie reared, and now, wickedly, he compelled her to bring her hooves down again and again upon the sprawled figure of the stranger. He could feel his own feet, iron-shod, striking repeatedly until the body was limp. He gloated, and his lips slavered. He heard himself chortling.

They rode around and around to trample the figure into the sand. Only the top of the head, with a spot bare and white as a clamshell, remained visible. Stevie was shouting triumphantly.

A train hooted. Instantly, he chilled. They were pursuing him. He was frightened; his fists clutched so tightly that his knuckles hurt. Then Katie stumbled, and again he was falling, falling!

"Stevie! Stevie!"

His mother was nudging him, but he was still falling. His head hung over the boards of Katie's stall; before it was sprawled the mangled corpse of the bearded stranger.

"Stevie, wake up now! We're nearly there."

He had been dreaming. He was safe in his Mama's arms.

The train had slowed. Houses winked as the cars rolled beside a little depot. "Po' Chavis!" the trainman called. He came by and repeated, "Po' Chavis!"

CHAPTER 6

Bong! Bong! startled him awake. The room vibrated as if a giant hand had rocked it. *Bong!* a dull boom and a throbbing echo. The walls bulged, the floor trembled, the windowpanes rattled. He stared at the far morning, expecting a pendulum to swing across the horizon. *Bong!* He raced to the window and yanked at the sash. *Bong!* the wood was old, the paint alligatored. *Bong!* A fresh breeze saluted him. *Six* o'clock!

He put his head out. There was the slate roof of the church; ivy climbed the red brick walls like a green-scaled monster. The clock which had struck presented an innocent face.

In the kitchen Mama was wiping the cupboards.

"There's a tower and a steeple on the church a million feet high. And the loudest clock in the whole world!"

"I know, Stephen," she smiled. "They say that our steeple is one hundred and sixty-two feet high. The clock you heard strike—it's really the town clock—was installed last April by Mrs. Shorter, on her birthday."

He dressed, and sped outdoors. He crossed Broome Street to Orange Square. The steeple leaned backward, while the church advanced like a headless creature in a long, shapeless coat. The spire seemed to hold up the sky.

Port Jervis, basking in the foothills, was the city of God. The Dutch Reformed Church, with two steeples and its own school, was on Main Street; the Episcopal Church was one block down Sussex Street; the Catholic Saint Mary's Church, with an even taller steeple and a cross on top, stood on Ball Street. The Catholics had the largest cemetery, near the Neversink River where Main Street ran south; Stevie whistled when he passed these alien grounds.

God was everywhere, in the belfry, in the steeple, in the clouds, in the trees, and in the mountains hulking on the horizon. Somewhere, beyond, where shadows lurked, must be the yawning pit of which Papa preached and the dreadful Lake of Fire.

So, walking in awe, he became familiar with God, who resided chiefly in Drew Centennial Church with its high steeple and clock. There was no church like Drew Church, no preacher like Papa, who was intimate with Him, and could consign sinners to hellfire. To know God he must follow in Papa's footsteps. He was fortunate, and proud.

The veterans, idling on their benches in the Square, beneath the soldiers' monument, got to their feet when Papa approached: "Morning, Reverend!" His being and His will—Stevie could not divide God from his Papa—illumined every parish face, turned the choir into a band of angels, and the pulpit into the tollgate to Heaven.

"We have nine hundred and eleven members in our charge," Mama announced, "and three hundred and eighty Sunday-school scholars."

When Papa went out to do God's work, Stevie often accompanied him in the buggy, which was drawn by Violet, the new black mare. Although they journeyed westerly as far as Germantown, beyond the Erie roundhouse and the machine shop, and along the Delaware and Hudson Canal, and northward to Brooklyn, below Point Peter, he could see the church spire wherever he looked back. Sometimes they went south and rolled past the tollhouse—"Afternoon, Reverend!"—and crossed the suspension bridge to Matamoras; that was Pennsylvania.

In the Delaware River, three long islands were overgrown with greening trees and underbrush. South of Laurel Grove Cemetery, and below the junction of the Neversink and the Delaware, was the Tri-State Rock, from which Stevie could spy New Jersey and Pennsylvania, as well as New York, simply by spinning around on his heel.

On these excursions, Papa instructed him on man's chief end, which was his duty to God and his own salvation. However, a boy's lively eyes might rove. Where Cuddleback Brook purled into the Neversink was a magnificent swimming hole. Papa pointed a scornful finger at the splashing youth: "Idle recreation!" Stevie saw no idols; it troubled him that he couldn't always see what Papa saw. He was torn between the excitement in the sun-inflamed waters and a little engine chugging northward on the Monticello Branch.

"Where you been today?" Ludie inquired every evening, pretending that he did not care. "He'll make a preacher out of you!"

"No, he won't!" Stevie flared. "Not me!"

"Somebody's got to be a preacher in the family. He made a will and last testament before we left Paterson. I heard them! Uncle and Aunt Howe were the witnesses."

"Will he die?"

"Everybody does."

Ludie could be hateful. To speak of Papa dying was a sin. It could never happen as long as God was alert and the Drew steeple stood guard with its peaked lance.

Stevie was constantly slipping into the church. He pulled with all his strength at the heavy, brass-bound door, and shuffled along the wainscoted wall. The cold, mysterious presence of God was all around him. At the end of a shaft of light, the pews appeared to be broad stairs in a long dungeon. Far away, standing before a curtained window in the study room, was his father, hands tucked under his coattails, and staring into the dark church. The figure was wreathed in an extraordinary luminescence.

The boy shuddered at the deathly pale countenance with its wrinkles and gray hair. Would Papa really die? The mouth was thin-lipped and wide, the long cleft in the upper lip like a slide. When Papa's slender fingers removed the spectacles, there were red indentations on the bridge of the strong nose.

"It's time you began to think on God, Stephen. Perhaps one day He will choose you as He chose me, long ago. Therefore, give Him your affection and store up His love for you. Open your heart to Him and pray, Stephen, pray! For His mercy and His guidance to spare you from evil and eternal punishment in the Lake of Fire."

Stevie had heard these words many times, yet on each occasion they caused him to tremble. For he feared the Lake of Fire. He strove to think of God and His eternal wrath; he must pray to be spared.

Papa was disappointed that none of the brothers had heard the Call. Not George, Townley, or Ted, certainly not Ludie. Burt was at Hackettstown and Will at Albany Law School, where they surely could not hear it. Someday God would choose *him*. He would hear the Call and would run to tell Papa. The stern face would relax, the black-clad arms would embrace him, "My son!" Yet how might he know the Call when it came? Probably, as in Scriptures, a still, small voice would whisper. It would summon him once; if he missed it, never again. What if it came when he was playing, or was asleep and dreaming?

He must not fail to hear it. He was Papa's chosen; therefore, nothing but good could happen to him, even in God's wrathful storms. When the skies grew dark and thunder rolled across the valley, he was unafraid. Aggie might fly into a closet, shut the door and bury her head in the clothes; he dared to wait for the lightning.

Lightning could strike you blind if you were a sinner! But he was good. He clenched his fists and faced the terror. Thunder crashed; barrels tumbled down the mountainsides, and bounced and bounced till their own fury split them open. Lightning might strike the steeples of the other churches; not of Drew Church. A flash illumined the trees as a crooked bolt twigged in several directions. Violet whinnied from the stable.

He ran out into the downpour, sped across the yard and into the buggy room. "Don't be afraid, Violet!" he shouted, and was aghast at the echoes. "Don't you be afraid!" He would save her. If there was a fire or a flood he would save Mama first and Violet next. Drenched and shaking, he stood near the sweet-smelling stall and dared to pat her muzzle. "Don't you be afraid, Violet!"

After the storm, the sky cleared blue and cool, and fragrant air swept the hills. When the sun came out, Stevie strode proudly into Orange Square, smiling like a landlord on industrious tenants. The fountain had brimmed over, the cannon were wet, the soldiers' monument glistened. Even before the benches had dried, the Civil War veterans were straggling back to their places. The great spire shone as if the lightning had polished it. He jumped. The pointed shadow had nearly touched him.

He trailed Ludie to the baseball game in the lot on Kingston Street near the Dutch Reformed.

"Go on home!" Ludie screeched at him. "Someone'll tell Papa!"

No one told on Ludie, not even when he slipped live grasshoppers into the mite-box. Ludie did as he pleased.

Ludie took his slingshot and climbed to the rooftop to shoot at crows. Ludie chewed roofer's tar. Ludie had a cigar box full of marbles and shooters, and a Roman candle from last Fourth of July.

Ludie hopped rides on freight cars, and was chased by Mr. Yankton, the railroad guard. He came home overheated, ran straight to the ice-chest, and gulped shivery cold water.

Stevie envied him. That Ludie! He, too, cocked his cap at a jaunty angle, jingled marbles in his pocket, and swaggered down Main Street. On the Christophers' lawn, little girls in white pinafores were playing grownups at a tea party. A Newfoundland sat solemnly beside a dog-house half his size. Stevie yearned for a dog. He wondered whether God had a dog in the sky.

He meandered down Pike Street, past the First National Bank with its green window shades. He crossed the tracks to Delaware House, where ladies in gay dresses and men in straw boaters and waxed mustaches crowded the verandah. A tall lady, with a ruffled collar very low on her bosom, turned insolent green eyes upon him. She was taller than Aggie. She was so beautiful with her rosy mouth and haughty air that she had to be wicked. Fiddles screeched; a piano tinkled.

"P. J."—as Ludie called the town—was crowded with summer people who came to the mountains to escape the heat in the big cities. They stayed at hotels and boardinghouses, or at private homes. Rich people went to Delaware House, Opera House, American House or Fowler House. Rich or poor, few summer people went to church. They stayed up past midnight and took their pleasures, Mama implied, in un-Christian ways; he believed that he understood what she meant. For bands played, and the visitors drove up and down the streets in open carriages into the outlying woods. Men with metal straps about their ankles rolled speedily down the hills on high-wheeled cycles, their leader blowing a bugle; but they had difficulty riding back up. Sometimes the cycles dashed lickety-split into the trees and the riders went sprawling, which served them right because they scared the horses half to death.

Papa disapproved. On his rounds, making his calls to members of the charge, he saw the frivolous, the picnicking in the woods, the merrymaking in the name of recreation, and the scandalous behavior on the part of couples who sacrificed their reputations for the pleasures of the moment.

"Poor sinners!" Mama sighed.

"The cunning of Satan at work!" he rasped.

A thrill of anticipation went through Stevie. Papa would surely preach on these wicked ones next Sunday.

Stevie now looked forward to Sundays and sermons. Papa fasted from Saturday sundown with only water to moisten his lips, spoke to no one, and, in the morning, sat grimly in the parlor until it was time to enter the church.

"He'll give it to them!" Ludie, too, could hardly wait.

In the pulpit, Reverend Crane began slowly, his voice so weak and low that the congregation, confident that these soft beginnings promised greater thunder, had to strain to catch his words. As he proceeded, he would draw on reserves of strength and, with the mounting sweep of his voice, gather every heart into one great heart to squeeze in the hollow of his palm.

Papa had two voices. The first, soft and gentle, was truly "Papa." The second voice, into which he could move without notice, like a locomotive switching from a siding to the main track, transformed him into a stranger. When that voice spoke he was not Papa but a Man of God. His blue eyes hard, his mouth thin-lipped and scornful, his sentences rolled forth with fiery eloquence.

"The forbidden. . . ."

Stevie tingled. Papa was expounding on how it despoiled mankind and robbed it of holiness. There were more ways to be bad than to be good.

"Vice!"

Stephen repeated it under his breath. Papa could describe the most frightful of sins.

"Hemp is hasheesh, or hasheeshen. From that vile word comes our modern term 'assassin,' for men who, under its debasing influence, will slay, murder, their fellowmen!"

Reverend Crane shut his eyes: "Assassin!" and his small son hissed after him: "Assassin!" A terrible, wonderful word!

"Tobacco!"

As the blue eyes of the preacher roved over his people, many a glance wavered and fell. Certain Indian tribes used to poison their war arrows with the oil of nicotine. Yet mature men, Christian men, smoked cigars, which were rolled of the pure tobacco leaf and could stupefy, or chewed the vile plug, which could cause cancer, blindness, dyspepsia, and delirium tremens.

Even the names of these vices were enlivening. Once Ludie had squeezed the oil of nicotine out of a cigar butt for his umbrella-rib arrows. He had shot all day at sparrows, and never got one. It had been an old cigar.

Snuff, a form of tobacco which men inhaled, could eat away the tissues of the lungs. Freddie Claghorn, the veteran, took snuff; he probably had not long to live, poor Freddie!

Cigarettes, more horrid than any of the other tobacco addictions were, fortunately, not used as widely as cigars, plug, and snuff. Many summer people, however, smoked cigarettes.

Every vice, declared Papa, was a trap for the unwary. But alcohol, whether in the form of wine, perry, mead, cider, rum, pulque, or whiskey, was the saddest of all.

Reverend Crane paused, for heads were nodding in agreement. "Lips that touch liquor!" a neighbor shuddered. Mama shot her a sympathetic glance.

45

Sadly, he went on, "The saloon is the charnel house with the swinging doors!"

Stevie jabbed Ludie. "Saloon-goer!" he whispered. Ludie had been *inside* Sam Schlund's saloon; he had admitted it to Stevie.

As Papa continued in a higher pitch, it was difficult to follow him. Civilizations had perished because their peoples, indulging in abominable vices, had sunk to the levels of Sodom and Gomorrah.

"Paris, that elegant city, is renowned for its vice," Papa informed all. "For vice and moral pollution of *every* description!" More heads wagged; everyone knew about Paris, which had become so wicked that "There a virtuous woman is not the rule but the exception, and one third of the children are of uncertain parentage!"

Ludie suppressed a grin.

"Dancing!" the preacher added softly. "Dancing."

Amusement crinkled his eyes and advised the people that humor was coming. "I am constrained to admit," he said drily, "that I am unacquainted experimentally with the art of the dance. But if the lovers of the pleasure dance should be tempted to deem this a disqualification for the task of discussing the subject from the pulpit, they will kindly remember that, as far as this species of ignorance is concerned, I am in the honorable companionship of the gentlemen who have penned learned disquisitions upon the subject of capital punishment. It is not needful, in my view, either to dance, or to be hung, in order to be able to come to conclusions touching the expediency of the performance!"

Mr. Cornfall, the lawyer, chortled like a half-emptied jug shaken violently. Smiles passed about. Reverend Crane was as witty as he was pious.

Papa did not disapprove of dancing, as the Bible recorded it of the Hebrews, in worship of the Lord of Hosts. However, he strongly condemned it in any countryside where it was employed for wanton pleasure.

"When Herodias received the head of John the Baptist, she took it into her hands, drew out the lifeless tongue, and thrust a bodkin through it!"

A shudder went through the church. Stevie could see the decapitated head of the Saint, with the dagger sticking through the dead tongue.

"Look at the whole transaction," Papa went on. "An adulterous mother sends her miserable daughter to obtain of a drunken king the head of a holy man, and the means upon which they rely for the success of their murderous scheme is dancing!"

He waited to let his words sink in, for there might be secret dancers here as there were secret drinkers and secret smokers.

"The dancing-master is the Devil's drill sergeant, just as the theater is the Devil's church!" Papa thundered. "Dance halls and theaters are dens of iniquity. The girls simper as they dance, and look so languishingly now on one side, now on the other, and end with an exhibit so edifying to all modest young ladies and nice young gentlemen of twirling around on one toe, with the other foot raised to a level with the shoulder, while the galleries thunder applause, and the rotten hearts of the wretches in the pit bound with ecstasy."

Stevie was confronted by an image of a dancer in veils, one foot lifted to a level with her shoulder. He shut his eyes tightly, for the sight was overwhelmingly wicked. His mind transposed the tall, beautiful lady he had seen on the verandah of Delaware House into the naked dancer. He writhed at his sinful thoughts. How beautiful she was, the sinner!

The preacher turned sternly upon the parents: "Your children may be taken from you in the days of your youth! You will not be able to cast from you the fact that you knew your duty and did not do it. The memory of your treachery to them will never depart from you. It will rise, like the grim specter of a murdered victim, from the graves of your loved ones, to haunt your path by day, and your dreams by night, till the hour that you lay down your head in the dust and go to meet at the bar of God the soul which you have helped to thrust into everlasting burnings!"

Stevie saw the veils catch fire, and the girl dancer, screaming, enveloped in flames that greedily licked at her naked flesh.

He was glad when people began to rise. He joined soberly in the closing hymn, struggling to shut out the vision of the beautiful dancing girl and her just punishment.

CHAPTER 7

At summer's end, Ludie was ill. Full-bearded Doctor Van Etten, in silk hat and frock coat, consulted gravely with the parents.

Ludie was frightened. "I don't wanna die!"

Mama reassured him: "Nonsense! Children don't die!"

Stevie wondered about Almira Blanche, and Elizabeth Townley, and the other Crane children who had died.

Doctor Van Etten decreed that Luther must stay in bed for six weeks and not exert himself in any way.

In one of the rooms that looked out upon Orange Square, Ludie was put to bed and propped up on pillows.

His constant companion was Stevie, who had hidden the slingshot and the cigar box and all the other articles that Ludie feared to have Mama discover, including the length of rope with a "hangman's knot"

47

—from a genuine suicide!—several shotgun shells, and a brittle copy of a pamphlet entitled *The Gods*.

The brothers were closer. Stevie had to report what he did, where he went, and whom he saw. Ludie, eyes glittering, asked interminable questions; his lips were bluish and his cheeks colorless.

Aggie arrived.

"Stevie, you're becoming so tall!"

"I'm getting strong." He offered his biceps for a squeeze.

"He's thriving," Mama agreed. "The mountain air. No more colds and sniffles."

Aggie had brought surprises, a fine long scarf for Ludie, and a new coat of red and gray checked wool for Stevie. "Your birthday is November first. But I wanted you to have it in time to keep you warm when you go to school in September."

He marched up the stairs to show the coat to Ludie.

"You get everything," the ailing boy grumbled. "She doesn't care for me any more."

"She does, Ludie."

"No, she doesn't!" Petulantly, he threw a crayon at Stevie's head. He had been drawing pictures on the manila paper. "Watch me!" Savagely, he made a little-girl figure with dots for breasts and a tiny v at the crotch of the legs. He bisected the triangle with a vertical stroke. "Guess who?" He gave a nasty grin and tapped the figure. "Your sister!"

Stevie paled. "You better not. Make her wear clothes. Go ahead!"

"I will not. That's her. Aggie, Aggie!" He mocked, "You can see her 'shame.'"

Stevie snatched at the paper. The two boys tugged evenly until Stevie leaped upon the bed and wrested it from the other's hands. He promptly tore the drawing to shreds. "You're bad!"

Ludie jeered, "You don't know anything. That wasn't Aggie. It was just a girl, any old girl. They're all the same. Did you think they're like you?"

Stevie blushed furiously. Ludie could always make him appear foolish. Yet he could not doubt that Ludie had told the truth. He was now uncomfortable with his sister even when she praised him, for the little naked figure remained vividly in his mind. When Aggie sat down with her journal, to enter her daily reflections, he watched her resentfully.

"What is it, Stevie?"

He hung his head.

"Have you mischiefed?"

He shrank from her.

"Tell me, Stevie." When she pressed him, he broke away.

She had become part of a gallery of figures that rotated in his mind and heated his senses. He tried hard to see her only in the long nightgown with its skirt wound tightly about her ankles. But she had become terribly alive in sinful and wanton ways, and he could not shut out the wicked images.

He dreamed that Ludie had died. In the morning, however, Ludie was quite alive; he could not be depended upon for anything.

He was sitting at the foot of Ludie's bed struggling with the letters on Aggie's new book, *Pendennis* by William Makepeace Thackeray. He heard Townley's voice, then a gruff barking, and shouted, "A dog!"

Townley called, "Ludie, I've brought you something!"

The sick boy rolled over and paid no attention.

Stevie thrust *Pendennis* under the bed and raced down the stairs. "Where's the dog?" he cried.

"You know better!" Mama was saying coldly to Townley. His big brother, his cheeks flushed, was hesitating on the threshold, like a sheepish boy, hat in hand.

Mama was incensed. "He'll not have it. He'll never agree to a dog. You've always known it. You've done it deliberately!"

"I'm not a child, Mama!" The auburn mustaches were freshly curled. He was dressed for a visit, in a dark suit and bow tie, and was neatly shaven.

"Deliberately! He is the master in this house!"

"Mama, I'm twenty-six years old!"

At Townley's heel stood a honey-brown dog of seeming great height, with wavy hair and large amber-brown eyes. The animal, slack-jawed, stared at the man as if he were dismayed.

Stevie squeezed past his mother. "Here, girl! Here, girl!"

"It's a boy," Townley said wearily. "Mama, I only wanted to do something to help Ludie to get well. I thought it might please him— and Stevie, too."

"I don't care what would please either of them. This is your father's house!"

"Here, boy!"

The dog's tongue was scarlet. He gazed at Stephen, wagged his tail, and stepped toward him.

"Look, he obeys me!"

"Besides, Ludie is in bed. I won't have it! Who would take care of him?"

"I would!" Stevie shrilled. "He's beautiful!" He was patting the splendid head. "A dog!" he gloated. "A real live dog!"

"His name is Solomon," Townley said.

"Solomel!" He knelt and shyly stroked the brown flank. "Do you like that, Solomel?"

"Solomon, not Solomel! Scratch behind his ears."

Stevie obeyed eagerly. He administered scratches with one hand and stroked as far as he could with the other. "Oh, Solomel!"

"Solomon!"

The dog lifted his muzzle and stared at Mrs. Crane. He was transported by the boy's soft attention, yet was attending the single person who blocked his entrance.

"Mama, he'll be a wonderful watchdog."

"We don't need a watchdog in a parsonage. We have nothing anyone would steal and——"

"We put our faith in the Lord."

"Townley!"

"I'm sorry, Mama, but the dog won't detract from the parsonage."

"I'm not sure people would approve of their minister owning such a big handsome brute."

"He's not a brute," Stevie chimed in. "He's beautiful!"

Townley grinned. "You like him, don't you, Mama?" He linked his arms in hers. "When you were a little girl in Wilkes-Barre, didn't you——"

The dog's eyes went to Townley, then turned sadly to the boy's face.

Stevie beckoned. Solomon hesitated, then followed warily, head forward over each outstretched forepaw as though waiting for the harsh command that would banish him.

Townley had engaged Mama in earnest conversation. He was wheedling. Townley always wheedled.

"We'll go see Ludie. Up! Up the stairs."

Solomon nodded and negotiated the steep stairs.

"Wake up, Ludie!" Stevie screeched. "Company!"

The sick boy stirred. He saw the dog and tried to be cheerful. "Who belongs to him?"

Solomon peered under the bed and sniffed at a brass leg.

"Townley brought him for you."

The listless eyes were closing. "I don't want him. I want a bloodhound."

"You can't have a bloodhound. He's a Solomel."

"I don't want him!" Ludie moaned. "Take him away!"

"I do! I'll walk him, I'll run him, I'll everything. Tell Mama you want him. *Please,* Ludie! I'll never ask you to do anything else as long as I live!"

Solomon stretched before the bed and, placing his muzzle on his paws, watched Stevie. His eyes moved slightly. He seemed to be listening to every word.

"I want a bloodhound," Ludie muttered.

"Sh! You'll hurt his feelings. I'll go tell Mama we're keeping him."

Stevie quietly descended to the kitchen, where Townley was being served a steaming bowl of pea soup.

50

"Ludie wants him," he announced. "Solomel is guarding his bed."

"Careful, Stevie!" Townley winked. "The guard is guarding you."

There he was. Solomon was standing beside him, his muzzle at Stevie's hand.

"I know," the boy assured his older brother. "He's hungry. Mama, do we have a bone?"

Solomon launched a tremendous tail-wagging.

Mrs. Crane suppressed a smile. "Tomorrow you may go to Fred Kunkel's and get a bone for him."

"If Papa doesn't insist that I take him back," Townley groused. The tail halted.

When Papa entered, Solomon uttered a bass yawp.

"Sh!" Stevie began to counsel. "Sh now!"

But Solomon had darted across the room, confronted the minister with head elevated and tail wagging joyously.

Reverend Crane frowned. "Well, dog, what are you doing here?" He observed the animal critically. "An uncommon fellow, you are. A retriever?"

"Mostly, Father." Townley appeared.

Solomon listened without resentment.

"Yours? A fine specimen!"

"I got him from a newspaper friend who's leaving for a new job in Boston. I'd keep him myself, but Fannie's not well and I'm away all day. He needs a good home." He paused with an air of innocence. "He has good lines, don't you think, Father?"

"Handsome!" Reverend Crane said. He patted the dog's head. "This breed is excellent at fetching and obeying commands. I've seen one pick a kitten up in its mouth and drop it unharmed at its master's feet. They get along well with horses, cows, other farm animals. They're very protective with children." He stroked his beard. "Here, boy!" He slapped his knee.

Solomon danced toward him, jaws open, revealing his fine white teeth.

"Not more than two years old. Good boy!"

"Three, Father."

"Mr. McKinney, the Baptist minister, has a dog," Mrs. Crane said.

Reverend Crane turned on her. "A mongrel!" he snapped. "I've seen it. This one is an animal of breeding, McKinney's is a wretched mongrel, poor thing." He sat down. "Come closer, boy!" He stroked Solomon. "Good boy."

"He likes you, Papa!" Stevie put in breathlessly.

"Yes, a dog likes a friendly hand. Don't we all? What is his name? Solomon? Excellent. Observe what a head this Solomon has, and a wise look." He suddenly stiffened. "Your mother rules this household. I daresay it would be too much for her."

Mama shrugged. "The dog, having no home, what is one to do? Shall we turn him out? He is a living creature."

Papa nodded. He had not taken his eyes from Solomon, who continued to wag his tail with admirable persistence.

"I would say, Townley, that if your mother approves—and the last word must be hers—Solomon might remain awhile. Strictly on trial, you understand. One misbehavior and off he goes, to anyone who will have him."

"I'll take him!"

"Silence, Stephen. Your father is speaking."

"Yes, Papa."

"I want none of your laggard ways here. You must attend to him punctually." He glanced at his wife. "It could be enriching, rewarding, this responsibility."

"I'll remember, Papa."

"Townley, you have done the merciful thing—if Stephen does not disappoint us."

"I won't, Papa, I won't! Here, boy!"

Solomon, alert, swung his head from father to son, and hesitated. He remained at Reverend Crane's knee.

The minister suddenly chuckled. "A dog knows its master. I can see McKinney and that mongrel of his!"

So the dog that had arrived as a gift for Ludie was tentatively adopted. Indoors, Reverend Crane demanded Solomon's attention. The retriever, with a curious wisdom, obeyed docilely. Through the day, however, he was Stevie's pet.

They understood each other, Stevie and his "Solomel." The boy groomed his coat, attended to his ears, delicately removing sticky burrs, and sensed that when Solomon blandly presented his hindquarters he required diligent scratching at the base of the tail where a muzzle cannot reach. Stevie declaimed and Solomon listened. Sometimes Solomon softly hissed or sibilated, as though he were shaping words, and greatly delighted his young master.

"He's learning to talk. Listen, he's talking!"

Mama laughed. Stevie observed that Solomon enlivened the parsonage. Smiles and chuckles, which had been rare in the household, became common. A modicum of levity, caused by an animal instead of a man, as Papa observed, would surely not offend the Lord, who had created the dumb beasts to serve Adam and his descendants.

With Violet, the black mare, Solomon could not come to terms. She glanced at him wild-eyed, bared her teeth and pawed the dirt.

"This is Solomel," Stevie anxiously informed her. "He's my friend."

Violet trembled.

"Go to her, Solomel. Violet likes you."

Solomon regarded the larger animal warily. As he moved forward, the mare reared in her stall.

52

"Take the dog away!" Papa said sternly.

"Come on, Solomel!" He was mystified. It grieved him that these two whom he loved should not be friends.

Solomon, in his devotion, was keenly aware that every morning the boy needed a long run in the hills, where the smells were delicious, and that, when the boy threw a stick, it must be retrieved in high style and offered with a gay, prancing step. He knew, too, that he must obey the older master absolutely, and mind the woman, too, although she rarely petted him. The boy, on the other hand, needed to be obeyed only when he gave commands in a final tone; other commands were merely wishes, to be carried out or not as befitted a dog of character who had his own boy.

Solomon comprehended that a dog must not bark inside the parsonage and, if possible, not at all on Sundays. Let Samuel, Mrs. Kindle's old tomcat, sire of a lazy generation that lurked in the fields from the Neversink to the Delaware, decide to stroll past and distress the vicinity with his unbearably feline aromas. Bristle and growl in a modest way, yes; nothing louder. Also, *never* cross the church lawn.

Alone with Solomon, Stephen hugged his dog. "You're the best dog in the whole world, Solomel! Do you know that?"

Solomon huffed. He knew that he was.

He slept at the foot of the boy's bed. When he had to go out during the night, he poked a firm nose under the sleeping boy's arm, or panted in his ear. There were times when a boy had to be informed that insidious fragrances had invaded the house; squirrels or rabbits were lurking outside, and should be dispersed with one surging leap. Then Solomon stood shining before his young prince, hind legs set and tail wagging like the pendulum of an excited clock. The amber-brown eyes communicated swiftly: *Out there!*

They had their best hours in the hills and the ravines. There the dog might bark to his heart's content and tear a hole in the morning with his deep bass voice. Ghost dogs barked back from every hollow, but dared not show themselves. Solomon gave Stephen a freedom he had never known before. "I've got to take him out," the boy could always say.

They explored Port Jervis from Cuddleback's swimming hole to Laurel Grove Cemetery, from the depot and the gas works out to Germantown, and up Mount William and Point Peter, "Bill" and "Pete," the twin mountain peaks, as high as they dared. They crossed the canal bridges. They roved through all of Deer Park Township, from Shin Hollow to Quarry Hill to Sparrow Bush. They rested under the open sky, and enjoyed a mutual affection that was beyond ordinary understanding.

Trees creaked. Solomon studied the green embrocations in the foliage where warblers flitted and squirrels deployed. A little sapsucker climbed around a branch, pecking and hopping. Solomon's brown ears lifted: a hundred yards away, a racoon was marshaling her brood for a trip to the brook. His tail thumped in the grass.

"What do you see, Solomel? What do you hear?" He wished that he knew what Solomon knew.

Solomon could lead to the secret places where quail assembled, or partridges clustered, where moles burrowed, or rabbits kept their young. But his companion was, by nature, sadly limited. A boy on two feet, with his weak nose elevated, cannot assess the wonderful knowledge that four legs and a nose with a powerful range can derive from the magnificent earth. Solomon could not say that a doe had nibbled tender shoots here, that a small bear had scratched his back against those round boulders, or that spoors that betrayed the passing of other creatures hours ago still lingered fragrantly. The silent, the stealthy, and the dangerous he could readily separate from the sweet grass-and-root smells; all these were his province. Despite his ignorance, the boy was worth owning.

"If only you would say something, Solomel. Just a word!"

Thump! Thump! Solomon lowered his great head. He knew what Stephen did not, that there are endless adventures that can be enjoyed by man and those devoted to him without the intrusion of speech; dogs have known that since they first domesticated boys at the dawn of human history.

CHAPTER 8

The incredible miracle of school unfolded before Stephen on a September morning. He was equipped with a black schoolbag, a red pencil-box, a writing tablet, and yellow scratch sheets. He carried his lunchpail and a bright two-cent piece for pocket money. He was excited to be going off to school at last, but he had to reassure Solomon, who eyed him dolefully.

"You take care of the house! Take good care, Old Sol, and I'll be back and tell you everything!"

Slack-jawed, the dog watched the boy depart, then clunked himself down near the kitchen stove, to sulk until Stevie returned.

The schoolhouse was of white clapboard, with broad windows and a wooden tower in which a black bell pealed morning and noon. Nearby was the playing field, once a cow pasture, now worn smooth by a decade of trampling young feet. The rooms smelled of chalk and clothes and children. The walls were hung with slates and maps, steel prints of faded historical occasions, and the stern likenesses of the statesmen who had forged the nation.

Stephen was assigned to Mr. Langley's room. A head shorter and ten pounds lighter than other boys his age, he was directed to the front bench, where the first and second grades were congregated.

Tall, long-legged Mr. Langley, with his beaky nose, his full set of red whiskers, and a worn tailcoat that attracted chalk smudges, presided over sixty pupils in the first four grades. In the morning, he devoted his talents to the younger pupils, who were seated on his right; in the afternoon, to the older pupils, who were on his left and near the cloakroom. The scholars at ease were cautioned to study for their next lessons. The girls applied themselves, or at least were meek; the boys shuffled their feet, rolled spitballs, carved their desks, and were generally restless. While one group recited, Mr. Langley, six feet of authority armed with deadly ferrule, ranged on the other side of the room to intimidate the unruly.

His closely-set green eyes, unusually large under coppery lashes, darted over the boys and girls on the double rows of benches. He was able, and willing, to administer one or more sharp slaps to the head with his bony hand or, in extremis, to deliver a series of hard strokes on the seat of any trousers that required correction. The little girls were, naturally, spared; the mildest reproof would send them into all-afternoon sniffling.

In this atmosphere, young Stephen felt lost. The lessons that were being assigned he had long ago, thanks to Aggie and to Mama, mastered at home. What he already knew bored him, so he listened craftily to the recitations across the room. It was difficult not to listen, for Mr. Langley roared; when he was not grilling some scholar he ordered the form to recite in singsong chorus.

The schoolmaster, however, permitted no exceptions. Any head not bowed in study was a head to be flicked, and the end of his brass-bound ferrule was a stinger!

"Crane! Are you so intelligent that it is not necessary for you to study your alphabet?"

"Teacher, I know it!"

"Indeed!" he sneered. "Then we have a gifted scholar in our midst. Pray then, Crane, embellish the blackboard with alphabets. Since you are so learned, add also one word for each letter. A—alphabet, b—brother, c—cloud, etcetera."

Sarcasm was wasted on a youngster who had been subjected to pulpit rhetoric all his years. Stevie approached the blackboard eagerly and, to Mr. Langley's surprise, wrote speedily. He faltered only at the letter q and, later, at the letters x and z. For s he wrote "Solomon."

Mr. Langley having boomed through a spelling lesson with the fourth graders, stalked to the boy's side. "Well, my fine-feathered fellow!"

"I don't know any of these——" He pointed to the q, x, and z.

"Ah, you don't! Then your education is not entirely complete?"

"No, Teacher."

"Your right hand, Crane!"

The ferrule came down. "For *q!* For *x!* For *zed!*"

The pain brought tears into Stephen's eyes.

"Do you think now that you may be able to shut your eyes and ears to recitations that are no concern of yours?"

Stubbornly, "No, Teacher."

"What!"

"I can hear them."

"So? You can hear them? Then your ears may need attention." The bony fingers reached for an ear, and twisted. Stevie rose on his toes and shrieked.

"Silence!"

"You hurt me!"

"Not I hurt you, but 'q' and 'x' and 'zed'!" Once more a cruel twist.

As the pain again shot across his cheek, the boy screamed, and clung to his tormentor's hand. He was flung against the blackboard. The class hooted.

"Stand in the corner, with your face to the wall! Class, be silent!"

Weeping, Stevie obeyed. He cupped the bruised ear and sobbed, his heart flooded with anger at the injustice. Soon he tired and leaned his forehead against the cool wall.

He jumped. The ferrule had snaked across the calves of his legs.

"I said 'stand,' Crane! Not 'sag'!"

Stevie stood erect, sobbing again. At the clang of the schoolbell, Mr. Langley called: "Dismissed!" The usual scuffling for the schoolbags and lunchpails began.

The boy turned about. Teacher was occupied with his papers. Stevie hurried to his bench, collected his belongings, and scurried after the others into the hall.

"Crane!"

He darted down the corridor and out of the building.

Mrs. Crane observed that her son had been crying. His ear was crimson. When he stroked Solomon, he favored his right hand.

She seized his wrist. The palm was raw and blistered.

"You misbehaved. You were bad!"

"He hit me—oh!" The flesh was tender.

"You must have done something," she sighed. "There must have been a reason. Oh, Stephen, I hope you won't disappoint your father!"

He was silent. They would not believe him anyway.

The ear continued to throb when Stevie went to bed and pressed his head into the pillow. Dam-ol' Langley! Damn his soul!

During the night, the hand swelled. He inadvertently threw his weight across it, and cried out. Ludie growled, "Go to sleep, kid!"

Stevie plotted terrible vengeance on Mr. Langley. Place a tack on

56

the schoolmaster's chair or, somehow, cut a round hole in the floor where Mr. Langley was sure to stand! Grimmer was the fantasy that possessed him as he began to drift off to sleep. Mr. Langley had mounted the wheel of his buggy and was taking the reins. Solomon barked, and the horse bolted. Mr. Langley fell headlong under the hooves and was dragged a mile. When the buggy came to a halt, the schoolmaster was a torn and disheveled body, with his whiskers sticking up under the animal's hindquarters. His ears were large and bloodied. He was good and dead.

Stevie quivered when Ludie roused him at seven. Solomon loyally trailed him as, lamely employing only the sound hand, he washed and dressed. At breakfast, he picked at his porridge and stared at the table. He would surely get it again in school today.

" 'Bye, Solomon!" Lagging down Broome Street, with his school-bag over his shoulder, he wished that he might take Solomon and go to live in the hills, maybe in some cave. He would find a box and shine shoes, and buy a loaf of bread and plenty of cold chicken. He would eat the meat and Solomon would crack the bones and they would keep house together. Old Solomon would protect him.

The first schoolbell, clanging, struck loud terror in his heart. The swollen palm throbbed anew. Soon he would be encountering other boys and girls from the class.

At the second clanging, he panicked. He darted into a yard, came out in a stable lane, and trudged close to the buildings.

A gig rolled from a stable. He loitered in the bushes until it was gone.

He came to stable doors and saw that they were slightly ajar. Henry Johnson, the Negro groom, worked there. Henry had concealed him once, when he was being chased by Marty Schermerhorn, the bully. He squeezed between the doors. A light shone from the harness room. He tiptoed in and dashed for the ladder. In the loft, he sank down upon a bale of hay and stretched out rigidly, his arms at his sides, the schoolbag under his head. The breakfast porridge had become a lump in his chest.

With a start, he realized that he had forgotten his lunchpail in the kitchen. Mama would be sure to find it; she would take it to school and Mr. Langley would sneer, "That boy hasn't been here today!" They would think that he had been kidnaped by gypsies. They would send out a searching party. If they remembered to take Solomon, he would surely be found.

The stable doors creaked.

Mr. Langley's footsteps thudded in the dirt. "Henry Johnson," he screamed at the groom, "are you hiding that Crane boy?"

"No, sah! I never even seed him."

"Johnson, don't you lie to me! I know that he's here somewhere."

The boy's heart thundered.

"Honest, Mr. Teacher, I never laid eyes on dat boy."

"Johnson, come here! Bring that lamp over and let me look you straight in the eye!"

"Yes, sah!"

"Turn up that wick. Now hand me the lamp." He heard Mr. Langley snicker. "You rascally liar, he's here! I ought to give you a taste of the ferrule." He raised his voice, "Crane, are you here?"

"No, he ain't."

"Silence, Johnson! Crane, come out, wherever you are!"

"Come out, come out, wherever you are!" echoed through the stalls like the call in a playground game. "Come out, come out, wherever you are!"

Stevie wanted to stir, but his limbs were paralyzed. "Oh, Lord, let me be dead!" he prayed. A shadow hulked on the beams overhead, rose and bobbed. "Let me be dead."

"Your last chance, Crane! I'll come up and get you and pull your ears right off!"

"Don't go up dere, Mr. Teacher. I know dat boy ain't dere."

"Stand back, Johnson. Crane, I'm coming up for you!"

Summoning all his strength, Stevie conquered the spell that had imprisoned him. He dashed to the edge of the loft. When the top of Mr. Langley's red crown appeared, he thrust his hands against the ladder and pushed. The schoolmaster uttered a wild cry, and toppled. Red whiskers gleamed as the lamp swung from his hand and fell with a crash.

Little tongues of yellow flame, a dozen, a hundred, a thousand, licked the dirt as the coal oil spread. They danced, sucked on threads of dried hay, ran speedily to fuzzy bunches of straw, crackled and stood up in full-grown veils of fire. They singed, hissed venomously and devoured everything in their path, with audible greed, attacking one bale, leaping to another.

"Crane!" the voice screeched. Mr. Langley was lying on his back, his legs twisted weirdly. A searing hedgehog of fire was eating at his red whiskers, gliding over his eyelids, annihilating the hated countenance. *He had no face!*

A roar shot up. Red and yellow and orange spears advanced and obliterated the walls. The ladder alone defied them. Slowly, the roof began to descend.

Stevie shrieked. The back of his head was in a vise.

Footsteps came running. Feet were climbing.

"Boy, what you doin' dere? Boy—dat you?—you come right down!"

He moaned. He was still lying on the bale of hay with his limbs rigid. That was his schoolbag tormenting the back of his head. Over him stood Henry Johnson.

"What you doin' here?"

"I—I—"

The strong arms lifted him. "You ailin', boy?"

His tongue felt charred.

"Can you stan' up?" The groom rubbed firm brown fingers over his temples and felt his limbs. He spied the schoolbag. "You playin' hooky?"

"Uh-huh!" he was gasping. Everything was the same. There had been no fire. "Mr. Langley——"

"Who dat? Wassa madder wid you, boy? You git on to school where you belong!"

"I—fell asleep."

"You sleep at home. Git me into trouble, dat's what!"

He descended the ladder. "I didn't mean to make trouble, Henry. I'm sorry."

He stood in the dirt, still incredulous. There was the spot where Mr. Langley had been stretched out. The lamp was still in the harness room.

It was too late to go to school now. Fearfully, he trudged to the parsonage. The stable doors were open! Violet was gone, Papa must be away.

Bong! The clock in the tower struck. *Bong!*

He dashed into the church and found his way to the narrow stairway that led to the tower. No one would think of looking for him there. After climbing several floors, he reached a platform where the broad stairs ended. He rested, and listened to the dark hush. Light filtered through crevices.

He glanced up: only the bluish air in the narrowing cone of the spire. A series of pine ladders, their resinous odors filling the enclosure with the fragrance of fresh shavings, led to the heights. The first ladder went to a narrow planking, which had to be crossed to reach the second ladder on the other wall of the tower, and so on and up, alternating.

He spit on his good hand and began, sturdily, to ascend. He ran a splinter into the sore palm. He winced and in the dim light tried to pick it from his flesh. His calves hurt; his thighs were stiff. Still he proceeded, one rung after another. They would never find him here.

Suddenly he looked down, and his head swam. The spider-webbing of ladders descended into a dark pit which spread wider and wider into a cavernous maw. Something was creaking, crawling. He strained to listen: the depths were reaching for him. A pain shot through the punished hand. He reeled, but clung tighter. Nothing could happen to him; he was in God's church and in God's spire. He looked down again, scornfully, and once more began to climb.

When he rested again, he caught a view, through a chink, of the blue sky with a cloud floating by and a snaggle-toothed mountain so near he could almost have touched it. Below were tree-studded hills, little farms and tiny cattle on patches of green meadow. A bird, which he took to be an eagle, soared over a peak. He clung to his perch. He was seeing the world as God had seen it the First Day, "And it was good." Far away, a river stretched like a silver ribbon across Aggie's lap.

A clang sent a dagger of fear through him. A whirring and another clang! Mrs. Shorter's clock was striking in the belfry below. Up here, although the sound fairly pierced his ears, its quality was sharp and metallic rather than gruff and booming. *Clang!*

He became frightened and, while the clock was still striking, began hastily to descend. The last clang was dying away as his feet struck the belfry floor.

He stared at a mass of toothed wheels, gears, and heavy weights that quivered and swung slowly. Strange hammers hung over the large bells. He was tempted to thrust in his hand, but the mechanism began to tick with deliberate, almost hostile, precision, like a monstrous heart. With each tick, a soft groan issued, as if some living organism were being stretched beyond endurance.

A distant barking reached his ears. He tried to peer through the chinks. That must be Solomon! Had the retriever, with his extraordinary hearing, sensed that he was here? Old Sol would fetch Mama after him. He hurried now. At the foot of the staircase, he was shaking. Solomon was still barking.

When he emerged from the church, Solomon came racing. He had been running madly around the edifice. His tail wagged and the amber eyes gleamed.

"Old Sol! You knew where I was hiding."

Solomon panted, lowered his head and looked wise.

He did not want to enter the parsonage, but he dared not go anywhere else, for Solomon would follow him.

"Mama, Mama, I got sick!"

"Stephen!" She paled and touched his forehead. "What is it? That dog hasn't let up barking for nearly an hour. Bad dog!"

"I got sick. He's not a bad dog. I forgot my lunchpail."

"I would have brought it to the schoolhouse at noon."

She examined his swollen palm. The climbing had caused it to swell to twice its size. Gingerly, she touched his ear. "He hurt you."

He buried his head in her lap.

"Come to bed, Stephen." He followed her contentedly. "Tomorrow you'll be well again. I'll put your lunchpail in the cold-room."

"I can't go back!" he blurted out. "Please don't make me, never!"

"Stephen, you must tell me everything. I am your mother. You must tell me."

With his arms around her, he sobbed out the whole tale of Mr. Langley's punishment.

She reflected. "Stay in bed, Stephen."

"Can Solomel be with me?"

"Oh, very well!"

After a while, he dozed.

"He needs discipline!" He heard Papa's voice. "Leave well enough alone. Helen, your anger is un-Christian."

"I don't care!" He had never heard Mama speak so sharply. "I won't have a bully of a man who, for all we know, secretly indulges in stimulants—mind how furiously he drives his buggy—mistreat our boy. His ear is swollen."

"Stephen must learn to respect authority!"

"He is my youngest," she continued. "I will not have him bullied. When my father went to school, he had a savage schoolmaster who gagged and whipped him and fastened a clothespin on his nose and beat him over the head, and called him 'Dunce' and 'Scoundrel'! I won't have it!"

"If you choose to intervene," he said with surprising mildness, "very well. I wash my hands of this."

Stevie's heart leaped. She loved him! She would protect him.

The next morning, she accompanied him to the schoolhouse. Her longish face was like Grandpa George's, her gaze clear beneath the dark eyebrows. He took her hand though a dozen classmates jeered and tagged after them.

"Mr. Langley," she opened bluntly, "it has come to my attention that Stephen has been abused." She pointed to her son's hand.

The red-whiskered man stiffened. "Madam——"

"I do not blame you for wishing to discipline him," she went on. She was pale and straight, nearly as tall as the teacher. "The best of us may profit from a little *inner* discipline. However, I will not tolerate inhuman treatment, sir. I want that understood! And now, I wish merely to inform you that Stephen has been taught at home and deserves to be promoted from the lowest grades."

"If that is your wish——"

"Such is my wish."

"He is bright," Mr. Langley agreed. "I have it in my mind to move him to the third division. I have it in my mind."

"Then let the deed speak for the thought," she said coldly. "You will do it at once."

He nodded. "That is my intention."

"Stephen," she addressed her son, "the teacher will give you your place. I want no more problems with you—or with the school." She swept Mr. Langley with an icy glance. "Good day, sir!"

"Crane," said the schoolmaster when he had composed himself, "I was much impressed with your knowledge of the alphabet. I will try you in the third division. It will require hard study to keep up with the others. You will do your best?"

"Yes, Teacher." He discovered that he could gaze calmly into the green eyes.

The ferrule advanced, but merely rested on his shoulder. Stevie did not flinch.

"I shall expect much from you." The schoolmaster's lofty smile revealed a crooked tooth. "If you require correction again, we may have to resort to a birch-rod. *That* leaves no marks!"

At noon, when the scholars were released and he went out to eat his lunch and to play in the pasture, he heard a gruff bark. Solomon was panting under the maple tree.

He caressed his dog. "Don't worry, Sol, if he ever does birch me, *he'll burn!*"

Solomon sniffed at the lunchpail. Stephen sat in the grass. Half of everything, he shared with the retriever.

At three o'clock, Solomon was again waiting under the tree.

A bevy of scholars admired the dog. "How does he know when school's out?"

Stevie pondered. "He hears Mrs. Shorter's clock—that's it."

He was confident however that old Sol hid in the fields, ready to come dashing into the schoolhouse if Mr. Langley dared—if he just ever dared again!

CHAPTER 9

His daytime world was a carrousel, on which all the family, his schoolmates, the neighbors, the hills and the rivers, and the joys they offered, revolved and passed him and his dog. Occasionally, an event snatched him aboard and whirled him about giddily to laughter or to tears, or simply speeded the elastic passage of the hours and days, bridging holidays and birthdays and cramming him with new bewildering experiences. Past and present interwove.

At night, the carrousel was peopled by bristling phantoms that roved and pillaged the dream terrain. Episodes developed without reason and ended without resolution; the scenes were hopelessly jumbled. He fell into wells that were bottomless, purple throats; he wandered into caves where the walls glittered with scarlet eyes and a thousand daggers held him at bay. Sometimes he fled all night from grasping hands.

The dawn, mercifully releasing, obliterated every dread adventure. Always, he was left morbidly aware that the dark held slimy dangers.

He prayed daily, and was on excellent terms with God. Papa was sufficiently pleased not to complain about his grades in school.

Knowledge of a large family, with branches dispersed over several states, expanded Stevie's horizons. He was the youngest of fourteen children! He counted on his fingers: Nellie, George, Townley, Will, Aggie, Ted, Burt, Ludie, and himself. That made nine. Five others were already dead.

"Why?"

"The Lord took them."

He wanted to ask why the Lord took little children when there were so many grown-ups. Perhaps grown-up people did not care to die.

"The first Stephen Crane came here from England more than two hundred years ago," Papa announced.

Stephen reflected. Had he been here once before, long ago, and not remembered? "I am Stephen Crane!"

"His wife was a Danish woman with red hair. Our seed has multiplied," Papa declared.

Stevie could see a sower in the fields, walking down plowed furrows, lifting his arms and tossing seeds to the winds. Wherever the seeds fell, tall Crane men, mostly bearded, some with only mustaches, leaped erect.

Stephen enjoyed the "love feasts" at summer's end when the whole countryside flocked to town. Early Sunday, every seat in Drew Church was occupied; the usual latecomers from Matamoras had to stand at the rear.

Reverend Crane, so pale from his fasting that he appeared purified for his task, recited a long prayer, and offered a call for love.

Stephen squirmed pleasantly, for when he heard the word "love" he knew that testimonials of sin would follow. Papa reminded the assembled that punishment was inevitable, that the Lake of Fire awaited sinners as surely as God had created Man in His own image.

When the way had been prepared, many in the congregation who had been saved went up and testified and affirmed. Some spoke in low tones, as though they were truly ashamed; others came out so boldly that Stephen shivered.

"I'm coming, Lord!" a voice boomed. Big John Travis, the brawny blacksmith who shod the brewers' horses, was on his feet. He was a huge figure in his shiny Sunday coat. When he pushed his way to the Mourner's Bench, others fell back.

Harrison, his youngest, came after him. "Gimme your hat, Pa, 'fore you bust it!"

Reverend Crane lifted his arms. The congregation stilled.

"Lord, I was wicked!" mourned Mr. Travis, and lifted his clenched fists. His cuffs shot from his shirtsleeves. "Lord, Lord, I was bad! Lord, Lord, I had a black heart. The Devil whispered at my elbow, and the Devil pulled at my sleeve. Lord, Lord!"

He roared, "I took His name in vain and did the Devil's own bidding, I did! Brethern, I was rotten through and through—to the core! Brethern, there wasn't no vice I hadn't tasted thereof, or yearned to get my fill of. Lord, Lord, I was corrupt. I knowed that great hellfires was heating up in wait for this sinful flesh of mine. But I didn't care. I was a scoffer, I was a doubting Thomas. I didn't hold nothing of the Lord. I was sliding down the wicked way."

A yellow butterfly flitted in through an open window.

"Then one night, after I had fallen off the pledge and been wallowing like a hog in a trough of this dee-pravity, I was laying awake thinking up new mischief—Brethern, I was!—when, with a clap of thunder, it came over me. Brethern, I heard it! It wasn't no tomfoolery. It was a voice. I began to shiver in a fever. I began to quake with the aguey. I was shaking like a leaf in a high wind. And, suddenly, a bright light broke in on me, even into the dark corners of my wicked old soul. Lord, Lord, I breathed deep and, Brethern" —he snapped his fingers—"I felt ree-leased. That there moment, I was free as a bird. The Devil and His Evil Spirit and all His Imps, they had been driven out of me. They had fled back into the Hell where they belong. And lo! I knew what had happened. The Spirit of the Lord had come breathing down, right down, on me, John Travis!"

"Hallelujah!" a woman shrilled.

"Hallelujah! Hallelujah!" the congregation chorused.

"Hallelujah!" roared Big John. "And that light grew white and wrapped itself all around me. And I prayed hard for guidance. How I prayed! I called out: 'Lord, Lord, look into my soul! It's coal black. It's wicked. It's no bargain, Lord. I've been a rapscallion, and I know it. I've been a plain, downright'"—he stamped his foot— "'scoundrel, and worse'n that, and I know it. But, I'm turnin' over, Lord, I'm turnin' over.' And sayin' this, I just ripped open my shirt and said, 'Go ahead, Lord, here I am. If you want me, you take me to the end of my days!'"

"Hallelujah!"

"Lord, Lord!"

"Hallelujah!" He threw back his head and stared at the rafters. "I waited, Brethern, for the lightning to strike me. I had a right to expect it. I waited for the brimstone to come pouring down on me. I waited for the righteous wrath to turn me into a pillar of salt, or a chunk of coke. Tears began to drip from my eyes. I was laughing and I was crying, and I was doing both together. For nothing happened to punish me, as I full well had it coming! Nothing. The Lord had just showed his mercy to me, the Lord had just saved me from being eternally damned. Lord, Lord, how can I thank you, Lord?"

"Hallelujah!"

"Hallelujah!" Big John shouted. "I was saved!"

"Saved, saved!" they shouted. "Hallelujah!"

He waved his brawny arms and, carried away by the responses, continued to shout for another ten minutes, with the congregation abetting him until great tears rolled down his cheeks and into the black mustaches. "Hallelujah!" he repeated hoarsely. "Hallelujah!"

Reverend Crane descended from the pulpit to embrace him.

Big John sobbed, "Hallelujah, Rev——" He could not continue.

People were jumping up and dashing into the aisles, shouting, "Hallelujah! Save, save, save the Lord!" They were jostling each other for the right to come forward. "Hallelujah! Let me tell how I was saved!"

The love feast continued for hours. Stevie watched the butterfly disappear and reappear. Big John Travis had started the procession to the Mourner's Bench and thirty sinners were inspired by his example. Stevie was astonished at the people—the banker, the lumberman, the conductor's wife—who threw themselves on their knees and whimpered out the stories of their sins and how they had been saved. Everyone was a sinner, everyone could be saved. Mama was weeping into her hands. Aggie sat stone-faced.

"We are sinners all!" thundered Reverend Crane, with outstretched arms. "All sinners! Come to the Lord and be saved!"

Stevie was brushed aside; Mama was rising. The butterfly appeared again. Was it the same one, or another?

She went forth into the aisle, her back military, her bosom sloping in black cloth, her prayer book clutched in her hand. From under her bonnet floated wisps of hair. She stared at the minister as though she had never seen him before. "Reverend!"

Stevie leaped to his feet. "Mama!"

Aggie restrained him.

"Mama!"

She stood at the Mourner's Bench, shrilling strangely: "Oh, God, have mercy upon Thy handmaiden. I, too, am a sinner!"

Aggie compelled him to sit down. "Sh, Stevie, she's coming right back!"

He could not understand his mother. The unearthly timbre of her voice sent shivers through him.

"Oh, dear God, have mercy upon me, a sinner!" Her cheeks, bloodless, became crimson, then waxen again. Tears streamed down her cheeks. "I have sinned, sinned!" The fingers at her breast were living claws, twisting as if they would rend the flesh.

Stevie, stricken, glanced at his father. A shaft of sunlight flashed across the spectacles. The face was a plaster skull dressed with lenses and silken beard.

"Lord, I have sinned in the morning, and in the evening, and in the dark hours of the night!"

A flood of suspicion assailed Stephen. "She is a sinner!" he breathed. "Mama!" He had to choke back his tears.

Above the tumult, he heard a raging sussuration that brought to his nostrils the smell and thunder of the sea. Gulping, he struggled to retrieve distant memories.

Ludie clapped his hands together and, with a grin, flicked the yellow butterfly from his fingers.

The love feast had ended. They were singing the final hymn. Stevie clamped his lips shut; he would not sing.

The pews were emptying. People were moving toward the doors. Some shook the minister's hand. "Reverend——"

"Praise the Lord!"

"Reverend——"

"Stephen!" He shrank as his Mama touched him. "What is it, son?"

He flung his arms about her waist and buried his head under her bosom. "Mama, Mama!"

"It was a long meeting," Aggie said coolly.

"Stephen, are you ill again?"

He could only utter tearless sobs that gave way to hiccoughs. He squinted at her through tortured eyes.

His father was still solemnly accepting the plaudits of his flock. It was Papa who had made her confess sins! He made everyone confess, yet never confessed himself.

Later, Ludie scoffed. "What were you carrying on for? Nobody's going to Hell, or to any Lake of Fire. Ask Will. There ain't no such place."

He scowled at his brother and muttered under his breath.

That night, Stevie dreamed that he was in church again. Everyone was hollering and screaming, "Hallelujah!" He looked for Papa. The pulpit was elevated. His gaze rose, but the higher he lifted his eyes the higher the pulpit ascended until his father was so high up that the point of the church steeple was just above his head. He saw the white beard distinctly and the flashing spectacles. "Sinners! Sinners!" The exhorting finger thrust out, farther and farther, like a dirk.

Suddenly, Papa leaned out too far. He lost his balance and hurtled into space.

Stephen screamed. It was too late. He heard the crash. Across the Mourner's Bench, sprawled Papa's figure. Stephen blinked: beneath it lay the broken body of his Mama!

He awoke in a cold, dripping sweat and stared incredulously into the darkness.

CHAPTER 10

It had been a hard winter since November 1st, his eighth birthday, when the first white flurries had come down. Light snows had fallen steadily through December and into the new year. In mid-January, a blizzard howled out of the mountains, and dropped six inches of fresh snow upon Port Jervis. Mount William and Point Peter had never loomed so splendidly. On distant ledges, snow-clouds appeared to stretch for miles.

The trees, majestic under the white pelts, creaked and groaned; branches crashed to the ground. For two days, no trains arrived or departed; the tracks were buried and the switches were frozen. Telegraph lines dangled from their stocks like blacksnake whips. The gasworks was a big frosty pudding.

Schools were closed for two days after the storm. Thirty or forty boys went coasting downhill on an assortment of cheese-cutters, skate-sleds and Lightning Gliders. A few of the veterans helped the older boys erect a snow fort in Orange Square. A hail of snowballs described wondrous parabolas. The church stood like a broken wedding-cake.

After two days of dry frost, the winds died down and the town sprang to life. Shovels clanged, sleighs appeared, bells jingle-jangled, and icicles depended from window sills and rain-gutters. Rifle shots sounded as more boughs cracked and fell.

Reverend Crane was nursing a chest cold. With a shawl about his shoulders, he stood at an open window and directed that crumbs be scattered and trays of water put out for poor birds. "God watches the sparrow's fall!" he said.

Chafing in enforced idleness, he wandered from room to room. He peered into closets. He spied Ludie's cigar box, which the youth, at end of term, had brought home from Hackettstown, and casually lifted the lid. He puzzled over a shotgun shell and the length of rope with the "genuine suicide's knot." He thumbed the worn pamphlet, *The Gods*, and muttered, "What have we here? *Ingersoll!*"

"Luther!" A paroxysm of rage seized him. "Luther!"

As he scanned the text, tears blinded him. "God, why hast Thou forsaken me, and punished me with such children?" In a terrible voice: "Luther!"

Ludie came in, stamping his feet. He saw the pamphlet in his father's hands and cried, "I found it!"

"Have you read this—this——?"

"No, Papa!" Snow dropped from his boots.

"Then why have you hidden it in your secret cupboard?"

"I thought some day I'd——"

"You'd read it."

"I never did, Papa."

"Who is responsible for the interlinings on these pages?"

"Not me!" Ludie paled. "There wasn't anything on the pages when I——"

"When you read it!" his father shouted. "I thought so. A vile, hideous vilification of Scriptures and religion—atheism and worse!—and my son Luther—what a mockery your name is!—reads it. With shelves full of books, have you ever tried to read the Lord's word?"

He ushered his son to the room the children never entered, and ordered him to remove coat, sloppy boots, and trousers. He plied the rod.

Ludie howled. No longer furious, but a cold, avenging angel, the father administered whipping justice. He left his son weeping and struggling feebly into his clothes.

Mama had secluded Stevie in the kitchen. The minister stalked in, raised a stove-lid and tossed the pamphlet onto the glowing coals. Flames licked hungrily; a blaze rose from the shrinking pages. He clanged the lid into place.

"In ten years at Pennington Seminary, I used the rod three times. Today, I wielded it again." He turned upon her. "Where were your eyes, Mrs. Crane, when your son was secretly reading a pamphlet by that arch-infidel, that anti-Christ, Robert Ingersoll?"

She bit her lip.

"And you—what do you know of it?"

Stevie was wide-eyed.

"A viper in my bosom, I nurtured. All vipers! Is there one who has followed in my ways?"

He thundered toward his study.

"I shall preach on this subject: 'Atheism Triumphant—What Does it Mean?' Nowadays, love has perished. Hatred is rampant in every heart. What would Doctor Whitney, president of Hackettstown, say if he knew! I helped raise the building funds for his seminary. He would expel Luther instanter to save other scholars from contamination. Think what an influence Luther is on Stephen!" He lifted his eyes. "I thank Thee, Lord! Even this storm was decreed for a purpose—to open my eyes to the horrors around me."

The frost relented the next morning. Dark patches appeared on the rooftops. A train hooted as it crossed the Neversink; the tracks were clear. Reverend Crane stamped his feet into his boots. "I shall sit here no longer to be mortified by my own. Out there God's work waits to be done."

Stephen and his father left in a rented sleigh, black Violet pulling staunchly in the shafts. The runners cut deeply; a fine powder blew.

The mare's breath came over her blanketed shoulders in a continuous gray plume.

Reverend Crane, securely bundled in a greatcoat and fur cap, with a thick scarf about his nose and mouth, drove moodily. Beneath the gray-fringed robe, Stephen felt Papa's boot jerking in silent anger.

They clopped across the Main Street bridge. The timbers were glossily treacherous with half-melted ice. Where the sun had cast its warm glance, single pines had recovered their green majesty. Yesterday the entire forest had taken refuge behind the white curtain; today it was advancing verdantly to reclaim its territory. Across the river, the hip of the ridge was studded with larches and hemlocks. Where the shadows of the range had thwarted the sun, the snow was still crusted.

Ascending the hills, the deep lines and the hoofprints they had been following vanished. The runners, crunching firmly, occasionally slipped.

They made six calls and were welcomed everywhere, even when they accidentally drove in at the Davidsons, who were Presbyterians, instead of at the Hartleys, who were Methodists and lived at the next farm. The Davidson children, trudging from the cow-barn with pails of milk, paused to regard them with puffing wonder.

At the Foxes, they stayed to supper. Mary Fox, fine Christian soul, had died of a heart ailment. Her daughter Halma had washed and dressed the body; the widower had laid it out on a table in the coldroom until Mr. Wellington could come by with the hearse-wagon from town.

The body was covered with a thin sheet; the sharp nose seemed frostbitten. "We ain't got no blanket to spare, but she knows that and I don't think she'd mind."

As Stevie ate hungrily, he thought how terribly unfeeling and cruel to leave poor Mrs. Fox out there to freeze. He stroked the ginger-cat, which was drawn up in a friendly ball near the stove, and listened to her purr. Over the farmhouse brooded a gray, frozen sorrow.

"We are late," said Papa as they drove away. The sky was briefly streaked with crimson and raspberry hues. A shutter closed on the setting sun and the light failed. The vast stretches of virgin snow turned faintly blue. Then, like a wall falling, the night dropped from the farther mountain peaks.

A fresh breeze whipped stinging particles. Something nipped Stephen's ears. He looked around as if the frost were taking human shape.

For an hour, they drove rapidly. The moon, like a dull-silvered ball on a Christmas tree, peered over a snow-ledge and sailed into the sky. Shadows threw dark logs across the road. In the open places, the snow rejected the moonlight.

The mare wearied, and her pace lagged. Ascending a hill, she finally gave out. The sleigh, surprised, slid off, and the back runners stuck firmly in a bank. The bells continued to tinkle.

Reverend Crane tugged desperately at the reins. Violet could do no more. He got down and, prudently treading snow, turned her about. The bells jingled weakly and became mute.

"Papa, are we lost?"

"God watches over us."

The roads were bound to be worse as they neared the town; they would have to cross more hills and frozen ruts. A mile back, they had passed the Bailey farm. Reverend Crane began warily to walk the mare, fearful that the sleigh might, on some patch of ice, capriciously shoot forward and upset them. He had turned the vehicle about and trudged a hundred yards when a blast of wind seemed to pierce his chest, and he halted to cough violently.

As he climbed back to his seat and bundled under the rug, a wheel of pain radiated through his breast. Frightened, he sat erect. The white world confronted him mercilessly.

Stevie said, "Mama will be worried."

"God's work cannot wait on women!"

"Solomon will worry."

"I don't think so, boy."

While the moon observed them coldly, man, boy, horse, and sleigh remained motionless on the spinning earth. The night throbbed, trees creaked, little cones dropped from the nearest hemlock.

Stephen became aware that his father was shivering. "We'll freeze!"

The man stirred as if just awakened. He lifted the whip over Violet's back, but would not bring it down. He clucked and tugged weakly on the reins. Violet's bells jingled, her hooves struck, and the sleigh swam ahead.

"Hooray!"

"So say I! Black Violet is a good beast." He coughed lustily, and tears slid from his eyes. From a woodlot, insolent echoes mocked him.

They saw the light at the Baileys long before they located the broad gate in the snow. Dogs began to bark.

A sharp stab in his chest doubled the man over. "Go, boy!" he gasped.

Stephen kicked off the rug and scrambled from the sleigh. He fell headlong into the snow, got up, admiring the gingerbread man he had made, and fell again. He brushed at his coat, ploughed through the drifts, and thrust his shoulder against the gate. He could not budge it, slipped, and fell again. His father's cough was like the complaint of a dull axe against a frozen treetrunk.

He shouted, "Yo! Yo!" as the door of the house opened and a lantern emerged, leading a man.

The Baileys did not often attend church. However, they tithed when crops were good. Fred Bailey, declaring that the sleigh could be left in the road, unhitched Violet and led her to the stable. Mrs. Bailey, a short, wide woman, appeared with a lamp and, shielding the top of the chimney, guided the callers into the house. The dogs continued to bark; Stevie was disappointed that the animals were locked in the barn.

A girl in faded brown calico, with a deer's solemn eyes, ladled soup from an enormous black cast-iron pot. The woman carried the shallow plates to the bare pine table.

Reverend Crane, clutching at his chest, insisted that he was not hungry.

Mrs. Bailey gazed at him reproachfully. "A little, perhaps! What of the boy?" She chattered in a coarse, unpleasant voice.

"Good friends," the minister said with a visible effort, "a few hours of rest—" He lowered his head; the pain was persisting in his left side and radiating down his arm.

So the Baileys put their guests to bed in their own barren room, and went to sleep elsewhere.

"Shall I take off everything?"

The man studied the little figure in the long drawers. "Enough, Stephen. It's bitter cold." He went on absently, "Before anyone is aware of it, you will be a man." He dared not draw a deep breath.

Stevie bounced on the mattress. "It's hard!"

"Sh! They will hear you. It can't matter. Your bones are young."

The boy heard his father's braces snap and garments being removed.

"Now we must pray."

He stared curiously as they knelt beside the bed. In his underwear, his Papa was a little old man.

"Pray, Stephen, pray for your soul!" He remained long on his knees. When he got up, he blew out the lamp. "Now to sleep."

They crept upon the lumpy mattress.

The man groaned as he stretched out. Stephen lay awkwardly at the edge of the bed; he had never shared a bed with his father.

Sometime during the night, he heard hoarse coughing and, rolling over, was surprised not to strike against his Papa; the bed was wider than he had thought. The coughing continued, tearing, hacking, searing. Long after he fell asleep, the rending sound continued in the hollow of his ear.

"Stephen!"

A wintry dawn was at the frosted window, which had been etched elaborately with white feathers and arabesques. Papa's face was haggard, his eyelids red. He was dressed and winding his watch.

71

Mrs. Bailey insisted that they breakfast on fried mush and hot milk. Stephen bolted his food and hoped that she would offer him more. The girl of the night before was standing at the stove, licking her chapped lips, watching hungrily.

"She is my niece," Mrs. Bailey declared in her brassy voice. "Her mother died, and we are saddled with her. She eats like a pig!"

The girl's pleading eyes fixed into Stephen's.

"A child—must—be fed!" Reverend Crane said sternly. "Let her share with us."

The woman knocked a fried slab of mush on a plate. "Eat, Hattie!" She seized the girl's arm.

The boy saw two pearly tears glazing Hattie's eyes. The minister gave her a tender smile. "Where—is her—father?"

"She has no father!" Mrs. Bailey grumbled, rattling the stove-lids. "That's her trouble, if you know what I mean, Reverend."

The girl colored. Her brown calico dress was shabby and torn. Stevie observed a red welt on the thin neck. Other welts scored the bare legs. She had been whipped!

"God is the—Father—of all children!" Reverend Crane insisted painfully.

The cold air affronted his cough. However, it did not affect him harshly until, with the sun shining brazenly on the frozen landscape, they were slipping swiftly toward Port Jervis. Black Violet, renewed by the night's rest, trotted briskly.

"How can she have no father?" Stephen asked shrilly.

"People can be cruel when God has no place in their hearts," his Papa replied, and went into a siege of painful hacking that did not end until they swept into Washington Street. He took shallow, labored breaths, his cheeks red, his eyes peculiarly lustrous.

He mustered enough strength to lead Violet into the stable. Mama, who had been waiting anxiously at the window, cried: "Jonathan!"

Solomon wagged his tail, and thrust his wet nose into the man's hand.

"We stayed over at the Baileys," he coughed. "Good dog!"

She beseeched him to go to bed.

Solomon followed him up the stairs. Mama placed two bricks in the oven, and warmed a fresh nightshirt. Stephen manfully pulled off his father's boots.

"I must write the sermon."

"There will be no sermon until you are well! You must get into your bed."

The silken white hair framed a deathly pale face.

"Stephen, sit beside your father! I must go for the doctor."

The dog put his head over the side of the bed, but Reverend Crane ignored him. He dozed fitfully, to be startled awake by new seizures of stabbing pain.

72

Solomon crawled under the tester-bed and stretched out with his muzzle on his forepaws. Stephen knelt and stroked the dog's head.

He sat on the cane-backed chair and listened to his Papa's stertorous breathing. A red globule oozed from the man's lips. Stevie searched for the handkerchief that was balled up somewhere in his pockets, but dared not touch the sick man.

"Helen!"

"Mama isn't here."

A film of thin gauze had slipped over each blue iris. "The orphan girl—Hattie—at the Baileys—should have—a new home."

The eyes were staring impersonally, as if their owner had retired far behind them. The fingertips picked restlessly at the faded red and green patchwork quilt.

Mama returned with Doctor van Etten. "You may leave now, Stephen."

"Come on, Sol."

The dog would not stir.

"Solomel!"

Still the dog would not move.

"Go, Stephen!"

Angrily, Mrs. Crane poked under the bed with a broomstick. The retriever snarled. She said, "Well!" and gave up. Reverend Crane seemed to hear nothing.

Resentfully, Stephen went out alone to play in the snow. He was forlorn. Below the porch, he shaped a supply of snowballs to store in the woodshed.

After supper, while Mama was in the kitchen, he stood watch at Papa's side. He secretly pushed Solomon's water bowl under the bed. The amber-brown eyes regarded him mournfully.

The dreadful, rasping sound of his father's breathing filled the room with an almost inhuman sound, as if a bellows were being pumped under the quilt. The waxen face was streaked with perspiration. The hands clutched feebly at the chest.

Early Sunday, Stephen heard his father descending the staircase. Solomon padded after him.

"Jonathan! Doctor van Etten is coming soon, and here you rise to go to church!"

"It is my duty."

"You have no sermon!"

"The Lord will provide."

Reverend Crane preached in the morning. His face was pale, but his voice seemed uncommonly strong. At intervals he halted, and perspiration exuded from his scalp and trickled down his forehead.

He had taken his text from Isaiah: "Woe unto him that striveth with his Maker" and, for his theme, "What infidelity must do before it can destroy the Christian religion."

Stevie was awed by Papa's strangely resonant tones. Mama wept. Even Ludie cried.

After the services, Reverend Crane again returned to his bed. Stevie saw him shivering under the covers. Whatever strength Papa had summoned for the preaching seemed to have ebbed from him. His lips had been traced with an indelible pencil. His fingernails had purpled as if a cruel hammer had come cracking down upon each joint. His breathing was one continued hissing, like gas escaping from an open jet.

Doctor van Etten called again. He drew Mrs. Crane into the parlor. "His heart is very weak——"

Stephen scowled; the physician was calmly sitting in Papa's chair! Mama covered her face with her hands, and sobbed.

"Mama, I'm here!"

"Yes, Stephen."

"Will he be better?"

"Soon, Stephen. In God's mercy, soon."

He was roused from a deep sleep. He was certain that he had been awakened. The darkness swirled and coiled; something had touched him. Faceless figures, looming in dimensions that threatened, peopled the room. He touched reality; he was at home, and Papa was ill. His nightshirt dragging, he crept down the hall and shuffled over the cold floor.

Soot had blackened the lamp chimney; the yellow cone of flame bobbed large and unruly. On the threshold, he heard a slow breathing, and reflected, "He's sleeping good!"

It was Mama dozing in a chair at the side of the bed. Her head upon her shoulder, she was respiring through her mouth; yet in her orderly way, her hands were clasped together in her lap.

The bed was empty! Papa was gone. Solomon had disappeared.

Stephen raced downstairs. In the parlor, where a small light burned in the night lamp, his father towered in his nightshirt. He was a figure all rumpled white except for the black family Bible in his fist and the amazing purplish color of his face. The fuchsia tint, which the boy had observed in the fingernails, had stained the hands and suffused through the skin of the forehead and the upper lip.

"Papa!"

Lifting the Bible as if he were exhorting, Reverend Crane abruptly sank into the chair behind him.

Stark dread overwhelmed Stephen. For the first time he was aware that his father was locked with a merciless foe, that he was desperately clinging to the Good Book by which he lived and preached.

"Papa!" But the word froze in his throat as a sigh shook the tormented figure and the eyes stared. The shadows behind the minister bobbed, and Solomon came forward, head raised and panting.

74

"Papa!"

Another wild sigh, and his father's jaw slackened. In the lamp, the flame wavered and went out.

Solomon began to whine and to trot around the room, sniffing as if he had caught the horrible scent. Only then did Stephen realize that his father had died.

CHAPTER **II**

Mama had screamed and torn her hair. She had embraced Papa and clasped his head to her bosom, as if she would save him from the final terror.

Not for hours could Stephen, hugging and petting—"Poor old Sol!"—persuade the creature to take a drink of water. Then the dog lapped so greedily that the sound was like the beating of eggs.

The house filled with neighbors. When the churchbell began to toll, Stephen hurried Solomon across Sussex Street. The day was bright; the spire flashed in the sun.

More people arrived. The men stamped the snow from their boots; the women cried freely even before they had entered the house of sorrow.

Back in the parsonage, someone said, "Take the dog to the woodshed, boy!"

Everyone had authority where the head of the house lay dead.

He marched Solomon into the yard. Not in that dark woodshed all alone! He led the dog to the stable. "You stay with Violet, if she'll let you."

Solomon brushed hard against his leg.

Violet hung her head. "My Papa is a dead man," he informed her. "He is all dead, Violet. I saw."

She gazed at Solomon, and nodded. The dog sank down before her stall. In this sorrow, the animals communed peacefully at last.

Stephen dashed out before their silence could make him cry.

What followed was a conglomeration of mechanical movements and a confusion of solemn faces as he wandered about in the deep gloom. When he was hungry, he hacked off a thick slice of bread and spread it with treacle. No one seemed to notice him.

Even after the undertaker had come and gone, many of the callers lingered. They sat in the room where Papa had died—he lay upstairs calmly under a white sheet—and talked of other dead men they had known. "He was only sixty-one!" Mrs. Cuddleback declared. People in black clothes drifted from room to room.

Unceremoniously, they shooed Stephen from their company. He

went to play with a handful of soldier buttons, but they were cold and meaningless.

In the morning, his uncles, aunts, cousins, and second cousins began to arrive. The train from Newark brought Aggie. In quick succession, there appeared also Townley and Fannie, George, Will and Ted, Burt, Ludie, Uncle Richard and Auntie Jane, Cousin Fred, Cousin Theodore, Cousin Ruth, and Cousin Phoebe. "My Papa is a dead man" went around and around in his mind.

Sometime later, he discovered that the rooms were empty and the blinds were drawn. He sped up the stairs. "Mama!"

On the threshold, he was greeted by a blast of cold air. The windows had been opened; the curtains on the tester-bed were moving. His Papa was gone! He pushed aside the curtains. The naked bed, stripped to the feather-tick, revolted him. His Mama would sleep alone now.

His Papa had been taken to the church, which looked like a vaulted dungeon with a bank of candles. Mama, in black, with a veil over her face, sat on the Mourner's Bench. Other women sat beside her, similarly veiled. Each pair of hands was folded peacefully in a proper lap.

Farther up gleamed silver handles, suspended above a black cloth that draped solemnly to the floor; the long casket seemed to float in the air. Men brought tall tapers in enormous candlesticks. The flames demurred till they were planted firmly at the head and at the foot of the catafalque.

His Papa lay asleep, with his head supported on a violet satin pillow and his black Bible clasped in his hands. His elbows were braced against the sides of the casket as if he intended to arise.

"Is that him?" Stevie asked aloud and stared into the casket. His Papa was dressed in his Sunday suit. His beard was spread, white and silky and neatly brushed; his upper lip was freshly shaven— when did he do *that*? All the wrinkles that had made wavy lines on Papa's brow had disappeared.

He leaned over. The eyelids were curved full, as if large marbles had caused them to bulge. He gasped. Papa had forgotten his spectacles!

Stevie lost track of the days. Papa had died on Monday; services were held in Drew Centennial Church on Thursday. Ludie swore that four ministers had preached and that 1,432 people had filed past the casket. No one had said anything about the Lake of Fire.

At the station, a row of black carriages waited in the snow. A silk-hatted coachman led a hearse with two black-plumed horses to the baggage car. His brothers and some others removed a big box. His Papa had been lying in that box, listening to the wheels clicking over the rails.

76

They drove away slowly; not a drum or a trumpet. Passers-by uncovered their heads; wagons and carts pulled aside. Everyone was kind to the dead.

Another church. "St. James's!" someone said. Another service must be held.

More than a hundred ministers had gathered. The organ played. A voice sang, "Servant of God, Well Done."

Reverend Doctor Hurst, president of Drew Theological Seminary, told about every charge that Papa had served in his thirty-five years in the ministry: "The Parsippany Circuit . . . Asbury . . . Port Richmond . . . Hope . . . Belvedere . . . Orange . . . Trinity . . . Haverstraw . . . Central . . . Morristown . . . Hackettstown . . . Cross Street. . . ."

Bishop Simpson spoke slowly: "He leaves a widow and nine children. The youngest is seven."

"I'm eight!" Stevie indignantly arose, and was promptly pulled down.

Again, minister after minister delivered a eulogy. At last, they were back in the carriages and the casket was safely inside the wagon.

Hours later—or was it the next day?—the cortege filed through a pair of iron gates and wound down a white, tree-lined road. Snow dropped from the branches. On either side rose large stone angels and massive crosses. One angel's cheeks were swollen with puffs of snow, another wore a little frosted cap.

He thought irrelevantly that it was Friday. Was he ever again to get anything to eat? He was famished.

His brothers and Cousin Fred were lifting the casket. Vapor swirled from their lips. At the long, gaping hole, he saw the raw, orange flesh of the earth.

Stevie gazed at the sod which, under the trampling of many feet, had been freed from the clutches of the snow.

As they gathered before the box and the grave, his glance roved to the rows of markers. So many dead! Was everybody's Papa a dead man?

The box was being lowered from gray ropes. Clods thudded. Two red-faced men in overalls appeared with spades and, industriously, began to fill the grave. Their arms swept back and forth.

He felt a withering blast of cold air from among the tombstones and began to scream, noting that his breath exhaled like a steam engine's.

Reverend Van Horne placed a fatherly arm about his shoulder. "He has gone to answer his Master's call, Stephen. He has gone to his reward."

The boy, momentarily, was silenced. Was that the "Call"? Some things they were surely not telling him. He could not fix his attention for long on the many perplexities. The dead must be glad that one more was joining their silent company; the living did not care.

They were withdrawing from the grave, retreating to the carriages, abandoning his Papa.

He was shivering. He had dropped a mitten. While his brothers and sisters clambered to their places, he retraced his steps between the tombstones.

"Stephen!"

He stumbled from one snow-spattered mound to the next. All the monuments seemed alike. He appealed to a silent angel. "Papa!" The stone image, snow on its eyelids, gazed at him blindly.

Townley carried him back. He tried to explain: "My mitten!" His brother would not listen.

On the long ride—to where, since they no longer had a home?— he wept as he snuggled against Aggie's shoulder. If Townley had not come after him he would have found Papa's grave. He could see it, the fresh mound, with his lone mitten stuck there, beckoning.

II. The Silent Dead

*H*E WAS LIVING the quick childhood days when sundown crowds hard on playtime. School, that thief of all leisure, snatched at the sweetest, brightest hours of the daylight. He drifted between games, chores, and book-study, better at the first than at the second, more willing at the second than at the last.

As long as she was officially in mourning, Stephen had his mother to himself. Then the moving began once more. Papa had taken with him to the grave their right to live in the Port Jervis parsonage; they had to give up the house to accommodate the new preacher and his family. Mrs. Crane fled to Roseville with her youngest son.

He grieved for Solomon and for Violet, who had been left with Will and Cornelia, his young wife, in Port Jervis. Stephen was angry with his mother and, vaguely, with his father. Will promptly sold Violet to Mr. Buchanan at the livery stable. And poor Solomon! Townley had been willing enough to take him, but Fannie was grieving—she had lost another infant. She sat home all day in her kimono, with her hair in strings, and complained about everything. Will and Cornelia had two babies, but welcomed Solomon nonetheless.

Stevie yearned for the retriever. He looked wistfully at every dog he passed, or that trotted by. He hoped that Solomon would run away from Will's house. One day, the dog would appear at the door, barking and wagging his tail, the amber-brown eyes shining. Stevie prayed for it.

Mrs. Crane journeyed so often to the cemetery to stand with her freshly-picked violets before the settling grave that Stephen, who went with her, became familiar with the peculiar stillness at Evergreen, each birch and maple and sycamore, and the hydrangeas on the nearby plots. The monuments stood like the bleached bones in some prehistoric wasteland.

He did not understand her. She could not tell him that her life was empty, the future terrifying. The little money that his Papa had left had been caught in the toils of a bank closure; the bit of acreage in Summit could not be sold. The coal shares in Luzerne County that Reverend George Peck had bequeathed to his children might bring in a solid annual income, if she did not have to sell them in a depressed market. This legacy must yield enough to pay for Ludie's and Stephen's education and also for the completion of Burt's medical training. Who would care for her if she became helpless? She, the daughter of one minister, wife of another, sister of a third, and the niece of three other ministers and a Bishop, was driven to apply to the Newark Conference for the paltry aid afforded the widows of deceased pastors. The five dollars for each year that Jonathan Townley Crane had served the church was her due, but she despised the cold odor of charity. Reluctantly, she went back to Port Jervis to live with Will and his wife.

Cornelia meant well. "Mother Crane, you've toiled long enough. Fourteen children, and never a home to call your own for more than two or three years at a time. Here I want you never to lift a hand. Let me serve you!"

Mrs. Crane shuddered. The threat of superannuation hung over her constantly. Hers was the quiet, resigned arrogance and the tight-lipped pride of the Peck family. She attended every service at Drew Church and listened closely to the new preacher. She was a bishop's niece, so Mr. Blakeslee was wary; Mary Helen Crane was an able speaker herself.

She took Stephen to Syracuse to visit her uncle, Bishop Jesse Truesdell Peck, who had fallen on an icy street while in Detroit, a grievous mishap for a septuagenarian who weighed more than three hundred pounds. Mary Helen Crane was his favorite niece.

Between coughing seizures, the white-haired giant with the bald dome and the great sideburns boomed at Stephen. He was so corpulent that he filled the entire bed from side to side and from head to foot. When his massive chest heaved, the bedslats creaked; when he coughed, the bedposts threatened to part.

The acrid odor in the room made Stephen think of Violet the mare. He stared at the enormous swollen ankles, swaddled in yellow bandages, which were elevated on a board.

The Behemoth sat up to the height of the bedstead and gave the boy his blessing. He wriggled his knobby fingers in the air, and the cough, as if exorcised, subsided.

Auntie Persis, a plump robin of a woman, served tea, which surprised Stephen. Tea in the house of a Bishop! In a moment of dry emotion, she clasped the boy's head in her soft little hands and kissed his forehead so determinedly that his temples throbbed.

For supper, Auntie Persis produced a large roast fowl, with a sage dressing, mashed potatoes, mashed yellow turnips, peas, carrots—swimming in cream—hot biscuits, apple butter, grape jam, and, for dessert, a fruit pie of astonishing dimensions.

Stephen was ready to sip his tea.

"You do not need it," his mother declared as Auntie Persis staggered from the room with a tray of second helpings for the invalid. They heard her puffing up the stairs, her tread camouflaged by the coughing of the invalid who was impatiently awaiting her. "A hearty man, the Bishop!" Auntie Persis said proudly.

In the morning, Mrs. Crane asked for hot gruel and milk. Stephen, who had dreamed of the enormous dinner all night, was disappointed. Upstairs, he saw his Uncle Bishop, defended by a napkin the width of a pillowcase, attacking a pyramid of buttermilk pancakes that dripped with melted butter and honey.

A week later, *The Christian Advocate* devoted a paragraph to the virtues of his Great-uncle. Bishop Peck had announced that he was bequeathing all his property to Syracuse University, which he had helped to found. The light in Mary Helen Crane's soul flickered unsteadily; one could not depend on relatives, not even a bishop.

Three months later, while Stephen played happily with Solomon and his mother nursed her grievances, the enormous Bishop, after another hearty meal, dropped off to sleep and went on to meet his Maker in Holy Triumph.

Mama decided to offer her services to several newspapers as a reporter on the doings at Ocean Grove. "I shall earn our bread," she informed her sons.

Will was hurt. "You shouldn't, Mother!"

"Writing is not employment when the heart and the spirit are in it, Will. Your Father and your Grandpa George both wrote. We come honestly by the gift of the pen." Grandpa George had been editor of the Methodist *Quarterly Review* for eight years and of the *Advocate* for twelve years.

When the New York *Tribune* and the Philadelphia *Press* responded favorably, she glowed and began to send out her articles. To Stephen's delight, checks for four dollars, sometimes for five, began to come in by post for "Mrs. Doctor Crane." She declined further aid from the Newark Conference.

She observed now that Cornelia, devoted daughter-in-law, was spoiling Stephen. What boy required a blue windmill jar of cookies marked "Secret" to dip into whenever it pleased him, which was five times a day? Furthermore, Mother Crane had her own proven methods of raising babies—fourteen, mind!—and if Cornelia thought it wiser to permit little Helen to shriek and to wail rather than to fall asleep at her grandma's bosom——

Will, thriving young lawyer, could have mediated with greater success between two railroads claiming the same right-of-way.

Back to Newark the widow went, pausing again at Evergreen Cemetery. While his mother communed at the grave, Stephen wandered among the soldiers' headstones, searching idly for familiar names. There might be one marked "Stephen Crane." At thirteen, soldiery seemed a sensible career. In Orange Square, big Rufe Coleman had boasted that he was not yet fifteen when he had served at Manassas as a drummer boy.

Through the trees, a rank of soldiers in gray advanced stealthily. He saw the smoke of their rifles and heard the crack of the balls. He clutched at his heart. "I'm dying, Mama!" She would bring violets to his grave, too. Suffering deliciously, he sank to his knees and fell headlong. The grass tickled his face. He would expire in a pool of blood. The phantoms vanished. Over an oak thicket, the red sun stared balefully.

An urgent summons from Nellie—"Please come!"—brought them to Asbury Park. Nellie's marriage to Van Nortwick had abruptly shattered.

Stephen heard weeping at his sister's door. The next morning, pale as a dandelion gone to seed, Van was leaving, with his trunks, his books, and his tennis racket. He kissed Mrs. Crane's cheek, waved to Stephen, and departed.

He knew what separated meant, but the word divorce, which came later, mystified him. Anyway, he liked Asbury Park better than Newark. They were near Ocean Grove, where the religious news was created daily for Mama to report to the newspapers.

Nellie kept to her room, toyed with her embroidery and her painting, and ate her way through hidden caches of cookies and marshmallows. In the back yard, she could lie for hours in the hammock, munching from a supply of sweets in her pocket as if voracious feeding could mend a broken heart.

Meanwhile, Mary Helen Crane consulted railroad timetables and whirled away on new missions as a lecturer on temperance topics. She traveled to address meetings in Philadelphia and New York and in thirty villages between these points. Frequently, she packed Stephen along; at least, there was the train ride.

However, the meetings at home irritated him. He missed the warmth of the old family gatherings. Instead, on Tuesdays and Thursdays, the "sisters" sailed into the parlor to sit on the edges of thin chairs, their Christian backs as rigid as their parasols. They inveighed against the liquor traffic, the tobacco habit, and other social evils. They extolled Miss Frances Willard, the temperance leader, as lavishly as Ludie praised "Bob" Ingersoll. "If Colonel Ingersoll came in tipsy," declared Ludie, "they would kiss him on his bald head and forgive him for being an infidel!"

Now and then Townley appeared, cheerfully unkempt. "You dress like a tramp!" Nellie said, shocked. Townley grinned. He looked unwashed; he shaved when it pleased him and left his mustaches untrimmed for weeks. His slouch hat, with its soiled crown, seemed to have been trodden by unfriendly mongrels. He often lacked buttons on shirt or coat.

Mama pointed accusingly at the stained fingers. "Nicotine!"

"Only cigarettes, Mother. Might as well burn in this world as the next!"

"And your clothing! What is Fannie thinking of to let you out in such a state?"

"Fannie," he drawled, "is thinking of as little as possible. When she isn't sick, she is sullen."

"What happened to you, Townley?" she moaned. "To the promise you showed?"

His grin implied that he had made defeat his triumph.

Her sons were rebels. As long as Reverend Crane had been alive, they had feared his iron gaze. Now, except for Will, who was an established lawyer, and for Burt, who was struggling through the College of Physicians and Surgeons in New York, they were all drifting. Ludie, the clever rascal, had announced that he would become a railroader. Even poor Nellie! A pity there had been no child to cement the marriage bonds. She was, however, reasonably proud of Aggie, who was teaching in the Red Bank schools.

Anyway, there was hope for Stephen. If the boy were not so changeable! One day a temperance meeting excited him; the next day, he yawned and squirmed, or fell asleep in the audience, while she was exhorting on the speaker's platform.

He was fortunate to have baseball. The game drew out the stings and soothed the rankling hurts. The singular virtue of baseball was that it absorbed him entirely. It shut out not merely the world of the dead but also the world of all the living who were not on the diamond. Step on the field, give a holler, "C'mon, play ball!" and the earth stops spinning; to watch a few innings, even the sun lazed in its course.

Never a poor game of baseball; played under the open sky, each game was its own supreme joy. Baseball inspired great deeds in running, pitching, sliding, throwing. It fired every player with a holy zeal—for more baseball. The game was everything; it leveled everyone. Even the final score was only a triumph of numbers. The pleasure was built into every play, from the catch to the pitch, to the running; nothing else mattered.

Stephen trotted to center field like a foal. He roamed, stretched, pulled at his cap, socked fist into leather, leaped up, shouted, grinned. "Pla-ay ball!" The batter took a swing. Crack! The bat met the ball which, surprised, flew back, back. "There it goes!" High, high— "Mine!" Stephen bellowed, and tracked it in the sun. The ball, sighting him, plummeted. *Zow!* It stuck in his glove. The gladness that comes with a first-rate catch! Now the throw. Smack at the first baseman! A yell of animal joy signaled that perfection had been achieved. Stephen, hugging himself, hooted at the sky and trotted around again. The sun smiled down.

CHAPTER 13

As Stephen entered the house, the night air whistled through the gap in his teeth. He had fought Charlie Zimmerman and had lost a front tooth. His stockings were ripped, his shirt bloody, his trousers covered with dirt and grass stains. Prudently, he had waited until dark to come home. He wished that he dared to climb to the second floor by the porch railing and the rainpipe and slink to his room. From the parlor, he could hear Aggie's voice.

"Mama, he's always wanted one."

"We have no money for luxuries," Mama was insisting. "A girl who has to make her living by teaching in high school, and has only the pittance she can manage to save against the lonely years ahead——"

"I may not have lonely years, Mother!" Aggie spoke as if she relished her loneliness; indeed, as if she anticipated impending spinsterhood. "I may not."

"Of course, Agnes Elizabeth, you may still marry."

"At twenty-eight, who will marry me?"

"Twenty-seven!"

Aggie shrugged. "Stevie is lonely. His dog was left behind. Every stray he brings in is at once driven out. Why shouldn't he have some creature of his own to love and care for?"

"He needs discipline, not a prize for wayward behavior. As for love, let him keep his heart pure and love the Lord. I have no time to pamper him. Your father's work, remember, Agnes Elizabeth, must go on as well as my poor hands and heart may continue it."

"I gave Mr. Randall ten dollars."

"Aggie!" Stephen bounced into the room. Mr. Randall was the owner of the livery stable where they had the marvelous pony. "Did you buy it?"

"Go to bed!" his mother called sternly. "You idled all afternoon and you failed to come to supper. To bed this instant!"

At the head of the stairs, he paused to eavesdrop.

"Did you see his clothes? Torn and soiled, as usual. Every day new mischief. Do you realize how disobedient he has become since your father died? And you wish to reward him! Besides, the pony costs fifty dollars."

"We will manage the rest."

"We!" the woman cried. "Not one penny from me!"

Nellie, walking in on the dispute, offered to contribute five dollars. "It will keep him from the beach. I don't need his sand on my sketches."

"I have nothing more to say!" Mrs. Crane shrilled.

"Mama!" Nellie snapped. "Even Papa let the boy have his dog."

Within a week, thanks to Ted, Will, Burt, and Townley, the money was raised.

The day Aggie was ready to pay the balance, Mama left to address a temperance meeting in Camden. "I've washed my hands of the whole matter," she announced. "Ask him where he lost his tooth! Walked into a pump handle, indeed!"

They watched Mrs. Handley, the pastor's wife, drive her off to the station. Mama sat erect, her traveling case up-ended beside her in the gig.

"Doesn't she like me?" Stephen clung to Aggie.

"Of course she does!" Her voice quavered. "She grieves and is so unhappy!"

The pony, small, white and chunky, with wild rolling eyes, was called Pudgy. Stephen inspected him while Aggie counted out the bills.

Mr. Randall, a sharp-nosed man who sported a black and white checked vest, reached for the leather saddle with the brass pommel.

"Saddle don't go. It's another ten, if he wants it."

Aggie clutched her money. "Heavens and mercy! I can do no more, Mr. Randall. That was the price!"

"Another ten dollars."

Her lips quivered. "Come, Stephen!"

The boy's temper flashed. "Listen, Mister, I heard you. You said 'pony and saddle'! What's a promise for?"

The man burst into laughter. "All right, young fellow, all right! Can't blame me for tryin'. Take the saddle."

"Thanks, Mister," he grumbled. He got one foot into a stirrup, waited for a boost up, and rode out proudly. With a curt nod to the livery-stable owner, Aggie tripped after him.

The sky was a flawless blue, with a light breeze wafting the briny smell of the sea. He tugged on the reins and felt himself growing taller in the saddle.

As he pulled up to let a phaeton pass near Steinbach Brothers' store on Main Street, he waved to the driver in a comradely style.

Pudgy decided to trot. Stevie bounced up and down, the street and the houses shattering into short views. The wind sang in his teeth. He shouted: "Pudgy! Pudgy!" He knew that he would become the boldest of riders.

On her return from the temperance meeting, Mama said coolly, "Remember to thank your brothers and sisters, Stephen. Their money does not come easily to them, nor to anyone. Not every boy has such a loyal family!"

That evening, he sat at the table with pen and paper and wrote his thank-you notes. Aggie watched him make his words large and clear.

"I'll be a writer," he declared, studying his first sheet, "like Townley."

"And Ludie," Aggie said loyally.

"You could choose a better example than either!" Nellie retorted.

Mama broke in, "Sign your letters 'Steve,' not 'Stephen Crane' as if you were twenty years old!"

"My name is Stephen Crane," he replied stubbornly. When he had finished, he covered another sheet of paper with "Stephen Crane, Stephen Crane, Stephen Crane," and admired it.

One night, not long after Aggie had bought him the pony, he dreamed that he was on a raft in a flood of waters. A shrieking wind blew. Houses were submerged to the rooftops; only the crowns of the trees protruded in the swirling flood. He bobbed up and down and heard the slurp of water at the edge of the raft, and saw it oozing through the cracks in the timbers.

"Stevie! Stevie!"

He dared to stand up, although the current of the river—it *was* a river!—threatened to pitch him overboard. "I'm coming!" he shouted. "Where are you?"

"Stevie! Stevie!"

Aggie was lying on her back, in her nightgown, on another raft! He looked for an oar, or a piece of wood. He pulled at a floating spar and paddled feverishly.

"Stevie! Stevie!"

He heard a great roaring of waters. They were approaching a waterfall or a dam. He felt the insidious strength of the raging white river pushing the raft.

"I'm coming!" he screamed. "I'm coming!" But she continued to lie there, calling his name, as if from some terrible distance: "Stevie! Stevie!"

He bellowed into the wind. Papa's silver watch floated by, the chain trailing; he could hear the works ticking. The black hands were as close together as the feet of a housefly.

The roar became louder. Aggie was trying to rise. Suddenly, the speed of her raft increased. It was lifted high into the air, and dropped. She gazed clearly into his eyes: "I told you, Stephen. I told you, you'd never come!" Then she disappeared from sight.

His raft continued to drift and drift. He stirred and awakened. It had been another hideous dream.

Ludie appeared. He announced that he had persuaded Townley to help him edit and publish a little newspaper for the resorts which they would call *The Summer Capital*.

Mama approved. Townley had occasionally given article assignments to Will and to Burt; now he would help Ludie, who strolled about in an ambling gait that mimicked Townley's and boasted that he would call upon every merchant on the Jersey coast to solicit advertising. He would make his fortune as a newspaperman.

In the stable, Ludie finally inspected Pudgy. "So that's your pony. Aggie gets you everything!"

He examined the animal closely. "He's not a pony!" He exploded, "He's a little horse!"

"He's a pony!"

"He's not! This Pudgy is a baby horse. You just wait until he grows up!"

Stephen gazed at Pudgy as if the animal had deliberately misled him. Pudgy hung his head.

Taking turns in the saddle, they went as far as Old Wreck Pond near Sea Lake, where people gathered each summer to celebrate Big Sea Day on the second Saturday in August. Ludie, who had grown tall, looked ungainly in the saddle. He sat hunched up like a jockey and made Pudgy gallop while Stevie had to chase after them.

When Pudgy had to be rested, they let him graze, and sprawled under a tree.

Stephen picked up the crop. "I say he's a pony. "I'm going to teach him to do tricks. "Pudgy!" he called, and touched the pony's hindquarters. "*Sit!*"

Instantly, Pudgy froze, lowered his haunches and sat down.

"Hey!" shouted Ludie.

"Good Pudgy! I knew you could do it." Stevie flung his arms out and did a cartwheel. "Hooray! I taught him a trick!"

Ludie advanced. The pony was sitting as docile as any trained dog. "You couldn't teach him that with one command!"

"I did! I saw a man do it in the circus." He touched the pony's shoulder. "Now, Pudgy, get *up!*"

Pudgy promptly got up.

Stephen howled. He rubbed his nose against the pony's muzzle ecstatically. "You're the smartest——"

"Shut up!" Ludie growled.

"He does tricks!" Stephen shrieked. "I'll take him to the circus!"

"You don't have to," Ludie grumbled. "He must have come from one. He's a trained pony."

"Do you think so? I'll bet——"

"He probably got too old for the circus, and was sold."

"You said he was a young horse!"

"Well, I didn't know. I hadn't counted his teeth."

"Oh," said Stephen, impressed, and slipped his tongue into the gap in his own teeth. "I could run away and make a pony show with him." He slapped his sides. "I'll go to Port Jervis and get Solomon, too."

"Let's sit down and think it over. Always sit down when you want to think."

Ludie placed something between his lips. A puff of smoke issued. He exhaled and, with a grin, held up the cigarette. "Sweet Caporal!"

Stephen relapsed into a stunned silence.

"Want to try?"

"Isn't it a sin?"

Luther shook his head. "If you're afraid——"

"I'm not afraid of any old thing you're not afraid of."

He got a mouthful of smoke, coughed, and waved his hands.

"Blow! Blow it out!"

"Is—that—all—there is—to it? What do you do it for?"

Ludie twinkled. "It's good for my corns."

"It's like smokehouse smoke, and not half as good." Stephen ruminated. If it was not sin, perhaps it was punishment. "Maybe there isn't any fire in hell either, only smoke."

Ludie roared. "That's good. They don't fry you, they only smoke your hams!"

They grinned at each other. The miracle of Pudgy had been temporarily forgotten.

CHAPTER 14

Aggie was lying in the hammock between the two trees in the yard. She watched them lead Pudgy into the stable, and beckoned to Ludie.

"Rose Sinnett and her family are giving a picnic, Luther. She wants you to come as her guest."

He tensed. "Are you going?"

"She didn't ask me."

"Then I won't go!"

"You should."

He reached for the hammock and gently rocked it. "I won't go without you."

"You must, Ludie! You're a man. Someday you'll be getting married."

90

"I won't leave you!" he muttered darkly. He pushed harder at the hammock. "I won't." They had been playing in that hammock, which had been transported from one home to the next, since their childhood.

"Don't, Luther! What if I should get married and go away? What would you do then?"

He gazed at her angrily and swung her higher.

"Don't, Ludie!" she cried. "Don't, I'm getting dizzy!"

"If you get married, I'll come to live with you!"

"Don't!" she shrieked. She tried to turn, floundered, and uttered a frantic appeal, "Please, don't!"

"Promise!" he called and sent her still higher. "Promise!"

At the highest point of the swing, Stephen saw Aggie's foot come over the edge. She was squirming on her stomach.

"Promise!" Ludie shouted, his hands open to send her back into the air again.

Suddenly the hammock seemed to tilt.

Stephen yelled.

At one end, the ropes snapped. The hammock dropped. They heard the thud as their sister landed in the grass.

Stephen came running.

Aggie was lying crumpled on her back, one leg twisted strangely beneath her.

"She's hurt!"

"I asked you to promise——" Ludie groaned. Tears streamed from his eyes as he knelt beside her.

"Ludie, she's hurt!"

The older youth pulled the hem of her gown decently over the black-stockinged legs. "Aggie!"

She did not reply.

He slipped his hands under her shoulders. A scream of pain tore from her lips.

"Aggie!" He kissed her cheek.

"My back!"

"Put your arms around my neck."

As he got her up, she sagged against his chest, moaning piteously.

"Aggie, what have I done?"

"Ludie, you're hurting her!"

The girl had fainted in Ludie's arms.

"Stevie, get somebody! Aggie, Aggie!"

He stood there, trying to support her, his mouth pressed to her hair, his features contorted from fear and anguish. "Aggie, I didn't do it. The ropes broke. Ask Stevie!"

Mama helped Ludie carry Aggie indoors. Later, Doctor Schwann arrived. Luther, weeping bitterly at the bedside, was dismissed.

Aggie seemed to have injured her spine.

Six months later, Aggie was walking with two canes. Doctor Schwann said that her vertebrae had been damaged in the fall. The injured area would never heal properly; she was fortunate that the spinal cord had not been severed. She *might* be able to return next year to her class at the Asbury Park High School.

Over family protests, she went to Newark to call upon Doctor Ordway, a bone practitioner who was reputed to have mended cases far worse than hers. Since extended exercises were involved in the Ordway course of treatment, she took a room at a local boarding-house. She proposed to live there quietly for the next sixty days.

Ted, who had married and settled in Lakeview, was nearby if she required help; he was devoted and called upon her every week. Mama, on her travels between New York and Asbury Park, brought fine curtains to hang on the single window; also a few green plants, an afghan, and a tintype of Papa to grace the bare room.

Ludie still blamed himself for her fall, although everyone agreed that the ropes had been frayed and that he was not responsible.

Over a holiday weekend, Stephen was permitted to take the train to Newark to visit his sister.

Mrs. Cornwall, the landlady, a thin-faced little woman, opened the door.

"It's time someone came!" She pushed steel combs into her hair. "She's been sick for three days, and not a soul has been near her!"

He took the stairs two at a time and raced down the hall to the back bedroom.

Aggie was asleep, bundled there under the red quilts, although it was the end of May and warm outdoors. Her head was tossed to one side; her lips were parted.

"Aggie!"

The green window shade was drawn halfway. He tiptoed, and sniffed. She had been taking medicine!

The room was furnished with a large brass bed that was sadly tarnished, an oak bureau with a dressing mirror, and a narrow ward-robe. On the marble washstand stood an ironstone ewer and wash-basin and Papa's silver toilet articles. Neat Aggie! She never left a stocking or a shirtwaist or a stray hairpin around. Across the trunk marched a row of books, her *Mill on the Floss, Pendennis,* and *David Copperfield,* in the center. On the bedside table stood a bottle of red medicine, a glass of water, the tintype of Papa, and her black leather Bible.

He sat down on the cane-bottomed chair. It creaked under him.

"Aggie?"

"Stevie?" she whispered. Her voice was weak.

"I'm here, Ag!"

He brushed his hand over the chestnut hair. Her lips tried to smile.

He lightly ran his thumb over her eyelids, as she used to caress him when his eyes ached.

She stirred feverishly. Her eyes were glassy; pink wafers had bloomed on her cheeks. "I'm—very—warm."

He pressed the back of his hand to her forehead. She seemed afire. Helplessly, "What should I do, Aggie?"

"In the bureau—Stevie—a nightgown."

Her undergarments were folded neatly in the drawers. "A nightgown?" He held it up before her.

She threw back the quilt, and gasped. "I'm so warm."

"You're already wearing a nightgown."

"I must change. Help me!"

He helped her sit up. With an effort, she tugged the other gown from beneath her. Her teeth were chattering.

"Please turn," she said primly. Beads of perspiration dotted her upper lip.

As he listened to the rustling and straining of the bed, a glint of light shot across his eyes. Facing the mirror over the bureau, he could see her undressing. The cords of her neck were rigid, her bosom white and divided. He stared at the pink aureoles. She was a different Aggie undressed; his sister was a woman.

"Help me!"

He turned back eagerly. She slipped an arm about his neck. He put his hand between her shoulder blades and was shocked to feel a hard lump. No wonder she could not walk erect.

She fell back exhausted. The nightgown she had taken off was drenched with perspiration. He hung it on a wooden peg behind the door.

The dark circles under her eyes alarmed him. Aggie had rarely been sick; before her fall, she had never been bedridden. He watched her mouth. The lips were cracked and split. He was suddenly terrified.

"Aggie!" He placed his ear against her bosom. Her heart was beating strongly. He poured water on a face-cloth and sponged her forehead. He patted the damp cloth on her eyelids and about her nostrils. "Good?" He held it gently against one temple, then against the other. She almost smiled.

A dray horse was clopping down the street; the heavy cart groaned. A sparrow flitted past the windowsill. Water was running somewhere in the house. A cat was meowing. A fly walked up the wallpaper.

He straddled the chair and supported his chin on his folded arms. She was lying with her legs apart, every curve of her figure outlined; she did not seem to know it. She was sleeping deeply now; he had come in time.

Her eyes opened.

"Aggie!"

"Is Papa home?" she murmured weakly.

He shook his head. Was she delirious? How could one tell?

"I'm hot!" she complained.

He pulled the red blanket away. Her gown was again soaked with perspiration. Moments later, she was trembling again, complaining that she was cold.

He strode from one side of the bed to the other. "What should I do?"

"Warm me!"

He pressed his cheek against hers. The room was stifling hot, yet she was shivering. He buried his lips in her hair; she smelled of a clothespress. "Aggie, Aggie, don't be sick!"

She was weeping.

Stephen felt himself quaking. "Aggie, should I call somebody?" He was frightened by the two thin streams of tears.

She did not reply.

He knelt at the side of the bed and prayed. The light was fading. He trimmed the wick and lit the lamp. The shadows clung to the wall as the flame bobbed, then crept away and let soft yellow light caress her.

He touched her forehead. She was burning.

"Papa!" she muttered.

Quaking now, and afraid of the unknown, he sped to the hall and thundered down the stairs. He hammered at the landlady's door.

"Who is it?"

"Stephen Crane. We've got to get a doctor for my sister."

Mrs. Cornwall came out in a long green wrapper. She had been putting her hair in curlers and looked like a cross little girl.

"I told you that she was sick all week. I said, 'Go home to your mother!' I pleaded with her."

He sprinted into the warm twilight. A bread-crust moon hung over the trees. Midges were clouding the streetlamps.

He rapped at the door to which Mrs. Cornwall had directed him. "Doctor! Doctor Mulhausen! Hurry! My sister! Mrs. Cornwall said to come!"

A half hour or more passed before the doctor arrived. He was a bony-faced man in a Prince Albert, with a waxed imperial and pince-nez, and a gold-braided watch-chain draped across his waistcoat. Black bag in hand, he marched gravely up the stairs.

At the foot of the brass bed, he growled, "Up! up! The lamp!" He looked grimly at the patient, and stroked his imperial; on his middle finger gleamed a diamond-studded ring. He turned to the landlady: "She has been like this how long?" He opened his bag and ordered Stephen to leave.

In the hall, the boy struggled with dark fears. He was vaguely bitter at everyone, at Mama for being away, at Papa for having died, and at the mysterious fever that had stricken his sister.

"Come in now." Mrs. Cornwall had stepped out. "What did I tell you? She's very sick! I say that she should be moved to a hospital."

Doctor Mulhausen produced a vial; one teaspoonful in water every four hours. "She must not be moved, Mrs. Cornwall." He pursed his lips. "Not be moved!"

He addressed Stephen. "You are the brother? You must tell your family to come at once."

The woman, glancing angrily at the physician, instructed Stephen to go to the telegraph office.

"I've only got my railroad ticket and fifty cents."

She kindly advanced him two dollars. "What shall I do with you?"

When he returned, the landlady was attempting to feed Aggie a beaten egg in warm milk. She forced two teaspoonsful past the invalid's lips. Then the girl was sleeping again, her head limp on the pillow.

Mrs. Cornwall offered Stephen the leather couch in the parlor.

He refused to leave Aggie's room.

"Well, you're not a child, are you?"

She brought him a featherbed and a pillow. "I'm a widow keeping lodgers for a living. I'll have to ask your mother for an extra twenty-five cents." She bit her tongue. "I'm upset, boy. I'm not well myself, and a thing like this is not good for lodgers. They come and go. Is she the only sister?"

He said yes, then quickly said no. "I've got one more."

"Anything I've said, you shouldn't worry. She'll be smiling again in a week or two. Don't forget to take off your shoes." Her voice trailed as she retreated from the room. "If you need me, knock at my door."

He was too weary to undress. He turned the lamp low and stretched out on the featherbed which the woman had placed on the floor. He was calmer now that the doctor had called. Aggie would get well. She was breathing quietly.

Somehow he counted the hours; when the clock struck for the fourth time, he got up promptly. "Aggie!" She would not open her eyes.

He sat numbly at her bedside until the clock struck the fifth hour. Again he could not awaken her. He forced the medicine into her mouth; the liquid dribbled down her chin. Through his tears, he pleaded and tried again. She moaned but did not swallow.

He would not give up. "The doctor said——" He could not reach her. The Aggie he knew, his Aggie, was hidden somewhere within the tortured flesh. He placed the glass on the night table.

He watched the dawn filter through the window. He blew out the lamp, and new shadows sprang alive in every corner.

His mother, stiff-backed and carrying a small brown satchel, arrived at eleven o'clock. Fortunately, she had returned to Asbury Park a day earlier than expected.

"Aggie will be all right, Mama," Stephen assured her. Then, wavering, "Won't she?"

At noon, Burt appeared. In the parlor, he talked importantly to Doctor Mulhausen. Stephen admired his comfortable manner as he consulted the physician.

Mrs. Crane was summoned to their conference. Burt urged her to call Doctor Vincent Graves, a Hoboken physician who had recently moved to Newark and was a friend of Doctor Darlington, his preceptor at the College of Physicians and Surgeons. They agreed not to send for Doctor Ordway.

That afternoon, a hospital wagon appeared. Two attendants fetched a stretcher. At Mama's instructions, the patient was removed from the bed and carried down the stairs.

Will and Nellie, who had just arrived, packed Aggie's belongings. Burt, bitterly disapproving of the transfer, argued with his mother inside the wagon. In two carriages, the others followed them for the ride to Ted's home in Lakeview.

Mame, Ted's wife, seemed to be expecting them. Aggie, who had not awakened since the previous evening, was put to bed in an upstairs room.

"Is she better? Is she better?" Stephen repeated.

"What the Lord wills, His will be done!" his Mama said in a hollow voice. She went to gaze out the window as if she expected a deliverer to appear.

In her prayer book she read silently, her features so placid that the boy was confident that Aggie would get well immediately. He, too, prayed, but through clenched teeth.

Doctor Graves, a tall clean-shaven man with furrowed cheeks and an aseptic smile, finally arrived.

Brusquely, he accosted Burt. "Crane, a full report, please!" He lowered his head as Burt spoke, frowned and showed the edges of his teeth. "Hm, hm! So!" Only then did he approach Aggie.

When he finally addressed them, it was in a thin, high voice, his tone melancholy. "Medical science, Madam, is, alas, a poor weapon against the invisible forces that harass the human frame. We walk in the night."

He took Burt aside and muttered, "Cerebro-spinal——" Stephen thought he also said, "Meningitis," or some word that sounded like that.

After Doctor Graves had left, Burt confronted his mother awkwardly. In the morning, he would consult his professors in New York. The woman did not reply.

The sick girl seemed to be deeply unconscious. Sometimes, frag-

96

ments of sentences tumbled from her lips. Once, in her delirium, she pleaded, "Papa, Papa! don't be angry with me!"

Mrs. Crane shuddered. "Hush, child!" Her face had set into a mask of grief. She ordered Nellie to the parlor to console the brothers, and swayed back and forth with the open Bible on her lap.

Stephen wedged himself into a corner and perched on a trunk where she would not notice him. For days now, everyone had been praying and nothing had happened. They were all here, why didn't they do something?

That evening, Burt complained bitterly to Ted and to Townley that Aggie should ever have been allowed to go to Doctor Ordway. He explained the complicated illness in medical terms. "Now she's having convulsions," he groaned. "Convulsions!"

Past midnight, Mame awakened Stephen. "Go to your mother, Steve."

Aggie lay peacefully, her face the pallor of a tallow candle. His mother, her eyes like glowing coals, was sitting upright in the chair at the bedside.

"Mama!"

She motioned him toward the bed.

"Aggie?" he called softly. He squinted at the waxen features. That could not be Aggie.

He spun about bewilderedly. "Is she—is she——"

His mother nodded, her shoulders trembling.

He stared blankly at the dead body of his sister, and rushed from the room and out of the house.

He tramped up one lane and down the next, staring aimlessly into the shadows. He walked, for miles it seemed, until, on the verge of collapse, he came out on a broad thoroughfare where the dark houses faced each other like two rows of up-ended trunks on a railroad platform. A red lamp shone at the far end. He raced across an intersection, and trotted over cobblestones. He fled past blind store fronts. A signboard overhead creaked a rusty warning.

Crickets were whirring. Against the glass, through which the pale yellowish-green of the streetlight shone, a moth was hurtling itself desperately. The wings fluttered and buzzed. At the base of the cast-iron pole, in the shallowly illumined penumbra, dozens of other moths lay stricken.

He raced on, his shoes echoing so loudly that he thought a battalion of hostile feet thudded after him. He was in total darkness, with a lamppost at one end of the street and another far away. He crouched in the darkness between a way to come in and a way to go out.

Velvety shadows brushed his cheek. He leaped to his feet, and began to run again. He had been walking, running, for hours; he felt nauseated, lightheaded. The night was lifting, the gray dawn denuding the buildings. The streetlights had shrunken. In the elms, a robin was laughing. His sobbing eased.

Somewhere, horses neighed and stomped, and wagon wheels groaned. The last shadows skipped away. In the early light, the houses were swelling, the trees growing taller.

His prayers had accomplished nothing. He would never pray again. Never! Never again!

Slowly, he retraced his steps to Ted's house. As he reached it, a fiery red ball emerged where the throat of the street narrowed before him.

CHAPTER 15

Aggie had died on Tuesday. On Friday afternoon, services were held at St. James's Church on Broad Street in Elizabeth. She had been laid out the evening before in the parlor of Ted's home, in the same white gown that she had worn for the valedictory address at Hackettstown. To Stephen, she was pale but beautiful with the Bible clasped in her stiffened hands.

At Evergreen Cemetery, the family stood in silence as the casket was lowered into the grave. Townley kept a firm arm about Luther's waist, for Ludie had hysterically threatened to fling himself into the pit.

Ludie's face, swollen from three days of weeping, was pasty white, his lips puffed. Occasionally, a lone tear slid down his cheek.

Death had struck down so many that Evergreen Cemetery was filling up rapidly. The nearby farm, part of the Lyons tract, had been transformed into additional acres of markers, shafts, crosses and angels. If Death continued to strike, Stephen reflected, the whole world might come to an end, because there would be no space for the living. If he wanted to lie beside Aggie, he would have to die early. With seven Cranes already interred, how would nine more, including Mama, be buried in such a small plot of earth? If the family died in order, Nellie first, then George, then Townley, then Will, then Ted, then Burt, then Ludie, where would they bury *him*?

Stephen wondered if anyone had found the mitten that he had lost on the day of Papa's funeral.

As they retreated to the carriages, the sky became deep blue with islands of white clouds floating dreamily.

Perhaps when the cemetery was deserted, Aggie would arise. She would fold her skirts beneath her and sit on a bench to enjoy the lovely summer day, or read a book.

Angrily, Stephen dismissed his thoughts. Aggie had died forever.

Ludie had kindled a bonfire, and was tossing papers and pamphlets into the flames.

Stephen watched the yellow shooting tongues. "You're burning up Bob Ingersoll!"

"Let him burn!"

"Why, Ludie, why?"

His brother gazed at him solemnly, fresh tears brimming. "I was wicked, Steve."

Stephen nodded gravely. He had known that about Ludie for a long time.

Ludie opened the precious cigar boxes that contained the forbidden trinkets he had amassed through the years.

"Everything won't burn."

"Take what you want, Steve."

Steve sorted the treasures with squeals of delight.

"Aren't you going to have firecrackers any more?" He was sorry about the fire-bombs, the rockets, and the pinwheels that Ludie had stocked around the Fourth of July each year since Papa had died. Without Ludie, there would be no fireworks in the family.

Stephen was awarded Aggie's dictionary. He read column after column and page after page of the words and definitions. Each new word was like a geode which, broken open, revealed wondrous formations and colors. Language was infinite in its pleasures, no end to its variety.

"You have a large enough vocabulary for a boy of thirteen," pouted Nellie. She conducted herself like a surrogate parent, yet there were moments when he loved her.

Returning with his mother from a trip to Scranton and Wilkes-Barre, they found the station agent waiting as they descended from the train. Nellie had not come because Ludie was ill. "They called Doctor Mitchell," the man said. "He's there now."

Stephen saw his mother clasp her hands together tightly. Her face had blanched, naked fear clouding the black eyes. At Fourth Avenue, she paused, he thought to catch her breath, but she was praying silently.

"Mama, should I run ahead?"

"Let us be calm, Stephen. The Lord moves in His mysterious ways." She squared her shoulders. "He will not forsake us."

The house was ablaze with light.

They swept past the curious who had gathered on the verandah. Several men were holding lanterns. Doctor Mitchell was still inside, in his shirtsleeves; so was Captain Baker of the Police Department, whom the physician had summoned, and two firemen. Ludie, his countenance greenish, his figure limp, was asleep on the sofa.

Her eyes fell upon the basins everywhere and their distasteful contents. Having assured herself that he was alive, she sank into a chair. Her hands twitched nervously at her pocketbook.

Luther had taken an excessively large dose of the laudanum which Doctor Mitchell had prescribed to relieve stomach cramps. Shortly thereafter, he had collapsed. Nellie, who had found him lying unconscious in the parlor, had been unable to arouse him. She had sent a neighbor's boy for the physician. However, not until Captain Baker had arrived and he, in turn, had sent for two firemen to assist him, did they succeed in reviving her brother. The quartet had labored over the young man for nearly five hours before he was out of danger.

"If Mrs. Nortwick had delayed calling me for another fifteen minutes——" Doctor Mitchell hesitated. "Luther had clear instructions to take only a half-teaspoonful for his cramps."

Nellie broke in: "He had been complaining all day. He's never taken medicine like this before. How should he have known?"

The physician lowered his voice. "His intentions were plain. He not only emptied this vial, he drank also"—he held up another bottle—"all this which another doctor had given your poor Aggie for her pain!"

Mrs. Crane gasped. She exchanged a single glance with Nellie and shivered.

She was glad when the men left and she could be alone with Nellie. They wept in each other's arms.

"With Aggie gone only three weeks!" Nellie cried. "Who would have dreamed that he——"

"Let us pray," Mama said, her bosom heaving. "Let us give thanks for his deliverance."

"Why did he do it?" They had forgotten Stephen, who was always forbidden to ask questions. He understood that the death of Aggie had cruelly affected Ludie.

Burt arrived from New York. "You fool!" he shouted at Luther, and shook his fist. "You want to disgrace the whole family?"

He acted swiftly. He spoke to Townley, George, and Ted, and the brothers closed ranks to protect the ailing youth. Ludie was not to be left alone.

Stephen, persuaded to be on guard most of the waking hours, regarded Ludie with admiration and awe.

"Did it hurt?"

He got a weak grin. "Not until Baker and those firehorses began to pump it out of me. They nearly killed me!"

"Weren't you already dead?"

Luther chortled. "A little." He wanted to continue his reading. "I've still got their bruises."

Stephen climbed upon the bed. "Read to me, Ludie."

"You wouldn't understand."

"Aggie used to read——"

Ludie paled. He lifted the volume. " 'I would give you some violets, but they withered all when my father died. . . .' " He became silent.

"What is it?"

"Ophelia speaking in Shakespeare's *Hamlet*."

"What has her father dying got to do with her giving somebody violets?"

"How do I know? Maybe violets mean something in connection with death."

More mysteries. They had had a horse named Violet when they had lived in Port Jervis. His mother dearly loved violets, and she took them to Papa's grave whenever they were in bloom. Aggie, too, had loved violets. He borrowed Ludie's book and read *Hamlet* from beginning to end. It told him nothing more about violets.

In late summer, when the last issue of *The Summer Capital* had been published, Ludie announced that he was leaving Asbury Park. Unable to obtain newspaper work for the fall and winter months, he had taken a job as a switchman in the Newark yards of the Erie Railroad.

A month or so before, Ludie had bought an English setter, a fine orange Belton whom he had named "Chester." The dog was left in Stephen's care. With his pony and Ludie's dog, he was as happy as a boy could be.

Burt had been dropped out of medical school; his thesis on typhoid fever had been rejected by the faculty. After three years of study, he was bitter and dejected. He bewailed his defeat as a gross injustice.

Mame, whose first child had been named Aggie, wept over Burt's failure. Nellie, however, bluntly called him lazy. If Burt had worked harder—Will had graduated from Albany Law School!—his thesis would have been accepted and he would now be licensed to practice. "A disgrace to the family!" Nellie tossed her head.

Loyal Townley came to Burt's rescue by introducing him to the managing editor of the New York *Tribune*. For a while, Burt, too, was a stringer for the newspapers. Then, one day, he decided to leave for upstate New York, where a manufacturer of patent medicines had offered him a job.

With the house half empty, Mama frequently brought guests back with her from her trips. Now and then, she boarded stray orphans until an asylum, or some kind family, could be found to adopt them. Hattie, the girl whom Stephen and his father had met at the Baileys after the snowstorm in Port Jervis, came to live with them.

Stephen remembered a thin, forlorn waif with deer-eyes who had ladled out the soup. The Hattie who arrived was a large, overgrown maiden, plump and heavy-breasted, with a faint down on her upper lip. He thought that she must be older than sixteen because her figure was so thick at the middle.

They gave her a little room on the third floor. She helped Nellie with the slavey work and, when not at her chores, sat in a corner and knitted scarves or winter stockings.

Stephen ignored Hattie. He had school, baseball, football, his pony, and Ludie's dog. On St. John's island in Sunset Lake he helped genial Mr. Harvey, who owned the boathouse. Sometimes he earned ten or fifteen cents, rowing a couple around the lake. He enjoyed the chance to be near the grown-up girls and their escorts. He strained to hear the rustling skirts and the whispering.

One Sunday morning, when Mama was in Trenton, Stephen decided to go swimming instead of to church. The sun was already hot, the sky that deep aquamarine blue of the coastal shore. He thrust his hands into his pockets and strolled to the beach.

The tide was out, not a soul visible. The beach stretched in a bone-white magnificence that was studded with a few gulls and sandpipers. Churchbells were ringing. Near the black boulders of the jetty, he undressed, folded his breeches, and tucked Ludie's bow tie into his shirt pocket.

With a hop, skip, and a jump he was in the sea. He swam easily. Over his shoulder were the piers and the orchestra pavilion, and beyond, like a golden crown, the dome of the auditorium in Ocean Grove. He fancied himself clinging to Ocean Grove's gleaming new fire engine while the bell clanged and the horses thundered through the streets. At a great fire, he would climb a ladder and rescue a beautiful girl.

He heard a cry. An arm flashed in the sunlight.

"Help!"

He rode a wave in. A dark head bobbed; a breaker engulfed it. Another wave crashed. Stephen braced his shoulders; the tide was moving in.

He spotted the figure face down in the water. A boy, or a young man, adrift in the frothing sea.

In the next trough, he lunged, swam and clutched. The breakers smashed savagely, but he got his arm about the inert figure.

The drowning youth's mouth was open, the sea maliciously striving to purge it. "He's dead!" Stephen thought. He should have swum faster.

The next wave struck him amidships. He was thrown off balance, but again held on. He struggled and clung. Soon his soles were scraping shells and the sandy bottom. He shot upright, shifted his grip under the armpits, and began to drag the body.

The force of the surf wrapped tentacles about his legs. He tugged and pulled. With a final heave, he tottered toward the beach, safely convoying his burden.

He knelt astride the body and delivered a series of hard resounding slaps on the back, under the shoulder blades.

"Come on!" he shouted, and pounded. Water gushed from the open mouth and dribbled from the nostrils. He pressed hard. More water issued.

The lad, long-legged and perhaps three or four years his senior, began to groan. Another series of pressures, and more gurgling and groaning.

The green eyes opened. Stephen grinned into the freckled face. The dazed youth rolled his head. His features contorted as a pain shot through his chest.

"What—what happened?"

He braced the boy's shoulders and sat him up. "You tried to swallow the whole Atlantic Ocean."

"I nearly drowned!"

"Not quite."

"You saved my life. When I tell my father, he'll give you a reward."

"Don't you dare!" Stephen's balled fist was at the other's nose.

"Hey! What's the matter with you?"

"It's Sunday," he declared grimly. "You can't go swimming on Sunday."

"You did! And lucky for me!"

"I'm supposed to be in church. Don't your folks go to church?"

"Sure!" The youth shrugged. "But I didn't go!" He coughed again and, as the pain diminished, tried to smile. "I wish I could do something. You saved my life."

Stephen relented. "Ho, hell, if you feel that way, you can buy me a plate of ice cream. Maybe two plates."

That afternoon, Wallis McHarg bought him one plate of ice cream in the shop next to the Surf Hotel on Kingsley Street, another at the Excursion House facing Wesley Lake, and a third at the Grand Opera Hotel on Emory Street.

The rest of the week, McHarg being liberally supplied with nickels and dimes, Stephen enjoyed the abundant rewards of heroism as they visited every confectioner's shop and ice-cream parlor in Asbury Park. He could not conceal his astonishment that anyone should consider being pulled out of the surf worth so many treats.

Wally smoked a pipe, a sleek little underslung briar that cupped nicely in the palm of his hand. "I can think better with a pipe." He offered to give it to his new friend. One day, when theMcHargs had been visiting New York, his father had bought it to dissuade him from smoking cigar butts out of the gutter. "Ever been to New York?"

"My mother lectures in New York. She attended the Young Ladies Institute in Brooklyn when she was a young girl."

"Next time, I aim to walk clear across the Brooklyn Bridge. I was there the week it opened."

Stephen emerged from a cloud of smoke. "Ho, hell!" he said. They had started to build the great bridge the year he was born. "One day, I'll have to see it for myself."

"See the Bowery," Wally advised. "Don't forget the Bowery. You've got to get to the roots to know the truth, even if it's ugly. And you can't know too much."

"Know everything, if you can," Stephen agreed. "Everything!"

Wally, who intended to study medicine, proclaimed his interest in frogs, mice, snakes, fishes, birds, and anything else that could be submitted to dissection. When he had his own office he would keep a real skull on his desk for an ashtray.

"With a little sign: 'My first patient!' "

Wally's burst of laughter gratified him.

When he came to supper, Stephen envied the ease with which Wally chatted with Mama and addressed Nellie, and engaged even the unsmiling Hattie.

Wally was critical of the books in the Crane parlor. "*Frank on a Gunboat!* Pretty bad. "Frank on This' and 'Frank on That'!"

Stephen disowned the lot. "My brothers gave them to me when I was little." He indicated Aggie's library. "My sister's. They're mine now."

"*Pendennis!*" McHarg approved. "Can't beat old Thackeray. Better than Dickens. That *Mill on the Floss* is good, too. Did you know that George Eliot was a woman?"

Stephen nodded gravely. He knew it now.

"President Cleveland's sister is writing a book on George Eliot's poetry," Wally smiled. "You heard about Cleveland?"

Everyone knew that President Cleveland had a bastard child; he had admitted it during the election campaign.

The guest inspected the special volumes on the mantelpiece. "Crane! Crane! Crane! Peck! Peck! Peck!"

"My father, my grandfather, my great-uncle. In this family, everybody either writes or preaches, or does both."

"You going to be a preacher, too? Or a writer?"

Stephen grumbled. "No, sir-ee! Writer maybe. Sometimes I think baseball is for me. A good player—Cap Anson or Mike Kelly—can make two thousand a year. Jim O'Rourke gets four thousand!"

"If you become a writer instead of a ball player you could go to London or Paris or Rome—or anywhere. You could write anywhere." He would attend medical school in Germany.

Stephen nodded.

"You should read the Russian writers and the French writers, and see how they do it."

"I haven't read all the English writers!"

He listened respectfully as McHarg recited the strange names: Tolstoy, Turgeniev, Balzac, Flaubert, Zola. "They cut through the skin and get into the nerves and bone. Real life, Steve!"

104

"How do they do that?" he asked slowly.

"I know only that they do. Father says so. We have them in translations. First, they *feel* it. They soak themselves in experience. They become stimulated, and can't wait to pour it out in words. They're not afraid of anything."

With a wink, as Hattie walked past, he asked, "Is she your sister-in-law?"

"Just a girl. Orphan."

"I thought——" McHarg was silent. "Is she fat, or is she having a baby?"

"Fat!" Stephen exploded. But Wally had jolted him to examine a suspicion that had been gnawing at his mind.

In the ensuing days, he observed the girl more closely. When the sun outlined her figure she seemed to walk with her shoulders back as if to balance a weight at her abdomen. McHarg had been right. Hattie was going to have a baby!

When the girl did not appear at the dinner table, he asked of no one in particular, "What's ailing her?"

Nellie clattered her fork, prepared to be hugely indignant. "A boy would not understand."

"Nell, you've never been a boy, but you always say that."

"It's not a subject for the table!"

"Should we go outside?" he prodded brazenly. "Is she married?"

Nellie sputtered, but their mother did not flinch. "I would not tell you an untruth, Stephen," she said grimly. "I have no right to discuss with you what concerns another's life and reputation. On the other hand, since you have asked, you must be answered. Hattie has had a tragic life for a girl so young. *Through no fault of her own,*" she emphasized the words, "she is in the saddest circumstances in which an unmarried girl can find herself. We will keep her with us until Thanksgiving. Then I shall find her a new home."

"She's going to have a baby."

"Stephen!"

"Quiet, Nellie. Is he a child? Yes, Stephen. And we must be kind to her."

He regarded her warily. She was not revealing much, but she was not lying; Mama never lied.

"We must be kind to her," she repeated. "This is our Christian duty. And if you hear idle prattle from neighbors or other boys, remember that we are doing our Christian duty."

At that moment, admiration and love for her courage and compassion flooded Stephen.

Before his eyes, Hattie was transformed into a maiden in distress, to be pitied and to be guarded since they had rescued her. He was proud now that she was their ward, and resentful of any slighting remark that might reflect on her character. Now that he understood the nature of her reticence, he sought to bring her into every family conversation. He was so eager to cheer her that he invited her to read the books that he had enjoyed.

"*The Mill on the Floss,*" he began, selecting Aggie's favorite, "is a story——" Then he hesitated, having remembered that Maggie Tolliver had been betrayed.

He might have spared himself, for Hattie, who had attended only four grades of school, was a poor reader. So he offered to read to her, as Aggie had once read to him. McHarg had praised Thackeray; very well then, *Pendennis.*

He was disappointed that Hattie seemed unable or unwilling to follow the least episode. He read slowly and distinctly, yet her face remained blank.

"Is it good?" she occasionally inquired and, when he smiled at a passage, frowned uncertainly.

He was baffled. He was beginning to be fond of her. Why could she not be a quick, sharp, clever companion?

To himself, he was reading *Pendennis* seriously, although he resented the style. Thackeray seemed to enjoy poking fun at his people. But the character of Arthur Pendennis appealed to Stephen. Laura, the sister, who adored "Pen," was startlingly like Aggie. In some respects, "Pen" was a dude. He fell in love with Emily, the Irish actress ten years his senior, and then with Fanny, a pretty servant girl who was like the girls Stephen had seen being squeezed by their escorts in Mr. Harvey's rowboats.

For a week, he read steadily. *Pendennis* was as long as a freight train. He was disenchanted when "Pen" went head over heels for Blanche, the rich girl. Then he was astonished to find that, in the end, "Pen" had turned back to Laura, who had continued to love him and to pay his debts. He had assumed that Laura was a full sister; happily for "Pen," she turned out to be only an adopted sister. Therefore, the two could become man and wife!

He wished for someone, anyone, with whom he might discuss *Pendennis.* If only Wally McHarg lived in Asbury Park! Nellie was occupied with church affairs and with the Reverend John Hamilton, who was courting her. Townley, busy writing for the New York *Herald,* the New York *Tribune* and the Philadelphia *Press,* declared that he had no patience with three-decker novels.

"Anything you want to write, Steve," he maintained, "you write clearly. Leave sermons to the preachers. If your novelists had to make linage for a newspaper, they'd learn soon enough to write to the point. Simple, concise, make every word tell!"

Stephen, having begun to write a long account of a dog like Solomon who had pined for his master, was dismayed by Townley's injunctions. He put the story away, and went outdoors to be alone in the dark with the booming of the surf and the voices of the night.

In the sky, a quarter moon was setting with visible reluctance. Aggie was out there among the unseen legions, observing gravely, perhaps writing in her memory book. When he was melancholy, as he was tonight, he thought of her so strongly that he could see her, alive and fair, with her eyes sad and her hair falling to her waist. Was everyone confronted by his dead? Did the dead never truly fade away? He searched the stars as if her image might appear to him up there in the constellations.

He was overcome by a sense of his minuteness before the immensities of life. He wished fervently that the years would turn faster and plunge him into the untold experiences that would anneal him into manhood.

CHAPTER 16

The mouth of tragedy, always fixed in a grimace over this household, opened to deliver a shriek of unbearable pain. Ludie, at work in the yards, was caught between two freight cars, his shoulder mangled in the marriage of the couplings, muscle, tendon, and bone crunched in the steel jaws, his body rising like a flogged dummy. His cries were muted by a passing switch engine which, intent upon its own crushing errand, blew a deafening whistle. When he was finally rescued, the boxcars forced apart, and was laid in the grass to heave like a dying fish, he had lost quantities of blood. Someone thought of a belt for a tourniquet, so he lived another day, hating the tortured hours to which they had compelled him to cling. Clever doses dulled his torment, strengthened him once to open his eyes and to recognize his mother and Nellie, Ted and Stephen. The good arm reached for the dismembered one and could not find it.

They took him to Hillside to lie near Papa and Aggie.

"Where is the other arm?" Stevie asked Ted.

His brother did not know. The arm had been forgotten at the trackside and later, incredibly, could not be found.

Will settled the estate. The Erie Railroad paid $35 toward the funeral expenses. Since Ludie had few possessions and there were debts to meet, George bought his brother's watch, alarm clock, and the meager personal furnishings of his room; Will turned over $50 for the dog Chester and for Ludie's books. The debit balance of $199.59 was divided among seven, Nellie, George, Townley, Ted, Will, Burt, and their mother, each paying $28.50 in cash to close the matter forever.

Burt, who could not be located for days and appeared only at the cemetery, was the most gravely shocked, for Ludie had been his favorite. He spoke with wild hatred of the railroad. There must have been some terrible negligence on the part of the hogger who had backed the train of cars. An action should be filed against the Erie. Mama would not hear of it; Ted, also employed by the road, would lose his job. "God's will!" Burt retorted bitterly, and stormed away.

Night after night, Stephen continued to dream that somewhere Ludie's arm, outstretched and bleeding, the fingers clawing convulsively, searched for the body to which it belonged.

The sun was flaming orange. Over the woods, the treetops were burnished. The pony clip-clopped. Deliberately, Stephen turned him down the path that led to the road-menders' camp. He had been forbidden to ride there because the road-menders were dangerous prisoners who were working out their sentences for the county. "Forbidden!" he grimaced. Everything was forbidden.

He wished that he was in the Far West. As he jogged along, he studied the trail and pretended that he was a settler stalking Indians. Wagons had passed, including a prairie schooner with pioneer men, women, and children. He caught a flash beyond the ravine and up the hillside, and tensed. Something had moved through the trees. "Whoa, Pudge!"

Figures were struggling: a man and a woman. He had arrived in the nick of time! The Indians were already attacking. Should he dismount or ride for help?

He heard cries. On the rim of the hillside, a huge Indian in black warpaint was assailing a settler-woman. The brave had his brown arms around her, but she was clawing and scratching. She tore away, and struck at his chest. Instantly, the Indian pulled something from his belt. A blade glinted. The woman uttered a long, terrifying scream. Stephen saw her gown rent and the gush of blood.

He gaped, but could not cry out. Was it real? Fantasy and reality had collided.

"Yo!" he finally shouted. It was not a dream.

The brave came crashing through the brush, spied the ravine, and halted. That was no Indian! It was a road-mender, stripped to the waist, in shabby trousers with a dirty cord around his midriff. The knife was still in his fist, the blade scarlet.

"Yo!" Stephen repeated, softly.

He shivered as the staring eyeballs glared down upon him.

The man bared white teeth, and made a threatening gesture with the knife. Stephen feared that he would spring at him, but the man turned and scrambled back up the hill. For a moment the brown giant was poised against the sky. Then he vanished.

Stephen swerved Pudgy around and yelled, "Giddap!" He must ride for help.

He had not gone thirty paces when several men dashed into the roadstead. Pudgy neighed in fright, and reared. Stephen kept his seat and reined in. He was unable to speak. The men were more road-workers, white and black, in ragged shirts and muddy pants. Several were barefoot.

A bearded man who was cradling a rifle shouted at him. A short, burly man was parting the brush with a cudgel.

A third man, in a broad hat, stepped from a thicket. "Hey, boy! There's a dangerous convict loose. Seen anything of him?"

Mutely, Stephen lifted his arm and pointed. Through the trees, the woman was lying like a heap of laundry with a red scarf flung over it.

Ten, perhaps twelve, other men, armed with staves and axe-handles, came thrashing over the brow of the hill.

"Here he is!"

A hoarse shriek of pain stabbed the air. Two men were struggling with the convict.

"We've got him!" one bellowed.

The ring of men slowly closed in. "Give up, Mose, or we'll kill you!"

Mose, the whites of his eyes rolling, his naked brown chest heaving like a bellows, tottered against the trunk of an oak. He dropped the knife. Still they advanced, staves brandished. He blubbered and threw his arms about his head. "Don't!"

A savage roar startled the woods as the weapons swung. Something thudded. A horrible abattoir groan came through the mass under which Mose had gone down. Dry leaves detached themselves from upper branches and, lazily, floated earthward.

"That's enough, Jack! Get them back!"

Stephen wished he could see more. Had they killed Mose?

The broad hat turned on him: "Go home, boy!" The eyes were bloodshot, the lips cracked. "Git!"

Frightened, Stephen jabbed the pony and dashed away. He was shaken and rode badly, conscious of a fiery turbulence inside him, as though every vital organ was in revolt against the cruelties he had witnessed. His brow ached; the bridge of his nose pinched. He must have become feverish from the sun. The dust had coated his tongue and the roof of his mouth.

He could see the scarlet lancing across the woman's gown as she toppled backwards. He wanted to vomit.

What he had thought could happen only at night had unfolded in broad daylight. Real terrors, he suddenly understood, did not have to lurk; they could come rushing out to overwhelm him in the sunlight.

That night, he overheard Nellie saying to Mama: "An atrocious crime was committed in the woods, near the road-menders' camp, today. I heard it from Mr. Bradley. A convict—one of those terrible men—escaped yesterday, with the help of a woman friend who had come to visit him—a white woman! They quarreled in the woods, and he assaulted her. They say she's dead."

"He slew his wife!" Mrs. Crane was shocked.

"I don't think they were married."

"I would not repeat gossip!" her mother said tartly.

"Mr. Bradley says that he thinks the man was under the influence of liquor, which the woman brought him."

Mrs. Crane bristled. "That would not surprise me! The question is how did she obtain the spirits, and from whom, since none may legally be sold in this area. I shall speak to Captain Baker!"

Their voices droned on. Images loomed from the dark, came into sharp focus and faded; others billowed out of purple niches and burst into colorful fragments. He was sinking. His skin tingled: a woman was embracing him passionately. He felt Hattie's hard abdomen pushing his own. Suddenly, he was on the hilltop where the murder had been committed. A woman was in his arms. She was replaced by another, and yet another. He struggled to escape them, but his arms were frozen.

He was a prisoner of his fantasies. Behind every action, he sensed dark, cruel, forbidding relationships. He was stroking a girl's hair, which fell into thick golden-chestnut tresses over her shoulders and down to her shoes; then he was lying like an infant at her round breast. The hot smell of lust invaded his nostrils; it became so unbearably sweet that his loins shuddered. He was torn between a sharp and insatiable desire to surrender and a deep loathing for sin, sin, sin!

He could no longer resist it. His body began to pulse and to throb; he clawed and squirmed, suddenly melted and knew a release that left him breathless and triumphant, and a sinner.

The soles of his feet were chilled: he was walking barefoot on a cold floor in a dark corridor. He reached for a door, and shook it violently. Between his fingers, from the very center of the porcelain knob, Papa's stern blue eye appeared. He turned and ran. He heard his own footsteps and fled before invisible phantoms. He would be safe when he reached Aggie and fell into her moist, warm arms.

CHAPTER 17

During his first term, Stephen had been miserable at Pennington Seminary. He had found the subjects dull and had rebelled against the discipline. He had written pleading letters to his mother and to Nellie, and had appealed to Townley. He had dispatched a long letter of woe to Will, whose reply, on new law stationery, read like a speech by Polonius. At least, Ted enclosed a dollar now and then for the hire of a riding-mare in the village: "Don't tell mother!"

On a free Saturday afternoon, Stephen walked the seven miles to Trenton. One of his classmates had boasted that the city had a red-light district where painted women waited under the lampposts. He had often thought luridly about such encounters; he lingered on the streets until darkness fell.

Near the Delaware, a large woman with a fringed shawl about her shoulders accosted him from a doorway. His heart skipped. "Yes, Ma'am?" Her eyes were black and outlined with kohl.

"Want to learn something?" She smirked; her mouth was scarlet. "Come on with me. I'll teach you."

He was frightened. "No, Ma'am!"

"Then what are you doing here? Does your Mama know? Ain't you ever been with a girl?"

"I'm just walking."

She offered her hand, palm up, as if he were a child.

He drew back.

"I won't eat you!"

He strode on. At a red light over a brownstone, he hurried faster.

A farmer driving an empty rick gave him a ride. Stephen was silent as the team creaked down the dark road.

"Been painting the town red, son?"

"No, sir."

The other chortled. "Why not? You're only young onct. Sow the wild oats!"

The moon leered over the trees.

At the crossroads, a mile from the school, the farmer halted. "As far as you go, son. 'Fraid of the dark?"

"No, sir."

The monitor reported him late. The next day, after Bible class, he was birched. The rod hurt. But the punishment was the price of the adventure.

Lying on his bed, he summoned a legion of resentments against the Seminary. He detested the restraint, he was irked by the boring textbooks, and worst of all, for successive breaches of discipline, he had been forbidden to play baseball next term. While he was wasting the days and nights at Pennington, exciting life was slipping from his grasp.

When the lights were out and the watch had trudged through the halls, he waited until his roommate was snoring. He dressed in the dark and, stealthily, crept out.

Once more he walked the seven miles to Trenton. When he arrived at the station it was 1:30. Not for hours would a train leave for Asbury Park. He curled up on a bench and fell asleep. At 6:30 he was aboard the train for home.

He was dismayed that his running away should stun Mama. He was aware of nothing dishonorable in his actions; having decided to leave, he had decamped. He could not fathom why school attendance should mean so much to her, or why it appalled her that he was repeating the pattern of his brothers' conduct.

For her youngest, she was prepared to make painful concessions. "Smoke your vile pipes if you must. *Not* inside the house. But to school you must go! If not Pennington, choose another school."

"I don't learn anything in school!"

"Have you tried? Stephen, are you determined to grow up unlettered as well as Godless, and break my heart?"

He was sorry for her, yet feared that indomitable will, against which he could pit only his obduracy.

"Is the Law hateful to you? It serves your brother Will. What of Medicine? Don't take Burt for your example. The way of the healer will always be blessed. You could teach school. And what of God's work? How will you spend your life? What of Eternity?"

He groaned.

"I am determined that you shall be educated. What will happen to you when I die?"

"I could write for Townley."

"Is he your noblest model?" The struggle was disheartening. "Very well. Spend the summer running his errands. We shall see."

He did not realize that she was temporizing and not yielding.

That summer he was Townley's shadow. He rode Pudgy everywhere to gather the news that must be fed to the city newspapers. He was too happy to give any thought to his future. He mingled with the summer people, studied their behavior, copied their speech, and admired their dress and carefree ways. He achieved a bright turn of phrase that often startled Townley. When the older brother's pencil occasionally struck out a line, Stephen growled to know the reason. He argued for the phrases and sentences that pleased him.

Nellie warned her mother. "To Stephen, Townley is Horace Greeley and Henry Stanley in one!"

Mrs. Crane pleaded with Townley to discourage the youth from journalism.

"Steve has the gift of words. He's grown up in a writing family. How can I deny it when the *Tribune* sets his copy into type without a complaint?"

"He's too young. He should go back to school."

By the end of the summer, the two brothers were inseparable. Stephen thought Townley worldly and clever, superior to anyone else he knew. Townley hummed snatches of popular songs; he whistled marches; he strolled about, hands in his pockets, as if he were the lord of the earth. "Free as a bird!" Nellie said scornfully.

Mama defended him. His untidiness she charged to his newspaper associates, for he had not always been unkempt and careless. She blamed Fannie in part; not for the loss of the two infants—God's will! —but for the woman's constant whining and increasing slothfulness. No wonder Townley was unhappy.

Stephen envied his command of words. Townley juggled them like dice, and grinned as though he were winning on every roll. He knew how to excite the boy's imagination with fresh, new phrases. He talked drolly about a lady he had seen struggling with her skirts in a high wind. Stephen, who was shy with girls, listened appreciatively. He was becoming a man; he was shaving once a week.

Townley had an ear for dialects, for the Irish brogue, for the Scottish burr, for the lilting, curiously punctuated speech of the Italian organ-grinder, and for the beery accent of the German brewmaster. He referred to his personal friends as Injuns. "You don't want to believe everything you read," he told Stephen. "It depends who's doing the writing!" He was no fool.

"If Townley spies a rock, he has to peer under it!" Nellie scoffed. "If he hears of a murderer he has to defend him, right or wrong."

Indeed, Townley was further endeared to Stephen by his espousal of unpopular causes. For Stephen was of an age when to be *against* was daring and to be *for* was conservative and spineless. Anarchists were not as bad as the press intimated. Atheists had something to be said in their favor. He had read Townley's articles on the Boonton episode four or five times.

"The blasphemy case?" Townley was pleased. "I liked the pieces myself. But only one paper would buy them from me."

"I wish I had heard Robert G. Ingersoll talk."

"A great orator," Townley expanded. "Little town of Boonton, New Jersey, had never seen anything like him. This man, Reynolds, the defendant, could have paid his fine for violating the blasphemy law and called it a day. But old Bob Ingersoll had decided to make the welkin ring. For days they postponed the trial because he had throat trouble. Finally, he came, in a black frock coat and a silk hat, with an army badge pinned to his lapel. You know Ingersoll was at the battle of Shiloh, Steve. The judge was respectful. He had asked two other judges to sit on the bench with him. Even Wilder Cutler, the prosecutor, was courteous to him. And the courtroom was packed!"

"What did he say?"

"You read my articles."

"I would rather have been there and heard him talk than listen to all the teachers at Pennington!"

"He's a big man, clean shaven, with a round bald head, and speaks in a husky voice. Eloquent? Even Henry Ward Beecher said that Bob Ingersoll is the most brilliant speaker in the English tongue.

'Blasphemy is what an old mistake says of a newly-discovered truth. Blasphemy is what a withered last-year's leaf says to this year's bud.' That's poetry, Steve."

"Uh-huh!"

"Sixteen witnesses trotted to the stand and testified that this man Reynolds had handed each of them a blasphemous pamphlet. Then, for the defense, Ingersoll talked from two o'clock until four-thirty in the afternoon. You could have heard an ash drop. 'What is real blasphemy?' he threw at the jury. 'I will give you a definition. To live on the unpaid labor of other men—that is blasphemy. To enslave your fellow man, to put chains on his body—that is blasphemy. To enslave the minds of men, to put manacles upon the brain, padlocks upon the lips—that is blasphemy. To deny what you believe to be true, to admit to be true what you believe to be a lie—that is blasphemy. To strike the weak and unprotected in order that you may gain the applause of the ignorant and superstitious mob—that is blasphemy. To persecute the intelligent few at the command of the ignorant many— that is blasphemy. To pollute the souls of children with the dogma of eternal pain—that is blasphemy!'" Townley's face shone.

"But why did he lose?"

"Easier to stop the sun in its tracks than to win on such a charge in Boonton. The old order changeth not, Steve, not if it can go on being foolish and cruel. 'Guilty!' The fine was twenty-five dollars, the costs were about seventy-five. A moral victory, anyway. Ingersoll paid the clerk and shook hands with everyone, judge, prosecutor, clerk, jury."

"I wouldn't have shaken hands with them."

"Ingersoll did. He's a man and a philosopher. Why, Steve, I've read that he once said, 'I do not hate a man that has rheumatism. I hate the rheumatism that has the man!'"

Stephen looked at Townley as if his brother had minted the phrases; from him, he expected amusing anecdotes and clever counsel every day.

His affection caused him to trail after Townley as he had once followed Ludie. He discovered that Townley drank beer or whiskey with the other newspapermen who came to Asbury Park.

"You shouldn't!"

"Are you going to be like Mother? Liquor, the social evil!"

"Town, she'd be heartbroken."

Townley slapped his thigh. "So you're to watch over me? All my life someone has been at my heels. Papa, Mama, Fannie, and now you, Steve? A man can't take a sip of beer or bourbon, or sit in a game of poker without being pilloried as a sinner damned to perdition. You've listened to too many of Papa's fire-eating sermons. Hallelujah!"

At the West End Hotel, Stephen met his brother's poker cronies.

Townley lost regularly, but Stephen accepted the poker meetings as a grand new experience. Cards and cigars, beer and bourbon, were also part of the great adventure.

In early September, he was still idling, doing odd jobs, trying also to write sketches. He dreaded mention of school. Mama rarely addressed him. He saw that she was suffering, and the tension between them mounted. He could not endure her reproachful glances; Nellie's disdainful airs only infuriated him.

Every day, on behalf of the *Press,* he tramped up one street and down the next, to call at the boardinghouses and the private guest-homes. He was after the curious items that the regular men passed by.

Under the eyes of Lloyd Dale, the whiskered editor with the hooded lids, another of Townley's cronies, he wrote his reports on yellow sheets. Mr. Dale, a green visor about his forehead, a dead cigar in his mouth, was more exacting than Townley. He drew a cold, blue pencil through half the words that Stephen proudly dovetailed into journalistic sentences.

"'A tall lady with beautiful white arms!'" the editor repeated gravely. "What's her name? Are they all anonymous, Stephen? Facts, boy, facts!" Cigar ash dribbled down his vest. "Why interview people? Who, what, when, why, where, and how—then, and only then, your descriptions. Facts! Don't be a Billy-be-damned poet!"

Stephen, though he listened sheepishly, was unconvinced that his writing was inferior to the stark sentences that Dale scrawled over his copy and sent on to the compositors. "I'm not a Billy-be-damned-poet!"

"You're as skinny as a poet," said the editor. The hooded lids made him seem impassive. "Well, keep it up. Write verbs, not adjectives, and work, work, work! That's the way."

He preferred to work at his writing rather than to idle where kindly people could pounce on him. "Are you still at home, Stephen?" Other lads his age were in school.

Neighbors who had heard him talk of baseball inquired if he would go into the big leagues. He was flattered, but he would have to become stronger and improve his wind and speed to reach such heights.

He forced himself to eat and tried to cram himself between meals. But he was a poor eater; it was hard to gain an ounce. He sought to hire out to toil in the fields from sun-up to sundown so that he might become as tough as nails. The local farmers laughed at him. He did bends, push-ups and squats, and considered the life of an acrobat or tumbler.

When the sun flashed across the sea, and people began to come out upon their verandahs, he saddled Pudgy and went cantering into the woods. Rabbits leaped from the brush. He wished that he had a gun.

He dismounted, let Pudgy graze and threw himself upon the grass to smell the earth and to hear the thousand tiny cracklings and stirrings. He was hurting Mama; he would surely be punished.

CHAPTER 18

In Library Square, Jeb Royal, the one-armed veteran, sat in the sun with his retriever and his cronies. Jason was not half as fine an animal as Solomon, but Stephen often stroked the head and scratched behind the animal's ears.

Jeb Royal was talking about the fighting at Antietam. Stephen admired Jeb, who reminded him of Ludie. Once he had asked Jeb what had happened to his other arm. Jeb had blinked and replied, tersely: "Buried!"

"How long do they live, Jeb?" Stephen broke in now. "I mean dogs."

"Dogs?" The veteran looked up impatiently; his armless shoulder jerked. "You're eddicated, ain't you, boy? Go look in the library."

"Jeb's trying to tell you the library's got his name printed in a book on his regiment," Carl Hick cackled. "'Corporal Jebediah Royal.'"

"It's there, Steve," Jeb nodded. "You can read, cain't you?"

Mr. Peterson, the portly librarian, who resembled a little walrus recently separated from the herd, was sleepily perusing a copy of *Harper's Weekly.* Stephen tiptoed about the room, peering at the titles on the bookshelves. The regimental history in which Jeb Royal's name appeared was probably locked in the "Reserved. Apply to Librarian" case.

He found the *Cyclopedia of Methodism* and carried it to a nearby table. Grandpa George, Uncle Bishop and Papa were all in these pages, with their pictures and biographies. In the article on Jonathan Townley Crane, the engraved portrait was real even to the tiny wart on Papa's upper lip. The spectacled eyes were cold.

Hastily, he closed the volume. The huge tome shut with a bang! "Oh, dear!"

On the other side of the table, in a white dress and a large wide-brimmed hat, sat Mrs. Marie Widdicomb, the tall, beautiful lady whose arrival he had noted in an item for the *Press.* She was the only other visitor in the room.

"I'm sorry, Ma'am!"

At her forgiving smile, he blushed furiously.

He had interviewed Mrs. Widdicomb for thirty minutes one day. Two hours later, Mr. Dale, his eyes masked by a green visor, had sternly decimated his long paragraphs to two spare sentences: "Mrs.

Marie Widdicomb of Montreal arrived last Tuesday. She and her servant are staying at the old Murchison house on Packard Street."

When he peered at the woman again, she was frankly staring, her lovely, cocoa-brown eyes sparkling. In confusion, he seized the leather-bound volume once more and flicked the pages. Again he came to "Jonathan Townley Crane, D.D."

She was a widow: Mrs. Marie Widdicomb. She had fallen ill after her husband had died in a mining accident in the Laurentian Mountains, and had come to Asbury Park to recuperate.

She had lovely round arms, and coils of reddish-brown hair. He admired the tiny beauty spot on her cheek. Her speech was not American but attractively English; she had the whitest teeth. She lived with her servant, Liliom, a dark, round-faced West Indian girl, in the Murchison house at Packard Street and Sunset Avenue.

He tried to read his father's biography, but the words swam away. Mrs. Widdicomb must be old, at least twenty-nine or thirty. In the white dress, with its all-over embroidery, she was probably very cool.

"Don't tell me you're reading *that!*" her mocking voice whispered above him.

"No!" His cheeks flamed.

She was at his side, several books on her arm, her parasol dangling from her wrist.

"No, Ma'am, I was looking." Around her waist, above the full skirt, was a wide pink satin sash.

"If you really care to read good books, there's a fine library at the Murchisons that no one uses."

He got up awkwardly, hoping old Peterson was asleep. "May I?" he mumbled, drawing back lest he inadvertently touch her. "I'd like to read them."

"Of course."

"Now?" he asked boldly and felt that a demon had taken possession of him. "I could come over——"

His gaze ran from her eyes to her lips, to the tiny beauty spot and to the curve of her cheek, and his pulses hammered.

He stood sheepishly, admiring her carriage, while Mr. Peterson charged the books. Her skirt flared at the hips; the wide pink sash was tied into a bow at the back.

The air in the gloomy room, which reeked of furniture polish, library paste, and the mustiness that prevails in long-shut chambers, had become oppressive. A horsefly was angrily buzzing at a lamp-chimney.

He went ahead to open the door. She swept forward like a vision in white issuing from some royal court. She caught the homage in his glance and bestowed another smile.

"I'll take them, Ma'am," he said. As she surrendered the books, his fingers slid across her hand. Her skin was as cold as Aggie's. On one

117

finger gleamed a strangely fiery ring, the cabochon milky with a profusion of orange and red pinpoints.

A blast of heat struck them as they emerged from the building. In the panes of the houses across Library Square, the sun flashed golden signals. On the broad staircase, she drew on a pair of crocheted white gloves. He grinned. She was fit to go to a tea party at Coleman House.

"Steve," Jeb Royal called, "did you see the book with my name?"

"Yep!" he shouted back.

Jeb was staring at Mrs. Widdicomb. She, with noble calm, ignored him; the other idlers, too, were gawking.

Jason trotted up to bark gruffly.

"Your friends?" Mrs. Widdicomb asked, gathering up the hem of her skirts.

"The dog is my friend."

Suppressing a smile, she opened the parasol.

"I'll hold it, Mrs. Widdicomb."

"You are already doing too much. In this heat—imagine!" Graciously, she lifted the parasol over his head. "We'll share it. After all, you are my escort today, aren't you?"

He threw a defiant glance at Jeb & Company and strode on at her side. The shade was gratifying, but he was still blushing; he could not tell Mrs. Widdicomb that he had never escorted any girls except his sisters.

On the back of his neck, he could feel the veteran's eyes. Jeb was probably rooted there, to ogle every wiggle of her shape, to wait for the sun to outline her figure, or the hem of her skirt to twitch and reveal an ankle. Jeb would let out a hoot and pretend to collapse; his friends would throw their caps into the air and crow as if they had never before seen a beautiful woman, the damn fools!

"Yo, Steve!" That was Clay Antheil, who played fullback. Clay winked broadly.

"Yo, Clay!" He would come face to face with everyone he knew in Asbury Park. Please God, not Nellie!

Mrs. Widdicomb was talking animatedly. He checked his pace. Most girls walked like chickens; she moved forward like a queen.

"I am so happy that I thought of coming to your delightful village-by-the-sea."

"Ho, hell!" he reflected. "She can't know Asbury Park."

He heard a padding on the walk. "Now, Jason, you go back!" If Jeb couldn't follow, he sicked on his dog. "You hear me!"

The dog ran into the street.

"Go!"

Jason fled.

"Dogs must be fond of you."

"Dogs and horses."

"What about girls?"

"I don't know."

Third Avenue. "Yo, Steve!" Arnie Bennett. At least, Arnie had the wit to tug respectfully at his forelock.

"You must know everyone. I suppose that a reporter's first duty is to know his community."

"Yes, Ma'am." She was right, of course.

His eyes roved far down Grand Avenue—not Nellie, please!—and darted into the side-streets as they passed.

At Packard Street, he heaved a long sigh and wiped his brow. Where had he left his handkerchief? He was scorched.

"You'll come in." Heat waves shimmered in the air. The street was blazing. "You must be terribly hot."

"I've got to——"

"Liliom will fetch us a cold drink. And you wanted to see the library."

He was curious about the interior. The Murchison place was a fine two-story structure with a mansard roof, blue spruces, hedges, and a sundial in the garden. The lawn was green, which meant plenty of water and a hired man to tend it regularly. Thirty was not so old.

Liliom greeted them with a sultry gaze as she accepted the books and the parasol. "My, my! More books when the house is full?" Her accent, too, was English. Stephen had never heard a dark-skinned person speak so distinctly.

"Be quiet, Liliom!" Mrs. Widdicomb said, not unpleasantly. "Can't you see that we have a guest?"

The yellow shades were drawn in the parlor. A large black and white tomcat was curled up peacefully in the rocking chair.

Stephen stood about, leaning on one foot and then on the other, surreptitiously drying his sticky hands on his breeches. He noted the silk portières and the crystal chandelier. He moved toward the bookshelves. The Murchisons certainly had a large library.

Sevastopol by Tolstoy. A row of volumes by Nathaniel Hawthorne. *Huckleberry Finn. The Luck of Roaring Camp. Miss Ravenel's Conversion* by De Forest.

"Here we are!" She had removed her hat and gloves, and was instructing Liliom to fetch iced tea and cookies. "You like cookies?"

He resented the motherly tone. "I'm not a kid!"

The enormous coiffure made her face seem girlishly small; she could not be thirty. The cocoa-brown eyes were lively. "Liliom baked some this morning. I'm afraid we have nothing else, Stephen."

He tingled to hear her speak his name. "Stephen." How did she know? But he had introduced himself—"My name is Stephen Crane!" —when he had called upon her and stood in the doorway with his pencil and notebook. He had not dreamed that he would ever return as her guest.

She was pointing to the books, pulling down volume after volume. "These are the books you should be reading."

While she whispered something to Liliom, he trod over the rose carpet as though he were a familiar of the household.

Languidly then, she took her place in the center of the blue-covered settee and, settling her gown, extended a hand to guide him to a chair. He sat before her silently, wondering if she could hear the thumping in his chest. What if she could read his thoughts!

The cat stretched and, as the rocking chair dipped, leaped to the carpet. With tail curling like a shepherd's crook, it stalked from the room.

"That's Tommy for you," she smiled. "Three's a crowd. He just said that. I heard him. Didn't you?" She laughed, and he laughed, too. A current of good feeling flowed between them.

He was searching her face. Since they had entered the room she had become younger. Twenty-eight or -seven. And beautiful! A sunbeam, lancing between the edge of the shade and the window sash, stroked the brown hair and glided across her cheek. Her neck was gracefully molded; a pulse throbbed in the hollow of her throat. Her sleeves fastened at the wrists with pearl buttons. He picked out the arabesques in the embroidery on her bosom; the same design appeared in her lap and in the long skirt. A lustful impulse streaked through him, and he wondered if women experienced desires like those that harassed men.

"A penny for your thoughts," she said.

"You'd be cheated!"

She cupped her hand about her mouth like a schoolgirl, intimating that she knew very well what he had been thinking. She spoke wistfully of her elegant home in Montreal. She said, "Moo-reahl." The Murchisons, distantly related, had offered her the freedom of their summer place while they were off to Egypt. "James has your fair hair and skin. Grace is dark like me."

James and Grace were her children. "Then Grace must be beautiful, too!"

She preened. Her girlish profile, with the small, upturned nose, was alluringly feminine. She *couldn't* be more than twenty-seven. Aggie had been twenty-seven when she died. With a start, he realized that Mrs. Widdicomb resembled Aggie—a little.

"I've been chattering and chattering, and you have said nothing," she murmured. "What do you plan to do with your life, Stephen? You are so young. The whole world lies before you, waiting for you to rise and demand and conquer!"

"I'll be a writer." Every word she spoke was enunciated with English crispness. "I've decided." The embroidery on the left side of her bosom repeated the same curlicues that were traced on the right. Every day, the shapes of women interested him more and more.

"A poet?"

A Billy-be-damned poet! he heard Lloyd Dale saying. "No. I want to write essays and stories."

"For the press?"

"Maybe."

"Tell me where you get your inspirations?" One eye winked, and the wink emboldened him. "Is there a little sweetheart of your own age who inspires you, to whom you address your finest efforts, who excites the best in you, the way the Muses of old used to inspire the great writers of the past? Every bard must have his Muse."

"Not me!"

"Where do you get it then? Do tell me, Stephen."

"Everywhere." He blinked. "I could write for you, Mrs.——"

"Marie! Please call me Marie."

"Marie!" he repeated. "I could write for you," he declared firmly, "if you wanted me to."

"Would you, would you, Stephen?"

"I might." The adoption of a Muse impressed him as a serious matter.

She told him that in Montreal many writers used to visit her home on Sainte Catherine Street and, on social evenings, read aloud to her guests.

"I've written—uh!—hundreds of stories."

"How wonderful! Won't you let me read them, or bring them and read to me? I'd like that, Stephen."

He shrugged. "I don't know."

A flicker of disappointment crossed her face. She arose and poured more iced tea into his glass. Silently, she offered more cookies.

He declined, and remembered that he must rise when she did.

His sudden action caused his arm to strike the silver tray. The cookies flew across the rug. He gasped, apologized, stammered.

She assured him that it did not matter. She knelt and her gown described a white pool against the rose of the carpet.

"No, let me!" He should have been the first to bend, to kneel. "Please!"

She had already gathered them. Lamely, he gripped her elbow. Something rose in his throat, and he swallowed hard.

Her hand touched his shoulder, then slipped about his back. As if she had bewitched him with a magic wand, he faltered. "Marie!" At the heave of the embroidered bosom, a surge of desire commanded his arms. Desperately, he planted a dry kiss on her cheek, and clutched her. Something animal had stirred within him.

Her body was warm and impudent. She did not resist. He realized that her mouth had met his, that it was soft and willing, and that the scent of violets had invaded his being. His hand, behind her, stroked the sash and its bow, speculating whether one swift pull might undo it and cause every stitch to fall away. She would stand revealed in seven veils.

Under the dark eyelashes, he caught the glint of the brown pupils. He vaguely knew that her lips were parted, that her nostrils were dilated. Hot and cold sensations, rising from his knees to his forehead, prickled his skin. He was melting, his spine was being extracted from his frame, and he was kissing her again, caressing her, dimly wondering at the rustling of her gown. She was marvelously rounded.

"Stephen!" she murmured, her eyes appealing, a frantic light igniting them.

"Marie! Marie!"

She became limp. Vaguely, he considered that she had surrendered because it was exciting to be held and be kissed and stroked.

"Hush!" She gripped his arms.

The back door had opened. He understood that she must have sent the servant girl away on some pretext.

When Liliom entered, he was seated again, the cold glass of iced tea in his hand. His cheeks were lobster-red. From under the settee, a broken cookie emerged.

He listened dully as the girl talked to her mistress. Mrs. Widdicomb replied nonchalantly, as if nothing had happened.

Liliom was humming as she left the room. Only then did Stephen dare to meet the woman's eyes. He was blazing hot.

Mischievously, she blew him a kiss.

With a rustle of skirts, she arose and excused herself. The bow of her sash was untied.

He searched his pocket for cigarettes as he heard her ascending the stairs. When she returned, he was defiantly smoking.

"Tobacco!"

He laughed. He knew that she was talking aimlessly for the servant's benefit. Liliom was idling in the dining room, tinkling glassware.

The woman's eyes shone greedily; her hands, open in her lap, appealed to him, but her words, spoken sharply, disguised the eagerness. "Yes, of course. How good of you to call it to my attention!" Her tongue was licking at her lips.

Stephen sat forward, one fist clenched. The ring was gone from her hand. She had taken it off when she had entered the house. She had intended that they should—— What had she intended?

"I do hope that we may have the pleasure of your company again very soon," she went on. Her eyes had become drenched in anguish. In a whisper, "Please go, Stephen!"

He got up, bewildered. On their way to the front door, she pressed a folded slip of paper into his hand. He looked at her inquiringly. She winked again.

122

At the corner, he paused to read the message: "Come back tonight —at ten—to the kitchen door."

His loins ached as he strolled homeward. He was exulting. He could have done anything to her—anything!

What would he do until ten o'clock tonight? The hours would drag on crippled feet until he was embracing her again.

She could not be more than twenty-five! She was young and firm; her thighs were strong. She might leave Asbury Park; he would follow her to Montreal.

He could still feel the texture of the pink sash in his fingers. When they had stood man to woman she had been as yielding as if he had known her all his life. What if Liliom had walked in and caught them?

He glanced back at the boy he had been. He was not the same Stephen Crane who had been a child; he was not even the same Stephen Crane he had been three hours ago!

CHAPTER 19

He told Nellie that he was going fishing after dark. She disapproved with blazing eyes. She had invited the Reverend Hamilton and his sister, and wished Stephen to remain through the evening.

"I promised, Nellie. You didn't say a word this morning."

Characteristically, she let her temper flare. It was cheeky of him to expect her to wait on his convenience to invite her friends; it was inconsiderate not to postpone an idle recreation to please her. "I insist!"

"No, you don't, little Nell!"

He made elaborate and noisy preparations. As he assembled the rods and tackle, she shrilled, "I'll never forgive you! With whom are you going? I'll talk to him or to them. I'll explain that you can't go tonight!"

A ball of fear, lest she contrive somehow to stop him, gathered in his stomach.

"You get into mischief once more and see if I'll speak for you to your mother! You'll be going off to school again, my precious brother. I'll see to it!"

He escaped into the yard, and concealed the gear in the stable. Pudgy clopped his hooves. He went to caress the pony. "I won't forget you, Pudge," he whispered. "I won't!"

He slipped out into the dusk like a thief. It was 8:30, an hour and a half to waste. He could have remained until Nellie's guests arrived, but his sister surely would detain him.

He ambled toward Sunset Lake. What would Marie be doing until ten o'clock? Nellie usually bathed before an important call and spent an hour putting up her hair. He gloated over a vision of Marie in her bath while Liliom snickered and scrubbed her back. He imagined a female figure of curves and jiggles and remembered toddling into a room when Aggie was bathing. She had seized her towel, and cried, "Shoo-fly! Turn around, Stevie Crane!"

He wished that he could have bathed, although he had had a swim in the sea that morning. He was wearing his best clothes, and his hair was combed. Nellie had been so furious that she had observed nothing.

He listened to the crickets and the katydids and a frog booming somewhere in the reeds. He would say that they had got an eel or two and thrown them back, and then had run aground in the dark. One lie must generate another and another.

On the bridge, he contemplated the dark waters. He leaned forward as a boat passed under. In the light from the lantern in the bow, he spied two figures.

A girl's voice tittered: "Willie, don't!"

"Willie!" he mocked. "Don't you dare!"

An oarlock rattled. "Sh!" A hand covered the lantern.

Instantly, he regretted his intrusion; he had envied their love-making. To inform the unseen lovers that they were safe, he shuffled his feet as he retreated from the bridge. He walked slowly toward Packard Street.

He was apprehensive about his meeting with Marie. Strange misgivings gnawed at his stomach. What would she expect?

He could spare himself a second encounter. He would go home; Nellie would welcome him. Ten o'clock would strike. Marie would wait and wait, and then retire to her room. He would, thenceforth, avoid her; if they should meet on the beach or in the library he would state innocently that his sister had forbidden him to go out. He saw the scorn rising in the cocoa-brown eyes. "How fortunate you could not come! I had other guests."

She had gone to bed; she had not expected him at all. She had not wanted him; she had been too kind to reject him. "Why, you're young enough to be my son!" He would find the door barred. He would stand there, futilely turning the porcelain knob. The house would be dark and silent; he would hear her rustling behind the jamb, grimly refusing to open. Eventually, Liliom would answer, and say that her mistress had a headache; women claimed headaches at any time of the month, whenever they could summon no other excuse. She would not dare! He rattled the doorknob. He would push Liliom aside and go shouting through the house: "Marie! Marie!"

He was churning between resentment and desire. She would not reject him. The door would be unlocked. He would tiptoe up the stairs. They would embrace and lie together, and he would fondle her.

Cold perspiration beaded his forehead. What if she asked him to stay all night?

He was standing before the Murchison house peering into the lighted parlor. Skirts swayed. Not skirts; those were the curtains billowing at the open windows.

He skipped across the street. In the upper story, the windows were dark. Where was her bedroom? What if she laughed at him? "I'm old enough to be your mother!"

The pianoforte tinkled, and something flitted behind the curtains. She had company! That was why she had set ten o'clock for their rendezvous! Jealousy coiled in his throat. She was so beautiful that she must have many callers, tall, handsome men in elegant clothes. He would walk in and catch them embracing. She would turn: "What are you doing here? Please go!" He fled, and did not halt until he had gained the bridge.

He clung to the railing. Everything in life was a fraud. Be good, be good, be good! He had heard nothing else since his childhood. But it was Sin that ruled the world, and not Goodness. His father had been right! Sin, sin, sin! Evil was everywhere; it devoured every human heart. The Devil's orchestra played the same seductive tune over and over, and frail humanity danced. He groped for a Truth to which he could cling. Where were the roots, where the anchor? Girls were no better than boys.

Birds shadowed past, twittering. Offshore, he heard more oars dipping and pulling.

A light rolled across the waters. The moon had risen, its reflection gliding silkily.

As he approached Packard Street again, the great silvery head appeared above the trees. The house was dark.

He went the long way around, behind the stable and through the back yard. He tripped on a long-handled tool and knocked his shin. He halted to catch his breath.

He stepped carefully upon the small porch. His feet struck the mat; mechanically, he wiped his feet. He tried the knob. The door was opening before him.

Something brushed against his ankle. The cat had darted out. "Come in!"

He crossed the threshold and fell into her arms.

She was wearing a soft nightdress. Her figure, which had been armored with straps and snaps and petticoats, was now, he exulted, freely, incredibly formed.

"Where is she? Liliom?" Their long, feverish greeting was momentarily suspended; wherever he touched her she seemed to be afire.

"Don't be worried. She sleeps like a log."

"Are you sure?"

"Even if she awakens she won't come out unless I call her."

Harshly, he reflected that it was her home and her responsibility if they were detected.

"You wonderful boy!"

"I'm not a boy!" he retorted, and endeavored to prove it.

She responded gratefully.

A pool of silver light fell upon the carpet as she led him toward the staircase. On each step they had to embrace again.

In her room, the lamp was burning low. A light breeze ruffled the curtains on the tester-bed. He stopped abruptly on the threshold. The bed had provoked a thin thread of frightening memory.

"Are you looking for someone?" she murmured and smiled.

Evasively, the fear slipped away before he could grasp it.

She was brushing out her hair. Every article on the bureau was neatly arranged. Confidently now, as if her voice had banished the fear, he strode across the room and buried his face in the brown tresses. He pressed his lips to her white arms and, sliding a kiss toward her shoulder, paused until she gave a delicious little shiver.

In the mirror, he saw himself supporting a beautiful woman in a revealing nightdress.

With a soft laugh, she leaned over and, with his hand still at her bosom, blew out the lamp.

Moonlight leaped across the window sill as he began to disrobe.

He was trembling as he crossed the floor, the rug whiskery under his soles, and climbed into the bed. Shyly, he wished he had not taken off all his clothes. The moonlight would become intimate with their figures.

"How far away you are!"

In the dark, he blushed. He raised himself upon his elbow and leaned over her. A silver finger touched the mirror above the bureau, leaped to her toes and glided over her nude body. He flung his arm across her breast.

The night opened to receive him. The bed was softer than sand. He was running toward the splashing waves. Shreds of some long-forgotten song skirled in the back of his mind. He plunged eagerly, brutally, engulfing himself with a shout in a primitive tumult that threatened to swamp him. The undertow! The surf drenched him, but he was swimming powerfully, his arms embracing each new wave. He caught his breath; he was not in the surf at all. Desires, shameless, gluttonous, overwhelmed him. He was free; the fetters had fallen away.

New fires kindled in his loins. He quenched them boldly. They kindled once more; he plunged into the sea again. From each chasm, he soared on the buoyancy of lust till there was no more need, and the waters lay becalmed around him.

126

Is this it? he reflected, pleased and weary. *Is this all there is to it?*
He was giddy. Sensations through which he had galloped now
slowly returned to him. The figure beside him throbbed—he would
never be sure who she was—and the house quivered. The night held
the moon in a purple nutcracker. Heaven and earth were one. He was
the dust before it had spilled from the Divine Hand into the shape of
Adam, and he was the First Man, lying alone, watching the stars
fall out of the sky, rising weakly to touch them. The great secret
was his at last.

He heard sighing and remembered that another had been his
partner in the enterprise. She had been joyful, sulky, then joyful
again. Now she purred and praised him. He started: she was speaking French!

A child was crying. He tensed. Someone at the door? It was distinctly a knock.

"Hush, Stephen!"

She broke the spell. It was he who had cried out.

"What is it, dear?"

Had Liliom been walking barefoot down the hall to listen at their
chamber door? A boy's shuffling tread, or a man's? He was growing
cold. He let her cuddle him in her arms, and listened. He thought he
heard the knocking again.

She left him. The bed creaked, then the lamp went up. "She lit
the wick with her glowing fingertips," he thought sleepily.

He spoke the next words aloud: "I love you, Marie."

Over her naked shoulder, as she studied herself in the mirror, she
returned gently, "Don't be ridiculous, Stephen."

Nellie knew something. When their mother became ill and pleaded
again that he go to school—to Claverack College and Hudson River
Institute—and he refused, his sister cornered him.

"I think it is time that you left home, Stephen. Better Claverack,
or any school, than to while away the days in the company of a
woman old enough to be your mother!"

He paled.

"I know that those books you've been reading are from the Murchison library. *Sevastopol!* Our public library doesn't have such
books, and they are not stamped either. Didn't that occur to you?
Ah, Stephen, being only a boy, you see nothing but kindness in this
woman." Her eyes hardened. "If I didn't know that her stay was
ending, I would call on your Mrs. Widdicomb and inform her in no
uncertain terms that her charms—the charms of a widow!—had better
be reserved for more adult swains."

"You wouldn't, Nellie!"

"No, I won't. But I'm not blind, Stephen, even if you are. I hope
you haven't spent any time with her in that house alone.'"

"I'm not a kid." She knew nothing, nothing!

"So you say." Nellie lifted her head proudly. "But I'm a woman, Stephen, and I know women as you never will. I don't trust your Mrs. Widdicomb."

He forced a grin. "You're smarter than I am."

"Undoubtedly. I don't want an older woman ensnaring my favorite little brother."

He quaked to think of the narrow escapes they must have had.

It had been a golden September, now turning somber. Marie, too, urged him to go to school. He resented her counsel. Except during their love-making, she, too, talked like a mother.

"You'll enjoy wearing a uniform and a sword, and marching on parade. The girls will swoon!"

She was thirty-three, she told him; he would be sixteen on November 1st. "I'm twice your age, Stephen."

"What if, one day, I should knock on your door in Montreal?"

She studied him intently. "Don't you *dare!*"

When their joys were indescribable, he prayed that they might die in each other's arms.

The week before Christmas he consented to have Mama write to Claverack College; the day after the holiday, Reverend Arthur H. Flack replied in hand. Because Stephen was the son of a late minister of the Methodist Episcopal Church, the tuition and charges for board would be reduced from $225 per year to $165.

He packed glumly. He had conferred with Pudgy a dozen times, explaining that it was not possible to take him along. Mama had agreed that he might, occasionally, hire a mount at the livery-stable in Hudson, if the rules permitted.

The rules! He had become adult, yet the rules that applied to children were to be enforced against him. He had written twice to Marie Widdicomb, long, chatty letters so formal that she might show them to her parish priest, if she wished. He had asked her to reply care of "General Delivery, Hudson, Columbia County, New York."

Nellie and his mother accompanied him to the depot.

"I don't know what to say," the older woman declared anxiously. "Study hard, Stephen. Beware of evil companions. I have asked Doctor Flack to give you a roommate of only the finest family. Read your Bible. Please, Stephen!"

He stared at his baggage.

"And write to me, son. You will write to me?"

"Yes, Mother."

"And say your prayers?"

"Yes, Mother."

"Mrs. Doctor Crane!" A voice came down the platform like a silver assegai. One of the temperance ladies was waving.

128

Mrs. Crane bustled away to greet her. "I'm coming, sister!"

Nellie pressed a silver dollar into his hand. Townley had given him a two-and-a-half-dollar gold piece. "If you ever get into New York, Steve!" He had winked broadly.

Nellie said, "Write to Mama, Stevie, write to her!"

"Morning and night."

"At least once a week. If you get good reports I'll let you take my banjo next semester. She's had so many disappointments."

He sighed.

"When your uniform is delivered, have a photograph taken."

"Yes, 'Mother'!"

"Don't be surly, Stephen. It'll please her. And remember to comb your hair. Don't forget. In your uniform."

"Does she think I'm General Grant?"

"God forbid!" The old war hero had been dead nearly two years. The train rolled in, hissing. Mrs. Crane hurried back.

"Embrace her!"

"Mama!"

"Yes, Stephen, your train. I see it. Do you have everything? I'll come up to visit you at Claverack whenever I can. If you need anything, write to me. Doctor Flack will have spending money for you. But, son"—she gazed at him sadly—"if only you would give up your tobacco, those smelly pipes!"

His arms had poised to embrace her. He could only say, "Yes, Mama. All right, Mama!" and peck at her cheek. She was still two inches taller than he.

"Are you sure that you packed your Bible?"

"Yes, Mama." He feared that she would cry.

She looked off into the distance and controlled herself.

He clasped her firmly and choked back a sob. " 'Bye!" he muttered.

Settled in his place, he wiped his eyes and peered through the window. Where was she? He located Nellie. Beside her stood a tall, graying woman in a bonnet and dark cape. She looked like a stranger. He waved his hand like a small boy until the station had slipped back.

CHAPTER 20

The day had quietly darkened. When the train puffed into the Long Branch Depot, snow flurries were dancing in the air, descending upon field and tree and the frightened houses. Wet flakes stuck to the windowpanes. An hour later, the Jersey landscape, cowering from the rage of the blizzard, had become ghostly, and the coaches were slipping through villages that were as white as geese.

When he stepped upon the ferryboat to cross the Hudson River, the skies were clearing, but an icy wind tweaked his nose and stung his cheeks. He stood at the railing, vicariously steering the ferry into uncharted seas while slabs of ice worked downstream. The river was cutting him from his past. As far as he could see down the Narrows, vessels, harassed by the howling gusts, were struggling on their courses with canvas reduced. Their masts appeared to be wobbling. An ocean steamer with three red stacks was frantically whistling outside her slip at Hoboken. Under her bow, two tugboats screamed back; the craft behaved like irate sisters.

Across the river the tall buildings of New York appeared to be mounted on a frosted trellis. Somewhere on the east side of Manhattan would be the new bridge to Brooklyn, a span of towers and piano-wires. On the right, he identified the back of the Statue of Liberty with the arm aloft. Wally McHarg had claimed that the giantess's head was fourteen feet high, the nose four feet long. Wally had, of course, exaggerated. Nothing could be that big.

In the Grand Central Station, he stood beside his baggage, one foot against his trunk, and watched travelers streaming by; not a familiar face anywhere. A wild hope tantalized him that Marie would be waiting at the station in Hudson.

He took a window seat on the left side of the coach. The train lurched. No one had asked to share his seat, although a pair of dark eyes had casually met his stare. With a sigh, he produced his notebook and pencil; Townley had taught him to carry the "tools" of his trade.

At Poughkeepsie, he went into the smoking car. He smoked calmly and scrawled "Stephen Crane . . . Stephen Crane . . . Stephen Crane."

"Hudson! Hu-Hudson!"

The river was choked with ice. They passed an island, a lighthouse, and commercial ice-houses. The little town on the western bank must be Athens.

Marie was not at the depot. He left his baggage at the Boston & Albany platform and hurried to the post office.

The clerk, who resembled his brother George, was gone several minutes. "Nothing."

He gripped the wicket like a prisoner gazing out at the free world. "Please, sir, would you look again? Stephen Crane. General Delivery. It would be from Canada. Montreal."

The clerk shrugged. "Maybe in the next mail."

Had she written to him at Asbury Park? Oh, God! It would fall into Nellie's hands!

On the train to Claverack, which wound pleasantly through white hills and across a frozen creek, he nursed his melancholy.

A slight, handsome lad, with a shock of closely-cropped black hair and a sharp profile, was perched on the window seat. Stephen, who had already formed a poor opinion of the environs of "Claverack College and Hudson River Institute," surveyed the tiny room. Upon leaving the station, he had wandered through the little village. Three churches, Presbyterian, Methodist, and Reformed, and, at the crossroads, a clapboard hotel. On the highway toward the barracks-like structure of the Institute stood another church. Beyond the parsonage lay a cemetery with rows of headstones like gray dominoes in the snow. He was in a dead and sterile world.

"I'm Crane." He dragged in his trunk. He pulled off his coat, flung open his suitcase, and began to unpack. Every drawer in the single bureau was crammed.

"You Earl Reeves? Professor Flack says you're my roommate." He amended, "I'm to be your roommate. That bureau is full."

Reeves ignored him. He stared over his shoulder and through the window. His fingernail scratched at a patch of frost.

Stephen inspected the closet. Every coat hanger was occupied. On the floor sat a row of new shoes. He counted six pairs.

"Reeves, where do I put my gear?"

He again pulled open the drawers. Fine shirts, crisp new underwear, two dozen or so white handkerchiefs, and almost as many pairs of new stockings. Three pair of braces! "You must be rich!" he called out. "But where do I put my stuff?"

In the next drawer were four nightshirts; in the bottom drawer, six percale pillowcases and several folded sheets and thick towels. "Hell, you must be Jay Gould!"

He returned to the closet: three suits, two heavy coats of soft, fleecy material, a raincoat, three caps, and a pair of ankle-high arctics in addition to the regular shoes. He crimsoned at the thought of his own meager possessions.

"Say! Where do I put my duds?"

In a surprisingly rich voice, Reeves drawled, "Not here, boy."

"I'm your roommate."

In the storage cabinet, new books were carefully arranged beside pads of writing paper, a box of red pencils, and a tall jar of ink.

The two drawers in the little table between the beds were also filled with personal articles.

Helplessly, he glanced again at Reeves, who had arisen and, hands in his pockets, was eyeing him contemptuously.

At a glance that roved from his tousled hair to his scuffed shoetops, Stephen bristled. "I've got to put my stuff somewhere!"

"Out the window, Crane!" Reeves replied coldly. He lifted the sash, and let a blast of cold air into the room. "Out!"

"Out the window?" Stephen repeated bewilderedly.

Reeves was strikingly handsome, the tiny mole on one cheek adding, in an almost girlish way, to the attractiveness of the lean features. He wore a brown wool cardigan, a fine white shirt, and a striped bow tie, neat breeches and polished brown shoes.

"Yes, my boy. As fast as you unpack, I'm going to heave your rags out. I don't want you here, thank you!"

Blind rage choked the newcomer. With a roar, he pulled out a drawer, seized an armful of shirts, and dashed for the open window.

"Don't you dare!" Reeves shouted, and blocked his way.

"Out the window!" Crane grated. "You said it!"

"Or fight!" The youth's fists went up. "Marquis of Queensbury rules."

Obligingly, Stephen halted. For a moment, he was poised with the shirts; then, deliberately, he dropped them on the floor.

"Hey, you! Pick them up!"

"Make me!" he snarled. "Make me! Duke of Asbury rules!"

"Who's he? Never heard of him!"

"You'll find out!" He approached warily, fists weaving. "Come on, you—you——"

"You'll step on my shirts!"

"Out the window with them! Come on!"

"You're hankering for a fight."

"Come on!"

"You're mad."

Stephen jabbed Reeves' shoulder. "Come on! I've had all I want. I've just had one loss, and I don't care any more. I'll knock you out the window along with your dude shirts!"

"You did?" Reeves inquired, ducking. He moved his fists expertly, and kept his adversary at a distance. "What loss? What happened?"

"A girl—a woman. Come on!"

Reeves shook his head and backed off. "Oh, no! No grudge fight. I've got nothing against you. I just wanted to mix 'em, and test you."

"Come on, mix!"

"Hey, watch it! Those shirts are five dollars apiece."

"Yeah! And I bet they're just my size." He struck the other's shoulder. "Come on!"

"No, sir!" Reeves, leaping forward, expertly pinned Stephen's arms to his sides. "I bet they're your size, too!" He grinned now.

They stood face to face. Crane's anger fled. Reeves had a grip of steel. "All right."

Reeves released him. "I didn't want to get a tenderfoot in here sharing with me." He began to empty the top drawers. "They said your father was a bishop."

"My uncle. Biggest bishop in the North, maybe in the whole world. Three hundred pounds of bishop, and cold dead."

"Who's the Duke of Asbury?"

Stephen chuckled. "I invented him!"

"Say!"

"I'm a writer."

Reeves smiled. "That's why you don't care how you dress. That old coat——"

Stephen studied his garments in surprise. Languidly, "Say, you're welcome to anything I've got."

Reeves beamed. "You, too. You can take anything of mine."

Together, they divided the storage and living space.

"That's better," said Stephen. He calmly produced his pipe.

"It's against the rules!"

"Rules?" He filled the bowl with tobacco and struck a match.

Reeves chortled. "You're all right. Can I try?"

Stephen fished in his belongings for a second pipe. "Pipe of peace."

"How! How!"

Now Reeves, the pipe in his white teeth, rummaged in his roommate's drawer. "Playing cards! Your family allow it?"

"Only poker." Stephen winked.

They sprawled on their beds, and smoked. Crane felt comfortable in his companion's admiring glances. He listened soberly as Reeves gave him the lay of the land. There was a poolroom at the rear of McKinstry's drugstore in Hudson; beer could be had.

"What about this girl, Steve?"

He shook his head. "Greatest love of my life. Can't talk about it. Her family sent her across the border to get her away from me."

"Beautiful?"

"Like an actress. Rich Canadian. They own half of Montreal. But it's all over."

"I know." They gazed into each other's eyes. "Steve, sometime if you want to, tell me more."

Crane studied the glowing coal in his pipe. "I learned a lot."

"Still hurts, doesn't it?"

He nodded thoughtfully. "I'll never forget her. One promise, Earl."

"Cross my heart!"

"Any letters come, never open them! If there's a crest or a seal on the envelope, don't ask questions."

"Hope to die!"

"And never mention her name to me."

Reeves' eyes opened wide. "I don't know her name!" He leaned across the bed and offered his hand. "Friends?"

"How!"

"Ugh, good!"

"How's the baseball around here?" Stephen inquired casually. "I can catch any ball anyone can pitch."

Having absorbed the information on the local athletics, he inquired about the newspapers in the vicinity. "I've got to write, Earl!" he said earnestly, touching his heart. "I've got to write to forget her."

Reeves nodded understandingly.

CHAPTER **21**

When the uniforms arrived, he accepted his with a grin. The stuff of the gray-blue tunic, the high collar, the tight trousers, the belt with its brass buckle, the cap with its insignia, warmed him with a new pride.

Military exercises might, as his mother had intimated, help to form his character. Military men had not been the worst of the nation's leaders. From West Point, up the Hudson, had come the shavetails who had fought the nation's greatest war: Lee, Grant, Meade, Sherman, Sheridan, McClellan, and their colleagues.

He could not yield unconditionally to the scholastic discipline. He skipped classes to go tramping in the snow down to Claverack Creek as far as the tollhouse on the turnpike, and to brood over the wintry landscape. He rebelled against attending chapel, and was the last to straggle into the dining hall. Every Saturday, until his money ran out, he rode the Boston & Albany into Hudson to call at the post office for the mail from Marie that never came.

He would probably never see her again. She had once belonged to him; she no longer did. Yet he relived their intimacies, and the sensual memories teased him. He marveled that he had been so bold.

She had showered him with useful presents: shirts, handkerchiefs, stockings, each article so fine that he had not dared to let them pass into the family wash; he had brought them to Claverack. When Earl Reeves fingered a monogrammed handkerchief, Stephen smiled mysteriously.

To flaunt his rebellion, he wore his old red sweater when he was not strictly required to be in uniform. After the first hootings and catcalls, it excited no comment, although Professor Landon quipped, "Yon Crane is clad like a flamingo!"

Reeves, jolly companion, sober student, and good egg, wore the red sweater on lazy Saturday mornings. Stephen good-naturedly yielded; he was welcome to any of the Indiana lad's garments. On one point, Earl, neat and orderly, quickly became cross: "Take a complete pair of shoes, dammit! Not a left from one pair and a right from another!"

The narrow corridors became familiar, the classrooms less like inquisition chambers. After the thaw, terminal buds appeared on the trees. The countryside was still drab, but spring was coming and baseball weather could not be far behind. His desire to make the school team compelled him to look to his studies.

As the temperatures rose, drill was no longer confined to the maple floors of College Hall. The entire brigade of four companies, equipped with the ancient rifles the government had passed on from stocks dating back to the Mexican War, was turned out to march and to counter-march. Professor Landon's pupils tootled appropriately on cornet and fife, while the huge music teacher, in mufti, rattled on a snare drum. Professor Flack, titular Colonel of the unit, appeared to review his troops.

The Colonel, five feet two, was in full dress including epaulettes, loops of gold braid, and a tasseled sword.

"The uniform that walks like a man!" muttered Stephen.

Colonel Flack received salutes with civilian eagerness, and returned them smartly. On the sidelines, with Mrs. Flack, stood the females of the institution.

"*Mira! Mira!*" whispered Francisco Eschemundias, the Cuban boy whom Stephen had dubbed "Chico." "Look! Garls!"

The companies performed sharply as the Colonel snapped commands. Not a file-closer escaped his attention. The cadets, who had expected a lark on this first outdoor drill of the year, were inspired to a new *esprit de corps*.

Even Crane agreed that the Head, though diminutive, was no tin soldier. Colonel Flack inspected the ranks with proper military competence and severity. As the brigade marched off the field, the ladies applauded.

The following afternoon, Crane, Reeves, Chico, and Stanton Grabill marched off in uniform to have their pictures taken. Beyond the depot, they waited for the daily freight, and climbed into a boxcar for the three-mile ride. In town, the quartette descended upon Mr. Glueckel, the humpbacked photographer.

Reeves proposed that they take turns posing with his sword and scabbard. Crane, elected to be the first to sit before the camera, was determined to look solemn in uniform. The others joshed and hooted to make him grin. Chico hopped about like a baboon, calling "*Mira! Mira!*"

"Qviet!" pleaded the photographer, appearing like a gnome from under his black cloth. "Qviet!"

Stephen reflected that the one person to whom he yearned to send a photograph would have it destroyed by her servant before the packet was opened. The finished portrait showed him unsmiling, with his hair slicked down as if he were Napoleon at Elba.

They walked the streets of Hudson, four abreast. At McKinstry's, they trooped in for ice cream. Sitting erect at the deal tables, they appraised the Hudson girls who swept in to admire their smart uniforms.

"That tall one with the red hair, Steve," Earl muttered. "I've seen her batting eyelashes at you before."

"Not interested."

Grabill muttered, "When you see a girl on the street, how can you tell if she's virtuous or——"

"You look in the eyes!" Eschemundias declared. "*Mira!* You watch how they walk." He wiggled his hips and sighed. "Ah, Habana, plenty garls!" He was a swarthy lad with eyes that gleamed like obsidian.

"I thought they had chaperones in Cuba."

Chico nodded vigorously. "I do not mean the good garls."

"There are no 'bad' girls," Crane frowned, spooning his ice cream. "If no man comes along to ruin them, they stay good. It's always the man."

"I mean garls who——" Chico's hands were so expressive that the others snickered. There was a certain house near the docks where "garls" from the New York red-light district came up every summer. "For the wis-itors! They are so wi-ild—like in Par—ris!"

Crane winked at Reeves. "How do you know, *amigo?*"

"I have seen!"

The conversation dealt exclusively with the qualities of harlots. Chico, whose home was in Santiago de Cuba, was a native of Havana, where hundreds—"t'ousands!"—ministered to visiting seamen.

"American garls are froze-up ice. In Cuba——" He described a party, which his older brother had attended, where the waitresses "wore aprons and not a naw-thing else! Not a naw-thing—like the day they were bored!"

The imaginations of his listeners were stimulated.

"Salomes without veils," Crane contributed.

"Beils! They got naw-thing on them, I tell you. You could see everything in front of your face. The men eat and drink and, when anybody likes, he takes a garl up the stairs. Then they come back and eat and drink some more."

"What do they do if they have a baby?" Grabill inquired.

"Many have babies!" Chico assured them. "Why not? They are womans, no?"

"Well," Stephen drawled, "if President Cleveland can have a bastard, why not a 'working' girl?"

The badinage, ranging over a dozen topics, returned always to the single subject that could not be tabled as long as boys, by nature's startling processes, were to become men. They sought mutually to ventilate the darkest corners of their minds.

Later, on Third Street, they encountered Mrs. Flack and a group of girls she had escorted into Hudson. "Hello, boys!" As they touched their caps, she scrutinized them suspiciously. "What have you been up to?"

"I guess," Stanton Grabill reasoned later, "that even if you only think about it, something shows in your eyes."

"I should keep mine eyes shut up all the time!" Chico laughed.

"Any married woman knows what you're thinking," alleged Reeves. "Once they get married——" He whistled.

"The young girls know, too," Grabill declared. "In the dark they're all grown up." He had sideburns and a swagger, and was reported to be a hand-holder and a waist-squeezer in certain dark lanes around Claverack.

"You can't say 'all'!" Stephen protested. "It takes a man to lead them wrong."

"What do you know about it, Crane?"

Reeves came loyally to his defense. "He could tell you plenty. Couldn't you, Steve?"

Stephen lapsed into a silence that he did not break until Reeves and he were back in their room.

"He's damn bad!" he said grimly of Chico. "He's just damn bad!"

Reeves, who gravely admired his chum, agreed. He was eager to hear Stephen expound, but his roommate had seized his notebook and pencil.

"I ought to write instead of grumbling about it."

Earl discreetly withdrew to the window seat. Soon he would tiptoe out.

Stephen, overwhelmed by a wish to create, was still uncertain, as he jotted down random reflections, of subject or form. There was no beginning and no end to the nature of his writing. He was sampling, prospecting, fumbling, but he was undisconcerted, full of zeal for a drive toward a goal desired but undefined. It spelled FAME, and was to be reached by his mind-force and his pen.

Vaguely, he was aware that he was different from the others, from Earl, Chico, and Grabill, even from his brother Townley; that he was related, as a nursling tree is to the giants of the forest, to the great names whose works he had tasted, that he was of their mentality and of their spirit. He was indeed set apart and chosen. The reportage and the sketches he had done were exercises to guide him to a greater purpose.

He had heard no still, small voice, yet the Call had come. He could not determine when it had reached his ears, not today but on some unaware yesterday. Blessed juices, of whose existence he had not known, were pouring strength into his brain and bloodstream, endowing him with acuity and new ambition.

A mystic dedication had arrived; all his life had been preparation. Confusion still abounded, yet the sounds of order were discernible and exhilarating. He knew that for him language would be the great tool. Life, in roughly-hewn blocks of experience, waited to be carved into figures and groups unlike any that had been sculpted before. Somehow, he would uncover shapes of vigor and great beauty.

So he sat, waiting for further inspiration.

In the dining hall, each group of ten was under the supervision of an instructor. Frequently, Stephen sat at the Reverend General Van Petten's table. The "Rev" frowned at the use of his military title. Once Stanton Grabill had addressed him as "Senator," alluding to his services in the State Legislature. The "Rev" had frowned: "Nay, boy, not that!"

His green eyes appeared so innocent behind the gold-bowed spectacles, his pink face so babyish-round in the center of the white mane and beard, that it was difficult to imagine "Old Pet" as a Brigadier General. Yet his voice had a baritone vigor, and could boom out when he became angry. Stephen had been assigned to his class in American History.

"Corporal Crane sits among us solemnly," the Reverend General mocked. "However, his active mind obviously is off in other fields. He has many fish to fry, has Corporal Crane. At this moment, he may be playing catcher beside the noblest athletes in the American League Association, or he may be following the footsteps of Henry Stanley, explorer, whom he admires, or he may be preoccupied with the merits of his new water-pipe. Speak softly, ladies and gentlemen, let us not awaken Corporal Crane from his reverie."

The chortling of his tablemates stirred Stephen. He glanced into the green eyes, and smiled.

"Ah, Corporal! The traveler returneth? Do you care to inform us where you have been wandering, what weighty problems bore so heavily upon your mind?"

Boldly, "I was wondering, sir, thinking of Chancellorsville, since we were talking about the twenty-fifth anniversary of the battle, if everyone who fought there was a hero. Didn't anybody on our side get scared and run like a rabbit?"

"An excellent query," Van Petten rejoined evenly. "Excellent!" He reflected. "We were, at different times, to be sure, all 'scared' as you say. All men, uniform or rank notwithstanding, know fear. Some men let fear conquer and destroy them, others strive against it."

"Sir, were you never afraid?" Chico blurted out.

"Mightily and often!" the General confessed. "The mark of a man is not whether he fears, but whether he can overcome his fear in time to save himself and those who look to him."

The youngsters listened respectfully. In Van Petten's class history became alive, at least in terms of the battles of Fair Oaks, Antietam, and Winchester, where the chaplain-turned-officer had commanded with distinction. He had held the 34th New York Regiment steadfast in the face of a rebel bayonet charge. With the 160th New York, he had, at bloody Antietam, reinforced another regiment and had maintained an exposed position in the face of incredible losses. It was also known that he had been seriously wounded at Winchester.

"Only cowards run away!" Chico declared. "In my country, a coward would be dee-spised!"

"Under certain circumstances, Captain Francisco Eschemundias," the General retorted, "all men may run! Brave men overcome their panic and return to the field."

Gravely, he added, "The line between the hero and the coward may be a thin one. No man can say how he will conduct himself in the face of fire." He clenched a fist. "Courage! The stout heart! Every man must pray to God for it."

"Sir, what is it like to be wounded?" Reeves asked.

Van Petten winced. "I do not know how it feels when a saber slashes at a man, or a cannonball strikes him. I have experienced neither." He stared over their heads. "I can tell you only what I felt. When a man hears a bullet whine, it has already passed him. It is not his. The ball that is intended for him does not announce itself. If it strikes the head, it may stun fearfully. If it tears off a limb, he may spin about from the blow. The ball that plows into the soft flesh may not give pain instantly. It does not maul, it slaps. It enters and, suddenly, the man is weakened!"

He mopped his brow. "He doesn't know what has happened to him. He knows that he is no longer a combatant, and he can't accept it. Something has taken place. 'No, not me!' He may go forward several yards, then feel that his strength is ebbing, and be grateful when he falls."

Beads of perspiration dotted his forehead. "The agony, the surgery, these all come later."

Stephen waited for him to speak of the hole which a bullet had gouged through his thigh. But the General concluded, "Brave fellows I had with me. God rest their souls!"

Mrs. Van Petten, eavesdropping from the next table, called sternly, "Reverend!"

He stirred, and said, "Pass the peas, boys!"

CHAPTER 22

At midterm, his mother met him in the train shed at Grand Central Station. As she advanced from the legion of blank-faced travelers under the great steel arches, he thought that she had never looked so regal. She was wearing a black bonnet with a purple velvet trim and a purple princess-styled gown with black velvet buttons from the high neck to the sweeping hem.

"You're beautiful, Mama!"

"I'm an old woman!" She hugged him. "I needed a simple gown for the speakers' platform. Nellie insisted."

She admired his uniform. "How you've changed! You've grown, matured. You're so much more confident of yourself, Stephen. I knew that Claverack would be good for you."

He peered at the throngs of passers-by, at the shop windows crammed with merchandise, at the victorias and cabriolets, and at the bicycles that rolled continuously at the curbs and brought curses from the coachmen. The noise of the city, a clacking, clinging, purring, rumbling concatenation, was impressive, the sum of the boiling rage of a metropolitan sea in which nearly a million persons swam daily.

"A man went all around the world on a bicycle." He had to raise his voice to be heard. "Stan Grabill has a book about it. From Yokohama to San Francisco he had to take a steamer, but he wheeled thirteen thousand miles. The Head won't allow me to keep Pudgy, but if I had a Columbia wheel——"

She wasn't listening; she had so much to tell him of Ted's new house on Sutton Avenue in Lakeview, and of Mame, who was a devoted wife and mother and kept four-year-old Agnes Elizabeth and two-year-old Edith in white dresses. "I've told her that dark clothing would save her the backbreak of daily laundry. But she is so proud of them that she dresses them like little dolls in white. Each has long, lovely golden hair."

She reported also on Will's family. Her namesake, Mary Helen, was eight, Agnes was four, Edna was two. "They lost Jessie. Your father and I lost two Jessies, a boy and a girl. How Will yearns for a son!"

Stephen, striving not to be bored, hoped that she would not talk of the family throughout the entire holiday.

They took a hansom cab to the hotel. On the way, she advised him that, unless he was willing to accompany her to a temperance meeting, he must spend the afternoon alone. "Since this is your first holiday in the city, I have prepared an itinerary for you."

He might visit General Grant's temporary tomb in Riverside Park. She had not changed; it was he whose horizons had widened. His classmates would flock to admire Lillian Russell; he was to gloat over the curves of a mausoleum.

They enjoyed Fifth Avenue from the top of a horse-drawn public coach. Then he was free to go on his way alone from the newly completed twin spires of Saint Patrick's Cathedral to the Battery at the southern end of the island.

The noise continued to fascinate him. "A noise of men beating upon barrels," he noted. "A noise of men beating upon tin." He boarded a streetcar to prowl down Broadway, and envied the gripman at the controls of the yellow monster. He tramped through side streets where beer wagons rattled horridly over the cobblestones.

New York drew him like a powerful magnet. Despite the din and the clanging, the city was a woman, a lusty, bawdy creature who strutted and swung her hips and kicked her voluminous skirts, and promised shuddering adventures. The passers-by were nameless, faceless. Not one said, "Good morning!" or "Good evening!" Not one cared to be recognized.

If the city was Babylon, he yearned to be part of it, to be lost in its labyrinths. Somewhere in these hostile structures, his fate skulked. He waited for a voice to call, for a hand to beckon.

The horsecars and the elevated trains swarmed with people. From afar, the vehicles seemed part of a grand carnival; the entire island was a carousel. Sitting or standing in the public transports brought no feeling of intimacy; poultry enjoyed as much privacy hanging from their hooks in the market. The elegant passengers in the fine carriages sat drawn into their corners as if any stranger might leap in beside them.

From the Bowling Green northward, he gawked as frankly as any of the newcomers in alien dress who, with bundles and children, moved like sheep in a new pasture. He must see Wall Street and Astor House, and the Post Office, which was supported by so many columns that it seemed to have been put together with slender bobbins. City Hall Park was a larger Orange Square. At Newspaper Row, he gazed wistfully at the buildings where the presses were throbbing.

He admired Grace Church, and the baked goods at Fleischmann's Vienna Model Bakery. At Union Square, he peered into the jewelry shops at the brooches and necklaces. Ladies in furs were being helped into their carriages by grooms in livery. Such fine women, soft, languorous, mysterious, were for the rich. Men without either fame or fortune must be content to feed on buns; their betters took the pastries.

At the hotel, he changed into his good suit. He had no right to wear the Claverack uniform in the by-streets. He dined with his mother at a little restaurant. He drew out her chair grandly, advised her on the table d'hôte, and asked the waiter to fetch water for her pill.

"You are a man, Stephen. So forceful."

"Yes, Mama."

She announced that she must travel to Brooklyn to visit Uncle Luther's church, where once she had taught Sunday School.

"It would do you no harm to come with me this time. He's a learned scholar. You would enjoy his library of Latin and Greek classics."

He raised an eyebrow. "I want to see the city."

"Be careful after dark. Satan's minions are everywhere."

She boarded the cars to cross the bridge, on which necklaces of light now twinkled. The elevated engine steamed and chugged and, with a trail of fiery ash, hauled the little coaches into the upper reaches and the darkness. The stone pillars loomed like dark giants; the cables were black pythons, the struts muted harp-strings that went nowhere.

He rushed away to meet the city as if she were a girl whose virtue he was eager to try.

On the Bowery, hundreds of people moved through the streets, on foot or in carriages; after dark, a new life had begun. It was too early to visit the Bowery Mission, where the breadline formed at midnight. He entered the dime museums and marveled at the cheap wonders. The famous Bowery was partly hurdy-gurdy, tinsel, and "secret sights." He ordered a glass of beer, sipped, and listened. Drabness and meanness, men who were ready to be aggressive, women ready to be friendly, while the bartenders wiped their bars and worked the taps, and the din grew louder.

Their speech tickled his ears. "Aw, g'wan!" Townley had mimicked it faithfully. It was not brogue and it was not burr; it was gen-oo-wine Bowery, dat's wot, comically swaggering, a true patois, rich in a sudsy poetry as native as the wash on the fire escapes, and wot de hell! suited to these cobblestoned lanes. Everyone spoke it, the little girl, the brawny teamster, the crook-backed peddler, the arrogant policeman, and the thievish pawnbroker. G'way with yeh! Go fall on yehse'f!

He listened keenly as they committed mayhem on the consonants, punished the r's, dropped the g's, sniffed at the haitches. Wot de hell! Any blokie kin talk English. Youse kin do it, too. Elsewhere, the vowels might wear kid gloves; here, they were stuck in torn mittens through which the grimy fingers poked. Outa sight!

The night had clasped the lighted houses in sinister arms. Behind closed doors, women were preparing for rites older than Astarte's.

"Wanna girl?" A lean man had stepped out of a doorway. The fellow was rat-faced, with a knife scar across one cheek.

"Suppose I do?" he retorted.

"What kind d'yeh want?"

"What you got?"

"You wanna Frenchie, huh? Do it t'ree way? I got a girl for you."

"No, no, thank you!" Fear had started perspiration on his scalp.

A policeman accosted the fellow. Stephen waited to see the procurer arrested. But the men chortled, and the officer of the law spun his nightstick.

"Give us a penny!"

A whining ghost in ragged drapery had touched his arm. The once-feminine countenance was like an apple that had wasted and shriveled. The nose was a caricature; the gums were toothless.

"Give us a penny!"

The dragging hem revealed bare, scabrous ankles, the feet housed in a tattered pair of men's shoes. He gave her a nickel.

Her mouth opened—the mouth of death!—and a fetid blast affronted him. "God bless yeh, sir!" The claw snatched the coin from his fingers.

Near an elevated pillar, he halted. Who was she? Probably a superannuated woman of the streets, the offal of sin. His heart ached for her and for every degraded soul. He wanted to shout into the night that the world might know of the existence of such creatures. Where could such a scarecrow roost? How did she subsist? On scraps and leavings, on cast-offs for the castaway. "God help us!"

But he had journeyed here to see Life, the squalid, the hideous, the unendurable that had to be endured halfway or more to ignoble death. Sharp yearnings prickled his flesh.

"Yeh wanna show me somepin'?" A plump girl with straw-colored hair and a brassy air halted before him swinging her purse. "Wot yeh say?"

"Ma'am?"

The bold glance pierced him. "Anyt'in' yeh got!" She licked her coarse mouth with a red tongue. Her cheeks were scarlet.

"I don't know——"

"Honey, I'll be good to yeh. I'm good to all'a boys. Wait till yeh see the time I give yeh!"

She pressed his arm to her breast. "Yeh ain' afraid?"

He bridled. "No, Ma'am!"

"It won' cost yeh n'more, yeh'll see. An yeh'll come back. They all do. Right upstairs."

He cast a beseeching glance down the dark street before he followed her into a vestibule. Bright lights in a parlor, and more women, tall, short, or plump, sprawling on divans. A man in a top hat was inspecting them like a buyer at a cattle fair.

He heard laughter through a wall, and a female voice cursing foully. A chair scraped.

"Where are we going?"

Her swaying rear went up a narrow flight of stairs. She led into a gas-lighted cubicle: a cot, a bureau, a chair, and a washstand. "We're home," she said drily, and shut the door. "What's yeh pleasuh?"

He shyly wiped his feet on the rag rug and watched her wriggling out of her gown. As she began to drop her petticoats, he pulled the chain on the gas-fixture.

"Doncha like what yeh see? Yeh're payin' fur it. Yeh didn' even look!"

"I want it dark!" The Welsbach mantle was outlined a fiery red.

143

She was reaching for his clothes.

Defensively, he clasped her hand.

"See? Like it?" She had flung her nakedness at him.

"Wait!" His temples pounded. "Wait!"

"Yeh're jes' a kid. I'll help yeh." He disliked the cunning hands.

"Yeh neve' bin wit' a goil?"

"Yes, I have!"

"G'wan!"

To prove it, he clutched at her; he knew where to begin. She squirmed and, in her grasp, he was, for a moment, left without purpose. She seemed incredibly larger in the dark.

"Say, I ain' got all nigh'!" Her arms were amazingly strong.

He struggled to elude the wet, devouring lips. He writhed, and the creaking cot startled him.

"Yeh sleepin'?" she sneered. "I ain' yer mudder."

A blaze of anger aroused him, and he forgot the bleakness of the surroundings. In the flesh of this woman was every woman. He cursed and seized her.

Impudently, he denied himself no pleasure. Marie's breasts had been smaller, her hair softer. He struggled to dominate, and vengefully assaulted the figure. "Damn you!" He lost himself; he was not a kid but a man. He gloated to hear her wheezing and grunting; she seemed to be convulsed. Then she was sighing, and her nails were scoring his neck. He wrestled with her as if she were his enemy.

The mattress was filled with straw. The complaining springs sawed at his eardrums. What if the door opened—"Stephen, what are you doing?" The images were gone; vague memories again, horrid, forbidding, loomed and faded.

His lust ebbed as suddenly as it had risen, yet he clung to her breast.

"Yeh all right, kid!" she panted. "Better'n I t'ought."

A scurrying at the wall alarmed him; he made out the shape of the washstand. The porcelain knob on the door was like a shining equine eye.

"Come off it now!" she said. "It's only a rat. Dere all oveh deh place."

He blinked. The instant she had pulled the chain, she had torn away the cloak of secrecy. In the garish light, he shrank from her. Nudity still astonished him; when it emerged from conventional costume, the human figure seemed loosely assembled.

He prodded the blue and yellow bruise that marred her thigh.

"Wotcha wan' now?" she asked grossly. "A big fellow did dat." Barefoot, she tripped to the basin. "Yeh're a schoolboy someplace, aincha?"

"How do you know?"

144

"Schoolboys kin be like monkeys. Dey t'ink the worl's gonna end tomorra, and theh'll be no more you-know-what. What's yeh name?"

"Sam. Sam Carleton."

"Yeh don' look like no Sam Carleton."

He grinned. "My real name is Huckleberry Finn."

She giggled. "Who's he? Yeh're a schoolboy, Sam, yeh are." She finished her ablutions. "Awri', I gotta move. I gotta git mo' customehs. Yeh can't eat and pay the house outa one blokie."

"How many?"

"I gotta woik. Maybe t'ree, fo', fi', six. Can't say how deh luck'll go."

"Six!" He was deflated. He watched the long, full breasts disappear into the chemise, the petticoats tumble down over the thighs.

"Yeh don' hafta go. Dey'll let yeh sit downstehs." Her eyes roved. "Mebbe yeh'll wan' some lateh, somefin' new."

"You have to go out like this every night?"

"Wotcha t'ink?" she demanded fiercely. "I gotta bring somefin' home, don' I?"

He reflected ironically that he had been assuming that she had been created only for his needs. She had to take her earnings home? Did her mother know? Her father? She required the bodies of many men to earn her living.

"C'mon!" She opened the door. "Yeh goin'? I like to keep dis bed warm."

Her eyes were as indifferent as if she had been knitting instead of lying under him ten minutes ago.

In the hall, an older woman was waiting. The girl quietly divided her money. "See yeh lateh, Madge."

Below, she paused to run her hands over her gown. As she pulled at the ruffled collar to elevate her bosom, she winked at Stephen.

"What if I want to see you again?"

"I ain't Nellie Bly goin' 'round the worl'. I'll be right heah."

"What's your name?"

She gave him a quick smile. "Ask for Grace. Jes' ask for Grace."

In the parlor, the women were sitting or lounging in various states of undress, their legs, he thought, unbecomingly apart.

Two men in bowlers were walking about.

A dark-skinned woman with protruding red lips and huge earrings pulled her skirts to midthigh, for their benefit. Stephen saw the naked, pale brown flesh. She turned about and wiggled honey-colored buttocks. A man stroked her and laughed.

Stephen rushed out of the house, clung to the railing, and took deep breaths.

Overhead, the stars were twinkling. Before each of the houses, a red light shone.

A block away, under a lamppost, he became sick in the gutter.

CHAPTER 23

He had been promoted to adjutant of his company, but it was baseball that kept him at Claverack the next term. He wanted to read, to reflect, and to write undisturbed by the narrow disciplines of the Academy, yet he was trapped in the student life. He had a profound respect for "Old Pet," who had displayed courage on the battlefield; the Head and the rest of his retainers struck him as amiable villagers equipped to teach small boys and nubile maidens. His newly-won knowledge of the secret world he could not share with anyone, not even with Earl or Chico, or his newer friends, Puzey and "Tough" Hathaway.

He had journeyed into that netherworld and returned safely. His feelings mingled distaste, pity, and savage triumph when he remembered Grace, the girl of the streets, her coarse mouth, her body with its mingling odors, the narrow bed and their struggles upon it. Certain repulsive details became startlingly alive when he dropped off to sleep, or reflected heatedly about girls and a man's need to be submerged in them.

His adventure had not exposed the secret of sin; it had reduced him to the rank of accomplice. The wicked and corrupt understood more of life at its bitter roots than the good and the innocent.

In April and May, the Claverack baseball team, for which Stephen was catcher, suffered a loss only to the Hudson professionals in the annual game on the Fair Grounds.

In June, First Lieutenant Stephen Crane, adjutant in Company C, which had been awarded the prize for the best drill during the Washington's Birthday ceremonies, was promoted to Captain.

For the final drill, Earl proposed a coordinated prank. Each officer was to march on the parade ground flaunting a colored ribbon.

Stephen wrote to Nellie for a long, red sash. "What in the world do you want it for?" her letter demanded. With the sash in his possession, he did not trouble to reply.

After the first three companies were on the field, Stephen slid the folded sash from inside his tunic and fastened it to the hilt of his sword.

As Company C moved forward, the wind whipped at his ribbon.

A shout arose from the sidelines. A yard of scarlet sash had swept from Captain Crane's regimental sword and fluttered grandly behind him. The spectators applauded.

As he gave his salute, he thought that Colonel Flack concealed a smile. Reverend-General Van Petten was frankly beaming. Captain

Crane marched on proudly. They would remember his farewell to old Claverack long after he was gone.

He was adamant. He would never return to Claverack.

Mama grieved. Nellie harangued him with a list of other schools. Townley, and even Ted, who usually took his side, argued that he must enroll elsewhere.

Cornelia proposed Lafayette College at Easton. "On weekends you can visit my parents in Riegelsville," she said.

His mother gave her consent to the Presbyterian college. "What you need is an institution where your father's good name does not pursue you."

"On holidays you can come up to Port Jervis," Cornelia added. "Will will take you hunting."

"Presbyterians are fine Christians, too," Mama sighed. "Your cousin Fred is a Presbyterian."

He had no sooner arrived at Easton than the Delta Upsilons, discovering that he had played baseball, courted him. At their invitation, he made the trip with the other pledges up little Mount Paxinosas to picnic with the upper classmates and to hear of the virtues of fraternity living. Munching a sandwich and sipping soda pop, he reflected that, on the Bowery, the denizens would have roared at the foolishness of the educated classes.

The Delaware River stretched below lazily like a curved shaft of steel. The sun honed a golden beam against Marble Mountain. Scotts Mountain was a green bulwark. Behind was Chestnut Hill; beyond the city of Easton wound the Lehigh River; seven miles away in New Jersey were the Musconetcong Hills and Hackettstown Seminary.

"There was nothing to that hazing story," a redhaired giant assured two troubled freshmen. "A pledge got scared and wet his breeches, so he cried for his Mama."

"There's no hazing at Lafayette!" another vowed. "A little horseplay maybe. That's all."

"I read that this pledge broke the soph's head with a baseball bat!"

The upper classmen swore that it had been a friendly scuffle. "Wasn't a D. U. in the first place. We don't do that."

Stephen turned a skeptical eye upon the speaker. Why was he lying? The fracas had been reported in the Easton Sunday *Call*. The chief of the hazers was said to have been seriously hurt.

"I heard that they were going to smear his privates with hot pitch!"

"Now who would do anything like that?"

"What about the freshman who was let down a well and kept there until he nearly drowned?"

Stephen knocked his pipe against the heel of his shoe.

"That talk isn't scaring you, Crane?" Ormsby, another sophomore, slapped his shoulder. "You hear those stories in every college. The D. U's don't want cowards. Just horseplay. A little paddling won't scare you, will it?"

He drawled, "I like to defend myself. I don't like to see people hurt. Got down to the Bowery one day and saw a fellow beaten up and his girl trying to protect his head from his assailants——"

He did not add that he had come running, and had received a smashing blow to the jaw. "Beat it, kid!" Two men had kicked the pimp as he lay bloodied in the gutter, while his girl, sprawling across him, had shrieked and tried to shield him. Stephen had shouted, "Help! Police!" and had been struck with a sashweight. Fortunately, the blow had glanced off his shoulder. He had gone staggering into the darkness. A policeman, watching from a stoop, had yelled, "Go run home to yer Ma! Mind yer own business, yeh hear?" The next day, he had purchased a .32 at a pawnshop. He had the gun at the bottom of his trunk.

Ormsby threw him a piercing glance. "Crane, I don't know where you've been raised. D. U. isn't opening its doors to the Bowery."

"I was passing through."

"He ain't afraid. Are you, Crane? Big Claverack athlete! 'Captain Crane,' wasn't it? You'll pull a few splinters out, but, next year, you get even with the new crowd. I bet you'll lay it on harder than we do. Pass it from generation to generation!"

"I don't want to get even with anybody," he retorted. "Maybe there are folks I'd like to paddle. But not around here, not yet."

They chuckled. "We'll see!"

"Why is a pledge like a locomotive?" posed Ormsby.

"Because he's got a tender behind!" the brothers chorused.

The badinage irked Stephen. "I didn't come here for that. I'll take on anybody in a fair fight."

"Who's asking for a fight, Crane? We only want to pull down your breeches and paddle your tail. Didn't your Papa ever skin you?"

"No, he didn't."

"Then it's time someone did. You'll be the better man for it."

All evening, he waited for them.

"You're next, Crane!" Ormsby had promised, and the sophomores had chortled. He had heard the Greeks tramping through the corridor of East Hall before. He had heard them knocking on doors, heard the howls when they entered and the moans as they worked over the pledges.

Lying in his bed, he raged silently. The strong punishing the weak! He wanted their good will, but the brutal hazing revolted him.

He shuddered at a knock on the door. "Crane?"

He could hear his own breathing. Fortunately, he had insisted on rooming alone.

148

"Crane, we know you're there. Open up!" Sticks played a tattoo on the jamb.

"Crane, damn you! Open up, or we'll break it down. Come on, take your paddling like a man, or you'll get worse!"

He scrambled out of bed. He was not afraid of the paddling. They thought it was great fun to humiliate a man; they had intimated that they would know if he had ever been with a girl. He scurried for his robe. It was not in the closet.

"*Crane,* damn you!"

Frantically, he pulled at the drawers of the bureau. He found the robe as he had crumpled it. Under his shirts lay the blue steel revolver.

"Come on, fellows! Break it down!"

They were battering at the door. He could hear them retreating, then rushing forward and pounding at the wood.

He ran to the window. The walk was two stories below.

The thin door was splintering. Then the lock gave. The door was flung back against the wall.

With a cry of panic, he faced them. He recognized Engels, Ormsby, and Craig brandishing paddles.

"Crane! Hey, hold it!" Engels waved at the brothers. "Crane! You're not going to use that gun, are you? Where'd you get it?"

He realized that the revolver was in his hand. Quaking, he swung the weapon from side to side.

"Never mind. Get out of here!" he snarled. "G'wan, or I'll kill yeh!"

They halted. Other youths were crowding in from the hall. "What's wrong? Get him!"

"Careful!" Engels called. "He's got a pistol."

Craig began to advance. "Let's rush him!"

"Doncha dare take—one—more—step!"

"Careful!" Engels repeated. "That's a revolver."

"Watch me and see!" Craig grated. Biting his lip, he tentatively swung his paddle. "I'll break your ass! I'll break your——"

"Not—one—more—step!"

At the cold hatred in his tone, Craig hesitated. "Put that away, Crane! Maybe it's loaded."

"*Not—one—step!*" He lifted his arm. "I'll fire!" His aim was steady as he sighted at Craig's forehead. "I'll give the Easton *Call* a real story! One more step, I warn you!"

Engels was edging along the wall. "You wouldn't dare, Crane, would you?"

He shifted the .32 from Craig to Engels and from Engels to Craig. "You'll see! Go ahead, take a chance."

"He's as green as cheese!" Craig faltered. "Ah, let him alone!"

"You're crazy, Crane!" said Ormsby. "We won't forget it."

He waved the gun. "G'wan, beat it! Get out of here."

They were nonplussed.

"Come on," Ormsby called. "We got others to work on."

They withdrew. "The bastard!" Craig growled.

"I'd like to go back and skin the balls off him!"

"Let him alone, Craig. Come on!"

"He'll wish——"

"We'll get him another time."

Stephen, listening at the door, quaked. In a nearby school, the hazers had hauled a boy off to a brothel and paid a French whore two dollars to corrupt him while they stood around the bed. The foul fiends!

Temporarily, at least, he was safe. Half crouching, he snarled again and muttered, "G'wan!" He waved the pistol. "You blankety-blank bastards, come on, I'll kill you!"

Hazing was officially limited to one week. They might bear him a grudge, but they could pursue him for only one more night. He bolted the door, and threw himself into bed.

The week ended without a further encounter.

He was sound asleep when he felt his arms gripped. A pillow was stuffed into his mouth. Outraged, he thought, "Hazing time is over!" He struggled and let out choked cries. The room was pitch dark.

"Well, Captain Crane?"

He was rolled over on his abdomen. In panic, he kicked his legs. A sharp, stinging whack across the buttocks made him leap. A hard hand ground his head into the pillow. He was suffocating!

After a long series of painful blows of the paddle, he was released, writhing and sobbing, his backside aflame. He coughed and began to retch.

Someone was searching the bureau drawers. "Crane, where did you put that pistol?"

He could not reply; a hand had once more ground his head into the pillow. He had hidden it under the mattress.

"Let's go! He won't be playing soldier for a while. Good-bye, Captain Crane!"

They had placed a ladder at the window. He heard them descending, and tried to get up. He would kill them! But he could not stir.

Three days later, when his wounds had healed sufficiently to permit him to drag along with a cane, he encountered Tom Craig.

"Hey, Crane, where've you been?" Craig regarded the cane with a flicker of amusement. "Did you have a fall?"

"Craig," he blazed, "you know I've got a gun! I know how to use it. You're too big to handle with my fists. You go buy yourself a pistol— I'll give you the money—and I'll meet you anywhere you say."

The other gaped. "You mean a duel?"

"Call it anything you please. I want to meet you and kill you! The same for the others."

"You're mad, Crane! You're not out West. This is Pennsylvania. It was only a paddling. We didn't do half of what we could have done. Why——"

"If you cross my path again, I'll assassinate you! Tell the others. In a fair fight, with a gun, I'll meet them. Otherwise, stay away from me!"

Craig retreated. "You're hot, Crane, hot under the collar. Wait till next year comes, and you can get even on somebody else's tail."

"I don't want to get even on the innocent. Besides, I won't be here next year."

The sophomore paled. "You don't mean that. Next spring you'll be second-string catcher on the team. At least that. Everybody knows your record. They need you."

"I don't need them!"

CHAPTER 24

He entered Syracuse University—"Sigh-rah-kyou-ss," as Uncle Bishop used to say—in January, and went to live in Auntie Persis' house on the hill.

As a one-time registrant at Claverack, he was required to pass only a written test. Once more, he was enrolled in Algebra, Chemistry, Physics, and in the abominable Drafting; he had skipped so many classes at Lafayette that the Dean had advised him to leave before he was expelled. He asked for German instead of French, and elected English Literature and English Criticism. It was mandatory to take Elocution.

Auntie Persis crowed, she was so eager to have him. Although she occupied the eight-room house alone, she allotted to her great-nephew a little room on the third floor. A dozen times each day, she climbed the stairs to knock: "Nephew, it's me! Your Auntie Persie, Dear One." She said, "Neffie." She kept the late Bishop's chamber intact, the great bed covered with a huge spread and bolster; no one must use his quarters. "He would not like it, Neffie, he would not."

Stephen had a good bed and a writing table, a bookshelf and a deep closet, and a fine view of the city. Every morning at six, the old lady managed the two flights of stairs with a vast tray of breakfast. At noon, she provided an ample dinner and quizzed him about school. For supper, she served a collation of cold meats. She aired and hung his clothes, she mended his seams, she sewed on missing buttons, and she brushed his coat.

One day, he came upon her blacking his shoes.

"Auntie!"

"I did it for the Bishop, your great-uncle—God keep his soul!—every day of his life, all our years together," she said wistfully. "He would let nobody else black his boots but me. See how I make them shine?"

He kissed the dry, wrinkled cheek. "Not for me, Auntie!"

"But I like it. Let me, Neffie, let me!"

He saw that she would be hurt. "Ah, Auntie!"

"Now if you would follow in his footsteps," she sighed. "I pray for you, Neffie, every night. Wouldn't your mother be pleased if you became a fine preacher and, maybe someday, were elected bishop? Oh, my!"

He was alarmed. "Auntie, I'm not worth your prayers. I'm a bad one. I'll never be a preacher!"

"Shoo, shoo!" she said with a flick of her wrist. "I'm praying to the Bishop to watch over you."

Her simple goodness affected him. He said grace and joined her in prayers. He could not bring himself to deny her his company to Centenary Church. "My God!" he thought. "She's making me backslide!"

"Recite your lessons," she pleaded after she had stuffed him with meats and goodies. "I may not understand, Neffie, but I listen brightly. The Bishop—God keep his soul—always said 'Persie, you listen brightly!' "

"No!" Was she really that simple, or was it artfulness?

"Yes, yes, Dear One. What will I say when he asks me when I've joined him up yonder? 'Persie, why didn't you listen on the boy?' I must."

She baffled him.

He stayed up past midnight, trying desperately to write sketches, filling sheet after sheet with false starts. Writing his brief pieces as city correspondent for the New York *Tribune*—thanks to Townley—was far easier work.

A scratch at the door.

"Neffie, Dear One!" In she came, carrying the ever-present tray: hot tea and eight slices of buttered toast. "For the inner man! The Bishop liked his bite of toast at night."

He could not rebuff the endless kindnesses. She sat before him. "Ah, the sight of a man enjoying his food!" Each slice of toast dripped butter.

He urged her to share with him.

"No, Dear One, I eat like a sparrow." She shook her head so solemnly that he could have written her next speech. "He always said, 'Persie, you eat like a sparrow!' "

"While you are writing, Stephen"—the brown eyes glowed—"I am praying for you!"

152

"My God!" he breathed.

"Will you read to me, Stephen? I like the story about the dog Jack. The Bishop—God keep his soul!—would never have a dog or a cat. And I so lonely when he was away traveling in Europe and everywhere."

Having visited the police court in the afternoon, he had written a report on three wife-beatings, two evictions, and an embezzlement. "Not now, Auntie, please."

She sniffed, her little nose wrinkling. "You are not employing the weed?"

"I am, Auntie." He had the pipe on his desk, he had never concealed it.

"I shall have to write to your Mama, Dear One."

"She knows it, Auntie."

The aged lady blinked. "In this house where the Bishop—God keep his soul!—lived and breathed! Are you addicted, Neffie?

"I use tobacco, Auntie Persis."

"My, my!" She put her hands to her cheeks. "I shall have to pray harder, harder. What would he say?"

She had faith in prayer, yet assisted it by gathering his pipes and depositing them in the dustbin.

"Auntie!"

"I must do the Lord's will, Dear One. It is evil, Neffie; we must root out evil!"

"I don't want to give up my tobacco, Auntie!"

She wagged a finger. "Oh, you will suffer for a while. But think how it will please the Lord. Besides, you may burn holes in my sheets."

When the old woman had gone to bed, he retrieved his pipes. How could he combat her goodness? No wonder his mother had settled on "Sigh-rah-kyou-ss."

He packed his trunk. In the morning, when Auntie Persis went to her marketing, he removed himself, pipe in his teeth, to the Delta Upsilon house at the corner of Ostrom and Marshall Streets.

The Varsity baseball team was uniformed in castoffs from the wardrobe of the Syracuse "Stars." As George Shepherd, the youthful manager, called the names, each member of the squad rummaged in the heap of garments and tried to outfit himself.

Stephen, third on the list, was so slight that nothing fit him properly.

"How did you ever play football? You didn't buck the line with those bony hips?" George Bond asked. "And no shoulders."

"He rattled his skeleton, and they got scared and let him run a hole through the line."

"I was sick," Crane groused. "I was sick all February." Belligerently, he demanded, "Do I play, or don't I?"

"Hey, he's got a temper, too!" George Shepherd said. "Go into town and buy a uniform."

In the evening, he rode the streetcar into Syracuse and went from store to store. Nothing was available in his size.

In a sour humor, he strolled toward the Criterion, the amusement center where the cheap shops clustered. New electric arc lights were being installed in the city. However, the wonders of the dime museum were still being hawked by the light of lanterns and hissing gas jets. He spent a dime potting targets in a shooting gallery, and a nickel hurling balls at a pyramid of milk bottles.

At "The Turkish Harem" he listened to the barker's spiel: "See the dee-lights of a see-rag-lio! Watch the gyrations of Madamoiselle Larsene who escaped a Pasha's passion and will show you—before your very eyes—the forbidden dance never before exposed in *all* its naked, shameless truth!"

A voice whispered. "Would you like to come home with me?"

The tall, dark-haired girl had kohled eyes and brightly rouged cheeks. She clung to his arm. "It's a few blocks' walk."

"I haven't any money."

"A dollar?"

"Not until next week. I haven't any to spare." She was eighteen or nineteen.

"You can stay as long as you want."

"I didn't mean that." He faced her. "Say, I just haven't got it."

"Too bad, Jack," she sighed. "Times is hard. Unless the college boys come into town, there ain't a free dollar around. Half the workers in the salt sheds got laid off."

"Why don't you try the saloons?" he asked.

"Not me!" she retorted. "That's the territory of Kate Skidmore. A copper would throw me in—unless he was a young one, and he'd want a piece free."

He frowned. "I didn't know there was anything like that going on in Syracuse."

She gave a short, bitter laugh. "Where did you come from? Off the moon? Say, you're a college boy, too! Where do your friends go when they get horny?"

He quailed. "You shouldn't talk like that." He thrust his hand into his pocket. "Look, I've got fifty cents. It's my last, but you can have it."

She shook her head. "I've got my price. If I can hold out to Saturday night, I'll get plenty of customers." She gave him a sidewise glance. "I've gotten as much as five dollars."

He pressed the money into her palm. "Take it, go ahead!"

154

Her fingers closed upon the coin. "What do you mean? Honest, I always get a dollar."

"Nothing! Take it."

"I don't want charity." She pouted, "I got a figure, I know my way. You from one of them fraternities? You ask them. Sometimes on a Saturday night I take on three or four of the boys for a party."

"Buy yourself some food. I don't want anything."

She shrugged. "You mean that, don't you? All right, I'll trust you. Maybe I shouldn't, but I ain't doing nothing. You can pay me when you get the rest."

He flushed. "Maybe I'll see you next time I'm in town."

Her eyes roved toward a huge man in overalls who was staggering forward. "Thanks! You look me up sometime. I won't forget you."

She swayed her hips. "Hullo, Jack!" she called.

The drunk grinned, and comically touched his cap.

"Bargain night, Jack! One iron man, huh?" She hugged his arm to her breast. "Come on, honey!" Over his shoulder, she winked at Stephen.

He was dismayed. In Syracuse! He had thought that soliciting on the streets was limited to the Bowery. For a moment he wished that he had accepted the girl's invitation. That drunk might beat her.

Freddie Lawrence, a Port Jervis boy who was planning to study medicine, was reading in the parlor at the Delta Upsilon house.

"Fred!" he called. "Do you know that right here in Syracuse, in the shadow of the University, there are girls walking the streets?"

Lawrence raised an eyebrow. "The Age of Discovery!" he mocked. "Wherever there are men who need a girl, there will be girls to fill their needs."

"This one who stopped me worked alone."

Fred smoothed his sandy mustaches. "Streetwalkers touch some mainspring in you, Steve. Don't waste your time thinking about them." He picked up his magazine. "*Lippincott's*. Their new serial. This line reminded me of you, Steve." He read, " 'How can you do anything until you have seen everything, or as much as you can?' "

Stephen located his pipe and tobacco.

"A new novel by Kipling: *The Light That Failed*."

"He must have forgotten to put a quarter in the gas meter."

"He writes brilliantly!" Fred countered. "Color and dash. You should read it."

"I'm writing, not reading!" Stephen retorted. "I've been living in the library. Except for Tolstoy, I could have spared myself the trouble. Even he writes too much, as though the world had nothing to do but read every word he sets down."

"Can a writer write any other way?"

"He can tell his story briefly, and move on to the next tale." He produced a match.

Lawrence lifted a warning finger. "Go up to the cupola if you want to smoke."

"My dark tower," he mused. He wanted to talk this evening. "I'm restless, Freddie. Sometimes a girl excites me and I want her. Sometimes it's baseball. The rest of the time I'm burned up by a fierce desire to write, to write. My heart aches and my fingers tingle. I feel it knotting in my solar plexus."

"A woman feels like that when a child is shifting inside her, waiting to be born."

"I've got to write, Freddie!"

"I see no chains around your fingers."

"If I could get nearer to real life! If I could climb on top of it the way I mount a horse, and ride—write!—ride, write, till I was exhausted."

"If you're serious, Steve," Fred quietly proposed, "come with me to New York when I go into medical school. Live with me for a while. You'll see what you need to see, just like Kipling's character."

Stephen pulled out his empty pockets. "No money. My mother wouldn't hear of it."

"I've got lodgings. So that won't cost you a red cent. You won't need much more. You think you've seen life? Come and see it as a medic does. The accident cases, the rot, the scum, the stink of living. Zola didn't imagine all his books. He had only to record a day in the gutter of a big city."

"Money!"

Lawrence scoffed. "Scrape up enough for bread and soup. That's all you'll need. There'll always be coffee on the gas-ring. You might get some work on the newspapers."

The blue eyes brightened. "I might sell an article here and there." He paused. "Say, for half a bean, I'd join you next fall!"

"Here's half a bean."

"If only my mother wouldn't take it so hard! She's getting older, and I'm a disappointment to her."

"Please her, or please yourself," said Lawrence. "You're not doing anything here."

Stephen thrust out his hand. "Shake, Freddie! I'll be there."

They shook hands gravely. "Welcome to New York, Steve."

In the cupola, relaxing with his pipe, Stephen dipped pen into inkwell and reflected that if he were to go to New York, he must be prepared to show a portfolio of stories as an artist showed sketches. *St. Nicholas*, to which he had sent his story about the dog Jack, had returned it with a kind note: too many similar pieces in their inventory. He must quickly construct three or four new short stories. He should also have one powerfully exciting long story that touched the "mainspring," to borrow Freddie's word, of universal experience.

He had long been thinking of himself as a writer. To turn the wish into fact would require application and perseverance. He must fix on a plot and a theme, create characters and resolve their problems. He wanted a romance, a story of love and abnegation, of tenderness and sacrifice, one that explored gentleness and affection, infatuation and passion. He remembered the devotion of Tom and Maggie Tolliver; he recalled how Stephen had betrayed poor Maggie. In the caldron where his story thoughts simmered, these long-buried elements stirred catalytically. When he reviewed his purpose in the light of his adventures he was disturbed. He had seen love mocked and abnegation a cynical exercise, tenderness become selfish and sacrifice a travesty. Undoubtedly, his mirrors were planted at angles of distortion. But the Pendennises he had known and studied were not polished scions of fine family, but crude, roughly-spoken lads and lasses of the Bowery.

He was unable to interweave his personal knowledge into that which he had read and held dear. Janus reigned everywhere, his faces love and hatred, goodness and sin, sweetness and hostility, life and death. "Love thy neighbor as thyself!" became ironical if one hated one's self, if love was merely an article of commerce.

Aggie, true, earnest, short-lived, had been the purest girl he had ever known; her innocence lived with him still. Marie Widdicomb had been the epitome of passion. The girls of the street, a bit of Hattie and her tragedy in every one, were less sinister than sinned against. The lotus flower blooming in the mud could be fairer than the rose.

He daydreamed of describing a girl, purer than the purest, adrift in an evil world, so innocent that, like Hawthorne's Hester, she was ignorant of the vile and the unclean. He struggled with the elements of the simple plot, yet resisted it because it was startlingly close to the surface of his experience; friends and family would be shocked. Then, blazing with conviction, he was writing feverishly, thinking only of the story.

The plight of the streetwalkers had affected him profoundly; he would never deny it. In eighteen hundred years of Christianity, society had not learned how to dispense with the services of the Magdalenes. The squalor in which these girls lived, the dangers they courted! Each night they went out like fisherwomen to bring back a catch of strangers to whose lusts they must subject themselves slavishly. The abominations men dared not practice upon their wives, or upon their sweethearts, they wrought upon these wretched harlots, forcing, bruising, and abusing, degrading and compelling carnal attentions that no animals dared require of each other.

To be a man was to be a sinning animal, endowed with, and limited by, hateful animal equipment, with the drive to copulate, the desire to ravish, and yet the awareness that carnal behavior was a mockery of man's spiritual destiny. Even he, wishing to be pure, was impure, seeking to be kind, was unkind, as the stallion mounting the mare is unkind with his loving, striking hooves.

The image of the street girl haunted him. What casual lapses had first reduced her to the whore's couch? Some girls were seduced by evil men, some lured by the promise of easy fortune, others goaded by poverty to support slothful, wicked, or indigent parents.

He was bemused with thoughts of the Bowery as the germ of the story crystallized. When it finally burgeoned, he was helpless; the decision seemed to have been made without him.

At the top of the page, he wrote firmly, "A Girl of the Streets." Only Christ had raised Mary Magdalene and restored her; perhaps she had once been as common as the girls who accosted him. "He that is without sin among you, let him first cast a stone at her."

After many false starts, he began: "A very little boy stood upon a heap of gravel for the honor of Rum Alley. He was throwing stones——"

CHAPTER 25

"Sit down, Crane, sit down!"

The elderly Chancellor was a smooth-shaven scholar with a pinkish complexion, a high-domed forehead and deeply set gray eyes.

"Thank you, sir."

"Crane, you baffle me." The Chancellor rubbed the little hairs on the backs of his hands.

"Yes, sir, Doctor Sims."

"I've judged you to be an able, diligent, and more than competent scholar. I graded you A in English Literature. But you have been astonishingly skillful in eluding every other course of instruction in this school. You have failed to produce a single piece of written study-work. Why have you never taken any of the examinations?"

"I did not think they suited me, sir."

The Chancellor's eyes widened. "Is it an incompatibility beyond hope of repair, or do you think that judicious application might cause you to be more amiably disposed?"

Crane caught a grin starting. "Incompatibility beyond hope of repair."

"You have even managed to escape the classes in Elocution. Hm! I have, more than once, had occasion to consult volumes from the pen of your illustrious father."

Stephen's blue eyes became flinty.

"An excellent writer, as he was an excellent man. A persuasive style, a genuine wit, and a happy turn of phrase. He was a preacher of great eloquence. But his son has no desire to follow in his footsteps?"

"None."

"Eh?"

"I have no desire to follow in his footsteps."

"I see. Mm, your great-uncle was our late Bishop Peck? A position of rank, a man of high purpose."

"I suppose so, sir."

"My dear boy, this is not a matter of supposition. A Bishop, well, is a Bishop."

"Of course, sir."

Doctor Sims studied him. "Your mother would not approve of this record. She would be grieved. Yet you are determined that it shall be no better?"

"I'm afraid so, sir."

"Eh?"

"I have no wish to make a better record in this respect."

Doctor Sims coughed lightly, and wagged a long forefinger. "Why, Crane, why?"

"I hope that this will finally convince my mother that I don't want to go to school."

Sadly, "Despite your record in athletics, which my colleagues judge to be the passion of your life, you have no wish to continue with us."

"None."

"Eh?"

"I have no wish to continue with us—here."

"And you have no other school in mind?"

"No, sir."

"You mean to confront the world with your athletic talents, such as they are?"

Once more the grin appeared, and subsided. "Not quite, sir."

"May I ask in what field of mundane endeavor you propose to launch yourself?"

"In writing, sir."

"In letters, that is."

"No, sir, in stories and articles."

"I meant letters as in *belles lettres*. You will write. Perhaps poetry."

"Perhaps."

"You will earn your livelihood by your pen?"

"I hope to, sir."

"A noble ambition. Other young men have nurtured similar ambitions. I recall that you have written for the Syracuse newspapers. This has encouraged you, no doubt."

"Yes, sir."

"And nothing that we offer here in the college, with the exception of, briefly, my own class in Literature, has been sufficient to hold you rapt and eager, as it were?"

"No, sir."

"We have reached an impasse then. You have, or your family has, private means at your disposal, while you assault the world with your verse and, eh, composition?"

"I don't think so."

"It is an adventure you are embarking upon, a challenge you are flinging at the Muse?"

"I suppose so, sir."

The long hands came to rest on a volume on the desk. The face seemed to have become gray.

"Then it would not confound you if you were advised to leave the University because of your scholastic deficiencies?"

"You mean I don't have to come back!"

"My dear Crane, the faculty has long been of some unanimity— with the single dissenting vote cast by myself—that you should be well on your way."

"Thank you! Thank you, sir."

The Chancellor sighed. "Your education is finished."

"Oh, no, sir!"

"Eh?"

"Only my going to college is finished."

Crow's-feet appeared about the man's eyes. "Good lad, Crane!"

"Doctor Sims, I should like to remain till the end of the June quarter."

"Indeed!"

"The baseball season has begun——"

"And you wish to remain on the team, and not disappoint your colleagues?"

"Yes, sir!"

Doctor Sims was thoughtful. "I have little sympathy for your plea. Yet to play baseball and to be exposed to the facilities of the University is not held unreasonable in the practices of our rival colleges. No doubt it would grieve your mother less if you finished out the term in some agreeable manner." He sighed again. "Very well, Crane, very well!"

Stephen listened indifferently when "Doctor John," the janitor, clanged his handbell in the Hall of Languages to mark the change of classes. He went his own way. He made the rounds of the police stations, called at the city's Poor Department on Market Street, and visited police court when Justice Tom Mulholland was sitting. He sent his dispatches to the New York *Tribune* and to the Detroit *Free Press*. Since he received three dollars an article when his material was used, he had money in his pocket.

The sprawling city of Syracuse, engirdling the lower end of Onondaga Lake, had become as familiar to him as Port Jervis or Asbury Park. The community lived on salt; for several decades, it had supplied most of the salt required for the entire country. On a bright day, he could stand on a hill near Burnett Park and see the salt crystals sparkling in the shallow wooden drying-cisterns; on rainy days, those vats, hastily covered, appeared like endless rows of checkers. Near Geddes, the Solvay Process Company was producing soda ash in a series of rambling buildings, the residual scum from which flowed over the company's dikes and spoiled the beautiful lake.

The trains of the New York Central Railroad rumbled through the heart of the retail district—at the Globe Hotel it seemed to thunder through the washroom—and the ashes from the fireboxes drove the idlers from the hotel verandahs into the lobbies. He favored the Yates Hotel for its superior plumbing. When the students came to town, to eat weiners and sauerkraut at Jake Klein's on James Street, they, too, patronized the Yates.

When the local guard met, he loitered around the State Armory. On one side of the building was the little depot of the "Delay, Linger and Wait"—a natural appellation for the sometime service of the Delaware, Lackawanna & Western Railroad. On the other side was a row of cribs from whose windows, or doorways, fifteen girls in open kimonos called their invitations: "Hey, soldier, ha's abah a li'l drill?" or "Ha abah some shootin' practice?" Over each crib shone a luridly red light.

Entertainment in Syracuse was not limited to the fifty cents and dollar cribs. Kate Skidmore, the buxom Madam with the carrot-red hair, whose carriage and pair was the finest in town, presided over a more lavishly furnished establishment for those willing to pay for clean sheets. Kate, once a fifty-cent girl on the Erie Canal stations, had pulled herself up, "by my petticoats," she said. She ran the best house between Buffalo and Albany.

Stephen, who came and went boldly in this area, knew that the girl sauntering down the other side of Railroad Street, in the little straw hat with the trailing ribbons and the shabby gray suit, was no professional. Her shoulders were hunched and her eyes cast down. If she was soliciting, it was with a faint heart.

She was appealing, with her yellow hair and pale cheeks. The poor kid! he thought, the poor little devil was frightened. He crossed the tracks.

At his approach, the girl shuddered and forced herself to continue her slow walk. He saw the scared eyes.

"Hello, Sis!" he began solicitously, pulling the wet cigarette from his lips. On second thought, he removed his cap. "Going somewhere?"

She looked at him like a cornered rabbit. "Yes, sir."

He wanted to smile. Hell, she knew nothing! "Can I help you?"

"You wanna spend the nigh'——" she hesitated. Her lips were trembling. "You wan' me, Mister?"

The yellow hair was suddenly lovely. If he put an arm about her shoulders, she would burst into tears. "Look, Sis, you're new at this."

"No, I'm not!" she cried. Then faltered, "I don' know whatcha talkin' about."

"Haven't you got a home? Where's your family? Look, I'll see you home!" He moved to take her arm.

She hugged it to her chest. "Lemme alone! Please lemme alone!" She stiffened. "Gee, Mister, I ain't es'pensive. Doncha wan' me?"

He lowered his voice. "You better watch yourself, Sis. The cops'll run you in." He dug into his pocket. "This life isn't for you. Here's a dollar. Better go home."

She seized the piece of silver. "Oh, gee, thanks, Mister!" Her eyes lowered. "Doncha wan' me?"

"No," he said kindly. "Look, Sis, you look like a decent girl. Stay off the streets. Want me to take you home?"

She withdrew. "Whatcha wan' from me? I'm min'in' my own business, ain't I?"

"You haven't got any business here, not on the street."

"Then take back your dollar!" She thrust it at him. "I don' wan' it for nuthin'." She was ready to weep.

"Who's protecting you? They shouldn't let you out alone."

"Huh?" she asked innocently.

He pushed the dollar back at her. "Take it, Sis. Get some groceries. Go home."

Now the tears brimmed. "You lemme alone! You lemme alone, ya hear?" She clung to the dollar. "I'm willin'—I'm willin'!"

"Don't get mad!"

She pulled at her suit coat. "I'm all righ', ain't I?"

"Sure you're all right."

"So what ya startin' up for? I'm willin' to make it with ya, ain't I?"

He put his cap on. "Good-bye, Sis!" She opened her hand on the silver dollar. "Ya wannit back?"

"It's okay."

At the corner, she turned. Idly, he waved his hand. She put up her chin, and strode on.

Some brute would take her all right, would take her apart, poor little devil!

He was still reflecting when a cold arm slipped into his. "Hello, Johnny!"

He would not turn. He had seen them all.

"Johnny, bet you can show me plenty. You name it."

He had the smell of her now.

"I'll bet you're a devil with the girls," she cooed. Her grip tightened.

"Not tonight."

"Why not, honey?" She pressed his elbow against her bosom. "Sleepy? I'll wake you up, Johnny. I'm a nartist."

He disengaged himself. The girl was a head taller than he. Her face was, of course, heavily rouged. The eyes glittered; the mouth was a red smear.

"Whatsa matter? You married or somethin'? I take good care of married men."

He stalked off.

"You don't have to get sore, Johnny, do you?"

He walked faster. God damn a world where women had to sell themselves!

A hand tore at his shoulder. "You insult that girl, Buster?"

He reeled. "Me? No!" A narrow rat-face peered at him. A fist with a cutting ring was lifted to strike.

"You give her the arm? I saw yeh. Why doncha try her? How yeh know yeh don' like her?"

He seethed at the pimp's intimidating manner, at the rakish bowler from which a lock of hair curled in an oily bang, at the diamond stickpin. "I'm not out for a girl. I'm a reporter looking for news."

"Oh!" The other laughed, and lowered his fist. He was smartly clad in a double-breasted coat edged with black braid. "I t'out yez insulted her. See, she's one of my girls, see? Yez insult her, I got to knock yer block off, see? Or break yer neck." He placed a meaty hand on Crane's arm. "You're a kid!"

"Yeah." The fingers were unpleasantly powerful. "Looking for a story. Say, maybe you'd give me one. How many girls you got working for you? I know Kate Skidmore," he added quickly.

"What fur I should tell yez?" The fingers again became a fist. "Look here, if you know Kate, whatcha standin' heah fur? Garwhan, beat it!"

At Matty's Cafe, Stephen pushed through the swinging doors and ordered a beer. Pimps and whores! Ten thousand years of human history had not changed man's behavior. It was a story no one—no American author—had written before in all its shabby truth.

His training as a reporter dictated restraint; he was not to preach or to exhort, but to state the facts and to let the naked drama stir the readers each after his own inclination. The characters had been shaping three-dimensionally: the girl, of course, must be called Maggie, as if no other name could suit a Magdalen; the family "Johnson," as ordinary as Smith or Brown; the mother "Mary," partly from his own mother and partly because Mary is the mother of the world. He could think of no Christian name for the father; as if, never having addressed his Papa by name, it was inconceivable that any father

163

should have a first name. Besides, the father in the story must die early. "His father died," he wrote, "and his mother's years were divided up into periods of thirty days." The sentence rang with a double meaning, but he would not alter it.

For the ultimate betrayal of Maggie, he prepared the figure of Pete, a lad with a chronic sneer, the very image of a Bowery bloke, with his hair "curled down over his forehead in an oiled bang." He gave him "a blue double-breasted coat edged with black braid."

Norton Goodwin, his roommate, glanced at the random sheets of manuscript. "You don't like Pete, do you? He's your villain all right! 'His patent leather shoes were like weapons'! I can see them even if I've never been on the Bowery. But what do you mean that Jimmie dreamed 'blood-red dreams at the passing of pretty women'?"

Stephen squinted at Norton and wrote on. Any D. U. should be able to grasp the underlying irony. Hadn't they ever dreamed of pretty women? In such dreams, did they behave gallantly, or did they fall upon them lustfully?

Every sophomore or junior who climbed into the cupola inspected his pages. The story about a streetwalker attracted even the haughty seniors.

Congdon demanded, "Where did you ever see people like that?"

"They exist. They're real. I've seen them."

He had been in Justice Mulholland's court when the cursing image of Mary Johnson had been haled before the magistrate for drunkenness and for beating her husband. Johnson, a sad sight in the courtroom, loyally maintained that it was turnabout and fair play; last week, he had blacked Mary's eyes. A bandage about his head, he sat beside her, and held the fist that had battered him. She, in a great hand-me-down hat with black feathers, sniffed to impress His Honor and made round, if slightly bloodshot, eyes at her lord and master.

The court attendant addressed a kindly word to their twelve-year-old boy, a sad-faced urchin in tatters, who had an arm around a runny-nosed little sister: "Eh, child, what is it dis time? Is it yer fadder beatin' yer mudder or yer mudder beatin' yer fadder?" Stephen had faithfully memorized the precious dialogue.

He had stood by while girls of the street, so frail that it was incredible that their bodies could bear the weight of a man in his passion, awaited sentences for prostitution. They were usually let off, and a sharp-nosed fellow who could only be a pimp appeared to take them away. He had seen "lines of vindictive hatred" in these faces. He listened as another girl lodged a bastardy charge against a bartender. The man vigorously denied it. What would happen to her after the court dismissed the charge?

Two miles from the police courts rose the buildings of the growing University, with Oakwood Cemetery behind it and the State Idiot Asylum beyond the low hills to the west. Did good Chancellor Sims know of this miniature Bowery in his university city, with its miserable shacks, its squalor, poverty, and vice? Had he ever stepped beyond his library and the black-clad ladies and gentlemen from whom he solicited money for more buildings? Was he aware of the beaches on Onondaga Lake after dark, or the shameful business in Cicero Swamp? Doubtless he believed in the existence of evil; did he know of its multitudinous forms? While students and faculty slumbered peacefully, a legion of women cavorted for hire like imps of Satan, bottles were emptied, heads were broken, and the simple-hearted, if not simple-minded, girls spread-eagled in skimpy beds to a trade older than Philosophy. The world of the whore and the world of the professor were unaware of each other.

Frank Noxon tapped his shoulder. "You've been sitting here for hours." He produced a sack of crullers. "Don't you ever come out for meals? You and your damned pipes! If you opened a window, you'd have so much smoke pouring out of the cupola that they'd send over all six fire engines!"

Stephen stretched and yawned. He munched on a cruller and nodded, his thoughts still far away.

As Noxon, with a grunt, threw open the window, he arose to look out at the night. A full moon rolled its white head through the clouds.

"Deh moon looks like hell, don't it?" he drawled.

Noxon snorted. "You're quoting yourself, Steve. I read it in one of your chapters. No one really talks like that, do they? Even on the Bowery?"

The first chapters of *A Girl of the Streets*, for which he had managed a crisp and stark style, each line as sure as the stroke of burin on copper, had appalled many of the fraternity brothers.

Stephen bit into another cruller. "Want an affy-davey with each speech? Hully gee!"

"Who would ever publish it? You'd go to jail!"

He scowled. "Who would publish it?" He dared not be concerned about publication until the story was completed. His cronies, who gloated over the works of Zola and Defoe, indeed over every novel about harlots and mistresses, professed to be shocked at his novel. They did not understand that he was writing a most unusual, perhaps a remarkable, certainly a unique, book.

Yet he was galled. He tossed the half-finished cruller aside. What if no one wanted to publish his truth?

He sat glumly before the little heap of manuscript. What if his story proved to be as much an outcast as its central character?

"G'wan fall on y'self!" he muttered. The world would accept his work because he was writing it for the world.

He was nearing the canal when he heard the horses and saw the ambulance dashing forward. The moon was milky opal on the water.

A fisherman's boat kicked gently at its moorings. Men were calling, running. Two roundsmen stood on the pier, holding lanterns and peering into the murky depths.

"What is it? What's happened, Officer?"

"Somebody jumped."

A torch flared. Three men in a dinghy were pulling something from the water.

"A girl!"

"Probably a whore," said the younger policeman.

"Naw!" his senior scoffed. "Whores don't jump in the canal. What for?"

An object sailed from the dinghy to the pier. Stephen strained to make it out: a hat of some sort, a woman's straw hat with ribbons.

"Got her!" a voice announced from the dark.

He stood beside the older roundsman. "Why do they do it?"

"Probably got knocked up! You never know."

"Living is tough around here."

The policeman glanced at him sternly. "That's a reason for jumpin' in?"

He was silent. Suddenly, he remembered where he had seen that straw hat. But there must be a hundred straw hats like it, a thousand.

"Give a hand!" came the call from the dinghy. "We don't want to be here all night!"

They were lashing something with a rope.

"Dead?" Stephen shouted.

A burst of ironic laughter drifted up. "Naw! Put your hands out, and she'll walk up!"

The policemen bent over. The girl's legs came up first. Her petticoats were dripping. There were holes in the knees of the stockings. The pantalettes clung to the thighs. Then the moonlight passed a pale hand over the distorted features, he saw the wet mane of soggy, yellow hair, and he knew her.

"Maybe," he said quavering, "if we squeezed out some of the water——"

"Listen!" barked the older policeman. "Get off a here! She's been in the drink for hours, can't you tell? You want to swipe a feel? Go find yourself a live one!"

The ambulance men came for her. Between them, they carried her away like a log, and thrust her into the rear of their wagon.

He stood awhile, shuddering.

Then a current flowed through him. That was how these stories ended! He walked hastily through the dark streets. Poor kid, poor devil! Poor Magdalene, poor Maggie!

CHAPTER 26

Neither his mother nor his sister would speak to him that first month after he left Syracuse. Townley quietly sent him out to gather news along the shore. Out of gratitude for the spending money that he would earn as his brother's leg man, Stephen showed Townley the one hundred fifty pages of *A Girl of the Streets.*

"So this is what you've been up to!"

"Will you read it, Town?"

"Sure thing!"

He was off to cover a lecture at the Albertis in Avon-by-the-Sea. The schoolteachers, a dedicated couple, who taught regular semesters in New York, conducted special classes for small groups of literate summer people.

Townley, quick to sympathize with any effort that seemed futile, had instructed him to report all the lectures as a legitimate shore activity.

The lecturer this afternoon was a tall Midwesterner with a full set of cinnamon-brown whiskers, a clever beaky nose, and good-humored crinkles under the deep brown eyes.

Stephen, ready to be bored, took a chair at the back of the room. However, he listened closely and found himself stimulated.

Unlike the majority of the literary speakers at Avon, Mr. Hamlin Garland, with his loose-limbed gestures and his rich, ringing voice, was a firebrand on the platform. Although his topic was "The Local Novel," he spoke as impassionedly as if every word he uttered must save the world. Now gentle, now oratorical, he elaborated the thesis that the novel was an art form with a higher mission to perform on the American scene. It could tell the truth about people in their several regions; it could, by deftly including accounts of their customs and by transferring their natural dialects to the printed page, portray them as living and real. The writer's central duty was to be truthful to his times. The keynote was "verity"; the artistic creed Garland had named, "Veritism."

Stephen chuckled. So the raw vernacular that he had used for the dialogue in *A Girl of the Streets* was veritism, and his story an example of local color.

Garland declared that young Rudyard Kipling was a "local color novelist," except that the color used by the Englishman was East Indian. He praised the American local colorists: James Whitcomb Riley, Bret Harte, and Bill Nye. These men and their peers were contributing live freshets to the mainstream of current literature by

167

drawing upon the simple, unvarnished speech of everyday folks.

A Girl of the Streets was evidently far better than Stephen had dreamed.

After the question period, he approached Mr. Garland. As a reporter for the New Jersey Coast News Bureau, he asked for the loan of the lecture notes to help him quote the speaker accurately.

"If you'll return them!"

"I promise, sir!"

Townley passed the copy, with the usual addition of the commas that Stephen had omitted.

When the Sunday *Tribune* arrived, Stephen turned to the resort news page. Fletcher Johnson, the day editor, with whom Townley filed the Bureau's news stories, had printed his article without an alteration.

"I'll take this over to Mr. Garland." Reaching for the scissors, he declared smugly, "Maybe I'll show him my novel, too. Have you read it, Town?"

His brother pushed up the roll-top of his desk and fished the manuscript from a heap of news proofs.

Stephen glanced at the pages, and exploded, "Did you sleep on it?" His neatly written sheets were wrinkled and dog-eared. He swallowed his anger and began to uncurl the corners and to smooth the pages. "Did you like it?"

"You're learning how to write," Townley returned drily. "I can say that much."

"Ho, hell!"

"Did you expect me to tell you to rush it into print? You're a beginner. It needs more work."

Stephen crimsoned. "It's my first draft."

Townley creaked in his chair. "Some of the sentences hit you in the face." He studied his shoetops. "For the love of Christ, why does a kid have to write about a fallen woman? What do you know about harlots anyway? Or were your classmates a bunch of blamed hellions?"

"How old do I have to be to write about a fallen woman? I'm nearly twenty. This isn't an assignment for the *Tribune*."

Townley's eyes narrowed. "You haven't seen this kind of ugliness and squalor. You haven't been anywhere. Brothels, vice and degradation! What do you know——"

"Isn't that part of life, too?"

"Part of life, yes," the other retorted, "but not all of it. You're too young. You'd have to get around more to know about that. You've got talent, Steve. You can do better than writing filthy muck."

Stephen was silent.

"Besides, old Steve, Mother would die of shame if you printed that story, even if the harlot came to a moral end in the river!"

"I don't have to clear with you. Or with her!"

"You should clear with someone. Besides, it's a waste of time. No one will publish it. *A Girl of the Streets!* The publisher would go to jail. This isn't France and you're not Emile Zola."

He was heartsick as he mounted his bicycle and rode off to Avon-by-the-Sea. He had left the manuscript behind. Townley, who was too lazy to write anything except reports on fires and trials, was almighty damned free with his opinions. Since Fannie had lost her second infant and had begun to suffer from Bright's disease, Townley was either hangdog, as if he feared that his wild behavior was responsible for Fannie's malady, or cocky, as if no one else could possibly know more about writing, or about anything else, than he did.

Stephen's temper cooled as he sped along. The manuscript *was* a first draft; it needed more work. "Why a story about a harlot?" Poe had probably been asked, "Why a poem about a raven?" and Hawthorne, "Why a novel about a seduction?" Evil existed; he had seen it, he was reporting it. The prophets of the Old Testament had thundered against evil; he was merely recording its presence.

The world did not care. Each man lived his own life selfishly, and the Devil take the hindmost. It was sickening. Man did not care, and God, who had averted His face from the horrid mess after the Sixth Day, evidenced no concern.

He was glum when he stepped upon the Alberti's verandah.

Mr. Garland was alone in the parlor, sprawled on the divan with a writing-pad and several books. Stephen returned the lecture notes.

"And here is the article from the *Tribune*. Arrived this morning."

Garland's whiskers, Stephen observed, were precisely the color of a brown thrasher's feathers.

"Rest yourself." The lecturer swung his long feet to the floor and reached for the clipping. "I'm obliged to you, Crane." He read. "Couldn't have done better myself. Couldn't."

"Thanks. And please call me Steve."

"Very good, Steve." He was still perusing the article. "You might care to look over those periodicals. They contain some of my articles."

Stephen thumbed through copies of *The Arena*. He had never seen the stout little magazine: fifty cents a month. In issue after issue, he noted enviously, there was a short story by Mr. Garland.

"Couldn't have done better." Garland rattled the clipping. "Mrs. Alberti says that you're writing stories. Have you published anything?"

"Only articles in the *Tribune*. But I've written a whale of a lot."

"Good!" Garland pointed a long finger at his books. "Send them out. Get them published. They do no good lying in your trunk. If you're rejected by one editor, try another. Look at my stuff. Arena published my *Main-Travelled Roads* in paper wrappers for fifty cents. *Jason Edwards*, also fifty cents. Now Appleton is publishing *Little*

Norsk. So keep them moving. Get them out, get them published. Published."

"I'm a beginner." Stephen fingered the fifty-cent books.

Garland stroked his beard and gazed at the ceiling. "So you are. Everyone is a beginner in the beginning. But if you're a writer, you must write, and you must publish. Send them out, and learn how to do better by writing more. Few editors will seek you out until you become so famous that you don't need them. So you must keep your manuscripts moving out to them."

Stephen nodded respectfully.

Garland fanned his brow. "As hot here in the East as it is in Dakota and Wisconsin." The air in the parlor was sultry. "Alberti tells me that you're a ballplayer." He stretched. "Care to pass a few? I found a baseball here. I don't get much exercise when I'm traveling."

Stephen leaped to his feet. "Yes, sir. Pla-ay ball!"

Garland swung his arm over his head. "I used to burn 'em in." They went out into the blazing sunlight.

"Mr. Garland," Stephen grinned, "you burn 'em in as hot as you like."

He was amused to see the older man lift both hands over his head, rock back and forth and, with a great heave of his frame, fling the ball.

He caught it easily. "Hey, I thought you said you'd burn 'em in!"

They passed the ball steadily for about an hour. Garland, warming to the game, worked hard over each pitch. His armpits darkened with perspiration. He called time to wipe his forehead and neck with his bandana handkerchief.

"He's pretty old," the youth mused. "Probably thirty."

At last Garland, pretending to sag, threw up his hands. "Enough for one day!" He came forward in his slow, measured gait. "Fine, Steve, fine. Enjoyed it fine."

They rested in the wicker chairs on the verandah.

"Say, have you read William Dean Howells?" he puffed. "Howells?"

"No, sir."

"Read him, Steve, read him. You quoted me correctly. By all odds, he's the most important and vital of our literary men today." He squinted into the sun. "He's editor of *The Cosmopolitan* right now. Why not send him a story? He encourages newcomers."

"Do you know him?"

"I know them all. That is, I try to meet the important men wherever I go. You've got to know the people in your craft. If I had stayed in the Middle West I would never have learned what I know now. Travel, meet people, and write. Now you, as an Eastern boy, should travel West some day. Of course, every writer must write sincerely about the life he knows best."

Stephen frowned. Townley would endorse that.

"And about the life that appeals to him the most. Write about what is true and fresh and exciting to you, no matter if it seems common-place to everyone else."

They agreed to play ball every day as long as he remained at Avon-by-the-Sea. When Stephen appeared at seven o'clock the next morning, Garland was already seated on the verandah, a writing-pad on his knees.

"I find it best to write early in the morning," said Garland. "I'm the lark. Everything that has been pressing on my mind all night pours out. Some writers—they are the owls—favor the very late hours, midnight to dawn. Important thing, lark or owl, is to get the writing habit and to slave away at it. Every day."

In his eagerness to be helpful, Garland often repeated the obvious as if he were announcing discoveries. "Write every day as you think every day." He scrawled a list of the authors whose works he recom-mended. Howells, first, then Walt Whitman and Tolstoy; always Tolstoy.

"The writer's life isn't always an easy life, but it can be good and satisfying when he is doing what it is in his heart to do."

He suddenly addressed himself to his deep convictions on the in-evitability of the Single Tax.

Stephen grumbled. "I leave religion and politics out of it. I don't hold with either."

"One man's fish may be another man's meat." Garland reflected. "Steve, if you get to New York, come and see me. My brother Franklin, who is an actor, lives in New York. I camp at his place."

After Garland had left Avon, Stephen read his stories in *The Arena*. The subjects were agreeable, but Garland's prose failed to excite him. He was convinced that he had written chapters in *A Girl of the Streets* which, for vividness and strength, were far superior to any-thing in Garland's work.

CHAPTER 27

At Asbury Park, Mama was seriously ill.

Burt, who had brought his new bride to visit his mother and his sister, diagnosed the high fever as typhoid.

Doctor Kaster flatly declared, with the calm that a practicing man exercises toward one who has failed, that it was not typhoid. Burt insisted; his thesis had been rejected, but he felt qualified on this disease and its variations.

Doctor Kaster ignored him.

Burt appealed to his brothers, whom Nellie had summoned. "Mama's been speaking in a dozen small towns where the water supply is unclean. I swear it's typhoid!"

Will contemptuously waved a lawyer's hand. "Trust the physician, Burt!" He could not forgive Burt the failure in medical school; to his friends he intimated that Burt had "given up medicine" to go into business.

As the fever mounted, Doctor Kaster prescribed remedies that made Burt splutter. But the patient's temperature suddenly dropped and, after five days, the physician proudly announced that she was "out of danger." The next week, however, even he reluctantly admitted that it might be typhoid. Mrs. Crane's spine had been affected, and her back was cruelly twisted. Her hair began to fall out.

"God has punished me, punished me!" Mary Helen Crane wailed.

She pleaded with her sons not to tell anyone of her baldness, not even their wives. She was bitterly ashamed.

In Jersey City, Townley secured a hairpiece from a theatrical wigmaker.

Mrs. Crane stared at the wig, and burst into tears. "It's reddish hair, like yours!"

So Townley made another trip and exchanged it for a black-haired peruke. They hung a mirror opposite Mama's bed so that she might see herself if, in shifting on the pillow, the hairpiece became ludicrously disarranged.

There seemed to be no end to their troubles. Fannie, returning from a visit to her parents in Morristown, came down with a recurrence of the old kidney ailment, and Nellie had to oversee both invalids. In a pet, claiming that she was being neglected, Mama demanded that she be taken to Ted's at Lakeview.

Nellie delayed as long as she dared. Mama had begun to suffer fantasies that assassins were trying to saw her back in two. One night, she screamed that she was lying helpless upon a railroad track, with a train thundering down upon her. Ludie—she had seen him!— had come running and had pulled her from the ties to save her life.

Stephen was deeply shaken. In her ravings, Mama had interwoven her pain with Ludie's cruel accident. Then she vowed that Aggie had mended her back by tacking it together with a shingle. When the fantasies abated, she remembered nothing of the delirium.

Nevertheless, good-hearted Mame agreed to take Mother Crane into her home.

Stephen, helping to carry his mother into the train, was shocked by her loss of weight. The eyes were sunken; the face was wan and cross-hatched with innumerable lines. The peruke had slipped rakishly over one eye. And this now-helpless creature had once preached from platforms and, on behalf of her causes, had threatened Governors and Legislatures. "Why punish *her*, God?" he appealed silently.

172

"What will become of you when I'm gone?" she moaned.

"I'll write, Mother. I'll be a writer all my life."

"If you had followed in your father's footsteps, you would be serving God, and have your livelihood, too. You could write, as he did and as your Grandpa George did."

He concentrated on the passing fields. His heart was heavy.

"Read to me, Stephen."

He reached for her Bible.

"Read what you have written," she pleaded. "Not since you were a child and wrote school compositions——"

"It's crude. It's not finished work, Mother. When I have something that will please you——" He could not read the story of Maggie, girl of the streets, to Mary Helen Crane.

Tears glistened at the dark lashes.

He spent the autumn in Lakeview. His mother, bedridden, occupied the room next to Mame and Ted. He wrote and slept in the attic study. When he was not at his manuscript, he played football. Sometimes he wheeled little Edith, who was recovering from the whooping cough, to the sidelines, and he and his friends took turns watching and amusing the pretty little girl with the long golden hair.

In the evenings, he played with the other children, or chatted with Ted. It vexed him to have to sit with Mama. In one breath, she bade him leave for his writing desk; in the next, she groaned as if he wished her death.

"What will become of you when I'm gone?" she repeated over and over. "It's a punishment on me. Retribution!"

To relieve severe pain, she had a dark-brown medicine that obviously contained distilled spirits. Nellie teased that the prescription was compounded of "gumfoozalum," but Mama was not to be consoled.

"The Lord has punished me for my pride. He has punished me!"

Mame described how the vertebrae in Mother Crane's back protruded, in the lower region, like a knuckled fist. The local physician agreed with Burt that the after-effects of the typhoid infection could have caused the crippling of the spine. This side the grave, her injuries would not be mended.

Stephen felt the last remnants of his faith dissolving. She had been so good, dedicated to God and His works and zealous for the welfare of all unfortunates. She blamed herself needlessly that Aggie had died because of her carelessness, and that she, therefore, deserved to be tortured with a spinal ailment. She was convinced that Luther— "He was only twenty-three!"—would not have died so horribly had she forbidden him to work for the railroad. A merciful God, who must surely know the heart of Mary Helen Crane, could not misjudge her.

Stephen paced the attic, smoking his pipe and thinking about her.

It was difficult to concentrate on *A Girl of the Streets*. He had twice rewritten the novel; he was revising a third time.

In late November, he traveled to New York to make the rounds on Park Row; he must find work as a reporter. But a blizzard swept down upon the city and kept him indoors at Fred Lawrence's for most of the week. He found no work. When he returned to Lakeview, Mama had been taken to the hospital in Paterson.

The next day, Ted whispered to him that, in Asbury Park, Fannie had died. Their mother must be spared that news.

Townley was already staggering drunk when they arrived. The dead woman had been laid out in the parlor, with good neighbors in attendance. The brothers, outraged, descended upon Townley, but he was wild, raving and shouting, and threatened to bolt from the house. They hid his clothing.

They forced him to sit in a tub of cold water. He roared and splashed them. When the effects of the alcohol began to wear off, they pulled him to his feet, rubbed him dry, and put him to bed.

In the middle of the night, he awoke sobbing that he had not wanted Fannie to die. He blubbered and pleaded for forgiveness as if Fannie could hear him.

Confronted by complexities in a nature that he had considered so simple, Stephen recoiled. There was more to a man's soul than banter, rough exchanges and brag. Townley intoxicated had been a man; this babbling hulk was a creature in whom the light had gone out.

They had no sooner buried Fannie than the telegram came from Paterson. Mary Helen Crane was expiring. The doctor said, "Blood poisoning!" The carbuncle from which she had been suffering had become infected.

Stephen glanced at his white-faced brothers. Would the curtain never fall upon their tragedies?

He derided himself for it, yet continued to pray for her, vehemently defying the Power to Whom he was appealing. How much she had suffered! Of her fourteen children, she had buried seven.

He leaned over the dark lips and thought, "This is the mouth of death!"

She recognized him. Would he promise to go to school, to complete his education?

"Mama!" How could he please her and not enslave himself?

"Your brothers will help you." The eyes were luminous, feverishly bright. "And I have provided for you in my will."

He could not speak. He was obtaining his education in a world as far removed from her experiences as the afterworld into which she believed her soul would be released like a white dove in flight.

"Stephen, have I failed you?"

174

"No, Mama, no!"

"Sometimes—I—have wondered."

He buried his face in her pillow. "Forgive me, Mama!"

The eyes opened wide. "I—forgive—you?" she whispered. "I'll forgive you, Stephen. I'll forgive you!"

Fannie had died the afternoon of November 26th; at ten o'clock in the evening of December 7th Mary Helen Crane was gone. Doctor William Nest pronounced her dead.

Stephen watched Nellie set the peruke over the waxen forehead. Only the sound of weeping filled the room. It was over; she had been the last tie to the old life. He slipped out of the room and walked down the empty corridor.

On the street, he plunged into an endlessly descending curtain of snowflakes. The sky was hidden in a gray mist. The trees were rimed with long white streaks; he tasted the snow on his lips and felt it on his eyelids. After such a storm, Papa had died. Now Mama was gone, and he was twice an orphan. He was free, unfettered, unshackled, a desolate figure among the undependable living, in the vast forest of the silent dead.

III. The Hungry City

*R*ICHARD WATSON GILDER was a tall sandy-haired man, with brooding black eyes that illumined a face of scholarly pallor; he could have passed for an English poet returning from memorial services for a younger colleague. Behind a great oaken desk, on which an assortment of page-proofs was neatly arranged, he sat like a judge whose bench had been lowered temporarily to the common level. He fixed and re-fixed the pince-nez on the fine, thin nose, brushed nervously at his mustache, and studied the youth in the gray ulster.

"Our readers expect unremitting excellence in the pages of the *Century*," he began cautiously, with a troubled glance at his caller. "Of course, there is promise here." Then the black eyes became stern. "However, nothing that we have ever published would prepare our readers for a story of seduction and street-soliciting."

Stephen listened glumly.

Mr. Gilder pushed the manuscript across the desk. "You must have known, Crane, that this is scarcely what the *Century* could buy." He said "this" as if he were referring to rancid butter.

"How could I know what the *Century* will buy?" Stephen asked wretchedly. "I have rewritten it three times, sir!"

The editor drummed sensitive fingers on the arm of his chair. "The irony and pity are superbly handled. The note of tragedy, struck early, is maintained throughout." He brushed again at the handsome mustache. "We could not publish tragedy, not if old Sophocles were to write it."

"Yes, sir." He was thinking heatedly, "Should Maggie be saved at the end by some kind gentleman who falls in love with her, marries her, and takes her away to live happily ever after?"

Mr. Gilder seemed to read his thoughts. "I assume that you are interested in my remarks."

"Please, sir!" An author must be interested in any editor's remarks.

The thin nostrils dilated. "The general harshness of the life depicted here——"

"I can vouch for its accuracy."

An eyebrow lifted quizzically. "Crane, I would assume as much. But you have carried accuracy to the point where you make the reader uncomfortable. Whatever the truth may be, the subject is scarcely palatable. It is shocking. Many of the scenes are cruel!"

There it was: the man's personal horror of blunt realism. "I'm sorry, Mr. Gilder." Politeness required that; he was not sorry, he was angry.

"One comes to the end—the old woman's terrible words, 'I'll fergive yeh!'—and sighs 'Poor Maggie!' but is downright depressed that such things may be." His hand reached for the schoolmaster bell; one finger poised to tap it and summon his clerk. "We, at the *Century*, strive, as far as we are able, to elevate our readers."

His cheeks flamed. "Mr. Gilder, what you are saying is that my story is too honest, isn't it?"

Mr. Gilder flushed. "We have a duty to the readers of the *Century*."

Stephen tucked the manuscript into its brown paper wrapper. "You don't believe that anyone would publish it?"

"I cannot speak for others. But if you ask my opinion, I am compelled to say No!"

Drily, "We can be honest in speech but not in print."

The editor remained calm. "I suspect that may be true, Crane." The deed done, he did not wish to give further pain. "Townley said that you were working for the *Herald*."

"I've already been fired," he returned candidly. "I did my best, but there, too, I must have been carrying honesty too far!"

Heavy-hearted, he again marched the streets of New York with the manuscript under his arm. At least Mr. Gilder, who had known his father and, in his thin-lipped way, had alluded to a call on the Cranes when Stephen was a child, had read the manuscript overnight; usually, an editor clung to it for days, like a drowning man to a spar, before he rejected it. No one else had been as forthright as the editor of the *Century*.

He had tramped from one magazine office to the next; he had visited every publisher in New York. None of the other editors would grant him an interview. Anonymously, his work was taken in, anonymously read, and anonymously returned. Did every author have to search blindly for a publisher?

His ears cocked at a familiar shushing. The walk trembled under the roll of a cylinder press.

ABLE JOB-PRINTERS. The entrance to the printshop was through a dark-green basement door. He remembered Hamlin Garland's fifty-cent paperbound books. The copy boy at the *Herald* had been reading *Gallegher* by Richard Harding Davis, in wrappers. Books did not have to be produced expensively in cloth bindings.

He ran down the steep wooden stair, inhaling the smells of kerosene and ink. At the rear of the shop, the press hissed as if it were sucking in each sheet of paper. In the foreground, men in green eyeshades stood at the cases, clicking types into composing-sticks. The shop was no larger than the office of the Asbury Park *Journal*.

At the stove, he accosted a small, bearded man who had paused to fix his sleeve-garters. "Mister, do you print books?"

"What?" He rubbed an ink-smeared finger across his temple.

Stephen raised his voice above the clatter. "Books! Do you print books?"

"We print anything. What do you want?"

The big press had suddenly halted and left a hole in the din. "Do you print complete books?" He peered at a galley proof. "DR. BROWN's HOME REMEDY."

"Don't shout!"

"How do I get a book printed?"

The smudged finger pointed. "See the office there? Talk to the boss. The jay with the celluloid collar, that's Mr. Able."

Stephen moved past a paper-cutter and three skids of paper. The walls of the partitioned office were festooned with galley proofs that hung from their hooks like sere funeral crepe. "The jay with the celluloid collar," a short, portly man, was scanning a press-sheet.

"Sir, are you the proprietor?"

"I'm the boss. Come in."

"What does it cost to print a book, a little book?" He hugged his parcel.

Mr. Able tucked his pencil behind his ear. "How many pages?"

He did not know. "In type? Maybe two hundred."

"How many books?"

He pondered. "A thousand. Eight hundred. Is that too many, Mr. Able?"

"As many as you want. Where is the copy?"

Silently, he presented the parcel.

"What is it?"

"A story, a novel." He undid the string.

The proprietor lifted the pages and, tentatively, weighed them. "We print jobs, not books." He waved toward the proofs on the walls and the printed matter that cluttered the roll-top desk. "Broadsides and handbills, circulars for medical companies. We do some printing for churches. Why don't you take it to a book publisher?"

"They don't want it. If it isn't too expensive, maybe I'll have it printed myself. I can't wait forever!"

"I see."

His indifference dismayed Stephen. "I'm getting ready to write a new one, so I'd like to see this one in print."

Mr. Able riffled the pages. "How you going to sell it?"

"Sell it?" He was perplexed. "Sure, I'll sell it. For fifty cents, in bookstores, everywhere."

The printer licked his thumb and once more flicked the pages. "A lot of work here, be pretty expensive, young fellow." He jerked his head toward the shop where the press was hissing again. "Those men want to get paid. It isn't like it used to be. They're not satisfied with a dollar a day any more."

On a galley sheet, Mr. Able jotted down figures. He stared at the column, made a finalizing stroke, and winced. "Might cost a thousand dollars."

"Wow!"

Mr. Able threw up his hands. "The labor and the paper! I'm working for them; the shop doesn't make much." He shook his head. "I don't know. A thousand dollars might not be enough."

Stephen laughed mirthlessly. "I'll have to begin to save my money."

"That's what I mean. Tell you, son, it wouldn't pay. Even if you had the cash, it wouldn't pay. Good binding costs money, too. You couldn't afford it."

"I could take it without a binding, in paper wrappers."

"Oh! You didn't say so!" He made more computations, then looked up sadly. "Might shave it a hundred or two, if you didn't have alterations in type."

"I wouldn't!" he promised. "This is my last revision and the way I want it in print."

"Writers are always changing their minds, even on these handbills and booklets."

"No, sir!" Stephen tapped the manuscript confidently. "I promise."

"Well!" the other spread in his swivel-chair. "Put it this way. You be prepared to pay a thousand dollars, and we'd guarantee the job finished, ready for you to sell."

Stephen frowned. "But if I sold the whole thousand copies at fifty cents each, I'd only get half my money back. Isn't there any other way out?"

"Not here," Mr. Able studied the sheet. "Look at the figures. That's the best we can do."

Stephen looked at them. He could gather more from his laundry ticket. "Yeah," he muttered. "That's the best you can do."

"You stand there all day setting a page of this in type, and then figure out how many days it would take a man. Then add up the cost of the proofs and the paper and the make-ready and the running-time, and the binding."

"I want a paper wrapper!"

"That requires some binding work, doesn't it? Sewing, glueing. Of course, you'd have your book in print. That's more than most young fellows, twenty, twenty-one"—he judged shrewdly—"are able to show. You'd be one up, as the saying goes. Might be worth it. But I'm not persuading you, son. We don't need the work. We make more money printing for churches and the medical companies."

"My father was a minister," Stephen said pointlessly.

"Then you know what I mean. Here, where's your string? Let me tie this up for you!"

Stephen halted him. "What if I leave the manuscript with you, and talk to my brothers? It would take a few days."

"Leave it if you want. Maybe I'll read it."

"You wouldn't lose it?"

"Why should we?" He dropped the string on the manuscript. "Son, you talk it over with anyone you want. But if you've set your mind to see it in print, don't wait too long. We might get a rush job, and I'd disappoint you."

Stephen's lips were dry. "I'll let you know quickly."

As he walked out, he took another deep breath: kerosene, ink, paper, and glue. If he could raise the money, every force and material here would be harnessed to produce his book. From the walk, he again peered through the window. The pressman had brought a growler for Mr. Able. The proprietor took a big swig, and began to turn the pages of the manuscript. A drop of beer spattered on a page. Mr. Able wiped it away with the back of his hand.

"A thousand dollars!" Ted said. "A fortune, Steve. Will can tell you that it's five per cent on an investment of twenty thousand dollars."

"I want that book printed!"

"Where will you get the money?"

"My part of Mama's coal shares."

Ted winced. Mary Helen Crane had left the Luzerne County coal shares, which she had inherited from her father, in trust to Will, with the net income to be divided share and share alike among all the children. The will also provided that Stephen was to receive three hundred dollars a year for his support and education if he entered upon a regular four-year college course before his twenty-first birthday.

"I won't go back to school!" Stephen was adamant.

"You've selected Ted as your legal guardian until you are twenty-one," Will said benignly. "If he approves——"

"I want Steve to follow his own wishes!" Ted retorted.

Their mother's intentions had been excellent, but the provisions of her will, requiring careful interpretation, had already caused a coolness between the brothers. The shares might not be sold until funds had been set aside not only for Stephen's education but also for a double monument on the Crane burial plot at Hillside. Will had borrowed money from a Port Jervis bank to buy out the interests of some of the heirs. In earlier years, Mary Helen Crane had derived a fine income from the shares; an improvement in business conditions might bring a sharp rise in values.

"I have to print the book!" Stephen maintained.

"If you must have the money," Ted said, "offer the shares as collateral. But don't sell them."

"I don't care."

"Your shares may some day be worth two thousand dollars. Don't give them away for one thousand dollars." Normally mild-mannered, Ted snapped, "I won't let you!"

Later, from New York, Stephen wrote to Will to ask for the loan of a thousand dollars. Early Saturday morning, no reply having arrived, he hastened to the print shop to reassure Mr. Able.

"My brother hasn't answered me."

"No hurry, son. We're not hungry for the work. Story about a chippy. Should go to one of those publishers that sell French novels."

Stephen crimsoned.

"They'd do it for you. I might talk to the printer who sets their type."

The blue eyes hardened. "Mr. Able, do you want to print it or not?"

"Got the money?"

"I'll get it."

"Hurry up then. We're getting rushed with work. It could be months before we got to it."

Stephen took the late train to Port Jervis. It was past midnight when he reached Will's home.

On his last Saturday night visit, Stephen had climbed to the second floor by way of the trellis. He had raised a window sash and pulled himself into the spare bedroom. Fortunately, the floor-boards had not creaked as he tiptoed about. He flung his clothes everywhere and went to bed. The family was breakfasting when he snatched Will's robe from the banister and thundered down the stairs, calling, "What's to eat? I'm starved!"

Will had nearly had a cat-fit. "Thunder, Steve! You try trespassing some places at night, and you'll get a load of shot in your backside!"

Now he stooped, picked up a handful of pebbles, and tossed them one by one overhand, high in the air. They dropped on the roof and rolled back into the rain gutter.

He heard hoarse coughing and cussing, and the dog Chester growling. A light went on.

A window opened and Cornelia's figure appeared. "That you, Steve?"

"It's me."

She slid the bolts on the kitchen door. She hugged him, not a word of reproach. She insisted on frying ham and eggs and warming leftover johnnycake.

He ate ravenously. "Cornelia, you're the best cook in the world!"

She put another slab of butter on the johnnycake. "Will you go to church with us in the morning? Your father's church?"

"No, Ma'am!"

"Will you be here when we return, or will you disappear, as you usually do? I'll make biscuits for dinner, and we have a standing roast."

"You make biscuits," he grinned, "and I'll stay forever."

He was fast asleep when Will and Cornelia and the four girls left for services. Vaguely, he heard the bells ringing, now from one church, now from another; he did not rise until the Drew clock struck ten.

Port Jervis was peaceful, so quiet, he thought, that he could hear the blossoms opening, the grass growing, the clouds sliding across the blue sky. The church spires were thin spears stuck into the aquamarine cushion.

He opened the cold-chest, ate bread and butter and drank cold milk. He admired the standing ribs of beef. Cornelia would serve an excellent dinner. Will liked to eat.

In New York, he could live for days on coffee and buns. Here, he would enjoy a thick cut of beef with natural gravy and plenty of mashed potatoes and butter, and hot biscuits; his mouth watered.

After dinner, the brothers went into the parlor.

"Will, did you get my letter? You didn't answer me."

"No hurry, is there?"

"I am in a hurry. I want my brook printed."

"We never hear from you unless you want something."

"Aw, Will!"

"A thousand dollars! Where do you think it's coming from?"

"Lend it to me."

"Haven't got it, Steve. Not cash."

"Raise the money for me. Sell my shares, if you can't do it any other way."

"Your shares?" Will ruminated. "I'm not a bank. The whole family's coming to me for money."

"You're going to them, too, aren't you? I've heard all about that.

185

Townley wouldn't have known he could get any cash if you hadn't——"

"Has he been complaining?"

"No, sir. All opinions expressed," he tried to grin, "are my own."

"Suppose you do print your book. Have you considered what you must do with the copies? How will you sell them?"

Cheerfully, "I'll go around to the bookstores."

"How do you know they'll buy them?"

"They sell books. They've got to take them."

"I suspect that they can do very well without yours. You may be throwing a thousand dollars down a rathole."

"They're my shares."

"Steve, I don't think you should sell them. The shares will some day be worth much more. You're not Townley."

"I can't wait!"

Will shrugged. "Very well, I'll find you the money. I'll give you the best price I can for the shares. You can draw as you need it."

"Thanks, Will!"

"But don't come to me when your money is all gone. Tell the printer to go ahead."

"What about the cash?"

Will was exasperated. "Tell them we guarantee the payment. I'll give you a letter. No one pays printers in advance. And tell them eight hundred dollars is all we can raise."

"Eight hundred dollars?"

"Bargain with the man. That figure seems very high to me."

"And they'll wait for their money?"

"Of course, they will. If they refuse, another printer will do it. I'll give you a hundred dollars for a deposit, and send the rest when the books are ready. This is business, Steve, not card games."

"You don't know Able Printers."

"You don't know anything about money, except to spend it. Have you ever earned more than five dollars at a time? Have you ever held a job for more than two months?"

Stephen clenched his fists. "Are you going to give me a sermon?"

"With Mother gone, who is there to look after you? In Ted's eyes, you can do no wrong!"

"G'wan!" he growled. "Come off yer horse!"

"Spare me!" Will retorted hotly. "Do you think that everyone has to cheer you because you've written a book about a streetwalker? *A Girl of the Streets* by Stephen Crane. Do you expect me to be proud of it? Or your sister Nellie? Why hasn't Ted made that clear to you? For the rest of your life, you'll be the boy who wrote a novel about a tart!"

"I'll write what I please. Can I count on the money?"

"Eight hundred dollars. Tell them that's all we can raise."

186

Back in New York, he returned to the printshop. "Best we can do is eight hundred dollars," he told Mr. Able.

"No, sir!" The printer hesitated. "What will you do with it, Crane?"

"Plenty of printshops, my brother says. He knows business, he's a lawyer."

"Did you bring the money?"

"A hundred dollars for a deposit. Rest when the job is finished."

Able blinked. "Why didn't you say so? Tell you what. I'll run a few extra sheets while we're on the press. Say eleven hundred altogether. You give us time and we'll do the work between other jobs."

Stephen cheerfully produced Will's check on the Port Jervis bank.

New York had never seemed so friendly. His book would be displayed in every bookstore. He would send copies to every editor or reviewer. Critical articles would appear extolling the virtues of *A Girl of the Streets* by Stephen Crane. He had launched himself on his career.

That night, in Ted's attic in Lakeview, he cleared the table, laid out his copy paper and writing implements, and prepared to start on his second novel.

A Girl of the Streets had concerned a single aspect of life on the Bowery. There were a thousand more stories to be written of the world of the tenements, with its poverty, squalor, and drunkenness.

He saw that the book wanted a stronger title. *A Girl of the Streets* might be taken for a sober essay by Jacob Riis, the police reporter. The great novels, *Anna Karenina* and *Madame Bovary,* had been named for their central characters. "Maggie Johnson." That was pallid. "Maggie" alone. Stronger. Just "Maggie."

Will was right that a story about a girl of the streets might embarrass the family. He would have this first book printed anonymously. When the reviews appeared and people inquired about the author, he would step forth: "I did it. It's my book!"

He could not abandon his Maggie like a foundling on the public's doorstep. She was dear to him, more than a girl of the streets. She was a princess of the streets, a wild untutored princess, like young Pocahontas who had saved Captain John Smith's life. He chuckled. There was a proper disguise; the country was overrun with Smiths. "By John Smith." He hesitated. He could have been John Smith's son. Then "By Johnson Smith." Johnson was Maggie's family name.

That suited him.

Since the printer still intimidated him, he would say nothing until the proofs were ready. Then he would instruct Mr. Able to change the title to *Maggie* and the author to "Johnson Smith." And he would wait for the world, awakening, to shout, "Author! Author!"

CHAPTER 29

Fletcher Johnson and Townley were lounging on the verandah of the West End Hotel. Both men had their feet up on the railing and long cigars in their fists.

Stephen sauntered toward them and accepted a cigar. He lit the end with awkward deliberation, as if he were igniting the fuse of a bomb.

"It's a ten-center," Townley said languidly. "Make it last. When an editor gives you a cigar, light it carefully, smoke it slowly. If he gives you two cigars, watch out. He'll be sending you to Africa to find Livingston, or around the world to trail Nellie Bly."

Johnson, a tall, sallow man with reddish mustaches and eyebrows, grinned good-humoredly. "Every time you send in a chit for a trip to Long Branch, you include a few cigars, don't you, Townley?" He yawned. "You've got everything here in Asbury Park, except good liquor."

"Thanks to Jim Bradley. He bought the land and laid out the town. Bradley's Pa was a heavy drinker, so Jim, taking his revenge, has been depriving everyone in town in his Pa's memory."

"What do you do to quench a thirst?"

"Go over to Shark River." He winked at Stephen, who had to journey to Slobacker's to drag him home when he failed to return by midnight. "Plenty of roadhouses."

"There are always the euchre parties at Spring Lake," Stephen murmured through a cloud of cigar smoke. "Also the poker games when enough reporters get together. Asbury Park is no dry gulch."

Johnson scrutinized him. "You've learned quickly, Steve."

"Had to learn to keep up with Townley."

"He's learned faster than I did in everything. He's a real writer, Fletcher. Not like me."

"You like writing, Steve?"

"Would rather write than eat."

"Your father wrote well. And so did your mother. You've got talent on both sides of the family."

"Preachers to the right of him, preachers to the left of him——"

"Don't tease him, Townley. If he wants to write seriously, encourage him."

"Don't I, though? But Father wouldn't approve of what his youngest son writes about. He's got a novel, Fletcher. Ask him. I read an early version that wasn't half bad for a kid. Zola pure. He got mad at me and won't talk about it any more. Brother Will hints that it may be printed some day."

"Maybe," said Steve.

"What did I say? He's way ahead of me. But he's got some sketches, Fletcher, that you should see. Steve's the genuine article." Townley was becoming garrulous; he had had his eye-opener this morning.

"May I see those sketches, Steve?"

"They're not as good as Townley says."

Johnson impatiently flicked his cigar-ash. "Let me be the judge."

"I called these the 'Sullivan County Sketches.' Little pieces I dreamed up, Mr. Johnson, or put together from experiences I had, or others had."

"That covers the writing of everything, doesn't it?" Johnson smiled. "Leave them at the desk, and I'll read them before I turn in tonight."

At breakfast, the next morning, the editor greeted him soberly. "Fine work, Steve, fine work!"

"They're not bad?" He flushed. "Do you think so?"

"I say they're good, Steve. We'll use some of them. Six dollars a column—space rates."

A chill went down his spine. "You think they're that good?"

Johnson chuckled. "We'll take five, Steve. Five Sundays in July: we'll publish one sketch each Sunday. 'Four Men in a Cave,' 'The Octopush,' 'The Ghoul's Accountant,' 'Black Dog,' and 'Killing His Bear.'"

"Jee-hosophat!" he shouted and shook the editor's hand.

"I've got to tell Townley." He burst into a smile, laughed, and sprinted across the lobby.

He leaped the stairs to the walk, turned left and collided with a girl.

"Excuse me, Miss! I'm sorry. Oh, I am——" He had his arm about her waist as he drew her to her feet. "Please excuse me. I'm so——"

The girl, a tall, willowy creature with ash-blonde hair, was ablaze with anger. "How rude!" she snapped. She jerked herself from his grasp and smoothed her skirts. "You hurt me!"

"Please, I didn't mean it. I was all excited. See, an editor bought five stories of mine and—nothing like that's ever happened to me in my life."

"Is that a reason for knocking people down?" she demanded, and touched her coiffure. The blue-gray eyes became soft. "*Five* stories, did you say?"

"Yes, sir! I mean—yes." He showed five fingers. He wanted to continue his explanation, but he was suddenly aware of the beautiful oval face with its strong straight nose and the lovely warm mouth. He mumbled. "I didn't mean to run into you. I mean not like that." Boldly, "Of course, if it's the only way I could meet you——"

"Now never mind that. You were rude and careless, and I don't know if I should ever forgive you. And look! All the ladies on the verandah are watching us."

He was forgiven; he knew it. With mock gallantry, he offered his arm. "May I? If we walk in the direction of Day's ice-cream parlor I can prove that I'm not a cad and a scoundrel but only a clumsy reporter."

She pouted. "I don't know if I should."

"On bended knee? I'll get right down on my knees in sight of all those ladies."

"Don't you dare!"

So he walked beside her toward the ice-cream parlor and chattered, while his heart thumped and he thought it the greatest day of his life.

She had a large vanilla ice-cream soda. He ordered strawberry ice cream in a dish.

"Do you always knock girls down when you want to meet them?"

"Always. I bowl them over. You're so beautiful, how else would I ever meet you?"

She laughed. "Weren't you bound on some important errand when you 'introduced' yourself to me?"

"Oh, that! I was off to tell my brother Townley about the stories. He thinks that I'm a kid, that I can write middling well. Wait till he hears that the New York *Tribune* will print five stories. Five! He'll become as green as grass. No, he won't, because he has no ambition himself and doesn't care."

"You do have ambitions."

"Big as the sky."

"You'll be famous, I wager."

The mirth left his face. "I think I will."

Softly, "Do you think that people will know your name if you don't tell them?"

He blushed. Names never rang with him; he had difficulty naming his characters; no name or any name would do. "I'm Stephen Crane."

She was Lillie Brewster Morrow. Her mother-in-law ran a boarding-house in Washington. "Comes summer, she moves most of the older folks up here. At least, she's done it since I've been married to Harris."

His jaw dropped. "You're married!"

She tossed her head. Of course, she was married. It was true that she and Harris Morrow, a government geologist, were separated, but they might be reconciled by the end of the summer. At any rate, she and Jennie Morrow were still the best of friends.

She was not wearing a wedding ring; how should he have known? "Every time I meet a beautiful girl, she's either married or engaged," Stephen growled.

"There have been others?" she twinkled.

He nodded.

"How many?"

"Millions!"

She pretended to sigh. "And you knocked them all down?"

"In a row."

Walking beside her, he forgot that she was married—she was "separated"—and could only think that she was the prettiest girl a benign Creator had ever set down upon this sun-drenched coast.

He was in love, thanks to a collision with a pretty girl, in love again. And Asbury Park, which he mocked daily when he could slip an ironic phrase past Townley's sharp eye, had become a sunlit Paradise. The boisterous vacationing crowds, upon the boardwalk, in the boats on the lakes, or in the surf, were no longer beyond grace. Even the pious bleatings at Ocean Grove were endurable. Life was sparkling, with sun on sea, vendors shouting, children cavorting, old people gossiping, and young people flirting. He was in an incandescent mood. A girl's merry eyes, her wit and her loveliness, had bewitched him. Lillie!

He met Mrs. Morrow, a shrewd, amiable, and loquacious little woman, who immediately suspected that the young man was not calling upon her daughter-in-law solely to read his newspaper articles for her edification. Yet she made him welcome.

"You children mustn't get notions in your empty heads," she said bluntly. "Lillie is a married woman. My son will come for her at the end of the summer. He will."

"Yes, Ma'am," said Stephen. He liked her outspokenness, though it embarrassed him.

"I want no nonsense. *No* nonsense!"

"Had you offered her any?" Lillie whispered when they were alone, standing before the sea under a lemon moon.

"Let's run away together!" he proposed. The cool night air, the moonlight, the sound of the surf and her nearness mesmerized him.

"Stephen! When?"

"In the morning."

"Where would we go?"

"To Texas or California. Out West."

She was silent.

"If you stay, you'll be reconciled with your husband, you'll have eight children and grow old."

"And if I go with you?"

"We'll live quickly, fiercely, and never grow old."

"What if I want to grow old?"

"Not me. Give me ten years and I'll cash in my chips."

"Sh!"

"It's true, Lillie. That's all I ask."

"Sometimes you look so grim and serious, as if you were reaching for something beyond your grasp."

"Am I, Lillie? Run away with me in the morning!"

"You know I can't."

"You're thinking of him."

She would not deny it.

He imagined that Lillie had been married against her will; that, on her wedding night, she had shut her door against her groom and was still chaste.

Townley said, "That girl walks like a queen. She's outa sight!"

"She's a looker."

"You're blinder than a one-eyed Jack. I tell you she's a Pasha's dream."

He told Lillie.

She clasped her hands to her bosom, threw back her head, arching that graceful neck, and laughed and laughed. The white teeth shone; the ash-blonde hair dispersed sunbeams. She radiated a vitality that was rare, fundamental to her being, the gift of gifts given unto womanhood.

Her father, who lived in Brooklyn, came in for a weekend. Lillie invited Stephen to dine with them at the Carlton.

Portly Colonel Brewster, retired soldier, was stony-faced through the first courses. Lillie tried to keep the conversation moving.

"Stephen is an author. My father once helped to write a history of his regiment."

The Colonel had been present at the last day's fighting at Appomattox Courthouse. "I supplied recollections," he said curtly. "Anyone could have done as much."

"Only those who had been there," Stephen offered.

"Of course. Are you writing about the War?"

"No, sir."

"Why not?" He tugged fiercely at his mustaches.

"Because I know very little about it, except what I've heard and read."

The other snorted. "Only subject worth a man's time. What do you write about?"

"He's a reporter for the New York *Tribune*."

The Colonel brightened. He was a partisan of Whitelaw Reid, the publisher. "May see him in the White House one day. Mark my words!"

"Stephen has also written a novel."

"Trash!"

"No, sir. It's very serious work." Defensively, "About the Bowery."

The man bristled. "Bowery! What can you know about that?"

"He's a realist, Father. He believes that the artist must render Nature as she is. As the French and Russians do."

Colonel Brewster was displeased. "There's no greater country in the world than your own, young man. Why write about the Bowery, a place of poverty and vice, when we have the finest, happiest citizens in the world, right here, all around us?"

"Because no one else does the Bowery justice, Father. Those people may be the 'dregs of society,' but they are the mute, the silent, and the degraded, condemned without a hearing. Isn't that so, Stephen?"

"You take a moral position then? Very well."

"Stephen's father was a minister. His great-great-grandfather, or some relatives, fought in the Revolution, didn't they?"

"I want to put down what I see and feel, sir. I don't want to reform anyone. I merely want to tell a story."

"He'll be famous, Father."

"Write about the War," the Colonel advised stiffly. "The country will never tire of hearing about the War."

Stephen knit his brow. "I may some day."

"Father could tell you plenty of stories."

The next day, Lillie confided, "Father likes you, but he's suspicious. He thinks we may be planning to elope somewhere and live in sin."

He guffawed.

She frowned. "I wouldn't laugh at that."

"You wouldn't dare!" he breathed. "You wouldn't dare."

The evening of the Fourth of July, Townley, returning from a hasty trip to New York, carried a copy of the *Tribune* under his arm. Casually, he tossed it to Stephen. "Page nine."

"Did Mr. Johnson use it?"

"Read for yourself!"

The title of his first story had been used as a head, with a sub-caption added in newspaper style:

FOUR MEN IN A CAVE

Likewise Four Queens
And a Sullivan County Hermit

"It's only the first," Townley said. "Fletcher will print four more. You're an author in print, Steve. Let's have a snort to it."

He produced a brown bottle and poured two drinks.

"Can't drink now," Stephen demurred. "Got to show this to Lillie."

Townley drank his whiskey in one swallow and, with a quick lift, drained the second glass, too.

Stephen found Lillie seated among the guests on the verandah of the boardinghouse. The sky was being rent by a holiday display of air bombs and rockets that showered sparks and colored lights over the dark beach and the sea.

193

She followed him indoors and, in the gaslight, inspected the printed columns.

" 'The moon rested for a moment on top of a tall pine on a hill,' " she read aloud.

"Children, hurry! You're missing the fireworks," Mrs. Morrow called.

Lillie pulled the chain on the gas fixture. "Come, Stephen."

"Don't I get a reward?" he asked hoarsely.

They embraced in the dark.

"Children, you're missing the fireworks," repeated Mrs. Morrow.

She was wrong. A whistling rocket burst and shed blue, red, and yellow lights.

CHAPTER 30

One morning Lillie was off to New York to visit her father. Stephen borrowed Townley's railroad pass, and tagged along. They sat facing each other in the dining car.

"You see we're running away together in the morning!" she smiled.

It was a jest to her. "I've got to see my printer," he said crossly.

"Father and I will lunch together. Then I'm free the whole afternoon." Her foot touched his under the table. "Show me your New York."

She went on to Brooklyn. He rode the horsecars, strolled down Eastern Boulevard and along the river toward Fred Lawrence's boardinghouse, which he had named "Pendennis Club." Lucius Button, another of the boarders, who had arrived to study medicine after a year at Yale, called it "Penurious Club." But the majority of the medical students, preferring Stephen's "Pendennis Club," had taken up a collection for printed stationery. "Who the hell is Pendennis?" someone had asked, and Stephen had loaned them Aggie's copy of the novel. It occupied an honored place on the mantlepiece.

Fred was out. Mrs. Van Sluys, the widowed landlady, greeted him effusively; "Pendennis Club" had given her lodgings a reputation in student circles. He skipped up the bare staircase to the big front room on the second floor.

He could hear the tugboats defying each other on the East River, the accusing shouts of teamsters and coachmen and, faintly, the thunder of the elevated cars. In an adjacent room, someone was scraping on a fiddle. Bells clanged; fire horses clattered by.

New York offered never-ending excitement; a unique set of promises to everyone who set foot on the island. Invariably, it disappointed, yet always it mollified with new and grander promises. Loneliness and anonymity it gave freely, today's circuses and yesterday's bread. A raucous, cocky, sneering, hostile city; sometimes genteel and almost friendly, occasionally hospitable. The capitals of the ancient world, Nineveh, Babylon, Athens, Rome, and Alexandria, must have been like Manhattan, with every language spoken, every crime committed, life cheap and death simple. The face of the city shone in maidenly innocence, the body offered the ugliest vices. He could not imagine that anything that men and women might do or produce, or destroy, should not be available in New York, where the co-regents were Money and Lust. Good and Evil were interlocked like a saint and a harlot.

Yet New York also promised recognition and fortune. Somewhere within these flats and residences were the people who would read and acclaim him. With their blessings, every line he wrote might become famous.

If only he might remain in New York until his book appeared! If Fletcher Johnson would publish five stories, other editors might take ten. One story a week at six dollars a column would bring in between twelve and sixteen dollars; he could live comfortably enough.

Anyway, the brass doors had swung open.

Six galleys of type had been set. He gloated over the proof-sheets. The first line on each galley read: "A GIRL OF THE STREETS—7-28-92."

He asked Mr. Able to insert "Johnson Smith" on the title page.

"Who's he?"

"The pen name I want to use."

Able gave him a hard glance. "Afraid of what they'll say?"

"Surprise for my family. And others."

The cylinder press was running with its usual rumble and sucking noise. Able shouted, "They read it, and they'll be surprised all right!"

The typesetting would not be completed until September, perhaps October. The compositors were busy on the fall work for the regular customers.

"It's taking a whole year!" He felt helpless. "People are waiting for it. The *Tribune* is printing my stories." He handed over a clipping from his wallet.

Able scanned it hastily. "Fine. We're a job shop, Crane, not a newspaper office. Be patient."

"I don't want to be patient!"

In an ice-cream parlor on lower Fifth Avenue, he showed Lillie the first galley proofs.

Her eyes brimmed. "It *is* in print!"

"Did you doubt me?" he retorted, ready to be hurt.

From the upper deck of an omnibus, he pointed out the sights as proudly as if the city were mortgaged to him. When the vehicle halted, people below looked up at the ash-blonde young woman. He was pleased that she lifted her chin to ignore the mashers who doffed their straw hats.

He was proud to be her escort. He would introduce her to his "Injuns."

The Needham Building was on 23rd Street. The Art Students' League having given up its quarters in the big, rambling structure for a new home on 57th Street, its old studios had been taken over by a horde of illustrators.

They encountered Jeff Carroll in the vestibule. Carroll, a muffler about his throat although the summer heat was intense, gazed impudently at Lillie and drawled, "Outa sight, Steve, outa sight!"

Lillie smiled.

He led her to Dave Eaton's studio, where he sometimes lounged and shared the coffee.

Eaton, curved pipe in his teeth, was finishing an illustration for a magazine. As he acknowledged the introduction, Eaton's pipe slackened in his teeth as if he had never seen a beautiful woman before; his technique had made him a favorite with all the models.

"I'll trade you a copy of my new book for a sketch of her," Stephen whispered as Lillie stalked about, admiring the drawings and the paintings.

"I'll trade you the girl for the whole Library of Congress," Dave returned. He snapped his fingers. "Miss, sit here, please!"

She came forward as if it were the natural thing to do; that was Dave's old magic.

Ignoring Stephen, he lifted her hat and studied her profile. "Your hair——" He had finesse.

"Steve, go bring us coffee and buns!"

"The hair-oil you say!" But he sped out obediently.

When he returned, Dave had Lillie relaxed and posing naturally.

"She has the lines, Steve. Excellent!" He was sketching with pencil. "A splendid chin. See the line of the cheek. There—the forehead. Ah!"

Eaton's murmured compliments—"Beautiful, beautiful!"—ignited new lights in the gray-blue eyes. Stephen was glad that there was a train to catch to Asbury Park.

"With a few more sittings, I could do you in oils. Next week?" He handed her from the dais.

She glanced at Stephen. "Shall we come back?"

He grumbled something. In a private moment, he said, "Damn your hide, Eaton!"

"Jealous?" Lillie teased at the station.

He denied it. But he had decided that women, whatever they protested, admired forwardness. He must break down the slight conventional barrier between them. Let his book appear, and she would discover the quality of his character.

He plunged into the composition of the new novel. It would be the second panel in a series of writings about life on the Bowery; ultimately, he might do many more novels and create his own world after the fashion of a Zola or a Dickens.

The most challenging question of the age, according to Hamlin Garland, was "the persistence of poverty, vice, and crime in an age of invention, art, and abundance." His intention was to follow the chronicle of Maggie, the streetwalker, with the chronicle of George, a weak youth who went to his ruin through the evil of drink.

He wavered in the selection of a working title. *Maggie* had been a tale of mother and daughter; the new book would be a tale of mother and son. He chose *A Woman Without Weapons;* in neither story was the father of any concern. The milieu would be the same, those blighted areas where life was raw, bleak, and pitiless.

The early scenes, in the tenements and on the crowded streets and in the saloons, flowed freely. With his senses brilliantly attuned, he produced short, etching strokes that set alive the speech and the speakers, the manners and the mannerisms, the smells and the squalor. In the jungle of the slums he moved confidently. The tragic mask of poverty grinned over the proceedings.

George Kelcey and his mother and George's cronies were denizens of the Bowery. They communicated in the argot of the Bowery, yet, under his pen, they throbbed with emotions common also to citizens in the higher economic orders. As he plunged into the narration and the plot unfolded, he perceived that he was borrowing as much from persons he had known intimately as from those whom he had met casually in the Tenderloin.

He had resolved to draw the figure of old Mrs. Kelcey after the wretched figures he had seen charged and committed in the police courts of Syracuse. But this woman, tender where Maggie Johnson's mother had been crude, solicitous where the other had been brutal and unfeeling, pathetic where her predecessor had been maudlin and coarse, was influenced by mixed memories of his own mother. And weak George was, unhappily, a distortion of Townley.

He had not planned it thus. He sought to retrace his steps to the impulse that had stimulated the portraitures. He had not deliberately seized upon subject and characters; they had grappled with him. He saw also that Maggie had been less his creation than that he, the author, had been commanded to create her. He was incapable of dissecting further. Designs seemed to pre-exist in his mind, to be brought into focus under circumstances beyond planning, and beyond his understanding.

He denounced any wish to lampoon; he would not be guilty of disloyalty. Yet the pen, like an Excalibur, was galvanically jerked by energies that derived from traumatic charges. He wrote on, pleased to see each scene falling naturally into place, each sentence supplying its essential mortar. As for any resemblance to persons living or dead, he defended himself that every writer borrowed; no bricks without straw.

On reading the first draft of the early chapters, his uneasiness mounted. He had bestowed upon old Mrs. Kelcey little traits, and had given her lines and actions, that were undeniably Mary Helen Crane's. His George was, in ample proportions, the very reflection of Townley. Mrs. Kelcey struggled to rescue George as Mary Helen Crane had striven to save Townley.

He defended himself. He loved the memory of his mother; in his visions, the glowing black eyes still adored, still reproached. If what he had written mirrored her anguish, it proved only that a slum widow might feel for her semi-literate son the same concern that the educated widow of a distinguished minister had felt for her wayward offspring.

In these muddied waters, Stephen floundered. "His mother was not modern," he declared of the old lady; that was the author's privilege speaking. Authors always peer out from behind their creations. He peered out from behind Townley–George.

Take the little scene in which Mrs. Kelcey asked George to accompany her to prayer meeting, and was rebuffed; that had been Mama talking. Once Stephen had succumbed and gone along. The way she had nagged at George to hang his coat on a peg; again Mama keeping after her youngest. Or her objections to swearing. He had exposed his hand in describing her, through a minor character, as, "spry as a little ol' cricket . . . helpeltin' aroun' the country lecturin' before W.C.T.U.s an' one thing an' another."

He had borrowed from Mama's final delirium: "She fought with some implacable power whose fingers were in her brain." So he had taken from one experience to enrich another.

He had not planned these strokes; he blamed the living, independent pen from which they flowed.

His characters lived on with him; not one ever died. If Maggie had perished, he resurrected her to piece out George's dream. George had encountered her on the stairs of the poor tenement and had yearned to possess her, at least to rescue her from something.

Mrs. Kelcey had died, and George had been left derelict. So be it: he would not alter a single sentence. What he had written of George might be more true of George's creator: "He was about to taste the delicious revenge of partial self-destruction." A little of an author must die with every story he creates.

CHAPTER 31

He was shocked to see Townley behaving by day as if he were following the lines written for George at night. Townley was not reliable. He could be gay and talkative, then suddenly morose and taciturn, withdrawn into a private world where the only pleasures were alcoholic. He would disappear in the afternoon and leave it to Stephen to file the daily gabble for the New York *Tribune*.

When he failed to reappear by nightfall, Stephen hired a carriage and made the rounds of the drinking houses at Shark River. He dreaded these journeys. "Who sent you? Your Mama?" He would have to support Townley, while he set off homeward at a brisk trot. Sometimes, the night air revived his older brother; more often, Stephen had to drag him into the house, undress him, and put him to bed. In the morning, Townley would scream that threepenny nails had been driven into his skull.

Stephen pitied him. Townley had taught him the delights of language; Townley had kept him employed; Townley, the handsome, quick-witted, and widely read, had been worth a dozen of those who now sneered at him.

They were checking the "Jersey Shore" columns on which the *Tribune* paid them once a week. Townley, wan and wretched, fanned himself with a newspaper, and listened indifferently.

"Here's the column on Ocean Grove: '7,000 AT MORNING SERVICE IN AUDITORIUM!' Doctor Hanlon will be sore. He swears 7,472 were there. Believe that, Townley?"

"Every word." He yawned. "Any news on the Fall River murders?"

Stephen searched the columns. "Do you think Lizzie and Emma killed Mr. and Mrs. Borden? Or was it Bridget, the servant?"

"I vote for Lizzie!"

"Why should any girl kill her folks?"

"Maybe a lot of sons and daughters would like to wield the ax in the old homestead."

"Have you ever wanted to kill anyone?"

"That's what dreams are made of. Wouldn't your Maggie have been better served to kill her mother rather than to drown herself?"

Stephen whistled. Townley was in a savage mood.

"Psst! There goes Isaac Meredith, the evangelist with the fiery eye. Watch him! Only twenty-three, Steve, and he has them hollering 'Hallelujah!' every time he wriggles his sideburns. Steve, now that you're an author, why don't you raise a crop of sideburns instead of that blond fuzz on your lip? Or did Lillie like it?"

Stephen fingered his new mustache. "I didn't ask her." Lillie had said that the mustache made him look older.

Townley mimicked Nellie, "Stephen, is that a married woman you're seeing again?" He went to the cupboard. The brown bottle of Monongahela was empty. "Got to go up to Hartwood tomorrow, Steve." He licked his lips thirstily. "Fish for pickerel for a day or two."

Stephen darkened. "Not Hartwood!" He could follow Townley to Shark River, but not to Hartwood, which was north of Port Jervis.

"Pickerel, I swear!" Townley grinned. "I'll row out to a stump and just sit and fish. Remember when we wheedled Mama to come out, and she caught more than you and I and Will and Ted? Pulled in six pickerel. She wouldn't have gone if Papa had been alive. I'll be back on Monday."

"Two more weeks and the summer is over," Stephen pleaded. "Johnson wants his copy."

Townley dropped the empty whiskey bottle into the trash basket. "You can cover the local gabble as well as I can." He winked. "I christen thee 'Assistant Manager of the Jersey Coast News Bureau.' That'll impress Lillie all right!"

On Wednesday afternoon, the New Jersey Councils of the Junior Order of United American Mechanics held their annual American Day parade on the boardwalk.

Since Townley had not returned, Stephen, shortly after midday, began methodically to gather data for his dispatch to the *Tribune*.

He was worried and angry. If Townley were nursing a bottle, he might topple from a fishing-stump on the lake at Hartwood and drown before he was pulled out.

With flags and banners, the workingmen marchers, clad in their best, some with their wives, a few with bright-faced children, strutted along, catcalling to their friends and gaily waving their pennons.

"Call that a parade!" a spectator hooted, and many on the sidelines sniggered at the straggling ranks.

Stephen turned sharply. The marchers, though obviously of modest means, had selected Asbury Park as the site for their festivities. They deserved as respectful attention as any businessmen who descended upon the resort.

"They're visitors, too!" he grumbled over his shoulder to Lillie, who swept after him. "The season is ending. They're putting cash into tills that would otherwise be empty."

Yet this was Mardi Gras, not marching. Only the bands, and a few proud units, were trudging forward in any semblance of order.

Except when the colors were passing, the hawkers continued to hawk, the vendors continued to sell, and the ladies from the hotels and the better boardinghouses commented audibly on the outrageous attire of the female marchers.

Asbury Parkers had no right to scoff! He was too irritable to be judicious. He was sick of Asbury Park and its trivia. He had been angry with "the summer people" before; now he was angry with everyone.

Back in the office, he began his article: "It was probably the most awkward, ungainly, uncut, and uncarved procession that ever raised clouds of dust on sun-beaten streets. . . ."

His pen was furious: "Asbury Park creates nothing. It does not make; it merely amuses. There is a factory where nightshirts are manufactured, but it is some miles from town. This is a resort of wealth and leisure, of women and considerable wine."

He returned to the workingmen. "Their clothes fitted them illy, for the most part, and they had no ideas of marching. They merely plodded along, not seeming quite to understand, stolid, unconcerned, and, in a certain sense, dignified—a pace and a bearing emblematic of their lives. . . ."

Cold anger, stored through ten summers, turned upon the residents: "The bona-fide Asbury Parker is a man to whom a dollar, when held close to his eye, often shuts out any impression he may have had that other people possess rights. He is apt to consider that men and women, especially city men and women, were created to be mulcted by him. . . ."

Then his anger slowly abated. He had written over three hundred words, far too many for a simple parade at the seashore; Fletcher Johnson would cut it by a hundred. He made a fair copy and mailed the dispatch to the *Tribune*.

Late Monday afternoon when he came in, hot and weary, from a trip to Long Branch, he found Townley pacing the little office.

Townley halted. His face boasted a three-day growth of stubble; his eyelids were swollen, his lips puffy. "So you're here! I thought you'd run away." He charged at Stephen with a copy of the Asbury Park *Journal*. "You blasted imp! Who told you to write college satire in your damned articles?"

Stephen blanched.

Townley clutched at his shirt and slammed him against the wall. "You devil, I ought to murder you!"

"Take your hand—— What have I done?" He flung him back. "What are you raving about?"

"You've ruined me! Ruined me!" Townley repeated with a dry sob. "Look!"

He tore open the paper and, in a tear-choked voice, read: "It is said that the *Tribune's* regular letter-writer, J. Townley Crane, was engaged in something else last week, and delegated the task of writing the usual Sunday gabble to another. This young man has a hankering for razzle-dazzle style, and has a great future before him if, like the good, he fails to die young. He thought it smart to sneer——"

Stephen snatched at the *Journal*. "What are they talking about?"

" 'Razzle-dazzle,' that's you! Read it! There was a mechanics' parade to write up. Who asked you to poke fun at it?"

"It wasn't a 'March Around Jerusalem'! It was only a 'pea-raid'!"

"I don't care, damn you! Did you think that Asbury Park wouldn't find out what the New York *Tribune* printed about that fool parade? Even *The Daily Spray* reprinted the whole miserable article and is shrieking for an apology."

"Apology!" Stephen growled. "What for?"

"You called these people exploiters of their summer visitors."

"It's true!"

"True! Ten Jersey papers are screaming for your blood!"

"Let them scream. It's true."

"Suffering catfish! Why did I ever let you write this piece?"

Coldly, "Because you were off somewhere with your bottle."

Townley sobered; his eyes were bloodshot. "You didn't tell anyone?" He nervously tasted his lips. "I was in Hartwood. That's all."

"I didn't tell. But who would believe you?"

Townley wrung his hands. "Dammit, Steve, who asked you to write this stuff? A report—that's what you were supposed to write." He was utterly wretched. "In type everything looks different. Call a man a bad name a hundred times with your lips, and it may not matter. Print one cuss-word and you're in the soup. By afternoon, Fletcher Johnson will have the protests of the Asbury Park *Journal* and of every other sheet in Jersey."

"He won't give a hoot what they say. He passed it to the compositors, so he must have read it and thought it all right."

Townley let out a deep groan. "Don't you understand anything except your writing? Whitelaw Reid, the publisher of the *Tribune,* is running for Vice President on the Republican ticket. Do you think he wants laboring people and businessmen up in arms about this?"

Stephen shrugged. "What have we got to do with Mr. Reid? Johnson is the editor."

"Oh, God!" Townley hammered his fist on the desk. "Reid's the publisher, the boss, dammit, the boss! He doesn't want Asbury Park, or the mechanics either, to think his paper mocks them."

"I wrote it as I saw it."

Townley jeered, "As you saw it! Steve Crane, authority on life and art! A few sketches printed in a newspaper and you think the world is waiting for your opinions. Reid's enemies are going to pick up this hoax of yours and make a bitter thing out of it. On the heels of these railroad strikes, steel strikes, riots of laborers, they'll use it to make him out an enemy of the workingman."

"I wrote it as I saw it. Poor simple folks marching and greedy ones watching them." Stephen was white-faced.

Townley brandished a clenched fist, then wearily lowered it. "Go away, go away, Steve! You're hopeless. Go write more clever stories about caves and pickerel and bear hunts. After this, not one line of copy do you file until I pass on it!"

"Then you'd better be around to give it your stamp of approval!"

"I'll be around!" Townley shouted. "I will! Drunk or sober, I'll be here."

In the afternoon, Stephen re-read his article. He had editorialized; that was the great sin. However, it was good reporting; it was solid truth. Everyone on the Jersey coast recognized that the summer people were the sole source of income. The tradespeople grumbled constantly about the visitors, but that was no secret. He should not have editorialized; otherwise, it was a tempest in a teapot. He wondered why Mr. Coffin, the editor of the *Journal*, had not dressed him down in private. "Razzle-dazzle style!" It was better writing than the Asbury Park *Journal* printed any day of the week. The *Journal*, opposed to Whitelaw Reid, was naturally taking advantage of the article to raise hell.

The next morning, he returned from the tabernacle in Ocean Grove to find Townley once more in a rage.

"You're fired, Steve!"

"Fired? You're crazy!"

"Fired! Cashiered! Sacked. The gate!" He waved a telegram. "Johnson got an avalanche of complaints. What did I tell you? Everybody is on his back. Mr. Reid must be spitting blood." His voice thickened again. "I spent ten years building a news bureau on this shore and, in one afternoon, you destroyed it!"

Stephen gulped, "I'm sorry, Townley."

"Sorry!"

"If I hurt you." Grimly, "But I'm not sorry I wrote the story. No, sir!"

Townley stared at him.

"Did you get fired, too?"

"That will probably be next. When this fracas gets to our other papers, who do you think will buy a line of our copy?"

"What did Johnson say in the telegram?"

"Read it. 'Whoever is responsible for the parade article is no longer acceptable to the *Tribune!*'" he shrugged. "You're the goat, Steve."

Stephen gazed through the window at the shimmering waves of heat.

"I can't help it, Steve. It's not my fault. You don't expect me to say that I wrote it?"

"No, Town." It was incredible.

His brother wrung his hands. "I should! It's my bureau. But I can't, Steve, I can't. I've got to hold on to it. It's all I've got."

"I know, Town." His stomach was churning. "I understand."

"Go in to New York, Steve. Here's the pass. Tell them you didn't mean it. Apologize to Fletcher, to Mr. Reid, to anybody who will listen to you. Maybe they'll give you another chance."

"I won't!"

"Steve, do it for my sake!"

"Let me alone, Town!"

"Do it, Steve, or the *Tribune* will never forgive us. I don't want them to think they can't depend on the Bureau." Townley was thirty-eight years old, and frightened.

"All right. I'll be there tomorrow."

"I've got a few dollars——"

"I'll make my way."

"Take it!"

Townley sped after him to thrust ten dollars into his pocket. Stephen hoped that he would never have to come back.

Fletcher Johnson thoughtfully rubbed his chin. "I knew it was your writing, Steve. It had your mark, no question." He rocked in his swivel-chair.

"It wasn't Townley's fault, Mr. Johnson."

"I didn't say it was. I told him that whoever was responsible for it was out. But I knew it was you."

"I should have held the article until he got back."

"Where was he? Drinking?"

"Sir? Guess he went fishing. To Hartwood." He knew that he had crimsoned. "I must have got the big head, Mr. Johnson."

"Why did you write that tomfoolery, anyway?"

Anger flashed. "That wasn't tomfoolery, Mr. Johnson. It was an ordinary parade at the end of the season. I saw Asbury Park making fun of its customers. I reported the whole truth, what I saw and what I felt."

Johnson moved with deliberation to select a cigar from the humidor on his desk. He bit off the end and spat. "What you felt? Townley is a skilled reporter. He writes a plain stick of type. You write as if this newspaper is a marketplace for your subjective feelings."

"Mr. Johnson, if it hadn't been for the politics involved, no one would have protested. Didn't anyone here, at the *Tribune*, read the article before it went to the typesetters?"

The editor was silent.

"Didn't you read it yourself?"

"Never mind!" Johnson replied. "There was hell to pay."

"And I paid it!" Stephen retorted. "Townley asked me to come in to New York and apologize, to say that I am sorry. Well, I'm not sorry! I didn't want to hurt Mr. Reid, and I didn't want to hurt Townley or you. But if you let the story pass, you must have thought it was good. It was the only readable column on the whole page!"

"Hold on, Crane!" Johnson said grimly. "You've been fired, that's all. You haven't been robbed of your talent. Go write your stories. But stay away from newspapers. As for reporting what you saw, you didn't even get the facts on the parade. Not a single name of a human being in the whole story!"

"Why did you print it then, Mr. Johnson?" he insisted. "If I was so wrong why wasn't a single word changed?" He lowered his voice. "I'm the same reporter who's been filing stories through Townley every summer for years, and you've known it, Mr. Johnson. You've known everything I did since away back when I went to Syracuse."

The older man stared at him silently.

"You've been good to me, Mr. Johnson, and I don't want to forget it. You published me. You helped me. If I'm the goat in this, then I'm the goat. But I'm through bleating that I'm sorry. I'm not!"

He threw the editor a mock salute and swaggered out.

"Steve!" Johnson called after him in a kindlier tone. But Stephen would not return.

He tramped into the street. He must start over, without Townley, without the *Tribune*. Probably the publisher had dressed down Johnson and the editor had passed the buck to Townley; Townley had passed it to him. He wondered ruefully whether even Lillie would sympathize with him.

He thrust his hands into his pockets and stared angrily at the lowering skies.

CHAPTER 32

He descended upon Mr. Able. Only twenty galleys of type had been set. The printshop had been busy.

"When will I have the finished books?"

"First of the year."

"My God!" he cried. "I'll be twenty-one years old before you get it bound and ready to sell!"

Able guffawed. "An old man, ain't you?"

"I haven't got time. I'm ready with another book. Time, time!"

"You hold your horses, Crane. Whatever you've got coming'll catch up to you quick enough."

He walked the streets. He must live in New York. He had been tempted before to pitch his tent—"A Tent in Agony"—here, but he had lacked the means. He still had no money. However, the mechanics' parade had forced the decision upon him. Between the Hudson and the East River and the Battery and 34th Street, or as far north as the Croton Reservoir at 42nd Street, was the battlefield upon which his struggle would be won or lost.

He made the rounds of the newspaper offices. He was nervous and gave his account of the parade story awkwardly; he would not disown the piece.

Editors smiled at the slight youth with the thin, blond mustache who slouched and assured them that he "could write anything!"

"You'd hardly think that a little innocent chap like me could have stirred up such a row," he said, with an effort to be droll, to Curtis Brown at the *Press*. "It shows what innocence can do if it has the opportunity!"

"Innocence!" exploded Brown. "Your innocence, Crane, strikes me as damn corrosive irony."

At the *Evening Sun,* where they were said to be hospitable to stories of New York life, the city editor promised to keep him "in mind." He marched from the *Journal* to the *Times* to the *World,* and called also at the offices of *Scribner's, Harper's* and *McClure's.*

He left the manuscript of "A Tent in Agony," one of the stories that Fletcher Johnson had rejected, in the editorial rooms of *The Cosmopolitan* magazine. William Dean Howells was no longer the editor; Stephen had waited too long, and Mr. Howells had been fired. It could happen to anyone.

At *Harper's Weekly,* Richard Harding Davis, author of *Gallegher,* was the new managing editor. But Mr. Davis, who had gone West to write articles on Oklahoma, Colorado, Texas, and the Mexican border, was now in Chicago for the opening of the World's Fair.

When he returned to Asbury Park, Mrs. Morrow was packing her linens and dishes; the boarders had left. She glanced at his somber features and said, not unkindly, "She's gone, Stephen. She's gone back to Washington."

He hung his head. "I came to tell her something."

"You're too late, Stephen, she left this morning."

Another "summer romance," he thought bitterly. All his life he would be destined to seek out and fall in love with women who either belonged, or had belonged, to other men.

He addressed a letter to the manager of the American Press Association proposing that he travel South and West to write special articles for them. A wild dream; he was not the lucky Mr. Davis. If he did obtain such an assignment, he would have to borrow the travel money from Will. He would tramp from state to state and send back dispatches that would make his name.

He had a two-word reply from the American Press Association: "Not interested."

He dreamed that "A Tent in Agony" was blown out of the windows of *The Cosmopolitan* and swirled away in a screaming wind. "Keep them moving!" a voice called. "Keep them moving!" He pursued the pages down the street. They descended into a gutter. He stooped to gather them and fell into a deep, noisy whirlpool of papers, each scrawled with his penmanship: "Stephen Crane . . . Stephen Crane . . . Stephen Crane."

He must live in New York. He confided his plans to Ted, who never reproached him. "I've got to get down to the real thing. There's nothing for me in Jersey."

"Don't be proud. Whatever we've got——"

"I've got to make it myself, Ted!"

He dared not fear hardships. Belly-pinch would not harm him. In France, artists and writers lived in garrets until the public recognized their great talents. If he could not find shelter, he would flop somewhere; he would not perish. Most important, he must break away, be his own master, and prove, dammit, prove!

Will said, "If you had gone back to college before you were twenty-one you would be getting that three hundred a year. If you hadn't contracted with that printer, you'd have another eight hundred dollars."

"If I were dead," he retorted wildly, "I wouldn't have to worry about anything, would I?"

Ted gave him an ulster, Mame a pair of mittens that were snug and warm. "Take your toothache remedy, Steve," she reminded him.

Townley pressed a black cardboard satchel on Stephen. "If you're to call on editors, remember to shave every other day."

He uttered a derisive laugh. "And you look like a gypsy's grandfather!"

The older brother's eyes blazed naked resentment.

"Sorry, Town!"

Like a lantern slide dropping, the mocking indifference returned. "Nobody expects any better from me, do they?"

He mustered the courage to urge the youth to write a few additional short articles. "It'll blow over, Steve. By next season, they will have forgotten, and you can return to your old beat as if nothing had ever happened."

A letter came from *The Cosmopolitan.* "A Tent in Agony" had been accepted! A check for fifty dollars would follow. The story would be published in the December issue.

"My God!" he whispered. He scorned to admit it, but he had been praying again. "My God!"

His first sale to a magazine, to a national periodical. And fifty dollars! Now he had all the money he needed to start in New York.

Will, who had kept his word and, in October, November, and December, had sent checks to the order of Able Printers totaling six hundred dollars, said, "Copyright the novel!"

On Pendennis Club stationery, Stephen addressed a request for copyright to the Librarian of Congress, and enclosed one dollar and a typewritten title page. He dared not wait for the finished copies of the book. He must have a record of the copyright in his own name; if the librarian noticed that the author of *A Girl of the Streets* was "Johnson Smith," he would surely refuse to issue the copyright to Stephen Crane!

He had visited the printshop at least twice a week in his six months in New York, but the books still were not ready. He had watched the pressman feeding the large sheets. The steel chase, which held eight pages of type, slid back and forth on the bed of the press; the sheets rolled off the cylinder and were imprinted with his words.

Mr. Zachary, the elderly, bearded compositor who had set most of the type, pitied Stephen's gaunt appearance and shabby clothes. "Buy yourself a new coat, kid, and a pair of shoes instead of those big old rubbers. What you want, is to eat three square meals once a week!"

"I must have this book printed, Mr. Zachary."

"There's a panic in the land, ain't you heard, boy?" He frequently passed Stephen an apple, and once a roast pork sandwich saved from his lunchpail. "Or do you think you're the only one starving? There's few fifty-cent pieces to spend for books. Take a look in the hallways at night and on the elevated stairs. You can buy any of those sleeping men for a lead quarter."

Stephen showed Mr. Zachary the December issue of *The Cosmopolitan.* "A Tent in Agony," handsomely illustrated, occupied three full pages. Fellow contributors were William Dean Howells, Henry James, Theodore Roosevelt, Bliss Carman, and Louise Imogen Guiney.

"You can't eat that fame, can you?" The compositor added warmly, "Don't mind me, kid. This is fame all right."

Stephen was living on forty cents a day and sleeping wherever he could find a spare bed. Fred Lawrence was hospitable, but the medics at the Pendennis Club thought it high-jinks to leave smelly bones under the guest's pillow or in the pocket of his ulster. The odors of the dissection table clung to everything he stored in the rooms on Eastern Boulevard.

Occasionally, he bunked at Riley Hatch's flat. When two unemployed actors came down upon Riley, he had to move over to Bob Vosburgh's on East Twenty-third Street. He was obliged to pay two dollars a week toward the rent and grub. In these times, many young men like himself, actors and artists, were tramping the streets, knocking feverishly at the city's doors. Everyone seemed to be sharing, or sleeping on a floor somewhere in the quarters of the rare friend who had a job and would spring a chum to coffee and cakes.

Fortunately, the artists were congenial fellows. Three or four illustrators, sometimes five or six, crowded into a studio; anyone who did not mind a shakedown in a corner was welcome. Artists—"Injuns," Stephen called them—were seldom strict about eating-money. Whoever made a sale threw a few dollars into the cash-tin; whoever went out for tobacco, or to call upon an editor, picked out the coins for the day's travel and purchases. When the money ran low, someone shouted for more, and everyone who was "heeled" dug into his poke for the kitty.

The studios were crammed with canvases, stretchers, old tables, credenzas, cans of turpentine, and boxes of brushes; everywhere, finished or half-finished drawings or watercolors. The floors were streaked with paint where brushes had fallen. The walls were stuck with illustrations, chiefly "scrap" from older periodicals, from which came the inspirations for new compositions. The wind wandered freely, its chill breath undisturbed by the potbellied stove.

Most studios had a sink and a shaving mirror, with a toilet-room somewhere down the hall or on the next floor. Some studios had a gas-plate and an enameled pot for coffee; on a shelf overhead would be canisters of sugar and tea, shakers of salt and pepper, and perhaps a sack of oatmeal, cornmeal, or rice. An early riser could steal a bottle of milk from any of fifty doorsteps. Within any group of six or eight, one man would be handy at cooking a stew that could simmer all day and feed a famished crew in the evening.

Sometimes a girl who had been a model came in to help with the grub. There was a fine familiarity as the male eyes trained on the female shape.

Stephen waited politely until the girl, having served them, lifted her spoon.

"You're a gentleman!" Florinda said.

"He's a writer," said Vosburgh in his flat Chicago voice. "No writer's a gentleman."

"I wouldn't say that," the girl returned earnestly.

Stephen thought she had a stunning figure. When they drew poker hands to see her home he won on three sevens. He remembered chiefly that she lived in a flat "with fire escapes written all over the front of it."

CHAPTER 33

To save carfare, Stephen walked the five or six miles to and from Park Row with his articles and stories. He bought day-old rolls to dunk in his coffee. From Ted, at the offices of the Erie Railroad, he "borrowed" reams of discontinued letterheads. To save recopying, he wrote slowly and carefully; his hand became larger and more legible as his funds shrank.

Cigarettes were costly. He was indifferent to the brands: Richmond Gems or Sweet Caporals or Old Judge. He enjoyed a cigarette when he worked at night. He tramped to Duke's factory on Rivington Street to buy the loose cigarettes that had failed to pass inspection for the slide-boxes. Townley had sent up his pipes. After two months, Stephen had to husband even the smoking-tobacco.

Mr. Wortzmann, the wizened tobacconist, saw him peering into his window. "Vy you no zmoke? Come in, boy!" He kept accounts in a little green journal that hung from a nail on his cupboard. "Ach! to go mitout zmoking tobacco!" He hovered over the bowls of cut tobacco and filled a paper sack. "Zmoke! Zmoke! You pay me later!"

Stephen accepted it humbly. The tobacconist started a new page: "S. Crane—20c."

He added Wortzmann's name to the list of the people to whom he must send complimentary copies of the book. A dozen for the family, two dozen for the artists and for school friends, about three dozen for literary editors of important papers and magazines; fifty for a reserve like Papa's in the bedroom closet. The list increased to one hundred and fifty names, and he had not allotted any for editors in Buffalo, Albany, Rochester, Detroit, St. Louis, and Chicago. He was dismayed. If he gave away any more he would not have enough to sell.

He would give one copy of A Girl of the Streets to some living girl of the streets. "Say, wot's dis? Aw, g'wan wit' yeh! A Girl of the—— Watcha take me fer?" The title might offend anyone.

Will had agreed that Maggie would be a far better title than A Girl of the Streets. Will had cautioned him not to frighten people from the book.

He now asked Mr. Able to change the title on both the wrapper and the title page. He should have done it months ago.

The printer flared, "The last form is ready for the press!" The wrapper and the title page had not been run, yet he insisted that the changes would cost extra.

The bill for the alterations was an additional sixty-nine dollars. Will complained. But the printer was running a full eleven hundred sets of sheets, so Stephen wrote, "Please send the money. Don't fail me now."

It was the second week in March when Mr. Able handed him the first, freshly bound copy of

MAGGIE: A GIRL OF THE STREETS (A TALE OF NEW YORK).

The wrappers were of yellow paper, the letters printed in black, with rules in red. On a skid in the pressroom sat hundreds of Maggies, each in yellow papers, each black and red.

He glanced at the cover, and wailed, "You spelled Johnson wrong! There's no *t* in Johnson."

Able studied the copy. "You were haunting us day and night, Crane, weren't you? Didn't you see it before?"

"I said *Johnson* Smith, not *Johnston* Smith!"

The other snorted. "What does it matter if neither one exists?"

Stephen could think of no reply.

"It's too late anyway." The printer pointed to the heap of smudged, dog-eared manuscript. "Want that?"

"Yes, sir!"

"Give it to your best girl?" Able chuckled. "If she reads it, 'Bye-bye Sweetheart!' Well, you've got your eleven hundred copies. Get them out of here!"

He took a deep breath, and burst into the studio.

Four men turned from their work. Dave Eaton peered out from behind an easel. Nelson Greene waved his arms.

"Look who's here!"

"What are you lugging, Steve?"

"Look at him! Smash your baggage, Captain?"

He hoisted the parcels to the table, and puffed. "Books!"

"Selling Bibles house to house?" Ed Hamilton groaned. "Sorry, Mister. Artists don't read."

"Where'd you get them?"

"If you've got to steal, boy, why don't you steal milk and fresh bread?"

"Just books."

Fred Gordon tossed him a jackknife.

They watched as he cut the twine, undid the parcel and pulled out the yellow-wrapped volumes. Carelessly, he tossed a copy to each man.

"Mustard-colored!"

"That's saffron!"

"*Maggie!* Who's Maggie?"

"*A Girl of the Streets.*"

Greene turned pages. "By Johnston Smith. Never heard of him."

Stephen whistled with an air of nonchalance.

"Who published it? 'Copyrighted!' But no date and no publisher on the title page."

"No pictures. Hey, Steve, don't you know any illustrators? Why don't you recommend a fellow?"

"Who's Johnston Smith?"

"Never heard of him."

"A new job? How much do you make on a copy?"

"Look at the smirk on him!"

"He sold a story, and some shark-editor paid him in books."

"Is it any good?" They were leafing the pages rapidly.

"If you Injuns would shut up and read it——"

Instantly, two copies sailed back. "Hey!" he shouted and caught one in each hand. "These books cost money!"

"Read it yourself."

"Wait! Steve, do you know the jay who wrote it? Friend of yours?"

He lifted his hand, Indian-style. "Peace! Me, Big Chief Steve, me wrote-um!"

A silence fell on the studio.

"I did it with my little hatchet."

They turned pages again. The copies that had been thrown back were retrieved.

"You pulling our legs?"

"Honest Injun!"

"Who is this Johnston Smith?"

"Me."

"Have some coffee, Steve," said Greene. "You'll feel better."

Awkwardly, he explained. "See——"

They listened skeptically.

"You going to peddle these books on street-corners? 'Guaranteed good for man and beast'? You're crazy!"

He talked on patiently, and they sobered; he was a friend.

"Brentano's has taken twelve copies. They'll sell them. Only fifty cents."

Dave Eaton tapped the bowl of his pipe on his wooden leg. "If I had fifty cents——"

"Only eleven hundred copies."

"How much did they cost?"

He ignored the question.

Fred Gordon inquired, "What about a notice in the newspapers? Steve, unless people hear about it, they can't ask for it in the book-shops."

Suggestions flew at him. He stood back proudly. They were good fellows, although artists proverbially knew nothing of books.

Gordon spoke up again. "One thing we can do, Steve, Everybody here has got to carry a copy wherever he goes. In the grocery, wherever we go."

"I think," said Eaton, "if we went everywhere in a pack, people would notice. That mustard yellow, with the red and black printing, knocks your eyes out!"

Nelson called, "Listen! 'Aw, what d'hell!' Steve, will your pastor recommend this?"

" 'Go t'hell!' " another read.

" 'Good Gawd!' "

"Is Maggie somebody you knew? A girl you really knew, Steve?"

His eyes narrowed as he unwrapped more books. He must send

copies to the reviewers. He must call on more bookstores. He must spread the news as if it were the Gospel.

"You'll have Comstock after you. You'll be lucky if the police don't run you in."

CHAPTER 34

The door opened warily.

"Mr. Garland? Remember me? I'm Stephen Crane."

"Crane!" The eyes flashed. "Come in, lad. Well! Come in!"

He stamped his feet in the hall. "My shoes are soaking wet."

"You walked? In this blizzard? From 23rd Street to 125th? My, it's been snowing all day! Take them off. Make yourself comfortable, lad."

Stephen entered the living room, awkwardly holding the wet shoes and trailing his muffler. He looked about the spacious flat with its bookshelves, oriental carpet, cushioned easy chairs, and the broad writing table. "Say, this is a library!"

"Get over to the stove and warm yourself." Garland raised his voice: "Frank! Company!"

From an adjacent room, a tall, clean-shaven, gravely handsome man, his shirtsleeves rolled up, stepped in. He hastily fixed his collar-button.

"Frank, this young fellow is Steve Crane. You've heard me talk about him. He picked the worst day of the year—— My brother Franklin Garland. He's the actor, Steve. Actor."

Stephen looked up respectfully. Franklin Garland was playing at Daly's Theater in *Shore Acres*. "I'm pleased to meet you, sir."

Franklin smiled. His grip was as powerful as his brother's. They resembled each other, too, Hamlin obviously the elder. "From what Ham says, you're a 'comer.'" He insisted on taking the wet shoes. "I'll put them back of the stove."

"Hoist your feet up on a chair." Hamlin Garland inspected the stockinged feet; a big toe had announced itself. "My slippers would be too large for you."

Stephen grinned. "Size seven!" He wiggled the bare toe. "I'll have to fire me valet."

"You're a kid," Franklin said amiably. He was removing his collar button.

"I told you, Frank. He's grown a mustache since Avon-by-the-Sea. Steve, the moment I read a dozen pages of that book I knew it was yours. Those descriptions! He can write, Frank! Didn't I say that?"

213

Again Garland's warm hand came out. "Best of luck, Crane. A splendid piece of work. Splendid!"

Stephen blushed.

The actor loomed over him. "Don't think he's flattering you. If Ham says it's splendid, it must be superb." He had a rich speaking voice. "He's not easy with the praise; ask around. I've read a few pages of your stuff myself. Honest, strong, and vivid. Ham is right. I'm going to toot it to my friends. I've already told Mr. and Mrs. Herne; he's the playwright." He beamed. "How old are you, anyway?"

"Twenty-two in November."

"Remarkable!" Franklin's eyes crinkled. "Did you hear that?"

"I told you, Frank. I call it genius. Genius! I mean to review this boy's book for *The Arena* in Boston. Boston!"

Stephen gazed from one to the other. Franklin was taller and handsomer than Hamlin, but he had the same brown eyes and the same imperious nose.

"Bet he's hungry, Frank. Aren't you?"

"Are you, Steve?"

"Don't ask him, Frank. He can eat. What's in the larder? In the larder?"

"I'll inquire of the cook," Franklin expanded. "An artist must eat." He made a mock salaam, and ducked into the kitchen.

Stephen heard the lid of an ice-chest drop. A frying pan rattled on a stove.

"Frank's a good cook, Steve. He'll feed you." He pulled his chair closer. "So you did it, Steve, you did it. Strange, the first time I saw you—where was it? at Avon—I thought you had talent. Remember how we passed ball? I thought you'd get lost there writing for the shore papers. How is your brother? Now this is a fine piece of work. *Maggie: A Girl of the Streets.* My!"

In the kitchen, something was sizzling.

Garland saw the appreciative gleam. "I said Frank would feed you. Steve, why didn't you scrawl a return address on your parcel? It could have been lost, and I'd never have known. And that inscription on the flyleaf, why didn't you sign it? 'It is inevitable that you will be greatly shocked by this book——' Of course, I knew right away that it must be you. I read your story in *The Cosmopolitan* in December. I said to Frank, 'I know that boy!' But when your book came and no name on it, I had to call on the Albertis to get your address. Even then, I had to track you from studio to studio. The janitor at the old Art Students' League Building said you often came around, so I left a message for you. Evidently you got it."

Stephen shrugged. "I've lived everywhere." Meat was frying!

"Have you really been down to Rum Alley, to Devil's Row? Obviously, you've spent a lot of time there, lived there. No need to be shy, Steve. That's vivid writing. Lord, Steve, that's vivid. You've got the gift! Frank thinks so, too. But why no 'Stephen Crane' on the title page? Who is Johnston Smith? And who is the publisher?"

Stephen explained. He concluded, "Couldn't wait the rest of my life for the damned publishers!"

Garland shook his head, sympathetically. "Difficult to get an audience. True in all the arts, and for everyone. Recognition comes dear, but you won't regret bringing *Maggie* out. You're not the first to publish a book yourself. Hawthorne, they say, printed his first novel anonymously, and Thoreau published his first book at his own expense. Walt Whitman told me he did, too, even set the type. Well, it's brilliant. *Maggie!* True realism, flavor of life. Veritism. Still, editors are fearful. My, they're fearful and cautious! Worse than when I began. Now that you've printed it, how do you propose to sell it? And what will you be doing for food and lodging?"

He did not wait for a reply. He cuffed his beard and went on. "Your pieces have got to sell, Crane. I say we've got to help you. I'll talk to Ben Flower in Boston, the editor of *The Arena*, excellent fellow, a man with a heart. He's paid me seventy-five dollars for many a story. And the syndicates. There's the Wilson Newspaper Syndicate, and *McClure's*. And Mr. Howells, you mustn't forget him. William Dean Howells. Part of his novel *A Traveler in Alturia* was in the same issue of *The Cosmopolitan* as your story. Did you read it? A great man, Steve, always interested in new writers. He can do more than anyone else. I'll talk to him first chance. Or you send him a book, Steve. Send it anyway."

The simple generosity overwhelmed Stephen. He stammered thanks.

Garland frowned. "This is what we owe to the new writers, every one of us. You've got the gift, you can do the work. We owe it to you. Owe it!"

There was a shout from the kitchen. Garland leaped to his feet and rushed out.

Crane sat limply, his cheeks tingling. Garland liked *Maggie!*

The brothers hurried in. Hamlin moved a little table before the guest. Franklin carried a tray and several steaming dishes.

"Come on, kid!" Franklin called cheerily. "Steak, fried potatoes. Eat! Fill the inner man. You've earned it."

Except at Christmas, on his visit to Ted and Mame, he had not sat down to so sumptuous a meal in six months.

"We should have a bottle of wine, Frank, to drink a toast."

Stephen was eating ravenously. "Boy, what steak!"

The two men made small talk while he devoured his food. Frank Garland produced a pot of fresh coffee and three large cups.

The actor cried, "To *Maggie*—in coffee!"

"To *Maggie!*"

"Boy, what a meal!" Stephen repeated. "To *Maggie!*" He clapped his hands to his abdomen. "I'm stuffed!"

Grinning, Frank took away the dishes.

"I'll help wash up——"

"No, you don't!"

"Now, in the same vein as *Maggie*," Hamlin Garland went on, "you could do many books."

"I'm already working on another."

"Good! No one, or hardly anyone, has been writing about the dispossessed of these big cities. No one has portrayed their squalor and their misery. Let the world know what goes on behind the facade of urban society. Tell the truth, and the public will have to turn to you. I've got to tell Howells. He's the great proponent of realism. Crane, you're on the road."

Stephen glowed. "I hope so."

"I say you're on the road. Frank, what's Howells' address?"

"Forty West Fifty-ninth Street."

"Send him a copy of *Maggie*. Tonight. Don't forget. You've got a future, Crane, a great future."

Wistfully, Stephen murmured, "Right now, I'd trade my whole future for twenty-three dollars in cash."

Garland wagged a forefinger. "Don't despair, Crane. Not now, you've got a great future." He paused. "Need a little cash?"

Pride crimsoned his cheeks. "Oh, no, sir!"

"The cupboard, as we say, isn't overflowing, but it isn't bare either. Do you hear that?"

"Thank you, Mr. Garland."

The blizzard was still raging when he left the Garlands. They had insisted that he accept a few coins for a hack or the horsecars, but the city was white and the streets were deserted. He set his face into the wind and plodded on. With the exception of Brentano's, none of the booksellers had taken any copies of *Maggie*. Not a single reviewer to whom he had addressed the book had responded. But Mr. Garland had praised him, and had promised to review him; and had offered him hard cash, too. Franklin Garland had asked him to come to the theater. He would meet the playwrights, actors, and managers. Doors were swinging wide open. He was, indeed, "on the road." He gazed defiantly at the white fairyland around him.

CHAPTER 35

He sat in the great man's presence, sipping tea from a painted china cup, while Mr. Howells, a copy of *Maggie* clasped in his small, plump hands, read aloud, in a grave and appreciative voice, several of the passages that had pleased him. Mr. Howells, having appraised the scope and style of *Maggie,* was, like a kindly old miner beside a tenderfoot, roughly assaying the fineness of the ore and judging its worth.

William Dean Howells, fifty-five or thereabouts, was neat and unwrinkled for a short, heavy man. The large, friendly face with its square jaw and iron-gray walrus mustaches, the unruly bangs over the high forehead and the solid neck upon which the big head pivoted, suggested a benign captain of industry rather than the most powerful literary critic of the day. He could have passed for a cleanly groomed Doctor Johnson; he was the voice of authority.

Garland, intimating that Mr. Howells had the gift of putting his juniors at ease, had prepared him for a hospitable reception, yet Stephen had not expected to be drawn so quickly into the field of the man's personal magnetism. Mr. Howells was a fellow novelist who, having suffered every pang of the writer-artist, could listen sympathetically and appreciate a younger man's plight.

While he appeared to be stout, round, and contented, something in the Howells manner bespoke the inner discontent. He had shown abundant grit and courage on the national scene; he had challenged orthodoxy in every field, from religion and law to government. Stephen remembered Townley's hurrah when William Dean Howells had dared to call for justice for the Haymarket "assassins." It was easy to believe that the once-United States Consul in Venice and editor of the *Atlantic Monthly* had, in thirty years, written two shelves of books, that he was the beloved and valued colleague of writers as unlike as Mark Twain and Henry James. But that he should also be modest and friendly was a pleasant surprise.

Mr. Howells had not replied to the note that had accompanied the copy of *Maggie.* The possibility of another rebuff had tormented Stephen. A week later, he had sent a plaintive message: "I see that you do not like it." Apparently, the busy Mr. Howells had not had an opportunity to examine *Maggie.* Now he read it and, indeed, did like it. "Immensely!" he said when he invited Stephen to call.

"What strikes me most in your story of *Maggie,*" he declared, "is the quality of the fatal necessity which dominates Greek tragedy. From the conditions it all had to be. There is present an ideal of artistic beauty in the working out of this poor girl's squalid romance, as in any classic fable. Yes, Crane, and all done in deceptively simple terms. The girl herself, with her bewildered wish to be right and good——"

"Thank you, sir!" Vindication clutched at his heart. Why had so many other editors and critics failed to see it that clearly? If only someone would shout Mr. Howells' words to the world! He would have liked to rub a dozen editorial noses in this praise. How much anguish he could have been spared!

"Her distorted perspective, her clingings and generous affections, her hopeless environment. The author has compassion for everything that errs and suffers." Mr. Howells spoke in a curiously melancholy tone. "The horrible old drunken mother, a cyclone of violence and volcano of vulgarity; the mean and selfish lover, dandy, rowdy, with his gross ideals and ambitions; her brother, an Ishmaelite from the cradle—a wonderful figure in a group which betrays no faltering in the artist's hand."

He gazed far over Stephen's head. "He is quite honest with his reader." He blinked; he was thinking of the young man's intelligent and ironical smile and the mystical blue, now clouded, eyes.

Stephen's spirits soared.

"A pity that it has to be so hard a study. Much here will shock the public," Mr. Howells added, stroking his mustaches.

"The profanities are there because they are part of the life, sir!" Stephen spoke up softly. He felt no need to defend himself; he was taking counsel with the Olympian who promised to be his champion.

Howells gave him a mild smile. "Yes, yes! The life induces savagery." He again pondered. "One wonders what faith might do for them in their plight." He hesitated as if the reflection was meant to quiz his visitor.

"I am not a believer, Mr. Howells!"

"A doubter?"

"No, sir. A nonbeliever. I see nothing in a cruel, harsh world to justify faith that either the cruelty or the harshness will abate in the foreseeable future. The universe is dark and silent."

The older man sighed. "Do you give way to despair? All men succumb to it occasionally."

"It is not despair. It is an absence of feeling."

"Resignation?"

"Not that either. It is a totally negative position of the universe toward me, toward mankind."

The gentle hand brushed that aside. "Hope must remain. Cherish hope. We dare not deny it."

"There is nothing to warrant it in all of man's history." He flushed. "Forgive me, Mr. Howells. You have encouraged me, and I've been carried away."

"Men must exchange ideas. The earth spins only from the force of the ideas that move it."

Stephen clenched his fists. "I wish I knew more, Mr. Howells. I wish I knew so much more!"

His host was breathing heavily. "Your complaint is less against religion than against dogma. You must read Tolstoy. He has influenced me. I can never again see life as I saw it before I knew him. Read Tolstoy! There is a divine essence in man which must be nurtured." He twinkled. "You demur?"

"It does not matter, Mr. Howells. God does not care."

Howells smiled. "Even when you deny Him, you speak of Him with passion. As if in your heart, you knew Him well."

Inquiring about the printing of *Maggie*, Howells confided that he had learned his alphabet from the printer's boxes in his father's printing office. "They say that I was eager to set the types when I was a little one. They had to stand me on a chair so that I might reach the letters. I had formal schooling only until I was twelve. After that, it was all work for me. For a time, we lived in a log cabin. We plastered it with newspapers against the wind and the snow. But there were books to read, always books. One worked, one read, and one wrote. A man who is hungry for knowledge will fill his stomach somehow."

Everywhere Stephen had turned, among the men he admired, he had found justification for leaving college.

Howells asked how the booksellers had received *Maggie*. He was not shocked when Stephen told him. He promised to help.

"Crane, you have the ability to penetrate beneath the surface. Compassion, penetration, sincerity, truth, and the great gift—these add up to mastery."

That evening, as he walked to his lodgings, Stephen gazed at New York like a conqueror.

CHAPTER 36

He was tempted to write to Lillie, to tell her that fame was within sight; she might have heard that he had been fired by the *Tribune*. He had Colonel Brewster's address, but he dared not send a letter in his care. Her young sister Dottie, whom he had met, lived with Lillie and her husband in Mrs. Morrow's boardinghouse in Washington; still, he hesitated to entrust an important letter to the youngster's mercies. He must tell Lillie that *Maggie* had appeared, that Garland had been overwhelming in his praise, that Howells had lauded it, that he had a future with Ben Flower of *The Arena*.

What if his letter fell into the hands of Harris Morrow? He addressed the outer envelope to Dorothy Brewster and enclosed a smaller envelope that contained his private letter to Lillie; he was cautious to write nothing tender or incriminating. However, when Lillie read it, she would know how much he missed her, how much he yearned for her.

Lou Senger came in from Port Jervis, and found him sallow and hollow-eyed. "How long since you've had any grub?" he asked Stephen.

"I can eat whenever I'm hungry!"

"Maybe so," Senger retorted wisely, "but do you?" He led him to his cousin's studio. "You Bohemians should know each other."

Corwin Knapp Linson, four years Stephen's senior, lean, long-jawed, and black-mustached, was a serious painter with a wholesome respect for young writers whose stories he might illustrate for the magazines. He was also keen to detect empty pockets. "Steve, you come and bunk here whenever you want. The joint is open house."

God bless friendly artists! Ceek Linson owned a couch, where a fellow might stretch out and write or sleep, or think, and never be disturbed by the man at the easel.

Linson and his cronies knew the cheapest eating-places. Lou Senger and Jim Moser preferred the *Boeuf à la Mode* when they had the price of a full meal. "Save it for Saturday nights when you can hang around the Buffalo Mud after dinner till ten o'clock!" The café was warm.

The rest of the week, the artists patronized Schneebuhr's Delicatessen on Second Avenue. The aromas of salami, bologna, boiled and baked ham, tongue, pickle, sour tomato, sauerkraut, and other fragrant dishes were enough to drive a hungry man wild.

"The potato salad is dependable," declared Moser. A five-cent helping would fill anyone—"with starch and glue," opined Ceek—from breakfast to noon, or from noon to suppertime.

At the delicatessen, Stephen tantalized himself. "I'll have herring and boiled ham and chopped liver and pig's feet, and a slab of that cheese with the holes and——"

"In zuh mornink?" Schneebuhr's round face, with its ice-tongs mustaches, became wreathed with onion-rings of smiles.

"Is it morning, Mr. Schneebuhr? Ach, zo it iss. Then give me five-cents' worth of your extra-special potato salad mit extra potatoes."

The proprietor waved the wooden spoon. "Ach, how could I gif extra boad-a-doze? Iss all cud up——"

"Yah, iss all cud up," Stephen mourned.

Schneebuhr stared helplessly at the artists. He mumbled and slipped a half-slice of ham, or a chicken wing, onto their plates. "Ach, for fife cents I gif away everyding!" Once he threw a heel of soft salami on Stephen's potato salad. "Zo zmall, I would only dhrow him out!" He winked broadly. "You are a *mahler*, a painter, no?"

"I am a paperhanger, *mein herr*."

"*Gott*, a paperhanger! Not you!"

"He's a writer, a *schriftsteller*," Linson put in.

"Zo! He does not hang up on the *papier*. *Er schreibt!*"

"*Ja wohl!*" Stephen grimaced. "I hang upon the *papier* all right!"

Schneebuhr bustled to their table with a tray of rye bread and pickles. "Mit all meals I gif rye *brot und* pickles." He dashed away, utterly embarrassed. "S'gooz me!"

"Somebody better make some money," Crane groaned. "We're breaking his heart!" Impishly, he called out, "*Mein herr,* forgotten de butter!"

Poor Schneebuhr spun around and delivered a wooden dish of butter. "Eggs-gooz me, gentlemens, I'm so mickshed upp!"

"Bring him a copy of *Maggie,*" Senger suggested drolly.

Crane snorted. "The most widely distributed book in all the delicatessens, tobacconists, roominghouses, etcetera, in Manhattan!" He had three hundred copies stored at Ted's in Lakeview, two hundred in the attic of the Pendennis Club, and a hundred behind the coal bin at Vosburgh's place. He had fifty more in Mrs. Armstrong's attic. Every day he sent off a few copies to more editors and critics across the country; each parcel required postage money that could have bought liberal servings of potato salad. He had even left copies at the rectories of the better-known crusading ministers, including Reverend Parkhurst's. None had acknowledged the book.

"Why don't you barter *Maggie* for a night with a girl?"

"Who would take the offer?"

The buyer at Brentano's informed Stephen that only two copies of *Maggie* had been sold. "No one knows about it, no one has reviewed it, and no one asks for it." He invited Stephen to remove the ten unsold copies.

Stephen carried them off unwrapped. On the horsecars he sat with the mustard-yellow books in his lap. He thought of his mother riding home on a train with her dead infant in her arms.

Mr. Howells glumly reported that the Harper brothers, whom he had urged to publish *Maggie,* had straightaway refused it.

Flower, far away in Boston, committed nothing except his enthusiasm. He sent free copies of *The Arena* and lists of the books he published, but he was in no hurry to buy the new man's work.

Garland sent Stephen to Blakely Hall, the editor of *Truth.* The large ten-cent weekly, which regularly featured the virtues of bathing girls, sometimes published articles of quality. Mr. Hall hemmed and hawed, and finally selected a minor sketch, for which he paid ten dollars in cash. Stephen felt that the editor had not really cared for any of the pieces, but had wished to be kind.

He called on Ted for five dollars. Ted silently took in the gaunt features, the shabby collar, the worn shoes, and the old ulster, and pressed him to accept fifteen.

"You can't spare it, Ted!"

"You'll pay it back when you come into your own, Steve."

"The Erie Railroad isn't making you rich. You've got your family."

"Birthday present in advance."

Stephen, light-headed from hunger, headed for the nearest saloon. He called for a schooner of beer and attacked the free lunch wolfishly.

In the evening, he treated Linson, Moser, Senger, Lawrence, and

Raught to a meal of oysters and beefsteak at the Buffalo Mud, and called for a quart of wine. After midnight, he walked to Vosburgh's, clinked three dollars into the cash-tin, and sat down to his writing.

He could do nothing more with his second finished novel, *A Woman Without Weapons*. He was convinced that, even if he found a publisher, the story would fail with the public. Garland and Howells might praise it; no one would buy it. To write a third story in the same vein would be folly.

He had been reading the authors whom Garland and Howells had recommended. The power of Tolstoy's novels and short stories sharpened his dissatisfaction with the writing on his foolscap sheets. He thought Victor Hugo overwritten; each sentence moved like a beer wagon. Flaubert was readable, but too solemn.

John Barry of the *Forum* advised him to lighten his stories. "Write more dialogue, Steve. You've got the ear for it."

It was difficult to explain even to Barry that he did not write to order. He composed best after a subject had flashed into his mind and, like a bursting rocket, so illumined the landscape that every figure was delineated, every line of action played out. Something had to well inside him, as though tremendous pressure below were forcing the narrative loose from his vitals; then he could write effortlessly, rapidly, the dialogue flowing as if dictated to his pen.

"My work," he told John Hilliard, another new friend from Park Row, "may not amount to a string of dried beans. I can only try to do the best that's in me. A man is born into the world with his own pair of eyes, and he is not all responsible for his vision. He is merely responsible for his quality of personal honesty." To cherish that personal honesty, to cling to it and to nurture it—he was borrowing from Mr. Howells—was his supreme ambition.

Lying on the couch at Ceek Linson's, he leafed through old issues of the *Century Magazine* and skimmed articles on the battles and leaders of the Civil War.

Although he had been born ten years after Fort Sumter, he had heard more of the war than of any other subject except religion and sin. He had been listening to accounts of the battles, of the passions and the hatreds, of the loyalties and the recriminations, of the tactics and the blunders, since he was old enough to stand behind Papa's chair.

Once the War had impressed him as exciting pageantry; now it seemed a monstrous dislocation in which the armies on both sides had been moved like pawns on a chessboard. He was touched by compassion, not for the generals, but for the nameless ones who had wandered from hill to hill and river to river on maps they had never seen, and had suffered loneliness, hunger, injury, and decimation. The real heroes were not the be-medaled survivors but the silent ones in the dark graves.

He wished that he had been a soldier and had a story to tell. Thousands might buy it, and thus feed him through the winter.

However, he must write of what he knew and of what he felt, not a potboiler for the sake of regular meals and a soft bed. The writer must be supremely attuned to his subject, the subject extraordinarily suited to the writer; only from such a marriage of author and material could the unusual be expected. One day, the lightning would strike and, in a blinding flash, convey the precise inspiration out of the unknown and the unknowable. The Bush would burst aflame, the Voice would speak. He would be endowed with that prophetic vision from which great art emerges, savagely.

He was sharply aware of the dilemma of the writing man. If he wrote only what he pleased, he risked being ignored, except perhaps by Mr. Howells and Mr. Garland; if he wrote what the public would buy, he risked the corruption and debasement of his talent. Yet he was ready to write any newspaper article to order at six dollars a column. A man need not consign his soul to the eternal flames because he wrote a piece for coffee and cakes!

CHAPTER 37

In the parlor at Scotch Ann's, center of the special commerce, painted boys wriggled their hips in sleek gowns, made feminine *moues* and skittered about in corrupted pride. Amazing how female they appeared when they were rouged and corseted! Stephen recoiled from their performances, yet could not help but pity them.

He fancied that many of the youths had been recruited, or trapped, by cunning reprobates. He had seen boys of fifteen in tow with elderly consorts; the centaur-like subtleties in these relationships baffled him. "It is disgusting to perceive aged men so weak in sin," he had already written. The abominations were incredible, as if they were the result of some devilish sorcery. These flowers of asphalt——

Moving through the night, he revisited the houses where he had once gone as a callow youth; he wandered from parlor to parlor. The common streetwalkers were poor stock. The better whores, often harassed and frequently beaten, by their protectors as well as by brutish policemen, were a more agreeable lot. Ultimately, the profession degraded everyone who brushed, or lifted, its skirts. Nevertheless, he had seen kindness among the cruel, charity among the avaricious, piety among the most lewd, and startling beauty on the dungheaps. It was blasphemous to charge God with the creation of Man in His own image.

Five of the girls at Dolores King's Seamen's Rest were newcomers.

Where Dolores recruited the fresh talent twice a year was her secret, yet she could boast that in her house were the handsomest women in the Tenderloin.

Dolores, a petite New Orleans woman who affected black silk and a huge black turban over a coiffure of bluish-white hair, knew him as a writer from San Francisco. She had viewed him through a gold-rimmed lorgnette and decided that he was harmless. Often he had a cognac in her private rooms.

When he told her that he planned to write a book about beautiful women, she opened a teakwood chest to show him photographs of herself when young. She drew a curtain to a full-length painting of herself lying as naked as Titian's Venus, with a black boy at her feet. As his eyes admired, she pulled up her skirts and petticoats to prove it. Her legs and thighs and belly were as fair and rounded as those of the woman on the canvas.

Her ringed hand caressed the flesh in the painting. "Men are dogs, the best of them!" The nostrils dilated; the rouged cheeks flamed. "With his breeches down, where is the gentleman?"

The man who arrived alone with his lust was no problem, she told him. The caller who asked for two girls obviously wanted a more extensive entertainment. The men who came in pairs lent courage to each other and usually departed in excellent spirits. However, those who descended upon Seaman's Rest in parties of three or four and chose one or more girls for their pleasure could be brutally demanding.

He wished that he dared to ask more questions. Where did she find her girls? How did she train them? Was it true that the cadets and the pimps broke them in? What hatred of men caused certain of the girls to become "artists"? Where did they go when they disappeared from the Bowery?

At Mabel's, he attended a circus. Three women and two men carried on revoltingly, while a dozen guests looked down from a balcony. He gaped at the wild contortions and the grunting, the flash of legs and the nakedness. He shuddered as the women shouted the vilest profanities.

A fat man with a cigar clenched in his teeth leaned over the balustrade, breathing stertorously like a bull in pasture. At his hideous gestures, Stephen cringed. He fled when the other began to shake and groan like an epileptic.

Mabel, a middle-aged strumpet who obviously considered herself a lady because she wore a feather boa and a pearl choker, followed him out. "What is it, honey? The sixty-niners?" Her teeth were gold-capped. "Those pigs make me sick!"

She gave him coffee from a silver urn. She had a "Turkish corner" with mother-of-pearl inlaid tabarets and rich Bokhara rugs. He picked up a copy of *Life on the Mississippi*.

"I used to read," she boasted and pulled her neckline down. As he stared, she murmured, "I don't work no more, honey. But I got a clean girl for you straight from the farm. She still smells of the milk."

Minnie, a sleek creature with tawny hair and a fair skin, deserved the good reports. He was amused when, still naked, she bent over and made up the bed trim and smooth. "I never could stand a mussed-up bed!" she giggled.

From the bureau, she offered him a red apple. "I get terrible hungry, don't you?" The drawer was full of apples.

As he munched, Minnie's gown swung open to her navel. She hastily covered herself: "Esscuse me!"

It was three o'clock, but he was still wide awake. He wandered past the Italian house and the Turkish house. The House of All Nations, on Thirty-second Street, was a yellow delirium, appointed in various decors to suit a wide clientele. Madam Charles, a mannish female, spared no cost; every summer she traveled to Brussels, Hamburg, and Marseilles to hire the best talent from the finest brothels. Her special attraction was Georgette; a customer had to buy her a magnum of champagne for the best results.

The famous house of The Seven Beautiful Sisters, where the proceeds were reserved for charity every Christmas Eve, was restricted to men in evening dress. The policeman at the corner advised him to move on.

He completed his tour at Maria Andrea's French House. Brazil Lily, the six-foot Amazon, was savagely stalking the parlor. Under the hissing, gas-lighted chandelier, her eyes were like black diamonds, her olive skin creamy. The nabob who had paid for her evening had not appeared, so she was accepting transients. Under her yellow silk kimono, she wore sheer black pantalettes.

He was tired and wanted only to talk.

Brazil Lily gritted her teeth. "I ain't got all night!"

He was intimidated by the huge nipples and their enormous aureoles.

She said impatiently, "Let me take care of you!"

He tried to wrestle with her, but she was the stronger. She smelled of fresh biscuits. He was alternately frightened, ashamed, and delighted in her skilled hands.

When he left the Bowery, a blind moon, with a single star to guide it, was shedding silver tears in the morning sky.

To please Nellie, he at last made the journey to Hillside to inspect the double gravestone for which Mama had provided in her will.

The block of gray granite was in place; CRANE had been raised in the border on the pedestal. Nellie had quarreled with Will about the wording of the necrologies. Having finally prevailed, she awaited Stephen's report whether her instructions had been carried out.

He read the legend on the front of the stone:

Jonathan Townley Crane, D.D.
1819-1880
Member of New Jersey and Newark Conferences
1842-1880
President of Pennington Seminary for Ten Years
His Wife
Mary Helen
Daughter of George Peck, D.D.
1827-1891

On the other side were the names of the children, with their birth and death dates. The gray stone had been placed directly above the bodies of the three infants who lay side by side like triplets in a cradle that would never rock again.

He strolled down the gravel lane, enjoying the curious stillness. The day was hot, but the oaks, willows, and maples cast a cool shade. A robin trilled.

He circled the family monument again. At least his mother had not asked for a stone angel, or for a huge, unsightly urn.

In time, every Crane would lie here; he, too, would be "gathered to his fathers." The piety, the love, the beauty, the anger, even the lust and the sin would have evaporated; nothing but the empty physical shells would be imprisoned beneath the red clay. Only the temporal and the insignificant were susceptible to capture; the real was the elusive. The breath, the spirit, the soul—where did that go? Earth could not contain it; no more than a closed fist could hold a dream. Death, he thought, keeps the strangest gardens.

In a plot slightly larger than the Cranes', stood forty limestone slabs, each like its neighbor's, each rounded at the top, each bearing a name, two dates, and some military attribution. In the weather of the years, the limestones had worn quickly; the inscriptions were already faded.

These tablets marked the graves of a band of Civil War Veterans whose ashes had been interred in a group; Townley said these were the remains of men who had perished in some rebel prison and had been laid in a common grave. Six years after Appomattox, the Grand Army of the Republic had collected the relics and brought them back to lie among their kinfolk in the county from which they had once marched out with flags flying and drums beating. They had departed in a company; and, in a company, they would lie here until Eternity, their bones interwoven as their brief destinies had been.

He used to marvel over the story. No parents or friends had claimed them; no one had wanted them. Or had all their kinsmen, too, perished? Perhaps they did not belong here at all, but in some other state or county.

He wished that he could decipher their names and offer them his kinship. He imagined them young fellows like himself, who had answered their country's call and said good-bye to their mothers, and with food and extra shirts and stockings in their knapsacks, probably a Bible, too, had marched away, jollying each other in the sunlight, while their mothers waved and called. They had never returned.

"Conklin." A Doctor Conklin had attended Ludie in Port Jervis. "Fleming." Mame's maiden name was Fleming. Mame's Uncle Henry had run away to war at sixteen, never to be heard from again. Perhaps he lay here beneath the green sod. He knelt to trace another name: "Wm. Wilson." The rest of the legends had dissolved into illegible strokes. Whoever they were, they were known only to the Great Keeper of Names. The dead required no passes, no badges, no identifications, indeed, no identities.

In what battles had they fought? What flags had they captured? If ever it had, it could no longer matter. Heroics were for the generals who survived to write memoirs and to march down cheering avenues. The men who had bled for their victories were ghosts who no longer heeded bugles or stirred to drumbeats, who no longer uttered savage cries at foes they could not see.

His heart ached. They could have been no older than the boys he had led across the parade grounds at Claverack.

On the train, riding back to the city, he dozed off, and dreamed that the youths lying there were not dead at all but, clad in tattered blue uniforms, were crouched under the soil, waiting for a command to galvanize them into action, to cause them to rise to some finer engagement than any in which they had yet participated.

"Going to be a battle, sure."

He heard the words clearly.

"Of course!" another voice replied. "You jes' wait 'til tomorra, and you'll see one of the bigges' battles ever was. You jes' wait."

As far as he could see, the dreamland horizon was crowded with great armies of men. In the trees, on a horse, sat old Reverend–General Van Petten waiting patiently.

"Think any of the boys'll run?"

He breathed shallowly, and listened.

CHAPTER 38

It was nearly four o'clock. His temples throbbed. He had turned up the gas-mantle; the room was suspended in a waxen light. Through the uncurtained window, the night peered in. The water-tap was dripping. Lou Senger was snoring.

A ball of distaste gathered in his throat at the half-scrawled sheets of paper. He had written six openings; each rang false.

He rubbed the small of his back and strode to the window. Sitting was as painful as thinking. He should have gone to Ted's this week end and tramped in the woods around Hartwood.

Who had ever said that he was a writer? To be a writer, a man must have assured power to summon and to apply all his energies to a single task and to persevere until it was finished.

Senger was sawing wood.

He grinned. At least, he had good friends: Lawrence, Senger, Linson, Hamilton, Raught, Greene, Button, Gordon; he was fortunate in his friends. In their eyes, he was of the brotherhood, not a sideshow freak. Men either belonged to the brotherhood or did not belong. Those who belonged understood the anguish of creation; those who did not could neither understand nor sympathize, and to explain was useless.

He had not lived enough. He must test himself against every experience of life, or his soul would shrivel and he would end his days writing gabble, like Townley.

In this hellhole of a city, a million people were lying asleep, temporarily dead. A few might be making love; he could see them bucking and heaving. Others might be rising; early workers would be stirring. In the Tenderloin, the girls would be talking it over with their madams, or handing their earnings to rat-faced pimps, or sitting moodily and dousing themselves with scent.

At the wharves, the fisherboats would be putting out, the freighters would be coming in. Strangers walking the streets at this hour might be waylaid, and beaten or murdered. Sin, sleep, murder, and death; the night was rich in these.

He gazed out of the window. The purple was lifting. Over the rooftops, a vivid streak hung like a lance poised to slay the night. He heard the metallic clang of fire-bells, the rapid clopping of horses' hooves. Somewhere, a fire, a disaster. The city was like a battlefield where the armies were rousing for tomorrow's struggle.

He was suddenly wide awake. It was indeed a battlefield, and those spires the tent-tops. Soon the sleepers would awaken, soon the fog of their dreaming would dispel, soon the bugles would blow. The armies would lie revealed in the dawn light.

His jaw dropped. He was staring into the paling night, but he was not seeing the night. From the mists, a whole army camp was emerging. Somewhere, a rooster crowed triumphantly.

"Hennery!" a woman's voice was calling. "Wake up, Hennery! It's near five o'clock."

"Git up, men! On yer feet naow!"

Horses neighed. He was here, listening to the hushed sound in the room and the scuffling in the flats next door, and he was there where the heart of the army, huge and raw, was beginning to throb. A tugboat hooted on the river, an elevated car rumbled, a coal-fired locomotive hissed like a kettle.

"Hennery!"

Men were being turned out in every tent. The cooks were on their feet, yawning, cursing, scarcely pausing to wash at the barrels. The fires, banked last night, were being coaxed with straws and bits of kindling. The flames crackled, flickered, and sprang erect with greedy, pointed tongues. Privates, shouting, swearing, were tumbling awake as the night reluctantly withdrew.

The sinews of the forest stretched. Dew glistened; grasses waved. A flash of light transformed a great black snake into a mercurial river. What had been a trembling section of woods became a regiment moving off on the flank of the encampment.

His heart began to trip like the works of the Drew clock. The campfires were the red eyes of an enormous monster. The steel of a bayonet traced icicles down his back.

"My God!" He stepped back as in a dream. His papers had blown to the floor; he gazed at them like a sleepwalker.

"Hennery!"

Thunder! Guns were firing. Puffs of smoke ballooned from the hills; musketry rattled. A flag appeared among the trees, was hidden in a cloud of dust, then issued again. A hoarse cheer went up. The earth leaped as another battery loosed a barrage.

"Hennery, are you gittin' up?"

Was the voice here, or over there?

"Naow, Hennery, are you gittin' up?"

In his chest, something tore loose; a chain had burst. The tension had evaporated; his panic had gone.

"Hennery!"

An explosion—was it the cannonading or the voice calling "Hennery!"—had broken the log-jam in his thoughts. He shivered. It was all clear, everything moving freely. Those hapless lads who had been lying in the tiny plot at Hillside were astir; the moment for which they had been waiting had come. There they were, by God! the soldiers and their officers, the huge batteries and their horses, and the stacked rifles. On a hillock, two bearded horsemen were conferring.

He retreated to his desk, the eye of his mind holding the scene firmly. Sentries were firing; more musketry, more clamor, and the renewed thundering of black guns in the hills. "A small procession of wounded men was going drearily toward the rear. It was a flow of blood from the torn body of the brigade."

Muttering, he shaped sentences as the impressions bled and coagulated into words. He slumped into the chair and grasped his pen. Methodically, he compelled himself to seek for a title. "Private Fleming." Better: "Henry Fleming and His Various Battles."

"The cold passed reluctantly from the earth, and the retiring fogs revealed an army stretched out on the hills, resting. As the landscape changed from brown to green, the army awakened. . . ."

A single sentence, and he had plowed into the heart of the opening scene. His pen moved rapidly, delineating the soldier comrades, then flashing back to Henry Fleming: "Ma, I'm going to enlist."

A rush of phrases and clauses marshaled with consistent predication into hard sentences and paragraphs. They brimmed over in his throat; they welled from throat to lips, which felt the texture and approved. He composed furiously. The words flowed into the steel nibs, and filed out in disciplined ranks upon the white parade-ground. He was at ease at every stop, comfortable inside each paragraph, never doubting that he could proceed from page to page.

He sought names for the characters. Jim Conklin, the "tall soldier." Jim Conklin, "J. C." for Jonathan Crane? The "loud private," William Wilson. The rest would be as anonymous as those beneath the sod at Evergreen. He lay on a bunk and listened, heard his voice taking part in the bickering, and recorded. "Sometimes he inclined to believe them all heroes."

He had no plot. The structure over whose architecture he had been brooding for many months was being projected from some mystic center within his brain. It was that way.

The penpoint scratched. Angrily, he picked it off and searched for another. Fixing the new steel into the penholder, he jabbed his finger. "Wounded!" he mused ironically at the bubble of blood, and raced on.

The first chapter ended naturally; he raced into the second. He suffered no more doubts; everything that he needed was welling within him. And, by God! it flowed. He had forgotten the city, the million sleeping or rising. He was composing on the tide of a torrential surging. Within his mind, which claimed unlimited vistas, the entire drama was alive, breathing, heaving and kicking, screaming and groaning in multi-dimensions and, appropriate to his design, there arrived aptly the speeches, the grunts, the curses, the sweet counsel, and the bitter exchanges.

Each scene, breaking like a wave, predetermined the nature of the scene to follow.

"How do you know you won't run when the time comes?" Henry asked, as legions of green soldiers had asked before him. "How do you know?"

Stephen's forehead pained. "No one seemed to be wresting with such a terrific personal problem." His jaws ached. He was Henry, and he was Henry's creator.

"Hey, you big Injun!"

"Ssh!"

"It's morning, man!"

230

"Ssh!"

He heard the window being lowered. Chapter three! "The insect voices of the night sang solemnly." No, they had stilled hours ago.

A hand tousled his hair. "Steve!"

He sat back in a daze. "I didn't say I was the bravest man in the world——" He had written the words; he was repeating them aloud.

That was Lou Senger, good old Lou! "One by one, regiments burst into view like armed men just born of earth."

"You've been up the whole night. What happened to you?"

His tired face was shining. "I've got it, Lou!"

"What have you got?"

He hugged himself, and chuckled. "I've got it, Lou."

Senger beamed and clapped his shoulder. "Whatever it is, I'll make the coffee."

"I don't care." He was trembling. "I don't care, Lou."

"Better get some shuteye."

"No, sir. I don't care about anything." He shouted: "I've got it!"

After a while, he subsided and read his pages. He corrected slips of the pen, hitched himself to the last sentence and went on. "He was in a moving box."

He paused for a gulp of hot coffee.

"It's boiling, Steve!"

"Sssh!"

"Your finger is bleeding!"

He lifted his hand as if it belonged to a stranger. His fingertip was scarlet. He laughed like a small child in the midst of the most wonderful game in the world.

When Lou had gone, he napped at the desk. He awakened, and went to sprawl on the bed. ". . . From the water, shaded black, some bubbly eyes looked at the men."

He slept until noon. His feet felt leaden, his soles tingled; he had forgotten to remove his shoes. "He expected a battle scene."

At the basin, he stripped and washed. Sunlight was pouring in. Had morning really come? Controlling an inner frenzy, he sat down again. "Once the line encountered the body of a dead soldier."

He remembered that Linson was expecting him. "The ranks opened covertly to avoid the corpse." Resentfully, he dragged himself to the cracked mirror and shaved with cold water. He stared at the bloodshot eyes that had peered into the past. He had not left his dead; they were all around him.

He walked Ceek to Schneebuhr's Delicatessen. They lunched on rye bread, frankfurters with mustard, and coffee. He did not recall having asked for the frankfurters.

Linson, amused, was talking: "Where are you, Steve? Come back!"

"Corwin" —he smiled; he rarely used Ceek's Christian name— "I've got something by the tail."

Ceek nodded. "You're deep in something. Steve, you write at my place if you wish."

Stretched out on the divan, he dozed off again. But he was tormented by the flow of the living narrative. It clamored to be released. "The invulnerable dead man forced a way for himself. The youth looked keenly at the ashen face. The wind raised the tawny beard. It moved as if a hand were stroking it." Suspended between sleep and consciousness, he listened to Jim Conklin and to the other soldiers.

He became fearful that he would forget their dialogues and, in a panic, leaped to his feet.

Linson pointed to the table. "There's paper, pen and ink!"

"He glared about him expecting to see the stealthy approach of his death." He covered six pages before his energy flagged.

Someone, not Ceek, was talking. He had not heard Johnnie Raught come in. "Shrill and passionate words came to his lips."

"So you're writing a new piece!" Johnnie cried gaily. "I was telling Ceek: 'Go down to that little hole in the wall where that fellow Ryder the painter works.' Ceek and I, and the whole pack of us, we're not artists, Steve. But Ryder is. Go see him; he has the gift, that old bear has. A giant with a great beard and a little voice, he sleeps in a buffalo robe, eats beans, and gets his reward from the warm glow in his belly when one tiny swab of color comes right on the canvas. He's an artist!"

Stephen listened impassively. Painters were lucky. Dark pigments against light pigments, and a man could stand back and assess the result. No writer was that fortunate. With words, the medium itself intervened between the creator and the effects he sought. He could never be certain that others read him properly or that, having read, their eyes, ears, and total mind assembled and assimilated and reflected truly the thoughts and visualizations he had striven to perfect.

"Go down the street," Raught nagged him. "Walk in on him. Tell him you're a writer, Steve. Sometimes he'll throw his rich patrons out on the street. He works all night," he winked, "and looks it, too. William Blake himself. Keeps his clothes in the bathtub, and his heart in his brushes. I've heard of him taking six years to paint a picture, and crying 'Damn!' to the fellow who had ordered it and paid for it, and then refusing to give it up at all. Why, he's got one oil, Steve— he had it there the last time—with Death carrying a scythe, dashing on a bony steed down a racetrack in the moonlight." He shivered. "I couldn't sleep that night."

Stephen dropped his pen. The spell had been broken.

CHAPTER 39

Albert Ryder's studio was up three flights of stairs on the top floor of a rickety old house. The dank, brown walls perspired; the saucer-worn treads of the staircase thrust at Stephen's soles. Sounds raced ahead, and lay in wait for him in the dark above.

A door whose paint was hideously alligatored stood open. Across the threshold, the spooled ribs of a brass bed shone from a cairn of old clothes, newspapers, and the remains of a fur robe. In a corner, dishes and utensils were heaped upon a gas plate. Jars of turpentine, brown crockery, unclean milk bottles, rickety chairs, and general debris surrounded a black lamppost from which the globe had been removed to expose a long gas-mantle like the stamen of a giant flower. He stepped over a tin of stiffened brushes. He spied the back of a tall easel near the windows.

Ryder must be out, or asleep. He made his way into the room. Under those burlap cloths must be unfinished paintings. The floorboards creaked. He hesitated; the disorder had trapped him.

On a bookkeeper's stool, a burly figure was hulked before canvas. The huge red head and beard were overgrown and shaggy; the coat was greenish, smeared with solvent and oils.

"I'm a friend of John Raught. May I watch?"

Ryder's deep brown eyes turned upon him indifferently. "Go ahead." The glance probed, and fell away. "Anyone stopping you?"

"Thank you, sir. I'm a writer. Stephen Crane."

"I'm Ryder," the man grunted slyly. With a rag, he brushed lightly at a corner of the canvas. He appeared to be nearsighted. He stared at his palette, where fat worms of white, green, and yellow pigments were coiled, selected something on the edge of his knife, and applied it cautiously.

Stephen drew closer. On the easel was the picture that Johnnie Raught had praised. A white skeleton, astride a horse and brandishing a scythe, was dashing down a moonlit racetrack. As he sucked in his breath, the painter murmured, "Death is the only jockey who never loses a race."

Minutes passed. Ryder sat so close to the canvas that it might have been a strange growth out of his flesh. He perched so motionlessly that Stephen sought the rise and fall of the broad chest. The illustrators worked feverishly; this man communed with every speck of paint he applied.

"What do you want?"

"Nothing, sir. I heard of your work and——" As his glance fell upon the other canvases, their supernatural gloominess silenced him.

A moon with a saturnine ring, presiding above a dark field, brooded grimly over the frozen world below. In a heavy impasto, moonlight smote a stream with heart-wrenching sorrow; three classic figures stood contemplatively, while a satyr pranced before temple gates. Glancing from the painter's serene brow and firmly chiseled profile to these haunting landscapes, he caught a glimmering of the man's purpose. Under those red locks tenacious genius sought to force open the Closed Fist of God.

He stared at a small, simple seascape in which a single-masted vessel sailed tranquilly under a greenish moon. Here, too, an innocent scene had been stripped to its bare bones. Reality had been transcended; the ocean had been halted while the moon, like the Divine Eye, scanned the face of the deep. The heavy ridges of pigment were not painterly caprices but impaled emotions. Ryder had caught the bird in midair at the moment the shot riddles it and the creature still hangs alive, for one instant defying the force that must, inevitably, plummet it to earth and death. Before these naked intimacies, this dark grandeur of turmoil, Stephen stood humbled.

"What do you want to know?"

"I don't know, sir." He had not intended to pry into another man's creative marrow. "I don't know anything," he confessed.

A streamer of wallpaper, uncurling from the wall, caused him to start. Ryder's shoulders quivered; a grin cut open the hairy red beard.

"Everything is alive!" Stephen whispered.

A warm glance from under the red eyebrows rewarded him. The fist holding the palette knife waved toward the grisly figure in the painting: "And Death is the liveliest of these."

"Mr. Ryder, may I come again?"

Ryder's head was sunk toward the canvas. Stephen tiptoed out, the lamppost leering over his shoulder.

Whether Ryder was a greater or a lesser painter, he could not tell; that he was a powerful, brooding spirit was beyond dispute. Stephen wished that the landscapes upon which his armies rested were as marvelously illumined. William Blake? Ryder was painting the Earth-to-Heaven phantasmagoria that had driven Poe from Usher and Coleridge from Xanadu.

He must finish his potboiler. That evening when he finally plunged into "Private Fleming" again, he was relieved to find that his writing, although he had deliberately eschewed the mystic, was, in its own way, rich and alive and colorful. The characters were firmly delineated, the scenes vibrant.

But "Private Fleming" was not a potboiler; he had held nothing back. If it was not veritism, it had a subjective quality that had

234

not appeared in his previous writing. Editors would view it with cold, saurian eyes. What if this story, too, were rejected?

He resumed his writing: "He had concluded that it would be better to get killed directly and to end his troubles. Regarding death thus out of the corner of his eye, he conceived it to be nothing but rest, and he was filled with momentary astonishment that he should have made an extraordinary commotion over the mere matter of getting killed. He would die, he would go to some place where he would be understood. . . . He must look to the grave for comprehension."

He wrote all night. As his fingers cramped, his penmanship became crabbed. To fight off the craving for sleep, he bathed his eyes in cold water and wrapped a wet towel about his head. When fatigue clawed at his shoulder blades, he exercised his arms. He fought prickling sensations in his calves and toes. By morning, his head was light, the hinges of his jaw pierced by wires. Excessive smoking had scorched his mouth.

He had hoped to write around the clock until the entire story was completed in first draft. But he had to feed himself crullers or potato salad and drink black coffee, fill his pipe and replenish his little supply of cigarettes. When a word or a phrase momentarily eluded him, he commandeered a rough substitute. After each pause, he revised his improvisations and corrected unhappy constructions before he struggled back into the saddle of the main work.

In the beginning, he had been possessed by no central theme; his purpose was to describe courage among men who were too shy to speak of courage. The story, therefore, was of the testing of a youth's mettle—would he run?—and of his profound relief that he was no less courageous and no more craven than his comrades.

No sooner had he created Henry Fleming than he perceived how much of himself he had wound around the armature of the character. The self-revelation pleased him, for had Destiny set him upon an earlier stage, he might have acted like Henry Fleming. Jim Conklin and William Wilson and their fellows, modeled on the dead, were equally real, more alive than the living. He sensed, as his pen moved, that he was at his best. The secret, was, indeed, to concentrate full powers, as the sun's rays are concentrated through a lens to start a blaze. He had his story superbly under control.

Day after day and night after night, the words sang to him and the pages filled. Twenty years ago this spring and summer, the battles of Shiloh, Chancellorsville, and Gettysburg had been fought. He was writing of The War, yet resting upon the terrain of no single battleground. He preferred to deny himself the comfort of historic names; these he left to the historians. Nor would he borrow the name of any commander to grace the narrative; a general is as remote from his ranks as a bishop from the worshipers in a village church. Henry

Fleming's battles had been fought in greater desperation within his soul than on the fields where he faced the enemy.

"The men dropped here and there like bundles." Upon the face of the captain of the company who had been killed and "lay stretched out in the position of a tired man resting," there was "an astonished and sorrowful look, as if he had thought some friend had done him an ill turn." Henry wandered among the bundles, clapping his rifle to his shoulder, firing, cringing, ducking, swearing, grieving as comrades toppled under the trees.

The fighting suspended, he could look out upon the field of the dead. "They lay twisted in fantastic contortions. Arms were turned and heads were bent in incredible ways. It seemed that the dead men must have fallen from some great height to get into such positions. They looked to be dumped out upon the ground from the sky."

Stephen had become so deeply immersed that it was a labor to retreat to his own personality. He felt like a deserter to be leaving the charnel-field while his comrades still fought and bled.

"He wished that he, too, had a little red badge of courage," he had written. Henry Fleming had yelled with fright and run away. He had wandered among the routed, covered with shame to walk among his wounded comrades a whole man.

Henry shook his fist at the battlefield and swore. "The red sun was pasted in the sky like a fierce wafer." Upon revision, Stephen deleted the word "fierce." The heavens had presented a sacrament; God will not mock the dead. Only *that* he believed.

On the sixth night, he created a scene in which a panic-stricken soldier bashed Henry on the head and so, at last, gave him the wound which he had craved. Returning to his regiment, he told his friends that he had been shot, and was restored in the esteem of his company. "There was a little flower of confidence growing within him. He was now a man of experience." Once more, Stephen whetted his irony. "And furthermore, how could they kill him who was the chosen of the gods and doomed to greatness?"

He wrote at Lou Senger's and at Ceek Linson's, and at Fred Gordon's.

Sometimes, he read aloud phrases that pleased him, and waited for their smiles and the nodding of heads. He was grateful for any encouraging words.

Vosburgh riffled a handful of manuscript. "It's longer than the Bible. How many chapters?"

"Twenty-four, I think."

On the tenth night, he was moving toward his goal like a locomotive which, having thundered down valleys and up mountains, steams proudly with its terminus in view. Baptized under fire, Henry had forgotten fear and had become a fighter. "He had fought like a pagan who defends his religion . . . he was now what he called a hero. And he had not been aware of the process. He had slept, and, awakening, found himself a knight."

When the color sergeant had gone down, Henry and his friend leaped to rescue the flag. "For a moment there was a grim encounter. The dead man, swinging with bended back, seemed to be obstinately tugging, in ludicrous and awful ways, for the possession of the flag." They had wrenched it from him. Later, Henry carried the flag with pride. Ultimately, he and Wilson were praised for their action and were happy.

Henry had come out of it a veteran. "He beheld that he was tiny but not inconsequent to the sun. In the space-wide whirl of events no grain like him would be lost. With this conviction came a store of assurance. . . . He had been to touch the great death, and found that, after all, it was but the great death. He was a man."

Stephen shaped the final paragraphs. He was bidding farewell to Henry Fleming and to Wilson, and to the bewildered but gallant lads of the company. When he had finished, it was morning again. He was empty.

He gathered his pages. He curved his arms about them as if they were a treasure he had mined.

What would those terrible arbiters, the publishers, say? He was wretchedly poor; he was penniless. He must carry his manuscript to the editors and plead for readings. When he had permitted *Maggie* to appear without his name, he had, like Henry Fleming, retreated from the field. That was the past. Like Henry, he was proudly carrying a flag now. He must not flinch or waver.

"He wished that he, too, had a little red badge of courage," he read again. The passage epitomized Henry Fleming's yearnings, as well as his own.

He dipped his pen into the inkwell. On the title page he struck out "Private Fleming: His Various Battles." He wrote instead in a firm hand: "The Red Badge of Courage by Stephen Crane."

CHAPTER 40

Leslie's Weekly said No. They had misplaced *The Red Badge*— was that the title?—but it would be found.

Stephen blanched.

"Surely you didn't submit a unique copy?" Stiffly: "You know that editorial offices accept no responsibility for authors' manuscripts."

"You've got to find it!"

"My dear Crane, we haven't lost it. Manuscripts are never lost. Someone must have it."

"I want to speak to Mrs. Leslie!" he muttered darkly. "I'll ask her——"

The editor, an elderly gentleman with mutton-chop whiskers, and pince-nez on a black ribbon, said heavily, "It's here, never worry. Mrs. Leslie would know nothing of it. But we are not responsible, Crane." He shuffled the parcels on his desk. "Keefler!" he bawled. "Keefler! What have you done with this man's manuscript?"

The secretary, a thin man in a black alpaca coat, came in nervously to accept the editorial abuse.

"We are never responsible for manuscripts," the frightened Keefler informed the young author. "It's the rule in all editorial offices. Imagine if we had to be responsible——"

The editor shouted, "Inquire, Keefler, inquire!" He cast a worried glance and tugged at his whisker.

"You must find it!" Stephen said weakly.

Half an hour later, Keefler returned with the manuscript. "It was perfectly safe all the time," he smirked, busily smoothing the wrinkled pages. "Our bookkeeper is fond of war stories and took the liberty——"

A coffee stain had made an irregular blob on the title page. The corners of the first sheets were like a beagle's floppy ears.

"If you could wait," the secretary declared, triumphantly shaking out his cuffs, "we would locate the wrapping paper. We are not responsible——"

Stephen was still furious when he reached the attic in Lakeview, and sat down to the battered pages. How close he had come to disaster! Had the novel been lost, he could never have rewritten it. He conceived an ignoble hatred for the dolts who passed on his labors, and cursed the whole miserable tribe.

Tortured by fear that he would lose his manuscript, he made a fresh copy, revising the text as he proceeded. He would leave the master copy at *McClure's*. Their syndicate, The Associated Literary Press, furnished literary matter to a group of newspapers; McClure's new magazine would not appear until May.

Stephen favored submission to Edward L. Burlingame, the editor of *Scribner's*. However, either McClure or Burlingame might misplace it as easily as the editor of *Leslie's*. He must have a typewritten copy.

Raught directed him to Earl Willoughby, a clerk in the Herald Building who owned a Caligraph typewriter and, for hire, copied letters and lawyers' briefs.

Willoughby, a thin, sharp-nosed young man with watery blue eyes, a narrow chin, and snaggled teeth, sneered as he flipped the pages. He said in a mincing voice, "What is it?"

"A novel."

"Indeed! Well, I'll do beautiful work for you, but I'm expensive."

"How much?"

Willoughby sniffed. "You're all alike. Why do you write so much?" His fingers were long, the nails neatly trimmed. "Why do you?" He adjusted a green visor to his forehead, crossed his thin legs with almost girlish ease, and rapidly tapped the keys. "I have all the work I can do, really I have. Very well. Thirty dollars."

"You'll be careful with the manuscript?"

"I'm sure that no one would care to steal it. People trust me with important documents! Five cents extra per page if you want a carbon copy."

Stephen assured him that he required only one copy. To placate him, Willoughby locked *The Red Badge* in his oak file.

After dark, the night being clear, he walked to 125th Street to show the second copy to Hamlin Garland.

Neither of the brothers was at home. He sat in the hall at the foot of the stairs with the manuscript in his lap.

At ten o'clock Hamlin Garland, wearing a black cloak and fedora and carrying stick and gloves, arrived in a carriage. "Crane! Never know when you'll come riding in like an Indian scout from across the plains."

"I've been working hard, Mr. Garland." He hesitated. "It's late."

"No, no! Always welcome. Anything to read?"

"Yes, sir. Here it is." He gazed at the other's clothes as if the Westerner had betrayed their common cause.

Inside the flat, Garland put on a pot of coffee and set out a loaf of rye bread, a dish of butter, and some cheese. "Put on the feed bag! Help yourself. I've been to a fancy dinner, and had to wear dude clothes." He studied the youth quizzically. "Why don't you come around more often? Frank asks about you."

Stephen lifted his boot. His soles were worn through.

Garland nodded sympathetically. "The way of the beginner is hard."

As he began to read, Stephen reached for the bread and butter. He was famished.

"Damn fine!" Garland grumbled, brushing under his bearded chin. "Fine! I like the opening. This is the first piece of imaginative writing I've seen from your pen, Steve. You lived *Maggie*, didn't you? But you know nothing of war, and yet this soars. Soars!"

Stephen bridled. Garland had posed that question before. "I didn't copy the girl from anyone I knew." His *Maggie* was far away; it might have been written by a stranger.

The room was silent except for the steady turning of the pages.

Occasionally, Garland's eyes narrowed, and he licked his lips or stroked his whiskers. Once he turned back to some earlier scene and vigorously shook his head. "Grand! Grand!"

"*Leslie's* has already turned it down."

"Some editors would turn down the Book of Genesis. It might offend their lady readers."

"I want to try *McClure's* and *Scribner's*."

"*Scribner's?* Burlingame is formidable. Looks like a Prussian general, yet he's a kind man." He reflected. "You'll break through, Steve. I wish you were continuing your social novels, but this is splendid work. What inspired you to write of the War?"

"It's any war."

"You're too young to know war."

"I may be too young to know anything!" he burst out. "It's the work that has to speak for itself, doesn't it?"

"Whoa, there, Steve!"

Stephen was disappointed that Garland offered no special praise. But the Westerner was reserved, as if he were vexed at this new turn in Stephen's writing and wished to consider it more thoughtfully.

"What else have you been writing?"

"Stories. No one will buy them."

"Go over to Wilson's Syndicate and tell them that I sent you. They need some Bowery pieces. Cash in the till."

He was silent. Garland was determined to steer him back to veritism.

When he called at *Scribner's,* he was received by a pale young man who said brusquely, "Mr. Burlingame is occupied. You may leave your manuscript if you wish."

"It's my only copy!"

The clerk gave him a faint smile. "We can only read one copy." At Crane's frown, he added, "It is customary to submit work to only one house at a time and to show it nowhere else until the editors have reached a decision."

He left the copy reluctantly. Walking down the street, he felt naked. *Scribner's* had the first copy, the typist had his master copy; he had nothing.

"I've written three books, and they haven't brought me a five-cent order of potato salad," he groused to Linson. "How many books do I have to write to earn the pay of a hod carrier?"

"Try *McClure's,*" Linson advised. "He needs material and he's clever. He'll succeed, if the money panic doesn't ruin him. Everybody in Wall Street is hoarding gold."

"Me, too," Stephen muttered. "I'm not spending a dollar these days."

"If you've got a quarter, we can both eat at Schneebuhr's."

He turned out his pockets. "Not a red cent."

Ceek drolly passed him a toothpick. "Try that, and pretend you've just eaten."

They went out to call at other studios. Raught, who had made a sale on Friday, offered coffee and a cheesecake. Later, five of the men played poker for high stakes. Each placed a note for one hundred dollars in the pot. Stephen lost nine thousand dollars. "I'll make it ten thousand dollars if someone will stake me to a fifty-cent dinner at the Buffalo Mud."

Gordon ripped the I.O.U's and threw the scraps up for confetti.

Linson had borrowed the June issue of *The Arena* from August Jaccacci, the art editor of the new *McClure's* Magazine. "Gus says Garland's review is in the 'Book Notes.'"

"Of *Maggie*?" He was stunned that Mr. Garland had not mentioned it.

His cheeks burned as he plowed through the first paragraph. Garland had declared that *Maggie* failed to achieve "rounded completeness. It is only a fragment." He read on and glumly tossed the periodical back to Ceek.

"It's a good notice, Steve!" Linson saw the hurt in his eyes. "He says it's 'a work of astonishingly good style.'"

Stephen raged. "He praised it to the skies when we were together! Franklin praised it. They couldn't find enough glowing words. Didn't he send me to Mr. Howells? Now he compares me to Richard Harding Davis and *Van Bibber*. He says 'Crane is a native of the city, and has grown up in the very scenes he describes.' He knows that I'm no more a native of New York than he is. I met him in Avon!"

"Listen, Steve: 'His book is the most truthful and unhackneyed study of the slums I have yet read, fragment though it is.' He is praising you. High praise! 'It is pictorial, graphic, terrible in its directness!' He says, 'It is important because it voices the blind rebellion of Rum Alley and Devil's Row. It creates the atmosphere of the jungles where vice festers and crime passes gloriously by, where outlawed human nature rebels against God and Man.' That's great praise!"

"I'd praise Sapolio stove polish in a louder voice, if I liked it. *Van Bibber!*"

"Merely comparison. 'Mr. Davis will have to step forward briskly, or he may be overtaken by a man who impresses the reader with a sense of almost unlimited resource!'"

"*Van Bibber!*" Davis was a dude with uncommon good looks and astonishing good luck. His father was the editor of the Philadelphia *Public Ledger*, his mother was a famous novelist, his friends the rich, the beautiful, and the powerful. Wherever Dick Davis went news seemed made to order for his special articles.

"'With such a technique already at command, with life mainly before him, Stephen Crane is to be henceforth reckoned with.' He says that, too, Steve. Listen: 'He has met and grappled with the actualities of the street in almost unqualified grace and strength.' I wish someone would say that of me. Steve, a critic doesn't start out with intent to praise a writer or a painter. He is first of all expressing himself *about* your work. He's like a batter working for a base hit. You're on first. In order to advance you at all, he's got to hit one safely for himself. It's a good notice."

"So this is a good notice!"

"A lot better than the scalping he could have given you. He's done very well by you, Steve. Be thankful for that."

"I thought he was my friend. How could Garland——?"

"He is a critic, Steve. A critic can't afford to be your friend until after he's finished his criticism."

"What will my enemies say?" Stephen mocked.

Scribner's said No! politely. He was not permitted to speak to Mr. Burlingame. The young assistant assured him that the editor had given the manuscript "First attention."

He tramped to the office of *McClure's,* prepared for another rebuff. Here, however, he was admitted at once into the editor's presence.

S. S. McClure had staring gray eyes and light eyelashes. His features were rugged, the mouth large and determined, the mustache heavy. Sandy hair rose above the forehead in a crest.

"I'm a writer, Mr. McClure. My name is Stephen Crane. I've written a novel, and I hope you'll like it."

The gray eyes widened at the dog-eared manuscript. "It has traveled."

"Yes, sir, but it hasn't found a home."

McClure wet his fingertip and, with crisp snaps, lifted page after page. "The public may not be ready for another war story." He looked away absently. "There have been many."

"Not like mine!"

McClure grinned. "That's it! Sell it to me."

Stephen dropped his eyes. Slowly, measuring his words, he talked about the youth in *The Red Badge,* of his fears and his baptism under fire.

"Good, good!" said McClure. "That's more like it."

Now he began to speak of his plans to bring the best of literature to the public at a price that the masses could afford to pay. "Our first issue was fifteen cents. The next will be ten cents. We'll publish the best." He was syndicating Kipling's *The Light That Failed,* which had been printed earlier by *Lippincott's.* He would include Stevenson, Meredith, Howells, Bret Harte, Thomas Hardy, Frank Stockton, and Joel Chandler Harris. "The best!"

242

"You'll like my book."

"I hope that I will. We'll pay the best prices, too. We'll ask first refusal from our writers on everything they produce."

Stephen walked out on a cloud. "The best prices!" "First refusal." McClure was a great editor, a great man. He might pay one hundred dollars, perhaps a thousand dollars. He would open the pages of his magazine to Stephen Crane. Each month: "A New Story by Stephen Crane."

To be fair to Mr. McClure he must exchange the worn manuscript for the typewritten copy. He hurried to Willoughby's office.

The typist gazed at him sourly. "Really, I've been very busy."

"I need that typewritten copy for S. S. McClure."

Willoughby stared at him archly. "You're ready to pay for it then. Thirty dollars, remember? I don't want to put everything aside and do your work unless you have the money."

"If you tell me the day, I'll come for it."

Willoughby scrutinized the unpressed clothes, the frayed shirt cuffs, and the skived shoes. "You come in with the cash, and I'll have your copy."

Stephen shuffled out. It had not occurred to him that Willoughby would want his money before he surrendered the typing.

He would have tramped to the offices of the Erie Railroad, but Ted had been bedridden for several days with another attack of his asthma.

He rode the day coach to Port Jervis and appealed to Will.

His brother reminded him sharply that he had Cornelia and four little girls to feed. "You look like a famished ginger cat! How long will you continue to knock at those doors on Park Row?"

Stephen made a brave story of his prospects at *McClure's*.

Will shrugged. "I'll do what I can. Ted's ill, and he and Mame have three small children and are expecting a fourth. George barely makes a living. Burt has a family of three. I'm the only one with a profession, and I can't help everyone." He gripped Stephen's hand. "Maybe the tide will turn."

Stephen was depressed. The members of the family had drifted apart, each with his own cares and responsibilities. He wished now that there was some way of repaying Ted at least the small sums he had borrowed. It occurred to him that dedication to his writing had made him selfish, that he cared only for the success of his work. Yet success, thus far, had eluded him.

CHAPTER 41

At the dinner table, Mrs. Howells, unobtrusively hospitable, had placed Stephen on her right. She smoothly moved him into the conversation, putting him at ease so swiftly that he forgot his shyness over the roomy suit that he had borrowed from John Hilliard.

He listened to the attractively gowned women and cultured men conversing of the books and the authors of the day. Literature was as much a part of their lives as good food and fine wines.

"Young Kipling has the golden touch."

"Talented, yet a bit shrill, isn't he? He waves the flag."

"Youth is the time for that," Mr. Howells murmured.

"At any rate, he is not as fiercely polemical as Zola."

"Zola is good for France, perhaps for the world at large."

"French characters are sometimes so deliberately unconventional as to be absurd. Yet American readers who would not tolerate the least slip from orthodoxy in a native writer devour foreign works."

Howells smiled at his plate.

A handsome, elderly lady declared, "For sheer mastery of vast galleries of characters, I would cast my ballot for Tolstoy."

There seemed to be general agreement on that. Mr. Howells crusaded for the Tolstoyan works and philosophy.

"We pay too little attention to our own," their host said, with a nod toward Crane. "We need to encourage their audacity. Talent they possess in abundance."

Mr. Crane, Mrs. Howells declared, had written a book that Mr. Howells had praised unreservedly "*Maggie,* isn't it, Mr. Crane?"

Stephen gulped and repeated the title. A few words about the circumstances of its publication excited sympathy; then the conversation moved on.

"What about Mark Twain?" The host's affection for the famous humorist was well known.

"Yes, yes." Loyally, he added, "But young Crane here can do things that Clemens can't."

After dinner, the men withdrew to the study for brandy and cigars. A tall, slender guest announced drily, "If George Washington had undertaken a novel he would have composed it in the style of Henry James."

Even Mr. Howells, selecting a small volume from his shelves, managed a smile.

"James' stock will rise, but I trust that it will not be too late for him." He peered over his reading spectacles. "As a nation, how much

244

we lose when talent goes unheralded until it is too late. How important it is for the artist or author to have recognition accorded early so that he, or she, may enjoy it to the fullest! Now the poet Emily Dickinson published nothing during her lifetime. Yet hers was a rare gift."

The company hushed as he turned the pages. "What do we know of the human heart who understand it only as a functional organ?" His glance again fell upon Crane.

> "A wounded deer leaps highest,
> I've heard the hunter tell;
> 'Tis but the ecstasy of death,
> And then the brake is still."

Stephen tensed. Emily Dickinson was a new name. However, he had often felt the welling of brief, fragile lines that were the equal of these.

"Miss Dickinson's poems are a distinct addition to the literature of the world," Howells went on.

Stephen bridled, as if the praise had been filched from him. Fine poetry conferred immortality upon itself, as upon its creator. He had scorned his occasional verses; disdaining rhyme and meter, he had called them "lines" instead of "poems," and had never submitted a verse anywhere. When his mind was at flood tide, poetic reflections had often been cast up, but their lack of conventional form had convinced him that they were of no account. Perhaps these lines, so personal in idiom, had a brighter validity than he could recognize.

At ten o'clock, he was the first to rise. Howells murmured, "To the writing table again? Good work, Crane!"

He hurried through the dark streets to Fred Gordon's studio. Already a verse was clamoring for expression.

He stumbled into the room and made his way among the easels. He lifted the glass chimney, trimmed the wick, and applied a match. The yellow flame bobbed, and rose to a soft, golden illumination.

"That's biting my eyes!" Gordon had been fast asleep on the divan. "Got work to do."

"Douse it, Steve, and turn in."

"Go to hell!"

He located the inkwell and the pens. Where had Fred hidden the writing paper? Quickly, quickly, before the words evaporated into the night!

With the pen fast in his fingers and every track in his mind cleared, the complete poem came pounding into reality, each line coupled to the next as surely as the coaches follow the locomotive.

> Many red devils ran from my heart
> And out upon the page,
> They were so tiny

The pen could mash them.
And many struggled in the ink.
It was strange
To write in this red muck
Of things from my heart.

Everything he had ever written and valued had poured from his heart in a bloody stream—"things from my heart."
He read under his breath and seized another sheet.

Should the wide world roll away,
Leaving black terror,
Limitless night,
Nor God, nor man, nor place to stand
Would be to me essential,
If thou and thy white arms were there,
And the fall to doom a long way.

"If thou and thy white arms were there . . . !" That verse had aged with him. He was filled with inexpressible yearning for all the women he had ever known.

Other lines formed from innermost recesses. He recorded them as quickly as the pen would move. He paused to reflect, and was once more inspired. To his friends, he was a youth of talent who never doubted that the world would accept him on his own terms; in his private night, his despair never ceased. As long as he lived, he would continue to pursue the horizon.

I saw a man pursuing the horizon;
Round and round they sped.
I was disturbed at this;
I accosted the man.
"It is futile," I said,
"You can never——"

"You lie," he cried,
And ran on.

He favored the cryptic. He was the man pursuing the horizon; he was the "I" asking the question. And he ran on because to halt is to die.

At eleven o'clock, he knocked at Hamlin Garland's door with a roll of foolscap sheets. "Fragments!" he grinned.

Garland read the poems gravely while Stephen ate a roll with marmalade jam. "When did you write these?"

"Last night. This morning. I haven't been to bed." He tapped his forehead. "I've got four or five more up here."

"Why didn't you write them all?"

"First, Fred Gordon made a racket, and then three other Injuns came in. All I need is the time and the place to draw them off."

"You mean that they're all arranged in your noodle, line for line, and all you have to do is to set them down?"

"Yes, sir."

A gleam of disbelief crossed Garland's eyes. "There's a desk, Steve. Sit down and go to it."

Stephen calmly accepted a fresh penpoint and a sheaf of paper. New verses were crowding his mind. He nibbled at the end of the penholder, and stared at the sheet.

After a while, he called, "Here's one!"

Garland tiptoed over, and read quickly. He was about to comment, but Stephen, lost somewhere in those invisible pastures where poets graze, was writing another.

Once more Garland read, and shook his head. He seemed powerfully impressed. "Any more?" The script was large and clear, not a word blotted, not a line altered.

For the next hour, Stephen continued to write. He finished a total of six poems, and Garland perused each carefully.

"That's all I can do now." He slumped in a chair. "Are they any good?"

"I'm not a critic of poetry——"

"Not poetry! I call them 'lines.' Fragments."

"Call them what you please," Garland declared thoughtfully; he failed to recognize the allusion to his review of *Maggie*. "I would say that it's poetry all right. Strange, militant, satirical agnosticism maybe, but poetry all the same. I've written 'lines' myself. Mine is doggerel and good of its kind. But this is poetry! How do you do it, Steve?"

Crane smiled wearily. That was Garland: how do you do it?

"I don't know exactly. They've been up there a long time. I've felt them seething, boiling. I used to be afraid of them. Now they seem better than anything I've ever done."

"It's inspiration then?"

"I don't know. They come up somehow. I don't plan them, and I don't design them." He tried to recapture the feelings that preceded the lines. "They're not contrived, Mr. Garland."

"You didn't memorize them before you came in?"

"No, sir!"

Garland walked the floor. "I watched you, Steve. As you sat there, you worked as though you had a ghost at your shoulder dictating every word. Can you do any more?"

He pondered. "I think so. Maybe. There seem to be more."

"Then get some rest, and do more." He shook his finger. "Don't you let up as long as the spirit of the thing is with you."

Crane gathered his sheets. "I think they give my ideas of life as a whole." He blushed. "As far as I know it."

Garland clasped his hand. "Do more, Steve, do more!"

"Do you like them?"

"I do, I do like them. But don't worry about what I think, or what anyone else thinks. There may be many influences here—Whitman, Coleridge, Bierce, maybe Olive Schreiner. What is important is that these are surging out of you. Some force that has been demanding expression is pouring through a break in the dam! This is real. That's all that matters."

He continued to work under the spell. He came to Garland's flat every morning to submit the new lines. Sometimes Garland made no comment; occasionally he smiled and patted Stephen's shoulder. "Go to it, lad, go to it!"

On the sixth morning, Stephen appeared with a single poem. "I'm empty."

"Sit down, and do more."

Stephen tapped his forehead. "All gone."

"You sure?"

"Yes, sir."

"Let the poems grow cold a while. Then study them. See if they remain alive. I think they will."

"I think these are my best."

He was proud and yet shy about the lines. He was not a poet. Yet what is a poet except one who writes poetry?

To his friends in the old Art Students' League building, he said, "If I can get you Injuns to sit peacefully for ten minutes, I'll read you something new."

"About a harlot?"

"The Return of Maggie?"

"Go ahead, Steve."

He stood before them with the sheaf of poems gripped tightly:

> "In the desert
> I saw a creature, naked, bestial,
> Who, squatting upon the ground,
> Held his heart in his hands,
> And ate of it.
> I said, 'Is it good, friend?'
> 'It is bitter—bitter,' he answered;
> 'But I like it
> Because it is bitter,
> And because it is my heart.' "

He had expected the usual banter with which they cloaked their dedication to matters of art, but he had their rapt attention.

Nelson Greene, who earned a tiny stipend as a proofreader, asked, "It's a poem, Steve, isn't it?"

Dave Eaton murmured, "Pretty bitter!"

"Read more," said Johnnie Raught.

Straddling a chair and resting his arms over the back, he read another and another. He had been right to come to the Injuns.

"Beautiful, Steve, beautiful!"

The papers crackled in his fist. "I like this one best.

> "Black riders came out of the sea,
>   There was clang and clang of spear and shield,
>   And clash and clash of hoof and heel,
>   Wild shouts and the wave of hair
>   In the rush upon the wind:
>   Thus the ride of sin."

"Read it again," Greene demanded.

When he had finished and was slipping his pages into order, they arose, one by one, and shook his hand.

"What will you do with them, Steve?"

"Publish them!" Vosburgh growled. "What else should a poet do with his poetry?"

"I'll have to make another copy," Stephen countered. He was perspiring, but happy. Not one had asked, "What does it mean?" or badgered him for interpretations.

"What will you do with them?" Eaton repeated.

To that question he had no answer.

CHAPTER 42

He was miserably famished: potato salad every morning, and then later and later each day to make it last into evening. Black coffee when he could get it free; a hearty meal once or twice a week. He was always cold. Hunger pangs awakened him at night; he drank water to quiet his stomach. His eyes glistened feverishly.

His hair was shaggy. The seat of his trousers had worn thin. His heels were run down. He scrubbed his shirts and underwear in cold water with a bar of yellow soap, and swore that he would marry the first model who promised to do his laundry. The cardboard satchel had been held back by his first landlady for four weeks' rent. He roved from Raught's to Linson's to Gordon's to Lawrence's, fearing that he would overstay his welcome with his friends.

He borrowed train fare to Port Jervis, and spent a week romping with Will's children. At mealtime, he ate earnestly. Each night Cornelia left a jar of cookies and a glass of milk at his bedside: "If you get hungry while you're writing, Stevie." She sewed buttons on his shirts, mended the ragged underwear, discarded the tattered stockings and replaced them with new hose.

He plotted to touch his brother for fifty dollars.

At the dinner table, Will regaled Cornelia with his adventures among his law clients. Stephen thought him tedious.

"Join us, Steve. You're moody and far away!" Will sounded as if he were a schoolmaster.

"He's thinking, Will!"

"He doesn't have to think so hard while he's working his way through the roast beef."

Stephen, easily injured when he was at their food, tried not to sulk.

"How do you spend your time in New York when you're not writing?"

"I gather material for new articles and stories. I call on editors."

"No regular hours, no regular appointments. I couldn't live that sort of life. Come and go as you please. What have you produced?"

"Three novels. A few poems. About ten short stories."

"In our Port Jervis bank you couldn't raise a hundred dollars on the lot!"

"No-o."

"How many copies of *Maggie* have you sold?" At the awkward silence, he snorted, "I warned you, didn't I?"

"You were right, Will, as usual."

"One day I'd like to read the book," Cornelia declared softly.

Stephen shot an angry glance at Will. "You haven't permitted Cornelia to read *Maggie*? It's good enough for Hamlin Garland and William Dean Howells."

" 'That old-time religion——' " Will hummed.

"S. S. McClure will take *The Red Badge*!"

"You won't have to pay to have it published?"

"Honest Injun!"

Will carved second helpings from the roast. "You're fortunate to have a family to keep an eye on you. Dozens of young writers starve to death in their garrets or drop by the wayside every year."

"They haven't got Cornelia to feed them."

"I wouldn't say that you were living off the fat of the land," Will remarked coolly.

"I'm Jack Spratt," he joked feebly. With an effort, he talked brightly of the artists and their exciting careers. He saw that Will envied the Bohemian life in New York, so he told about stubborn old Ryder and his canvases. "He lives for his art, and strives to perfect it."

Will pointed across the table with the carving fork. "The world owes him a living because he's an artist! I hope that you're not entertaining such nonsense."

"No one owes me anything," he replied coldly. "Not even a dinner."

Cornelia tried to draw them away from the painful subjects.

"Aren't you lonely in such a big city? Have you met any young girls?"

"I've called on a few."

Will, suspicious, glowered at his plate. "Is McClure firmly committed to publish this book?"

"Do I have to have a legal document to bind it? He reassured me again before I left New York."

"It would be better if you had his promises in writing."

"It would be better if I had his promises in cash, wouldn't it? Any bank would welcome me."

The next morning, when they were alone in the law office, Will said stiffly, "With McClure ready to buy the new book, you'll have all the money you'll need."

Stephen gulped. Dare he ask for twenty dollars? "I'm not likely to turn into Andy Carnegie or J. P. Morgan."

"Nor I." Will pawed among his papers. "Need a few dollars?"

He drew a deep breath: "Can you spare thirty? It would help me, Will."

Silently, Will took out his cashbox and counted out a twenty and ten new ones. "You're so darn proud that I suppose you'd rather make the loan formal." He scribbled something on a pad.

"I'd rather!" Stephen retorted. "If I die this will be collectible through my estate, won't it?" He signed the promissory note.

Will detached the note and neatly deposited it in the box. "Maybe we will still see you now and then after you've made your fortune."

"Will!'

Appalled at his own waspishness, Will murmured, "I don't want you to forget us when you're moving among your artist friends and your Garlands and your Howellses. Even in a small town like Port Jervis, if a man is bound to remain intellectually alive, he can do it, and be as good as your swells in New York!"

On his way to meet a client at the bank, he walked Stephen in the direction of Orange Square. The day was dull and humid. "You wouldn't visit the old church, would you, Steve? You could stay on until the last train. You haven't seen the memorial window to Father. Everyone is proud of it."

Stephen peered down Broome Street at the spire of Drew Centennial. "I should pay a call on the Sengers before I leave. Lou Senger has been good to me in the city."

The sky had turned leaden gray. Birds flitted past rapidly, but the air was very still. A woman was watching them from a verandah.

"A storm is coming up. It's been a strange August and a dry September. We need the rain badly. With the panic and all, the farmers have been——"

A high-pitched whine pierced their ears. Dirt gritted in Stephen's eyes. Leaves danced in the gutter; loose shutters banged; screen doors slammed. A tabby cat ran fearfully across the street and scurried under a hedge. A gust of wind nearly upset Will.

"If we hurry we'll get to the church before——" Will went after his hat.

The sycamores, elms, and maples were bending and soughing. A nest fell from an oak tree. The clouds were churning over Orange Square, the light withdrawing as if some great breath were sucking it in. The mountains were hidden behind a black curtain.

"It'll start to pour. Come on, Steve!"

At the next corner, another gust knocked them both against a fence.

The whine had mounted to a thin keening that wavered, fell, and rose in an unearthly pitch. It seemed to herald the march of unseen spirits. Thunder should have rumbled or lightning flashed; there was only the increasing velocity of the wind and the eerie sound.

The brothers faced each other. "What is it?"

Children were scampering to their homes. A small boy was lifted and hurled flat. A girl was fighting to pull a perambulator up a porch step. Down the street, a horse stumbled and threw its rider. The man scrambled to his feet and frantically pulled the animal into a yard.

"Steve, let's go home!"

With a sharp crack, a branch fell across their path. Panes of glass shattered.

"Cornelia and the girls——"

The day had turned into a fearsome night. Will shouted something, then was driven a dozen feet before he could check himself.

"Steve!" Will shrieked. He was pointing at the sky. "The church! Church!"

Out of the semi-darkness, the spire on Drew Church suddenly loomed. *It was moving!* Stephen braced himself against a treetrunk. The steeple was swaying back and forth like an up-ended pendulum.

"Steve——"

The keening had become a fiendish howl. Steve felt his feet lifted from the ground, and clung desperately to the tree. More glass shattered. Above the whistling, a woman's voice screamed, "Tommie! Tommie, where are you?" Another blast flung him against the bark.

"Steve!" Will's voice seemed to be coming from a distance.

A bugle sounded. Men would come running to man the fire engine and the horse carts. The chief's bugle call echoed like the trumpet of doom.

The spire was still swaying. "Will!"

Before his eyes, the steeple was drifting from the belfry! He saw the entire cone of the spire step away from the structure beneath it, hover without visible support for an instant, and then, leaning backward, describe a great arc and come down full-length across the roof of the church beneath it.

He heard himself bellowing, "Papa! Papa!" His mouth opened in horror. Minutes seemed to elapse. Then came the crash and the reverberation; the spire had really fallen. Timbers thudded; glass tinkled. The impact lifted him and he was thrown violently. When he recovered his footing, he heard a loud groaning: the dying voice of the stricken church, or the cyclone recoiling from the wreckage?

It began to pour. Through the rain, Drew Church stood truncated, the belfry a giant, broken molar. Weirdly now, the hour was tinnily striking; the town clock was still running. Then it stopped short, as if some vital part, necessary to continue the *bongs*, was not there but below, in the bowels of the fallen steeple.

He did not know how long the rain fell. His heart was palpitating, and he was weeping hysterically, "Papa! Papa!" He was still whimpering when Will reached him.

No sooner had they taken shelter than, with a finale of sharp thunderclaps, the storm ended. By the time they had skirted Orange Square, the clouds were lifting. The skies were still roiled, but Mount William and Point Peter were emerging. The black masses retreated swiftly northward.

The fire bugle sounded again. The carts were rolling. People were running and shouting, pointing toward the amputated church tower.

Stephen could not catch his breath. His hands were chilled.

"I've got to . . . Cornelia," Will muttered. He tugged at Stephen's soggy coat.

Stephen shook him off. The earth tilted, and threatened him with an attack of vertigo.

People were milling about on Sussex Street. Firemen in oilskins, wielding long axes, were parading in and out of the open doors of Drew Centennial, striding in the rubble, climbing over the fallen spire like Lilliputians over Gulliver's lance-head.

The demolition had been complete. The steeple, which had crushed the top of the church auditorium and lay buried in the ruin, had thrust its tip into the roof of the parsonage next door.

He lowered his head to overhear several women who were mournfully consulting under their umbrellas. No one had been injured, either in the church, which had been unoccupied, or in the parsonage, where the minister had been napping.

Stephen walked into the ruin. Altar and pulpit had been crushed. The base of the spire lay like a giant rocket, with the apex, where it rested on the parsonage, elevated as if ready to fire. He recalled that day when he had climbed into the steeple and, through the chinks in the slats, had peeked out at the entire countryside.

He heard Solomon barking furiously. Through the shattered memorial window, a large black dog was racing wildly around and around the edifice. But it was not Solomon.

He was still breathing with difficulty when a silver coffin handle ascended. "Papa!" Only the reflection from a large silver candlestick which a fireman had lifted from the rubble.

After several minutes, he became calmer. People were again pointing. The steeple of St. Mary's was intact; likewise unharmed were the twin steeples on Deerpark Reformed. The rest of the town had sustained but minor damage. Only the spire of Drew Church had fallen and completely demolished the church.

The hand of God had reached out of the whirlwind to obliterate his father's tyranny. What force, what decree of destiny, had commanded the destruction? Reverend Crane, looking down, would behold and deny that it was the Devil's work. How could he explain it, citing chapter and verse? Unless God lay dead in His Heaven and anarchy ruled the cosmos.

When the shock of the event had passed, a burden lifted from his heart; his father's long reign had ended.

IV. The Fourth Violet

*T*OWNLEY had married again. Melinda was a pale edition of the shy and silent Fannie. When she spoke, her voice was tinged with a note of bitterness, as if his brothers and sisters were responsible for his careless habits.

"He promised he would turn over a new leaf," she said drily. "He turns it over every day."

Townley burst into laughter.

"Cards and liquor. He told me that he was a minister's son, and I believed him."

Her husband was only amused. To Stephen, "Friend of yours is in Asbury. Outa sight!"

His pulse quickened. "Lillie?"

Townley nodded. "Just the family, no boarders."

He rushed over to the Morrow cottage. Dottie Brewster, her pigtails swinging, dashed into the parlor. "Did you come to see the baby?"

He followed the girl to the screened porch. In a walnut spool-cradle, a tiny infant in a blue fleecy robe was asleep on its stomach.

"That's Jimmie. He sleeps all day and hollers all night."

"Babies do," he returned solemnly. "Jimmie who?"

"James Brewster Morrow. Didn't you know?"

He grinned, still failing to comprehend. "Small baby for a three-barreled name."

He recognized a footstep.

"Stephen!" Her voice was cool. She gave him a limp hand and

tucked the frills of her wrapper firmly about her waist. "How nice of you to call!" She turned to the baby, tenderly lifted it, and faced him with reddening cheeks. "He's six weeks old."

"You've had——" he began wonderingly.

"He didn't know, he didn't know!" Dottie chanted.

"It's his feeding time," Lillie said and, with the baby nestling at her breast, swept from the room.

He was left standing before the empty cradle.

He felt as if she had betrayed him. That there was a baby impressed him ominously. He roamed the deserted beach in a daze. Why hadn't she told him that she had become reconciled with her husband?

He cursed himself for a fool.

He sat humbly while Mr. Howells read his lines. The older man leaned his cheek on two fingers of his right hand, a characteristic pose, and gazed out of the study window. He read on and stroked his mustaches. "Are there more?"

"Only these, sir. There are more waiting to be written."

> " 'In heaven,
> Some little blades of grass
> Stood before God.
> "What did you do? . . ." ' "

"I like that one," Howells said. "I like them all, those you have shown me. I like also:

> " 'A youth in apparel that glittered
> Went to walk in a grim forest.
> There he met an assassin. . . .'

"Yes," he went on, "I like them. Irony. Allegory. I wish you had given them more form. They are so striking in content that they would have found a public ready-made for them. As it is, they will have to make their own public." He gazed into Stephen's hopeful eyes. "May I show them to Mr. Alden, the editor of *Harper's Weekly?*"

"If you would, sir!"

"Will you stay to lunch, Crane?"

He was too proud to accept another invitation to the Howells' hospitality. "I must get back to my writing table."

He was obtaining an occasional newspaper assignment; twice he earned ten dollars a column. He haunted the police headquarters in Mulberry Street and the Jefferson Market Police Court.

The novels might one day be published; he dared not count on them. He wrote more "lines" when the mood was upon him; when he was calmer, he worked on a story entitled "An Ominous Baby."

On Nineteenth Street, he saw a dirty-faced slum child kicking a little fox terrier. "Yo, kid!" he called and gave the toddler a penny. "Be good to him, or he'll run away. Then you'll be sorry, won't you?"

The child, dark-eyed, ventured mistrustfully, "Pa says he'll t'row him outa window!"

Stephen brooded over "such a small rug of a dog." At night, he went back to Ninteenth Street. The windows were lighted; a woman's voice cursed her husband.

He stood below, waiting for the father to catapult the little dog into the gutter. He expected a window to be thrown open in any of the flats and the cruelty to take place.

He opened door after door, and scanned the treads in the light of the flickering gas jets. "Here, boy!" he whispered softly.

At last, he found the animal crouched on a stair.

"Here, boy!" He tucked the dog inside his coat, and fled.

"The landlady will throw him out!" Vosburgh cried.

Stephen set the fox terrier on the table. "Look at him. A nose like a black bead. I'll bet he's got a pedigree. He's mine."

"Where did you get him?"

"I stole him."

He wrote a story in which the child's father, "in a mood for having fun," grabbed the little animal by a leg, "swung him two or three times hilariously about his head, and then flung him with great accuracy through the window."

Vosburgh, always tender-hearted, wiped his eyes. "When you write about kids and dogs——. The pathos: 'Down in the mystic, hidden fields of his little dog-heart bloomed flowers of love and fidelity and perfect faith.' God, Steve! What do you call it?"

"'A Dark Brown Dog.'"

"Any story about a dog and a kid," Greene insisted, "is cash in the bank. You'll sell it sure."

Yet neither *Leslie's Weekly*, *Scribner's*, *Harper's*, nor the *Century* would have it.

Stephen asked Hamlin Garland, "What do I do that's wrong?"

"What you do is right, Steve. Send it to Ben Flower."

Because Garland continued to sell stories and articles to Flower, he insisted that the publisher of *The Arena* must respond to Stephen Crane.

"You keep on sending him manuscripts! Truth will prevail."

The prevailing truth, Stephen thought despondently, was that his damned shoes were worn through and he had holes in his stockings.

Suddenly, he was in a frenzy of expectations. Ed Marshall, whom he had met at the *Post*, had recommended *Maggie* to Harry Wright, the city editor, and to Mr. Linn, the managing editor. If only Mr. Godkin, the editor-in-chief, approved of it!

Meanwhile, *Harper's Weekly* rejected the poems. When Stephen delivered another batch, even Mr. Howells had lost interest. "These things are too orphic for me," he sighed.

The criticism depressed Stephen.

The next day, the *Post* said no to *Maggie*. All doors seemed to have shut. McClure was still clinging to *The Red Badge*, but he had gone away on a long trip.

"I rushed your work," Willoughby complained shrilly in the lobby of the *Herald* building. "Publishers were waiting, you told me. Now you let them wait, and make me wait, too!"

"I ran out of money."

Willoughby stamped his foot. "How dare you? Didn't you know it would cost money?" He surveyed Crane's shabby appearance. "Of course, you haven't a sou. I should have known." His parting shot was, "Remember, I'm not responsible after thirty days!"

In his room, he sat glumly, fearing that after thirty days, Willoughby would destroy both the typewritten copy and the manuscript.

"Mr. Crane, do you have an old newspaper for the lighting of a fire?" The landlady's maid appeared in the doorway. "It's bitter cold, and the kindling wood is out."

"Not a scrap, Jenny."

She peered around the room. "Are you going to save all these books? I can never push a broom under the bed. *Maggie, Maggie, Maggie!*"

"*Maggie, Maggie, Maggie!*" he mocked. Then a sardonic grin crossed his face. "Take one. Here. For the fire."

She fingered it dubiously. "Will it burn?"

A wild thought possessed him. "*Maggie* was made for burning."

"You don't mean it, Mr. Crane. I'd have to tear it."

He ripped off a cover. "She'll burn." He tore the front pages from the stitching, and a dozen pages more. "There!"

He gathered an armload of *Maggies*. "We'll make a big fire, Jenny."

In a fury, he ripped and tore signatures loose while she stuffed them into the stove.

She applied the match. The flames licked at the paper and turned it brown. The sewing threads went like fuses. The pages ignited with a roar.

"Burn, *Maggie!*" he cried. "Burn!"

Yellow and blue flames shot forth; they churned in the belly of the little stove.

"Here's more."

The fire ate hungrily. He dropped in an entire volume. The mustard-yellow wrapper resisted. A girdle of fire encircled the book, the fierce light threatening to scorch his face. The lines imprinted red seemed like a harlot's sneering mouth. The paper, which had refused to curl, finally crisped and buckled, and the fire huffed and roared.

"No more, Mr. Crane. I'll toss in a few coals."

He was disappointed.

"I'll save a few for tomorrow, if you don't mind. I can burn a few every day."

"Burn a few every day. Burn them all!"

"Did you know her, Mr. Crane?"

"Who? Maggie? Yes, Jenny, I knew her."

"Poor Maggie! One gentleman said it was a story about a girl. How did she die?"

"She was betrayed!" he said fiercely. "The whole world betrayed her."

Maggie was dead. He had made his sacrifice.

He scrawled a note to John Henry Dick, who wrote for the ladies' magazines, and asked him to "beg, borrow or steal" fifteen dollars to help ransom *The Red Badge* from Willoughby.

He sent identical notes to other friends. None would have an extra thirty; but if he could raise the total in fivers and tens, he would peddle the story somewhere else should McClure continue to procrastinate.

Only Dick produced fifteen dollars, and he had borrowed it from his managing editor against his salary.

Willoughby surrendered half the typewritten copy. "I shouldn't let you take only half," he groused. "I really shouldn't."

Reading *The Red Badge* in typewritten form excited Stephen. The narrative seemed infinitely more alive than in handwriting. He hurried off on the long walk to Garland's place.

"Where's the rest of it?"

He explained that the balance was in hock to Willoughby.

"How much?"

"Fifteen dollars."

Garland impatiently cuffed at his beard. "I'm going to Chicago, Steve. I'd like to read it all at one sitting before I leave." He reached for his clasp pocketbook. "I'll lend you the fifteen if you bring me the rest of the manuscript tomorrow."

His face fell. He did not want to "touch" Garland; he had been careful never to borrow from him, except small sums for carefare.

This money would be for the typewriter and nothing else. "One day you'll come into your own, Steve. Maybe you'll help others. Take it!"

At noon the following day he returned with the rest of the typewritten copy.

Garland, still in his dressing-robe, sat down to read. Stephen repaired to the kitchen for the leftover breakfast coffee.

A shout startled him. Garland's eyes were sparkling.

"Steve, I say you've writen a great story. And I've just thought of another try. Go to Irving Bacheller. Ever hear of him? He wrote a novel a few years ago, *The Master of Silence*, a passable thing. He's been involved with a little advertising periodical that he and his brother and a friend call *Brains*. Now he's starting a newspaper syndicate as Bacheller, Johnson & Bacheller. He knows good writing. Tell him I sent you."

Stephen swayed dizzily.

Garland caught his arm. "Don't weaken now, Steve. For God's sake, in this business you need perseverance more than talent!"

In Stephen's ears, the sea was pounding. Lights flashed, hooves thundered.

"What have you eaten in the last forty-eight hours?"

"Coffee. Yours."

Garland found cold beans and bread and butter and pickles. Stephen wolfed the food. Licking the gravy from the bean pot with a crust of bread, he felt his strength returning.

"Say, I'm better!" he smiled.

"You get *The Red Badge* published and you'll be as fit as a fiddle," Garland growled. "Never saw the writer who couldn't be healed by being published."

CHAPTER 44

At 154 Nassau Street, he climbed the stairs to the office of Bacheller, Johnson & Bacheller. He knocked, turned the cold doorknob and entered.

A gust of wind sent papers skittering across the small room. A beer-pail stood on the sill. Through the open window he saw a red-funneled steamer at her mooring on the Jersey side of the river.

Heaps of manuscripts and periodicals covered two old roll-top desks. At another desk, beyond the low railing, a broad-shouldered man was hunched over an open newspaper.

"Mr. Irving Bacheller?"

"That's me." The big man looked up. He ruffled his blond hair with an ink-grimed hand. "Come on in."

"I'm Stephen Crane."

The brown eyes kindled.

"Oh, Crane! Glad to see you. Come on in, come on in!" His voice was high but pleasant. "Somebody was talking about you recently. Ed Marshall maybe. Sit down. Talk to me."

"Mr. Garland said you might be interested in some of my writing."

"Garland? Yes, sir. Always interested in writers. What have you got?"

Stephen produced his manuscript.

"Here it is, sir. Mr. Garland liked it."

"Shouldn't you wrap it in a clean piece of paper?" Bacheller asked helplessly. He peered at the parcel as if he expected a fish to be done up inside. "This copy the cleanest you've got?"

"No, sir."

"Do you have a fresher manuscript?"

Stephen lifted his head cockily. "I've got one typed script, Mr. Bacheller. Cost me thirty dollars cash, and I had to borrow the money to get it out of hock. If you like the story, I'll bring you the good copy."

Bacheller once more ruffled his hair. He seemed to be amused. "You're saving the good copy to send on to the printer?"

"Yes, sir."

"*The Red Badge of Courage.* Not much of a title."

"I like it."

"Of course you do. You wrote it, didn't you?" He took the manuscript in both hands and settled back into the swivel chair. "Let me read it."

His eyes galloped over the lines. "How old are you?"

"Twenty-three."

Bacheller read steadily. "Is the rest as good?"

"Better!"

He read on. "Did you ever paint?"

"A fence now and then."

The man chuckled. "I mean in oils."

"No, sir."

"Fresh, vivid. You've got a lot of color here." Over the manuscript, he stared at his visitor. "Crane, I don't know what Garland may have told you. I'm not a publisher. I sell to newspapers. Syndicate rights." He weighed the pages in his hands. "How long is it?"

"About fifty thousand words."

"This would make a book. Too long for us." He caught the disappointment in Stephen's face. "Could you chop it down to, say, eighteen thousand words?"

"What for?"

"That's the maximum length we might sell as a three-part serial to newspapers. You would still own the full-length rights to sell to a book publisher."

"I like it the way it is, Mr. Bacheller."

The other rocked thoughtfully in his chair. "Since *Trilby* became a success, everyone wants more Trilbys. However, if the rest of *The Badge* is as good——"

"It is!"

"I might be able to sell a cut-down version to the papers. It would get you attention, Crane. You might cut it down yourself. Think about it."

"You don't even know that you'd like it."

"No, I don't know. Can you leave the manuscript overnight?"

He was silent.

"I'd promise to have an answer for you in the morning."

Stephen's defenses collapsed. "Go ahead, Mr. Bacheller. If you like it, I'll bring in the typed copy."

"Good. Tell me," he went on gently, "is there excitement in it?"

Stephen became grim. "As you said, sir, I wrote it."

Bacheller grinned amiably. "Nine o'clock in the morning?"

"I'll be here at eight-thirty."

Bacheller was already at his desk when Stephen arrived the following morning at eight twenty-five.

"Morning, Crane. Is that the typed copy?"

Stephen laid a neat brown parcel on the desk. He had not slept all night; his eyes were bloodshot. "What's the verdict?" he searched Bacheller's eyes. "You didn't read it!"

"I did. Fact is, Mrs. Bacheller and I took turns last night reading it aloud. Fine work, Crane. It may be great work. I like it. We both liked it."

Proudly now, Stephen undid the parcel.

"Would you say this is your best work?"

"No, sir, My best is in some 'lines' I wrote."

"Poetry?"

" 'Lines.' Don't rhyme, and no meter."

"Can't use it. Newspapers want doggerel."

"I wrote this story because I needed the money."

"You mean that the only reason you turned it out is because you need ready money?"

"That's part of the reason. After I started it, and it became mine, the story became serious. So it is a potboiler, and it isn't."

Without rejoinder, Bacheller glanced at the fresh copy.

"Thirty dollars to type that!" Stephen said bitterly. He had lived an entire month on less. "Can I get that much from you?"

"I can't afford to pay a big price, Crane. Best I can do——" He glanced at the disappointed youth. "Hold on, I wasn't talking about thirty dollars. I'll give you a fair price. Not a great price—you're not Kipling or Davis—but a fair price. Ninety dollars."

"What!" Stephen exploded. "You said ninety?"

Hastily, Bacheller went on, "It's a risk, Crane, a pure risk. I've got to sell it to the newspapers, to three or four or five, or six, I would hope. I need several papers to cover expenses and my payment to you. If it goes well, Crane, I'll buy more of your work. Maybe I'll send you out to do special articles and speculate on selling them around. We'll see; I'd like to do that. There would be certain expenses before even a nickel comes back, but you needn't worry about that. The ninety dollars are clear to you." He paused abruptly. "What do you say? It's a good offer and the book rights remain yours."

Stephen was regarding him narrowly, as he used to regard Aggie when she read an incredible fable.

"A good offer!" Bacheller repeated.

"Ninety dollars?"

"Best I can do."

"Sold!" He thrust his hand out.

Bacheller sighed as if he had expected Crane to demand an outrageous figure. "It's a fair price. Ask Garland. In the newspapers more people will see your story than ever might see it in a book. Your name will become known, if you catch on."

"If I don't?"

"You'll still have your ninety dollars." He sobered. "Now to cut the story down. From—how long is it?—55,000 words to about 18,000? Can you do it? You'll find it painful; some authors do. Like cutting off an arm."

"It's mine," he said coldly. "I don't want anyone else to cut it."

"As you wish, Crane. How quickly can you deliver it?"

"How quickly can I get the ninety dollars?"

Bacheller laughed. "As soon as you bring in the cut-down."

"I'll do it tonight, if it takes all night, and tomorrow. I'll work until it's ready." He licked his lips. "I need that cash. I owe for the typing."

"As soon as you bring it in."

Tentatively: "How about a few dollars on account?"

A panic gripped Stephen as Bacheller hesitated. He might refuse and call off the deal.

But Bacheller counted out five silver dollars from his cash box. "The rest when you bring in the cut-down."

They parted with another handshake.

"I suppose the first thing you'll do is to read through and decide——"

"First thing," Stephen grinned, "I'm going to eat till I bust!"

Snow clouds hung in the blue sky. The February wind whipped about his legs and penetrated the worn ulster; he wished also that he had earmuffs. Withal, New York had never seemed so friendly. Here, in the great literary marketplace of the nation, he had arrived at last. Ninety dollars!

CHAPTER 45

"You did it, Crane. Eighteen thousand words, more or less."

"Do I get the money?"

Silently, Bacheller wrote the check. "Eighty-five and five you received in cash makes ninety. Sign this paper making over the syndicate rights."

Stephen signed with a flourish.

"I've talked to the men at the *Press*. Edward Marshall, who says he knows you, is on your side. His brother Isaac is an old friend. Said to come around and he'd put you in the way of a few assignments."

"I've haunted him, and no luck!"

"Different now, Steve. Let an outsider praise you and their perspective changes. So get on your horse. I said 'Give the lad something regular. He can't live on speculation.' I'll talk you up to others. Toot the horn, and people listen. They can't help it."

Stephen was dubious until Ed Marshall received him with a broad grin.

"Bacheller says you've written a masterpiece!"

He replied offhand, "You've seen my gabble."

"To hear Irving tell it, you're bound to be a runaway success."

"He couldn't be wrong, could he?" Had his talent increased since he had first come knocking at their doors?

"I knew you'd make it, Steve," Marshall beamed.

"Any assignments?" he prodded. "That's what I need."

The *Press* was prepared to take several articles on the missions and the lodging houses that were feeding and sheltering the hordes of the unemployed who were streaming into the city.

"Steve, a lot of the action is on the Bowery, your old beat."

"I'll go there and live the life, and write it as I see it."

Marshall smiled. "We'll run your copy as you write it. G'bless you!"

"I don't care for *The Red Badge*." Mr. Howells declared heavily. "I do not wish to discourage you, Crane. But to me, *Maggie* is everything. I have said it again and again."

Stephen stared numbly at his erstwhile champion.

"*Maggie* is worth everything," Howells repeated. "*George's Mother*, which you have mentioned to me, may be another panel in the same mural, perhaps also unique, and as unrelenting as *Maggie*. Now *The Red Badge* is excellent work, but others have toiled in that field before you." He paused. "But *Maggie* is *sui generis;* it will have its imitators."

"I can get nowhere with it."

Howells hunched his shoulders. "Ah, Crane, don't be discouraged. The public will yet, I hope, find your true worth. And don't be offended with me. What value is a friend and critic unless he speaks the truth?"

Stephen reeled from the house on 58th Street. His new confidence had been rudely shaken. If Mr. Howells was right, *The Red Badge of Courage*, too, would fall stillborn.

At Fred Lawrence's, John Barry, the editor of the *Forum*, was waiting. "Steve, you've been invited to read your 'lines' before a meeting of the Uncut Leaves Society. They meet at Sherry's. Saturday evening, April fourteenth."

"Swells?"

"The best, Steve. Literary ladies. They buy books. Frances Hodgson Burnett will be the guest of honor."

"She wrote *Little Lord Fauntleroy!*" He wrinkled his nose.

"You must, Steve."

"I'd sooner go into a cage of lions I'd sooner die. I can't talk on my feet."

Barry persisted.

"Then you go in my place and read for me."

"Mad, Steve! This is an important step for any writer."

The prospect of facing the ladies in the little ballroom at Sherry's made him ill. If Howells had thought the lines too "orphic," people less sophisticated would certainly not understand them.

"A great opportunity. Yes, I'll get up and read them if you insist, but you should be there. You must be seen, Steve. Evening dress. We'll hire you a suit."

"Not on your tintype!"

The good-natured Barry went as his deputy. Fred Lawrence, Louis Senger, and Ceek Linson, as friends of the poet, were permitted into the rear of the hall. Stephen, a cigarette dangling from his lips, waited under a lamppost down the street.

"Mrs. Burnett was in white silk. Regular 'Little Lady Fauntleroy.'"

"What did they say about the 'lines'?"

"Barry told them that you would rather die than read your poems in public. He read beautifully, Steve. You would have been proud. We clapped like hell!"

The editor had remained to attend the reception for Mrs. Burnett.

Fred roused him the following morning. "Wake up! The *Press* has an interview with Howells by Ed Marshall. Are you awake? He quotes Howells as follows:

"'Mary E. Wilkins, Mark Twain, Sarah Orne Jewett, Hamlin Garland, and George W. Cable are the most strikingly American writers we have today. There is another of whom I have great hopes. His name is Stephen Crane, and he is very young, but he promises splendid things.'"

Stephen thought, "If I'm as good as that, can *The Red Badge* be as worthless as Mr. Howells implied?"

"Here's more—a puff for *Maggie*, 'There is unquestionably truth in it, the kind of truth that no American has ever had the courage to put between book covers before.'"

Stephen blinked. At least Howells had remained steadfast in his admiration for *Maggie*.

"You should be proud, Steve, proud!" Fred pounded his back.

When he called to thank Barry, the other declared soberly, "I want to take these poems and send them off to Herbert Copeland and Fred Day in Boston. They're young publishers and they're not afraid. They take to experimental poetry like yours. I think they would print it attractively, too."

"The 'lines'? They're too 'orphic'!"

"Orphic!" Barry grunted. "I don't even know what the word means."

The "lines" went into the mails to Boston.

When he next saw Garland, the other was leaving for Chicago. "Remember that I said, 'Truth will prevail.' Steve, you watch and see."

Suddenly he thrust a volume into Stephen's hands. "My own poetry. Not at all like yours, Steve. *Prairie Songs*. Stone & Kimball, a little firm in Chicago, published it for me. Something like Whitman's, all grass and wheat."

Stephen thanked him profusely.

"Read the inscription, Steve."

On the flyleaf, Garland had scrawled: "To Stephen Crane, a genius."

Ceek Linson said, "Steve, time you sat for a portrait. I want to be the first to paint the 'genius.'"

He grimaced. But when Ceek had arranged the easel and began to make his sketches, he sat upright.

"Ceek," he drawled, "I guess I've got everything now except a girl."

CHAPTER 46

The long, semi-dark hall was like a hospital ward, divided by a narrow aisle into two rows of canvas cots. Upon each bed a male figure was stretched, ghostly in the light of the few gas jets that hissed yellow, blue, and orange from cast-iron fingers in the wall. Most of the sleepers were stark naked; a few were clad in singlets or undershirts.

The odors of the fifty or more unwashed bodies, competing like the fumes of cheeses from rival ageing vats, assailed him. A dormitory in Hades!

He stumbled over a shoe. With a hoarse cry, a burly lodger, bare flesh gleaming, flung himself over the side of the cot. " 'S mine!"

Stephen mumbled an apology and hurried on.

He found a vacant bed and hastily sank down upon it. On the next cot, the man had covered himself with a newspaper; a section having slipped to the floor, the lean buttocks were exposed. Wherever he turned he encountered more bodies without faces, naked males in startling attitudes, lying prone in the antechamber to the Pit.

The fragrance of smoking tobacco would have screened his nostrils from the awful stench, but smoking was forbidden. He pulled off his ulster and his sweater. He unbuttoned his shirt. Others had managed, by balling their jackets and pants into their outer garments, to improvise pillows. He shivered and decided not to remove his underwear. He dropped his shoes and tucked his stockings inside the heels.

The cement floor was cold. Something gritty crept over his big toe.

As the canvas bed gave under his slight frame, a cry caused him to lift his head. A child was sobbing! No, a man in his sleep.

Slowly, he distinguished more shapes, up and down his row, and several, their feet startlingly large, on the cots across the room. All these creatures were homeless and jobless. How long since they had slept in beds on soft mattresses with clean sheets? He wondered from where they had come, and where they would be bound in the morning.

"Hey, Buster, lay down!" Over him loomed a monstrous attendant. "You don't get out of here now!" He brandished his nightstick.

"I've just come in." As he rose on his elbow, the taut canvas threatened to pitch him over.

"I catch yeh stealin', I brain yeh! Strip and get yeh shut-eye! No funny stuff, yeh hear? We don't go for that!"

He finished undressing. Nearby, the nightstick cracked the naked shoulder of a figure on its knees. The man hopped to his feet. "I wuz sayin' me——"

"No crawlin' to udder beds!" The guardian, his brass buttons shining, flitted like an avenging angel down the aisle, a raging Morpheus among the shades. He had only to rap his stick against the foot of a cot to make the sleeper galvanize into an approved position. Except for his random presence, Stephen suspected the ward might have been a place for assault and assassins.

The hall was damp. He gawked at the high ceiling and the strange veins meandering across the plaster. High up across the wall, below the dado, a row of small-paned windows marched. In the bobbing gas flame grotesque shadows pulsed and stretched, rose, quivered, and bounced. Glimpses of wall, sleepers, and cots flickered in the magic lantern.

A sleeper loosed an agonizing shout as if a spear had been thrust into his side.

"Shut up!" someone bellowed.

The warder came running. "Quiet! Or I t'row yeh out!"

Again silence, interrupted by steady snoring, an asthmatic wheeze from somewhere, and a loud flatulation.

In the fetid air, he remembered the dank odors of stables. Here, where the rankness was human, the atmosphere became unbearable; he felt drugged. His neck cramped over the lumpy ball of clothing. A pencil in his coat pocket seemed determined to jab into the base of his brain. Too tired to care, he began to breathe shallowly, seeking to ward the foulness from his lungs.

He dreamed that he was lying in a field of tall grasses. Crickets were chirping. Above, stars glittered. He heard the grasses bend; someone was approaching. He lay rigid with fear, listening. Whatever it was moved stealthily for several feet, then halted, moved again stealthily, then halted. Transfixed, he observed a lozenge-shaped head appear above the grasses. As it swayed, he recognized a cobra with the forked tongue darting in and out. Slowly the long slimy length, its scales burnished, lifted higher and higher. He wanted to cry out, but his throat froze as the serpent's head wagged evilly above him. He was aware that he was dreaming, and struggled to awaken and banish the hateful reptile. However, the image of the loathsome head was frighteningly clear; he could not escape it. He was behind an arras, imprisoned between the dream and the reality. A bellows pumped; it was only his breathing. Bewitched, he watched the cobra swaying, gliding, threatening. Suddenly the head lowered, the fangs licked greedily, and a slithering force entered Stephen's flesh. He screamed and sat up, wide awake. He was alone on the cot.

"Shut up!"

"Git down!" the attendant boomed. "Down!"

He lay back drenched in sweat. For a long time he trembled, and dared not fall asleep until daylight filtered into the room.

"Git up! Everybody up! Time! Everybody up! Git up, git up!" The night man was walking up and down the hall, beating a pan with his stick.

The cots creaked. He lay wide-eyed as the men around him, cursing aimlessly, began to dress. His gaze roved among the hollow-eyed masks: red faces, yellow, bearded, stubbled.

They had called upon his sympathy, yet he feared them. Some were destitute because of the collapse of will power; others were depraved on diseased purpose. The majority, without friends, family, or employment, were the victims of the times; the nation's march to prosperity having halted, they had been left to forage on the countryside.

270

They were of concern to no one; if they died they would be buried in Potter's Field or be hacked by the nervous hands of Pendennis Club medics on some laboratory slab.

He was separated from this rabble only by the single rung of his talent. "Brothers! Comrades!" They were his equals in loneliness. They traveled the great desert of life with their souls their only baggage; he was burdened with his manuscripts and tantalizing mirages in which the name "Stephen Crane . . . Stephen Crane . . ." was scrawled over and over in the sand.

A tap at the foot of the cot shocked him.

"Git up, kid! Time! Hurry up, kid!"

Hastily he dressed. His garments were clammy. From the next cot, a bloated countenance confronted him. "Dincha hear me, kid?"

The torrid light in the stranger's eyes chilled him.

"Whassa matteh, kid? I wanna be yer frien'."

He was suddenly afraid.

The cold hand touched him. "How yah know yah won't like me?"

"Lemme alone!" With loathing, he got up, thrust the ulster over his arm, and pushed toward the center of the room.

The men who were already dressed loitered about; a few still sprawled fully clad on their cots. He reached the queue at the door.

"Hold on!" The night man blocked his way. "Everybody got his gear?" He swung his stick. "Before yeh go, look around. Take yeh own gear an' nobody else's!"

No voice protesting, he opened the doors.

They began to file out. "Goo'by, Max! Goo'by, Jake!" The majority trooped to the latrines and queued up again. The smells were less offensive there.

His erstwhile neighbor leered. "Hey, kid!"

Stephen fled from the premises.

Curtis Brown of the New York *Press*, to whose desk Ed Marshall sent the article, paid eight dollars per column: sixteen dollars for "An Experiment in Misery." The Wilson syndicate would dispatch proofs to newspapers outside of New York.

"Very good, Steve. We'll take more of the same."

While he could not sell stories that were riven out of his heart, his descriptions of hunger and privation had become saleable.

In the great blizzard that descended upon New York, he prowled the snow-swept streets, peering into hallways at men who lay like sides of meat wrapped in newspapers. His lungs became congested. He coughed up masses of phlegm as he trudged through the drifts, but he was like a hound on the trail as he searched for vivid descriptions to transmute his impressions. He must spend the evening and the night on his quest, sleep with the men in their holes in some charity

271

house and eat whatever they ate; a bed for the night and coffee and bread in the morning: price, five cents.

He began to hate the city, which had closed its doors to the blizzard and smugly sat in warmth, while the desperate breadlines formed before Fleischmann's Bakery and dispirited queues wound before the crowded lodging houses.

"The full dinner pail!" cried a tree carrying a great weight of snow upon its hat and shoulders; it shook, and a man emerged.

A group trailed off to a Gospel mission, where listening to the sermon and joining in the hymns would bring a reward of thin soup and bread. "There'll be pie in the sky when you die!" they muttered.

He huddled before a tenement where the tables, chairs, cradles, and beds of an evicted family sat under weirdly shaped masses of snow. A hand rocked the cradle, and snow clumped. "Move on!" a policeman called from a sheltered corner. "Move on, now!"

Stephen thought that he had done his best writing in "The Men in the Storm." Ed Marshall liked it; Curtis Brown did not.

The rejection infuriated him. His feet still soaked, his clothes damp, and his head burning feverishly, he had waited in the anteroom for a draft on the cashier. Since the article had not been ordered, it was returned without compensation.

Marshall frowned. "Why did you do it, Steve? Wait for an assignment. You don't have to write on 'spec.' A day and a night and you have nothing for it."

"It's good!"

"It is, Steve, but the *Press* didn't order it."

"Take me on for a regular," he pleaded. His chest was aflame; needles pierced his shoulder blades. Each cough was an anguish. "Haven't I proved that I can do it?"

"Can't, Steve. Haven't a place for you." He shrugged. "If I had, I don't know that I'd give it to you. You're an imaginative writer, not a reporter. Tying you down to a job would not improve your style. I'll feed you as many commissions as I can. That's all I dare to promise."

His pockets were empty; he had been paying off old debts without regard for tomorrow. He had spent his last five dollars on breakfasts and handouts for the men with whom he had spent the night; now he lacked a nickel for carfare. He would not borrow from Marshall.

Shivering and coughing, he tramped uptown in the snow. When he reached 23rd Street his feet seemed frozen; each coughing spell threatened to dislodge his ribs. He tottered into Fred Gordon's studio.

"Into bed with you!" Gordon shouted when he saw him trembling. "You damn fool—in this storm!"

Meekly, he let his friend put him to bed. "Dammit, Fred. I can't fight them any more, I can't! Not all of them!"

He remembered hazily that light came and faded. He was lying on a pallet of nails. When the fever abated forty-eight hours later, he was weak and bathed in perspiration. Fred was offering him a milky gruel.

He muttered wearily, "What am I doing here?"

"You're better, I guess!" Gordon snapped. "I suppose trying to kill yourself is just 'getting experience' to you!"

"It was fierce cold in those streets."

"So cold they were taking in the brass monkeys! And who is Lillie? Your old sweetheart? A great interview you had with her. My, my! She's still married, isn't she?"

He crimsoned. He had tried to forget Lillie and her child. He wondered what he had said in his delirium. He no longer cared that she had returned to her husband. Every girl or woman he had ever loved had belonged to someone else.

He sent "The Men in the Storm" to Copley Square; perhaps Ben Flower of *The Arena*, with his partiality for social reform, would be kind to it. Flower promptly replied that he considered the article "a powerful bit of literature" and would publish it in the fall.

When he displayed Flower's letter to Ed Marshall he received more assignments from the *Press*. Irving Bacheller, who had sent the abridgments of *The Red Badge* to thirty newspapers, as yet had no offers, yet he urged Stephen to find quarters where he might write undisturbed.

"What shall I use for cash?"

"Have some faith in yourself!" Bacheller growled. "You're not in Coxey's Army, you're being published!"

Emboldened, Stephen rented a furnished room at 111 West 33rd Street, with sink and closet and a bathroom to share down the hall: $1.25 per week.

"Some people are getting rich," Vosburgh teased. "Soon as you get a private toilet you won't be talking to anyone."

He wrote to Hamlin Garland at the Elm Street address in Chicago that he was eating "with charming regularity at least two times per day."

"I guess anyone could have written *The Badge*," he grumbled to Ceek Linson.

"You haven't heard from McClure," Ceek pointed out. "Never say die!"

CHAPTER 47

Mr. McClure finally returned the manuscript. "We tried to find a place for it," he declared, sober as an undertaker. "But we're stocked up."

"It took you six months—or is it a year?—to find that out?"

McClure gave him a severe glance. "Hold your temper, Crane. You knew that we had a syndicate, yet you sold the newspaper rights to Bacheller & Johnson. That was not correct while we were still considering it."

Stephen sputtered. "You never said you were interested in syndicate rights. You—you said nothing! Should I have waited and starved?"

"No, Crane, of course not. Anyway, we can't use it. Next year perhaps, if it is still available."

"I hope not!"

"For your sake. But you'll do well. I saw Howells' praise of you in that *Press* article."

"Praise!" he sulked. "I need money for coffee and buns!"

McClure blinked. "Say, Crane, why not an article for *McClure's?* Your friend Garland has written a piece on the Homestead Mine. I could use an article by someone who's been down a coal mine and has seen the real thing."

"Me?"

"With this coal strike on, a piece like that would be widely read."

"I'll go," he volunteered. He had already forgiven McClure. "I could take an artist with me to sketch on the spot. C. K. Linson would come if I said the word. Your art editor, Mr. Jaccacci, thinks he's very good, Mr. McClure."

McClure laughed easily. "Go ahead, Crane!"

Cautiously: "Any expense money?"

The publisher shook his head. "We couldn't do that. No. But you have my word that we'd use the article."

"You wouldn't be 'stocked up'?"

A faint smile played about the other's lips. "No!"

"A little expense money would be 'earnest' money, Mr. McClure."

"Take it or leave it."

He felt that McClure, whose efforts to acquire the works of Stevenson, Meredith, and Kipling at high prices were the talk of Park Row, was taking advantage of him.

"If I can borrow the money, I'll go," he returned woefully. Someday he would get even with every man who had ground his face in the dirt.

Linson, elated at the prospects, managed to raise the travel money. The two men left for the Pennsylvania mining town the following week.

Stephen was awed by the scene at Scranton. He thought that the coal-breakers squatted upon the hillsides and in the valley "like enormous preying monsters, eating of the sunshine, the grass, the green leaves." He stared, open-mouthed, for the giants "sat imperturbably munching coal, grinding mammoth jaws with unearthly and monstrous uproar." During the descent eleven hundred feet into the Stygian darkness of the Dunmore mine, he reflected that "Man is in the implacable grasp of nature. It has only to tighten slightly and he is crushed like a bug."

On the lower levels, the sight of the little-boy slate-pickers, black as imps, who earned fifty cents a day, wrenched his heart. He turned to Linson: "Do you suppose God ever gets down here?"

Moving through the galleries, they came upon the battalion of mules that lived underground in stable dungeons. He would never forget their wild and glittering eyeballs. "They resembled enormous rats," he noted pityingly. They had been imprisoned here for years; many would never see the light of day again.

Later, at Raught's home in Dunmore, he wrote his article, "In the Depths of a Coal Mine," at a speed that astounded his friends; he did not pause to change a line or to correct a phrase. He was still seething from the impressions that had been etched indelibly on his mind.

Ceek, too, had been affected by the incredible horror of an existence where men lived, breathed, and chopped coal, and died either in some crushing or suffocating accident, or survived to endure the malicious grip of "miner's asthma." As he toiled to complete twenty-four sketches, he scanned Stephen's copy and shook his head. "You can get it down in words faster than I can draw," he grumbled. That was a bone of contention between the illustrators and the writer: which art was the more difficult.

"Johnnie," Stephen asked of Raught without lifting his head from his pages, "you've got faith, haven't you? Do you think that the same Jehovah that watches over you and me also keeps his eye full-time on those miserable urchins down below, and the poor scared mules?"

McClure approved of the work. So quickly did he send proofs to the newspapers served by his Associated Literary Press that the St. Louis *Republic* printed the text before the last of Linson's illustrations were ready for the engravers. Only then did writer and artist receive payment—fifty dollars each, not as much as either man had hoped but better than they had feared the canny McClure would pay.

"If we could do one article a week," Stephen crowed, "we'd be in clover."

"Or down in more coal mines. No, Steve, you're headed in other and finer directions."

Stephen was silent. The confidence of his friends was stimulating. What did they see in him that editors could not, or would not, see?

The following Monday, Copeland & Day wrote briefly, in a stiff Boston style that addressed him as if he were a purveyor of green groceries, that his "lines" were acceptable.

Gordon chirped, "Now I'll do you a cover design!"

"They'll have their own artist, Fred."

Gordon appeared so crestfallen that Stephen wrote to the publishers that his friend must draw the cover. To celebrate the acceptance, he invited eight "Injuns" to sit down to a fifty-cent table d'hôte, and furnished two bottles of red wine.

"You'll be famous!" Vosburgh promised.

"I'll settle for never being hungry, and for an extra pair of dry shoes."

"And a girl when you want her."

The day the temperature registered ninety-five degrees, and his little room became a bake-oven, he fled for a two-week camping trip in Pike County.

At Twin Lakes, his chest cleared. Every morning Fred Lawrence and Lou Senger and one or two of the girls, whom the older couples chaperoned diligently, would march with Stephen three miles to the O'Day farm, on the road to Parker's Glen, for the daily supply of fresh milk, butter, eggs, chicken, and produce. In the afternoons, they rowed or fished, sometimes boxed, sawed or chopped wood, picked wild berries, played baseball in the sun, and consumed the enormous dinners that the colored boy, "Energetic" Brinson, and his grinning sister Charlotte, cooked over open fires. In the evenings, the campers sang to the twanging of Stephen's banjo, or danced in the clearing while their shadows sparred with the firelight.

With Lou Senger, he edited a spoofery in the form of "The Pike County Puzzle," a four-page newspaper for which, over several long evenings, they wrote articles, dispatches, editorials, quips, personals, fillers, and advertisements. They indulged their whimsy and impishness. They listed all the campers as the proprietors, with Stephen Crane "Office Boy" and Louis C. Senger Jr. "Assistant Office Boy." Subscription nine thousand dollars a year; rattlesnakes, in which Pike County abounded, and bluestone from the nearby quarry, acceptable in exchange.

One dispatch reported that Senger and Crane, passing through Bradner Woods, had killed a rattlesnake ninety-three feet long and possessing three hundred and sixty-two rattles.

An "accident," Stephen himself drolly recorded: "As Stephen Crane was traversing the little rope-ladder that ascends the righthand side of the cloud-capped pinnacle of his thoughts, he fell and was grievously injured."

Back in New York, Linson greeted him with a copy of the August *McClure's*. "Steve, they gave us sixteen pages! Used sixteen of my illustrations, one on every page. Five are full-page drawings!"

He congratulated Ceek. "In the Depths of a Coal Mine" was the lead article. A moment later, Stephen was cursing explosively. McClure had deleted the passages that were critical of the lords who operated the coal mines. "They didn't want the whole truth, did they?"

"The prose is still beautiful, Steve. It's a strong article."

"How would you have liked it if they had redrawn your illustrations? Or chopped off pieces of a figure here and there?"

The packet from Copeland & Day, which arrived the next morning, dismayed him even more. The publishers were willing to bring out Mr. Crane's poetry, but they proposed deletion of all the "lines" that were irreligious.

"They want to cut out the ethical sense!"

"Only the anarchy, they say," Linson countered.

"It's the anarchy I *want*. There would be no satisfaction for me in 'a nice little volume of verse by Stephen Crane.' I am obliged to have in those lines they want to take out."

"Steve, you're in no position to dictate to the publisher."

He became gray-faced.

"Substitute other poems."

"No, sir! That's utterly impossible to me. I can't write them to order, I won't destroy them to order. I won't be offended if they reject them all. No, sir!"

"Think about it, Steve. Didn't Mr. Howells write you that he did not think a Merciful Providence meant the 'prose poem' to last?"

He would discuss it no further. A week later, in a curt "Dear Sir" letter, he invited Copeland & Day to return the "lines." He would not yield.

His satisfaction, then, was real, grim, and throat-filling when the Boston publishers, who blandly continued to sign themselves "The Editors," far from rejecting his poetry, forwarded a contract and a sample type page for his approval.

It was a rare pleasure to carry the entire story to Mr. Howells, and to accept his congratulations.

The lines had greater meaning for him now than when he had originally drawn them off. He felt as if he had had his ear to a door behind which he stood, as a small child and as a bewildered boy, seeing vaguely, hearing faintly, all the life he knew passing in terrible mystery.

He informed Irving Bacheller. "*The Black Riders* is the title, and I plan to dedicate the book to Hamlin Garland. I've waited a long time for this."

Bacheller twiddled his thumbs with the air of one who is in possession of a great secret. He smiled at the youthful face. "You're an old man, Steve."

"I figure to live until I'm about thirty-five," he replied seriously. "I wouldn't care to go through this much longer."

Bacheller laughed. "Fortunate that the decision isn't up to you.

Now, Stevie, hold on to your bowler. The *Press* has bought *The Red Badge*."

Stephen gazed at Bacheller in stunned silence.

"I mean the Philadelphia *Press*. They will run it serially in six parts beginning December third."

He studied Bacheller's lips under the blond mustache, and could not speak.

"And your friends on the New York *Press*, Curtis Brown, Ed Marshall, and the others, like it, too. They will run it a week later in a single issue. December ninth."

A pigeon settling on the window sill was peering into the beer-can. Across the river a steamer was shrieking like a girl with a mouse under her skirts.

"Steve, did you hear me?"

"Yes, Irving," he replied hollowly. "Two papers will run *The Red Badge*. Yesterday nobody wanted it, nobody wanted anything. Today —two papers. And *The Black Riders* will come out as I want it."

He thought that success, too, could be sad. He stared as if, over the river, he were seeing his Destiny riding forth "in the rush upon the wind." He was afraid to move, to turn, or to blink. It might disappear and leave him stranded upon a deserted beach.

CHAPTER 48

It was a beautiful world. Even Boston, cold as a codfish, threatened to smile. In October, *The Arena* published "The Men in the Storm." The note on the author stated: "This young writer belonging to the new school is likely to achieve in his own field something like the success Hamlin Garland has attained in his."

Copeland & Day, as deliberately as if they were taking rubbings from the original tablets of Sinai, finally moved into the production of *The Black Riders*. They proposed, in addition to five hundred copies for ordinary sale, to print a special edition in green ink on Japan vellum.

"What is Japan vellum?"

Gordon assured him, "It's de luxe, Steve. Expensive paper. Outa sight!" With an eye to Aubrey Beardsley's style, Fred had elected an orchid for the cover design.

In successive letters, Stephen pleaded for the specific date of publication. Boston—"Dear Sirs"—intimated that the book would be issued "sometime in the spring."

"I wrote the 'lines' faster than they are setting the type!" Stephen

278

cried. "They're as slow as Able Printers!" He would receive fifty dollars on publication.

In December, the Philadelphia *Press* ran the first part of *The Red Badge*. "Stephen Crane is a new name," a *Press* notice read, "but everybody will be talking about him if he goes on as he has begun."

Irving Bacheller decided to introduce Stephen to his new public. In Philadelphia, the reporters crowded around the visitors and asked, "Which is Crane? Not the kid!"

Stephen blushed as they clapped his back and wrung his hand.

John Duffy, the managing editor of the *Press*, read a quotation from another article: ". . . He is quite likely to gain recognition before very long as the most powerful of American tellers of tales."

"He's gone redder'n a rose!"

"You keep it up, Steve," Duffy glowed, "and everybody will know you in a few years. Bacheller, give us first look at all of his stuff."

"This is only the cut-down," Stephen apologized. "The complete book is even better."

On the train back to New York, he concluded that, if nothing good ever happened to him again as long as he lived, he would never forget this day of triumph. Everything Garland or Howells had ever said was in the shade.

Bacheller, who had been snoring, stirred and put his feet up on the seat facing them. "If I had the money, I'd send you around the country. The New York *Press* would take your pieces and, you heard Duffy, so would the Philadelphia *Press*."

"I'd like to go to Europe!"

"Couldn't afford Europe, Steve. Might go as far as Mexico. I'll talk to my brother Wilbur. Maybe to Willis Hawkins, too."

"He's got *Brains*," Stephen returned drolly. *Brains* was the little magazine for advertisers that Willis Brooks Hawkins edited; the Bacheller brothers were his partners.

"A big undertaking for a new syndicate. We've got very little cash."

"McClure could do it!" Stephen said savagely. "But I'd never go for him. He was a beast about *The Red Badge*."

"Steve, do you know that McClure had his back to the wall last year? His first issue came out at the wrong time. Twelve thousand copies of his first twenty thousand were returned. Conan Doyle, the British writer, Pope, the bicycle man, and another friend bailed him out. He would have gone under."

It had seemed to Stephen that everyone in the world, and certainly S. S. McClure, must have unlimited supplies of money. "He should have told me."

"Give him time. Never turn your back on a market."

Remembering Garland's counsel to keep his stories moving, he sent out every manuscript in his trunk, even to such an unlikely periodical as the *Plumber's Trade Journal*. It was the latter, to his glee, that bought a hideous scrap of an article, "Christmas Dinner Won in Battle," and paid fifteen dollars. At *Truth*, Blakely Hall accepted an old manuscript about an Irish wake and paid twenty-five dollars. Stephen enjoyed these crumbs of success.

At Appleton's, he called upon Ripley Hitchcock.

As the editor looked up blankly, Stephen realized that he did not remember having rejected *Maggie*.

"I'm a reporter, Mr. Hitchcock. Some people have been nice enough to say that I'm a good one!"

"What do you think?"

"That I'm a good writer."

"That's fine. What have you got to show me?"

He opened his envelope. "Cuttings of the pieces I've been doing for the newspapers."

Mr. Hitchcock glanced at the clippings indifferently. "Have you anything longer, something that might make a book? We're a book publishing company."

Crane paused. "Sure thing, Mr. Hitchcock. I wrote a long story a while ago. Irving Bacheller wanted it for the Philadelphia *Press*, so I cut it down to fit. They ran it in six parts. The New York *Press* printed it last Sunday on three pages." How could anyone have missed it?

"I'd like to see it, Crane."

"I could send the cuttings. If you liked it, I'd find the manuscript." The rejection of *Maggie* still rankled.

"What's the title, Crane?"

He stiffened. *"The Red Badge of Courage."*

The editor reflected. "Umm. Longish, isn't it?"

"I suppose so. I've got a book of poems appearing soon."

Hitchcock raised an eyebrow. "Have we seen any of the poems?"

"No, sir. They're different."

The editor said tersely, "We're stronger on prose. Bring that."

"I'm likely to go off on a trip for the Bacheller Syndicate. If I could make a contract for the book before I leave——"

"Crane, you send in your manuscript. We'll read it. I can't promise more. What are you to do for your syndicate?"

"See the world and write it up!"

A flicker of amusement crossed Mr. Hitchcock's lips. "We'll not detain you."

Bacheller waved a sheaf of railroad tickets and two hundred dollars in cash.

"Then I am going!"

"Westward ho! Here's a list of the newspapers with whom we correspond. Call on all of them, but don't travel too slowly or your money will give out." He sobered. "This is a big risk for us, Steve. Everything depends on you. I'll work hard to sell what you send me, but you've got to write lively pieces. I can market good articles right off. Stories will take longer. Keep that in mind."

His finger charted a course on a tinted map.

"Big country!"

"So they say. It's the West you want to see, isn't it? Go straight to St. Louis. Then west to Omaha and Lincoln, Nebraska. Move around on those prairies. Here's Texas. Don't get lost there; it's as wide as the sea. San Antonio. Cross the border. Spend a week or two in Mexico City and the territory around it. Come back by way of Chicago. Of course, you'll want to see Garland there. Then come home as quickly as you can before your impressions fade."

Stephen grinned and studied the map.

"How soon can you leave? By Christmas Day?"

Apologetically, "I'm waiting for Copeland & Day to send proofs on *The Black Riders*. Maybe Appleton's will offer me a contract for the damned *Red Badge*."

"Waste no time, Steve." Bacheller nonchalantly tossed cash and tickets into a pigeonhole. "They'll be waiting for you."

Through the holidays, he looked anxiously for the proofs of his poems from Boston and for word from Ripley Hitchcock.

By the second week in January, Copeland & Day had forwarded less than half of the galley proofs.

As for *The Red Badge*, Appleton's was silent. Surely, Mr. Hitchcock, a trained reader, could read the fifty thousand words in less than thirty days! Or had he lost the manuscript?

He waited another week. The last of the galleys came in from Boston. He promptly read and returned them. He would leave the page proofs to the mercies of the publisher. Still no word from Ripley Hitchcock.

Disconsolately, he packed, drew the tickets and the cash, and left for Philadelphia.

In the Broad Street Station, waiting for the train to Pittsburgh and Cincinnati, he impulsively decided to go to Washington. He must see Lillie Brewster. She was probably absorbed in her child, if not with her husband, but he must see her.

He misdated letters, forgot overcoats in restaurants and umbrellas on trains, but he clearly remembered her address, "150 A Street, N.W."

His heart pounded as he rang the bell at Mrs. Morrow's boardinghouse. He would ask for Dottie first. To the colored manservant who opened the door, he said, "Will you tell Miss Brewster that her friend Stephen Crane is calling?"

"Miss Brewster is away, suh."

"Perhaps someone can tell me where she is. I've come all the way from New York. I'm on my way to Mexico."

His pulses hammering, he waited in the parlor. If Lillie's mother-in-law came out, he was lost. He stared at the drab furnishings.

"Mrs. Morrow will see you directly, suh."

He heard the swish of a skirt. It was too late to retreat.

"Mr. Crane!" the voice said politely.

He gulped. He had forgotten that "Lillie Brewster" was also "Mrs. Morrow."

To the servant, she murmured, "Thank you, Horace." Then, "I am so sorry that you have missed Dottie, she's——"

As the man departed, she clasped his hand. "Stephen! Stephen!"

They kept a rendezvous in the Botanic Garden across the way, moving side by side in a humid hall where the fronds of great tropical plants scarcely stirred and some rare creation—"Bird of Paradise," the card read—eyed them with pelican disapproval. In the dull light that filtered through the glassed dome, they held hands and whispered. How beautiful she was! She had not changed at all. He could not glance to the right or to the left, only into her eyes. He dared not ask about her husband or the state of their relationship.

"It's true, Lillie. The 'lines' will be out in a month or two. My new novel will be published; someone will have to publish it sooner or later." He showed the tickets in his pocketbook. "I go to Mexico!"

"Be careful, Stephen!"

"If I thought I might come back to you, I would be very careful."

She held him off guiltily. "Be careful for my sake——"

"Will you ever be free?" The words rushed out.

She was silent.

"I would ask you again what I've asked so many times before. We could be so happy——"

She shook her head. "The child—little Jimmie——"

"Am I just a memory to you, Lillie? A mere figure in the landscape of the past? My love for you——"

"Stephen, you mustn't!"

"You are the dream of my life. Your face with the lines and the smile that I love is always before me. I can't free myself from my love for you. And I wouldn't try to escape from it. It's better to have known you and suffered than never to have known you. You may value me as a straw——"

"I don't, dearest!"

The hour sped swiftly. The February gloom descended. Behind a fig palm, he held her and kissed her.

"Don't forget me, Lillie, never, never!"

She dried her eyes. He stared at the rigid green fingers of vegetation.

"Closing time, sir," a guard called. "Closing time."

He was in Lincoln when he received Mr. Hitchcock's letter: Appleton's agreed to publish *The Red Badge of Courage*.

A month earlier, he would have danced through the Injuns' studios and taken them all to the Buffalo Mud to celebrate. Now, after his travels across the country and the tryst with Lillie, he accepted the new triumph soberly. Mr. Hitchcock thought the title too long; Stephen promised to reflect on it.

He was cold, proud, and eager as he left the American West. He had seen blizzards raging on the plains, cattle starving, families suffering. All his pores were open to impressions. Articles flowed from his pen, his prose hardening as he forged one piece after another.

In New Orleans, he was driving himself, burning up more energy than he readily commanded. By the time he reached Mexico, he was a seasoned traveler. He wore a sombrero, carried a serape over his shoulder, and was bronzed, his blue eyes flinty as he studied the people and their villages and cities. He permitted himself no rest; he was tumbling upon his pallet at night in utter exhaustion, writing feverishly at dawn, rushing to the nearest post office with his dispatches. He was spending hours in the saddle, and camping alone, or with some rascally guide, on terrain where bandits roved freely.

Often he rolled into his blanket to lie awake and watch the Unknown watching him through a thousand pinholes in the sky. No one cared whether he lived or died; he cared least of all.

CHAPTER 49

At Ted's house in Hartwood, with the little volume of *The Black Riders* fast in his hands, all defenses collapsed and he was down with a fever. Doctor Cranmer said that it might have been caused by bad drinking water in Mexico.

While he was convalescing, Will came to visit. He brought with him the first issue of *The Bookman*, which contained a long and favorable review. The brothers vied in their pride for Stephen, Ted reading the lines softly and shaking his head, Will louder and perversely critical.

Harry Thurston Peck, editor of *The Bookman*, and a professor of literature, stated, "Mr. Stephen Crane is the Aubrey Beardsley of poetry." He declared that *The Black Riders* was "the most notable contribution to literature to which the present year has given birth." He compared Stephen Crane to Walt Whitman.

Will remarked severely, "Beardsley is that decadent English artist!"

Stephen sighed. "He is." He had admired Beardsley's strange black-and-white drawings, with their adoration of the harlot, in the copies of *The Yellow Book* that Fred Gordon kept in his studio. Beardsley was all right.

Will went on, "Perhaps more praise—if *this* is praise!—may encourage sales of the book. Seventy-six pages, and small type at that, for one dollar!"

It had become important that *The Black Riders* should sell. Newspaper publication often ended with a one-time appearance. Books must sell and sell and continue to sell.

"Any word from Garland?" asked Will. "You dedicated the book to him. He might acknowledge it. I would have felt honored if you had dedicated it to me."

The galley proofs of *The Red Badge of Courage,* the title unrevised because Hitchcock could not improve upon it, were waiting to be read.

"There isn't a woman character in the whole book!" Will grumbled. "Except Henry's mother. If you ever make up your mind to write books that the public will buy, with a bit of romance in them, you'll do better."

Stephen was weary of his brother's sententiousness. "I want only enough money always to have two pairs of pants with a separate pair of suspenders for each."

"Howells made twenty thousand dollars out of *A Hazard of New Fortunes.* I've looked into this. If you tend to your writing, Steve, you can become an independent man."

Back in New York, at the flat on 23rd Street, John Barry burst in, waving a copy of *Munsey's* magazine. "What did I tell you, Steve? Have they editorial sense at *Munsey's*? 'Stephen Crane is one of these newly heralded geniuses!'"

Stephen read thoughtfully. "What they say is that I'm 'one of the fads among certain classes.'"

"Someone there believes in you, or envies you. They don't have to use the word 'genius,' Steve. Admiration and envy; one goes with the other as boy does with girl. Maybe the praise is grudging, but it is praise still. Think what Harry Thurston Peck said: 'Bold and original.' Also, a 'powerful writer of eccentric verse, skeptical, pessimistic, often cynical; and one who stimulates thought because he himself thinks.'"

"And the *Tribune* pilloried me for 'futility and affectation.'"

"Let the yawpers yawp. You go on with your stories and write more poems."

Copeland & Day appeared to be satisfied with the reception of *The Black Riders,* and promised to go back to press for another printing.

Irving Bacheller invited him to join the new Lantern Club, which he had founded. "Take your lunches on credit, Steve."

The weird approach to the Lantern Club on Monkey Hill, between Fulton and John Streets, delighted him. Irving gave him the directions, "At 126 William Street there's an ironmonger's shop. On the side of the shop there's a hanging iron stairway with a chain. Pull the chain and the stairway comes down. Climb to the top, and you land on a broad roof that covers an old stableyard. At the rear end of the roof, you'll see a door. Watch for a three-four step-up. Knock twice. If no one answers, knock again. Walter will let you in."

Inside, at the long dining table, Stephen enjoyed the quaintness and informality of the surroundings. The ceiling, low-beamed, was hung with lanterns; ships' lanterns, miners' lanterns, Oriental lanterns, and jack-o'-lanterns. The old wooden house was said to have been one of Captain Kidd's haunts.

Bacheller, Willis Hawkins, Ed and Isaac Marshall lunched there every noon; Frank Verbeck, the artist, and Charles Hooke, who wrote humorous articles under the pen name "Howard Fielding," attended at least twice a week. The Lantern Club dues were two dollars a month. Every second Tuesday night the members listened to each others' compositions. Approval brought only silence; usually there was a free-for-all of sharp criticism.

"Steve, make a clean breast of it. How did you come to write free verse?" Hawkins' eyes, widely set, smiled at Stephen.

"It seemed the perfectly obvious way of expressing what I felt," he replied. "I couldn't have written those things in straight prose any more than I could have chewed up green paper and spit out ten-dollar bills!"

He was at ease with Hawkins, who was an unusually handsome man, with a well-proportioned figure, a cool, dignified air, and a singularly pleasant voice. Willie, too, had attended a military school, Immanuel Hall at Lakeview, Illinois. He, too, had once been a seminary student. He had served as a train boy and as a telegrapher, had been a reading clerk in the Assembly at Springfield, had, briefly, been a member of the detective force in Chicago, and had worked for six months as a pilot on a Minnesota river packet before he had gone into newspaper work. "Once owned a half interest in the Aurora, Illinois, *News*." On the Chicago *News*, his desk had faced Eugene Field's. He still wrote a minute hand that perfectly imitated Field's penmanship.

Stephen was fascinated with his yarns. "Willie, what haven't you done?"

"Nothing of real importance! I've been a dabbler and a tramp most of my life." He took part in amateur theatricals; he could sing and tap dance. He played excellent poker, and beat Irving Bacheller regularly at pool. He was forty-four and married, and lived in a house on Greene Avenue in Brooklyn.

"How did you turn up in New York?"

"Knocking about from city to city." He frowned. "Nothing I care to talk about." He rarely spoke of his wife; he was devoted to his son and daughter, for whom he wrote reams of clever doggerel. "Steve, you're doing the writing that I and a thousand other reporters once dreamed that we would do. 'Maybe some day!' Never did it."

Whenever they parted, Stephen felt that he was leaving a devoted friend.

In early September, Stephen brought the first copy of *The Red Badge of Courage* to a poker game in the offices of the Brains Publishing Company.

Hawkins examined the book and crowed. "I sweat days to do five pages of readable copy, he turns out two hundred and thirty-three pages and it's a masterpiece. They've done it handsomely, too; a tan binding with stamping in red, black and gold. You have arrived, S. C. *Maggie, The Black Riders,* and now this one. Not many men even twice your age have three books in print."

"It's only a potboiler, Willie," Stephen said humbly. "I'll get forty lashes on my bare back when the critics catch up with me."

Hawkins retorted, "If Shakespeare published *Hamlet* today, some critic would rant that he was ludicrous because every one of the major characters gets killed."

From Hartwood, he wrote to Hawkins every week. He tramped in the woods, went after partridge, sailed Ted's catboat on the lake and settled down to work on a new novel before the critics could lay down their deadly barrage on *The Red Badge.*

He wrote swiftly. His brother Will should have his romance. *The Eternal Patience,* light and airy, was about unrequited love. Sometimes it seemed clever, sometimes nonsensical; at least, it was not serious.

One morning, an envelope from his clipping service sat against the sugar bowl on the breakfast table.

With a display of nonchalance, he slit the flap and scanned the clippings. He muttered, "Great guns!" and sat dazed.

"If I had my way——" Mame began warmly. She saw the mist in his eyes. "What is it, Steve?"

"God!" he breathed. "My God, Mame, they're good!"

He divided the clippings between Mame and Ted, got up and stalked from the room. He feared that he would burst into tears before them.

The sharp November air calmed him. By God! he had known all along that it couldn't happen otherwise. He wiped his eyes, and began to laugh hysterically.

The *Home Journal* and the *Transcript* of Boston, The Detroit *Free Press,* the St. Paul *Globe,* the Chicago *Post,* the Minneapolis *Times,* the Cleveland *Plain Dealer,* the Providence *News*—the whole pack were hooting that *The Red Badge* was all right. Justice, after all!

He thrust his hands into his pockets and strolled rapidly into the

286

woods. Now what would Howells say, and the *Tribune* and the *Nation?*

He felt light-headed, and rested against the trunk of an oak tree. No, he had not believed that it could happen. Yet it had happened. Oh, but he had known that it would, deep in his soul, he had known it, for he had believed in himself, in his talent.

Exuberantly, he leaped for a branch, caught it, and hung there above the ground, swinging until the bough cracked and brought him down to earth.

CHAPTER 5O

Outside, snow had begun to fall again in Buffalo. In the pleasantly warm Colonial parlor of the Genesee Hotel, a long table had been set with snowy napery and silver candelabra. Elbert Hubbard, publisher of the small butcher-paper-covered periodical, *The Philistine,* was honoring Stephen Crane with a banquet.

The twenty-eight guests were chiefly editors and newspapermen who had come in from New York, Scranton, and other nearby cities for the first dinner of the Society of the Philistines.

As the men seated themselves around the table, Stephen glanced at the cover of the eight-page stitched menu: "The Time Has Come, the Walrus Said, To Talk of Many Things." Below were the four black riders, cloaks fluttering, as they descended out of the rays of the setting sun. They were mounted not on steeds but on polka-dotted hobbyhorses. A figure that he recognized as a crude caricature of himself was running toward the horizon.

"Dwight Colain over there is the artist," boomed Harry Taber, the jovial editor of *The Philistine.* "Tried to get the spirit of your poems. Hubbard thought it was good."

Stephen agreed that it was clever, yet the representation irked him. Since September, the press had been printing various parodies of his lines. Colain, mocking Aubrey Beardsley's style, must have read many of the satires.

Ed Lawrence, the Buffalo manager of the Associated Press office, called attention to the new Crane poem which Hubbard had printed on the back cover: "I have heard the sunset song of the birches."

"We sent out two hundred invitations," Hubbard said, his round, friendly face beaming under the Buster Brown bangs. "Many more would have come except for this foul weather. Bliss Carman said he couldn't find East Aurora in his railroad guide! Rudyard Kipling sent his regrets," he added proudly.

In the buzz of conversation, the guests read the greetings of the many who had declined. Four pages of messages were included in the souvenir booklet under a quotation from Dryden: "Fate frowned upon them and they could not come."

Mr. Howells had written: "I am very glad to know that my prophesies are being realized and that Mr. Crane is receiving recognition at a time in life when he can most enjoy it." McClure: "I admire Mr. Crane's work, and I admire the man. I also admire the valiant Philistines—from a safe distance." Garland: "I take a very special interest in Mr. Crane, as I was one of the very first to know about *Maggie* and *The Red Badge*." Ambrose Bierce had written from San Francisco: "Were it not for the miles which separate us, I would be with you."

"A tribute to the Philistines!" Willie Hawkins declared.

"A tribute to Steve Crane," Hubbard generously insisted. "Note that in most of the replies the reference is to his work. *The Philistine* is being read, but these prove that Steve is getting attention everywhere."

Stephen blushed and picked at his food. It was still hard to believe that anyone should have wanted to honor him so far from home.

Hubbard's invitation had come in the mails: "Recognizing your merit as a man and your genius as a poet, and wishing that the world might know you better——" It had stated candidly that the dinner might be "of very great value to your books and will lead to wider recognition of your talents!"

He had feared that he was being guyed. But Hubbard, who had printed several of his "lines" in *The Philistine,* had three novels on the Arena Publishing Company's list. He would not be engaging in a prank on a fellow author.

Will cynically pointed out that Stephen was probably being used to promote Hubbard's *Little Journeys* and *The Philistine.*

From Hartwood, he appealed to Willis Hawkins, and was gratified that his new friend urged him to accept. When he confessed that he lacked the clothes for a fancy dinner, Hawkins agreed not only to accompany him but to hire a dress suit and to send along a decent overcoat.

"In your old age," Stephen wrote gratefully, "may you remember how you befriended the greatest literary blockhead in America from himself."

Hubbard, presiding like a jolly friar, at last arose. Before he introduced Stephen, he read a clipping from the Port Jervis *Union* that quoted ecstatic praises from reviewers in Chicago and Cleveland. The round of applause made Stephen's collar tighten. He had dreaded having to make a speech.

For several minutes, as he talked about his work, they listened gravely: "I've been a free-lance during the years I have been doing literary work, writing stories and articles about anything under heaven that seemed to possess interest, and selling them wherever I could.

It was hopeless work. Of all human lots for a person of sensibility, that of an obscure free-lance in literature or journalism is, I think, the most discouraging."

He paused for a gulp of water, and was no longer afraid. "It was during this period that I wrote *The Red Badge of Courage*. It was an effort born of pain—despair almost; and I believe that this made it a better piece of literature than it otherwise would have been. It seems a pity that art should be the child of pain, and yet I think it is." He was quoting himself as he had described his career in a letter to an editor of *Leslie's Weekly*.

"I suppose I ought to be thankful to *The Red Badge*, but I am much fonder of my little book of poems, *The Black Riders*. The reason, perhaps, is that it was a more ambitious effort."

"Caesar was ambitious," someone drawled. "*Et tu*, Steve?"

The banter had begun. Grinning, he tried to go on.

"Crane, isn't it true that *The Red Badge* is autobiography?"

"Every line!" he retorted.

"What battle were you wounded in?"

"Chancellorsville. I got it in my 'wounded knee.'"

Just like his Injuns! The hecklings multiplied until, helpless with laughter, he gave up and sat down. A burst of applause made him lift his hands clasped together like a prize-fighter.

"Very good, Steve," Hawkins whispered.

Suddenly, Claude Fayette Bragdon, the Rochester architect and an impassioned advocate of a new esthetics, swayed to his feet. "I am here to honor Stephen Crane, not to ridicule him." He was white-faced. "I regret to take this step, but I can no longer remain in this room."

A silence fell on the table.

"Crane, you weren't offended?" Taber muttered. "No disrespect meant."

"No, no!" He was pained that anyone should think that he had been hurt.

Thoughtfully, Hawkins, the tallest man in the company, got up. As the glowering Bragdon made his way toward the door, Willis laid both hands on the architect's shoulders. "Whoa, my friend! I'm the oldest man in this room. I know Stephen Crane better than anyone else here. I know him through and through, every mood. I've taken part in all this banter, too, and he knows that I love him and admire him. He knows that you all do, or you wouldn't have invited him from a distance of four hundred miles or more. I assure you that he feels more complimented by the spirit of this meeting than by all the solemn eulogies you could have pronounced over him. Is that right, Steve?"

Stephen nodded vigorously. Again the men, sobered now, applauded.

Bragdon hesitated, then apologized and returned to his chair.

The evening continued with more speakers rising to their feet to be heckled amiably. More bottles were passed, and the stories flowed as agreeably as the liquor.

As they were waiting for Hubbard and Taber to say good night to the guests, Hawkins tapped at the printed quotations on the menu.

"Remember what I said, 'A few good reviews and the ladies would be paying attention to you?' Here's a nice regret from Louise Imogen Guiney, the poetess. But this one from Amy Lee of the Chicago *News!*" His eyes narrowed. "Did you meet her in Chicago?"

Stephen frowned. "Briefly at the *News* when I went to call on Eugene Field. He was ill, but I met others on the staff."

"'My most gentle thoughts are tinged with envy of you who are so lucky to meet Stephen Crane.' Signed, 'Amy Lee, of the Chicago *News.*' Sounds like a crush. Are you sure, Steve, that it was briefly?"

"Briefly!" he repeated, and was irritated. Amy Lee, a small buxom woman with lively green eyes, had reminded him of Nellie. She had pressed his hand and praised *The Black Riders*. She had intimated that since she often came to New York to write dramatic notices on the important shows, she might ask him to inscribe her copy of the book of poems when she came East again. That had been six months ago; he had forgotten about her.

"Any woman who makes up her mind to catch Stevie Crane will land him like a prize fish!" Hawkins grumbled. "Watch out. Fame is a bitch!"

Willis left Buffalo the next morning. Stephen went to East Aurora with Hubbard and Taber. He enjoyed their easy hospitality and was eager to see the printshop where Hubbard produced his own editions of the pamphlets in the *Little Journeys to the Homes of the Great* series.

Hubbard, with his Windsor tie and the Buster Brown haircut, was a complex character. Warm and outgoing, with an infectious grin and a hearty manner, he seemed to be obsessed with the self-educated man's compulsion for perfection. He could talk as vulgarly as a longshoreman, yet in a trice become as sober as a college president and sprinkle his declamations with quotations from the learned dead.

Together, they rode the wintry countryside, Hubbard shouting into the wind. "I made a little money in the soap business, and I could have made a lot more. One day I decided that money wasn't all I wanted. It wasn't getting me where I wanted to be. Steve, I needed a formal education. So I washed my hands of the soap business, literally. Sold it to my partner. At thirty-nine, I went off to Harvard. Damn, but I found that I couldn't take that classroom moonshine! Too much chaff to too little wheat. Stood it as long as I could, then packed and went abroad. Looking for destiny. In England, I called on William Morris at his Kelmscott Press. I saw what he was doing, trying to revive the good old crafts. Then I knew what I wanted. So when I got home I set up The Roycrofters' shop. Now I write what I please and I print it, too. That's the important thing, Steve. Do your best, but be your own master."

When they returned to the stables, Hubbard showed Stephen "a young peanut of a horse" nuzzling its mother in one of the stalls.

"A good saddle-horse is the greatest blessing in life!" Stephen gazed longingly at the beautiful colt.

"He's too young to be saddled. By spring, maybe. Look here, Steve, would you like to have him? You'll never come upon a finer animal. That boy of mine who's been following us around, his chums call him 'Butch,' will break him in if you say the word. You can have him for a hundred dollars. Just say the word and he's yours."

"If I could raise the cash——"

"You've got until spring. We'll ship him down to you as soon as you're ready."

"I'll take him!"

Riding home on the Erie Railroad in a snowstorm, Stephen thrilled in anticipation of the glorious days ahead when he and his "peanut" steed would roam the woods around Hartwood. Surely the tide had turned. A banquet in his honor, praise from the critics, and, now, his own mount! Later, he could not remember whether "the peanut" was male or female. He chuckled. It made no difference. A horse is a horse.

With Bacheller after him for a work of novel-length to serialize in the newspapers, he was like a reporter with a copy-boy at his elbow. The first chapters had flowed so smoothly that he should have become wary. Then he blamed Willie Hawkins who, determined to learn the craft of fiction, had urged him to talk about each character and to reveal the general plot. He had lost the fine edge of surprise that creating his story as he moved along used to give him. He had staled on the romance.

In retaliation, he had threatened to name a character after Willie. His friend had thought it amusing. Well, he had named his chief character "Hawker," close enough to Hawkins.

He was convinced that the New York studio scenes were his best. However, the romance between Grace Fanhall and Hawker had developed lamely; it avoided a satisfactory conclusion, as had his own with Lillie Brewster Morrow.

Ted read the first ten chapters, and asked, "Do they get married?"

He replied soberly, "How do I know? The story isn't finished."

The story wove in and out of his affair with Lillie. He had changed the locale from Asbury Park to Port Jervis, had made the little boy the son of the sister instead of the child of the woman Hawker loved. Still, his characters flitted palely, refusing to alight.

He hastily finished the manuscript and sent it off to Ripley Hitch-cock. He could do no more with Grace Fanhall, his disguised Lillie, than he could do with the living Lillie. She was a married woman with a child and would never leave her husband. He altered the title to "The Third Violet." Let Hitchcock puzzle over it.

He was angry with his editor. In declining the invitation to the Philistine dinner, Hitchcock had sent a strange message to Hubbard: "I am glad to know that our puppets, when they prove themselves prophets, are not without honor in their own country." Hitchcock, who must have thought better of the phrasing, had written a private letter of apology; he had not meant it unkindly. Stephen had assured him that he was not offended, but he was deeply hurt.

CHAPTER 51

He started the New Year placidly, walking the woods in his old corduroys with Judge, the Gordon setter whom Ted was training for a neighbor, prancing ahead and sniffing at the snow. They crossed a white field pitted with rabbit tracks.

Judge, who was gun-shy, bounded off as Stephen began to pot-shoot from the hip with the big Smith & Wesson revolver he had brought from Mexico. He tired, for the pistol had the kick of a mule, and started back across the fields in search of the dog. Whistling as he went, he heard an answering whistle. Ted was coming toward him, waving a long envelope.

Standing in the snow, Stephen slit open the letter forwarded from William Heinemann.

"They've published it in England!" he cried. Heinemann, who had contracted to issue an edition, had been undecided whether to offer it in wrappers in the "Pioneer Series" or in a cloth-bound volume at two and six. So he had published it in both formats simultaneously.

Steve read the clippings aloud. *The Red Badge of Courage* was charming readers in England. Critics there were "wild" over it. George Wyndham, presumably an important British voice, had de-clared: "Mr. Stephen Crane, the author of *The Red Badge of Courage*, is a great artist." Furthermore, "Mr. Crane's picture of war is more complete than Tolstoy's, more true than Zola's."

"Ted, you hear that?" Stephen, his eyes shining, shouted at his brother. Here, in the woods, he could strut. "You hear that? Tolstoy! Zola! They're crazy, of course, to say it, but, you know, Ted, I like to hear it, I like it, I like it!"

Heinemann had other reviews, equally praiseworthy, that would follow "in a subsequent post."

"I never doubted it!" Mame cried tearfully when they told her. She kissed Stephen's cheek. "Never, never!"

Crossing the threshold at Appleton's, he reflected how different his entrance had been on his first visit. They had kept him waiting; he had been gawky, awkward, ignorant and afraid. Today, no sooner was he announced than Ripley Hitchcock came forth. "Ah, Crane!" They shook hands. The editor led the way to his private office.

"People are buying your books, Crane." Hitchcock smiled and offered the cigar of hospitality. "We've sold two printings and are preparing a third."

"A third printing!"

"We ordered the paper last Monday. Now, it seems, we may need a fourth printing."

"That's good, isn't it?"

"I should say so."

"Who—who buys the books?"

Hitchcock stretched and studied the ceiling. "Always difficult to say, Crane. People, the cultured, the half-cultured, the uncultured. Some who read for the simple pleasure that any good story offers; some who read suspecting that it can't be as good as they've heard it is; some because they read the way sheep chew grass, cropping off to the ground and leaving no sign either on themselves or on the landscape that they ever saw the book; some because they hope they'll find something to disagree with; some because they're always waiting honestly for anything that promises to have merit and leap at the opportunity to enjoy it. Some read it and like it because it has been hailed as worth-while, and it behooves them to praise it lest they be thought behind the times. All sorts of reasons. That, Crane, is the public for you, the mass for which you write, for which everyone writes."

Stephen studied the end of his cigar. "Haphazard."

Hitchcock smiled again. "You write because you want to, perhaps because you must. The drive within you will not permit you to cease and desist. The fate of a book, though, lies in the lap of the gods."

The fact was that Stephen had never seen anyone reading *The Red Badge*, except his family and personal friends. It had dropped into the great American sea. *Maggie* had plummeted to the bottom; *The Red Badge* was somewhere afloat. He had strolled past bookshops and not seen a single copy on display. No one with the book in his hand, not on a park bench or on a stoop, not on a trolleycar or on an elevated train, not in a restaurant or on a ferryboat. If multitudes were reading *The Red Badge*, they were doing it in dark cellars or behind locked doors.

"How many printings can a book go into?"

Hitchcock laughed. "Who knows?"

"There's no way to tell?"

"None at all."

He thought this success as transitory as a harlot's affections. He had fame, but feared that it resembled the Emperor's clothes in the Hans Christian Andersen story: some little boy would show up and cry out, "He ain't got none!"

"Our treasurer has a draft for you," Mr. Hitchcock said. "Money is also due from Heinemann in England."

A little shiver passed down Stephen's back.

"Now about *The Third Violet*. Do you think it is your best? The public—you've got a public now, Crane—expects your best."

Stephen crimsoned. "I can't write everything with the intensity of a war novel! I want this published."

"Very well. Of course, Crane."

"I'd like to have *Maggie* published, too, Mr. Hitchcock."

"It would have to be revised."

"No, sir."

"A few minor touches perhaps. I advise you to reread it first, Crane."

He dropped his eyes. "Mr. Hitchcock——" It was difficult to address his editor as "Ripley" or "Hitchcock." He would always be "Mr. Hitchcock." There was a certain gulf between them.

"I have *George's Mother*, too," Stephen said.

"If we publish *The Third Violet* and perhaps *Maggie*, you should follow with a completely new book. If you care to add to your reputation, we would rather not take *George's Mother*."

Stephen frowned. *George's Mother* was not to be despised. Harry Thompson, an old school friend who was manager of the American office of Edward Arnold, the British publishing house, had said, "Anything you've got, Steve!" He would give *George's Mother* to Edward Arnold and press for American and English publication simultaneously. If that mystic public was in the mood for his work, he would give it the opportunity to buy as many books as could be rushed into print.

"Very well. I'll revise *Maggie* for you, Mr. Hitchcock."

"A few of the curse words might be taken out."

He winced. "Don't you see that with my characters those words are necessary?"

"They may be necessary, but not so many. Crane, don't forget your readers!"

When they shook hands again, Stephen avoided Mr. Hitchcock's eyes. The editor had once seen him as a naked, callow youth trying to peddle stories; but he had changed, he was not the same lad. He was an established author.

As he cashed a draft for four hundred dollars into new banknotes,

294

he reflected that Hitchcock was not responsible for his success at all. That elusive public had made him.

John Phillips, Mr. McClure's syndicate partner, proposed a series of articles on the Civil War. Expense money was now available. Evidently the success of *The Red Badge* had not gone unnoticed; perhaps they regretted having refused it.

Stephen favored Fredericksburg, the most dramatic of the battles in his estimation, as the subject for the first article.

In Virginia, he tramped over the battlefield and stared at the glittering Rappahannock. Fifteen thousand men had died in the assaults on the stone walls in this area. Then the old distaste for the stuff of history lessons returned. To hell with Phillips and McClure! Any undertaker could set down names and dates.

He disdained generals, even the great ones, and the adjutants, colonels, and majors, with their echelons of braid and brass. But the little stone markers, always the little stone markers, were eternal. Beneath them lay boys who had never given a command. Whether they had worn the blue or the gray, they were his kind, his little regiment.

He would not dishonor their memory by writing diluted history in which they became pallid statistics. The ghosts on the Fredericksburg battlefield were whispering; his duty was to give voice to their truth.

Some day he would face a real battlefield and meet the bleeding reality. Meanwhile, McClure could take the story as he wrote it— or leave it.

McClure was not disturbed that the trip to write a battle article had brought forth a battle fiction. He read it and grinned as if he had planned such a coup. He would publish "The Little Regiment" in his June issue. "Got any more of these, Crane? We'll make a book of your war stories."

Meanwhile, more reviews arrived from England. God bless them! The *Saturday Review*, too, had said that Crane was better than Zola. When they compared his irony to that of old Sophocles, he wished that his instructors at Pennington, Claverack, Lafayette, and Syracuse could read their praise. Why, the book was, in a long word, "an inspired utterance that will reach the universal heart of man." *Pall Mall's* did as well. So did *St. James's Gazette*, calling *The Red Badge* "a revelation." The *Daily Chronicle* reported: "In the whole range of literature, we can call to mind nothing as searching in its analysis."

Harold Frederic, London correspondent of the New York *Times*, described the triumph to his paper: "Stephen Crane's Triumph— London Curious About the Identity of America's New Writer."

Hawkins crowed: "Six months ago they were slandering you. Now that you've stormed England, they'll be singing a different tune!"

Excellent reviews now appeared in certain domestic papers. In the *Literary World* of Boston, John Barry gloated that he could not think of another American writer who had been accepted as a man of consequence in England "before winning marked recognition in his own country, and I doubt if Mr. Crane's recent experience now has a precedent." *The Bookman* put the question: Why were American critics less sure and American readers slower to discover a good book? Even the *Literary Digest* moaned that it was scarcely to the credit of America that England had been the first to pronounce *The Red Badge* a work of genius. A month later, the *Digest* pulled all stops and stated bluntly that it was "now pretty generally admitted that Stephen Crane is a 'genius.'"

Stephen settled back to enjoy his fame.

Bacheller reported that a certain General A. C. McClurg, in the "Letters to the Editor" columns in the *Dial,* had given him a stiff lacing. Under the title "The Red Badge of Hysteria," the veteran, an important Chicago bookseller, had bellowed that the Crane book was "a vicious satire upon American soldiers. The hero is without a spark of soldierly ambition." He lambasted Henry Fleming as if he were sitting at Henry's court martial: "No thrill of patriotic devotion moves in his breast."

Stephen growled, "My namesake was a delegate to the Continental Congress. A dozen Cranes fought in the Revolutionary War. We've served our country as well as any general in the land!"

Hitchcock agreed that the attack was savage and unwarranted. "But he attacks your hero, not you!"

Stephen, carefully revising *Maggie,* was dispensing "with a goodly number of damns," and heaping them upon the editor's head. Truculently, he appealed for a hundred-dollar advance to pay for Peanuts, the riding-horse that Hubbard was ready to ship to him. "If I am worth $100 in your office——" He expected a polite refusal, but Hitchcock quietly forwarded a bank draft.

Money began to trickle in. To the end of the year, forty-five hundred copies of *The Red Badge* had been sold; now four thousand more had been shipped, and a fifth printing was on the press. He began to pay off old debts. He bought lunches and dinners for the Injuns. He played poker twice a week.

He had new contracts to sign. The Edward Arnold firm was eager to publish *George's Mother* in May, in New York and, simultaneously, in London. Heinemann would issue the English edition of *Maggie* and, in conjunction with Copeland & Day, a third printing of *The Black Riders.*

McClure urged him to go to Washington to write on political themes: "An article, a story or a novel. Do as you please!"

Willie Hawkins applauded. "I'll come with you, Steve. I know everybody in Washington."

Stephen was nonplussed. He must be free to meet Lillie. Willie, who envied the license of a writer's life, was eager to get away for a week or two.

"Meet you in the morning at Bacheller's!" Willie said. "We'll leave whenever you're ready."

Determined that Hawkins should not be at his side in Washington, Stephen calmly took the night train. Not until he was safely at the Cosmos Club, courtesy of Irving Bacheller, did he write an explanatory note, "It was a woman! Don't you see? Nothing could so interfere but a woman." Hawkins would be blazing mad. To placate him, he would send him the handwritten manuscript of *The Red Badge of Courage*. Willie, who treasured scraps of Eugene Field's writings, would be elated with a complete manuscript.

His obligation to McClure required that he concentrate on the national political carnival. He dutifully called upon Senators and Congressmen from the Middle and Far West and listened to their plans for the salvation of the Republic, while he waited for Lillie to fix their next rendezvous.

One morning, the clerk at the Cosmos Club handed him an envelope: "Urgent, Mr. Crane." The message read: "Library of Congress. March 18th. Ten o'clock. Reading-room gallery."

The Washington springtime had come early. The sky was blue; the trees were in bud, water purled in the fountains. The avenues were crowded with rapidly moving carriages and messengers on bicycles. The Library of Congress structure, with its splendid Italian Renaissance style and Greek wings, had not been officially completed, but the reading rooms were in use. Workmen still clambered about the wooden scaffolding at the bays of the central pavilion.

Inside the bronze doors, a beanpole of a man in a brown smock was sketching the main hall and the grand staircase. Stephen, absently studying the mosaics and the Pompeiian decorations in the ceiling, climbed to the mezzanine.

The instant she appeared, he knew from her pallor that she was alarmed. "Lillie, are you well?"

She glanced about warily. "Your note," she whispered, "fell into his hands. Oh, Stephen, go quickly. Leave Washington." Her eyes were red from weeping.

"Why?" he asked in bewilderment.

"You must go!" she insisted. "He's insanely jealous. When he found your note, he searched my closet and discovered the manuscript of *Maggie* and several of your letters. He tore them all up in a wild rage! He—he knows that we used to see each other."

He chilled. "My letters!"

"All but a few I had given to Dottie to keep. He destroyed the others." Her voice quavered.

With a sinking heart, he said, "I don't care. I'll call on him. I'll tell him that I love you."

"Don't be ridiculous!" She caught his hand. "Stephen, don't do anything foolish. You have your work. I must return to the child."

He stared at her speechlessly. The child, of course.

"You'll do nothing," she pleaded. "You'll be prudent and take care of yourself."

He returned bitterly, "We who are condemned to live are not allowed to die."

As he moved to embrace her, she turned and left him standing there with his arms outstretched. He watched her walk swiftly away.

"Good-bye, Lillie," he whispered. "Good-bye, my violet!"

He lay on his bed at the Cosmos Club and wished that he were dead. Life to him was no more than a mouthful of dust.

He dreamed that night that the house on A Street went up in flames. He saw Lillie, in a white gown, screaming frantically to the upper story: "Jimmie! Jimmie!" He watched himself rush into the blazing structure. He ploughed through billows of smoke and snatched the child from its bed. The little hands clutched at his chest; the small voice cried: "Papa!"

Suddenly, he was outside the dream but still within the dream, and Ludie appeared. In his brother's arms lay his own body charred beyond recognition.

CHAPTER 52

McClure was undismayed that the trip to Washington had produced nothing. He seemed to have infinite patience with creative men.

"Something must have seeded in your mind. One day it'll burst out like popcorn! You do more war stories, Steve. They're fine." He jingled his keys. "Write more adventures about your hero in *The Red Badge*. In more battles, eh?"

Stephen shrugged. As often as McClure had urged stories in sequel, he had ignored it. He mused that Henry Fleming had been not a hero but a callow youth who had been annealed under battle conditions. After the war, like the veteran Jeb Royal, Henry might sit in the square of his home town and spin windy yarns of his baptism under fire. The joust with the great Death had been the only dramatic act of his life.

Determined to lay the ghost of Henry Fleming, Stephen conceived the central idea for "The Veteran." Savagely, he compelled Henry to tell the truth to his admirers: "Why, in my first battle I thought the sky was falling down. I thought the world was coming to an end. You bet I was scared." Henry went on, "Yes, siree, I thought every man in the other army was aiming at me in particular, and only at me!"

Stephen lingered over the scene. He, too, had once thought that everyone in the world was aiming at him in particular, looking at him, talking about him. He knew now that the universe did not care. Henry Fleming might plunge into a Lake of Fire for his sins and the sky would not shed a star, or drop a meteorite.

He pondered that in such a "lake of fire" might occur Henry's final act, his only heroism. Instantly, the destruction of Henry was illumined. The Swede, a hired man, fashioned after some gawky type he had seen in Nebraska, overturned a lantern in the barn. "Fire! Fire!" he screamed.

Vividly, Stephen described the panic and the conflagration. Henry must rescue the cattle and the horses from the barn. "He took five horses out, and then came out himself, with his clothes bravely on fire." He was running lamely, "as if one of the frenzied horses had smashed his hip." He even dragged the Swede, who had become paralyzed with terror and screeched like a maniac, into the open air.

The church bell was pealing its tocsin note. But the horses were safe.

"De colts! De colts!" the Swede cried.

Two colts had been forgotten in the box stalls at the back of the barn. It was suicide to go back into the flaming structure. But old Fleming would not be dissuaded. "The poor little things!" he said, and rushed into the barn. "When the roof fell in, a great funnel of smoke swarmed toward the sky, as if the old man's mighty spirit, released from its body—a little bottle—had swelled like the genie of the fable. The smoke was tinted rose-hue from the flames, and perhaps the unutterable midnights of the Universe will have no power to daunt the colour of his soul!"

Stephen sat with his hands folded as if he were praying for this creature of his mind whom he had destroyed. In the end, Henry Fleming had proved himself; in the panic and flame he had towered above his fear and subdued it. That he had perished was of no consequence, for all men must die. Henry Fleming had died, he thought ruefully, as his copies of *Maggie* had died, in flames; a punishment, an expiation, a redemption and a victory. And he had died rescuing not men but horses.

The next day, polishing his prose, he was proud of "The Veteran." In effigy, he had purified himself. He was done with Henry Fleming forever.

McClure, who now read his stories immediately, hugged the pages to his vest. "I like it! A curious tale, but I like it. You seem to favor it, too, Crane."

"I do." He could not explain that a great burden had lifted from him, as if he, too, having shared Henry's experience had conquered fear. Henry had, indeed, conquered, but only in death, the ultimate triumph.

The police business began innocently. Once more, it was the restless, volatile McClure who urged him to take the new road.

"Crane, there's a quiet war going on every day and every night, never a flag of truce, never a treaty of peace. The city is the battlefield and unlawful forces roam it at will, sometimes to loot, sometimes to pillage or rob, sometimes to murder. By day and by night, a thousand crimes are committed. There would be thousands more if a division of skilled troops were not here to defend, to strike back, to maintain order, to hold the wolves at bay. These troops are your metropolitan police. The roundsman is your soldier. I say that, if you drew your sights on that blue-coat with his nightstick and his badge, you would find enough material for a dozen articles or stories, or both."

Stephen had no kind thoughts about the guardians of the law. He had seen them openly extorting petty graft from pushcart peddlers, storekeepers, householders, streetwalkers, pimps and madams. He had witnessed individual acts of courage and heroism, but the majority of the men patrolling the Tenderloin were sturdy, well-fed buzzards in blue who wore their uniforms as a license to prey.

"I never saw one pay for his own meal or glass of beer, or even for the girl he mounted in her crib!"

McClure ignored him. "There are good men and there are bad. You've met Theodore Roosevelt, the new president of the Board of Police Commissioners. I hear that he admires *The Red Badge* and your Mexican stories. If you went down to Mulberry Street, and told him that you wanted to study the life of a policeman, he'd pave the way. He's young, too, older than you, about thirty-seven, and ambitious. He's sworn to drive the grafters out. He prowls the city at night like a Haroun al-Raschid to see what goes on. If you wrote a few good stories or articles you would be helping him, and he would help you. For *McClure's* exclusively now!"

Stephen scratched his head. It was true that Roosevelt, as president of the Board, had promised many changes. One day, he had chased a policeman whom he had caught loafing in a saloon, had collared him on the street and had hauled him off to the nearest station. He had forced "Clubber" Williams, notorious for beating prisoners, to resign. The average man on the beat would enforce the law honestly if the higher officials set him an example.

Eddie Mayhew, the young tough whom Stephen had befriended and whose rooms he shared, screwed up his eyes at the proposal. He put a finger to his battered nose. "Yeh go write about de police an' every copper in N'Yawk will have the finger out fer yeh!"

Stephen spluttered.

"Yeh go down to opium hells, awright! Yeh go down to whorehouses, awright! Yeh go down to write about coppers, an' yeh'll git a bad name—wid de coppers!"

"Roosevelt's cleaning up the city."

Eddie sneered. "He's cleanin' up a stable wid ten t'ousand horses. So what happens? He cleans over here, an' dey do it over dere! Dey can lay down de turds faster'n he can sweep dem away. Stay off from coppers!"

Stephen hesitated. The tough, wiry ex-fighter, who earned a meager living around gymnasiums and, sometimes, on the docks, had come up from the Hell Gate quarter and knew the "coppers." Eddie was devoted to him.

When Doris Bowen, who had been his mistress, had decided that she wanted to marry him, Eddie had begged Stephen to intercede. "I wouldn't dass marry that broad if she was Lillian Russell an' workin' steady!"

To quiet Doris, Stephen had paid her various sums, for a total of one hundred and fifty dollars, out of his Appleton royalties. Then Doris, seeing in Stephen an easy touch, had set her cap for him. When he repulsed her, she threatened to come to Hartwood. Thoroughly alarmed, he had marched to her flat to warn her off. Doris had thrown a knife. Fortunately he had ducked; the blade had quivered in the door jamb. Doris was a "heller."

"Eddie, it's true the city is an Augean stable. But that doesn't mean——"

"Don't blame it all on de Irish!" Eddie snapped, a glint of humor in the clouded eyes. Stephen was never certain whether Eddie was clever, or whether he stumbled on word-plays like "O'Geon." "Jes' yeh keep off de coppers. Opium is one t'ing. But not coppers. Yeh oughta know betteh!"

Stephen had not feared the opium dens. The first time he had donned shabby clothes to shuffle into the colorful Chinatown quarter, with Eddie for his escort, he had been ill at ease, but unafraid. That he no longer flinched before danger astounded him.

He and Eddie had slipped into a shop where a tall, bronze Buddha presided over cabinets of carved teakwood. By a glimmer of lanterns, they had wandered through a maze of corridors that must have wound under the street. They came out in an underground dormitory where men who looked like deacons, except for their pigtails and quilted coats, enjoyed stuporous dreams on cots as narrow as a girl's waist. Twenty-five thousand addicts or casual smokers frequented similar dens in the bowels of Manhattan.

To experience the sensations he wanted to describe for the editors of the *Sun*, he had paid for a pipe and watched skillful yellow hands mold the pill and light it in the tiny bowl. His first sensation, inhaling a smoke that reeked of scorched linen, was of having "swallowed a live chimney-sweep." Later, the simple languor followed, resignation and the bought peace. What others might smilingly dream he could not tell; he seemed to be lying on a warm beach with his arms pinned and sand up to his chin, while the surf thundered and black riders rode back and forth, beyond his reach, in a violet sea.

The second and third time, he returned alone, not to smoke, although he bought a long pipe and the "makings" in a smooth black case, but to absorb more of the catacomb atmosphere, while he lay cramped in a narrow bunk and watched figures flitting about, heard men cry out or sing, and listened to music that drilled little holes into his skull. He learned about "yen-yen," the ultimate craving whereby the confirmed smoker "placed upon his shoulders an elephant which he may carry to the edge of tomorrow."

That had been adventure in Chinatown. But Eddie had shown him the way. He was baffled how to learn of police life without wearing the uniform and carrying a badge and a nightstick.

When the Lanterns gave a dinner for Commissioner Roosevelt, he bluntly stated his purpose.

"Dee-lighted, Crane!" Roosevelt punched the table with his fist. "Dee-lighted! Go to it! 'Seek and ye shall find.'"

He had a closely cropped head, a walrus mustache and small, piercing eyes; he wore his pince-nez on a black ribbon. The large white teeth, enormously impressive teeth, flashed with every sentence he rasped. He might be a "dude," as his critics called him, adolescent and noisy, but he was genuine, a rare kind of official in the big, corrupt city.

In July, Stephen dined at the Roosevelt home.

At his own table, however, the Commissioner was inclined to defend his department.

"Watch them in crowds. They have to be good-humored and yet please everyone, control and do it gently." He peered through his spectacles, the large mouth open as if the teeth were ready to bite the nearest foe. "That's no mean task! But you find me a bad policeman, and I'll run him off the reservation."

"He's not going to put me on to anything," Stephen told Eddie. "I'll have to go after it without him."

"Whaddid I say?" Eddie demanded triumphantly. "All coppers stick togedder."

George's Mother had been published and, instantly, attacked in the press. Even Harry Thurston Peck trampled it as "old bones and junk." The *Tribune* maintained its record for hostility by assailing it as coarse and dull.

"See, if dey praised yeh, even den yeh'd get nowhere," Eddie said wisely. "Now yeh'll get double nowhere. Stay away from de coppers."

CHAPTER 53

Amy Lee had arrived from Chicago, and had invited him to "tea and talk." The address was in a 25th Street brownstone. An older woman, with gray hair and a haughty nose, surveyed him sternly before she let him in. In the parlor, the shades, drawn against the heat of the day, made a yellow sky.

The furnishings were simple, but expensive. A Mason and Hamlin piano, with popular music—"Daisy Bell" and "Linger Longer, Lou"— on the rack; a fine Turkish rug in a small animal pattern; old chairs with tapestry covers. Above the mantel hung an oil portrait of a lovely golden-haired girl in a filmy gown. The shoulders were splendid, the eyes green and frank.

On either side of the fireplace, above the glassed bookcases with their sets of Shakespeare, Jane Austen, Byron, Browning, and stacks of music sheets, were large playbills framed in oak. Evidently they were for light operas: *Olivetti, The Mascotti,* and others of which he had never heard. He recognized a portrait of De Wolfe Hopper beside a smiling study of the girl in the portrait. She had been in the theater, no doubt a singer. The inscription read, "For Lily West." He scanned the playbills once more. Lily West had sung the role of Amelia in *Olivetti* and of Fiametta in *The Mascotti.* She had also appeared in *The Mikado* and *Pinafore* and in several other Gilbert and Sullivan operettas. She had sung opposite De Wolfe Hopper in *Castles in the Air.*

"Stephen Crane!"

Between the double doors, the woman he had met in Chicago now entered. A glimpse of the staircase beyond her revealed more framed playbills ascending to the floor above.

"Miss Lee!"

Small and lissome, with a wealth of reddish-gold hair, she swept forward in a flaming Oriental robe of red and gold silk—he noted the golden slippers—and warmly extended her hand as if she had known him all her life. "We meet again at last! How good of you to come."

"How good of you to ask me!" he smiled.

Her perfume dazzled him. He looked into the cool sea-green eyes, and tingled at the clasp of her hand.

"I knew you would come, Stephen." She pressed his fingers to her bosom. "Pitty-pat! Can you feel it? I've been excited all day. I was grieved that I could not travel to attend that dinner in Buffalo. I nearly came anyway, you know."

While he sat like a small boy, she was moving nervously, flicking this lamp and that cushion, talking and bending and compelling him to follow her magnificent figure. "You don't know how much courage it took to write that letter inviting you here." She seated herself. "I've never written a letter like that in my life, although I've received letters from hundreds of men." Her hand gracefully took in the wall of playbills. "One expects that in the theater. But mine—mine to you was like a mash note!"

"I didn't think so." He tried to be cool. "I get lots of letters."

She laughed. "You must! Since your books appeared, beautiful women must be knocking at your door. I nearly didn't send it."

"I'm very glad that you did."

"No, you're not glad, Stephen," she returned gently. "Why should you be? You're a poet and an author and, of course, you were curious. 'What does *she* want?' you thought to yourself. 'Another female. I'll go and see.' And here you are!"

"I was flattered."

"Honestly? Stephen, honestly? I'm already addressing you by your Christian name!"

"Most people do."

"Women and girls, do they?"

He grinned.

"Will you call me Amy?"

"Amy!"

"We're less formal in the theater." Again she glanced at the play-bills, and now also at the portrait.

At last he understood. "Lily West! You are——"

She feigned a curtsey. Her hands, never at rest, made little flourishes. "You're too young ever to have heard me sing."

Mischievously, "I thought it was your sister."

"Teresa? She's much older than I am. But for years I sang, light opera mostly."

"Why did you give it up? Your voice is enchanting."

"Oh!" She lowered her eyes. "There were reasons. Shall I tell you? I had wanted a career, everything for my career. I loved my roles, I loved the applause; I was young and greedy for fame. We were on tour. My baby became sick, mortally, though I didn't know it."

A chill went through him. She, too, then was a married woman!

"But I went on, and left him with friends. I promised myself that I would leave the company as soon as the manager could replace me —city after city. One night, when the curtain went down, a telegram was waiting." Her voice choked. "I had no baby, only——"

"I'm sorry." He saw the fists clench fiercely.

304

"I had lost Frankie. He was four. I vowed never, never again! I was through with the theater. They came to me with new offers, but I would never go back to the stage." She became pensive. "It may have been my grief that destroyed our marriage. My husband was an excellent comedian. He had played Lorenzo the Thirteenth, the unlucky king in *The Mascotti*, with me. Have you ever heard of him? Harry Brown. He was stricken. Everything—we blamed each other!—was destroyed. Soon we were divorced, and I had my living to earn. Six years ago, I tried drama reporting for the Chicago *News*. My parents, dear and old-fashioned, were still alive, so I became 'Amy Lee' to shield their privacy. And here I am."

He was silent.

She mused, "How odd of me! I rarely talk of the past, and here I have blurted out my whole story. Now you know me. I wish you could have known me when I was the girl in that portrait." She preened. "I was a bride then. Lily West, once a singer, once a mother, once a married woman."

The sister who, Stephen surmised, had been listening at the door, came in with a silver tea service. Amy introduced her: "Mrs. O'Brien." The woman gave him a cryptic smile.

"She pampers me, she worries over me. I am the little sister. She's never so happy as when I am here where she can look after me. This is partly my vacation, but I also send back pieces on the New York stage for my column, 'Echoes from Mimic Land.' "

The tea was hot; the cakes were freshly baked. He enjoyed her nearness; she was a bold and clever woman.

She spoke of her dull girlhood in Iowa. Her father had been a journalist and, later, a banker. She had graduated from St. Mary's Academy in South Bend. "A convent," she added, as if that explained everything.

He was at ease with her; she was a strong, emancipated woman.

The chattering had ended; she was eyeing him soberly. Her bosom heaved and a flush came to her cheek. "I'm much older than you, Stephen, ten years your senior."

"Does it matter?" He was suddenly eager.

"Ten years can be a great deal between a man and a woman."

"I've never thought so."

Her voice became low. "It can be. But I'm a sensible woman, Stephen, and not demanding. Shall we be friends?"

"I hope so!"

"Why haven't you married?"

He crimsoned. "I suppose that I'm afraid of women."

He said it so drolly that she laughed. "Don't be afraid of me. I was educated by the good sisters, and sometimes I think that I could take the veil myself."

"You won't, Amy!" he said warmly, his eyes stripping the robe from her. "You won't!"

The light in her eyes had become frankly lustful. Who was the hunter and who the hunted?

As her head went forward almost imperceptibly, he understood the unspoken invitation. She was waiting; she was available.

Calmly, he put his arms around her. Her lips were soft and pliant, her body mature, knowing.

Lost in the passionate embrace, he murmured, "Lillie!"

The eyes opened. "Lily is the past and dead. Call me Amy, Stephen. And love me, oh, please, love me!"

CHAPTER 54

"Stephen Crane," observed the Literary News column in the August *McClure's*, in which "The Veteran" appeared, "has been for some time giving a good share of his days and nights to study the life of the metropolitan policeman, in the hope of giving it finally a literary presentation equal in reality and dramatic power to the presentation of the life of the private soldier in *The Red Badge of Courage* and 'The Little Regiment.' He has undertaken the work especially for *McClure's* magazine. The president of the New York Board of Police Commissioners, the Hon. Theodore Roosevelt, has taken particular interest in the matter and is giving Mr. Crane his personal aid."

Eddie Mayhew said, "Leadin' wid yer chin! Every copper will be watchin' fer yeh!"

"They don't read *McClure's*."

"Why doncha' wear a Roman candle in yer hair, so dey'll see yeh from far off?"

He was standing in the shadow of the turrets of the Jefferson Market Police Court, chatting with Ed Marshall, when Clancy, an elderly police sergeant known to both men, emerged from the gloomy structure.

Clancy nodded to Marshall, but he gave Stephen a sneering glance. "Marshall, is that boy-spy a friend of yours?"

Stephen flushed angrily.

Marshall said, "Wait, Clancy, you've got Crane wrong."

"Have I?" the sergeant barked. "What's he nosing around here for?"

As Clancy strode on, the editor murmured, "I don't like it, Steve. They think you're a spy for Roosevelt."

"The Commissioner doesn't need me and won't help me. Anyway, he's off on a jaunt in the West."

"Ever since the Lexow Committee they're jumpy. You've written about the Bowery and about Chinatown. They think that now you're going to write a story to make fools out of them."

"That isn't the way I would write it, Ed. McClure is right. The man on the beat is a sentry. I——"

"They'll never believe that you mean it. The word has gone out that you're 'bad medicine,' Steve. Forget Roosevelt, There's still a core of rough, hard men on the force. Don't go down into the Tenderloin alone at night. They would raid a place if they thought they might catch you with some woman. They'd give plenty for a chance to discredit you."

He decided to be wary. Violetta, the boisterous Corsican girl at Dolores' place, had offered to tell him of her experiences with the police. He prevailed upon Eddie to ask her to the flat late Saturday night after work.

On Saturday morning, he remembered that Willie Hawkins had promised to round up five or six friends for a "fiesta da poke." He hurried out for the Pilsener, cheese, frankfurters, ham, bread, butter, pickles, and mustard. He cleared the large room for the poker game by pushing the extra furniture into the partitioned sleeping area. He would cut the festivities short; he would say that he must leave for Hartwood in the morning.

The players straggled in around eight o'clock. Hawkins brought an old colleague from his Chicago *Daily News* days, Harry B. Smith, the librettist whose *Robin Hood* and *Rob Roy* had become musical successes. Smith had written *The Tzigane* for Lillian Russell.

The evening was devoted more to talk than to poker.

At eleven-thirty, after the beer and the sandwiches had been passed, the game became serious. It was two o'clock when Smith, who had lost fifteen dollars but had evidently enjoyed himself, called it a night.

The chips were cashed in. Hawkins groaned about the long trip to Brooklyn; on other occasions, Stephen had invited him to bunk on the sofa.

Leroy Fairman tiptoed from the bedroom; he toured every flat he visited like an old furniture buyer. "Shh!" he hissed. "Someone has been sleeping in Stevie's bed. And *she* is still there!"

At the laughter, Stephen started. "Gosh, I didn't hear her come in!"

"Is it Maggie?" Hawkins inquired.

"Some of her." He added, "Good night, Injuns."

Fairman chuckled. "She's got an interesting birthmark! Come and see for yourself."

Stephen tried to discourage them, but Leroy, with a wink, led the way. "Hey, do your other girls know about this one?" *Sotto voce,* he asked, "Does Amy Lee?"

Violetta, having found the door ajar, had gone into the sleeping area. She had undressed, strewn her clothes over the floor, chair, and dresser, and had fallen asleep, stretched out like a nude by Ingres. On her left thigh was a large yellow and blue bruise. The admiring spectators had to be cajoled to leave.

Stephen suspected that Violetta had feigned sleep while they stood over her. When the guests had departed, he roused her. They talked until dawn.

He was dismayed that Leroy Fairman should know about Amy.

After a day on the beach with the Howells family at Far Rockaway, Stephen returned to the city in the early evening to dine with Amy.

"What are you thinking, Stephen?" Amy asked, fondling the bunch of flowers he had brought her.

He had sent "A Man and Some Others" to Paul Reynolds, a literary agent whom he had met through Bacheller. Reynolds, who represented Heinemann in the United States, had intimated that he might obtain as much as three hundred dollars for the American rights.

"I have learned that a story has both English and American rights. That if I am not a boob, I can sell my work many times, in different ways. But to earn more I must have a clever agent working for me. I can't do it myself."

She confessed that she, too, had consulted an agent; she sought a wider market for her critical articles.

As they left the dinner table, there was a quick patter of rain on the windowpanes and a rumble of thunder.

"'O Master, thou knowest the wherefore of raindrops——'" Amy began, quoting from his poem in the March issue of *The Chapbook*. "Every word you've written is precious. To me, you're the greatest writer that ever lived."

He protested.

"To me!" she repeated. "I don't care about the others."

She had been an easy conquest. Or was it he who had been conquered? Certainly Amy had been the aggressor in their love affair. No one had ever praised him so lavishly, embraced him so earnestly, wooed him with such passion. A hundred times he told himself that hers was the extravagant speech of theater people.

"I set my cap for you long ago," she smiled. "If I could I would never let you out of my sight. I am jealous of every hour you spend with anyone else."

"I value my freedom, Amy."

"I know, Stephen," she sighed. "I am airing my dreams. You owe me nothing. You belong to many people. Everyone must adore you. But I could be of great help to you," she added. "If you trusted me."

He ignored her offer and talked of his current assignment for McClure. Jamieson, the elderly roundsman on Park Row, had passed him a friendly warning.

"I've seen you around since before you learned to shave, ain't I,

Crane? You used to work for Mr. Johnson on the *Tribune*. And Mr. Marshall when he was at the *Press?* Well, lad, I'll tell you. *They* don't like you writing about the Department. *They* don't, and they can be damn bad to a jay that gets in their way."

Amy shuddered. "Do be careful, Stephen!"

He assured her that he had nothing to fear. "The President of the Board of Police Commissioners would skin them alive!"

"I would die if anything happened to you."

Later, on the couch in her room, she whispered, "When we first met, did you dream that I would ever be your mistress?"

The word offended him.

She clasped him to her bosom. "I was testing you. We are lovers, aren't we? I'd do anything in the world for you!"

He was pleased with her passion, yet wished that she would not speak so boldly. He had not seduced her; she had come to him of her own free will, as had Marie Widdicomb, the first woman whom he had ever known intimately. It was incredible, especially when he remembered Lillie Brewster, the only woman he had loved with every fiber of his being.

CHAPTER 55

After an opening performance at the Broadway Gardens, he went backstage to meet the players. Later, he escorted three girls of the chorus to the Broadway streetcars.

He handed the tallest girl, whom he knew only as Myra, aboard the cable-car.

"Good night, Mr. Crane." She had promised to dine with him next Wednesday.

Stephen turned to the other two. "Now, how do you go home?"

A burly, mustached man in a bowler hat had seized their arms.

"Here, now!" Stephen protested.

"Move along!"

"Wait, you! I'm with these ladies!"

"Ladies!" the other snarled. "A couple of whores! Get along!"

Angrily, Stephen thrust himself against the man. A blow to the chest made him reel.

"I'm arresting these two. You'd better get along yourself, Crane, or I'll run you in with them!"

He was astounded. "But they're with me!"

The man's beefy face darkened. "Are you defying me? Go home, Crane!"

One of the girls was already weeping.

"Where's your authority?"

A terrible hand choked his collar. "You damn fool, I'm Detective Becker! West 30th Street Station. Now will you run home to your mama, or do I have to beat you up?"

He tottered. "I'm a reporter, Detective. And you know it. These girls are with me. I've just taken them from the Broadway Gardens —they're in the chorus. If you run them in, I'm coming along as a witness."

Becker glowered. "You come along then! I'm not letting your little whores off." He uttered a shrill whistle.

As a blue-coat appeared, a crowd began to gather. Becker marched the girls, who were both crying now, to the curb.

"There's no reason to pick on them, Detective," Stephen insisted. "If you're after me, run me in. But let them go."

Becker seemed enraged. "Be quiet, or I'll take this man's billy and rap your skull. I'm throwing these whores into the cooler, and I'll have no sass from you, Crane!"

In bewilderment, Stephen addressed the girls. "You were with me every minute since we left the Garden!"

They trembled in the detective's rough grip, and continued to weep.

The Black Maria arrived. "Get in!" the detective shouted. "You, too, Crane."

In the gloomy patrol wagon, Stephen sat between the girls and held their hands.

Becker, sneering, thrust his foot against the door. "That little whore I arrested before. Didn't I, sister? You're Dora Clark, you——"

The girl sobbed. "He arrested me because he knows that another policeman, Patrolman Roseberry, did when he insulted me and I wouldn't let him touch me. The judge let me go free. Now they arrest me every time they see me!"

"This time you won't get off, you tart!"

"Detective, there's no call for that language!"

"Crane, one more word!" Becker shook his fist into Stephen's face. "I'll teach you what you never learned in your goddam books!"

At the station, the girls were prodded toward the desk. Stephen tried to intervene. A uniformed man thrust him aside. "Stand back, you!"

Sergeant McDermott listened calmly to the stories.

"I'm charging these two," snarled Becker. "Soliciting in public."

"You lie!"

Becker snatched a club from the policeman. "Take it back, or I'll split your skull!"

Crane paled. "Sergeant, he's threatening me!"

"Better take it back," McDermott advised sternly. "He's an officer of the law."

"I'm going to appear as a witness for these girls. I——"

Ellen Day, Dora's companion, began to sob wildly. "Please don't arrest me!" A policeman caught her as she toppled in a faint.

Becker snapped, "Let her go! I'll hold the other whore. That's enough for a start."

As Dora Clark was booked, she, too, was sobbing. "I'm not bad," she wailed. "Give me a chance!"

"How old are you?"

"Twenty-one."

"Where do you live?"

"137 East 81st Street."

"Why don't you book me, Sergeant?"

"Crane, don't go looking for trouble. You've been doing it all summer," the Sergeant declared. "Everybody knows you."

"Dora, don't you worry!" He sickened at the phrase "all summer." Had he been under surveillance? "I'll be in court tomorrow."

"If you've got any sense," Becker roared, "you'll get out of town." He addressed the Sergeant. "I'd like to work him over downstairs, the skinny little bastard!"

Sergeant McDermott shook his head. "No reason for that, Becker. I'll talk to him."

Stephen urged Ellen Day to wait until he was ready; Becker, with a hard shove of his fist, commanded her to go. She screamed and ran from the station.

"Is this justice?" Stephen raved. "How can you treat a girl like that?"

"Be quiet, Crane," McDermott advised again. Three policemen moved closer. "No one is hurting you." He ordered Dora Clark taken downstairs and waved Becker off. "Listen to me, Crane. You're a fair-haired lad in this town, ain't you? Everybody says so. Don't butt in where you don't belong. The detective did his duty and arrested the girl for soliciting——"

"She was not soliciting, Sergeant. I swear that I walked her out of the dressing room at the Broadway Gardens. She was never out of my sight half a minute!"

"Be quiet, Crane! Don't let me, too, get mad at you. I advise you to go home and forget you ever saw anything. If the detective says he saw the girl soliciting——"

"He's lying!"

"Crane, you're going to be sorry. That's all I got to say. Go home and forget it, or you'll wish you hadn't been borned."

He struggled with phantoms that night. In the morning, Eddie Mayhew pleaded with him to leave for Port Jervis or Hartwood.

"You mean that I have to run away because the police—not **crooks** or criminals, but the police!—are going to persecute me?"

"Steve, don't be a damn fool!"

"I won't run!" He cursed. "I'll die first, but I won't run!"

On the witness stand, the following morning, with Detective Becker, who had already been examined, sitting below and glowering, he told his story.

"Then how do you account for Detective Becker's testimony being contrary to yours?"

He clenched his fists. "Your honor, the man lies!"

Magistrate Cornell re-examined the detective. Becker was adamant. He swore that he had seen the girl soliciting two men in a single block. After a reiteration from Stephen, the magistrate said simply, "There seems to be more than sufficient doubt here. Case dismissed!"

A court attendant muttered, "Mr. Crane, watch out for yourself! That Becker don't like it when anybody crosses him."

As soon has he could get away, he hurried uptown. Bacheller was out, but Hawkins listened sympathetically.

"McClure shouldn't have printed that notice. Now they've got it in for you. Go away for a few days. Go, Steve!"

He called on S. S. McClure.

"How did you manage to get into this scandal?" the publisher demanded. "And why didn't you let Roosevelt know?"

"First," he replied drily, "I guess it was your notice that alerted the whole police department. Second, I couldn't run to Mr. Roosevelt until I went up before the magistrate."

McClure stroked his mustaches. "Won't be much more you can do if the police have their number on you. Well, have you got enough material to start your articles? The fat's in the fire, let it sizzle. People will read these articles."

Jamieson, the friendly old policeman, nodded to him on the walk. "They didn't wait long to get after you, did they, Mr. Crane?"

The press the next day carried brief accounts of the scene in the magistrate's court. The *Journal* said, "Stephen Crane as Brave as His Hero." The *Tribune* used three sticks of type under the heading, "Saved from a Fine by Stephen Crane—The Novelist Testifies in Behalf of a Woman Accused of Soliciting."

At Eddie's place, a messenger had left a note from Amy: "Pray God you are safe. Come to me, please!"

On the street, he thought that eyes were upon him. Was he being followed? When he paused, and a man who had been walking behind him abruptly halted to tie a shoelace, he was convinced that he was being shadowed.

"Stephen, Stephen!" Amy cried, and embraced him. "I thought I'd die when I read the *Tribune* this morning. Why did you have to defend her? Galahad!"

"I'm not a Galahad. The girl was innocent."

"You know that if she had been arrested before she couldn't be a complete innocent."

Wearily, "She's a girl trying to earn her living in the chorus. She's prettier than most, so she's fair game. Anyway, she was with me, and I was her only witness. Could I leave her to those wolves?"

"What would they do?"

"Harass her, I suppose."

Amy shivered. "They might force her to do their will."

"They might," he returned calmly. Amy was eager to know how Dora Clark might be humiliated, less out of pity than from a morbid curiosity. Women approached the conjugal act variously, some with animal delight, some in terror, some resignedly, as if they expected to be stabbed to death. "Poor kid!"

She bit her lip. "You're defending her even to me. Are you sweet on her, Steve? No, don't tell me. I can't bear it. I'm jealous." She held him closer. "Steve, darling, I don't want you to leave tonight. I would die if anyone hurt you. We have a spare room. You can work there and sleep there. No one will go near you. Teresa will bring you your meals. I wouldn't breathe a word."

"I think I've been followed, Amy."

She drew in her breath, and strode to the window. "There isn't a soul visible on this block anywhere. Besides, I don't care. You must stay here, Steve. I won't come near you unless you wish it."

He shook his head.

"I'll talk to Teresa this minute. She won't be in your way."

"No, Amy!"

She blanched. "Don't you care at all what happens to you?"

"There's no need to risk your own safety and reputation for my sake."

"But I love you, Steve," she said simply.

He put his arms around her, "I don't deserve your love."

"You're good, Steve, just good. If I had my way, I'd never let you go."

In the upstairs sitting room, she renewed her plea. "This can be yours for as long as you wish. I want you to be free to do your work as God ordained that you should. No chains, no claims. Even if we were married, I shouldn't want you to be anything but free."

Her possessiveness alarmed him, yet he did not leave until nightfall. She swept him away with her adulation and made him feel reckless, manful, and domineering.

CHAPTER 56

As he opened the door to Eddie's flat, the odor of cigar smoke drifted to his nostrils. He hesitated; Eddie seldom used tobacco in any form.

He pulled the chain on the gas-fixture. Someone had been in the room. His sharp eyes detected that strange hands had untidied the papers on his desk. He opened the drawers of the bureau; his clothing had been disarranged!

In the closet, he removed his folders and fingered the brown paper parcels. He located his bankbook. His cash reserve of fifty dollars was intact. Was he imagining that someone had been in the flat?

He examined the lock on the door. A simple skeleton key, or even a thin strip of metal, could have opened it. As far as he could determine, nothing valuable was missing.

Eddie, who arrived after midnight, stalked about, hands in his pockets. "Dey came on purpose, Steve. We bin ransackled."

"We lost nothing! It could have been a curious neighbor with a skeleton key."

"Not in my place. Dey know I'd maul 'em." Mayhew pinched his lip. "C'mon, Steve!" He led to the janitor's flat. "Jake, did you see dose men who wuz here today to take me old clothes?"

The janitor scratched his head sleepily. "They didn't take no clothes. They said they were your friends and wanted to look at the furniture. Are you selling out, Eddie?"

"Did you give them a key?"

"They had a key. They weren't sure which was your room. So I showed them."

Stephen, concealing his alarm, described Detective Becker.

"Yeah, that was one. He is a friend of yours, ain't he? Said so."

Eddie said, "Sure. Did you see dem go out?"

"Yeah, sure." He pinched his brow. "One was holding a little black case."

Stephen tugged at Eddie's sleeve. "The pipe!"

They hurried upstairs again. The only items that had been removed were the opium pipe in its case and the little opium lamp, souvenirs of his journeys to Chinatown.

The following day at the Lantern Club, Hawkins cautioned him, "Be careful about being seen with any girls on the streets. I've heard that they again arrested your Dora Clark and another magistrate released her."

He groaned, "How can anyone fight back at them when they have the power to make that poor girl's life miserable? They'll force the manager to fire her from the chorus. They'll drive her into the streets!"

Hawkins shrugged. "I care only that you don't make it worse for yourself. Garland says that it was a mistake for you to write that opium story, that you shouldn't write or publish any police stories. This notoriety is bound to hurt your reputation. Even Howells will think it strange that you're always in trouble."

"My friends will understand."

314

"Your friends are like other people," Willie maintained. "Soon they will be saying that where there is smoke there must be fire. Go away for a month or two."

The next evening, as he strolled out, the policeman at the corner waved him on. "No loitering here!"

"I'm going for a walk."

The man's fist went to his nightstick. "Are you refusing to obey my orders?"

"You've seen me a hundred times, Officer. You know that I live here."

"I don't want you on my beat. Get along, or I'll run you in!"

Four blocks farther on, a meaty-faced roundsman who was posted before a saloon deliberately crossed his path. "You stop making a disturbance on a public street! I seen you."

Stephen stared in cold anger at the brass buttons and the shining badge.

"If you don't move along, I'll run you in. You hear?"

After an uncomfortable night, Stephen called on Sergeant McDermott. "Sergeant, I can't go anywhere without being stopped."

"I warned you not to be a hero. The Department don't like it."

"Call off your boys, Sergeant. I've got a right to walk the streets."

McDermott yawned. "It's not the likes of me, Crane, that you got to talk to."

"To whom do I have to talk, Sergeant? You know Becker's after me."

"Right now you're talking to yourself. Stay out of here if you know what's good for you."

As he left the station-house, Detective Becker jostled him.

"What do I have to do to get straight with you, Detective?"

Becker surveyed him contemptuously. "Go cut your own throat! Big reporter, ain't you?"

"Somebody in the Department raided my room without a search warrant."

"Maybe the next time they'll come with a warrant for your arrest," the detective sneered. "You want material for articles, don't you? We'll teach you what you never learned in school. Your little whore-friend, Dora Clark, is locked up again. How do you like that? But if you don't know what station she's in, and if she ain't booked, you couldn't get a writ if you wanted to, could you?"

"Are you beyond the law, Becker?"

The other spat at his feet. "Keep it up!" he ground out in a deadly tone. "We'll fix you!"

Stephen was shaking. New York, which in the last year had seemed friendly, had turned overnight into a hostile camp. Becker would persecute Dora Clark until she collapsed. And why had they stolen the opium pipe?

In the morning, he hurried to the Pennsylvania Station. He was certain that a plainclothes man followed him as he boarded the train for Philadelphia. The same burly fellow passed him several times in the coach. At the Broad Street Station, Stephen lost him in the crowds.

In Fred Lawrence's office, the young physician asked worriedly, "Have you been sick, Steve?" He reached for his stethoscope. "Take off your shirt. I want to examine you."

Stephen's eyes were bloodshot from lack of sleep, and he had another hacking cough.

While the doctor tapped his chest and listened to his heart, Stephen recited the whole story of Dora Clark and Detective Becker.

"Have you told Mr. Roosevelt?"

"I couldn't get near him at the Mulberry Street headquarters without arousing every spy on his doorstep. He's president of the Police Board, but his colleagues resent him bitterly. I can't get to him. I'm a marked man."

"Send him a telegram."

Stephen was dubious.

"Unless you do something, you can never return to New York without being in danger. If you put Roosevelt, who admires you, on notice, the others may think twice about persecuting you."

At the telegraph office, Stephen wrote, "Confidential. Protest police abuse of powers in maltreating innocent women on city streets. Suggest investigation Dora Clark case. Situation incredible."

After three days with the Lawrences, he returned to New York. A heap of mail awaited him. Theodore Roosevelt, upon receipt of Stephen's telegram, had read the riot act to his police captains on the mistreatment of women. Once more Dora Clark had been released. Now, through her attorney, she had preferred charges against Becker, and Stephen was subpoenaed to testify at the detective's trial before the Police Board.

Stephen was dismayed. The girl, seeking to protect herself, was involving him in another scuffle with the Department.

There were three frantic letters from Amy. "Where are you? Steve, darling, please come to me!"

"I haven't deserved this from you!" she said reproachfully when he appeared. "Thank God you're safe!" She wrung her hands. "Not a word, not a line. I thought the police had you locked in a cell somewhere and were beating you!"

"They wouldn't hurt me."

"Not a word," she moaned. "You just disappeared. I asked Bill Fairman, but he hadn't seen you in several weeks."

"*Bill* Fairman?" he asked, puzzled.

"Leroy. I call him Bill. He knew nothing, nothing!"

316

"I left hurriedly. I told no one." Had Fairman told Willie Hawkins about Amy?

"Not a word to ease my heart. You could have got a message to me. Oh, Steve, I've known so much tragedy in my life. You could have spared me. I can bear anything except not knowing where you are." Her eyes narrowed. "You weren't with those women?"

Coldly, "I'm not a child."

"Forgive me, Steve!" she pleaded, watching his fingers as he lit a cigarette. "I care so much that I forget that I can't mean to you what you mean to me."

He skirted the challenge. Why did women give freely, pretending to be generous, and then in return expect full meed as if they were affianced?

"You're angry with me."

"No, no!"

"I'm so proud of you, I could shout it to the whole world: I love Stephen Crane!" The green eyes glinted. "Oh, Steve, I must be a burden to you. Sometimes I think you feel that I trapped you, and I hate myself for it!"

Trapped! The word made him cringe.

"You've never given me a word of encouragement. I've done all the wooing and the courting."

"Not entirely," he lied.

"You're afraid of falling in love with me. You've always been. It's true, Steve. With you I've had no pride. I surrendered completely, and now I wait for crumbs of your time, of your affection."

"Amy——"

"If you cared for me at all you wouldn't leave me. You would stay here and write. You'd be safe. You wouldn't care what anyone thought. I've told you——"

"I can't be a——" He halted at "prisoner."

"You can't be tied to one woman!" she concluded wretchedly. "You've been accustomed to 'the others' and the quick liaisons. Is that it? Do you need them, Steve, these girls of the street? Are they so important to you? If only I understood your fascination for these vile, ugly harlots!"

He protested that they meant nothing to him.

"Hush, Steve, don't tell me. I shouldn't ask or want to know. You can't belong only to me, or to anyone. Your genius belongs to the world. Yet I'm so torn. Give them up for my sake? We could be so happy together!"

Her persistence alarmed him. Still he knew how to placate her. He stopped her mouth with kisses, the only effective weapon. She moaned and clutched at him in her ardor. She seemed at peace when he left her.

CHAPTER 57

Upon entering the courtroom for the Becker hearing, Stephen was dismayed to see Commissioner Frederick D. Grant, Roosevelt's bitterest opponent, on the bench.

He had naively hoped that, after his telegram, Roosevelt, instead of either of his colleagues, would preside at the trial.

"Outside!" the clerk snapped. "You'll be called in your turn."

Through the next six hours, he leaned against the wall in the corridor and waited impatiently. The only bench was occupied by several patrolmen who chatted in undertones. When he addressed two of the roundsmen from his district, they pointedly ignored him.

As the court recessed, he headed for the staircase. A patrolman barked, "Here, you!" He asked his way to the washroom. Two policemen, talking derisively, accompanied him.

At four o'clock, when he was finally called, he was relieved to see Willie Hawkins inside the courtroom.

No sooner had he been sworn in and asked the usual preliminary questions than Mr. Hinkle, Becker's attorney, assailed him. "Mr. Crane, is it true that, while you were out there in the corridor, you made every effort to eavesdrop on this hearing?"

Stephen flushed. He glanced at the presiding Commissioner, but Grant's heavy features were impassive. "No, sir."

"Isn't it true that you tried your best to overhear what was being said?"

"Through that thick door?" he reported. "And with policemen watching me every minute, for six hours?"

"The witness must answer the questions civilly!" Grant reminded him.

"I couldn't hear anything, sir. Nor did it occur to me——"

Becker was watching him with a knowing leer. Dora Clark, in a dark hat and frock, was whispering to her attorney. He alone had appeared without anyone to advise him on his rights.

Becker's attorney, a stout, florid man with a gravelly voice and an accusing forefinger, fired personal questions: "Are you a native of New York? Are you a graduate of any school? Are you married or single? Do you live alone? What is your roommate's occupation? Have you ever been arrested? Have you ever been fired from any job?"

Stephen protested. "I'm not on trial, your honor!"

The Commissioner grunted. "The witness must answer the questions!"

318

It became apparent, after another barrage, that the defense contended that an author who wrote about prostitutes and alcoholics, and traveled freely among the denizens of the Tenderloin, must be as depraved as those whom he described.

Stephen saw Hawkins pass a note to Arnold Davis, Dora's attorney. Thereafter, the lawyer sought twice to interpose objections. Commissioner Grant advised him sharply that Mr. Crane was not his client.

Hinkle resumed smugly. "Do you have any regular income at all from wages or salary, Mr. Crane?"

Stephen's jaw dropped. "No, sir, but I have published five books——"

"The witness will please answer the question only."

"Your honor, I have no regular income from any source. I am a free-lance reporter and writer. I earn my living——"

The gavel pounded. "The witness is not to make an outburst. It will not be tolerated."

"I am not on trial, your honor."

"Your credibility as a witness is a proper area for examination," Grant ruled.

"But I haven't been permitted to give any evidence, sir. Wouldn't it be proper for me to be allowed to testify first?"

"Mr. Crane, I will not permit you to behave with contempt, either for the Department or for this hearing."

Stephen was breathing heavily. They were trying him for his audacity in gathering material for the police articles, for his telegram to Roosevelt, for his appearance before Magistrate Cornell.

Becker was grinning. Hawkins rose again to whisper to Arnold Davis. The lawyer shook his head.

"Will the witness identify this article?"

It seemed to rise before him out of a mist. "That's an opium pipe."

"And this?"

"A lamp which is used together with the pipe."

"Will the witness examine both of these articles and tell the Commissioner if he recognizes them as his property?"

"They belong to me," he admitted, and turned in his chair. "Your Honor, isn't this entirely irrelevant? I bought this pipe and this lamp as souvenirs when I was writing an article for the *Sun!*"

"Mr. Crane," the Commissioner returned grimly, "I will not tolerate your insolence. You are a sworn witness. Answer the questions."

"You admit then that these 'souvenirs' are your property?"

"I do. And that they were stolen from my room!"

Grant once more pounded the gavel. "If they were stolen from your room, did you immediately report the theft to the police?"

"No, sir. Because I learned from our janitor that police, pretending to be friends, raided my place—without a warrant—and 'confiscated' them. That is, they stole them!"

Hinkle smiled. "Mere surmise, Mr. Crane. I think that we can show that the police would have had sufficient reason to raid your room, as you say. I hand you now a newspaper article on the opium dens of New York, written by you, at least signed by you, which indicates that you have yourself taken opium. Is that correct, Mr. Crane?"

Stephen squirmed. "I sampled it once, as an experiment——"

"Are you an addict?"

"No, sir!"

"But in your article you describe the 'yen-yen' which is known only to the confirmed addict. Is that true?"

"I gathered the impressions. I used my imagination——"

"Mr. Crane," the attorney asked softly, "is it not also true that you have accepted money favors from various of the women in these places of infamy that you have described?"

A cry of rage escaped him. "No, sir! I swear that isn't true!"

"Is it true that you have known prostitutes and madams and other persons of low reputation?"

"Yes, sir."

"Is it not true that you have long known Dora Clark and that you have taken money from her?"

"No, sir!" he shouted. At Grant, he bellowed, "I won't answer any more questions if what he is trying to prove is that I am the wrongdoer instead of Detective Becker!"

Grant angrily hammered the bench.

Dora Clark's attorney, at last, succeeded in calling the Commissioner's attention to the fact that the witness' activities, whether they related to opium or to girls of the streets, could have no bearing on Becker's repeated arrests of the plaintiff.

The Commissioner reflected, and directed Mr. Hinkle to proceed with more pertinent questioning.

In a hollow voice, Stephen recounted once more the story of the arrest at the cable-car tracks on Broadway. Coolly, the attorney led him again and again over the details, implying that Crane must have had a sinister interest in the two girls of the chorus to ride with them in the patrol wagon and to defend them before Sergeant McDermott.

When he was finally dismissed, his collar was drenched and his hands were shaking. He tottered from the stand.

"Don't let those bastards break you, Steve," Hawkins muttered hoarsely. "Hold on now!"

"I walked into—an ambush!" he gasped.

He refused to leave until he had heard Becker testify. Led adroitly by Mr. Hinkle, the detective declared that, as a police officer, he had a right to judge any woman a prostitute if he saw her talking at night to any man on a public thoroughfare.

Stephen groaned. "Pity any woman at the hands of that fiend!"

"How did I get into this?" he moaned again and again to Willie that evening. "I wanted to help that girl. Now they're branding me as a dissolute cad!"

"The girl will lose her suit against Becker. They'll stop at nothing, false testimony or intimidation of witnesses, and Roosevelt can't help you. To defend yourself properly you'd have to hire counsel and fight a long-drawn-out battle. Steve, get out of the city until this quiets down."

"If that girl needs me as her witness, I can't run away."

"Then they'll smear you until you won't have a friend left in the world. They'll put a dozen madams on the stand. They'll— Better go away."

The next day, his spirits lifted when Hawkins produced a copy of the Brooklyn Daily *Eagle*. Under the title, "Mr. Crane and the Police," an editorial that extended two thirds of a column described the entire Becker hearing as a ludicrous farce. Commissioner Grant was severely criticized for permitting Crane to be attacked "without comment or protest." The Department, which had been shielded, was bluntly described as one that had been shown to be, collectively, "one of the most corrupt, brutal, incompetent organizations in the world."

"Everyone doesn't believe that I'm a monster."

"Leave New York," Willie counseled gravely.

CHAPTER 58

Below the editorial in the Brooklyn *Eagle* had been a brief report on a new outbreak of guerrilla warfare in Cuba. The revolutionary Junta, with committees in New York, Washington, and Florida, raised funds from American sympathizers, and landed men and arms on the island. The Spaniards constantly reported victories over the filibusters, yet the expeditions continued to flow across the waters to Cuba. Frederic Remington, the artist, had gone off with Richard Harding Davis to execute illustrations of activities in the field. Ralph Paine, whom Stephen had known in Asbury Park, was listed as a correspondent for New York and Philadelphia papers. Every important newspaper was sending special writers to the Caribbean.

He decided to ask Bacheller to send him to Cuba, and to syndicate his dispatches. He was, at last, convinced that he must leave New York until Becker and his colleagues had forgotten him.

The prospect of traveling out of the country excited him, particularly with the clouds of war swirling so close to American shores. He had written about bloodshed, but he had seen none. On a real battlefield a man might have an opportunity to test his courage. He would be confronting an enemy of unknown dimensions; he would be advancing, rather than retreating, to taunt this grinning Death whom he had derided so often.

"What do you say, Irving?"

Bacheller, his eyes lighting, got to his feet and, hands in his pockets, slowly walked the floor. "The best idea you've had since *The Red Badge*." He pointed a finger at Stephen. "Better than this damned police mess of yours!" In his customary fashion, he discussed the proposal as if the idea had originated with him. "You go over on a filibuster boat. The Junta will tell you how to do it. You get down to Key West, probably, or to Tampa, and hang around till you can buy yourself a place on a gun-runner. That's it!"

"Great idea, Irving!"

"You write and I sell."

He cherished his secret for three weeks before he was prepared to tell Amy. The New York committee for the Junta advised him to wait in Jacksonville; when a filibustering boat was ready a message would reach him.

Meanwhile, Dora Clark, having lost her case against Becker, had, wisely, left both the chorus and the city. Occasionally, the police annoyed Stephen, but he was careful to skirt Becker's precinct and to avoid the Tenderloin.

One night, he encountered a roundsman who had threatened him. Desperately, he pretended to have lost something in the gutter.

"You still looking for trouble, Crane? What did you lose?"

"I think I've lost myself somewhere in the dark," he replied grimly. "If you find me, let me know."

The man twirled his nightstick. "Report it to Lost and Found! Why doncha go back to your hills? That's all they want. Go hang yourself, but don't do it on my beat."

He related the episode to Amy when they dined together that evening. She was wearing a new gown of some sheer green floating fabric.

"They will never forgive you as long as they find you loitering on street corners, or squiring Dora Clark."

"Dora has 'flown the coop.'"

"There will be others. 'Sir Stephen' to the rescue. The easiest way for any woman to attract Stephen Crane is to appear to be in some sort of trouble or danger. Some day you will rescue the wrong woman." Archly: "How many have you known?"

"Hundreds!"

"Deeply, intimately."

He tallied on his fingers. "Three or four."

"Thirty-four, more likely."

"The others wouldn't have me."

"All young and pretty?"

"All women are pretty," he replied. "All women are young."

Crimson wafers appeared on her cheeks. "Must you continue this way, foot-loose and fancy-free? The police will never give up as long as you wander about like a bird, with no home and no ties." She dropped her eyes. "Now if you had your own home and a wife, what reason could they have to pursue you? Everything would be different. You would take your place in the literary scene, with your own study and your own library, a place to entertain your friends, and regular days or evenings when you could be 'at home' to all New York."

"I'd be in harness for fair!"

"You couldn't bear it to belong to one woman only."

An urge to spring to his feet and to run from her seized him, yet he sat as helplessly as a child before its mother. "Some day, Amy," he sighed. The cleverness of women appalled him; against their cunning, a man had no weapon except flight.

"Some day," she mocked. "Don't wait too long."

Teresa entered, bearing a frosted cake that had been decorated with a host of lighted candles. "Ready?" she called.

"Happy birthday!" Amy trilled. "Happy birthday, dear Stephen!"

He remembered with a jolt that it was, indeed, his birthday, November 1st.

"Now blow out the candles and make a wish!"

He paused, thinking, "What shall I wish?" Traitorously, he thought only of Lillie Brewster. A dozen candle-flames resisted. He blew harder until all were out. He stared at the smoking wicks.

"What did you wish?"

"Many happy birthdays together."

He kissed Amy and, impulsively, bussed Mrs. O'Brien on the cheek. "I've never had such a big cake."

"Twenty-five years old!" Amy glowed. "Our young genius."

As he cut the cake, he was musing, "A farewell party!" He would not break the news to her until they were alone in her sitting room.

"Irving Bacheller has ordered me to stand by to leave for Florida. He is paying my way. I'm to board a filibuster boat, run the blockade and get over to Cuba."

Wild terror filled her eyes. "Steve, you'll be killed!"

"No, I won't."

"Steve, I've dreamed it!"

"Amy, I've never seen any real fighting. This is my chance, the real thing. And, meantime, the police will cool off."

She covered her face. "Steve, don't go. You can't. You can't, you mustn't!"

"You're needlessly alarmed," he returned icily. "I've promised

Bacheller I'm going." He put his arm about her waist. "Amy, you'll be proud of me."

"I'll never see you again," she whimpered. For an instant then, hope flickered. "I'll take the train to Florida, and wait for you."

He became sullen.

"You don't want me!" she cried. "It's not Florida or Cuba that you're going to. It's me that you're running away from!" She clutched at his arms. "If you only knew, if you only understood——"

"What are you trying to say, Amy?"

"How much I love you!" she whispered. "How much I love you!"

A wave of fear engulfed him. "Is that all?" he demanded. "Is that all, Amy? Or are you concealing something?"

She turned away and began to sob.

"What is it, Amy, what is it?"

"I'll never see you again."

"Of course you will."

"I should have known that I could never hold you."

"When I come back," he promised tentatively, "we'll be together again."

"Will you return?"

"As soon as I've seen what there is to see, and have written about it. A month or two, maybe three, four."

She dried her eyes. "Where shall I write to you?"

He paused. "If the boat is ready and waiting in some inlet, they'll be leaving the moment I come aboard. I'll write to you." He was lying grimly. "I may not spend more than a night on the coast."

Another tear dropped. "And if I should need you, if I should become ill, or be in trouble——"

"Trouble!" he repeated hollowly, the terror clawing at his throat. He thought that her face had become ghastly pale.

"Willie Hawkins will know where to find me. I have no secrets from him—except about you. If you need anything——" The screw was slowly turning in his entrails. What was she trying to tell him? "Are you——"

"Leave me!" she whispered. "I wish I were dead!"

A lump rose in his throat. "I'll leave money with Willie Hawkins." He was parched and frightened. "If you should need anything."

"Go!"

He threw himself upon his knees and buried his head in her lap until she comforted and forgave him. He could feel her terrible will commanding, drawing with inexorable force. If he yielded, he would never be able to leave her.

"Good-bye, Amy!"

In the night air, he leaned for support against a lamppost. Down the street, a red lantern flickered over an open excavation.

He came bearing gifts, a copy of the fourteenth printing of *The Red Badge* and of the fourth printing of *Maggie*. He was reluctant to tell Willie, but he had no choice.

Hawkins, slumping in his chair, listened like a granite image. He accepted the five hundred dollars that Stephen counted out, and tucked the bills into his cash-box.

"I know how you've worked and starved," he muttered. "Hard rolls and black coffee, sometimes potato salad. She'll have to convince me to get a dollar of this money."

"If she's in trouble, I must help her."

"Trouble! She's been nothing else for you, that man-eater. She's forty-five if she's a day. She's acting her best role, and you've fallen for it."

"Why should she want me?"

"Because you're Stephen Crane. She came here to catch you! I would give her nothing."

"What if she's telling the truth?"

"She has told you nothing. She has hinted, implied, and wept. Oh, she knows you, Steve. She's counting on you to yield."

"I did, Willie," he confessed. "I'm not innocent. That's why I've come to you. You should have seen her. She sat like a statue. She might collapse and die."

Hawkins snorted. "She can take care of herself. Women can, women do!"

"What if she can't? Her sister is a weak woman, and would be of no help to her. If she should need money, I must provide it."

"If you are so certain, why didn't you give her the five hundred dollars yourself?"

He threw up his hands. "I couldn't offend her!"

Hawkins uttered a shout of derision. "Women aren't offended by money! Not harlots or queens. Haven't you learned that yet? You had better go off to Cuba, go anywhere! You're not fit to be left alone with any strong-willed female. Let her open her thighs, and you pass into her as if you were going to your doom in your father's lake of fire!"

"What if——"

"What if nothing! You've told her to call on me, and you've given me the money. You didn't ask me, Steve."

"Willie, you're about the only man I could trust."

Hawkins sniffed.

"Willie, how can I ever repay you?"

"By keeping away from predatory women who clip your wings, truss you up like a fowl, and shove you into their ovens."

As Stephen sat hunched over in his misery, Hawkins relented. "Ah, Steve, when a man has your gifts, who has the right to ask more of him? Anyone may lie at a slut's tit and think himself a hero for the night, but to hug that tit and to see in it the breast that nourishes all mankind, and imagine her a goddess couching strangers in defiance of old Zeus, that takes a poet. If you could be callous with these women, you'd be another kind of man, instead of a dark rider on a mysterious mission that never had a beginning and may never have an end. To make fantasies out of realities and realities out of fantasies is a game for champions. To ride yesterday, today, and tomorrow, as if they were three bareback horses in a circus, and to drive them across a rope-bridge, with a shout at the sky and a spit into the chasm——"

"Whoa, there!"

Hawkins shouted, "Damn, but I envy you!" He waved his fist. "And could beat you for it, too!"

He rubbed his chin, and sighed. "You know, Steve, I've seen her column in the Chicago Daily *News* week after week. All the time she's been here in New York. How does she do it? And you two, cozy as a pair of rabbits. A tricky woman; I remember her. There was a story around the newsroom that on one of her first assignments she reported on a play or some opera. But she didn't attend the performance; she stayed home and wrote her review anyway. Unfortunately for Amy Lee, the play was canceled that opening night for some reason. Next day, all Chicago rocked with laughter. Old White, our managing editor, was ready to maim her!"

He sighed again. "Steve, I'll do my part. I'd say, 'Stay clear of women in Florida.' But not one man in a million can do that and remain a man."

Stephen bought his ticket on the New York & Florida Special, the through-train on the Atlantic coastline. He sat in the outlook car at the rear, and as the wheels pounded, "Amy! Amy!" and the tracks, extruding from under the speeding train, made a ladder to the sky, he fell into a sleep of exhaustion.

V. Hotel de Dreme

*J*ACKSONVILLE, tucked inland twenty-five miles from the sea on the north bank of the St. Johns River, was a blazing outpost among palm trees and coconut groves.

The St. James Hotel, covering an entire block, was a proud little village under a single roof. It boasted spacious rooms, electric lights, a band to blare in the sweltering afternoons, and an orchestra to play in the evening for dancers young and old. Thick rugs and high ceilings absorbed unwelcome sounds; the waiters were as solemn as doorposts. Every human function seemed to be carried out with starched crispness, on fresh linens, and with decorum. The wine steward wore about his neck a magnificent metal chain that would have staggered a knight of the Holy Roman Empire.

Stephen, registering as "Samuel Carlton, New York," waited for a visit from agents of the Junta. He listened to conversations in the lobby and in the barbershops. Every colloquy seemed to be spiced with the languorous Spanish phrases, and the hated name of Captain-General Weyler, "the Butcher" of Cuba, and the sacred names of Maximo Gomez and Antonio Maceo, the courageous leaders of the insurrection.

He bought, against Bacheller's account, a brace of revolvers that would have impressed Henry Fleming, a grand supply of bright cartridges, an ugly machete, a razor-sharp sheath knife, the world's heaviest boots, two pairs of breeches, a raincoat with roomy pockets, and three soft-collared shirts. He deposited Bacheller's gold doubloons with the hotel cashier, but continued to wear his money-belt as if St. Christopher had blessed it.

On the wharves, mysterious craft steamed up the river, took on cargo, and disappeared. Offshore, the American Navy maintained swift patrol boats that skimmed about like outsized beetles. Farther at sea, the Spaniards were said to be lurking in heavily armed ships that waited, with gun decks cleared, to discourage Yankee gun-runners.

The atmosphere of conspiracy delighted him. At the bars, men drank often and deeply to *"Cuba libre!"* as if a course in oblations must help the cause. Outside the customhouse, sailors swaggered and landsmen with lobster-red faces mimicked them. Each morning there was new talk of some saucy steamer, like *The Three Friends,* which, laden with guns and panting rebels, had darted from a swampy inlet, outward bound for the great adventure.

His alias fooled no one at the St. James, for on the fourth day, mail addressed to "Stephen Crane c/o Samuel Carlton" arrived from Irving Bacheller and from Ed and Isaac Marshall.

To conserve his funds, he considered moving to the New Duval or the Everett. However, he was enjoying the pretty faces and the narrow-waisted figures at the St. James. Frugally, he took his meals at any lunchroom on Bay Street or Forsyth Street, or at some dockside saloon. He drank cool beer and, for small stakes, played dice or poker with any available strangers.

The clerks and the bellboys suggested female entertainment. But the shoeshine boys, to the *menage* born, had been touting the brothels: "Cheap, cheap!" since the day he had arrived. Every correspondent had been adopted by at least one boy, some by three or four, who were sworn to trail him, and to polish his boots the instant a grain of dust settled on the gleaming leather.

Sancho was Stephen's shadow. The lad, about twelve or thirteen, with a face the hue of strong tea and eyes like polished jet, breathed advertisement: "Know all houses on Ward Street." He was as persistent as a lottery-ticket vendor who peddles only winners. "Hoohouses, no?"

"No!"

"All collah, all style, two-way, t'ree-way, how about?"

"Go away!"

"Got a sista. Bee-ooruhful!"

Stephen licked the end of his cigar and studied the glossy black hair. The ready rag was already wiping his boots. "Sancho, how old is your sister?"

"Fo'teen." The face turned up; the eye-agates rolled. "Too ol'?"

"Sancho, you got a mother and father?"

"No fatha." Hesitation. "You like motha betteh like sista?"

330

"Go chase yourself, you rascal!" He flipped a nickel into the air and swatted it with his palm.

The urchin shouted and scrambled in the dirt.

That evening, a Cubano in a Panama hat knocked on his door at the St. James. "Señor Carlton?" Captain Edward Murphy, skipper of the *Commodore*, would soon be steaming southward.

He found Murphy, a strapping, redhaired and freckled Irishman, playing whist at Kelly's Occidental Saloon. Stephen offered to sign on as an ordinary seaman.

"At twenty dollars a month?"

"I'll pass up the money."

"I've got a full crew," Murphy replied. "And I'll be carrying a dozen or more, uh, passengers. Haven't got the space."

"What's it worth, Captain?"

"A hundred in gold."

"Sold!"

"Got to wait till the cargo is ready and the *insurrectos* give the signal." The Navy had halted him on an earlier venture.

While Stephen nursed a single whiskey, the Captain amiably tossed down three: "*Cuba libre!*" They visited several neighboring bars to become better acquainted.

As the evening aged, Captain Murphy proposed a visit to the Hotel de Dreme on the outskirts of the city in the La Villa district.

"There can't be a joint with a name like that!"

Murphy chortled. "No place like it from Boston to Tampa. Strictly a boardinghouse, you'll hear, with roulette and dice." He winked. "The usual circuses in the bedrooms. Beautiful trollops." He contributed choice descriptions.

"Why 'Hotel de Dreme'?"

"Named after Ethel de Dreme, the former owner." Murphy let out a guffaw. "It could only happen in Jacksonville. Cora Taylor—Miss Cora, please!—is the owner now."

Through the palms, the large semicircular lighted sign was visible for three hundred yards: HOTEL DE DREME. A player piano was tinkling. The rooms on the first floor were brilliantly illuminated; in the upper stories, the shades were drawn.

A dark-skinned groom, attending the line of hacks at the porte-cochere, helped them down. At the door, a pretty mulatto maid smiled, "Welcome to Hotel de Dreme!"

A Florentine mirror observed them as they crossed the lobby. The stairs were carpeted; large chromos in ornate gilt frames hung on the walls. Hotel de Dreme was surely an example of that gracious living of which Jacksonville boasted.

"Good evening, gentlemen!" A bright crimson velvet gown addressed them.

Stephen looked into the bluest eyes he had ever seen. The small face was so youthful that she might have been a schoolgirl who had wandered upon the dance floor in search of a partner, but the fiery velvet hugging the figure was a blazon of defiance. The golden coiffure gave her style and height; she was a small girl. Finely-shaped eyebrows, a petite nose, and a small, firm mouth that threatened to pout, and coils of golden-blonde hair wound again and again to a bird's nest.

The Captain was at his politest. "Good evening, Miss Cora. Came to play a little roulette."

The blue eyes probed. "Your pleasure, Captain!"

"My friend, Samuel Carlton."

"Welcome to Hotel de Dreme, Mr. Carlton." The pearl choker sat above a milk-white skin that came alluringly to the swell of young breasts. Her gown, narrowing at the waist, extolled the line of the thigh.

"Thank you, Miss Cora." A large diamond sparkled on her hand.

"I trust you enjoy your visit." She held a gold fan to her white teeth. The eyes continued to probe.

Her speech was not Southern; English perhaps, more likely Northern, with traces of Boston and New York. Stacking his chips at the roulette table, following the little white ball as it skipped in the numbered shallows on the turning wheel, Stephen murmured, "A cool little lady, the madam. Thoroughbred."

Murphy was pleased. "Cora Taylor? Smart. Mind, it's hands off Cora! She's taken. Also got a husband somewhere. You hear different stories, that he's the son of a lord or a general, that she led the big life in London until she up and left him."

Miss Cora was observing the players at a dice table. The dealer, in green eyeshade and black alpaca coat, was chanting: "Eight! The point is eight!" A moment later, softly: "Place your bets, gentlemen! I've got a new shooter."

"Easy to believe any story, except why she's here!"

Murphy chuckled. "Don't get a sweet tooth for her. She'll have a girl for you. They don't board in, a matter of pride with her. But she'll give you anything you want. Quietly. She don't like the noise and the cussing, Steve. The lady herself? She's taken." He heaved a mock sigh. "I'd like to peel off that red velvet and give her a tumble, wouldn't you? The rich always get the best pieces, don't they?"

Miss Cora caught Stephen staring brazenly. She swam toward him, silver slippers kicking the crimson velvet.

"Shift for yourself, Captain," he muttered. "I'm heading out to sea."

"Mr. Carlton, is there anything you wish that you do not see?"

"Yes, Ma'am," he grinned, and let his gaze rove impudently.

The blue eyes froze. "Try your luck, Mr. Carlton." The fan gestured toward the roulette wheel. She tapped his shoulder and swept away.

"Polite and cool," he reflected. "A fine back, too." Addressing Murphy: "A vestibule virgin?"

The Captain frowned at the pun which, apparently, was beyond him. "She arrived here last year and settled down in a suite at the St. James, with a woman companion and a maid. Then she bought this establishment from Ethel de Dreme. The place has been booming since she took it over."

Stephen disliked roulette. Tonight, he won four times on number fifteen. He suspected that the wheel was controlled somehow. He slipped the chips into his pocket and wandered toward a blackjack table.

A servant approached with a box of Havanas: "Compliments of Miz Cora, sah!"

Bored players were strolling into an adjacent room. On a giant buffet sat hot and cold dishes in gleaming silver; two black men were carving roasts of beef and ham. At a small mahogany bar, a servitor was pouring champagne. No money changed hands. Free lunch! Hotel de Dreme's clientele was not drawn from the poorer classes.

A murmur ran through the assemblage. On the staircase, a tall, generously proportioned female in a black sheath gown was descending on the arm of a stout man in evening dress. Stephen noted the rouged cheeks and the ample bust which threatened to pop from the bodice. The kohled eyes shifted with that calculation that comes naturally to women who have stripped many men to their boyishness.

In the gaming room, the stout escort bowed; the girl was already drifting away. At the roulette table, she caught a glance from the dealer and placed herself beside another player in evening dress. As her bust grazed his shoulder, the man swung about, beaming. He was evidently next.

A redhaired girl in a green gown entered the room. She, too, was followed by an escort whom she here discarded. By some prearranged signal, she too sailed toward a new patron.

Everything seemed cleverly administered. The earlier admirers headed for a door marked "Office."

He sauntered closer. Miss Cora, seated in a carved teakwood chair, was jotting down figures. He revised his estimate of the youthful madam as the customers paid from well-filled wallets. The girls, assembled to accommodate the prosperous clients, were offered with finesse; the hire-money was turned over as smoothly as at a bank.

He leaned against the doorjamb. Miss Cora was totaling a column of figures; her diamond flashed as her fingers moved. Curiously, he peered at the figures. The smallest set of digits was twenty dollars; the largest, including perhaps food and wine, was fifty dollars.

His gaze went to a book on the window seat. The light tan cloth binding jolted him.

"Sir!" She was sitting back, indignant. "Mr. Carlton, I must ask you not to intrude!"

"My apologies, Miss Cora." He suppressed an urge to tell her the joke. "Do you permit poker games in your establishment?"

She winced. "There are plenty of establishments in Jacksonville where poker games are welcome. Not at the Hotel de Dreme." She resented his smile. "Mr. Carlton, may I ask what you find so amusing?"

"I see a book by a man I know."

"*George's Mother!* Have you read it?"

"I've read all his works."

"Our bookseller had only this one." Defiantly, "I wept over the last scene."

"He might be pleased to know that you were so affected."

He was prepared to mock-describe Stephen Crane.

"Excuse me, Mr. Carlton." The blue eyes had risen to an approaching client.

Stephen crossed to the window seat. While she concluded the transaction, he picked up the volume. As he thumbed the pages, he was amazed to hear Miss Cora present charges totaling thirty-eight dollars, the eight dollars "for a quart of iced French champagne."

"On twenty-four hours' notice, we can arrange suitable entertainment for any number of your guests. Our ladies are carefully selected; I choose them myself from the big cities. They know how to conduct themselves."

"A whore is a whore——"

Her face became livid. "Sir!"

The man pretended to cringe. "Now, I didn't mean anything, Miss Cora. I spend a lot of money here, don't I?"

Stiffly, she bade him good night.

On the flyleaf of the book, the amused Stephen wrote: "To an unnamed sweetheart. Stephen Crane."

"Mr. Carlton, what are you doing?"

He passed the copy.

"I do not consider this a jest I can appreciate!" She glanced at the flyleaf. "You said your name was Carlton!"

"Alias Stephen Crane."

She regarded him distrustfully.

"Shall I quote from it? 'When he entered the chamber of death, he was brooding over the recent encounter and devising extravagant revenges upon Blue Billie and the others.' That's the first sentence of the last chapter."

She turned to the last chapter. "I should have known." A blush came to her cheeks. "I dreamed that someone like you would appear."

"You believe in dreams, Miss Cora?"

Earnestly, "They have rarely failed me. Wherever I have been, the big, the important, events of my life have been telegraphed to me in predictions, forebodings. You would not believe it."

"I might. What was the nature of your prediction or foreboding about me?"

A smile sat in the corner of her mouth. "Can you wait till we close?"

At three o'clock, when most of the guests had departed and the doors to the gaming room had been shut, he lingered in the drawing room.

Captain Murphy peered in and winked. "Don't forget the *Commodore*. I won't wait for you!"

Miss Cora was consulting with her staff. From the window, Stephen counted eight or nine girls leaving in two carriages; evidently, only a favored few had lodgings on the premises.

He strolled back to the office. Miss Cora was stuffing a packet of banknotes into a wall-safe. The mulatto maid handed her a cash-box.

In her apartment, they shared a supper of lobster salad, cold roast chicken, and a bottle of white wine. He studied the small, bejeweled hands as they skillfully carved the fowl and deposited choice pieces on his plate.

"At this hour I'm always famished," she sighed.

She told him that she was a native of Boston. Her father had died of tuberculosis when she was six; her mother had remarried, but since the child had disliked her stepfather, she had been raised in the home of her grandfather, a restorer of oil paintings. With the inheritance he had left her, she had bought the Hotel de Dreme.

She had been married when very young to Thomas Vinton Murphy, a dry-goods merchant with whom she had traveled through Europe. She had divorced him and married Captain Donald Stewart of a distinguished English family. Life at Harrington Gardens in London had been delightful, but she had been bitterly disappointed in the Captain.

"Life rolls the dice and the numbers fall where they will."

"Fate gives one few choices," he agreed.

She lifted her head appealingly. "One is fortunate to make a point anywhere." She added the last with a note of resignation.

He stifled a yawn, and apologized.

"You may stay overnight. Rooms are available."

His eyes kindled. He had already disrobed Cora Taylor mentally. The soft voice, the blue eyes, the honey-blonde hair, and the milk-white skin excited him.

"Do not misunderstand me," she said firmly. "I am not inviting

335

you to share my quarters." She folded her hands. "We can be friends, can't we?"

"Shall I dwell among mine enemies?"

"Dwell among friends. Perhaps God will show us the way."

He viewed her skeptically. She, the mistress of an elegant brothel, considered herself above her occupation, and talked of travel and literature as if she were a learned spinster. Yet within that lovely head must reside every skill in vice that any madam in the Tenderloin had at her command. She might weep over the death of Mrs. Kelcey in *George's Mother*, but she was a madam still, and probably the sweetheart of the Taylor whose name she used.

The suite to which she led him included a large sitting room, two gleaming mahogany bureaus and wardrobes, a leather-covered lounge, and several deep chairs. The zinc tub in the bathroom was as large as a rowboat. "Fit for the Prince of Wales! Has he been here lately?"

"We often have guests from the finer families." She produced towels and soap from the linen closet, and smartly pulled back the tufted bedspread. "I trust that you will not smoke in bed. Men are careless. It distresses me to find holes burned in my sheets and pillowcases."

As she placed a nightshirt on the bed—"This will fit you"—he slipped his arm about her waist. She was tightly corseted.

"Mr. Crane!"

He pressed his lips against her mouth. She accepted the kiss wide-eyed.

"Stay with me?"

Color flooded her cheeks. "Good night, Mr. Crane."

Lying in the dark, he wondered about Cora Taylor. No one could force a strong-willed woman to accept a responsibility abominable to her. She had sought the ultimate in degradation. She could not blind herself to the acts her girls performed; she hired them, perhaps schooled them. Had she been trapped in the quagmire of her own rebellion? How much of her story was credible? Harlots always spun romantic myths to please naive clients. The lies were so much more pleasant than the truth that the girls often believed their own fictions.

The wind was in the palm trees. He heard horses neighing and stomping. From the stables? Or were there riders in the woods tonight?

They breakfasted at noon. She was pale and somber: a little gold cross depended between her breasts. Twice before dawn he had heard footsteps at his door, and had lasciviously anticipated her weight on the bed, her warm bosom against his back.

"I dreamed that you came to me," he said, "that we were together."

She tossed her head angrily. They finished the meal in silence.

336

Later, riding in her carriage, they paused near the river under a blue sky that was streaked occasionally by the slow flight of herons and clumsy pelicans.

She was melancholy. "Is the world real?"

He was silent. At night a sinner, at noon a penitent?

"It must be since we suffer in it," she replied to her own question.

"Or do we dream that we do?" he murmured, to encourage her.

She told him that she kept a commonplace book in which she recorded random thoughts and quotations from Shakespeare, Byron, Burns, and Keats. She esteemed the women writers, George Sand, Elizabeth Barrett Browning and George Eliot.

In the marshes behind them, he heard shots. Greedy plume-hunters were murdering the egrets.

CHAPTER 60

At the St. James, a Western Union order for ninety-five dollars was in his box. He had been spending freely, and had asked Hawkins to send him one hundred. With a sinking heart, he noted that the money had been dispatched by Leroy Fairman.

The clerk said, "There's also a letter, sir."

Fortunately, Willie's brief note explained. Amy, instead of calling upon Hawkins, had appealed to Fairman. The latter had reported to Willie that she urgently required help. Immediately, Hawkins had paid over thirty-five dollars.

Stephen sat beside his bed, too dispirited to undress or to remove his boots. Amy must, indeed, be in trouble.

He could not guess how much Bill Fairman knew. Yet Willie had entrusted him to dispatch the money to "Samuel Carlton." Willie—canny Willie!—had deducted the cost of the telegraph service and the transfer of funds, and so had transmitted a balance of ninety-five dollars instead of one hundred.

He slipped the bolt on the door, drew the window shades, and tried to sink into bottomless night. At intervals he awakened with a start. Orange and blue lights flickered before his eyes.

He could not still his apprehensions. He feared the worst, yet dared not face what the worst might be. The image of Amy swept his mind like a figure on a gallows.

That evening Morton, the night clerk, slipped another letter under his door. Again from Hawkins.

Fairman had told Willie that Amy must have one hundred and twenty dollars in a lump sum. She must have it positively on a certain day! Cautious Willie had insisted on a formal request for the

337

money. Amy had complied in a note to his office by "District Messenger No. 2022." Willie had promptly handed over his check.

Stephen reeled to the basin to cool his feverish lips and forehead. His cheeks were stubbled; he looked weary, gaunt, and disheveled. One hundred and twenty dollars could only be the fee for some special, perhaps illicit, medical treatment. What if she died?

At midnight, he hired a carriage to take him to the Hotel de Dreme.

Cora Taylor paled when he strode into the crowded gaming room. "Were you ill?"

"I'm perfect." He tried to smile. "I am per-fect!"

"You were secluded——"

"Thinking. Worrying——" How did she know?

"Will you stay tonight?" She saw his eyes follow a tall, redhaired girl. "Do you want company? Is that it?"

"No." He hesitated. "Will you put me up?"

"The maid will show you to my rooms. You don't want——"

"No, Miss Cora."

She rewarded him with a little smile.

He dozed on the canopied bed. When she joined him, she seemed pale and agitated. She handed him the Jacksonville *Times-Union. The Three Friends,* which had gone off to Cuba to run munitions, had been seized by the Navy as she had tied up at the foot of Ocean Street. The charge was piracy. *The Three Friends,* fleeing the enemy, had fired its howitzer and had damaged a Spanish patrol boat.

"Is this what you are after? Death or capture on the high seas?"

"How can you guess what I am after, Miss Cora?"

"I have the right friends in the right places. I know precisely why you are in Jacksonville."

He grimaced. "No one has died yet."

She stamped her foot. "I'll never understand you men who run to court death! You so much fear being restrained that you would tempt fate and risk imprisonment in a Spanish dungeon."

"Shall I stay here with the girls? I must go to meet the enemy somewhere."

Her eyes narrowed. "So there *is* an enemy! In New York? I suspected that you were running away from someone!"

"Only a woman," he returned roguishly.

"I thought so! Stephen Crane wouldn't run from a man."

"She threw herself at me, and now behaves like a woman scorned."

"Ignore her!" she snapped. "Forget her! Women always do that. I know more about them than you do. And about men, too." Shrewdly, "She must be older than you."

"How can you know that?"

"You would not be smitten with a girl younger than you. You are

338

the kind of man who is always attracted to someone older." Half-seriously, "I am older than you. By two years. Is that enough?"

"You're wiser than I am by twenty. And so is this woman in New York."

"I should like to talk to her," Cora said grimly. "We would understand each other."

"Thank you."

"You wouldn't permit it, I know. But I could promise that your problem with her would vanish after I spoke to her."

In the suite that he had occupied on his first visit, he made a feeble effort to detain her.

"I choose not to be another woman on your list. If I ever held you, Stephen Crane, I'd never let you go."

"I dare you!"

She did not accept the dare until several hours had passed and he was fast asleep.

He awakened and, as he clasped her warm figure in the dark, knew that he had won.

At dawn, she wheedled, "What is her name? Tell me more, Steve. You need to be protected from such women! I would scorn to hold a man who didn't want me."

"Even if he had wronged you?"

"I would curse his ghost and forget him!"

"Not everyone has your audacity." There was the word for Cora: "audacity."

She gazed at him simply. "Isn't it self-respect that you mean? Is she accepting your money?"

"Modest sums."

"There is no modesty in money!" she retorted. "Harlot for a pound, harlot for a thruppence!"

He saw that she had conceived a hatred for the other woman. To defend Amy, however mildly, was to outrage Cora.

"How a man could grow up, with sisters of his own, and sweethearts when he went to school, and girls here and there, and know so little about the female creature that was driven out of Eden, is beyond my understanding. A woman uses every charm, from the roots of her hair to the tips of her toes, to attract a man. And when she gets him, she brands him: 'This man is mine!' She would sooner see you dead at her feet than surrender you to another woman!"

"That can't be true of all women," he demurred. "I've known of a woman who sent her young lover away——"

"She was done with him then, or had something better to turn to, her social position, or some older association."

"And I've known of a woman who denied her love because to continue it would be to expose her lover to the jealousy and wrath of her estranged husband."

339

"She was choosing the stronger horse!"

"Also a woman who came a thousand miles for the love of a man she hardly knew, whom she had seen only once——"

"Like a hunter going after the rare antelope!" she concluded triumphantly. "Steve, you can tell me nothing about the breed. Envy, avarice, greed, and lust. You see her with her eyes shining. I see her as she is, vengeful, cruel, merciless, with her claws out; beneath the décolletage, I hear the belly purring. You're safer with one of my girls who is what she is and damn-the-world! than with one of those respectable wrens who bobs her tail meekly but, at heart, is a bloodthirsty tiger!"

He was awed by the strength and the drive in her. "All this because Adam gave up a rib!"

"Taken from him while he was asleep. The creation of woman began with a piece of thievery, you see, and, endowed with her feline gifts, she can't help being what she is, half-goddess, half-harlot."

He winked. "Exception?"

She planted a kiss on his mouth. "Be warned, Steve. If I were free, you'd not get free of me."

"Captain Stewart?"

"He'll never give me a divorce."

"The other man, whatever his name is?"

"Al Taylor befriended me and advised me at a time when I was sorely beset. But for him I might have——"

"Where is he?"

"Away—for the moment. He'll be back within the month."

"And when he returns? What about us? Is this the end of the road?"

She sighed.

She was Cora Taylor, born Cora Howarth, legally Cora Stewart. She had also been Cora Murphy. How many other Coras had there been?

"I was a terrible little liar. Maybe that's why I've always enjoyed romances, stories better than any I could make up. Grandfather never punished me; I could outwit him. My aunt Mary Holder, I lived with her before I married Murphy, is a dear soul. She is still in New York." She paused. "She believes that I run a boarding-house."

"Tell me more."

"Father died when he was thirty-five. I wish that he had been alive when I grew up. I often pray for him."

"You are religious?"

"I need God, Steve."

"Did you love Stewart?"

"With all my heart. Love is a candle that will burn forever if it is sheltered from the wind."

"What happened?"

"He blew it out."

Where was Stewart? In India? No, in Africa.

"In those days I had a frightful temper. We quarreled. He had been severely wounded. I liked to gad about, he did not." Quickly, "I've changed, Steve."

"And the Hotel de Dreme?"

The little foot tapped the floor. "You can be hateful! I had no choice."

"You made this choice. The black truth is the best truth."

Her bosom heaved. "Is the black truth the best truth for you, too?"

"Always!" he growled. "I'm clay, common clay. But Cora knows better. She does, doesn't she?"

"Yes." She threw her arms about him. "Yes, I knew. I was wicked, I hated everything and everyone."

Her softness and warmth thrilled him. "Yes, I knew," she repeated. She was an exciting woman, even if a dozen men had sported with her.

At peace, they praised each other.

"You have authority, Steve, and you are so handsome. Your profile is strong, your mouth is sensuous—I love your mouth!—but everything else about you is gentle, sensitive, and brooding. God was good to send you to me."

He basked in her admiration, comforting himself that he was too solidly armored with skepticism to be affected. He could not forget her profession, not even when, at their flood-tide moments, they achieved the physical communion that, with thunder and eruption, shatters order into chaos and slowly reassembles the fragments into happy mosaics. He had never known this total, draining, peremptory satisfaction that a woman's yielding can deliver to the man who lies over her.

CHAPTER 61

Christmas Eve was revelry at the Hotel de Dreme. The verandah was strung with lanterns; a large green wreath had been fixed over the doorway, lesser wreaths hung in the windows. A fir tree that had been brought from Georgia by coastal steamer, brushed the ceiling in the gaming room. Cora and the girls had trimmed it with candles, tinsel, and colored balls, and decorated the branches with silver garlands.

Stephen wondered if Al Taylor would appear this evening. By nine o'clock, nearly fifty guests were at the roulette wheel and at the other tables. The girls, gaily dressed, descended the staircase at the usual intervals, and moved with their studied languor toward new customers. If Cora's lover was on the premises, he was incognito. Stephen wondered when Cora had her liaisons, and whether they met at the Hotel de Dreme. Perhaps Taylor had shared the same bed in which he and Cora had made love together.

A sumptuous dinner was served, at a banquet table set with silver and crystal. Silver wine-buckets stood on the sideboard; the champagne glasses were filled again and again. Cora had placed Stephen on her right and Captain Murphy on her left. Fifteen girls, flanked by guests he had encountered either in the gaming rooms or in the lobby of the St. James, ranged on either side.

Turkeys, crisply browned and garnished, were carved, and the servants passed huge tureens of vegetables, and cranberry sauce.

"I ordered everything to be prepared as I remembered Grandfather's Christmas dinner, including the mince pie and the brandied sauce."

Stephen drily offered a toast "to Miss Cora's Gran'daddy!"

On the stairs, Jessica, a raven-haired lass with an appetite as sharp as her tongue, was having her stays released by little Doctor Flinders, her table companion, who was now agreeably tipsy.

"I feel as if I'd swallowed a stowaway," Stephen groaned, refusing the dessert.

Cora promised that he should have another banquet on New Year's Day. She boasted that she knew that the *Commodore* would not leave until after the holidays.

Captain Murphy put down his brandy glass. "You know more about my plans than I do, Miss Cora."

"I know and hear many things." She smiled.

In her room, Stephen murmured, "At Christmas holiday time you will not have a visit from your friend?"

In an instant, dark anger flooded her face. "I do not choose to discuss it!"

"I have told you of my affairs."

"I won't talk of him." She stamped her foot. "I won't!"

The next day, Captain Murphy called at the St. James. "Be ready any time."

"You said January 2nd."

"Any time, Steve." He wagged a finger. "This date will not leak out unless you give it away."

On Wednesday, a seaman hailed him at the newsstand. With a tug at his forelock, the man whispered, "Captain wants you aboard at noon tomorrow."

"At midday!"

"Aye, aye, sir."

Stephen chuckled at the nerve of Murphy to leave in broad daylight. He packed and drove off for a last visit to the Hotel de Dreme.

Cora had strung Japanese lanterns across the verandah. She had secured a supply of paper hats and party favors. A van had delivered ten cases of champagne that had come in by steamer from Nassau.

"Cora likes parties," Stephen said.

She clasped her hands like a child. "They are something to look forward to and something to look back to." She became sober. "In a few days, you'll be leaving me as you left the woman in New York. I wonder if I shall ever see you again."

"You'd never give this place up."

Cautiously, "Where would I go?" The blue eyes softened. "If you said, Come with me, Cora! I'd go with you to the ends of the earth."

"If you were free."

She became wistful. "Try me."

At nine o'clock in the morning, he breakfasted alone, and asked for a carriage.

"Miss Cora ain't awake yet."

"Don't disturb her."

He was lighthearted again when he reached the St. James. It was always the same: a feeling of relief when he escaped a woman; the regrets, if any, would come later.

He had telegraphed Hawkins for another fifty dollars. The Western Union money order was there, also a letter.

Hawkins wrote that he had been paying out additional sums to Amy Lee; he had receipts for every dollar. He enclosed cuttings of her column "Echoes from Mimic Land" from the Chicago Daily News. On successive days, when Amy had presumably been in New York, her newspaper had carried articles over her signature. She had reviewed E. H. Sothern's performance in "Enemy to the Kings" as if she had been present in the theater. Hawkins had scrawled: "How does she do it?"

Stephen grasped at the hope that Amy had left New York, and was merely feigning illness. Yet that was unlikely unless she had persuaded Bill Fairman to go along with the game. At least, she had survived her mysterious ordeal.

He was on the wharf at high noon.

Although the revenue cutter Boutwell lay at anchor downstream, a procession of Negro stevedores carried boxes of ammunition and bundles of rifles up the gangway to the hatches of the Commodore as calmly as if they were loading oranges. A file of Cubans stared at him impassively as he went aboard.

"Cuba libre!" Stephen saluted them.

To a man, they replied, "Cuba libre!"

343

While they were waiting for Captain Murphy to return from the customhouse, Morton, the night clerk at the St. James, ran up the gangplank.

"Mr. Crane!" He waved a bottle of cognac. "Miss Cora's compliments. She says that she'll have dinner ready for you whenever you get back."

"Thank you, Morton." Her informants had finally caught up with him. "Tell her I'll come to claim it."

It was six o'clock before the brawny Murphy reappeared. Several armed Cubans trotted at his heels. Someone whistled, and other Cubans suddenly sprinted aboard from the dockside. To the first mate, the Captain shouted, "All ready. Get under way!"

Soon the *Commodore* was swinging clear of the dock. She uttered several long blasts of her whistle, and slipped away. Downstream, a light fog reached out to receive her.

The old tug had no sooner entered rough waters than she was waddling like a drunken beldame; she seemed to know better than her handlers that she was no match for the open sea. The deck heaved. The fog thickening, rolled down the companionway and fleecily insinuated itself into the bowels of the craft.

Stephen, with the damp in his lungs, went below to his bunk. He sprawled on his stomach, with his arms wrapped about the mattress, and pitched with every convulsion that shook the boat. Twice, he was rudely tumbled to the floor. He vowed that if he ever reached dry land again he would confine his journeys to trains and carriages.

He discovered that a vessel like the *Commodore*, bored with the years of steaming upright in the St. Johns River, had a childish desire to ride the ocean waves on its side. The engines, which should have been pounding rhythmically underneath him, also pounded overhead. The bulkhead thumped at his crown.

Twice before reaching the sea the *Commodore* had stuck in the mud. Stephen wished that they had stayed there.

Sometime during the second night, the *Commodore* gave a sudden hideous lurch. He heard frantic shouting and rushed to the pilothouse. There was trouble in the engine room.

Eight inches of bilge water swirled in the hold. He staggered to a place in the chain of Cubans who, knee-deep in the gray, sloppy stuff, were passing buckets up and out, while the machinery, one oily steel forearm visible, clanged and banged and clattered. Jets of steam hissed.

"'Ere now! This way." Higgins, the oiler, showed him with one strong swoop how to get a bucket full. "Don't want to drown us, do you? She's leaking bad!"

The Cuban Rojo, evidently a leader, was giving the commands. Stephen obeyed willingly. "*Alla voy, señor!*" "I'm coming, sir." He was sent to the afterhold where the steam pumps had fouled. He followed Higgins, who dashed wide-legged, as if to proceed thus in a heaving, sliding ship was as natural as strolling down Bay Street.

Midway, Stephen sagged. *"Que tiene usted?"* "What's the matter with you?" They held him up. He had not been giddy in the heat of the engine room; he was ashamed of this weakness in the afterhold. Rojo ordered him on deck.

The sight of the ocean at night, with a gale blowing and white seas rolling, alarmed him. He had not thought, while working below, that their peril could have increased. The wind thrust invisible hands at his chest. He seized a grab-rail.

A boat was being lowered. He stood aside, dumfounded. This was madness! But Cubans were dropping into it. As he shouted scornfully, the crest of a wave reached over the side and drenched him.

"She's sinking!" someone cried.

The *Commodore*'s whistle began to scream like a hysterical woman. He turned about aimlessly. Where was Captain Murphy?

"Man the lifeboats!" the mate bellowed.

The faces of the men, struggling aslant the deck, were blanched by terror. A stranger toppled over a huge valise. Stephen hesitated; he had no desire to desert the tugboat for the howling caldron of the sea.

Someone jabbed him. He must climb to the lifeboat on top of the deckhouse. *"Lancha salvavidas!"* they screamed: the lifeboat. He did not remember the strain of climbing, yet he was suddenly up there, bending in the wind beside Higgins and the two stokers. "Push!" The boat seemed to weigh, he thought, as much as a Broadway cable-car. Montgomery and others appeared and rigged a tackle to a leeward davit. Still the lifeboat refused to budge

Mr. Granes, the first mate, cursed like a prophet condemning Sodom and Gomorrah. "Push, you——"

From his perch, Stephen was surprised to see the boat launched at last, surprised greatly to see men frantically leaping into it. *"Alza los remos!"* "Hold on to your oars!" The first boat was already being tossed on the waves like a toy. At intervals, the gale, lashing at the figures, froze them motionless as if they were part of an illustration.

A fist nudged him to jump into the boat. He refused angrily. Lowering himself to the deck, he muttered, "Damn fools!" He could not leave Captain Murphy. He beat his way among the panicked men.

The Captain had evidently injured his arm, for it was bound in a sling. "Stand by!" he shouted at Crane. He was pale but calm.

Stephen found himself accepting a five-gallon jug of water. He danced about helplessly with his burden.

"Shift for yourself!" Murphy boomed.

Stephen kicked off his shoes and watched them slide overboard. "If we're going to swim I won't need them, will I, Ed?"

Murphy gave him a comradely slap on the shoulder.

Told to help launch the ten-foot dinghy, he went on with his jug like a comical dancer hugging a short, stout partner.

He saw men wearing life preservers. When the Captain shouted that he must wear one, too—"*Cinto de salvamento!*"—as if Stephen could not understand English, his jaw dropped. It must be true that they were "leaking bad."

Nursing his arm, Captain Murphy tried to assist with the dinghy. "Get in!"

He stood dazed.

Murphy shoved him. "Get in!"

As the dinghy was lowered, he had a desire to leap out and cling to the tugboat, but the ocean came up violently and he was riding up and down in the little craft. He clutched at his money belt as a snarling wave slapped his face.

They lowered the water jug, which he could not remember having surrendered. Again he clasped it in his arms. The cook came down and was thrown against the gunwale. There was blackness, but he could see no sky; only a roaring, raging sea in which the dinghy bobbed beside the tug like a feeble calf near its mother.

He spied the crowded lifeboat far ahead, and the oars pulling.

Now a spar of light defined the horizon. It came to him that a whole day had passed and another had arrived—where had the hours gone?—and he had had no sleep.

Billy Higgins dropped into the boat and, exhausted, sprawled at the bottom. The band of pain about Stephen's midriff proved to be the money belt. He unclasped the buckle and let the belt drop at his feet; the gold doubloons rattled like chains.

The Captain, bundled in his overcoat, joined them, pulling on a lead line. They began to row into the wind.

Higgins cried out, "Look!"

Stephen hugged the jug of water, and stared.

Seven men were poised in the stern of the doomed *Commodore*. The Captain bellowed an order to jump.

Dawn swept the seas as four men went over the railing. Three dropped safely to the rafts. The first mate wavered.

"Jump!" Murphy shrieked.

The mate suddenly threw his hands over his head, and plunged. His face slid by with an expression of horrible rage; he plummeted into the sea and did not come up. Stephen tried to rise; the cook held him down.

The three men left aboard the *Commodore* hesitated near the deckhouse. The Captain pleaded, but they would not jump. For a while, the sea, too, hesitated as if it were watching the drama; then it resumed its boiling.

"There she goes!"

346

The *Commodore* appeared to have come alive. She struggled, lurched, and righted herself as if she were eluding giant hands. Her stern sagged; the bow rose. Then she slipped her entire length unprotestingly into the sea.

A wave rose high, and blotted her out. In Captain Murphy's eyes, grief struggled with incredulity.

Morning spread across the Atlantic. Mosquito Inlet was twenty miles away.

CHAPTER 62

"None of them knew the colour of the sky."

While rowing desperately in his turn, the words echoed in his ears. He sat midway on the ocean, midway in life, midway on the seething journey to Cuba.

Six inches of gunwale separated them from the ocean, which came over the sides to inquire. Gulls flew near and far; one, beady-eyed, threatened to alight on the Captain's head. He gently waved his free arm to dissuade it; any brute gesture might capsize the boat. Slavering waves flung their wet shapes aboard and left spittle at the men's feet.

The cook took one end of the Captain's overcoat and Stephen the other, and thus they made a sail.

They were finally within sight of a lighthouse. But the wounded Captain, lying in the bow, ordered them to head out to sea again. That lighthouse had been abandoned last year. They were too far from shore to swim, and the dinghy would not live three minutes in the raging surf.

They saw a man on shore, another on a bicycle, and then a hotel omnibus. They were that near. They waved, signaled, and shouted themselves hoarse. Someone waved back, as if to indicate that the dinghy had been seen; he must have thought it friendly to wave to loony fishermen who were bobbing in a small boat.

The light began to fade, and a chill wind cut through their wet clothes. The shore vanished; the lighthouse sank. Another night at sea.

They were hungry and weakened from exposure. None had slept for two days; Stephen reckoned that he had not slept for three.

That night, as he rowed, and the others, lying in three inches of water, slept the sleep of the near-dead, sharks probed the boat, circled about, swishing astern and leaving a silver trail in their wake. It occurred to him that many creatures, not out of the sky where no one seemed to care, but out of the deep, must be watching.

They spelled each other rowing. At some time, for what seemed no more than a minute, Stephen slept groggily.

A new day came. It no longer mattered. His chest was racked with fiery pain, his head was feverish. Inside, he felt shrunken with hunger.

The green, vomiting sea, he reflected, had long sought conversation with him. He had avoided it these many years; now, boiling, hissing, roaring, it had him at bay. It was spinning no riddle, making no conundrum, posing no enigma; its speech was coarse. It was time for a reckoning.

He shivered. The fires within his frame were slowly being quenched.

He had never before given serious thought to dying. Birth came in with trumpets, fanfare, and shrieking demands. The littlest unwanted orphan popped into the world with a bit of drama, a gasp of victory, a statement of affirmation: "Lo, I have arrived!" In Death there was only dying. Men never died well; not even a king could manage it nobly. Men did not exit, but toppled from the stage like awkward louts.

He feared the storming waves. They would not release him gracefully when his turn came. He would lash and thrash, choke and cry, and die like a harpooned fish.

A white windmill, a row of dunes and squat cottages. The Captain said they must try a run through the surf. If they waited longer they would be too weak to do anything for themselves. The moment had arrived: life or death, and no turning back.

They shook hands as ceremonially as the seas and the rocking boat would permit.

He stripped off his wet clothing and trembled in his singlet. His bare feet crunched something hard: the gold coins in the money-belt.

The great combers began to charge. Higgins wearily pulled off his shirt. White-faced and shaking, he refused to lower his breeches. The cook shook out of his clothing. The Captain gazed helplessly at his own wet garments.

In that instant, Stephen saw the windmill ashore as a tall and peaked structure. It became Drew Church risen halfway out of the earth; the steeple was swaying and swaying as in that windstorm. He found its action first terrifying, then ludicrous.

As a huge wave moved forward, Captain Murphy shouted. Obediently, they tumbled into the sea.

Frantically, Stephen began to tread water. In the next trough, the oiler was swimming; the cook was swimming; the Captain, his sling tossing like a scrap of sail, was clinging to the keel of the capsized boat while the ocean hurled wet maledictions.

He began to swim toward shore, and tired. When he sought to tread water again, the undertow caught him. He was engulfed as if a shark had seized him in its jaws. It was over, all over, nature's final encounter with him.

He heard, above the sea, as clearly as if he were far from the boiling surf, the clang and clang of spear on shield, the clash and clash of hoof and heel.

He gasped, for there beyond him, within sight of shore, rode four black riders, with wild shouts and the wave of hair. Magnificent muzzles lifted above the spray; mantles stiffened in the breeze. The fourth steed was riderless.

He flung himself into the rush upon the wind. He must see their faces. A wave swept him under. In his drowned eyes, they were familiar. He choked: "Can it be possible? Can it be possible?"

He emerged spluttering. His chest was bursting, sand gritted under his feet. He was safely ashore. But the riders had vanished.

Moments later, he was staring at a head in the sand, a head with a battered crown. He tottered and, hysterically, felt his own skull. He was looking down upon the corpse of Billy Higgins, oiler, lying at his feet.

He grieved, then reeled as a dread thought struck him. Could that have been *their* mission? Was that why a single steed had been riderless? Billy Higgins had been his surrogate. He tottered, helplessly clenching and unclenching his fists.

His knees gave. As the beach embraced him, he was grateful for the firm earth. The thirty hours or more of exposure seemed to have disordered his mind.

A cup or a flask was pressed to his lips. He drank greedily of some searing liquid, and opened his eyes. All about him, people were standing or kneeling, men and women. The Captain was safe, smiling wanly; the cook was safe, hobbling with the support of a bearded man; and he, the correspondent, was safe.

Gulls stood in a wake beside a solitary oar. Eels of fire writhed on the waves, kindled and quenched, and kindled again.

He waited for the great foam-lipped white horses to rise four abreast on the crests of the sea; on their gleaming backs would sit black riders. They would shout and brandish silver swords.

They were not there. Aggie was not there, either. Suddenly, the earth was moving beneath him and, with the sound of the surf alive and seething, he was up and running down a dark corridor, his hands groping before his face, searching for the door that was still closed to him.

CHAPTER 63

He had been without sleep for more than eighty hours, except for two snatches on the tug and a cat-nap in the open boat. He had been without food for nearly seventy hours.

The rescued men were wrapped in blankets and carried to a nearby house. The cook, and the Captain, except for his sore arm, were in fair condition. Stephen remained in a state of semi-shock. His teeth chattered; his lips were bleeding and cracked, his skin sunburned, his eyes bloodshot.

A woman's hands washed the salt from his matted hair and mustaches. He smiled dreamily, and lost consciousness.

He awoke babbling about horses and calling "Aggie!" Captain Murphy, in the next bed, addressed him. Stephen's replies were confused. During the night, he shouted hoarsely, "Get up, Billy!" and "Ludie! Ludie!" The Daytona physician ordered an iron tonic.

He slept fitfully, groaning and tossing. When he awakened again, he accepted tea and hot soup. He was weaker now than he had been when cast ashore on the beach. He lay horror-stricken as he relived, in deliberated sequence, the events that had swept past him so furiously. He licked at his cracked mouth, stared at the ceiling, and wondered why the sky was so white. The joints of his fingers ached. His palms were as puckered as a child's after a long hot bath.

Gradually, the chills ended; the gooseflesh disappeared. Then, as the fever abated, the old hacking cough returned.

The physician examined him again. The skin was still very cold. Discolorations had appeared about the sunken eyes, yellow bruises along the thighs and ribs.

"You won't die," the doctor assured him. "Two, three weeks of rest, sunshine, and plenty of good food, red meats and milk, and ten, twelve hours of sleep a day." He frowned. "I don't like the sound of that chest."

Captain Murphy was sitting up on his bed. "A miserable old washboard he's got for a chest. And he told me that he'd been athletic!"

Stephen was appalled at the effort required to smile. His arms and legs seemed detached from his body.

"But you'll be off on another filibuster as soon as you're well enough to travel, won't you?"

He tried to nod. He was honor-bound to make good for Irving Bacheller's gold doubloons, now at the bottom of the sea. If he could write the story of the disaster and send it off to Irving, Ed Marshall would surely buy it for the *Journal*. Murphy said that the local papers, from statements of the survivors who had reached Port Orange and New Smyrna, had blazoned accounts of the sinking of the *Commodore*. Several of the New York correspondents who had been on the coast had already sent stories northward. Most of the dispatches had praised "Stephen Crane, the novelist." He was achieving undeserved fame; so Henry Fleming had been admired by his comrades for a wound that he had not received in actual battle. He must write his story within the next twenty-four hours, before it grew too cold for newspaper use.

Telegrams arrived from Bacheller, Hawkins, Marshall, and from Ted and Will. From Cora, a fervent, "Thank God you're safe. Have been almost crazy."

Murphy, who was shaving with a borrowed razor, uttered a long whistle. "She was that upset!" He blinked at Stephen. "Why does she stay on with it? The Hotel de Dreme? She could do anything a man could."

Forcing himself to concentrate, Stephen wrote through the afternoon. He finished his dispatch in a single draft and begged Murphy to send it to Bacheller. Until the last paragraph, the writing went smoothly. But the picture of Billy Higgins lying dead on the beach tormented him. Poor Billy had been buried at community expense.

A telegram that had been addressed to the Florida *Times-Union* in Jacksonville and had been forwarded to the St. James was finally delivered. It phrased a tender wish for his safety; signed, "Amy." Dismayed that she had found him at last, he wrote a brief reply, promising more news when he was better.

Murphy chortled. "Cora, and now Amy! How many girls do you have on your string?"

With an effort, Stephen left his bed. Murphy helped him dress in the clothes that the charitable women of Daytona had provided. He smoked cigarettes, which the doctor had forbidden, and walked the floor. He must find another filibuster and go on to Cuba. He recalled vividly the flash of the ominous fin as the shark had circled the open boat.

A second telegram from Cora pleaded that he return to Jacksonville: "Come surely."

He dreamed that Amy, clad in a billowing gown, with the dread fullness at her abdomen, was in the room. She pleaded that he come back to her. "Stephen, I need you!" He cowered in an agony of apprehension.

Captain Murphy rattled a stack of newspapers. "Mr. Stephen Crane, author. Because you went down with her, the poor *Commodore* has obituaries in every paper in the country."

He quoted a dozen lamentations on the demise of Stephen Crane. The story of the sinking of the tugboat had reached print before the news of the rescue had been telegraphed. "Are you alive or dead?"

"I wish I knew."

They talked for hours of the events on the *Commodore* and of its twenty-eight passengers and crewmen. Four lives had been lost. Some accounts implied sabotage in the fouling of the steam pumps. Murphy maintained that the old tug had probably sprung her seams when she had run aground in the St. Johns and near Mayport. Furthermore, she had been overloaded with coal and munitions.

As they reviewed their experiences, Stephen vowed that he would write the full story of the open boat.

He was still scrawling preliminary sentences when another telegram was delivered. Cora would arrive on the noon train.

"I wonder if Al Taylor knows," said Murphy.

After a while, Stephen asked, "What would you do, Ed?"

The Captain stared at the blazing January sunlight. "No woman has ever chased me like that. Maybe I'd wait until she caught me."

Stephen was on the verandah when her carriage drove up. He watched her, in dark traveling habit, step down and stride forward like an Amazon bound for battle. With a bounce and a flash of the blond hair, she was up the wooden stair.

"Steve!" She flung herself into his arms. "Thank God you're safe!"

Cora thanked Murphy as profusely as if he had dragged Stephen from the sea. "I had called upon the Navy to send out a search party. I tried to get a special train——" She shivered. "Thank God you weren't shipwrecked off the coast of Cuba. Now, I've come to take you home. I can't bear to have you so far away among strangers when I have the room and the servants."

Murphy discreetly slipped away.

"The Captain and I were together all along."

"I'll take him with us." Her eyes narrowed. "Morton told me that you had a telegram signed Amy. Is she the lady?"

"Yes."

The small face set sternly. "Come home!"

When, at ten o'clock that night, they reached Jacksonville, Murphy elected to go to a seaman's lodging house.

"Whoa, Ed! I've got to see you. I've got to write that story, and you've got to help me."

Murphy promised.

"He'll be safe with me," Cora assured him.

He wrote the story "The Open Boat" not at Cora's, but in the saloons and cafés of the waterfront, sometimes with Ed Murphy sitting before him as he described how wind and wave and terror had shaken the boat and its hapless occupants. He wrote it as fiction, to be free of the bonds of journalistic style, as an act of homage to the sea and to the men who sail it, and as a tribute to dead Billy Higgins and to all who come to an end in watery graves.

"Don't they feed you at the St. James? Or at the Hotel de Dreme?" Murphy demanded. "Look at you, Steve!"

His eyes, bright when he was reading, had become listless. He was sallow and gaunt; his skin clung to his cheekbones. Cora had nursed him, set a table to tempt princes, mothered him with extra breakfasts and snacks at midnight, and amused him in every way. But her attentions oppressed him; one morning, without notice, he had fled back to the St. James to pick up the shards of his privacy.

If Cora was angry, she cloaked her feelings. "Whatever is best for you, Steve!"

She knew, of course—Morton would be sure to tell her—of the letters from New York.

Hawkins informed him that, on January 7th, he had paid Amy Lee twenty dollars. On January 13th, Amy had sent a note asking for thirty-five dollars, "for I am broke and need the money very much." Willie had given her fifteen dollars one day and twenty dollars the next, for he still would not believe her. On January 22nd, she had again pleaded, and he had again paid out twenty dollars. On January 31st, another request. Six days later, he handed her another twenty-five dollars. Then Willie had obliged her to wait two weeks before he would release an additional thirty-five dollars.

Stephen was tempted to write a stern letter to Hawkins, instructing him to give Amy everything she asked for, but he feared to intrude; Willie might throw up his hands. Besides, he had not written to her as he had promised.

With Cora, he had journeyed as far south as Tampa in search of other filibusters. He had achieved nothing but another fever and a closer view of moss-draped cypresses and the royal poincianas at Palm Beach.

On his return, Murphy said, "If your *Red Badge* didn't make you famous, Steve, this shipwreck did. Go back North and enjoy it. Or can't you ever admit defeat?"

Glumly, "Defeat is the only thing that I can admit."

"If you've got to have a war, pick a live one!" advised the correspondent Ernest McCready, who had come in to Jacksonville with Ralph Paine. "The Powers are rattling their sabers over in Europe. Watch the Greeks and the Turks; there will be more trouble with them. But before you go off to try to die again, Steve, you ought to fatten up. No bullet could find a place to lodge in that skeleton of yours."

Stephen confided that he had asked Ed Marshall to send him to Crete where a new insurrection, fomented by the Greeks against Turkish rule, was under way. Marshall maintained that the fighting in Crete would be stalemated. However, the Greeks, counting upon

353

European support, were massing forces on the Turkish frontiers. At Mr. Hearst's expense, Stephen might sail for Europe and proceed to Athens via London, Paris, and Constantinople.

"What are you waiting for?" McCready hooted. "Off with you!"

"Steve won't go anywhere because Miss Cora wouldn't like him to leave her," Murphy teased.

The afternoon post brought more mail from Hawkins: an envelope of cuttings of Amy's articles in the Chicago *Daily News*, chiefly prose parodies of *The Black Riders* under the title "Our Own Steve Crane." She must be in Chicago! He telegraphed to Marshall that he would go to Greece for the *Journal*.

When he told Cora, her eyes sparkled. "I'm happy for you, Steve." Wistfully, "Unhappy for myself."

"Where will you be, Cora, tomorrow and tomorrow?"

"What if I were to say that I'd go with you?"

He sobered. "Follow the fortunes of a wanderer?"

"What if I said Yes?"

He became vague. "I've got a fever in me. I must keep moving." "Chasing wars?"

"Running away from the wars inside me."

"Running away from the women who pursue you. Will you return to *her?*"

"I'd sooner go back to my shark swimming around the open boat!"

She snuggled in his arms. "What do the Spaniards say? 'Go with God!' "

Once more, he stayed the night. She was like an eager bride in his hands, praising, pouting, adoring. "We'll see the sun rise together."

They were both weary, yet neither would admit fatigue. As the sun burst over the trees, she shut her eyes and said, "Go quickly now! Alex is waiting with the victoria."

CHAPTER 64

He was reading the New York papers in the lobby of the St. James when a woman dropped heavily into the chair beside him. He gazed into the terrified eyes of Mathilde Ruedy, Cora's housekeeper.

"Miss Cora says to leave at once! By the afternoon train if you can." He seized her wrist. "Why, Mathilde?"

She sobbed, "He's beaten her! He came, and they quarreled about you. You must go away, Mr. Crane. He's a bad man!"

He stared absently at their reflections in the ormolu mirror on the opposite wall. Al Taylor could have burst in on them any night when he had been in Cora's bed at the Hotel de Dreme. What mad stories had she been telling her lover about the trip to Daytona to bring Stephen Crane back, and the journeys with him through the Southern swamps? She must have hoodwinked him in some way.

"Go, Mr. Crane!"

"I've got to see her first. Wait for me."

In his room, he slipped cartridges into the Smith & Wesson revolver he had bought at a pawnbroker's. He considered scribbling a note to Hawkins, to indicate where he had gone, if he should not return alive. He grimaced: unnecessary heroics! If he should die, it would not matter.

He sauntered into the lobby as calmly as if he were going out for a stroll. To the clerk: "If there is a telegram this afternoon, send a boy out to Miss Cora's."

In the carriage, as they moved swiftly up Bay Street in the brilliant sunlight, he listened to Mrs. Ruedy's story and questioned her sharply. Taylor had appeared after the guests had departed and Cora had retired.

Stephen shuddered. Had the man expected to find him in Cora's arms?

A loud and bitter row had followed. Taylor had grated accusations. Mrs. Ruedy could not, or would not, say whether Cora had confirmed or denied them.

She had been playing a dangerous game. By what legerdemain had she been able to shuttle her men back and forth so that one had never encountered the other? Grimly, Stephen believed that she had been truthful in his embraces, that her protestations of love and passion had poured from a full and honest heart.

Taylor had resumed the quarrel the next morning. Suddenly, Cora had begun to shriek in terror. Mrs. Ruedy had run to the door and hammered to be admitted. She could hear the man raging and Cora pleading and weeping. When Taylor finally admitted her, Cora was lying unconscious on the floor. He had beaten her with a riding-crop.

Mrs. Ruedy had revived her with spirits of ammonia and had put her to bed. As soon as she could speak, Cora had beseeched the housekeeper to drive to the St. James to warn Mr. Crane. Victoria, the maid, had been attending Cora when Mrs. Ruedy dashed out. The doctor had been summoned.

"Was he—Taylor—there when you left?"

She did not know; the hotel was so large that he could have concealed himself anywhere. "You shouldn't have come with me, Mr. Crane! He may kill you."

He tapped his holster. He had no desire to shoot any man, but he would defend himself. If Taylor threatened him, he would act accordingly.

"You could go in by the back way, Mr. Crane."

He was scornful; he might also disguise himself as an old woman.

As the carriage rolled to a halt, he leaped out. The sunlight on the house reminded him of a tiger.

He stood exposed. He squared his shoulders and dropped his hand to the holster. The other man, probably armed, certainly vindictive, might be lurking at any window. Yet he moved deliberately, contemptuously daring to offer himself as a target.

The door creaked. Not a servant was in sight. His eyes sought the pillars, the divans; his ears strained. He tiptoed up the stairs, harkening for the pulse of the house. The walls seemed to throb.

At a swift tread at his heels, he whirled and drew the pistol.

"His carriage is gone!" Mrs. Ruedy whispered.

He disavowed any sense of relief. His foe might be waiting behind some portiere. He followed the woman as she stoutly plowed toward Cora's rooms.

Victoria and Hortense, the maids, were leaning over the bed, applying salve to a naked, bleeding back. In a basin lay crimsoned cloths.

Two of the girls, Angelica and Myna, standing by like caryatids, modestly closed their wrappers.

"Miss Cora!" Mrs. Ruedy called.

"Did you tell him?"

"He's here!"

With a groan, Cora dismissed the soothing hands and turned her head. "Steve, why did you come? Her face was hideously swollen, ugly abrasions under the eyes, the lips puffy and bleeding.

Angelica, hastily flinging a kerchief over the victim's bosom, murmured bitterly, "He wanted to ruin her looks!"

Cora moaned, "Go, go!"

"Hush, child!" Victoria arranged the golden hair. "Hush, Miss Coah. The doctor goanna come any minute."

"Go!" The left eye was shut. The lovely features had been battered, perhaps by the man's heavy ring.

Stephen clasped her limp fingers.

As the others withdrew, he laid the pistol on the bedside table.

"I look hideous!" She moaned. "You shouldn't have come, Steve. I told Mathilde to warn you to leave!"

He bent over her. "Poor darling Cora!"

"He'd kill you, Steve, if he found you here."

"I won't leave you!"

"Go away!" she pleaded.

"I won't leave you."

"Yes, you must." A dry sob shook her frame. "You must go."

He hesitated, aware that the invisible jaws of a velvet trap were closing. He did not truly want her; he must not tie himself to her apron-strings, nor to any woman's. But the compulsion was stronger than his own wishes. "Come away with me, Cora!" he whispered. "Come with me."

"You don't want me."

"Yes, I do. Come with me."

She was like a beaten child. "You'll regret it. You will. He heard talk in a bar. Your—newspaper friends."

"Yet you still belong to him."

"Belong to nobody—to everybody."

"You belong to me now. Come with me. I won't leave you," he repeated. Eagerly, he went on. "If you can travel, we'll go this afternoon. If not, as soon as you can. We'll take the Special to New York. I won't let any harm come to you."

Tears glistened on her eyelids. "Don't pity me! I can't stand pity."

He knelt, and pressed his lips to her hair. "Cora, dearest, come with me to New York. At least to your Aunt Mary Holder's. You'll get well, and you'll never return here to this life."

She was listening.

"By the time I am back from Greece you'll be well, everything will heal—and we can," he added lamely, "decide later."

Both eyes struggled to open; her gaze settled upon him uncertainly.

"Didn't you say you had a foreboding about me?" he added persuasively. "That we'd be safe as long as we were together?"

Tears trickled down the swollen cheeks.

CHAPTER 65

She wore a heavy black silk veil to conceal the battered features, and a gown of blue cashmere with puffed sleeves, velvet collar and cuffs, and steel buttons down the middle. Her injuries were still painful; she winced and twisted her head, for the welts on her back were agonizing under the corsets and petticoats. She shrank from the scrutiny of the passengers who sought, by sharp glances as they roved the aisle, to pierce the identity beneath the veil. He covered the little, gloved hand.

Victoria, Hortense, Angelica, and Myna had accompanied her to the station. He saw their coachman guide a porter, who was struggling with two large trunks, to the baggage cars. She must have packed her entire wardrobe.

The women embraced her tearfully, as if she were departing on her wedding trip.

Victoria began to weep. "You'll nevah come back, Miss Coah!"

"Stop that sniveling!" came through the veil. "Angelica will take care of you and be good to you."

357

To Angelica, she whispered, "Wear my red gown. I'm holding you responsible. Send the money to my lawyer's office every morning. Fail one day, or hold out a single dollar, and you'll wish you'd never been born. And with the gentlemen, be firm. With the gentlemen, always be firm!"

"Take good care of her, Mr. Crane," Angelica murmured. "Please take care of her." Her lashes glistened.

He was startled to receive her sisterly kiss.

Sitting beside her in the Pullman, Stephen admired Cora's grit. The Special was shrieking over the rails. When the train jarred and ground around a curve, she moaned softly and leaned her head against his shoulder. Otherwise, she sat erect and silent.

An amused glance from the porter alerted Stephen that her veil conveyed such an air of mystery that the man assumed that they were, indeed, a couple bound on their wedding journey!

When dusk fell over the savannahs, the conductor, to whom Stephen had appealed, informed them that a compartment was available. Cora, clinging to a leather case that she had let no one carry for her, went quickly to the new space. Stephen asked the dining-car steward to bring them two large dinners and a bottle of wine.

As usual, he had no appetite. Cora, however, was famished. Her facial muscles moved painfully and compelled her to chew slowly, but she consumed a shrimp bisque, a porterhouse steak, fried potatoes, black-eyed peas, and an artichoke salad. He marveled at her capacity. Her will to survive was unimpaired.

At a knock on the door, she dropped her veil. The Pullman conductor asked for their tickets. "Holiday in New York?"

Stephen ignored him.

From behind the veil came sweetly, "Conductor, my husband is very shy."

The man grinned, and touched the bill of his cap. "I was shy myself, ma'am."

Stephen glared at her.

"A nimble wit is sometimes more useful than the black truth," she murmured when the door had shut. She lifted the veil again and poured their coffee.

He collected himself. The old Cora! She had forgotten how cruelly she had been beaten, how monstrous she appeared.

Suddenly, he understood, with the curious illogic by which odd impressions are rearranged logically, that the black leather case at her side must contain her valuables.

"Heirlooms?" he mocked and prodded the case with his foot.

"My jewels." She returned his gaze defiantly. "The girls gave me everything they had. I have a right to everything I took. Did you think that I would come along to take money from you like that other woman?"

He dodged his reflection in the window and peered at the occasionally illumined night scenery. He would leave her in New York. Thank God he was sailing soon.

Cora, who fell into slumber easily, muttered and groaned as the welts and bruises distressed her.

He dreamed, as the whistle screamed and the train hurtled into the night, that they were, after a trip through a long, dark tunnel, coming into Manhattan.

They slowly climbed a vast height of stairs and came to the hem of a woman's gown. His eyes ascended, and there was Amy, severe and pale, towering wrathfully above him, her hands crossed over her protruding abdomen.

He pressed Cora aside. With a swift motion, Amy produced a small, blue revolver, the muzzle pointed at his chest.

"Amy!" he shouted.

They faced each other. Amy, shrinking to normal proportions, advanced with a tigerish ferocity. "So you would have walked right past me!" she cried, and thrust the revolver at him. "You would have ignored me. No, Stephen Crane! The time has come to settle with you."

He was thinking regretfully that he had left his pistol in his baggage. "Go ahead and shoot," he returned nervously. "I have no defense. I am unarmed."

Her cheeks livid, she swung the revolver to and fro before his chest. "Don't you lie to me, don't you dare lie to me! You've always been able to defend yourself." The green eyes blazed. "Why, I ought to tell your mother."

He crimsoned. "Go tell my mother," he said hotly. "I tell you that I am unarmed. Tell my sister, too, if you like." Suddenly, he was no longer afraid.

She drew herself erect as if to take aim. "If you're not going to defend yourself, tell me why not, Stephen?" She sneered.

"Because I've just arrived from Florida with my family. I'm married now."

She did not understand at all. "Married?"

"Yes," he said distinctly. "Yes, Amy, I'm married."

"Married?" she repeated again. For the first time, she saw that the woman, drooping at his side, belonged to him. With a swift gesture, she flung Cora's veil back and exposed the bruised countenance. "You're married to—to this——?"

She stepped back as if she had glanced into a dreadful chasm. The arm with the revolver fell weakly to her side. "To this creature with —with no face?" she asked in a whisper.

"Yes," he replied, "to her."

They stood in an isosceles triangle, in utter silence. Cora's swollen features, with the yellow and blue bruises, might have been borrowed from Maggie's mother after the old woman had drunk herself into a stupor. But Amy's face was shining, as if she were wringing triumph from an ignominious defeat.

"To her," he repeated.

She murmured, "Then it's finished, Stephen?"

With a heavy heart, he glanced from one to the other. "I'm afraid so." Harshly, "I didn't start the trouble."

"Married!" Amy repeated once more, with a haughty toss of her head. The simple word seemed to dissolve her anger.

She turned away.

He heard Cora laughing sarcastically and, with an angry sweep, brought the veil down over the battered face.

When he awakened, it was dawn. The train was thundering into the outskirts of the city. Across the river, a yellow sky hung over Manhattan.

CHAPTER 66

He settled Cora at her Aunt Mary's flat on West 128th Street, and headed for McClure's.

The fame of newspaper headlines had granted him his own red badge of courage. He was the Crane who had been thought lost in the sinking of the *Commodore* and then had appeared from the sea.

They greeted him with the February issue of *The Philistine*. Hubbard had gone to press with a tearful obituary:

> I have gibed Stephen Crane, and jeered his work, but beneath all the banter there was only respect, good-will—aye! and affection. He is dead now—Steve is dead. How he faced death the records do not say. . . . Within the breast of that pale youth dwelt a lion's heart. . . . *He died trying to save others.* So, here's to you, Steve Crane, wherever you may be! You were not so very good, but you were as good as I am—and better in many ways. . . . And so, Stevie, good-bye and good-bye!

Stephen said, "Son-of-a-gun!"

"See the next page," smiled Jaccacci, the art editor. "Hubbard must have been on press when the good news came."

Stephen read Hubbard's addendum:

> LATER: Thanks to Providence and a hen-coop, Steve Crane was not drowned after all—he swam ashore.

He said wistfully, "After an obituary so touching it seems a shame to have spoiled it for him."

He avoided 25th Street; he had no wish to encounter Amy or her sister. Perhaps Amy had returned permanently to Chicago. He yearned for the full truth about her, yet feared it, too; even his suspicions drove a spear into his side.

Willie Hawkins settled the matter in short, sharp words. "You walk in on her, and I wash my hands of it, Steve. I've had her on my back ever since you went away."

"Do you think she went to a doctor?"

"I don't know. Whatever she did was best for her. Leave that to Amy Lee."

"She needed one hundred and twenty dollars that one day. For what else if not a doctor?" He faltered. "Surgery!"

Willie snickered. "She wanted money. She hoodwinked Fairman, too, but not me." He produced a sheaf of papers. "I have her letters and a receipt for every dollar I gave her. She tried to hook you."

"I don't believe it."

The other swore thoughtfully. "Don't you dare go near her! I sent her a last check for $12.95, the balance of the money left from the sum you gave me. I told her it was the last. No more! So stay clear of her. One glimpse of you, and she'll start all over again. She'll drag you into the hay before you can say 'William McKinley,' and this time you'll never get away from her. To a certain kind of woman, you're a blessed meal-ticket."

"What if——"

"Dammit, Steve!" Hawkins shouted. "Go to England, go to Greece! Don't you know how to cut away from any woman's apron-strings?"

He collected three hundred dollars, less the agent's commission, from Paul Reynolds, the price paid by the imperial Ned Burlingame at *Scribner's* for "The Open Boat" story. He called on Appleton's for his accrued royalties on *Maggie* and on *The Little Regiment*. In London, he would ask Heinemann and Edward Arnold for the English money from his books.

Ed Marshall gave him his travel expenses and his instructions. The *Journal* would also have Julian Ralph and John Bass in Greece, but he was to cover the war in his own style; Mr. Hearst was eager for fresh, vigorous reporting.

"Don't get into trouble with the police before you leave," Marshall pleaded.

"No danger." He was spending the long evenings with Cora.

She was healing rapidly. "I was not born to be ugly," she preened. She was wearing a black silk gown, her pearls and the diamond ring on her finger. "Have you seen Amy?"

"No."

"Swear!"

"Honest Injun!"

"If I thought that you were seeing her again, I'd find her and scratch her eyes out!"

"I've forgotten her."

"Oh, no!" she retorted. "Not Stephen Crane. Not until you've interred her in some story. Only then will she be dead for you."

She demanded to see his passport and his steamship ticket. "How else can I know that you are really going across the ocean? You might be leaving for Chicago with your Amy."

"Will you be here when I return?"

She smiled cryptically.

"Shall I ever see you again, Cora?"

She nodded. "There will be no mystery about what I do."

He smiled, too. Once he left the country, he would be totally free to do as he pleased. He might linger in Europe and not return for several years.

He wrote to Will that he could not come to Port Jervis; he must sail at once: "My time is tragically short."

Aboard ship, the sharp wind improved his appetite. He ate heartily and might even have gained weight on the voyage had he not made the acquaintance of several merchants who fancied themselves fine poker players. Subsequently, he earned more in the smoking room than he had received for "The Open Boat." The passion of the game kept him from the dining rooms.

When the players wearied him, he retired to his stateroom to work on a new filibuster story. In wry homage to Captain Murphy, about whom it centered, he called it "Flanagan." His tale of the open boat had been written hastily, feverishly, with emotions left over, it seemed.

When the Irish coast was sighted, Stephen hurried on deck. A beautiful young woman crossed his path.

He stared at her. "No!"

She laughed and held out her hand. "Well, Stephen Crane!"

"Cora!" he paled. "You've been aboard?" He confessed that he had been playing poker the whole voyage and had not even glanced at the passenger list. "Why didn't you send me word?" Over her shoulder, grinning happily a few feet away, stood Mrs. Ruedy.

Cora seemed ready to fall into his arms. He hesitated; other passengers were eyeing them.

"Should I have sent you a card?" she chided. "I don't believe that you can read, Steve, at least not the signs in a woman's heart, or you would have known that I would follow you on this steamer. Oh, I would even have invaded your precious smoking room to find you now that I'm presentable again. Or am I still hideous?"

Her face had healed. The hair was golden; the eyes were blue, mischievously blue and alive.

"More beautiful than ever!" He was nervous and bewildered. Had she followed him, or had her own affairs—Captain Stewart!—brought her on this voyage?

They moved toward the stern. Ireland was a leaden coastline in the north.

"Oh, give me your arm, Steve!" She was the old gay Cora. He searched her countenance again for the signs of the injuries. The simple animal vitality of her!

"We're not strangers, are we?" she trilled, and her eyes were full of malice. "Let's parade before those tight-lipped ladies there. From their grim faces, they expect me to flirt with you and with every other man aboard this ship."

As they strolled about, arm in arm, he saw that every glance pursued them. The admiring, coveting eyes of the men made him sharply aware of her loveliness and the elegance of her carriage.

"Shall we run away together in the morning?" she murmured.

"Haven't we already done so?" he retorted.

He decided that, whatever the reason for her appearance, he was glad she was aboard. He preferred not to think of the long road to Greece.

CHAPTER 67

After noisy Manhattan, London was an astonishingly silent metropolis. On the streets, past parks and monuments and small-paned shops, the omnibuses waddled as quietly as if the horses wore felt slippers. The bobbies strolled under their helmets; nothing concerned them except the dignified keeping of law and order. The girls were pink-cheeked; the men carried tightly furled umbrellas even on sunny days. In the clubs and hotels, English was spoken with a celery crispness that he envied.

William Heinemann, publisher, received his American author coolly. *The Red Badge* had done nobly. *Maggie* had not done as well, nor had *The Black Riders*. Yet, stoutly maintained Mr. Heinemann, he was proud to have them on his list. *The Little Regiment* had sold "nicely." On *The Third Violet*, which was still in press, he planned a rise in price from three shillings to six shillings.

Heinemann, perceiving that the young American was inclined to accept his publisher's every word as the ultimate in wisdom, forthwith, became as avuncular as if his nephew had arrived from the colonies.

"The house looks forward to publishing all of your future works, Mr. Crane, whatever they may be."

Sidney Pawling, Heinemann's partner, proposed to introduce Stephen to the editors of the various periodicals. "Good markets," he said. "*Cornhill Magazine, English Illustrated, Pall Mall Gazette, Cassell's, Blackwood's, Strand.*" A few had already published Crane stories. "Your name is quite good with us."

Thanks to Pawling, he was given an appointment at the *Illustrated London News*. In their chilly offices, he accepted a cup of strong tea, a thin bread-and-butter sandwich, and a promise of forty pounds for "Flanagan."

The next day, the *Westminster Gazette*, equally hospitable, agreed to buy his correspondence from Greece at better than space rates. His name was indeed good in England!

"Excellent fellows!" said Pawling. "Now you must meet Frederic. Fine fellow. American."

Harold Frederic, who filed the local news for the New York *Times*, had spread the English praises of *The Red Badge* to American readers a year ago.

"Crane!" Frederic boomed. He was a big man with a gruff voice and large, fierce features. He had the grip of a navvy and teeth as prominent as Theodore Roosevelt's. "Time you got here. England's been waiting for you. *The Red Badge* is splendid. God's trousers! England hasn't seen its equal in a novel by an American in a year of Sundays."

Frederic, high-spirited and hail-fellow, had been born and raised in Utica, but he impressed Stephen as more English than the Englishmen. His unruly black hair was parted to the left side. His cheeks were carelessly shaven, but the heavy mustaches and the small beard were neatly trimmed.

When Stephen thanked him, Frederic beamed, "Didn't say half enough. You deserved every word."

He carried Stephen off to the National Liberal Club and stuffed him with whiskies and dinner, while he sipped Apollinaris. In the lounge, he asked a myriad of questions and, while Stephen was still framing his replies, asked more questions and flung his opinions like darts.

Other club members, dozing on their necks in adjacent chairs, harrumphed and clucked; they could hear every word. It was evident that Frederic, though loud and eccentric, was understood and accepted. Even when he whispered, his eyes and gestures shouted. He leveled a finger, generally the little finger, which struck Stephen as an odd digit with which to emphasize, and delivered heretical dogmas.

Stephen enjoyed him. Frederic was genuine; Hawkins, Bacheller, Ed Marshall, and the other Lanterns would have a rooting evening with this forceful and boisterous fellow.

Frederic lambasted the British for a lot of selfish imperialists and, in the next breath, celebrated the delights of Devon strawberries and clotted cream, the beauty of the Scottish moors, or the rare quality of some obscure village that had remained unwashed Tudor.

He, too, was a novelist. Stephen confessed that he had not read *The Damnation of Theron Ware.*

"God's trousers!" Frederic sputtered with no effort to conceal his disappointment. "Published by Stone & Kimball in Chicago—also by Heinemann, under the title *Illumination*—survived several editions and you haven't read it! Dammit, I read yours. . . . Mine's about a minister. Certainly another minister's son would appreciate it. Read it. It's not half bad."

"God's trousers, I will!"

Frederic guffawed. "That always shocks them. Thirteen years I've been here. Most Englishmen like to cuss, but in cipher, y'know. I give it to them out of a cannon."

He had small, handsomely shaped ears, and white, neatly-groomed hands. Although the voice was harsh and the manner was belligerent, Stephen recognized that there was a warm and gentle soul in Frederic.

The other lauded *Maggie,* and insisted on riding Stephen off to the Empire Theater promenade where the fashionable prostitutes sauntered.

"I hold that sex is man's only power to deal a counter-blow against his enemy, Death." The little finger prodded the air. "It is the main-spring of human activity. It is only base when one indulges without due regard for the self-respect of the other party." He snorted. "Most people regard sex as something so sacred that they cannot bring themselves to discuss the conditions attending it—hence our present muddle. I say that those who regard it as base and despicable are those who don't give a hang with whom they satisfy it." He assumed that Stephen must be in absolute agreement with him.

He took Stephen to Whitechapel to visit the gin-dives and to see women lying drunk in the gutter. "The upper classes turn their backs on all this as if the God of the Established Church meant it to be."

He overwhelmed Stephen, but he was an education on the mores of these islanders who ruled half the world.

The next day, he brought an invitation to meet Richard Harding Davis. "Wants to give you a luncheon at the Savoy. Don't say no! Under the boiled shirt"—Frederic, who refused to wear any formal attire, affected a soft tie knotted loosely in artist's style—"is a good fellow. His gifts are small, but he's done well with them. He has the luck, he has the looks, and the connections. But the boy works. He gets to the coronation of the Czar in Moscow; where were you? He gets to Budapest for their Millennial; where were you? He gets in everywhere, and one damns the fellow for it, but you like him when

he's with you." He shrugged. "He said he admired *The Red Badge.*
I say, God's trousers, he'd better!"

Stephen proudly told Cora, who was at the Cecil with Mrs. Ruedy,
that England was receiving him hospitably.

"Why shouldn't they?" she pouted. "England's the place for Stephen
Crane."

"And you?"

Her mouth quivered. Captain Stewart was on duty somewhere in
Africa. At her request, his solicitor was forwarding her plea for a
divorce.

"What now, 'Nellie Bly'?"

"I don't want to stay in London and run into the old crowd. I don't
want to languish here alone in a hotel. I'll go to Paris when you leave."

He hesitated. Her eyes had become longing.

"I'm off to Greece."

"Until there is some word from Donald, there is nothing to keep
me in London." She threw herself into his arms. "I have the money,
Steve! I'll take a separate compartment on the same train, a separate
room at the same hotel. I won't come near you unless you want me.
Take me with you!"

"God's trousers!"

She stood off frowning. "Is that necessary?"

He laughed. "What shall I do with you in Greece when I'm off to
the battle lines?"

"I'll stay in Athens. I'll go to the Parthenon. I won't be underfoot.
We could see Europe. I could show it to you, and I'd be near you."
She gave him a lingering kiss. "Don't you want me?"

"I want my freedom," he replied, and was surprised to hear it from
his own lips. "I don't want to be tied to anyone, not even to you."

"Can you ever be more free than you are with me?" she asked
tenderly. "I'm still married. I can make no demands on you, as the
others have done. Or are you so fearful what people will say? 'Who
is she? Where does she come from?'"

"I'm afraid of no one!" he retorted, and believed it.

"And I love you, Steve!"

He gazed deeply into her eyes. In their lovemaking, she yielded to
him utterly, as if she had never known a man's sly hands under her
skirts. They could be wickedly happy together; her attention could
be constant and ingenious.

"I don't want to lose you, Steve. Don't you see that I followed you
across the ocean?" The blue eyes were pleading.

"I don't know what I'll do, where I'll go after Greece."

"You'll be free!" she breathed. "As you're free now, you'll always
be free."

She was magnetic, and he was susceptible. She was spirited and modish. It might be a lark to wander across Europe with Cora Howarth–Murphy–Stewart–Taylor.

The luncheon on Wednesday was at a great round table in the center of the Savoy dining room. In addition to Stephen and Harold Frederic, the guests were Anthony Hope, author of *The Prisoner of Zenda,* James Barrie, the shy author of *Sentimental Tommy,* and Justin H. McCarthy, the sober critic and novelist who had recently returned from Greece.

"Crane, a great pleasure and an honor!" Davis said, clasping Stephen's hand in both of his. "I've long wanted to meet you. I say, and I've said it to everyone, that you've written the last word as far as battles or fighting is concerned. In *The Red Badge of Courage,* of course."

Stephen was flattered. Dick Davis, seven years his senior, was "pretty," as those who disliked him said; no wonder Charles Dana Gibson posed him for the dudish characters in his fashionable drawings. But he was a man, and likeable.

"Crane and I hail from the same stretch of Jersey coast," Davis announced to the other guests. "You are an Asbury Parker, aren't you? Our family spent great summers at Point Pleasant and on the Manasquan River."

Stephen sparkled. The reference to the little summer resort put him at ease. He took a deep breath as if he were inhaling the smell of the ocean.

"As kids, Nora, my sister, and Gus—my brother Charles, I mean—and I played on the chunk of sand beach island that Stevenson described, or they say he did, for *Treasure Island.*"

"Crane resembles Stevenson," McCarthy put in.

Barrie, who had been a personal friend of Stevenson, shook his head. "No, not really."

Davis clapped his shoulder. "R.L.S. was better than anyone thought, the poor devil." He confronted the other men as though he and Stephen were inevitably on the same side. "He sped around half the world seeking his peace and his health, only to be trapped by that fiendish tuberculosis in the South Seas."

It was difficult to resent Davis' permanent air of confidence. He was an estimable, straightforward chap.

Stephen, toying with the excellent food, admired his conversational skill; the man had polish and charm. Davis drew Frederic, who seemed taciturn today, into the conversation by speaking of *Seth's Brother's Wife* and *In the Valley* as novels he had enjoyed. He addressed himself to Hope and to Barrie, and assured them that America loved their works. Hope was soon to leave for a tour of lectures in America; Barrie was planning new writings of whimsy that dealt with young people.

He turned once more to Stephen. In December, Davis had tried to reach Cuba on the steam-launch *Vamoose*. A violent storm had driven it back to Key West, and he had not seen Havana until January.

"Crane was luckier," he said wistfully, as if any kind of adventure, even near-disaster, was good fortune for a writing man.

Stephen nodded. "But I've still not seen an honest-to-goodness war."

The Englishmen expressed surprise.

Again Davis sprang to his defense. "Crane doesn't need the actual sights. He's done better than any of us."

Stephen was at a loss to repay the praise. He had forgotten the twinges of envy that he had suffered when he had heard that Dick Davis had been paid five thousand dollars for *Soldiers of Fortune* and five hundred dollars for reporting the Yale-Princeton football game. Even for the Cuban jaunt, which had not come off, the *Journal* had paid Davis a flat three thousand dollars for the month's work.

A commotion near the door disturbed the diners. Men and women were rising, straining to see the maître d'hôtel protest the entrance of a uniformed lance-sergeant. The man had a large envelope for "Richard Harding Davis, Esquire." Sir Evelyn Wood of the War Office, the sixth guest, had been detained and thus sent his apologies.

"Thought they had declared war on you," Frederic murmured as the soldier clanked away and people crowded about their table.

Davis was calm. "Fellow had orders to deliver it into my hands." He passed the letter to the guest of honor. "Memento?"

Stephen accepted it. Cora would enjoy the souvenir.

Davis was on his way to Florence, where Gus was Consul. He planned also to pause at Monte Carlo to try his luck at the tables. "And you, Steve?"

"To Paris tomorrow."

Davis proposed that they cross the Channel together.

Before parting, they chattered once more of common experiences. Davis, too, had found school onerous; Swarthmore, Lehigh, and Johns Hopkins, but he had not graduated. "Decided to write for a living. It's not easy, is it? But you get the satisfaction deep down. Sometimes."

The next day, Stephen could not locate Dick Davis until the boat-train had left the Admiralty pier in Dover, and the town, the castle, and the cliffs were receding in the distance. He muttered an excuse to Cora and stepped away.

Davis, standing before a deck cabin, greeted him cordially, but the keen dark eyes were scrutinizing Cora. Stephen had hailed him as if she did not exist, and Cora had turned about angrily.

Davis said, "The London *Times* asked me to be their correspondent in Greece. I refused. I'll get there later. Hope the war doesn't start till I arrive."

Stephen, conscious that he had been discourteous to Cora, made a feeble attempt at small talk. Shrewdly, Davis, whatever he was thinking, discussed the Greek–Turkish embroilment. His sympathies were with the Greeks. "If they should arrange a truce to accommodate me," he said cheerfully, "I might return to London to cover the Queen's Jubilee in June."

Stephen rejoined Cora when the boat entered the harbor at Calais.

She was scornful. "You have made it obvious to your friend, haven't you?"

He apologized, but she would not forgive him. "I am not a camp follower!" She remained sullen during the luncheon in the buffet of the depot of Chemin de Fer du Nord. Stephen silently picked at his omelet. Davis had disappeared.

They had a glimpse of the walls of old Calais, then quaint Boulogne and Abbeville, and halted for refreshments at Amiens.

When he went out to smoke, Davis reappeared.

"Say, Steve, if I should miss you, since we're off in different directions, remember that I've got a little flat on 28th Street in New York. When you get back, come and see me." The hard grip conveyed genuine camaraderie. "A pleasure to be with a real writing man." With a sober smile, he added, "Good hunting!"

What the devil did he mean? The Greek War, of course. He must have been referring to the war.

Waiting for a brougham to take them to the hotel, Cora snapped, "What must he have thought?" She faced him suddenly, a light dawning in her eyes. "You didn't want me to meet Mr. Davis because you were jealous!"

He took refuge in the excuse that she had so guilelessly presented.

"Stephen Crane!" She smiled behind her eyes. "Jealous!" She took his hand. "He is a beautiful man. But I want no one except my Stevie. For the rest of my life, I don't want to look at another man, as long as I live, as long as we both shall live!"

He smiled over his victory, as Paris, wisest of cities, opened its broad avenues and embraced them.

At the Hotel Campbell, on Avenue Friedland below the Arc de l'Etoile, he signed the register with a flourish: "M. et Mme. Stephen Crane."

CHAPTER 68

She rebelled at his haste to reach Athens. The war, if Davis, Frederic, and the London editors had predicted accurately, would not break out soon. She considered it a silly business, Greece pitting her two and a half millions against Turkey's twenty-eight millions.

But he was a reporter, not a critic of the insanity of nations; he had come to see a war, not to disown it before it was waged.

"If *The Red Badge* is not all right I'll sell out my claim and take up orange-growing!"

"Maybe there won't be a war."

"War is God's ironic revenge on Man for having failed to become a better creature than he was created."

She fingered the little gold cross at her throat, and stared out the window of the Orient Express. He was not godless; rather he was displeased with the Creator for having abandoned Man to his own destiny. She was not a formal adherent of the Church, yet she prayed for him in every cathedral they visited, from Paris to Budapest.

"All the world, which believes, is wrong, and you alone are right!"

"All the world is sick," he mocked, "and I can't find a corner in which to hide myself from the sight of it!"

"How can anyone predict that a war will take place?" she asked hopelessly.

"Generals have already estimated the casualties; munitions makers have already made their deliveries. Sooner or later, this war will be fought. Quickly, because neither side has the resources for a prolonged struggle. Short and swift, like death."

They registered at the Hotel d'Angleterre in Athens on Palm Sunday. The broken Acropolis, which remains forever witness that gods once dwelt among men, shone in serene glory. He left Cora to unpack and rushed to Constitution Square to wander among the cafés. The streets were crowded with reservists and volunteers in baggy pants and tasseled fezzes. A company of *evzones* debouched from a side street, singing some traditional marching song. People rose from the café tables, and cheered.

Walking under Homer's sunlit sky, he reflected that it was a pity that his father had never visited this myth-drenched soil. Papa had been devoted to *The Odyssey*, and its account of Telemachus who had searched so many years for his lost parent. Hercules, Hector, Achilles, Solon, Pericles, Aspasia, and Helen of Troy had trod this earth, shouting, struggling, teaching, loving, dreaming. Somewhere in the vicinity of the old market place, Socrates, a valiant soldier in his time, had quietly sipped death rather than deny his principles. The ultimate in heroism, he thrilled, to drink a toast to death and, slowly, to grow cold.

The Greeks had humanized their gods and deified their men. When the gods are leveled men may become their equals. How the ancients had understood the vanities in the fragile human heart!

He met other correspondents. Young John Bass, who was to manage the *Journal* crowd, gave him a letter from Hawkins sent "care of the *Journal* correspondents." Fairman had evidently told Amy that Stephen Crane had passed through New York and had avoided her;

that he was on his way to Greece. Fairman said that she was in need of more money.

Stephen crushed the letter in his pocket. Would he ever learn the truth about Amy?

In the square, he came upon Cora chatting gaily at a table in the sun, with young Mrs. Bass and several of the British correspondents.

He was strolling toward them when he heard a voice address her: "Lady Stewart!"

He gritted his teeth. Cora was in her glory. They must have been delighted to discover that she was married to an Englishman who was the son of the former commander of Her Majesty's forces in India.

He turned back to the hotel. He had needed this jolt of recognition. At Cook's, he bought a draft for one hundred dollars and mailed it to Hawkins with a simple note: "One hundred for Amy."

Cora spoke wistfully of Mrs. Bass, who was a new bride. "She's so young, so innocent, that I see myself in her as I was a few years ago. She likes me, I think." Her eyes narrowed. "I've proposed that she urge John to invite me to write for the paper."

He exploded, "For the *Journal!*"

"From the view of a woman who sees war for the first time."

"He will ask what you've written before."

"I've told Mrs. Bass that I've written many stories," she replied defiantly.

"In your memory book?"

"Your Amy is a writer, isn't she? From singer to writer?" She pouted. "I can do anything she can, Steve. You'll not oppose it?"

He sighed. "I'll not oppose it."

"Oh, Steve!" Instantly, her manner became feminine again. "Since Fate has brought us together, perhaps we may work together, too. I could never write as you do. I am not gifted. But serviceable impressions I surely might produce. And you would help me, read my copy, advise me?"

He promised, without enthusiasm. He hoped that Cora would not seek to do everything that Amy had done.

The night when rumors reached Athens that the Turks had bombarded Arta, he decided to move quickly. He had not traveled to Greece to escort Cora to the battlefield and correct her commas under shellfire.

"I'm leaving for the field. First to Nikopolis, then to Arta, and from Arta wherever the road leads."

She was dismayed. "John Bass wants to think it over. He may cable the home office. I couldn't go with you as a correspondent until he gives me the assignment."

He shook his head. He dared not wait. "I must be there. Hearst is expecting my copy from the front lines, not from Constitution Square."

"And you're leaving me behind?"

The Turks withdrew toward their headquarters at Janina. The Greeks pressed onward. Stephen was as elated as if he had a right to share in this success. When he saw Turkish fezzes lying upon the road "like drops of blood from some wounded leviathan," he smiled until he remembered that he had no quarrel with the fleeing soldiers.

He was delighted to come upon other correspondents, mostly Englishmen who had covered the Sudan, India, and South Africa, and a few who were here to learn what they could, including the art of writing.

Some provoked him by speaking of death vulgarly; he judged that those men were afraid and feared to have their fears suspected, as the man who is vulgar to a harlot deep in his soul fears her, and rants obscenely lest that fear be discovered.

He did not have to force his prose; his sentences seemed to be born of themselves when the artilleries barked like savage dogs and the cavalrymen and foot soldiers slashed angrily at the foe.

He saw that the callousness of soldiers and correspondents alike was an armor for innermost anxieties. He, too, strove to appear indifferent when he viewed the ruins of churches, came upon houses burning and flocks of sheep straying, and saw the miserable civilians rushing for their cellars and stables when the troops appeared.

One night, he awakened to find that he and his dragoman had been left behind. The battalion with which they had been bivouacking had been withdrawn without notice. He and his servant had to stumble down mountain paths in pursuit of the dying hoofbeats of the retreating cavalry. He tried desperately to make his way, never daring to show a light along a road that went nowhere in the pitch dark. The night was longer than any he had ever known, yet he felt brave because, Anatol, his dragoman, had melted in his cowardice into a creature who, if he could have mustered the nerve, would have clung to his employer's hand.

Some distance away, volleys cracked. The shells exploded and little rattles of lead played tattoos on innocent boulders. Stephen, concerned that they were being followed, carried his revolver in his fist. He had never killed a man; in the dark he might do it. The prospect both angered and encouraged him.

He shouted, "Halt! Who's there?" and again "Halt!" and thought how silly he had become. The correct word was "*Stasu!*"

He waved his revolver at shapes of nothing that loomed out of the blackness.

"Steve!"

"Cora!" Fear for her safety mingled with disbelief. Was she a captive of the Turks? Had she followed him with a rescue party? Anger welled that she, willfully, capriciously, had pursued him again.

"Cora!"

It was dangerous, but he was insanely provoked. In the midst of a sharp desire to clasp her in his arms in the dark, he struck a match. In the quick blaze before the flame died, he saw her in an enormous cloak, with a tiny felt hat on her head and a revolver and canteen strapped to her hips. Men, other correspondents he recognized, were behind her, and horses and more men.

"Crane, that you?" That was the impudent fellow who had called her Lady Stewart.

"Put out the light!" a voice growled. "Before someone shoots it out."

He embraced her, while someone chuckled. He enveloped her as if to protect her from her rascally escorts, and himself from the night and the enemies lurking in it.

"Crane, where are we?"

He was suddenly self-assured. They had been plodding ahead like fools; they were not his rescuers, he was *theirs!* He felt taller in the darkness.

Later, they lay on their blankets and listened to the night and the sporadic firing in the distance. Cora told him that she had been so worried for his safety that she had challenged the correspondents to accompany her. Fearing that he had been captured, she had threatened to go on alone.

"You might have been captured by the Turks!" A blond Christian woman would have been carried off to Salonika.

"So much has happened to me, Steve, that I no longer fear anything. I couldn't think of myself. Only you."

She had spent one night in a village where the only sleeping quarters available to a woman were in the town billiard hall. She had made her bed on the hard table and had laid out her hatpins to use against anyone who tried to molest her. The mayor had promised to stand guard outside the door; twice during the night someone had attempted to force entry. Oh, yes, John Bass had approved; she had already written her first war dispatch under the name "Imogene Carter." She pleaded, "Steve, will you please copy-edit?"

No longer resentful, he winked drolly at the stars.

CHAPTER 69

Back in the capital, after the fighting around Janina had ended, the rumor was that the big campaign would be fought in Thessaly, in the east. With Crown Prince Constantine in command, the Turks would surely be beaten.

"If the Greeks fail now," Stephen said grimly, studying his map, "the Turks will surprise them as they did in Epirus."

Meanwhile, waiting for Bass to give instructions, he edited Cora's

373

meager dispatches and instructed her in composition. When he was beside her, she took his guidance soberly; her prose, grammatically correct, was colorless. However, as soon as he left her, she relaxed and was ready to read her articles aloud to any correspondent who inquired about her progress.

Seeing her golden head in the sunshine, as she read from her writing-pad to the tall men crowding around her, he thought her foolish and presumptuous. She could not observe the ironical amusement in their eyes. "Imogene Carter!" The *nom de plume* delighted them; they applauded as if she were George Sand or George Eliot. With an effort, he concealed his vexation, wondering how much of the Jacksonville story, familiar to several of the American correspondents, had become gossip in Athens.

It struck him that she might deliberately have come after him across Europe to indulge a fancy that she, too, could become a writer. She was capable of having plotted it.

On the other hand, he admired the cool nerve that had brought her stumbling up those dark roads out of Arta. No perils dismayed her. Whatever her tragic past, she had the will to triumph over it. In that respect, she was much like Amy, but finer, more sensitive. Perhaps, if she persevered, Cora might learn to write passably well; Amy had not been a born writer either. And thinking of the other woman, he sentimentalized for her condition and bought a draft for twenty-five pounds to send to Hawkins. "I love Amy," he added and, for a postscript, "Tell Fairman go to hell."

"Crane!"

It was Dick Davis, in Athens at last, and representing the London *Times* after all.

"The war has waited for you."

Davis wore a smart cap, a trim coat, a shirt with a wing collar, riding breeches, and puttees. "You're not hurt, Steve? Thank God!" In Florence, he had heard that Stephen Crane had been wounded in Thessaly. "Gave me a jolt."

Stephen pointed to the ribands pinned to the breast pocket of the other's coat.

Davis only grinned. Then the grin faded. He was staring at Cora who, with writing-pad in the lap of a broad skirt and a tiny hat upon her head, was again reading to the correspondents.

"Woman correspondent at the front," Stephen said drily. "Friend of mine."

The Davis gaze was curious but not unfriendly. "Striking!" When Stephen introduced him, he bowed.

Cora glowed. She said, "I've read everything of yours, Mr. Davis, since *Gallegher*." Breezily, she ran on, "Stephen is determined to make a writer of me. Unfortunately, I haven't the talent ever to make more than a scribbler."

Davis returned gallantly, "Anyone who has the friendship and esteem of Stephen Crane is already more fortunate than most mortals."

He won her with that. However, she was his match, for she praised the Van Bibber stories and other Davis achievements.

"He is very handsome," she declared after Davis had bade them good day, "but it's easy to see that he envies you. He wishes that he could write as well as Stephen Crane."

When John Bass advised his correspondents to get ready to leave for Velestinos and Larissa, he announced that Davis would accompany their party.

"And Imogene Carter?" Stephen asked.

"I hope that she will come with us." Bass was eager to take his bride along, and she would be more at ease if another woman were present.

They boarded the steamer *Thessalia* out of Piraeus. The cargo consisted of rice, flour, correspondents, and bleating sheep. In the evening, when the aromas of roasting lamb drifted from the galley, Stephen groused that they were lucky not to be carrying goats. The Greek cuisine, with its emphasis on olive oil and garlic, disturbed him more than the pitching Aegean.

The next morning, they entered the Gulf of Euboea and slipped through narrow straits where the black capes came down to stand in the bluish waters.

Stephen was suddenly ill. He blamed the daily offerings of lamb and pilaf, the wine, which tasted of molasses and tar, and even the peerless sky and the spangled night. He could no longer endure the interminable conversations in which his colleagues argued which god had dwelt on the passing shores, where the centaurs had been tutored and the nymphs had been ravished. However, he felt better after fasting a day, and was much improved when they steamed into the Gulf of Volo and saw snow-capped Mount Pelion stretching down the Magnesian Peninsula with white villages on its shoulders.

All agreed that the Powers would not let the war be waged indefinitely, for at Volo, German, French, Italian and British gunboats were anchored not far from the Greek flotilla. At night, searchlights from the warships wandered over the countryside. Signal fires burned in the hills.

The train to Velestinos, which climbed a gently rising slope between two ranges of undulating hillocks, came to a halt in the midst of a herd of sheep milling across the tracks. The fireman clanked his bell for the shepherd. By the time the other had appeared, like a figure out of a picture Bible, in his sheepskin and sandals, with crooked staff in his fist, the steam was down. Passengers and crew adjourned to eat a late lunch in the grass.

Cora said, "Mr. Davis thinks now that he has seen me somewhere."

He was silent until they reached Larissa. "*Has* he seen you, Cora?" She shook her head. "I would have remembered him."

Walking the arched bridge over the Peneus, the next day, his knees began to give. He hurried to the nearby Turkish cemetery and rested on the fallen gravestones. Sitting there, he wrote a dispatch; he was not filing enough copy to suit the *Journal*. Regiments moved to the right and to the left; the skirted *evzones*, sweeping by, lifted their rifles in salute.

Returning to Velestinos, Bass and Davis decided to wait for a clash of arms. Stephen was obliged to remain beside them. However, Mrs. Bass was suddenly unwell. Her husband, eager to send her back to Volo, asked Stephen to take both women under his care. Imogene Carter, too, must have become fatigued on these roads.

Stephen obeyed, but Cora was as hardy as any of the men. He marveled how easily she had adapted herself to the rough life. No sooner did they halt anywhere than she was laundering, either her garments or his, in the small basin which she had wisely added to their luggage. She complained only that she missed her bath.

"You would have been more comfortable in Athens."

The blue eyes were as sapphire as the sky. "I am with you, Stephen, and that is where I want to be."

In Volo, he was grateful for the soft bed at the Hotel Minerva, but Cora would not rest. She tramped to the Red Cross Society hospitals and made beds, carried bedpans, comforted the wounded, and gave away bits of Stephen's precious chocolate. In the evenings, she helped Mrs. Merlin, wife of the British vice-consul, who had thrown her house open to the civilians evacuated from the north. Several cases of dysentery had been reported.

At midnight, Stephen and Cora walked out into the moonlight where the bay ran silver. Mount Pelion was a sprawling giant brooding over the town.

They strolled hand in hand as if they were children. "There is so much pain and terror in the world, Stephen, and one can do so little."

A wave of tenderness swept over him. She had quality.

"If the world would forget us, we might be happy," he murmured. Impulsively, he proposed that they hire a boat to take them sailing. They had seldom been alone since their arrival in Greece.

The rest of the night they sat on the deck of the little craft and watched the moonlight gliding over the ancient landscape.

In the morning, they breakfasted under an awning. She taught the man in the galley to make Stephen's coffee American style.

With the boat anchored in the middle of the gulf, they bathed over the side. He swam out so far that she became frightened and shouted for him to return.

"If anything should happen to you, what would my life be?"

He looked deeply into her eyes. She did love him! And he recog-

376

nized, at last, that he loved her dearly. They stayed together upon the Gulf a second night.

Lying in each other's arms, they felt the mountains rocking. He stirred. "Artillery!" Had they missed the battle? The hours of serenity had ended.

Volo was swollen with new hordes of refugees. He must push on to Velestinos where the battle was being fought.

Cora refused to remain behind: "Wherever you go, Stephen!"

Together, they hastened northward, then in a westerly direction, first jostling in a cart for several miles, then slogging on foot over muddy roads, while streams of panicked villagers tumbled from the hills and away from the cannonading.

It was incredible that, on this fear-tossed countryside, they should come upon a single familiar face. Yet, at the first battery, they sighted John Bass. "Where were you?" They had, indeed, missed the first day of a great battle.

Davis, nearby, merely grinned. As Cora mounted the hilltop, struggling under her saddle bag, he called, "Nearly missed the whole show!" His eyes gleamed in acknowledgment of the woman's pluck.

Stephen sensed that both Bass and Davis charged Cora with having detained him, as if the war would run out of slaughter for him to describe. He drew her after him into an adjacent sector.

He was utterly absorbed as he looked on and penciled his notations. Cora, lying prone, busied herself with the field glasses.

Writing *The Red Badge* had been art; here was the brutal reality.

An explosion, too close for safety, caused his heart to ricochet against his ribs. He seized Cora's arm and pulled her under a tree. He stared at the woods as if the mouth of hell had opened.

"Stay here!" he shouted.

The barrage was dropping toward a fortified place on the next hill. "Don't move from here!"

Her face drained of color. Her stricken eyes pursued his figure.

As he plodded on, past the men in the slit trenches, he saw that they were calmly eating bread or polishing their rifles. Some stood in pools of water from the rainstorms of the first day.

He entered a grassy area for which, it seemed, Death had as yet made no plans. Reserves waited under vegetation that dripped from a recent shower.

He gazed in astonishment at the wounded. They were cast in all poses of agony or coma, some lying in puddles or in bloody patches, others sprawling with limbs mangled or limp, or jaws so crushed that the supremacy of the human countenance was reduced to a hideous apparition. Never had simple survival seemed so important.

He shuddered. He had reached a peak of excitement in which he could make no move without bursting, like a man in the most intimate moments of love.

Upon a vast mound, he sighted Dick Davis, his strong profile against the clouding sky, standing behind a battery of howitzers and calmly observing the guns loaded and fired, clapping his field glasses to his eyes to judge accuracy and effectiveness. Once, as a distant hill vomited dirt and scraps of metal and the earth quaked, Davis turned to shout approval.

In the late afternoon, Stephen rejoined Cora. There was no time to compare notes. The enemy infantry was advancing again. He shared the quiver of dismay running through the lines as the defenders, seriously outnumbered, understood that they were facing fresh troops.

Then the bugles were blowing the retreat, and he shared the shame of the Greek forces.

Bass had guessed earlier that the Crown Prince would order a withdrawal. From Pharsalos, he would be falling back to Domokos; from Velestinos, General Smolenski would retreat to Halmyros on the Gulf of Volo.

Stephen instructed Cora to hurry back to Volo to pack their gear. He halted a wagon and boosted her up among the wounded. She could take refuge with the Merlins, under the protection of the British flag.

He had become parched in the heat. His canteen was empty; not a drop. He looked for a water bottle that some fleeing soldier might have dropped. He kicked aside empty wineskins, cooking utensils, and articles of clothing.

Near a rivulet, he came upon the stiffened body of a large black dog. Three puppies lay rigid at her teats; a fourth, with a white body and black markings, still whimpered. Tenderness flooded Stephen as the surviving puppy whined.

He gathered it into his hand. The little tongue came out to lick his fingers. The creature needed water.

He spied a soldier sitting upright with his back against a tree. Two arms seemed to be holding the man; someone had him captive against the trunk.

He stammered, *"Hydros!"* Water for the little dog.

The soldier was contemptuously silent.

Stephen shouted again before he saw that the man was dead. The two arms about his chest were the crossed bandoleers in the waning light.

As he dropped to one knee to undo the canteen, the body bent forward as if to embrace him. The mustaches were blue-black and bristling, the eyes, a mild, wondering brown.

He poured a little of the water into his palm. The puppy lapped eagerly. He put the canteen to his own lips and drank.

"The puppy was thirsty!" he explained to the air, as if the dead

378

man were witnessing his act. He was surprised at the hoarseness of his voice.

He intended to return the man to his upright position. But the open eyes, in glazed brown astonishment, were staring, between the spread knees, at the earth that would soon cover them with immortal darkness.

As the Greek armies engaged in a general retreat, Stephen now went back and forth to various sectors of the wavering front. The line officers and the foot soldiers were confident that the enemy could still be halted. He interviewed Greek wounded and Turkish prisoners-of-war in hospitals and camps.

Cora, following him wherever she could, wrote more dispatches as Imogene Carter. She rode with him on the riderless horses he caught; when these were reclaimed by the cavalry, she tramped beside him with her saddlebags over her shoulder. Her costume had become torn and muddied. The pert hat was gone; instead, she wore a peasant woman's kerchief. At night, although Turkish patrols tramped nearby, they camped on the hillsides. They shared hard biscuits, figs and goat-cheese for their supper, and divided the watch, for pillagers roved the battlegrounds to rob the dead and the wounded.

They were ready to board a fisher-boat from Agria to Athens, ten gold francs a head, when Sylvester Scovel appeared in a hired launch.

They were in Chalkis with Scovel when the news came that the Turks had triumphed at Domokos; the Crown Prince was again withdrawing.

As an atmosphere of gloom and defeat blanketed the nation, Stephen felt himself sagging. He was relieved that an armistice was to be signed. He had held out longer than Dick Davis, who had been seized with an attack of sciatica at the front. But he walked about like a gray corpse, too stubborn to heed Cora's pleas and go to bed. At least, he had not failed the *Journal.*

The next morning, he could not get up. It was only dysentery, he assured Cora. He felt as if he had suffered a personal defeat and no longer needed his weary body. He smiled wanly at her panic.

A German physician from one of the gunboats in the harbor prescribed blackberry brandy and chocolate: "As good as anything!" As he percussed Stephen's chest, he made a long face. "A man with such a bronchial apparatus should absolutely not lie down on damp battlefields!"

There was no chocolate. Cora gave Stephen the powdered chalk that Doctor Freidrich had secured. Anything that might check the dysentery would be welcome; some patients died from extreme weakness. Scovel toured every bar in Athens until he had located a bottle of blackberry brandy.

Stephen, acutely mortified by his illness, feared that Cora, who tended him day and night, might be infected. So might Scovel, who faithfully called every morning to help Cora in the sickroom. The story of her courage at Velestinos and her devotion to Stephen had reached Athens; noble hostesses now asked her to their teas. Someone intimated that the Queen might receive her; Her Majesty had expressed a wish to meet all the war correspondents who were still in Greece.

Alone with Scovel, Stephen candidly admitted that he had no desire to return home. He could not take Cora back to Port Jervis and Hartwood; they could not marry as long as Captain Stewart refused to grant her a divorce. He had no hope.

"She's a good influence for you." Scovel had known the Hotel de Dreme. "She's an ambitious woman, but she's ambitious for your sake."

Stephen had considered moving from capital to capital as a roving correspondent: Constantinople, Cairo, Rome, Vienna, Berlin. He might do special articles for the *Journal*, the *World* and the *Herald*. Stories were simmering on the back stove in his mind; possibly a novel on this Greek business. Paul Reynolds would represent him in America; he would find an agent to sell his work in London.

Scovel said, "A man needs a place to turn back to. One day you'll have to come home."

Furthermore, according to Doctor Freidrich, foreign cuisines were not for the Crane digestion; more travel would expose him to more infection.

"In time, she'll hear favorably from her husband. The fellow will give up. What has he to gain?"

Stephen said impatiently, "I'll be twenty-seven in November!"

Scovel guffawed, "Old man Crane!"

CHAPTER 70

He arrived in England with a mistress, a sickly constitution and a perfectly sound reputation as a successful, and therefore well-to-do, American author.

"Joseph went down into Egypt with less."

"You are Stephen Crane," she reminded him. "You're not living on your Bowery now. England will pay you according to your station. I shall manage."

He could scarcely complain, for at a London bank Cora had received funds from her attorney in Jacksonville for her equity in the Hotel de Dreme. He did not inquire; she enjoyed her secrets. He came upon her one day counting pound notes as if they were cabbage leaves. He laughed when she tucked them into her bosom.

"Not a secure hiding place."

"Never mind. You write, and I'll find the money."

They agreed to be "Mr. and Mrs. Crane."

"Will you be hearing from Captain Stewart soon?"

"Whether I hear soon or late, Steve, it is better that you and I be together than apart. Our friends will understand."

Harold Frederic greeted him with a bear hug. "Come to stay with me at Homefield. In Surrey. Large house."

Stephen murmured, "Traveling with a lady."

"Wife?" He probed shrewdly. "God's trousers, Steve! A Greek princess, or a Turkish harem girl?"

"A Boston girl married to an Englishman who won't give her a divorce. I met her in Florida. She came to Europe with me, and to Greece."

Frederic uttered a short whistle, and became silent.

"You don't approve," Stephen muttered. "We'd marry if we could."

"Thinking of my own problems, not yours!" He gestured with his little finger. "Listen to me, and I'll fill your ears."

Frederic had a fine house at Brook Green in Hammersmith where he spent weekends with his wife Grace, whom he had married at her mother's bedside when he was twenty-one. They had raised a family —his first-born, Ruth, was his favorite—but had drifted apart. Now, during the week, he lived in Surrey with Kate Lyons, with whom he had raised three other children, Helen, Heloise, and Barry.

"You'll like Katie," he added simply. "I love her. But Grace will never give me a divorce."

Stephen loyally suppressed a feeling of shock. For, in that flickering instant as Frederic eyed him warily, he had seen the anguish, the plea for understanding, as well as the defiance. "It's not as you would want it."

Harold grimly struck the table. "By the Eternal, no!" His voice lowered. "What shall we do in these situations, Steve? Do we live, do we die? I say that we live and make the best of it, damn our souls! I couldn't go back home either, could I?"

He was saying that the situation with Cora could be, must be, endured. Others had it worse.

Stephen computed gravely. "You have seven children."

Frederic pretended to be amused. "No credit to me for all that. A stable groom could do as much." He repeated, "You'll like Katie. She's my Mrs. Harold Frederic to everyone."

Stephen did like Katie Lyons. He could see her devotion to Harold in the quiet gleam of her dark eyes, hear it in the softness of her rich, throaty voice. When Harold became boisterous, she laid a finger to her lips, and he subsided. Cora, too, liked Katie; Stephen had not yet confided that there were two Frederic households.

Harold, rushing about London like a Guards regiment in full war panoply, got them out of the tiny rooms they had rented and into a villa at Oxted. Above the house rose the sails of an old windmill that no longer turned; in the cellar were the great stones that had once ground meal. The little hamlet, with a church, a smithy, a pond, and a common beyond which green fields dropped away into a haze, stood, with the windmill behind it, like a knight with upraised arms.

When they first approached the house, Stephen declared whimsically that he felt like Don Quixote.

Harold, ever ready with barbs even for those to whom he gave his affection, rejoined, "England is the place for broken lances."

He was a man who, expecting offense, elected to give it first. He tossed off skewering opinions on every subject, on Aubrey Beardsley and *The Yellow Book*, on wretched Oscar Wilde in Reading Gaol, on Meredith, Swinburne, Henley, Kipling, and even on Henry James, whom he called a friend.

The rooms in the villa were small and dark; the coal cookstove was primitive. They sheltered Mrs. Ruedy, Velestinos, the foundling puppy brought from Greece, and Aristotle and Adoni, two Greek servants. They had no room for Aristotle and had to find him employment in the village. Cora complained that Adoni alone could not administer to their wants.

"I've never had one servant, much less two."

She flared. "I've always had servants!"

She resented being taken from London, where she had friends and could attend gay parties. Old acquaintances had arranged for choice seats outside of St. Paul's for the Queen's Jubilee Festival. He pretended to scorn spectacles, so she went alone; he suspected that she preferred it. He would not listen to her description of the coaches of state, the austere dignitaries, and the march of the colorful regiments.

"Did Captain Stewart appear?" he asked darkly.

The solicitors said that he was still in Africa. "Would I not tell you immediately?"

In a fury, he wrote new poems that reflected his current chagrin, and angrily pursued the old habit of writing late at night.

Cora asked to be permitted to sit in his room. He consented until he found her staring at him.

"What were you thinking then?" she asked. "A cloud passed over your brow."

He dropped his eyes to his papers. "I didn't realize that I was on view."

She withdrew with a hard clack of heels across the bare floor.

He would not come to bed. He sat up, as in the old days, smoking and thinking, writing his prose with controlled reluctance so that each phrase bit into the stone of his narration like a sculptor's chisel.

He slept late and disrupted the routine of the household. When he arose, his mind still churned from the stream of images that had seethed through the night. He grimaced at the hot breakfast. He chafed to be at his writing table again.

He was writing a story of the Greek War, "Death and the Child."

"Do you think there may have been a child?" she asked.

His heart fell. She was thinking of Amy; in one swoop, she had plucked him naked.

"Of course not."

"To whom will you sell the story?"

"I am not a merchant," he replied coldly, and sulked the rest of the day. The work had its own right to exist and to be published. He wished that she had not reminded him of Amy; her image would now haunt him.

They had differences about money. She had been spending her own funds on the household. He expected money from McClure's and Appleton's; none arrived. At last, Pawling sent an advance from Heinemann. He gravely turned the draft over to Cora.

The next day, she filled the house with flowers and hired a pair of saddle-horses for a ride into the country.

"I don't know when the next check will come. We mustn't go into debt."

"We agreed that I should manage," she replied curtly. Then, relenting, "Oh, Steve, trust in me!"

He saw that she must live in her own style, and was troubled. He had never supported a wife; he had never supported anyone except Stephen Crane. In the old days, he had made five dollars last a week and more; now five pounds would not do it. He dared not complain, for Cora would reply that she spent her own money quite as freely. On the Jubilee trip to London, she had purchased a vast quantity of gowns, shoes, and hats, including garments for Mrs. Ruedy. Well, Cora had promised to manage.

Sidney Pawling spoke to Edward Garnett, who lived nearby at The Cearne, and soon there was an invitation to tea.

The Cearne was a fine newly-built house of stone and oaken timbers which sat midway up a hill of beechwoods. Behind it was an apple orchard. From the windows, Kent stretched in a lazy vista.

The Garnetts were a rare couple. Edward was over six feet tall, with thick-lensed spectacles on a sensitive, poetic face, and a chrysanthemum shock of hair. Spilling ashes from his cigarette on his tweeds, he came forward shyly, "Welcome, welcome, Crane!" His wife, Constance, frail beside him, was bright-eyed and equally friendly. "Mrs.

Crane, we've longed for the pleasure of greeting you and your husband."

Garnett freely admitted to an admiration of *The Red Badge*. It had, of course, been influenced by the masters. But which masters? he pressed Stephen.

He asked also for estimates of the contemporary French writers. Stephen, always uneasy under interrogation, blandly denied acquaintance with any of the Frenchmen. Garnett was nonplussed.

Mrs. Garnett amused Cora with anecdotes of her early travels in Russia. Fascinated by the language, she had resolved to translate the great masters. She was aware that Harold Frederic had been to Russia in the year of the famine. She had visited Tolstoy at Yasnaya Polyana.

Her husband approved of her translations of Tolstoy and Turgeniev. However, he held that it would not be worth her while to translate Dostoievski. She gaily declared that she would translate him anyway.

Stephen was profoundly impressed by their erudition. Edward Garnett was only three years his senior.

"See how respectfully they received us!" Cora chortled happily on the way home. "My Stephen Crane!"

Through Edward Garnett, they met other figures in the literary world, among them Ford Maddox Hueffer, a tall blond man with an amazingly receding chin. Hueffer, whose father was the music critic of the London *Times,* was in many ways like Harold Frederic, an explosive young man with positive opinions on every subject. He lived in a stone cottage that seemed to have been thrown together by lazy Druids, and was confident that the world owed him a better place. He spoke of *The Red Badge* as if it were Deuteronomy.

Stephen was content to enjoy his fame in the homes of others, but Cora, restless unless she was the hostess, insisted on returning the hospitality.

"Our little brick villa is only temporary, everyone knows that. Until we find a house worthy of Stephen Crane, we must receive here."

"I know only Harold and the Garnetts and a few others."

"Robert Barr, the Canadian novelist, who is a friend of Harold's, lives nearby. And the moment that England becomes aware——"

He groaned. She spoke of "England" as if it were a living organism that would come riding into his courtyard to lap up the whiskey and eat all the biscuits.

"You are Stephen Crane!" she concluded smugly. "I remember it, if you do not."

She made him a study overlooking the garden. "You can see the flowerbeds when you work."

"I work at night."

"You might work better in the sunlight."

"I am a creature of the dark," he replied drily. "I like the night."

One evening, she burst into the study with a cry that Velestinos was ailing. The little dog was in convulsions. Stephen ran for the animal doctor. They spent the next eleven days nursing the creature, which lay in Cora's bed with pillows all around and under him.

Stephen stroked and stroked the poor creature and faithfully administered the potions that the doctor had prescribed.

"He'll live!" he insisted. "I won't have him die. Listen to me, Velestinos. You must live!"

Neither his praises nor his caresses elicited the feeblest lift and thump of the tail. The large brown eyes glazed in the grip of death.

"You must brace yourself, Steve." She saw him crushed as the animal slowly expired.

They buried Velestinos in the rhododendron bed in the garden. Cora placed the collar that Scovel had bought him in Athens around the stiff neck.

"It's unjust," she said wearily, clinging to Stephen. "Unjust!"

He wanted no comforting. Death was at its cruelest when it descended to slay dumb creatures.

CHAPTER 71

He had upsetting news the morning they were to drive to Homefield for Harold's birthday. Burt wrote from Binghamton that Townley, who had been with him for several months, had disappeared and gone on a drunken spree. He had run down the streets, shouting and frightening the passers-by. The police had finally caught him. Now Townley was restricted to the premises and small boys came every day to hang over Burt's fence and watch him ranting and raving.

Stephen was shocked. He had known that Townley was ill, that alcohol seemed to have destroyed his moral fiber, but he had not suspected that the mental deterioration was so advanced.

He decided to send word to Harold that he could not appear at the luncheon. Cora insisted that they must go.

"After all, you could do nothing for your brother."

"Nor for myself!" he retorted bitterly.

As they drove to Homefield in a hired trap, a fox crossed the road. Stephen, still bemused over Townley, saw the little beast lope before them. Suddenly the horse bolted and the carriage careened. Stephen rose to his feet and shouted. A harness strap broke, and the vehicle went over into the ditch.

Cora shrieked. She was unhurt, but Stephen had been pitched out. A shaft had fallen across his chest.

He was unconscious for several minutes. He awakened to find her screaming over him.

"You're alive!" she gasped. "Steve, Steve!"

His eyes lighted mockingly, although the stabbing pain made him fear that his ribs had been broken.

Cora and Adoni helped him sit up.

"Is the horse hurt?" he demanded.

Adoni caught the runaway. Despite his agony, Stephen, leaning on Cora, tottered to his feet to calm the animal. He threw his arms about the mane and pressed his cheek to the quivering muzzle. "Poor girl, the fox frightened you." He felt that the mishap might not have occurred but for his preoccupation over Townley. "The foxes in this world frighten everyone."

Now Cora was for turning back. But, after a nearby physician had bandaged his chest, he insisted that they go on.

They were three hours late reaching Homefield. Katie, whose faith excluded any belief in disease and injury unless it was caused by evil thoughts, assured the suffering guest that, if he rid his mind of everything but God, he would soon be hale and hearty.

"I'm full of bad thoughts!" he rejoined, as Harold supported him indoors.

"Don't say it, Stephen!" She would offer silent prayers.

Harold fetched a tumbler of brandy, his favorite remedy for any ailment.

He would not permit Stephen and Cora to return to Ravensbrook. A villa on the Irish coast had been put at his disposal by Mrs. Rice, an admirer. As soon as Stephen was able to travel, the Cranes and the Frederics left together for County Cork. Harold grandly promised to foot the bills.

"Dear Stephen, if only you will remember that God is love," Katie pleaded.

"I'll try," he promised. She was so dear that he was loath to offend her.

During their days at the Irish villa, Harold, Katie, Stephen, and Cora rode out to visit the fishing villages and tramped the hills. In the evenings, after they had dined together, the couples separated. Harold was driving through the revisions of his new novel, *Gloria Mundi*. In an adjoining room, the Cranes could hear him intoning passages to Katie.

Stephen made notes on the Irish scenes. He had planned to write a story while in County Cork, but he was depressed, despite the pleasant surroundings and Harold's boisterous efforts to keep him amused. Katie might pray for him, but his ribs still pained and any sudden cough or sneeze sent a radiation of needles through his chest.

To please Cora, he retired early. When she was asleep, he arose again, slipped into his robe and tried to write by lamplight. The

386

words were sticky; the sentences dragged. He went to sit in the wing chair by the fireplace.

The nights being foggy, the servant had brought in a huge log and, with Harold's help, had wormed it into place. The timber had been damp; it had smoked for several hours before the bark would begin to sputter. Finally, little blue flames began to dance from underneath, licking the furrowed edges. Soon yellow tongues emerged and an orange blaze crackled; at the sides, smoke still curled feebly.

He heard Cora stirring. She came out in a green wrapper. The Frederics must have retired; someone was snoring.

"It's eerie!" She took the wing chair on the opposite side of the fireplace and watched the shadows dancing on the walls.

"Ghosts!" he replied, and opened his notebook.

The draft on the floor chilled her ankles. She tucked her feet under her.

He enjoyed the lights burnishing the tresses at her shoulders. Cora was like a schoolgirl in this pose.

The log shifted, and sparks shook out.

"Oh!" It had startled her. She saw him bemused. The presence of the notebook prohibited small talk.

A blaze shot up from the back of the log. The flames were blue with cones of green. He observed how the carved escutcheons on the stone mantel had blackened through the years.

"I love you, Steve!"

He heard her, and smiled. As he looked up, a charred fragment exploded in the fireplace. Something began to smoke on the rug at his feet. He peered down intently. The smell of burning wool assailed his nostrils.

"Steve!"

As the rug burst into flames, he sat paralyzed with fright. He should be flinging his robe upon the burning spot. Instead, he sat rooted while the blaze sped toward him. With a greedy roar, it reached his slippered feet. He wanted to jerk his arms free, but they were fixed against his chair. He could not stir! The hem of his robe lighted fiercely. He felt the sharp tongues licking at his ankles. As he smelled the hair burning, he uttered a wild cry. The cruel heat enveloped him. Tiny vipers of coral and blue and orange wrapped around his legs and hissed upward. He writhed. His knees were charring; his thighs were scorched. A ring of fire engirdled his hips. He felt the snakes slithering on the inside of his thighs, and gritted his teeth for the pain of the viper-bite to come.

He heard a fearsome explosion. He sat in a cloud of stifling smoke, and coughed. He was blackened from the waist down; where his genitals had been was a large gaping hole. He began to sob uncontrollably. The fire had castrated him!

"Steve!"

He gasped, tears rolling down his cheeks. His hand reached timorously for his flesh.

"Steve!"

His gaze shot toward the rug. The sparks had burned a neat round hole in the rug, and had gone out. His robe was untouched, his thighs, his legs—everything was hale and sound. The fire had never reached him; he was unharmed.

"Steve, how can you sit there and watch the sparks burn a hole in the rug?" She was stamping her little foot on the place. "What will Mrs. Rice think?"

He threw her a sickened glance. His body was whole, although in the twinkling of an eyelid, he had been the victim of a monstrous fantasy. "I guess I dozed off!"

"Dozed off!" She was furious. "Your eyes were wide open!"

A shudder wandered down his spine. It had been a weird nightmarish hallucination!

He was trembling again. One side of his face was heated from the fire, the other cool.

"Are you a man?" the child in "Death and the Child" had asked the correspondent. He searched for the trigger that had exploded into this hideous punishment.

A dark figure loomed over him. Again he was frozen, convinced that he had projected a fantasy of a man whose potency had been obliterated by fire.

"Steve!" Cora was screaming. "What is it? Your face is terrible—like a face in ashes."

Again, in a trice, it was gone. He stirred uneasily as she caressed him.

"What is it, dearest?"

He regarded the shadows of helpless men cavorting on the walls, and the shape of the story that had been lurking in his mind clicked firmly as though he had locked it in a strongbox.

"Come to bed, Steve."

"Got a story——" he mumbled.

He followed his shadow to the table, and took up his pen.

He wrote until the gray dawn found him spent. The tale was strange, paradoxically of a dark Caliban imprisoned behind a face destroyed by fire. Its meaning was clouded only because he could not bear its overtones. He continued to work on the story the next evening and the next, feverishly anxious to purge himself utterly.

When he read the manuscript to Frederic, the other grimaced. "Revolting! Story of a man who lost his face! What do you call it?"

" 'The Monster.' "

Harold snorted. "Must be another of your 'orphic' secrets, Steve. I don't understand it, and I don't like it."

He nodded glumly.

388

"Tear it up!"

"Not on your tintype!" he exploded. "The Monster" had cleansed him of a fear that he could not believe now had ever possessed him. It was too painful.

CHAPTER 72

Cora, reading the *New Review*, came upon *The Nigger of the Narcissus*. She brought it to his attention because Mr. Garnett had praised it. Indeed, Garnett had discovered the author, Joseph Conrad, while reading for T. Fisher Unwin, the publisher.

Stephen became absorbed in the chronicle of James Wait, the towering Negro seaman. He relished the descriptive passages: "The whites of his eyes and his teeth gleamed distinctly, but the face was indistinguishable. His hands were big and seemed gloved."

Narcissus, like "The Monster," was the story of a Negro. Except in the writings of the Southern tellers of tales, no one, to his knowledge, had treated Negro characters seriously.

However, the resemblance ended with the color. "The Monster" was the story of the hostler Henry Johnson whose face had been destroyed by flames while rescuing little Jimmie Trescott from a burning house. Stephen's unfortunate black man had been rejected by society because he had become repulsive. "The Monster," swept on by his disenchantment with a community that created outcasts and savagely beached them, was a social study, his first since *Maggie* and *George's Mother*. *The Nigger of the Narcissus* was a story of the sea and men who lived by it.

He admired the rhythm of Conrad's prose. Every roll of the sea, every heave of the deck, was recorded in thick verbal strokes. James Wait was a proud, cantankerous man, ailing from consumption, alternately despised and feared, accepted and rejected by his shipmates. Evidently, Conrad both loved and hated the sea. In his best sentences, crystals of brine glistened, spume rose, and sea birds screamed.

At Heinemann's, Stephen enthusiastically recommended the novel to Sidney Pawling.

The editor beamed. They were to publish *The Nigger* in December. "He's quality."

"We're of the same opinion." Pawling confirmed that Edward Garnett had brought Joseph Conrad to light. "When Unwin froze, because of the failure of Conrad's first two books, Garnett brought him to us. I took *The Narcissus* to Henley at *New Review* for the serial rights."

"Quality," Stephen repeated.

The delighted Pawling arranged for a luncheon with the new author.

"He's a Pole. A dreamer fellow who went to sea, got his master's certificate at twenty. Korzeniowski: Joseph Conrad Korzeniowski. English is his third language, Polish and French the others."

When Stephen, unpunctual as usual, finally appeared, the editor was already seated beside a man whose bearded face rose like a dark spade. Conrad's hand, strong and knobby, greeted him warmly.

The eyes were dark brown, the lids somewhat folded over. The cheekbones were prominent, the high forehead sallow, the hair neatly combed. The pointed beard accentuated the almost oval shape of the face.

"I liked your work!" Stephen declared.

The brown eyes kindled. "I am honored." The voice was husky, the pronunciation foreign.

"Best I've read in many moons."

Conrad glowed. "Many moons!" he repeated. He had read *The Red Badge of Courage*, and been greatly moved. "You are so young, now I am ashamed of myself."

Stephen grinned. He had been awkward with the English authors; with this man he was at ease.

Pawling, playing the good publisher-father, ordered generously. He ate well, and listened proudly as his guests became animated. Conrad, the morose, was sparkling; Crane, the taciturn, was talking swiftly, yet enunciating carefully for the benefit of the alien.

"You've sailed to the places that I've always wanted to see: the Horn, India, Singapore, Borneo, Australia, the Congo. I'd give my right arm——"

Pawling signaled to the waiter to bring port and an old brandy, and fine Havanas. At four o'clock, he took his leave like a happy midwife. Authors, who work owls' hours, might spend their afternoons in talk; editors, to afford such authors, had to keep business hours.

Still talking, the two men strolled the London streets. Conrad limped from rheumatism in his left leg; Crane, his hands in his pockets and a cigarette dangling from his lips, nonchalantly kept in step.

They reached the Embankment. The autumn sun hung defiantly over the Thames.

"The red wafer!" Conrad pointed.

Stephen blushed.

"Ay, that *Red Badge!*" Conrad said. "They say you were twenty-five and had never seen a war. I am forty."

"I was twenty-three." He glowered at the river. "I should have had a better education in life and in living, in everything."

"I am fourteen years older than you. Crane, you have got the time to learn."

"That's it," Stephen replied gloomily. "I haven't got the time."

"Also, I have paid for my education." Conrad tolled off his ailments: malaria, neuralgia, liver trouble, gout; in damp weather he limped and his legs swelled. He had spent months in sanitaria, at Marienbad and at Champel. "There is one gift—you call it?—that I have, that nobody else can have the same. My wife, Jessie." They had married a year and a half ago when she was twenty-two and he thirty-nine.

Stephen was silent. He was unaccustomed to hear a man praise his wife.

"To me, yes, to me, in my youth a devil with women in every port, to me has come this quiet jewel of an English lady who loves me. When I write, she knows how to leave me alone with my world and to stay in hers. She knows soon as I will finish my work, I will come to her. When she marries with me, I have no shillings even for the flowers. But she believes in Joseph." He shook his head. "What do I do to deserve the love of such a woman?"

Stephen was thinking of Cora.

"When there is no money, she does not say, 'Joseph, you promise me this on my wedding day, you promise me that.' She takes what there is from me, and she brings happiness to my unhappiness."

Stephen murmured that he, too, had married recently. "In Athens." That was far enough away. "Come and visit us."

Conrad spread his hands. "We must wait for the baby soon." He said "bebby."

Stephen colored. There it was, in the natural course of marriage. But he and Cora would never have a child. "Then you and Mrs. Conrad must come to see us as soon as the baby is born."

"You will like Cora. My wife." Stephen went on. He found the words as lame as they were untrue. "My wife."

Conrad, unlike the reticent Englishmen, talked freely of his personal life. His father, a Polish poet and revolutionary, had been a skilled translator from the French and the English. The family had been intensely patriotic, also romantic. One uncle had been killed in a duel, another in a rebellion against the Czar, a third had been sentenced to Siberia for his political activities. Conrad's mother had died when he was seven, his father when he was twelve. At seventeen, he had gone to sea. In Marseilles, he had been wounded in a duel "because of a lady." He had also been a smuggler of arms to the Carlist insurgents in Spain.

"I have lived," he declared modestly. He cracked his big knuckles and sniffed at the wind, which had become damp. At Green Park, he studied the sunset, and pronounced, "Fair weather tomorrow," as if he were addressing his first mate.

London twilight turned to London dusk. At Kensington Gardens, they realized that they had missed their trains. Neither minded; the rare communion was precious. They were colleagues who must share experiences and barter those random bits of technique that artists, like artisans, acquire by trial and error. Crane, with his newspaper training, preferred direct narration: tell it clean, tell it quickly. Conrad, the sea captain, approached each story as if he were embarking on a long voyage. He favored the slow unfolding of complex relationships, as might be expected from a man who had spent months aboard a ship with a mixed crew to command, instruct, and subdue.

In the studios, Stephen had shunned talk of art as an indecent exposure of the mind. Here he listened gravely as Conrad speculated on the need of every novelist to create a world in which he could believe. This *was* the man; no pretense and no sham. An author's world, if it was to have any lasting value for its creator, must be "individual and a little mysterious."

"Do you agree," asked Joseph when they reached Piccadilly Circus, "that the artist must speak to our capacity for delight and wonder, to the sense of mystery surrounding our lives, to our sense of pity, and beauty, and pain?" He threw his head back as if he were addressing the London night. "He is dedicated to a feeling of fellowship with all creation, and to the subtle but invincible conviction of solidarity that knits together the loneliness of innumerable hearts . . . in dreams, Stephen, in joy, in sorrow, in aspirations, in illusions, in hope, in fear, which binds men to each other, which binds together all humanity—the dead to the living and the living to the unborn." He turned tear-glazed eyes upon his companion.

"Yes, Joseph," Stephen replied soberly, and stole another glance at the craggy countenance. A man's head is his castle.

Conrad, who had roved far in the literature of several languages for his models, declared of the *Comedie Humaine*, "This Balzac has made his own world." It was his goal to create a similar world.

They walked in an emotional silence, content with shared honesty, under streetlamps where midges gathered, past lawns where swirls of gray mist coiled eyelessly. It was nearly ten o'clock, with the air foggy and cold, when they remembered dinner.

They had to meet again soon. Conrad, confessing that for a writer there was forever doubt and fear, "a black horror" in every page he wrote, gave him a copy of *Almayer's Folly*, inscribed, "With the greatest regard and most sincere admiration," and a set of the proof sheets of *The Narcissus*.

"Only another writer," said Conrad, "can understand the misgivings, the doubts, and the reproaches that accompany the elation and the arrogances of creation."

Stephen was awed by the controlled mastery with which the death of James Wait was unreeled in *The Narcissus*. He wrote to Garland

and to Bacheller and, for the first time, he urged his friends to read another man's work.

He invited Conrad to Ravensbrook. However, since Mrs. Conrad was "not presentable," he accepted their counter-invitation.

At Fenchurch Station, Conrad was waiting in a fly. The intense, dark features lighted. "Stephen!" He flung his arms about him in the Continental fashion. "I think almost you have forgotten the day!"

On the drive to "Ivy Walls" farmhouse, Stephen felt that he had known this man with the Polish accent all his life.

"Crane, my wife Jessie. Jessie, our good Stephen Crane. He likes the death of James Wait."

Stephen thought Jessie Conrad beautiful, with her charmingly girlish face and the wealth of fine dark hair.

"You did not bring Mrs. Crane? I wished to meet her!" she pouted. "You must bring her soon."

He knew instantly that Cora would like her. She sat entranced while he talked about America and of Sponge, the black poodle that he and Cora had acquired.

"Dawgs!" she repeated impishly. American speech was as strange to her ears as to her husband's. Her family had never owned a dog.

He promised that, if the baby were a boy, he would present it with a fine little dog. "Every boy should have a dog!"

Conrad, beaming throughout, glanced proudly at his wife and at his friend: "See how well I have chosen!" His white teeth gleamed.

Elegant in his dark coat and wing collar, he good-humoredly presided over a dinner table of twelve, including his mother-in-law and eight of Jessie's brothers and sisters. During the meal, the Georges indulged in so much private conversation about persons and places dear to them that Conrad seemed like a foreign visitor calling at an English home instead of the master of the household.

After dinner, the family withdrew and the two men were left alone, to sit up half the night, smoking and talking. They went upstairs to enjoy the view of the lights on the Thames from the upper windows.

Joseph among his familiars placed him in a new dimension for Stephen. The world around Joseph might be adolescent; he remained adult and self-possessed. He had unswerving opinions and could be ironical, often as caustic with others as with himself. Remorselessly examining his own states of awareness, he tortured himself for meanings beyond meanings. He never left the seven seas of reflection.

"Every novel, every tale, is it not so, contains an element of autobiography?" He walked the floor as if it were his quarter-deck. "How else should we write except from the resources of the self?"

Stephen considered the strong differences between them. He strode through his dreams like a somnambulist; Conrad sleeping and waking, critically evaluated every vision. As to autobiography, was *The*

Red Badge autobiographical because it had been a wished-for adventure? A man's wishes and dreams, though unrecorded, might be the most significant part of his autobiography.

"Most important, Stephen, is to be true to the conscience!"

Joseph praised "A Man and Some Others." He vowed that it was an amazing bit of biography. "I am envious of you—horribly. Confound you—you fill the blamed landscape—you—by all the devils—fill the sea scape." He liked "The Open Boat" less, for the sea was his private world. To him, the wonder was that Stephen, out of a single experience, had made so much. He agreed with Edward Garnett that Stephen Crane was "a complete impressionist." He professed to be shocked that the American was only half aware of the exceptional quality of his achievement.

Stephen, richly pleased, said little. Even when Joseph moaned about the long, tormented hours at the writing table, he said nothing of his own tribulations. When the writing would not go, Conrad had attacks of neuralgia and gout. "I am like a damned paralyzed mud-turtle—I can't move—I can't write—I can't do anything."

Suddenly, Joseph was speaking of his courtship of Jessie. One day, he could no longer endure the casual meetings, first with Jessie and her mother, later with Jessie and one of the sisters. He eluded the chaperone and drove her to the National Gallery. He piloted her through rooms of paintings, sat her upon a bench and declared, "Look here! You must marry with me at once!" Then they went to lunch and ate something that gave them both a violent food-poisoning. "The bride, she came home ill!"

Stephen, still attentive, relived, in that meteor speed with which memories defy the laws of time and space, the circumstances of his own "courtship." Cora was again sitting beside him, under the dark veil, on the Florida-New York Special.

Conrad saw him bemused and, considerately, fell silent. They could share silence, too, while each fished in his own meditations.

CHAPTER 73

Since the return from Greece, he had entered an astonishingly creative period. "The Monster" was a strong story; so was "Death and the Child," still unpublished. The tale of the trip from Jacksonville to New York—"The Bride Comes to Yellow Sky"—he thought a daisy. He rushed the manuscript to Paul Reynolds before he showed a copy to Cora.

She read it suspiciously, for the title irked her. "Who is the bride?"

He had disguised the personal elements by placing the scene in

394

Texas: a simple sketch of Jack Potter, the town marshal, bringing back to Yellow Sky a bride who was neither pretty nor young, and fearing the opinions of his "innocent and unsuspecting community." He had introduced conflict in the person of Scratchy Wilson, the town bad man, who had come gunning for the marshal. But Potter had carried no gun, and Scratchy, faithful to the code of the West, was unable to satisfy his passion for a gun-fight. Whereby the tale ended, with the bridegroom saved because he had concealed himself behind the skirts of marriage.

"Do you like it?"

"Of course," she replied, with a little frown. Certain passages had struck jarring memories. She sat over it uneasily, searching "The Bride" for the special meanings it must have for him.

Yet, once he had shown it to her, he would not read it again. Joseph would have struggled until he had compelled every phrase and sentence to reveal its ironic secret. But Joseph would never believe that a demon drove him when he worked; when the demon relented, he laid down his pen. Cora might think that "The Bride" had drawn upon Joseph and his bride—or upon Amy—or upon her. He concealed a fragment of himself in every story; palimpsest or cryptography, he defied her to unwind his riddle.

Cora would not protest, because the money problem was pinching, and he needed stories to earn money. She had been right. English writers had suddenly become aware that he was among them. He was being invited to teas and to luncheons. He was also a fair target for random callers who descended upon Ravensbrook. That encouraged Cora to lay in additional supplies, for he must live the part of an American man of letters. Wine and whiskies; fruits in season—or out; flowers when available—or when not; pieces of silver and fine napery to grace the table. He was distressed, but he had no choice. She set up accounts with the local tradesmen.

People burst in from London with notes of introduction, youngsters brought stories for his praise, and Harold, dear fellow, thundered in at any hour with as many friends as he had corralled on the way. Since they had no cook, Cora and Mrs. Ruedy were kept busy in the kitchen. Frederic, big, bluff, good-natured Frederic, persuaded Stephen to show the guests the revolver he had carried in Greece and to demonstrate his skill by shooting at a target nailed to a tree. He must adjust to the penalties of fame while the children of the neighborhood hooted from the bushes.

Reynolds informed him that Gilder, at *Century* magazine, had declined "The Monster," declaring that they dared not publish "that thing" with half the expectant mothers in America on their subscription list. Stephen growled that he had not been aware that expectant mothers read the damn *Century* for either solace or information. But there was no appeal from the decision.

He had four in the household, and now four dogs to feed. He had wanted one dog; Cora, characteristically, had assembled a court. He loved them, but he would rather have had a horse than three extra poodles. Whereupon, Cora hired a riding-mare and vowed that they would buy their own as soon as money came in.

"As soon as money comes in!" McClure was demanding that he send his entire output to his syndicate to settle his balance. He was so aroused that he decided to withdraw from McClure's. He would give them a collection of stories to make a small volume under the title *The Open Boat and Other Stories*, and be done.

Appleton's would not make an accounting until January. At Heinemann's he was overdrawn, thanks to Pawling's kindness. However, they would satisfy themselves with an English edition of *The Open Boat* volume and with a reissue of *The Red Badge* and other war stories under the title *Pictures of War*.

He was down to his last ten pounds. He wrote a series of articles on his impressions of England and Ireland, and dashed off another on an engine ride from London to Glasgow. He discovered that when he moved from an article to a story he was tortured before he could come to terms with the substance of his fiction. The articles turned out easily, but they blocked the creative flow.

He was tempted for the sake of ready money to sell the English rights in "Death and the Child." Harold crossly reminded him that it would not do. "God's trousers, the American magazines won't touch it!"

Harold's counsel on copyright matters was sound. Moreover, his fortunes as a novelist had improved, and he was behaving like an arrogant Spanish grandee. The new novel, *Gloria Mundi*, rejected by two publishers, had found a home with Stone & Kimball, who would publish it in Chicago.

The Damnation of Theron Ware, which was selling slowly in New York, was doing surprisingly well in London. Harold claimed that it was outdistancing *The Red Badge*, and presumed to advise Stephen on his manuscripts.

"The Monster" ought to be destroyed. "If I don't understand it, who will?"

"Conrad thinks it is haunting."

"Bah!" Harold cried. He strutted about with one hand in his pocket and the other stroking his beard. "You do a new *Red Badge* on the Greek War. Take my advice. You've seen the real thing now, the dripping bloodshed, you've smelled it, wallowed in it."

Because the till was empty, Stephen tried to direct his thoughts to a plot about the Greek experience. He could not force himself. He must wait for that magical inspiration that had saved him before. The surface would heave and the story would come forth, like the hand rising from the deep with the sword Excalibur.

Perhaps if he committed himself to a contract, as he contracted to write articles, his brain would produce it.

He asked McClure's for an advance of two hundred pounds on "a Greek novel."

New Year's Eve, the Cranes spent at Homefield. Katie served a collation, and Stephen played with the three children. He wondered how Harold had managed to be away from the other wife, and the grown daughter Ruth, who loved him, on this ending of the old year and the beginning of the new.

Robert Barr opened the bottles of champagne, filled glasses for the adults, and tuned up for the inevitable "Clementine." Katie brought tiny glasses of pink lemonade to the children who, at their father's insistence, had been permitted to stay up.

"Everyone, everyone!" Harold bellowed, pulling out his silver pocket watch. "A toast to the best year of all! And may we, everyone, forever and a day, be happy together." He glanced at his watch, stamped his foot and shouted, "*Now!* Happy New Year!"

They chorused, "Happy New Year!"

Stephen slipped his arm about Cora's waist, and kissed her mouth. "I love you, Steve!"

"Happy New Year!" he, too, shouted.

An hour later, after a direct question, he replied that McClure's had turned him down on the Greek novel.

"They're idiots!" Harold shouted. "With your reputation, you can get any publisher." He picked up *The Nigger of the Narcissus*, which had just been issued. "Conrad got an advance even on this. Over-written and purple."

"I don't think so."

"God's trousers, Steve, don't defend it. The best passages show the influence of *The Red Badge*. Have you read that article in the *Daily Telegraph?* Who is it—Courtney?—comes out and says so!"

"He's wrong!" Stephen glowered. The article had mortified Joseph, who had immediately written to him, "Do you think that I tried to imitate you? No, sir! I may be a little fool but I know better than to try to imitate the inimitable." Stephen had been pained by his friend's anguish; he saw no resemblance between Conrad's style and his own. "Not true, Harold. Conrad is first-rate and original."

Frederic threatened to work himself into a rage. "Two other critics say your influence is there."

Stephen scoffed, "It's a game the critics play. 'Who influenced whom?' Mr. Garnett asks have I read much of the French writers, especially Maupassant. Mrs. Garnett wants to know have I read much of the Russian writers, especially Turgeniev and Tolstoy. No one asks have I read the American writers, Hawthorne and Poe. What about a man shaping his own style from the day he first heard words spoken and stories told? Conrad is Conrad!"

"Nonsense!" Harold sputtered. "You're overvaluing that fellow because the poor devil's struggling with his English."

Stephen smashed his fist upon the table, and shouted, "Damn it, Harold! You and I and Kipling together couldn't have written his *Narcissus!*"

At his show of fury, Frederic became calm. He said blandly, "Hell's acre, but you've got a black temper! I meant only that you're better than he is, that you should get your damn two hundred pounds. God's trousers, Steve, Happy New Year to you!"

CHAPTER 74

A terse note from Appleton's stated that the next royalty accounting would be delayed because of a writ of attachment being sought in the Supreme Court of New York against his property and funds. The publisher had been advised that an action was pending and had been cautioned not to disburse Mr. Crane's earnings.

He was stunned. Confound it, he owed nothing to anyone that would warrant a writ of attachment! He remembered no loan outstanding for more than fifteen dollars.

He had been depending on the payment from Appleton's. Now he was embarrassed for ready money. He wrote to Paul Reynolds for a quick transmittal of funds: "My English expenses have chased me to the wall." If McClure's did not want "The Monster," let Harper's have it. He urged a special effort to sell "The Bride Comes to Yellow Sky." He wrote to Acton Davies to collect the several hundred dollars that he had loaned to the American correspondents in Athens, if the fellows could be located.

Cora said frigidly, "There could be no writ of attachment if there were no debt." She gazed at him as if he had been keeping a criminal secret.

The next day, a letter from Willie Hawkins solved the mystery. It was Amy Lee. She had filed suit in New York for the recovery of $550. In her complaint, she had alleged that Stephen Crane owed her that amount out of a sum of $800 which she had given him on or about November 1, 1896, to deposit in a bank to her account! She had stated that he had not only failed to make such a deposit, but had put the money into a bank to his own credit. She further alleged that, at various times, he had returned sums aggregating $250. She now demanded that the balance be returned, with appropriate interest.

He was dismayed. He had never received any money from Amy. On the contrary, he had left funds for her with Hawkins, which

Willie had faithfully paid out to a total of $352.95. He had twice sent her money from Greece. He owed her nothing; contrariwise, he had given *her* roughly $550.

Cora read the cuttings that Willie had enclosed. The New York *Tribune* and the *Times* had both reported, "Stephen Crane Sued." Her eyes narrowed. "I should have called on her in New York. But you were still protecting her."

"I took nothing from her."

"Of course not!" she snapped. "She would have given you nothing. I said that she was predatory."

She read Willie's letter carefully.

Hawkins was annoyed because George Mabon, Amy's attorney, had sought service upon him as agent for the defendant. Fortunately, he had receipts for every sum he had paid out. He was able to satisfy Mabon that he had merely served his friend by dispensing certain monies in a prescribed manner.

"What could she gain?" Stephen asked wretchedly.

Her lip curled in disdain. "A jilted female? She filed suit when she learned that you were with another woman, perhaps had married her. She's showing her claws. When did you last write to her?"

Stephen hung his head. While in County Cork he had thought of Amy remorsefully. Although he had faithfully promised not to write to her, he had sent a letter anyway.

"You were writing 'The Monster,'" Cora said thoughtfully. On one of those nights they had quarreled about Stewart, and had failed each other. He had avenged himself.

"She calls the attention of the world to her. No one will believe that you have taken her $550, or even the $800. But she announces that you and she were friends, probably more than friends. She pulls the cloak of Stephen Crane over her shame, and leaves you exposed. She punishes you for trifling with her, for going to another woman."

"But she lies!"

"Oh, Steve!" she replied impatiently. "Of course, she lies. What is a lie to a woman in wrath? But to answer her, you have to take action or to plead with her. Meanwhile, she has cleverly shut off a source of your income."

"In a week I can be in New York——"

She stamped her foot. "You will not go to New York! To fall into her arms? Oh, no, Steve. I do not leave you to her mercies."

"I must reply somehow."

"Reply in no way. She has merely filed suit. If she has lied, as you say——"

"She has!"

"I believe you. She will do nothing more. She will not make a spectacle of herself by appearing in court, will she? Your friend Hawkins' receipts would prove her a liar."

"She signed the receipts. How did she dare?"

Cora sighed. "She dared because she wanted to hurt you. And you are hurt, aren't you? She remembers how appalled you were about the police embroilment and the Dora Clark girl, so she has struck at you in the same fashion. All the people whose opinion you respect and value will know that Stephen Crane had an affair with Amy Lee."

"And I have no recourse?"

"Only to be silent." A little smile played about her lips. "One does not have to be guilty to suffer, to be besmirched and humiliated."

He groaned.

"Another payment on account of fame."

In her eyes, he saw, unspoken: "We are of a kind, aren't we?"

He fled to Dover, although a snowstorm howled over Surrey. He must be free to think and to work. To go to Dover had become a romp from the tensions of the villa at Ravensbrook.

As the carriage slowed before the Lord Warden Hotel, the sight of purple crepe and a row of mourners wearing armbands greeted him. The hotel seemed blue against the snow-hung town. He watched a coffin being carried out by six pallbearers past a bank of wreaths.

Johnnie, the porter, taking his shining valise, explained that an Eastern nabob had died, one of those fearsome men who had helped to carve an empire from the benighted lands on the other side of the globe. Johnnie uttered the name and the titles; the personage, having served his Queen well, had come home to die.

Mr. Patrick, the clerk, an eager little Irishman, apologized for the inconvenience. Stephen, tempted to seek another hostelry, was dissuaded by the howling storm.

From his window, he looked out at the funeral hearse and the carriages. Men in "gafftopsail hats," as Conrad called the silk toppers, were walking solemnly under flakes of snow. In full regalia were high military officers; aides leaned out with umbrellas that were buffeted by gusts of wind. A troop of black horses bearing plumed and uniformed riders trotted forward. When he shut the window, muffled drumbeats continued like the footfalls of a reluctant doom.

He had come to work again on the Greek war novel, but his thoughts were with the cortege that would be moving the dead man to eternal peace. He watched the snow falling in thick streamers. A casement rattled as if a lost soul was pleading to be let in. He was as isolated as he had been three years ago in a snowbound prairie town in Nebraska.

He remembered that he had failed to lift his hat before the cortege. Those who feared death always paid homage to its trappings. Life flowered only in the womb; the long surrender to death was begun the day the newborn was ejected. Men stupidly feared death because they cravenly considered it a punishment; if they remembered that death was inevitable and a blessed release, they would have nothing to fear. For Death conquers fear; that was the supreme commandment. And he craved this conquest.

The stranger who had died might have expired in this very room, he mused; doubtless, other men had. In the long history of the Lord Warden, men might have been slain within its walls.

A knock on the door shocked him. It was Patrick again. "He resembles a murderer," Stephen thought in his anguish. At the guest's blanched face, the clerk stuttered that a new blizzard was sweeping in. A fire would be lighted; a toddy before dinner was available. If this room was not satisfactory another would be provided. Below stairs, a group of men, indoors because of the storm, was playing cards. If Mr. Crane would care to join them——

Stephen glared, and shut the door.

He forgot the Greek war novel. The happenstances had lit another fuse. . . . The title was clear, "The Blue Hotel." A stranger, an Easterner, alighted from a train and came to this place seeking death. The man was lighthaired like himself, "a Swede," who feared that he would be killed, perhaps wished it.

The frenzy taking command, he wrote steadily, scarcely aware that the storm was battering at the windows. He made the innkeeper not Patrick, but Pat Scully. He peopled the house with a few Western characters. Johnnie, the porter, became Pat Scully's son; he gave him a daughter Carrie, with a figure like Cora's.

He wrote wildly, tearing at his fears and passions. The Swede, fear-ridden, shaky, and wild-eyed, was spoiling for a fight. He sat in on a card game with a cowboy who was a "board-whacker." The Swede went crazy with suspicions, tantalizing the others, affronting them, swearing and prodding.

He glanced over his shoulder, expecting to see his characters staring from the shadows. He was panting; his breath had become short.

He pulled on his coat, wound his scarf about his throat, and hurried down the stairs.

The streets were deserted in the bitter cold of this night. The snow had stopped falling, but the wind was still howling with the voices of wolves. When, around a corner, he jostled a tall bobby who emerged suddenly, he trembled, as if it were Becker again. He wanted no extraneous figures to violate his ready-furnished landscape; Dover had become the fictitious "Fort Romper," the Lord Warden his "Palace Hotel."

He found a pub, pushed open the door, and entered. He slipped upon the floor, wrenched his side, and came up with fists clenched. There was no one to blame. Four men sat at a table drinking. At his footsteps the owner appeared, snapping a sleeve-garter.

He asked for a whiskey. He poured himself a large drink and

swallowed it in two gulps. The bartender eyed him furtively and remarked that it was a bad night.

"Oh, it's good enough for me," he replied and, because it was expected, poured himself more whiskey. He threw several coins on the bar. "I like this weather. It suits me."

The pub-keeper picked out two coins and turned away to his cash-machine, which was nickeled and adorned with keys. A bell rang, a drawer shot open; a card with the sum recorded leaped up behind the glass. Above the machine was a legend printed black on an orange strip, "THIS REGISTERS THE AMOUNT OF YOUR PURCHASE."

Stephen read the seven words, and laughed.

He wanted someone to drink with him. The men at the table had recognized an American and were staring. One, a slim, little man, said something; the others laughed, then seeing the stranger eye them, fell silent. The far player seized the opportunity to glance casually at his neighbor's cards.

"You're cheating!" Stephen wanted to cry.

There would be a tumult, perhaps a fight. He felt arrogant, profane, disdainful. One man would be sure to produce a knife. He was in the fracas. The knife shot forward . . . "a human body . . . was pierced as easily as if it had been a melon."

In a twinkling, the scene unfolded and collapsed again. He wished that he had not drunk the whiskey; liquor always made him slightly ill.

He returned to the Lord Warden, walked angrily about the lobby, as if he were the Swede, studied the card-players—they were at whist instead of high-five, as his people would be in the American West—and tramped up the stairs.

The interlude had not cooled him. His story had remained suspended as if the six figures he had summoned were seated in the open boat. At such a time, from every cranny in the universe precisely the correct sequences filed past him. Before morning, he had embroiled the Swede in a fight with Johnnie and made him victorious, then led him to a saloon and a brawl. A knife had shot out, and the Swede had crumpled; he "fell with a cry of supreme astonishment." He had come begging for death and had reaped his reward. "This registers the amount of your purchase."

CHAPTER 75

In London, Harold lay ill. In the midst of haranguing several journalists at the National Liberal Club, he had been stricken. The doctor had diagnosed it as a heart attack and had ordered him to bed.

After five days, the stubborn man had dragged himself to Homefield. He had shut himself in his room with his books and his papers, and pretended to be working.

He forbade Stephen to tell Katie. "She doesn't believe in disease," he said calmly.

Stephen walked the floor beside the bed. He was shocked at the pallor on the high forehead and the sagging flesh under the eyes. "Send word to Ruth, if not to your wife at Hammersmith."

Harold, in an enormous flannel nightshirt, with a tasseled nightcap over his head, merely sneered. He sprawled upon the covers, unwilling to slip his body into comfort beneath the blanket. How could Katie, unless her faith had blinded her to reality, fail to see that her man was mortally ill?

"Katie has a right to know."

Harold gave him a broad wink. "Why? Because it is customary to share one's troubles? Because it is conventional to punish loved ones with news of impending disaster? How shall I say it: 'Katie, I am dying!'"

"You won't die, Harold."

"I will, Steve," he returned heavily. "The sun rises, the sun sets. Can any wish, hope, or prayer seduce it from its course, or cause it to hesitate? I would not be Joshua even if London were Jericho. No, Steve, I am dying. The sawbones bleated like a billy goat, but I got it out of him. He said, 'Six months, lad, if you don't mend your ways.' I asked, 'And if I do?' He was as silent as Commons the day after Parliament is dissolved. Well then, I won't mend my ways. God's trousers, Steve, I can't!" He clasped a fist to his chest. When the pain had subsided, he swore profanely.

"I've got two families to mourn me," he went on. "What more can a man ask? And from neither do I deserve a tear, Steve. If I should tell Grace, she'd come to smother me with forgiveness. How does Rostand say it in *Cyrano*? 'No, thank you!' God, she'd thank heaven to be able to forgive me at my dying bed, as I married her at the dying bed of her mother. What a scene to write, Steve! But I couldn't bear it. Poor Ruth, I love her. Shall I burden her with a secret that will wither the bloom from her cheeks while I comfort myself that someone dear to me knows? No, thank you. That would be a course for a self-pitying wretch, and I'm not that, not yet, thank you. Should I tell Katie, she who's got three youngsters that don't have a proper surname under our damned laws? What kind of man would I be? She, with her faith, if you please, smoking her little pipe of holy opium, should I wrack her? I'm not so gone that I want to test her without cause. At best, she'd sit the livelong day and shoot good thoughts into me out of an invisible forty-five. No, thank you!"

"You're a wretch, Harold. Someone must know."

"You know, and a few others do. Don't tell Cora; never trust a woman you love." He made an effort to grin at his mockery. "I'd like to die with my boots on, but I won't. The end will come in some rumpled bed, as it should, since I was born in one. If it comes quietly, I'll light a candle in the next world; they need the light out there, I expect, in the God-forsaken darkness. I've tried to make a bargain with the Old Fellow to let me go in my own way, but He's got me by the pectorals and won't bargain."

"Follow the doctor's orders."

"Bah, Steve, you can't mean that! I'm not a child. I'm forty-two in August. I'm a man ripe for the plucking, neither too young nor too old. This is His chance, and He knows it. If I beat Him now, I might live forever, ghastly thought!"

"Harold!"

Frederic's grin vanished. "I've got about six months, the sawbones says. Maximum-um. So I've got to work. I've got to provide, Steve, provide! I've got to lay by a few shillings for the toddlers. If I lie on my back the muscle may give out anyway. What's the odds?"

"If you rest, you may get well."

He made a wry face. "I've got to write, to write and to die. There it is. Shall I weep about it, or run with my tail between my legs? 'Look at Frederic, the big bastard's afraid to die!'" He sighed. "When there was cholera in southern France, I went down to investigate. Others became infected and died like beetles, turned up their toes. I was not afraid, and I survived. Some said it took courage. Nonsense! When there was famine in Russia, I wandered about the countryside. Typhus was on the loose. They used to bring the bodies to town in carts; I helped to unload them. Ugh! But I survived. Now a pump of muscle smaller than my fist is inflamed. I've never seen it except in medical books, but it's turned on me. And I can't do anything about it, except curse."

He had over-exerted, and was forced to rest. At his frantic gestures, Stephen opened the commode and produced a brandy bottle and a glass.

Harold sipped thoughtfully. "Heart stimulant!" he gasped. "And after all the years I've drunk it without reason."

Stephen pointed to the cigar humidor. "Won't you give up anything?"

Frederic snickered. "Life! Isn't that enough? Know what I shall do with these six months? I shall do as I please, as I've always done. I'm going to smoke my cigars and drink my brandy. I'm going to go to music halls and eat at Frascati's, and buy hot potatoes on the street, and play dominoes with Ruth when I go next week to Hammersmith. If I'm still here when spring smiles on this blasted island, I'm going to stand before that rosebush in the garden and wait for the buds to form and see how many different colors I've grown from those new grafts. I'm——"

"You'll kill yourself long before your time is up."

"Come, old Steve," he winked again, "don't we all now? Don't we all?"

Conrad approved of "The Blue Hotel." He suggested submitting it to David Meldrum, the literary adviser to *Blackwood's Magazine* of Edinburgh.

"They are always open to me at *Blackwood's*," he said almost apologetically. "Garnett turned me there. They've paid me forty pounds."

Stephen was committed to send the story to Paul Reynolds who could do better than forty pounds, fifty or sixty, in America. Reynolds had sold "The Monster" to *Harper's Monthly* for an excellent price. He was also soliciting the Harper firm for an advance on a volume of short stories.

"You have published many books here and in America," Joseph remarked. He believed that greater frequency of issue would solve his money problem.

"And I've been one jump ahead of the sheriff. I've managed my success like a fool."

Conrad spread his hands. "Who is wise?"

Their friendship was warmer because of the regular exchange of confidences. When the Conrad baby arrived in the middle of January, Cora sent a bouquet of flowers that cost three pounds.

"Fifteen dollars!" Stephen protested.

"Can Stephen and Cora Crane do less? Should I save ten shillings on the baby? Jessie loves flowers, and so does Joseph."

In a spending mood, she bought quantities of the most expensive tinned delicacies for the pantry against the appearance of those random guests who plagued them. On the frugal days, she sat with Mrs. Ruedy and ripped the seams of old gowns and painstakingly sewed new garments, to save a few pounds.

"I am not earning enough to keep us," he worried.

She scoffed. "Let one book or story become a sensation and sweep England, and every debt will be paid and the world will be at our feet." She looked at him adoringly. "Steve, how can anything, or anyone, defeat us as long as we are together?"

With five-week old Borys, the Conrads finally came to visit. To Stephen, the infant was a miracle. His rapport with "The Boy" endeared him to Jessie.

Conrad confessed to Stephen that he had only ten pounds in the bank, and yet Jessie's two orphaned nieces were coming to live with them and to be educated.

"We ought to pool our intellectual resources, since we have no other," offered Stephen, "and write a few books together."

The spark in Joseph's eyes dimmed. "What have I to offer *you?*" He was humble and bitter, but with a perverse pride beneath the surface.

Cora said, after their guests had retired, "When I see you together, you and the child, Steve, I could wish that we had one of our own."

He ruminated. "I have thought of going to Africa on some assignment, to call upon Captain Stewart and persuade him to divorce you."

She flung her arms about him, crying, "You care, you care!"

"Yes, I care." He reflected again. "Haven't you heard from him at all?"

"Yes," she admitted. "I have."

"His decision?"

"He'll never grant it."

Coldly, "How long have you known?"

"Two months."

He scorned her in the half-dark.

"I don't want to lose you, Steve."

A ball of anger rolled in his chest. "How long can we go on like this? Mrs. Stewart to your friends, Mrs. Crane to my friends?"

"What shall I do?" she asked wretchedly.

Lying beside her, alone with his hostilities when she had fallen asleep, he mused how the tables had turned. The suspicion seized him that, for some unnamed reason, Cora did not want to be divorced from the other man. They must once have been very happy together, and somehow she still cherished Donald Stewart.

He spent the rest of the night on the couch in his study. Restlessly, he began to cough. The sound punctuated the silence in the sleeping house.

When he came to breakfast, hollow-eyed and sullen, he had a plot ready for a collaboration with Joseph.

Over his grilled sausage, kidney, lamb chop, and scrambled eggs, Joseph listened. "Continue, continue, Stephen!"

"A man impersonates his predecessor, who has died, in order to win the love of this girl."

"Your setting?" He speared a bit of kidney.

"Anywhere. In the Rocky Mountains, I would say. It could be in the Congo, if you wished."

"You have a title?"

"'The Predecessor.'"

The gleam in the guest's eyes and the effort he made not to glance at Cora betrayed that he, too, had heard rumors. "'The Predecessor,' eh? A story of an impersonation. The spirit of the dead man, of the departed, is between our hero and his romance." He munched. "It is ready-made. How could I be of help?"

Cora had crimsoned.

"Write a play about it with me."

406

"What do I know of plays, Stephen?"

"Nor I. But together——"

"We will talk about it," he said hastily.

Jessie gazed quizzically at Stephen. "You men think of such stories!"

"I think it is an excellent plot," Cora spoke up icily. "But first, Stephen must see a physician. He was coughing all night. Persuade him, Joseph, for my sake."

To Borys, they gave Soap, one of the black poodles from a new litter.

"What kind of name for a dog is Zoap?" Conrad frowned. "I will call him Escamillo."

The carriage was ready. Stephen accepted the sleeping infant from Cora and tenderly handed it to Jessie. "Take care of the boy."

Joseph pulled Stephen aside, "The boy is a nuisance," he whispered, "but is it not good for a woman to have children? Many problems vanish when there is a child to cement the bond between the two people. You, too, my friend."

Stephen, smiling with an effort, agreed.

CHAPTER 76

Spring had come early; the trees were budding. The lawns were turning green. He had seen violets at the flower stalls; he must remember to buy some for Cora.

In this mood, he decided that, on such a day, with nature reawakening, he ought to surprise Cora and visit a physician. With the help of a bobby, he located the Harley Street address of Doctor M. H. C. McKenzie, who attended Harold.

The doctor, a dour little man in tweeds, glanced at him disapprovingly from under bushy eyebrows.

"I have a persistent cough, sir." Drily, "It annoys Mrs. Crane."

"How long has this cough persisted?"

He became vague. "Six, eight months. I've had it often before that, too. More than a year."

"Remove your jacket and shirt, please."

Stephen, who had settled back for a chat, bestirred himself.

"The undergarment, too, please."

Medical men the world over, whether in such dingy offices or in well-lighted clinics, conducted themselves as though they were the direct legatees of Aesculapius and Hippocrates.

"Come here, my boy!"

McKenzie was older than he appeared to be at first glance. Stephen noted the intermingling of gray hairs on the brown shock as the physician drew him to the window and applied the cold disc of the stethoscope.

"Relax, please! Now, inhale. A very deep breath. Hold it. Now exhale. Again! Thank you. Inhale—exhale! When were you last seen by a physician?"

"Last May."

"In London?"

"In Athens."

"You were ill in Athens?"

"Dysentery."

"Then you had some loss of weight. Did you regain it, or have you lost more since your return to England?"

"Perhaps fourteen, fifteen pounds altogether, I believe."

"A stone."

"Yes, sir."

On a sill, across the street, a tortoise-shell cat was sunning herself. Before the window, a boy chased a large hoop. A victoria swept by.

The physician applied two bony fingers of one hand to the flesh and, with the fingertips of the other hand, tapped smartly. The fingers moved across the chest, tapping from the shoulders to the rib cage. The process was repeated on the patient's back. "Please cough. Again! Thank you."

Stephen was suddenly aware of his scrawny arms and flat chest. The room was cold.

Minutes seemed to pass while the physician percussed. He examined the eyelids and the skin, the throat, ears, and nose; he pinched the fingernails. He asked the patient to remove his shoes and to drop his breeches; he examined the veins in the legs.

At last, he stood back. "You may dress. Ah, but wait!" He nudged Stephen to the scales, and expertly slid the weights. "Seven stone ten."

Stephen calculated: one hundred and eight pounds.

Seating himself behind his desk, the doctor studied his caller. "How is your appetite?"

"Poor."

"Any night sweats?"

He frowned.

Doctor McKenzie explained.

"Yes, sometimes. No, often."

"Did you have a chest condition as a youngster?"

"Coughs and colds. So I've been told." Pridefully, "I was a good athlete at school.

"No doubt." He idly rolled a pencil between his palms. "Mr. Crane, are you aware that you have an activity in your chest?"

"Only a cough!" He uttered a dry, hollow cough as if to verify the statement.

408

"Precisely. Have you ever noticed any blood streaks in this phlegm that you cough up?"

Stephen's heart began to pound. "Occasionally, Doctor. What do you mean, sir?" The significance of the battery of questions was dawning slowly.

"Have you ever suffered a hemorrhage?"

"No, sir!"

"Never? Are you certain?"

"Yes, sir!" A shiver passed down his spine. He heard himself repeating Cora's question, "What shall I do?"

Doctor McKenzie's eyes were turtle-green in the fading light. He had reason to believe that a tubercular infection was present in Stephen's lungs. It might have been acquired in Greece or, with the system weak, as easily in England. "We have it here; it is everywhere."

The light was going. Stephen's throat was dry. He craved a cigarette. Doctor McKenzie, producing a pipe, reached for tobacco from a blue Delft jar.

"May I smoke, Doctor?"

"It doesn't matter." The reply came regretfully as he sank into thought again.

Boldly, "Is it fatal?"

The doctor, exhaling a cloud of smoke, absently regarded the bowl of his pipe. "All infections may become fatal. Medicine fences with them. Sometimes we are prepared to destroy them. Often we can only parry the lethal thrust."

"Is mine fatal?" He was pleading for the sentence. His temples were moist.

"In time, unless its course can be arrested. It is not encouraging, I should say. Our task is to shore up the defenses." The doctor smoked again. "Of course, I have examined you hastily. There is always human error to reckon with. Always."

"What shall I do, sir?"

McKenzie sighed and stared out the window. "I could prescribe a little tincture of creosote. However, I would strongly recommend a warm, dry climate, fresh air, the outdoor life, and a diet of high nutrition. By outdoor life, I mean that you should sleep outdoors, in any climate, with this condition. Above everything else, complete rest. Complete rest!" He got to his feet. "I recommend that you come in again, let us say next week, for a more thorough examination. I shall ask a colleague to have a look at you."

Stephen arose. "Doctor, I would prefer that no word of this reached my friend Mr. Frederic."

The doctor stiffened. "Naturally!"

"Is there any danger to my wife?"

"If it is what I think it may be," he said cautiously, "and she has already been exposed to it, she may have a certain natural immunity.

Some persons seem to be able to expose themselves to the disease without contracting it." He patted Stephen's shoulder. "I shall look to your visit next week. Meanwhile, think of a long holiday somewhere. You are a writer? How fortunate! You may do as you please. Think of the poor fellows who are miners or factory workers, and cannot take their employment with them."

The sun was setting. Red streaks defined a great wound in the western sky.

He slept well and dreamlessly that night, as if the visit to Harley Street had never occurred. He awakened early, and took the dogs out for their walk. He watched them yiping and barking, tumbling joyously as they raced into the morning. He cut a switch for the stroll through the woods, to slash at the grasses and plants. The air was winey, the sky a robin's-egg blue. When he whistled, Flannel and Sponge swerved about and raced toward him; Ruby, as usual, became entangled in a brake and squealed until he came up and released her.

Cora was waiting when they returned.

"Stephen," she asked, "do you know how much I love you?"

"No."

"More than life itself!" She searched his face. "You're so fatigued. You're away somewhere on a new story. I can tell by that faraway look. You're in another world. Is it exciting?"

"Dramatic!"

"Does it end happily?"

"It ends as life itself does."

He was still unable to accept the diagnosis, as if the obstinate will to live could admit nothing hostile to its existence. Yet he had written enough of death to be familiar with it. What could man fear in dissolution that he, as soberly as an executioner, had not meted out to his characters? Maggie had died in the river, George's mother in her bed, Jim Conklin on the battlefield, Henry Fleming in the stable fire in "The Veteran," the Swede by a gambler's knife in "The Blue Hotel."

The shadow of the scythe passed over his head. He thought, "So I'm going to die!"

He stared out at a Stygian black universe. From the Eternal Silence he could expect no mercy. He had written it in one of his lines: "God is cold."

He would not return to Doctor McKenzie. He knew everything that he needed to know. An insidious foe was lodged in his chest; it devoured tissue or dissolved it, and left hollows that only skilled percussing fingers could detect. One day he would begin to hemorrhage and would spit his life away.

Since the sinking of the battleship *Maine* in the harbor of Havana, everyone was talking about war with Spain. To die in Cuba would not be difficult. A chance bullet, and the tale would be ended.

Cuba then; let the die be cast.

To get back, to leave money for Cora, and to pay his passage out of England, he must have at least sixty pounds. *Scribner's*, which had been so pleased with "The Open Boat," had declined "The Blue Hotel." He would accept assignments for war articles, or for pieces on the West like those that he had written in '95. If he earned enough, he would send funds to Cora.

"I must go home," he told her. "War will break out, I should be there."

She blanched. "Is it Amy?"

He was exasperated. "Not Amy, or any other woman. The war! I can earn more there in three months than in a year in England."

"How shall we live there? Where? In New York, where everyone knows you? In Port Jervis or in Hartwood, with your family?"

"I must go alone," he replied stubbornly. "I'll be off for Cuba at once, as soon as I've arranged for assignments with the *Journal* or the *World*."

The light went out in her eyes. "How long would you be gone, Stephen?"

He avoided her gaze. "Two months, three. As long as the war lasts."

She sighed. "Couldn't I go with you as Imogene Carter?" She provided the answer bitterly. "No, we have the household and its debts. Unless we paid everyone, we couldn't leave together. And the dogs, what about the dogs?"

He was silent.

"There is no money," she concluded with a frown, "either for your passage, or to keep me while you are gone. I could borrow from friends in London."

"No!" he shouted, so quickly enraged that she flinched. "I'll raise what is needed without them."

He appealed to Heinemann's, but he was overdrawn there. He called on the *Westminster Gazette*; they would offer no advance until war was declared.

He told Harold that he was bound for Cuba. Frederic applauded. On the first of April, he had been felled by another attack; only John Stokes, his secretary, and a few others knew. Blind Katie! She could not see that the man was becoming more gaunt and wasted every day.

Stephen said, "Your Doctor McKenzie has told me that I've got holes in my lungs. Consumption."

"God, you've not told Cora!"

"No. She'll be better without me. Why didn't you tell Katie?"

Harold lifted his glass. "Brother Crane, have a brandy!"

"I'd sooner have one of Katie's silent prayers than your vile firewater, which makes me sleepy."

The other cocked an eyebrow. "Need a few pounds? I've twenty to spare."

"Save it for Katie and the children."

Frederic pondered. "You'll beat it, Steve!" he growled. "You will!"

Stephen gave him a crooked smile. "If I do, it will only be to do one more book, maybe a few stories, a few poems."

Harold lifted his arm in a mock holy sign. "My blessings, Saint Stephen, the martyr! God's trousers! when I pass the pearly gates, I'll leave them ajar for you."

As they parted, Harold clung to his hand. "Beat the bastards, Steve! Turn the rascals out. You're only twenty-six. Beat them!"

Desperately, Stephen raced about London. But London was not New York, where any of his newspaper cronies would have been good for a touch. The "rich" American author humiliated himself by pleading for loans to take him home while his wife remained in England as a hostage for their debts.

By the end of the week, only Conrad was left. "To leave, Joseph, I need sixty pounds."

Conrad wrung his hands. "I haven't sixty shillings to spare."

"What of your Mr. Meldrum and *Blackwood's*? Would they advance me against stories to come?"

Conrad did not hesitate, although he was personally leaning more and more on *Blackwood's*. *Youth* was in the last stages of composition, and he lived on those advances from Edinburgh.

At the Paternoster Row offices, Joseph twisted his hankerchief in his fingers and pointed to his friend. "Crane here leaves for Cuba this week!"

Meldrum smiled. "You are in great haste, Mr. Crane, to be off to your war."

He replied simply, "I should be there before the hostilities begin." He would write sundry articles on both the island and the fighting; he would send *Blackwood's* any stories with a war background.

Meldrum pondered. Mr. Crane had so many commitments, to Heinemann's and to his American publishers, that the advantages that might accrue from making an advance to him were very slender. Now if a book were involved and the serial rights might also be pledged——

Stephen declared that he could not abrogate agreements of long standing.

Conrad, meek in his own behalf, gruffly declared that he would go surety for his friend, with his own work, if necessary.

Meldrum calmed his author. He would have to consult Mr. Blackwood. But surely Mr. Crane did not require as much as sixty pounds for ordinary passage to America.

Conrad became agitated. "He must leave certain monies for his wife, no?"

412

At last, Meldrum promised forty pounds within a day or two; twenty more would follow as soon as he had clearance from Mr. Blackwood.

When the two friends, arm in arm, emerged into Paternoster Row, Stephen laughed, "I swear that you've done better for me than you've ever done for yourself."

They halted at a nearby shop for a long tea while Conrad expatiated on his technique in the story *Youth.* It was going well, far better than he had expected. "But it is not like your work, old pard, upon my word and honor!"

Stephen envied the decades from which Joseph could draw material for his tales of the sea. "Maybe I'll meet my big adventures in Cuba."

Their last few days together, Cora hovered over him as she had not since Athens.

"My heart tells me that I shouldn't let you go!" She shook her head. "You won't be heading for Jacksonville?"

"Probably to Tampa, or to Key West." He was impatient. "Congress has demanded that Spain withdraw from Cuba. How long can it be before the war breaks out?"

"Come back to me, Steve!"

Fortunately, Harold, still pretending that he was well, invited Cora to join him and Katie at the villa in Ireland. To simplify their household arrangements, he also included Mrs. Ruedy and Adoni.

"Shall I go, Steve? If I stay here I'll go mad without you!"

He urged her to accompany the Frederics. He had been perplexed how to bid her farewell. She was so attuned to his moods that she might sense that this was his last good-bye.

She rode quietly at his side in the train to London. He would change for Liverpool to board the *Germanic.*

"When America throws her arms around you," she murmured wistfully, "will you remember that I am Mrs. Stephen Crane?"

"I want no one else," he replied truthfully. He held her and kissed her. "All that is past, Cora."

"Come back to me, Steve!" she repeated frantically. "Come back to me!"

He saw her walking beside the railway carriage, waving her hand. Then the train jarred and she was moving away. He had a strange sensation of having lived through this scene before.

CHAPTER 77

He checked into the Fifth Avenue Hotel, but did not stop to unpack. As he hurried downstairs and crossed the crowded lobby, newsboys were shouting, "War Declared!" It was still unofficial; the *Journal* and the *World* were anticipating. Troops were being concentrated in the Southern states. The North Atlantic squadron, strung out below Key West, was said to be moving to blockade Cuba.

A line had already formed outside the Navy recruiting office. He took his place at the end of the queue of brawny men. He had been an alien in the Greco-Turkish War; he belonged here.

"I want to get me a couple of them Spanyers!" a neighbor was saying. "Then a couple of senoritas. That's all I want."

In a large room, partitioned into tiny booths over which cloths had been draped halfway so that naked legs struggling out of trousers were revealed, several petty officers were shepherding the would-be enlistees. In a corner stood a large grain and feed scale. At a window, a bearded doctor was looking down open throats. "Say Ah!"

"Ever been to sea?" a petty officer asked Stephen.

"Not exactly. But I've been shipwrecked once."

The man grinned and handed over an application form. "Fill 'er out!"

At the stand-up table, he filled in the questionnaire, with many blotches of the cheap pen. He placed a check mark beside "Married." For next of kin, he wrote "Cora Crane, Ravensbrook, Oxted, Surrey, England," and instantly regretted it. He should have given Ted's name and address.

The doctors worked deliberately. "Bend over. . . . Now cough!" A petty officer tramped to the door of the hall, and bellowed, "Quiet down, men! The war's jes' starting. You'll all get your chance."

A grinning applicant walked naked across the floor, and beat his chest with his fists. "You can send the rest of these jays home, Admiral!" he shouted. "They're taking me!"

"Stow it!"

"Next!" A hand took Stephen's papers.

He stripped off his clothes, and was suddenly chilled. He choked back a desire to cough.

"Crane!"

"Whee!" someone whistled as he strode out. "They're taking skeletons!"

"Quiet, men!"

He trembled as the stethoscope clamped to his bare chest.

"Any recent illnesses?"

"No, sir."

"At ease, man!"

"Yes, sir!"

Perspiration was dripping from his temples. The doctor in the next row was wheezing hard: "Bend over!" Something smelled of freshly scorched linen.

His physician, who was not in uniform, wore steel-rimmed spectacles; he had a scrubby little beard and a tiny mole on his upper lip. The Reverend Doctor Jonathan Townley Crane!

As the bell-shaped end of the instrument moved quickly, he felt gooseflesh rising. Now the fingers were percussing. Fear tightened the muscles of his throat. He saw the heavily-lidded eyes open wide; abruptly, the fingers left him.

"You can get dressed." The fountain pen scribbled something on the form.

"Is that all, sir?" He was pleading. "Did I make it?"

"Crane, why not go to see your family doctor, or any doctor?"

"I'm all right, sir. I know I am."

The other peered severely through the thick lenses. "You see that line of men? This is costing your government money. I haven't the time to hold your hand."

He blanched. "What's wrong, Doctor?"

"I can't pass you. You're not physically fit for the Navy, or for any other active service. Get dressed!"

He beckoned to another applicant, a burly fellow with a hairy chest who swaggered across the bare floor.

Dressed, Stephen elbowed past the waiting line in the hall and down the stairs. "Did you make it, kid?" The queue now stretched around the block.

As he reached for a cigarette, he was seized by a coughing spell. He had to stand at the gutter for several minutes before the spasms ceased. A policeman turned to watch him.

Grimly, he headed for the offices of the *Journal*.

Ed Marshall received him cordially, but Mr. Hearst had already hired a large staff. Furthermore, Ed had decided to give up his desk and to leave for Cuba himself. "This is one war that I don't want to miss, Steve. A man owes it to himself to take some part in the biggest thing in his generation."

At the *World*, Stephen asked for Sylvester Scovel. Fortunately, Scovel was in. By nightfall, he had been hired and given his expense money. Within twenty-four hours he must be on his way to Tampa.

He called at Appleton's. Since Amy's suit had not been pressed in the courts, her claim had no standing. He drew the entire balance in his royalty account. How shrewdly Cora had estimated the other woman's actions!

At the little desk in his hotel room, he toyed with the fresh pen-points. He must write to Ted and to Will. He should write to Burt to inquire after Townley. He brooded, and wrote to no one.

He walked Manhattan, and passed the house on Twenty-fifth Street. He paused and listened sharply, as if the next click of feminine heels might bring Amy.

He could not sleep. In the dark, he was borne around and around on a carrousel of sounds and fears. He leaped from the bed and by the light of the streetlamp, which had ventured through the curtains, regarded his scrawny figure in the mirror. He was woefully thin-chested. He flexed his biceps. Where had his strength fled? He lifted his right arm over his head, but dropped it weakly to his side. "S. Crane" would never make that toss to second base now.

In Washington, the next afternoon, he dashed through the station toward the row of hansom cabs, and gave Lillie's address.

Would she recognize him? "Stephen, you've been ill!" At this hour, Harris Morrow would be in his laboratory or in his office. What if Lillie were out strolling with the child? He yearned for her tall figure; he could see her pushing the perambulator. But he had forgotten; time had sped so swiftly that Jimmie would be a big boy. He would be four years old!

He ran up the stairs and rang the bell. The clanging echoed through the house. He waited, and rang again. Then again and again, gazing angrily at the door. Only the silence stretched toward him.

CHAPTER 78

Somewhere a village was burning. The fiery light turned the palm trees into "enormous crimson feathers."

When the whaleboats and the cutters bearing the First Marine Battalion were towed ashore under cover of a barrage from the *Marblehead* and the *Yankee*, Stephen followed doggedly. Other correspondents elected to return to Port Antonio to file their dispatches. He was drawn to the dark beach of Guantánamo.

He shared the apprehensions of the men in the boats. Death, surgeon who commanded many instruments, was shrieking overhead. He was relieved when they reached shore and could dash for cover in the flame-splintered night. Death could come in a sudden explosion from a three-inch projectile that scattered men to bits, in the sharp flut-flut-fluttering of a rapid-fire gun, or with the insect whine of a soft-nosed bullet. The Navy .45 tore a jagged hole and could eat through bone; the Lee-Medford made a clean hole. He had made inquiries about these agencies of destruction.

On the third night after the landing, the enemy opened heavy fire. Until dawn, Stephen listened to the tortured dying of Johnnie Gibbs, the young surgeon.

In the morning, Captain Elliott was at his elbow. "Crane, I could use an adjutant. Want to come along? We're short of officers."

He stirred as if he had just heard the Call. "Yes, sir!"

A group of Cuban scouts, swinging their long machetes, led the way into the hills. Soon a wood dove cooed. "Cover!" The men ducked and moved faster. Bullets zinged; guerrilla observers had signaled their presence to sharpshooters in the trees.

He recognized that he was afraid, but also that every man beside him was afraid. The detail began to run up the incline. No one knew why except that the Captain had waved and grunted, "Up!"

Weird green cactus with thorny paws confronted them. Stephen found himself gasping from the exertions as he dug his toes into the sandy earth. Thorns caught at his clothes.

"Up!" Ugly sharp prickles protruded from every vine and stalk; no one dared to seize at any plant for support. "Up!" More of the misshapen thorn-men leaped into their path. The shadow of a broad-winged bird crossed over them.

He tagged stubbornly at the Captain's heels, waiting for some adjutant instruction. Once more, a wood dove cooed; once more, Death sputtered, although no foe could be seen.

"Faster!"

The climb became steeper. The sun was blazing. "Up!" His chest filled to bursting. How high must they climb? He could hardly breathe. A terrible resentment overwhelmed him; he would fall and the Captain would go on without him. "Where's Crane?" He plowed on desperately.

An hour later, he saw the tops of palm trees far below, and puffs of smoke that indicated *our* firing; the enemy enjoyed the advantage of smokeless powder. A valley appeared. There was the sea, and there the *Dolphin* sat like a toy boat of gray lead.

A knock at his shoulder made him fall obediently. The men were squirming on their bellies into firing positions. Directly above hung the placid blue sky, but the sun had flung open another furnace door.

"Crane!" The Captain speaking. "Go down to that hill and satisfy yourself who those people are."

"Yes, sir!" He sped. "Those people" might be the enemy.

He plunged through the brush, scorning the cactus, gathering needles in his fingers. He must identify these people. At last, approaching them, he recognized the uniforms. They were "ours" after all, not the "canaries."

Hastening back, he scampered the last yards on his hands and knees. "They're ours, sir."

"Good! Now go over to Lieutenant Shaw down below on that side. Tell him to move over thirty yards to the left."

A snake emerged from a scraggly plant. A bullet kicked up the dirt, and the creature vanished. Stephen ground his teeth. The spitting and buzzing that came so uncomfortably close to his ears related to the passage of bullets; merely spitting and buzzing.

Wounded men were being dragged to cover. Over the next ridge, vultures, soaring and banking, were writing mysterious messages.

He lost count of the errands he ran or crawled. He was the Captain's voice. The riflemen who saw him coming and going marked his coolness; he was as good as they, as fearless, as useful.

A shout went up. The enemy was breaking; the "canaries" were fleeing the thickets. The young Marines, rising or kneeling, were firing easily, as if dogs had flushed a covey of birds.

The foe was rushing toward him. On a bearded man's shirt, a red stain appeared, and still he climbed until Stephen could see the horror-stricken eyes and the clenched teeth; he was becoming crimson from his chest to his knees. "*Madre D——*" he cried. He paused, gazed back at the wide sky, and, dying, dropped out of sight.

Captain Elliott's company, having raced six miles to seize the crest of Cuzco Hill, had outmaneuvered the foe. There was a sounder logic to this business of war than a man might suspect.

The fleeing Spaniards were being cut to pieces by fire from three directions. Some were trudging in with arms lifted. The vultures were screeching.

He stood idly at the Captain's side while the prisoners, begging, "*Agua!*" were being interrogated.

On the descent to Camp McCalla, captors and captives alike moved silently. Every Marine face was dark as beet-root, from the sun and the labors at the higher altitude.

"Steve!" Sylvester Scovel, sporting a yatching cap and his unpressed pea-jacket, greeted him with a hug. "You old son-of-a-gun! Elliott says you were as cool as newly-made ice cream. He says he'll mention you in dispatches."

He shrugged. He had done no more than he had been told to do. The near-misses had thrilled him. Scrambling on all fours, often in full view of the enemy sharpshooters, had heightened his enjoyment until it had become almost unbearable, as if he were stroking a responsive harlot and could not wait to get inside her.

> I went to the animal fair,
> The birds and the beasts were there;
> The little raccoon by the light of the moon
> Was combing his auburn hair.
> The monkey he got drunk,

And sat on the elephant's trunk,
The elephant sneezed and went down on his knees
And what became of the monk, the monk, the monk?

That was the Rough Riders' mocking chant, introduced at Tampa and repeated on the long voyage to Daiquiri Bay: "The monk, the monk, the monk!"

Somewhere the enemy lurked; somewhere west was Cervera's fleet, bottled up in Santiago harbor.

Although his sympathies were with the unpedigreed regulars, Stephen, like most of his cronies, was eager to follow the Rough Riders, that flamboyant hodgepodge of cowboys and clubmen, of unlettered daredevils from the West and of college-trained scions from wealthy families in the East. The eight troops of men, mustered in six weeks ago would somehow manage to be in the center of the hottest fighting.

He tramped alongside them that night, when they made a forced march to Siboney. He slept in one of the hastily-pitched tents, and at five in the morning was roused to march again. The order was given for silence as they entered a defile between towering curtains of vines, trees, and chaparral.

At about nine o'clock, with the sun blazing, firing broke out up the trail. "Cover!" He flung himself into the jungle thickness. The rat-tat-tat! indicated that the enemy was using machine guns. On every side, the blanket rolls and haversacks were being discarded as the men aimed their new Krag-Jorgensen carbines. Firing in the general direction, they were running forward and dropping as the vines crackled and snapped and bit. It was impossible to see through the densely green foliage for more than a few feet, yet the enemy fire was effective. Wounded men were being dragged back by their comrades. He caught a glimpse of Colonel Roosevelt, shouting and swinging his arm. Men charged when he shrieked, then fell flat in expectation of the next volley.

Stephen stumbled over a canteen. The grass glittered from the reflections of hundreds of empty Mauser cartridges. That was the first evidence that they had driven the enemy from his original position.

"Steve!"

He reeled about at the familiar voice.

Ed Marshall had been hit! With horror, Stephen saw his friend crumple into the dirt. Another sputtering volley caused Stephen to throw himself headlong.

By the time he had crawled over, a regular had pulled Marshall against a tree. He was supporting Ed's head against the trunk and waving toward a man with a kit. "Here's another, sir."

A young surgeon hastily examined the wounded man. "He has a

bullet through his back. Just missed the spine. He shouldn't be moved." He glanced at Stephen's garb. "Correspondent?"

"We're friends."

"Don't let them move him. If they drag him off, he'll die. He needs a stretcher."

"Will he——"

"I don't know. He must not be moved!"

Other men were calling. Nearby, two men were covering a body with a blanket.

On his knees, Stephen gazed into Marshall's haggard features. The editor had given up his post on the Sunday side of the *Journal* to see war at first hand. "Ed!" he pleaded, and lifted his canteen to the parched lips.

The water spilled from the chin. The eyes opened and rolled. "Steve!" the hands jerked spasmodically. "Steve, I'm dying," he muttered. His chest heaved; his jaws gritted violently.

"No, you're not!" Stephen assured him. "The medic said you'd be all right." He could not watch the agony.

From the shouting, he surmised that the troops were charging the hill; they could not be far from the junction of the trails where the other column would surely flank the enemy. Men were still running forward; others, bleeding, were staggering back. As the firing continued, the wild cowboy-yelling of the Rough Riders became audible.

Marshall was gasping.

Stephen opened his collar. "What shall I do, Ed?"

The wounded man drew a deep breath, and his eyes began to clear. "I don't know, Steve. I'm afraid——"

"You're not going to die," he repeated. "You're not!"

"This is my first story. I wanted to send it back——"

Stephen wiped his face tenderly. Squatting beside his friend, he took out his notebook. "Give it to me, Ed. I'll take it down."

A little smile came to the twisted mouth. "You're on the *World!*"

"Never mind, Ed." Marshall had been his friend for nearly five years. "Give it to me. I'll get it through." He wheedled, "Try!"

Laboriously, Marshall composed: "To the New York *Journal*, June 24. At La Guasima with the Rough Riders on the way to Santiago. This morning at nine o'clock——"

At intervals, Stephen crept out upon the blazing trail for news of the progress of the engagement. Big Sergeant Hamilton Fish, with a bullet through the heart, had been the first man to die. Young Captain Capron was dead. The roll of fatalities was disheartening. The enemy, though he had succeeded in ambushing the invaders, had been driven from his fortified position. "Ed, we've won!"

Marshall shuddered as a land-crab scuttled over his hand. "When will you write your own—story?"

"Go on, Ed," he urged. "Mine's already written in my head." He sat in the grass and again took dictation, while Marshall, eyes bulging, forced the words through his teeth.

Suddenly, he faltered and his head dropped.

"My God, he'll die!" Stephen thought. He shouted to a dresser who was covering another figure in the brush.

The man obliged by placing a dressing on Marshall's wound. "I got nothing else here," he mumbled. "Not enough doctors. Don't know where the supplies are."

The sound of the fighting had subsided.

Marshall groaned, "You'll get the story to the *Journal?*"

"I promise, Ed."

He scrawled a note and slipped it into Marshall's belt: "Bullet near spine. Stretcher needed. *Do not move!*"

"Ed, don't let them move you."

"File the story!" Marshall pleaded. His lips shaped, "I'm a goner, sure."

Stephen ran and walked, ran and walked, the seven miles to the encampment at Siboney. He met two correspondents who listened incredulously. They had been told that Ed Marshall had been ordered back to New York.

"I saw him!" he heard himself bellow. "I've just left him!"

He sped to the field hospital and, frantically, told his story again and again. Finally, he convinced a Major who had heard of Stephen Crane that bearers and a stretcher must be provided.

As they were leaving, he encountered a *Journal* man.

"Marshall's hurt!" he gasped. "He gave me this story. Send it!"

The man glanced at the dispatch. "What's the game, Crane? You're a *World* man, aren't you?"

"Can't you understand a man doing something for a friend?" Perspiration streamed from under his hat; in the entire skirmish the cheap hat he had bought in Florida had not deserted him.

He raved on the way back to La Guasima: "Hurry, hurry! He may be dying!" The men with the stretcher trotted after him in the grueling heat, cursing.

Marshall, weak from loss of blood, was still sprawled at the foot of the tree. One of the bearers gruffly declared that the wounded man would probably die anyway. When a hospital wagon came by, they tried to find a place for him inside.

"No!" Crane screamed. He insisted that they carry the wounded man over the jungle trail.

Marshall roused. "The story——"

"It's on the way, Ed."

For the fourth time, he walked the seven miles in the glaring sun. It was six o'clock in the evening when he delivered Ed Marshall into the hands of a surgeon.

Stephen staggered away. Someone found him wandering aimlessly, and led him to the correspondents' camp.

Acton Davies had heard of the Marshall episode. "What about filing your own story, Steve?"

He sprawled on a cot and buried his face in the bare mattress. "Steve, you've done everything you could for Marshall. You're behaving as if you'd been shot in the back instead of him."

He sat up to glare at Davies. "Do you know how many different ways a man can die?"

When he was calmer, he swiftly wrote a dispatch for the *World*. He thought the skirmish at La Guasima had been a blunder, and said so. He was bitter because of the death of so many men; he was bitter about the lack of attention for the wounded. He wondered if, when his turn came, he would be able to write his story as Ed Marshall had done, while death leered in his eyes.

CHAPTER 79

At the banks of the San Juan River, the men leaped in up to their waists. A fusillade swept the water. The badly wounded collapsed; some were drowned. Through this leaden hail, the regiments splashed to the other side. They rested, until the enemy guns found them again. They rushed into the woods and did not halt until they reached several fences of barbed wire.

Now they could see the hill. It rose like a perpendicular dune that had been strewn with rocks and tufted with grasses. The crest emitted bluish puffs; it was from this eminence that the foe was decimating the ranks with rifle and machine-gun fire. To reach the hill, the attackers must cross a level grassy plain that stretched for half a mile.

In the harsh, burning sunlight, he had to repeat to himself the precise location: they were at the foot of San Juan Hill, three miles from Santiago, whose streetlights they could see on the western horizon at night. That structure at the top resembling a Japanese pagoda was a blockhouse; that line of sandy dirt below it consisted of rifle-pits where the enemy was entrenched. When the moon rose, the coconut palms, mangos, and lime trees whispered softly. The stars twinkled like fireflies.

Bugles tootled. Men ran across the plain. Figures slipped in the grass and toppled. Some shouted, others cursed foully to purge themselves of the terror. A hat rolled back as if it could not bear to face the volleys from the top of the hill. A soldier in a blue blouse halted momentarily; one of his suspenders had snapped loose. Then he sped on as if mad dogs were after him.

The sun sparkled on a black rock. A belch of flame cut a neat hole in the ranks. One man glanced over his shoulder; another fell to his knees. The rest, yelling savagely, dashed on and upward. Roosevelt, on foot now, with a blue polka-dot handkerchief about his neck and gauntlets on his hands and wrists, charged madly. He waved the host on. The sun glittered in his eyeglasses.

The wavering line was being reinforced by men in blue and men in brown, white-skinned men and dark-skinned men. They came cursing and shouting as they swarmed up the slope. Their blanket rolls made superb targets.

Suddenly, a silence came down, so swiftly that it disturbed the forward skirmishers. What were the "canaries" up to now? The firing had ceased. A trumpeter gleefully played his call.

Isolated figures of enemy soldiers appeared against the sky. The assault troops leveled their weapons, but the Spaniards were fleeing down the other side.

The carbines fired. Pent-up emotions released, the sky was rocked by triumphant shouting.

A young Rough Rider tottered toward the scarred walls of the battered blockhouse. Broken fragments of shells were scattered about as if a meteor had exploded. He spread his arms to embrace the white stones.

Flags of victory were rising. The men who hauled down the enemy banner were tearing it to shreds. A cheer broke out as the Stars and Stripes was unfurled.

On the slope, bodies remained in curious postures. The later arrivals raced past them to join those at the top who were firing after the escaping foe. The bodies in the curious postures, white men, dark men, did not stir. Their brass buttons glittered; the insignia sparkled in the sun.

Returning across the field, Stephen saw the wounded being lifted, or helped, into the rickety hospital wagons. A man with a heavy mustache and blood streaming down his face collided with him, and said, " 'Scuse me!" as if he had jostled a stranger walking down Main Street.

At the bend of the Aguadores and the San Juan, most of the dead had already been laid to one side. He searched their faces as if they were mirrors.

The light was driving heated needles through his pupils. How many hours had he been in the sun? "Que hora es?" "What time is it?" San Juan Hill had been taken at one-thirty. Three hours ago. Or had that happened yesterday? He tried to smoke a cigarette, but his throat was raw; the roof of his mouth seemed aflame. His back itched; he had not been out of his clothes in sixty hours.

He labored over his next dispatch. He struggled to capture the feeling of the simple courage that had goaded the men to rush across the plain and up that hillside. "It was the behavior of the men. One cannot speak of it. . . ." His emotions choked him. Only those who had died or been carried off in litters could bear witness. The dead deserted the living all too eagerly.

As he wrote, the blistering sun became a blood-red orange. Odors identified with latrines and decay assaulted him. Over the positions on both sides, the vultures circled neutrally.

He rode mechanically from San Luis de Caney and back to Siboney for the sake of more dispatches. Under the arch to the entrance of a gloomy church that had been transformed into a hospital, he saw a figure clad only in a loincloth stretched out upon an altar turned into an operating table. Blood spurted from a wound in the thigh. He paused humbly, as at another Calvary. He stood bowed in anguish for the poor sons of God.

He was babbling hysterically when he tottered from his horse in the correspondents' camp. In the middle of a sentence, he halted abruptly. George Rhea was eyeing him.

"A touch of the sun!" he pleaded. The top of his head was being pounded by invisible hammers. "A touch of——"

Rhea summoned Sylvester Scovel. "It's Crane."

Scovel clapped a palm to his brow. "Dammit, Steve, you're burning up!"

The Army doctor said cautiously that it probably was not yellow fever, which was going around. He could not be sure; he had never seen a case until he had landed in Cuba three days ago.

The following morning, he heard Scovel talking. "Maybe it's nothing, Steve. But yesterday you thought Ralph Paine was Harold Frederic, and you called someone else your father. I thought that you had sunstroke when we went over the mountains to spy on Cervera's fleet, but you were all right the next day. Now I'm sure you've had sunstroke. Damn if you haven't been walking around in a delirium!"

"I'll take some more whiskey and quinine."

"Whiskey!" Rhea scoffed. "You never drink enough whiskey to wet your whistle. Sylvester is right. Dick Davis said that at San Juan you were stalking before those rifle-pits like a sleepwalker. A miracle the canaries didn't pot you. He had to pull you down."

Scovel placed his big hands on Stephen's shoulders. "*Mando usted vaya.* I order you to go home," he pronounced solemnly. "*Pronto!* You've written a dozen good articles, and you've been cited by the Marines. Enough. I'll tell the office you're on sick leave. Go home." He paused at the woebegone expression. "Steve, when you're better, you hurry back and catch up with us. The war won't be over."

Stephen held together until they got him into an enormous night-shirt and put him to bed in the Siboney Army Hospital.

"Anything you want, *hermanito?*" Scovel asked.

He grinned feebly. "Pickles."

By evening, Scovel had obtained a jar. "Stolen from a general officer's mess. Eat hearty, mate!"

With that craving satisfied, his resistance to hospitalization diminished. He lay quietly under a wool blanket and shivered, although the temperature in the room was ninety-eight. The hacking cough returned.

He dreamed that he was riding a horse that was thirty hands high. The jungle parted to admit a crooked trail. He dashed into a dark, tangled undergrowth where the cries of the birds were like the gulls and terns screaming over the beach at Asbury Park. He could not separate the impressions, except that he was riding hard and his bones ached. He heard Mama's voice, but could not catch her words. Two riders wheeled out and trotted ahead; another galloped at his side. He could not distinguish their faces. The sun flashed into his eyes, and glittered from their swords. He rode on and on until the darkness engulfed him.

The *City of Washington,* a whaleback transport that dipped and rose with the tide, was waiting.

"Here's your permit to go aboard, Steve," George Rhea said. "Scovel's been called to Admiral Sampson's headquarters. Here's some money, too, you lucky stiff! Get well, and hurry back! *Adios, companero!*"

His next memory was of gazing at the receding shore.

Coughing, he drifted aimlessly about the ship. His legs were unsteady.

Later, a doctor found him. "A correspondent?" He glanced at him sharply. "Say! Do you know you've got yellow fever?"

"No, sir. I——"

"By God, you have, man! You shouldn't be aboard here at all. They've got dispatch boats for you fellows. You isolate yourself, do you hear?"

He was surely hearing this in a new delirium. He cursed at the doctor's retreating back. "Isolate yourself!" That might have been good advice years ago. It was too late now.

The ravens, those poor scarecrows of men with bandaged heads or amputated limbs who crept up from the bowels of the ship, fed him. No one had told him that he was required to bring his own food aboard, so he shared their tinned stewed tomatoes and bread. They did not resent his civilian status.

The transport steamed at a miserably slow speed, but the sea was kind and, except for a single line squall, the weather disturbed them little. When the ocean was calm, green as a mermaid's eyes, and the sun shone, as many as could clung to the rail.

Other men died as, for lack of drugs and surgical attention, their endurance snapped. They were nailed into pine boxes and lowered into the hold.

It seemed three weeks, but they were at sea only five days. When they passed the Chesapeake lightship and Cape Henry, and entered Thimble Shoal Channel, Stephen was feeling stronger.

Fearing that the doctor who had given the isolation order would detain him, he went ashore hastily at Old Point Comfort.

He hired a hack to Chamberlain's Hotel, then remembered his moldy boots and scarecrow garments. He asked the way to the nearest clothing store. For twenty-four dollars, he purchased a complete outfit, from underwear, shirts, and handkerchiefs to a linen suit, hat, and boots.

The verandah at the hotel was as crowded as a reviewing stand. Girls and women in light summer dresses and picture hats mingled with smartly dressed men and neatly clad officers from Fort Monroe.

Suddenly, the crowd in the roadway was bisected, rudely thrust aside by soldiers clearing a path. Through this narrow avenue limped a procession of the returnees from the *City of Washington*.

Stephen gawked at the wounded he had left two hours ago. The lines were so orderly in a halting, hobbling, crippled way that the sight wrenched his heart. Amputees were being supported by comrades who were sadly emaciated, the sightless were clutching at the arms of men who could see, gaunt creatures with bandaged heads shuffled bravely, others treaded stoutly, all tattered, all ragged, while behind these broken ranks came the stretcher cases carried by the sick-bay attendants. Each prone figure, with only the pale head exposed, was covered by a grimy blanket, each unit appeared to be a two-headed apparition, for the stretchers, between the bearers, extended like thin limbs, and the heads of the wounded lay like garish trophies being transported as offerings to the temples of the God of War.

The same military band that had blared the national anthem at the dock swung into a marching song until some sensitive officer ordered a halt. The band moved on silently, the sun flashing from the brass. The silent anguish of the wounded was sufficiently tragic music; the compassion of hearts melting to their pain the only acclaim the arrivals could welcome, if they were aware at all of the stunned spectators observing them.

Stephen thought that he heard the wind moaning. But it was not the wind. A tremor had run through the dignitaries, a shudder through the people in the streets. The sound, a single giant sound of awe and horror, came from a thousand throats as the sobbing civilians endured vicariously the terrors of war. At the tears on the faces of the girls and the women, his lips moved: "Do not weep, Maiden, war is kind."

426

He was in a better frame of mind when he reached New York. To the news editor of the *World,* he turned in a general article that he had completed at Old Point Comfort.

"They want to see you, Crane," the other said blandly. "You're walking into a lion's den."

"I've just left it. And, as soon as I pick up another advance, I'm going back."

"Puerto Rico?" The campaign to take the island had started. "Better see the financial manager. Don't say I didn't warn you!"

The financial manager sniffed contemptuously at his list of expenses. "Crane, don't you think you've had enough of our money without earning it?"

Stephen gasped, "Sir?"

The man ran his finger down the little column of figures. "Twenty-four dollars for a new outfit? No, sir! Nothing of the kind. You've caused us more grief——"

"Hold on!" Stephen retorted. "I've just come up from hell and——"

"If you plan to go back there, you'll not do it on the *World's* account."

His knuckles went white on the desk-top. "I cabled enough stories to make good my advance and more. Sylvester Scovel put me aboard the *City of Washington*——"

"Never mind Scovel! Your story on the New York 71st has embarrassed Mr. Pulitzer. We're quite happy to terminate our association with you here and now."

"The 71st?" He was bewildered. "I wrote no story——"

"Crane, you accused the regiment of cowardice. Is that so unimportant in your mind that you've already forgotten it? The article appeared on Saturday. You cabled it from Port Antonio."

"I wrote no story about the 71st. It wasn't my dispatch! I've been aboard——"

"Never mind, I said!" By his fingertips, he picked up the sheet of expenses. "Not one cent. Good day, Mr. Crane."

Stephen crumpled the paper in his fist and hurled it into the other's face.

The injustice of the charge sickened him. He could not have purchased a new outfit in Virginia and been in Jamaica two days later. The miserliness of a paper that would not pay for a cheap outfit, when his own clothing had been ruined in its service, disgusted him. As for the 71st, either Scovel or one of the other men must

427

have sent the dispatch. The harassed Scovel had even failed to inform New York that he had sent Stephen Crane home.

He was received warmly in the offices of the *Journal*. So he was the man who had aided Ed Marshall and sent through his dispatch! The Hearst officials demurred against nothing; if Mr. Crane was ready to return to the battlefields, he had only to present himself to the cashier for any advance he required.

Before he left New York, he called on Doctor Trudeau, the consumption specialist.

The physician, a stern little man, began the usual examination with a sharp scrutiny of his caller and a series of short, crisp questions. He had spent little more than five minutes in listening and percussing when he lifted the bell of his stethoscope from Stephen's chest. He pulled the binaura from his ears and said bluntly, "Sit down, Mr. Crane. Unless you spend the next year in bed doing absolutely nothing, you may find yourself seriously ill."

Stephen gripped the arms of the chair.

"You have a very productive cough, with blood-streaked sputum, fevers, and night sweats. You are markedly underweight. It appears that you have had pulmonary problems before. If you were my patient I would place you in a sanitorium for at least a year."

"And if I did not choose to go?"

The physician studied him with severity.

"Doctor, I don't want my wife to know anything about this."

"Look here, Crane. I have no intention of letting your wife, or anyone else, know what I have told you. But I cannot advise you too strongly to change your way of life. Go home and rest."

"Would a stay in the West Indies aggravate the condition? I am obliged to go there."

With an air of finality, Doctor Trudeau folded his stethoscope. "Crane, I am a physician. I am not a travel agent. Go home!"

After the Santiago campaign, Puerto Rico was as calm as a chess game. General Miles feinted before he made his thrusts; he moved to outflank the enemy and to render the prepared positions untenable. Guanica was taken, Ponce surrendered, and village after village on the southern coast greeted the American troops as deliverers from the Spanish yoke.

In Stephen's opinion, Puerto Rico, although there was heavy fighting at Coamo and Guayama, and in isolated areas, was a lark that promised a dozen interesting articles for the *Journal*. However, in mid-August, Spain signed a protocol of peace, and the fighting was over.

He lingered in Ponce for several days before he returned to Key West. Since he had not worked off Mr. Hearst's advance, he had no desire to return to New York.

A letter from Cora, forwarded through several hands, reached him as he was waiting for new instructions. She was in dire need of funds for the creditors. Furthermore, what of *Blackwood's?* Had he written any stories to apply against the account? Meldrum, who had been dunning Conrad, should not be kept waiting. She was anxious to lease and to be settled in Brede Place, an old English manor-house in Sussex, before he came back. Would he instruct Reynolds to cable more money? The move to Brede Place would be costly.

On another sheet, evidently scrawled in great agitation, she advised that Harold Frederic had suffered a stroke. Although the physician had diagnosed endocarditis and an embolism of the brain, Harold had peremptorily dismissed him as soon as he could stir. Would Stephen write to Harold urging him to heed medical advice? She added that it was important that he cable acceptance of Brede Place.

Poor Harold! He could do nothing for him. Frederic would leave two broods of children, and neither wife provided with enough money to raise them.

Brede Place! The name chilled him. If Cora had debts at Ravensbrook, how many more would she incur in a larger establishment? Besides, the tone of her letters exasperated him. Did she think that he was dawdling in a saloon, observing the war through field glasses? She could not have forgotten their hardships in Greece. Did she expect him to dedicate evenings in the slit trenches to stories for *Blackwood's?* Brede Place would be a drain down which every dollar he earned would be poured to support them in the style she thought fitting to their station in England. He sent no reply.

By the terms of the armistice, in effect while the peace negotiations continued in Paris, Havana remained under Spanish authority. Correspondents were expressly forbidden to enter the city; several newspapermen who had attempted to land had been arrested. The *Journal,* however, urged Stephen to gain entrance "somehow." The American public was eager to learn of the state of affairs inside the capital of Cuba.

By invoking the names he had used in Jacksonville, he reached the local committee of the *Junta* in Tampa. He gave an account of the filibuster trip which had ended with the sinking of the *Commodore,* and a detailed report of his newspaper services in the field. He pleaded for help in traveling to Havana. He was met with stony silence; Cuba's leaders had been ignored in the American occupation of Santiago and, at this hour, were being denied a voice in the peace negotiations with Spain. Why should they help this young correspondent?

As he trudged back to the hotel, he paused at a cigar-maker's stall to purchase a box of cigars.

"You no longer have any with the fine Havana tobaccos?" he inquired casually. "Not until Havana is free again."

The cigar-maker grumbled, "All our cigars are strictly Havana."

"But you can't get tobacco out of Cuba."

"Our buyer returned yesterday. We will have enough leaf for a month."

He frowned. "Is he an American then, your buyer?"

The man retorted, "Do you think that General Blanco would permit a free Cuban to enter his city? Our buyer comes with American papers, and for gold we buy what we need. Their warehouses in Havana are overflowing."

Stephen calmly lit the end of a cigar. "*Gracias, Señor!*" He had heard weird tales of the trading behind the lines in wartime; that had been true in Greece and in Turkey. But how to obtain the necessary papers to enter Havana safely?

Again he intruded upon the committee. "*Señores,* I must confess to you. It is not for the sake of my newspaper that I am so eager to enter Havana." He spoke dolefully; he must appeal to that sentimental Latin tenderness. "There is the beautiful girl I love who is in Havana. She has promised herself to me. Since I have been unable to enter the city, her family has resolved to marry her to another."

Stony silence greeted him once more.

"Unless I can appear before her soon, I am undone. My life after that would not be worth a tobacco leaf."

A pair of dark eyes glistered, and a voice compassionately addressed the other men in Spanish.

"She has sent word to me," Stephen added, "that if I love her I must surely come. How can I prove it?"

Softer glances were exchanged. They were angry at the high-handed American government in Washington, not at this romantic young man whose heart was breaking for the love of his *muchacha.*

He went on slowly. "She has informed me that there is a way to open the doors of the city. If I appear as a bona fide buyer of tobacco, with the necessary papers, the police will permit me to land. As a *corresponsale,* I would land in jail. Yet, if I do not appear in a fortnight, all will be lost and she will be another man's wife."

"Your passport?" the chairman asked gravely. "*Pasaporte!* Is it in order?"

He produced it. "My occupation is given as 'author.' What help would it be to me in Havana unless my name were Miguel de Cervantes Saavedra?"

"You are not Cervantes," a second committeeman informed him gruffly. "But—*quien sabe?*—for the sake of this woman we may help you."

"*Gracias, Señores! Muchisimas gracias!*"

Three days later his passport was returned. His occupation had been altered to "tobacco buyer." He was provided with correspondence from a Tampa cigar firm; he was authorized to obtain information on the current crop, prices, and quality.

He sailed on a Swedish steamer. When he arrived in Havana, the police official studied his papers, and smiled. "For this product you Americans have no other avenue. You must come humbly to our doors, hat in one hand, gold in the other."

"*Sí, Señor.*"

He relaxed as he drove through the narrow cobblestoned streets of the beautiful city and out upon the sunlit avenues toward the Hotel Pasaje.

The next day, with his first dispatch cryptically worded, he headed for the cable office. Calmly, he placed a gold eagle upon the pages and slipped them across the counter.

The operator pocketed the eagle, and read and reread the text. "It is a report of conditions, Señor," he murmured.

"My friends speculate on the tobacco. If conditions are very good, the price will be low. If conditions are bad, the price will be high."

Within the week, he sent two additional stories, each at the price of an eagle. Then the operator's soft inquiries began to disquiet him. A hint to the police would send him to jail. Besides, as soon as the *Journal* printed his pieces with a Havana dateline, he would be a marked man.

In the early morning he packed, paid his bill, and fled from the Pasaje. The *Junta* had given him the address of a boardinghouse run by an American woman who could be trusted.

He found 75 Calle del Aquacate on a street of old white houses.

A large woman in a flowered wrapper appeared in the doorway. The face, with its dark lashes, smooth skin, and pert turned-up nose, was serenely handsome, but the black eyes were troubled and mistrustful. She might have been forty.

"My friend, Señor Rojas in Tampa, said that you took in American boarders."

At the male glance, she pulled the wrapper tightly about her figure and studied him warily.

"I'm trying to hide out, Mrs. Clancy, to do a piece of writing. You'll not turn me away from your door?"

She said at last, "Look at me straight now."

"Yes, Ma'am." She must have been a beautiful girl in her youth. The trace of brogue in her voice pleased him.

"Señor Rojas was sure that you took American boarders."

Curtly, "Sometimes I take them in, Señor, if I've a good mind to, and sometimes I don't."

He dumped his suitcase across the threshold. "My name is Stephen Crane, Mrs. Clancy. I'm sick of hotels—the Pasaje—and short of money. If I don't write, I can't eat, and I can't write in those fancy places."

"Upstairs!" she said laconically. She picked up his case as though she had been carrying such burdens all her life. Inside the house, with the shades drawn, the air was cool.

"What are you doing in Havana, Mrs. Clancy?"

"I live here," she replied. "I'm a widow, and I mind my own business. Do you?"

The room on the second floor was small but neatly furnished, with a white bedstead, a stand with ewer and basin, a chair, and a small table against a window that looked out over the street. Several religious pictures hung on the whitewashed walls.

"You'll take those holy faces away, won't you, Mrs. Clancy?"

She dropped the case at his feet. "It's my home! You look at my pictures as they hang there, or you sleep somewhere else in Havana. Savvy?"

He grinned disarmingly. "Mrs. Clancy, I've never seen pictures so beautiful!"

"The name is Mary." She handed him towels. "Don't waste my soap. I don't have to give it."

"Yes, Ma'am!"

"No *muchachas*. No lady visitors."

"I wouldn't dream of it, Mary."

"What you dream is no business of mine," she retorted sagely.

When she had left, he took off his boots and his whites and lay on the bed in his singlet. In the heat, he smoked and stared at the ceiling. A millipede—or was it a centipede?—came out of a crack in the plaster. He heard the noises of the street: wagons, carriages, horsemen. He was pleased to be alone again. No one would find him here.

At siesta time, when the city had quieted and even the carts that rolled down the streets like barrels hurled from a rooftop had ceased their racket, he unpacked and spread his manuscripts and notebooks on the table. He was comfortable in the little room. For a writer, it was an admirable sanctuary. He would soon be through with the *Journal*. After that, if he could write day and night for three months, Reynolds would sell the stories, and he might accumulate a thousand, or two thousand, dollars.

Reynolds had recommended James B. Pinker on Arundel Street in London to arrange for the sale of the British rights. At thirty-six pounds a story, six stories, less commissions, would bring nearly two hundred pounds, enough to keep Cora, too.

Dick Davis was planning a book on the Cuban and Puerto Rico campaigns, a rewrite of his dispatches. Ed Marshall, who was making a slow but painful recovery, was writing a volume on the Rough Riders. But he had no heart for such rehashes. He would be better served to write out the short stories that had been welling in his throat.

Hastily, he created "The Price of the Harness," drawing upon the

Cuban experiences as if he had been the only witness at Armageddon. He mailed it to Reynolds, and launched a new story.

He strolled through Havana, from the sea-wall at Calzado del Malecón to the Arsenal, from La Machina wharf to the Botanical Gardens. He studied the wreckage of the *Maine,* which was still visible in the harbor. He walked the Prado every afternoon when the promenade was deserted in the heat. He haunted the markets, admired the statues, and, when he tired, rested in the cool churches. Often he sat in the café near the Parque Central, hoping for a glimpse of a beautiful face or figure.

"Where were you last night?" Mary Clancy demanded.

"I walked."

The dark eyes fixed upon him jealously. "I know you men! *Muchachas!*"

Her proprietary manner made him uncomfortable. It was true that he visited Havana's cribs and brothels. The girls were plump, some placid, some tigerish, their ways startling to a Northerner. He made the acquaintance of Francisca, whose Madonna-like features belied her talents. However, he patronized her for the sake of feminine company; he did not mean to be unfaithful to Cora.

In the following weeks, he fired more stories at Reynolds. The agent sold "The Price of the Harness" to *The Cosmopolitan,* and sent a copy of the manuscript to *Blackwood's* to apply against the debt. When John Brisben Walker, *The Cosmopolitan's* editor and publisher, changed the title to "The Woof of the Thin Red Threads," Stephen was furious. The fool! "The Price of the Harness" referred to the price the men had paid in blood, hunger, and fever.

He was sitting in a café, staring at the passers-by, when an American halted before his table. "Crane? You Stephen Crane? I heard General Wade asking about you. Better get over to see him."

He finished his coffee, nervously sloshing it on the table, and went off to La Machina, where General Wade, who was in charge of evacuating Americans, had his headquarters.

An aide ushered him in.

"Your wife has been looking for you for weeks, Mr. Crane."

"My wife!"

"She wrote to the Secretary of War two weeks ago. About ten days ago she sent him a cable from England. And she communicated with the British Consul. He, too, has been after us. She must be frantic with worry, Crane."

He crimsoned. "I regret if I have caused you trouble, Sir."

"No trouble," the other replied tersely. "It's your affair. Only we'd like to know that you're alive. No one could find a trace of you. Some paper in Florida, the *Times-Union* in Jacksonville, said that you had disappeared. Evidently, the news reached her."

The General, a handsome, middle-aged man, twirled the end of

433

his mustache. "I'll report at once to the Secretary of War that you are alive and well. I assume that you will write to your wife, or notify her somehow."

"I will inform Mrs. Crane," Stephen replied stiffly.

Outside, in the sunlight, he stood on the wharf and gazed across the harbor at Casa Blanca. Only Cora would dare to write to the Secretary of War and state that her "husband" had disappeared. Reynolds had informed him again and again that Cora had been badgering him. She was determined; Cora had always been determined. She would rouse everyone. Soon she would cable to Mr. Hearst. She would cable to President McKinley!

Sullenly, he sent a brief cable to Ravensbrook. He was well; he would write soon.

CHAPTER 81

Stephen worked feverishly for two weeks, and finished four stories. He mailed them separately to Reynolds, each with its special burst of enthusiasm: "I am now sending you a *peach*. I love it devotedly."

Reynolds forwarded the news that Harold Frederic had died on October 19th. Cora wrote that she had immediately invited Katie and the three children to come to live at Ravensbrook. She was forming a committee to raise a subscription to support and educate the three youngsters. She was appealing to everyone: to Joseph Conrad, to Robert Barr, to Hall Caine, to G. B. Shaw, to Henry James, to Kipling, to the whole literary pack. Trust sentimental Cora to ring a tocsin for orphans who had no legal status! Grace Frederic and her four children were also to be pitied, but they had their position before the law; Katie and her brood were under a cloud.

The death of his big, blustering friend numbed Stephen. Harold, cold in his grave, was free, while Death now exposed the whole sorry tale of his dual menage. Fortunate that there was an impulsive Cora Crane who understood, as she had often put it, "the supreme egotism of women who have never been tempted," and would fight like a lioness to protect and shelter his little ones. Stephen mused over the paradox that Cora, the sinner, should have more charity and forgiveness, even more humility in her soul, then the virtuous women of society.

Harold's death remained a blow; like the big "Swede" in "The Blue Hotel," he had begged for death.

Suddenly, the wind went out of his sails. Becalmed, he sat for hours at his table, bored and unable to lift his pen. He was empty, drained. The prospect of writing more stories loomed as a flat and insipid chore.

The short story vein having played out, he decided to concentrate on the novel about the Greek War. He must produce, once again, a "potboiler." If it were a long narrative Reynolds might obtain a sizeable advance. He cabled to Reynolds: "For Christ's sake get me some money here!"

He had no theme and no plot for a novel. He could add nothing to the statement on mountain warfare that he had made in "Death and the Child." Yet he must write a novel.

Ruminating on the Greco–Turkish fiasco, he considered describing a correspondent who had been accompanied to the battlefront by a woman. But a man's problems, it seemed, were never solved by one woman, unless she were his mother. An ironic smile played about his mouth. Let there be a correspondent accompanied, or pursued, by *two* women.

His thoughts drifted to Amy. Had there been a child? Would he ever know? Was it alive or dead? Was it somewhere, in Chicago perhaps, being reared in obscurity, a child who would one day curse its father?

Stern shadows compelled him to view his conduct with distaste. His behavior had not been beyond censure. True, he had made no bold decisions, yea or nay. He had let the tide of Amy's emotions carry him.

When he had left Amy, he had traded her for Cora, another mistress. Still, no ordinary woman would have given up the security of the Hotel de Dreme for the wandering existence of a writer's paramour. He was withdrawing from Cora, but he had never given himself completely to any woman. His letters had never been romantic or passionate, or even blissfully touched with ardor; he had written to his beloveds as if Aggie or his mother were standing at his shoulder, as if he were writing under the surveillance of an unseen audience. Only with the unredeemed fallen was he utterly free. The lustful freedom of the early days with Cora had ended when she had asserted her mastery, or when his own had failed. The same force that led him to the outcasts, the violated, the divorced, and the unhappily married, later repelled him from them.

He consoled himself with Francisca, but she aroused nothing in him. Her sister Carmelita, who seemed half savage, tempted him. He had dreamed of burrowing into her, falling, clutching, and sinking into the primordial cave.

Someone opened the door. Francisca, naked as a brown nymph, tripped across the threshold with little cups of steaming coffee. They both reeked of butter and violets, the sinning sisters. He was spent when he went downstairs.

A thunderstorm was lashing the city. The proprietor, a lean, sinewy villain, invited him to his room for a glass of rum.

On the threshold, the blood drained from Stephen's face. A photograph of Cora in a Spanish wedding gown hung over the bureau.

"My sister!" said the man, crossing himself. "She was a good woman."

The way the light had struck the photograph! He had always feared that, one day, he would find Cora's picture in another man's quarters.

With patient amusement, he constructed his puzzle in "Active Service." A light and romantic novel about a newspaperman who was a Sunday editor, like Fletcher Johnson or Edward Marshall, from the *Eclipse*, not the *Sun* or the *World* but the *Eclipse*, who went off to the Greco-Turkish conflict. His hero would be "Rufus Coleman," the surname after the Asbury Park hotel.

Cora would be "Marjory," a pleasant little girl, as close to Maggie as he dared; her father, a professor who forbade her to marry Coleman. Sardonically, Stephen shaped him after Jonathan Townley Crane and Willis B. Hawkins. "W.B.H." He twisted the initials to "H.B.W." for "Harrison B. Wainwright." An excellent name for a sedate professor; Willie would chuckle.

To foil Coleman, who was wooing his daughter, Harrison B. Wainwright—was there a trace of Captain Stewart in this character, too? —plotted to take his wife and daughter, along with a group of his students, on a study trip to Greece. For the school, Stephen created a comic name: "Washurst College"; "Was-Hearst" College.

To plot a contrived novel was a child's game. Coleman, dismayed at being rejected by Marjory, sped to Greece where the war was brewing. On the boat whom should he meet again but Nora Black? None other than Amy Lee in disguise—an old flame, an actress on her way to London to appear in a new play. As Cora had done on their way to Europe, Nora had remained below deck until they neared Queenstown. Stephen chortled as he commingled the actions of the two women.

He relived the trip across the continent to Athens. He wrote swiftly, accurately recording his experiences, deviating only when he introduced his personal characters.

The encounter with Cora in the dark, as she had sought him on the road to Arta, he transplanted without elaboration, except to add her "father" and his pack of students. To Marjory, he gave the little lines of dialogue that only Cora would recognize as deriving from the flight from Jacksonville.

Ironically, he twisted the realities. Nora was to write an article on the war from a woman's point of view; whereas it had been Cora

436

who had written as "Imogene Carter." He referred to his disguised Amy as "this queen of song and the dance."

He scorned himself by permitting the students to comment on Nora's effect on Coleman. One said, "She has got him somehow by the short hairs and she intends him to holler murder. Anybody can see that."

Into the novel, he could pour his long-suppressed anger. When Amy–Nora laughed insolently, he wrote, "She could see that he wished to strangle her." She goaded him until he burst out, "Confound you, Nora! I would like to kill you!"

She taunted: "You know what I can do when I get started, so you had better be a very good boy. I might take it into my head to say some things, you know." To the core of his soul, Rufus Coleman hated Nora Black. The novel had become a ritual of vengeance.

As he continued, chapter after chapter, the Greek war served as a scrim for his private story, for the confession that would never see the light of day in any other form, that even here would lie masked in an underbrush of prose.

Night after night, he fought his battle with Amy–Nora. What had finally defeated her was the news, transmitted by some good soul in the newspaper world, that Stephen Crane had been traveling in Europe with another woman.

He was aware, as he reveled in this fantasy, that his portraits of Cora and Amy were intermingled and interwoven. They were two women and they were one; they were every woman.

His portrayal of Cora–Marjory as a delicate girl was a mask. Cora was neither helpless nor tearful; it suited him to contrast Cora and Amy when, in fact, they were so frighteningly alike.

To round off his plot with a devilish jest, he had Nora come upon a little Greek officer–prince who wanted to marry her. So, by proxy, he wished Amy on Cora's Captain Stewart!

The novel would not be completed for weeks, perhaps for months, but its architecture had been determined.

Then two letters from Cora in a single day, one in the morning, the other in the afternoon, both forwarded by Reynolds, derailed him from further work.

Cora wrote that the year's rental on Ravensbrook, the colossal sum of ninety-one pounds, had never been paid; the landlord demanded his money. The grocer, who had not had a shilling in nearly six months, threatened an action. Payment was also due on the furniture she had bought to furnish the villa. She begged for money; meanwhile, she was appealing also to Joseph Conrad and Robert Barr. "Come home, Steve!"

He fumed. Cora and her debts! The effrontery to appeal to poor Conrad, who was living from hand to mouth! Barr was a good fellow, but to knock at his door was cheeky. She would do anything, *anything!* He stormed, and hurried out to cable money.

The second letter advised that Katie and Mrs. Mills, the Christian Science practitioner whom Katie had called in to visit the stricken Harold before his death, were under arrest on charges of manslaughter. Everyone who had known Harold Frederic intimately was wanted to give testimony that the two women were innocent, that the sick man had rejected all aid and that he alone was responsible for his professionally unattended demise.

He reread the letter with a heavy heart. Poor Katie! He vaguely recalled Mrs. Mills as a pleasant woman who had frequently been a week-end guest at the Frederics'. If he was needed as a witness he would have to return at once.

He told Mary Clancy that friends in England required his testimony to save them from prosecution.

"To be a witness?" she scoffed. "You go to an attorney and make a deposition and swear to it, and the post carries it off. I did it once to help a friend in Jersey City."

He was convinced, as of old, that women had the shrewdness that men lacked. He would not have to return to England to be overwhelmed by his creditors.

Mary located the attorney. Stephen explained the circumstances and gave his deposition, which was notarized and sent off to Katie.

He was back at Mary Clancy's when he realized that he had betrayed himself. The deposition carried his address: 75 Calle del Aguacate, Habana, Cuba.

"The jig's up," he said to Mary. "They'll be after me for fair."

They were. At the end of the week, he received a long cable from London. Against his future books, Heinemann had advanced fifty pounds to bring him home. A second cable from John Stokes, Frederic's ex-secretary: the money was being dispatched through General Wade. Canny Cora! If the money was paid to Stephen specifically for his passage, he would have to leave Havana.

CHAPTER 82

He trod the pavements of Manhattan in high spirits. A noisy, dirty city, but he could live here. The fire engines clanging, the ambulance wagons and the beer wagons rattling, the steam engines on the elevated lines hissing, newsboys shouting, people arguing, garbage cans on the sidewalks—New York, loud and brassy, had not changed.

He sat with Paul Reynolds, who soberly passed over more letters

438

from Cora. "She wants you back, Crane. She thinks you have a great future in England. She says she has a wonderful home waiting for you at Brede Place."

Frederick A. Stokes Company had taken *War Is Kind*, but Heinemann had not reached a decision. Although poetry sold poorly, Stokes was willing to make a special edition.

The conversations thawed him. No one had put the direct question, "Are you married?" Not even at the newspaper offices. What he had assumed to be common knowledge was apparently not known at all.

Ceek Linson, he learned, was in Europe, so he decided, at last, to call on Willis Hawkins. He climbed the stairs to the office of Brains Publishing Company.

Hawkins spied the slight figure on the threshold, and stared in disbelief. A choked cry, "Steve!"

"Willie, the prodigal returneth."

Hawkins hugged him, pumped his hand, and repeated, "Steve! You're alive, you skinny, pale ghost!" He turned away to clear his throat.

Stephen admired the big, handsome figure. Willie had put on weight.

Hawkins slapped his abdomen. "Life's been dull since you went away. Remember our poker games, the long walks and the talks, the trip to Hubbard's dinner in Buffalo? Steve, the times we had!"

"And you got me a suit to wear at the banquet."

Willie's eyes filled. "You remember!"

They went to the Lantern Club to eat with the old crowd: the same mad climb to the rooftop, the same bare entrance, and the large, warm room with its fireplace and a hundred lanterns glowing from the rafters.

Irving Bacheller exhibited a dozen copies of *The Lanthorn Book*. For several years he had goaded the members to contribute to a volume of the best of the stories that they had read at their gatherings. Irving, persistent fellow, had completed the collection. He had included Stephen's "The Wise Men." *The Lanthorn Book* had been printed on fine deckle-edge paper and bound in green cloth with the backbone in sheepskin.

Stephen gravely signed his name in each copy at the bottom of the last page of his story. The book was a keepsake; only a few would go on sale.

Long after the others had left, he and Willie lounged before the fireplace. He told of his adventures in Greece and Cuba; he avoided mention of England and Cora.

"Now you'll stay on this side, won't you, Steve? We'll start the poker games again. Until you're settled, you're welcome to my office any time."

Stephen referred casually to his lungs; he was considering residence elsewhere than in New York.

"You need a dry climate then. Texas or the Arizona territory. Regular living, good food, and plenty of sleep will fix you, Steve. But I wish you could stay in New York. I'd keep an eye on you."

"Got to write, Willie. I'm flat."

His gravity silenced Hawkins, who slowly nodded in recognition of the marked changes of these two years. Stephen Crane's horizons had widened. He was no longer a youth who needed protection; he belonged to many people.

A familiar bearded figure strode from McClure's office. As the man flung a fur-lined cape around his shoulders, he suddenly noticed Stephen.

"Mr. Garland."

Effusively, Garland wrung his hand. "Well, well! I didn't know that you were back. All I ever know about Steve Crane is what I read in the papers."

"I'm a poor letter-writer."

"No matter. The important thing, Steve, is that you're back! Now you'll get down to some real writing, real writing. You had got off to such a splendid start. What a start! Then you got lost in England. Let the British have Henry James and the others. You belong here, Steve, in the U.S.A."

"I was in Cuba——"

"So I read. But the war's over. Don't let them spread you thin with more newspaper work, Steve. You need the time to think, to write at your best level." The old voluble Garland. "The fleshpots aren't for plain folks like you and me, are they? Hard writing is the best writing. I'll never forget *The Black Riders* and watching you at my desk while you poured out those lines. I thought it remarkable. I still think so. Take my advice, Steve," Garland concluded with another powerful handshake. "Go back to your hills! You'll be safer there, away from things that can do you no good. Don't let them get you off the track. Go back to your hills!"

The meeting with Garland encouraged him to pay another call.

Mr. Howells seemed slightly grayer and slightly stouter as they shook hands.

"Crane, Crane, well!" A smile played over the heavy features. "What a rare pleasure!" The knotted fingers vigorously pressed Stephen's palm. Slowly, "You've been ill?"

"An inconvenience in Greece. A fever in Cuba."

"You're not over the effects."

"Not entirely." He tapped his chest.

They took deep chairs at the window. Howells offered a cigar.

"Tell me how goes it in your world? You've been down there in the fighting, in the excitement."

"Yes, sir." He stared out the window. "Blood, death."

He wanted to talk, to confide, to open the sluiceways. But he felt estranged from Howells as much as from Garland.

"Are you staying awhile, or are you going back? Crane, tell me." His affection for the younger colleague was obvious. "Going back, eh?" He was thoughtful. "England's gain. A man must find his home. To a writer, home is where the brain works best and the pen moves smoothest."

"But I don't want to go."

"Eh, why not?" With a grunt, he crossed his legs. "Why not, Crane? Good company, I hear. James now, and that Conrad, young Wells, Garnett. England can be hospitable."

"It's not England. I've raced everywhere when I could, the West, Mexico, Greece, Cuba." He faltered.

"Tired?" Howells muttered. "With your name now, Crane, no need to trot to England if your heart tells you to stay here." He blinked. "No need. Unless you have new cakes on the griddle?"

"A few, sir. Half-baked, mostly."

"They'll come through. You do your best. The fate of the work lies in others' hands. Your physician," he asked brusquely, "have you seen him?"

For the first time since he had entered the room, he gazed directly at Howells. "I'm sturdier than I look."

"Yes." He searched the drawn countenance. "I suppose you are. Have you been happy, Crane? Your fame should please you."

"Sometimes I've been pleased."

"The nature of letters. A word pleases and the sentence does not, a sentence seems right and a paragraph is upsetting. The paragraph is right, and the chapter disheartens." He appeared lost in his thoughts. "Yet it is not a bad life. A man can think, a man can work. Live long enough, and the world comes to its knees."

At last, Stephen arose. "I don't know when I'll be back. I wanted to say good-bye."

"Not good-bye, Crane." Arising, he spoke now with a show of heartiness. "As the Germans say, *Auf Wiedersehn!*"

"I've never been to Germany."

"You'll get there. Give yourself time, Crane."

Cora's letters fell upon him like meteors. If he did not return soon, she would be dispossessed. She had raised nearly fifty pounds to support the Frederic orphans, but was keeping them until she could persuade a family in the country to take them in.

The Crown had dropped its case against Katie, and Mrs. Mills had been acquitted, but Cora still had the children. Katie's health, and no wonder after the series of shocks she had suffered, was in a poor state.

Edward Garnett had written an appreciation of Stephen Crane which was to appear in the *Academy*. Much of it was excellent; Mr. Garnett was a good friend as well as an excellent critic. It was Garnett who had recommended her to Moreton Frewen, the owner of Brede Place.

He read the letters stolidly. Cora must be dramatizing her plight. He was comfortable in New York; he would persuade her to abandon Ravensbrook and come here. They would rent a house somewhere on Long Island or in New Jersey.

By evening, he was vacillating. They could not live as man and wife. Will, Ted, Cornelia, Mame, Nellie, Burt, George, would ask questions; the women would be embarrassed for their new "sister-in-law."

The next day, he wavered again. He would neither go back nor ask her to come over. If she preferred England, she must remain there.

Mrs. Sonntag, a crippled lady whom he had met through Clyde Fitch, invited him to *The Serenade* at Abbey's Theater. She met him in the lobby, with Father Hartmann, her cousin.

"I wish that your wife could be with us," the woman said wistfully.

For a moment he was speechless. Where could Mrs. Sonntag have heard that he was married?

He answered quietly, "She is in England. We are debating whether she should come to me or I should go to her."

He had been reluctant to attend an operetta, since any musical reminded him of Amy. However, the libretto was by Harry B. Smith, who had once appeared at a poker game with Willie Hawkins, and the music was by Victor Herbert. He became absorbed in the music and found himself enjoying the performance.

Father Hartmann, who sat unimpressed throughout the scene in the convent garden and the chant by the monks, warmly applauded the performances of Alice Nielson and Hilda Clark. Stephen gazed curiously at his neighbor. He had known only one priest, the kindly old Father Harrigan to whom various of the girls in the Tenderloin went to confession. When they exchanged views during the intermission, he warmed to Father Hartmann. The priest was amiable and well read.

"London has an excellent stage. Does your wife enjoy the theater?"

Stephen explained that they lived in the country and rarely went into London. The term your wife no longer rasped in his ears.

After the performance, he guided Mrs. Sonntag through the crowd, and suggested a visit to Sherry's. They stood at the curb behind the policeman who was waving the carriages forward.

"Crane, glad to see you back in New York!"

Harley Jackson, a newspaperman whom he vaguely recalled from Athens, tugged at his arm. "Say, Crane!"

The policeman turned his head.

In the instant of recognition, Stephen remembered Patrolman Morrison as one of Detective Becker's men who had intimidated him during the trial before the police board.

The man growled. "So it's you again? Back to make more trouble? All right, all right, you come along then."

Stephen panicked. He would have stepped back to escape in the crowd, but he dared not leave Mrs. Sonntag unsupported.

The rough hand gripped Stephen's collar. "Here, I've got you! Don't you try to get away from me!"

"What's wrong?" Harley Jackson demanded. "Crane here——"

The woman, swaying on her crutch, protested, "Why, officer, Mr. Crane's with us. He's been with us all evening."

With a curse, the patrolman lifted his nightstick. The sight of the crutches halted him. "You shut up, lady! I know what I'm doing." To Jackson, "You, too, there!"

The milling crowd had frozen around them.

"What's going on here?" someone demanded. "This man's just come out of the theater."

"We know him," Patrolman Morrison retorted. "I'm taking him around to the station."

Father Hartmann thrust himself between Stephen and the policeman. "Say now, Officer, you've made a mistake, haven't you?"

At the sight of the Roman collar, Morrison flushed. "He's got a record with us, Father."

"Never mind!" the priest snapped. "I'll vouch for him. He's a friend of mine."

Morrison touched his helmet. "If you say so, Father." He bellowed at the crowd, "Move on now, move on! Don't block the sidewalk."

Stephen was perspiring. He mumbled an explanation to Mrs. Sonntag and to Father Hartmann. "I had trouble with them before, years ago."

In the carriage, they stared at him silently. He told of Commissioner Roosevelt and of Becker and the police trial. His voice was hollow. He was certain that the more he said the less convincing he sounded.

"I'd keep out of their way," Father Hartmann said kindly. "They can be vengeful men."

He became morose. Memories of the Becker episode haunted him that night as he tried to work on the revision of *Active Service*.

However, he could not remain indoors. He had to take his solitary walks. Several nights later, another patrolman confronted him. "Come around to the station, Crane."

"Can't I live in my own city, in my own country?" he protested. "I've done nothing."

"I don't know about that," the man replied. "All I know is that if I catch you on my beat, I've got orders to run you in."

"I'm minding my own affairs," he pleaded. He added, "I'll be leaving New York in a few days."

The policeman hesitated. "Well, if you are—— But you stay off my beat, you hear?"

He crept back to his room. He was, indeed, a marked man. If the patrolman had taken him in he would have been kept overnight in the bullpen with drunks and thieves. In the morning, the judge would no doubt have ruled for him, but if Becker was thirsting for revenge, the men on the beat would harass him every night. He could imagine Cora cabling to the Police Commissioner: "Where is my husband?"

The day before Christmas, Reynolds gave him another letter. Cora's distress seemed to be genuine; Stephen could no longer doubt it. If she were dispossessed, what would become of Frederic's waifs?

At midnight, walking down Broadway, he saw a policeman waiting for him under a lamppost. Prudently, he retraced his steps. It would not do. He would have to struggle for his freedom wherever he went, either on these streets or in England. Here or there, his forces seemed unequal to the task.

By morning, he had made his decision. He had overstayed his welcome in New York. He reserved passage on the S. S. *Manitou*, which went directly to Gravesend, Port of London. He would return, settle his debts, and save Cora from the sheriff's men. But he would not remain at Oxted. He and Cora would part company. He would reveal the truth about his health. The prospect jarred him; he had almost forgotten the red devils in his chest.

He cabled Cora that he would arrive on January 5th.

VI. The Red Wafer

*A*S HE STEPPED from the gangplank, Cora thrust her way through the crowd. She ran toward him, a tiny bunch of hothouse violets in her hand, a perky flowered hat over her golden hair. He felt a wrench as the sight of the small, harried features.

She opened her arms, and cried, "You've come back to me!"

The violets dropped, and the new hat went askew. He had not kissed her so passionately since Jacksonville. "Steve, Steve darling!" she was sobbing. She wound her hands about his neck and covered his eyes, his cheeks, his mustaches, with more kisses. "Oh, Steve!"

"Cora——"

"Hush, hush, my beloved!" She brushed away her tears. "You're here, that's all that matters." She clutched at him so fiercely that the past, his angers, his frustrations, his moody, mixed feelings, slipped away. "I knew that you wouldn't leave me, Steve, I knew that you wouldn't. God couldn't punish me so!"

A hundred pairs of eyes might be on them; they ignored the world. While she arranged her hat, he picked up the violets; they had no fragrance.

When they reached Ravensbrook, he greeted the squealing, yiping dogs and the three Frederic children, Mrs. Burke, their governess, and the servants, and strode to his desk.

Cora pleaded, "Not today, Steve. Let me enjoy this first day with you without these miseries coming between us."

Her eyes appealed so ardently that he relented; tomorrow would

447

wait. "I've missed you so," she murmured. "Been so famished for you."

Later, fluttering about him worshipfully, she insisted that he read the dozens of clippings that had accumulated in his absence.

The reviews were uniformly exciting: praise for *The Open Boat* volume, for *The Little Regiment,* and even for *The Third Violet.*

He said cheerfully, "I would gladly import these critics into New York to write notices for me."

A tinkling on the piano in the next room jarred him. Cora had ordered the instrument on trial from Whiteley's Department Store last February, but she had promised to return it to save the sixty-five pounds.

"Harold urged me to keep it," she countered defiantly. "I played it when I was lonely. When we took the children in, it was there to amuse them. Heloise is very clever and quick to learn." She threw up her hands. "Now those wretches at Whiteley's won't take it back. They say that it has been used, but, of course, I've used it. They've directed their solicitors to compel us to pay. You'll talk to them, won't you, Steve? They're behaving abominably."

Her fear of dispossession had miraculously evaporated. His return had freed her of it; *ergo,* it no longer existed.

"I didn't spend a penny on myself, except for the new hat to meet you in, and I've pawned the last of my jewelry, so I really have a right to it."

"Angel child!" he mocked.

She pressed her bosom against him, and pouted. "Say that you love me, Steve!"

He kissed her eyelids. "I do."

The evening meal was a miniature banquet that must have cost three pounds. When she placed the wine bucket on the buffet, he glumly scanned the label: a vintage burgundy!

"For your homecoming!" she declared, gaily lifting her glass. "I saved it out of the household money." Then her defense of the extravagance struck her, too, as incongruous, and she giggled.

That night they renewed their love with an eagerness that exhausted him. He had forgotten how they used to try each other to the limits of desire and passion. Soon he wanted only to drift in the warm, pleasant sea that laved gently as the breakers subsided.

She whispered, "You didn't intend to come back to me, Steve, did you? I knew. So did the Conrads, the Hueffers, Robert Barr, the Garnetts, everyone." As he was silent, "Why ever did you come back to me at last?"

He buried his face in her hair.

"Because there is a bond between us, isn't there?" she concluded fiercely. "Because sometimes I've been everything you've looked for in a woman, even the girls you've taken to bed for a night, and sometimes I've been someone you needed to protect. And sometimes I've been someone you've wanted to beat to avenge yourself for I-don't-know-what." She spoke sadly and without reproach, as if she had studied their relationship night after empty night. "I used to think that true love was a clean, strong, electric force like the current that lights the new lamps. Now I know it's that and also the flickering, and even the hours between of coldness and dark."

He caressed her.

"I'll never leave you," she murmured. "Never! In sickness and in health, for richer, for poorer——"

"I'll never leave you again," he promised, and rocked her in his arms. He was not thinking; he was suspended.

He dreamed that the golden hair became alive and the strands moved like tendrils under his jaws and about his throat. A noose wove itself around his neck. His hands were tied. He struggled futilely against the wildly meshing hairs. He wanted to call out, but choked. Then a gleaming blade appeared. With incredible swiftness, it hacked at the noose and he was released. But his own hair, like Samson's, had been shorn!

He awakened to find Cora's warm body squirming over him. She was kissing his lips and his eyelids. "Steve, love me! Steve, love me, love me!"

It was noon before they rose to meet the day. Cora could postpone the reckoning no longer. Before breakfast was finished, he had the full disheartening story: the bills from the butcher, the baker, the grocer, the dairyman, the florist, the vintner, and, of course, from Whiteley's, and the threats and summonses. Three hundred pounds!

"What shall we do?" she appealed, as if the children had run up the accounts. She walked the floor while he labored over additions in pounds, shillings, and pence. "I offered a chattel mortgage on the furniture. Robert Barr said I dare not because it isn't all paid for. Steve, don't look at me so cruelly!"

On the one hand, she was shrewd, clever, and hard, on the other, incredibly naive and reckless. Extravagance! Half the debt could have been avoided by careful management, but what could a Cora Taylor know of frugality? He swallowed his chagrin.

"We'll manage," he declared stoutly. It would take time, but he would pay off the creditors, every one.

She embraced him as if he were a new St. George. She said that she had never doubted that he would solve the problem. She was pleased with James Pinker, the new agent, because he shared her optimism. Let Pinker deal with the editors and publishers, and the money would flow in.

Fortunately, the Frederick A. Stokes Company, as Stephen's new publisher, was ready to help. Dominick, the Stokes representative in

London, advised that his firm would advance one hundred pounds if *Active Service* would be available for early publication.

Pinker said to Stephen, "You stay at your writing desk. Business is my province. You produce and I will sell."

"He would write better," Cora pointed out, "and write more, if he did not have to wait and fret from the time he finishes a story till the time the money arrives from a publisher."

Stephen was mortified. Because they were penniless, their agent should not be pressed like a rich uncle.

"You have no patron to give you money."

"I need no patron!" he retorted.

She maintained that few authors could subsist without patronage or independent means. "If Pinker believes in you, as he says he does, he will advance what we need. In Paris, the gallery owners do it for their favorite painters."

"How can he be certain that he will sell everything I write?"

She stamped her foot. "Of course, he will sell it. Every word!"

To Stephen's surprise, Pinker agreed that, at least until several large sales had been consummated, he would assist with reasonable advances. He immediately supplied a draft for forty pounds against the next sale that Reynolds might make in America.

"Pinker's a good fellow," Stephen declared. "He's risking his money on simple faith."

Cora snapped, "I say that you are Stephen Crane, not a beginner but an accomplished writer. If they have a regard for you, it is because they know your work is good. They will make oceans of pounds on you. Let them open their moneybags when we need it!"

He thought that he had made a good beginning in the negotiations with Dominick. Now he confessed that she was the shrewder bargainer. Without qualms of modesty, pride, or fitness, she forced results that he could not hope to obtain.

"You must command attention," she went on, like a general devising a strategy. "Live like a hermit and everyone will forget you. You are Stephen Crane. First, you need more space in which to write. Brede Place—"

He groaned, "We have no money."

"We will get the money!" she insisted regally. "Money can always be gotten. The world will give it to us. It must."

He was sometimes amused at her eloquence about money, but the depth of her conviction and that unshakeable faith that they would get what they needed never failed to impress him.

He continued to meet during the day with the creditors and the solicitors. At night, he retired to *Active Service*. Morrisons and Nightingale, who represented Whiteley's Department Store, were courteous but hard as flint; they must have ninety-eight pounds in full for the piano and for the other goods, or guarantees in writing from Mr.

Pinker. They badgered him also on behalf of the owners of Ravens-brook. When they were satisfied on the rental account, they announced that the landlord would require an advance payment if Mr. Crane was to occupy the villa another year.

Once more, he turned to his agent. Pinker advised him to retain a solicitor: "You must not risk an action in bankruptcy."

Alarmed by the legal phrase, Stephen consulted Alfred Plant, who handled the problems of other authors. He spent an agonizing afternoon with the solicitor, but thereafter he could send Morrisons and Nightingale to meet with their dialectic equals.

As quickly as the money came in, he parceled it out. Cora, watching the drafts come and go, stormed that she had no ready funds for current expenses. "How shall I run the household?"

He clenched his fists. "I won't be pushed under!" He was an alien in this land, and feared its cold laws and bewigged institutions. Bankruptcy! The word had chilled him.

The burst of anger startled her. "We have a solicitor to serve us, Steve. They won't, any of them, frighten me. We'll do what we can and, for the rest, ignore them, defy them!"

He stared unhappily, then stamped out, with the dogs at his heels.

She diligently sought means to shield him inside the household. If he were to produce with regularity, he must have solitude. Mrs. Burke was to take the children early each morning to the Peases' house or, if the weather was inclement, keep them amused in the parlor. He must have his seclusion when he required it, and church silence when he slept late after writing all night. Everyone, on pain of dismissal or punishment, must move on tiptoe.

When the three youngsters trooped in cheerily for the noon meal, he came to sit with them, for he enjoyed their company.

Cora signaled to Mrs. Burke to leave him with the children. "Have a care," he heard her say. "He can fly into a temper when he's creating."

At midnight, she brewed fresh coffee and made him partake of a light refreshment. "You must, Steve."

"You should be asleep at this hour." He was pleased to be waited on.

She sat before him in the deep chair, with her golden hair falling to her waist. "I'm so glad that my husband is home that I don't care if I stay up all night to be with him."

He gazed at her lovingly. He told her that, sitting thus, she might be a model for a Renaissance painter of the Botticelli school.

A flush of pleasure mounted her cheeks. "That is your love speaking." She asked naively, "Am I trouble for you?"

"You're an angel child," he returned, with a half-smile. He finished his coffee. "Now to bed with you!"

He was alert in these quiet, dark hours. He stood at the window when snow fell. The house, never adequately heated, creaked from the cold. He listened to the sleepers, sometimes to the children crying out, and trudged back to his desk. He wrapped his legs in a blanket, lifted his pen, and stared at the copy paper.

He was troubled by the legion of promises. They could not remain in Oxted; he must look into the suitability of Brede Place. He must provide short stories for both Reynolds and Pinker, and he was still obliged to Meldrum. He was irked with *Blackwood's*. The Scottish lairds in Edinburgh had refused "The Blue Hotel" as "too strong and brutal" for their readers. They had said nothing to him; Conrad had it from Meldrum that Mr. Blackwood's maiden sister, an austere lady, had disliked it.

"If maiden sisters are also to be our judges," Cora said vehemently, "I would never give them another story!"

Every rejection dismayed him.

Shortly before dawn, when he was in the midst of revisions in the tenth chapter of *Active Service,* a brief tale about a mischievous youngster suddenly flowered in his mind. He was startled; the entire piece was ready. His young girl character was patterned after Cora in her childhood on Long Island. Once, on her birthday, she had wheedled money from her grandfather, who, absorbed at his easel, had handed her a crumpled five-dollar note instead of one dollar. She had corralled the children of the neighborhood, and had bought them as much candy and ice cream as they could hold. A great deal of silver was left. So she had led the band to the barbershop and ordered their hair cut. "My beautiful blonde hair—shorn! The twins, who lived next door, and had lovely brown curls—shorn! Three other boys and two more girls—shorn like lambs!"

Out of the episode, which his fancy refurbished till only the core of the original incident was left, and transplanted into a Whilomville–Port Jervis setting, he created "Angel Child."

She listened proudly as he read the manuscript. Together, relying on delicious memories, they increased the variety of sweets that the Whilomville children had consumed.

She objected to a single line, where he had "the queen," whom he had named "Cora," declare, as she led her subjects up the street, "We must think up some way of spending more money."

"I never said that!"

He replied blandly. "I wrote the whole story for the pleasure of that single line."

"Steve, one would think that I was extravagant by nature! You know that I haven't any more clothes than a rabbit!"

He chuckled. "Paul Reynolds will sell it to Harper's, and we'll include it in a volume of 'Whilomville Stories.'"

She beamed. "I have dozens of stories!"

She would never understand that he could not work his magic upon every anecdote she related.

CHAPTER 84

On Tuesday afternoon, after an unfruitful session at his desk, he proposed the trip to Brede Place. She was reluctant to start out so late in the day, with the weather blustery, but he said, "Now or never!" They hurried away as if they were eloping.

They had tea in Hastings. He sat woodenly, still out of sorts, while she chattered about the historic countryside and Norman the Conquerer. "Come now, lass!" he said drily.

In the hired sleigh, they drove out of Hastings into a snow-covered Sussex valley where a flock of sheep was moving slowly toward a fold. Heavy snow-clouds were massed on the horizon; a bitter cold wind blew from the east. "We're not far from the sea, and Henry James lives at Rye, five miles from Brede."

They dashed through an oak woods where a few brown leaves, like little curled hands, clung stubbornly to the white-rimed boughs. They slid down a narrow road that was patrolled by overgrown snow-burdened hedges, moved cautiously across an iced-over bridge, and emerged upon a vast snowfield of a park where a gray stone fortress with two huge chimneys that flared at the top like medieval trumpets presided in glacial loneliness.

"There it is!" she cried proudly. "Brede Place."

Clammy fingers touched his heart. He was ready to turn about at the next crossroads and run for Hastings. The structure seemed like a strange, prehistoric monster frozen into the valley.

"Isn't it magnificent?" she breathed, and, the next moment, as his face became ashen gray, "What is it, Steve?"

He had expected an English manor-house in the grand style, conceived for rich and gracious living. Brede, low and sprawling, was massive, stone on gray stone a fortress in which some cruel baron might have confined prisoners of high rank; the walls had certainly been planned to discourage attack and siege.

As they drew nearer, he saw that the winter light had tricked his eyes. This country seat was neither as large nor as forbidding as it had appeared at a distance.

In the foreground, the peaked creations that stood like cozies over teapots, or bell-gowned matrons without heads, were old boxwoods that had been cut and trimmed into grotesque sentinels. Through some artistic whimsy, the top of one boxwood had been transformed into a hen sitting on a nest.

Cheerily, Cora rattled off the story of Brede as if she had been preparing for an examination in Sussex history. One wing had been erected in 1378, and another in the time of Cromwell. In Elizabethan times, Brede had been expanded to embrace a third wing so that the structure would form the letter *E*, a pretty conceit in honor of Elizabeth Regina.

"The Oxenbridges, who built it, are buried at St. George's in Brede. The name 'John Oxenbridge' is cut in stone over the doorposts."

"For the sake of the postman!"

She ignored it. "Privacy, Steve, room to spread in, space to write in. Enough for the children, enough for the dogs, and far enough away from everyone we don't want to see." She added, "There's a family chapel, too, and a great hall, and more chambers than we could ever use."

"A damn fine dungeon," he said noncommittally. The entire structure was sad, desolate, and mournful. The huge stones were joined by fat seams. The doorways and windows were arched with Gothic forethought and variation; the place lacked only crenelated battlements and a drawbridge.

They mounted a worn brick stair and passed under an arch. Before they reached the door an eye of light wavered through the glass.

"Here he comes!"

"John Oxenbridge?"

"That will be Heather, the caretaker."

She was already the mistress of Brede Place.

A figure out of *Wuthering Heights* stood in the doorway, the long, gaunt face pale as a jail-warden's.

"Mrs. Crane? Welcome, Mum."

"My husband. Mr. Crane, this is Heather."

The evening light fell in halberds of topaz across the stone floor. The air was dank.

In the great hall, the walls were paneled in oak; the few pieces of furniture were overpoweringly heavy. The fireplace was enormous and dark, broad enough to roast an ox.

He trudged after her like a visitor at a museum, while she pointed and described. Heather followed, with his lamp held high. Stephen saw no gas-fixtures in the beamed ceilings.

"That's the charm of it, Steve," she exulted. "It hasn't been spoiled by conveniences." She indicated the iron torchieres. "We'll use lamps and candles. It'll be a lark. There is much to be done, but we can do everything ourselves, can't we?"

There was no running water.

454

"But there's a well. A good well!" There was no ghastly modern plumbing either. "It's like a step back into olden times."

"A step in the dark," he muttered. Brede Place was an elegant old ruin.

"There's no heat, Mum," Heather put in, with a sympathetic glance at the frail young man.

"Fireplaces everywhere!" she said airily. "And a wonderful Tudor kitchen with a brick floor."

They wandered about until it was pitch dark, with Cora now carrying the lamp, and Stephen trailing her doggedly. The wind whistled through windows that had not seen glass in a decade. There were thirty-four rooms!

When they began to prowl on the second floor, Heather reappeared to warn them that various floors were unsafe. Furthermore, they must not open certain doors. The room that had once been the private Oxenbridge pew gave directly upon the chapel twenty feet below. A misstep would bring them crashing down upon the dirt floor.

"Listen!" Cora touched his hand. "Do you hear footsteps?"

He had heard nothing.

"There's a legend that Brede Place is haunted by a ghost who comes in two parts."

"Serially?" he jibed.

"It is quite true, sir," Heather verified. "Quite true."

Sir Goddard Oxenbridge, who had flourished in the sixteenth century, had been a wicked ogre who had taken an occasional meal off any unlucky child that crossed his land. His rude practices had given him a bad name with the neighboring parents, but they were cowed by the old rascal. However, the children in the vicinity took counsel and, in a sortie unparalleled in Sussex annals, had waylaid Sir Goddard on his stone bridge and, after a mighty struggle, had overcome him and sawed him in half.

The death of Sir Goddard had rid the countryside of an unattractive nuisance, but, alas, it had not driven him from Brede Place. Here, upon occasion, his spirit made apparition in two halves, each section rattling and groaning and creating an unseemly row. He was not to be feared, for Sir Goddard, as might be expected from a miserable child-eater, had also been a coward. Yet his ghostly presence was enough to discourage the servants from sleeping in.

In the old kitchen, they rested on a bench and toasted their feet before the fire, while Heather fried ham-steaks and eggs for their supper.

They drove back to the village in the starlight to spend the night at the cottage of the Tanners, an elderly couple who had once been employed at Brede. In their cozy attic, Cora pressed him to agree to the next step.

"Think of the privacy! In six months of regular, uninterrupted work we could be out of debt."

He demurred weakly, for something about Brede Place had enchanted him.

"We cannot stay on at Ravensbrook, and we are too poor to live in London. Think how it will be in spring, with the blossoms and the trees, and the sun shining.

"And the two-part ghost!" That would make a story.

The next morning, Heather had laid a fire in the great hall. Stephen warmed his back, while Cora, with pencil and paper and a seamstress' tape, took measurements and sketched the placing of their furniture.

"We'll try it for a year. If you dislike it, we'll look elsewhere. By then our fortunes will have improved."

"Or worsened."

"Where else can we have a home of our own?" she put to him, and, as he yielded, "I'll make you a study to be proud of!"

"The Duke of Brede," she sang, and with a flounce of her skirts, went whirling across the floor, while the log crackled and sputtered and the firelight traced lively patterns on the oak walls. "Stephen, Duke of Brede!"

He felt unaccountably saddened.

CHAPTER 85

They arrived at Brede Place after a four-inch snowfall had transformed the estate into a virgin wonderland. Because the roads were buried in swirling drifts, the wagons could not get through with their household goods. Mrs. Burke moaned, but Cora was prepared. The children were bedded on blankets on the refectory table. The adults slept on old tickings that Heather placed on the floor before the fireplaces. The dogs were restricted to the kitchen. When they whined and scratched, Cora relented and each furry animal was snuggled against a grownup.

Cora bullied the carters. She dashed to the village and hired a carpenter. The first chamber to be put in order must be Mr. Crane's study.

Half an hour later, all hands stopped for tea. She walked the great hall like a lion-tamer whose charges had deserted her in mid-act.

By the time the wagons finally rolled into the courtyard with their furniture, he had lost four days on the makeshift arrangements. If they were to keep out of further debt, he would have to complete at least one story a week for the next six months.

456

Stephen rambled over the grounds. He paid his respects to the lead bas-relief of a mitred bishop that was mounted under the rain gutter on the stone wall beside the kitchen chimney. His Worship, snuggled in capacious robes, with his crook and his Book, looked down placidly, more comfortable in his niche than any of the living denizens of Brede.

He strolled past the topiaries and the poor hen which, after decades, was still sitting on her empty nest. He scooped up a handful of snow and hurled it against the roof-tiles. He peeked into the smuggler's passageway which wound underground for nearly a mile and emerged at the dikes of the River Brede.

By evening, the study was ready. The woodwork had been painted red, the floor had been scrubbed. A table and chair had been provided, with his boxes of books and papers stacked neatly.

He relaxed slowly into the new serenity. The sensation of imminent creation made him wary, as if he were lying along a front where firing might break out in any angle of the sector. He picked up volume after volume. His eyes read inattentively as flashes akin to heat lightning darted through his mind.

He would ask Ted to forward his Claverack swords, the Mexican serape, and his Western spurs and belt. From Will, he would request the books left to him by Mama. Somewhere, probably with Nellie, there were photographs of his parents.

Still on the shores of reflection, he came upon Conrad's *Youth* in an issue of *Blackwood's*. So, at forty-two, Joseph had hit his stride and no longer needed to fear that the critics would accuse him of the influence of *The Red Badge*. The sea, its ships and its men, were his province. Stephen envied him the rich knowledge of the East and that Slavic eloquence.

He owed Joseph a visit. He had been vexed to learn that Conrad had undertaken a collaboration with big, blond, amiable Ford Hueffer from whom he had rented Pent Farm. Poor Joseph, to tremble before the formidable English language when he was a master of it!

Cora's account of Joseph's frantic efforts to raise money to bring him back from Havana had embarrassed him. On his gout-stricken legs, Conrad had hobbled about London, pleading with Meldrum and with John MacQueen, another British publisher. It was Cora's fault for having alarmed everyone, as though he were being held for ransom in Cuba.

He sent half of *Active Service* to Pinker. The agent was true to his word and advanced two thirds of the expected cash on every story Stephen placed in his hands; but new material must reach his office regularly. Stephen hopped from the novel to new stories, and back again. He must feed the periodicals if Pinker was to feed him.

Spring burst over Sussex. Through the window, he watched the buds fatten on the trees and open to blossom. He craved to be free and outdoors, yet dared not wander for more than an hour each day to walk the dogs or to play with the youngsters.

Cora guarded his door. He saw the Frederic children at noon and before they went to bed. His poodle Sponge was admitted for regular visits. Otherwise, he was secluded in the study.

Each Friday morning, Cora stood at his elbow. "Is it ready?" She was waiting to copy the story before it went to Pinker. One story each week; he had promised.

"You have a story, Steve? I saw you working."

He stared moodily at the walls.

"One every Friday, Steve. You made the schedule, and we promised Pinker."

"It didn't go." He struck the flat of his hand against his forehead. "I'm flat, stale. Another week maybe."

"Where is it?"

He rattled a manuscript.

"Give it to me."

He grated, "It's thin, shabby, weak. What would you have? I'm working like a threshing machine."

"We agreed," she returned curtly. "They're buying your linage in London, not your genius. Every story can't be an 'Open Boat.'"

Helplessly, "Another hour."

She withdrew while he reread the pages. A simple anecdote, pleasant enough but lacking any reason for existence beyond his need, the never-ending, all-devouring need! It failed to clutch at either heart or mind; it was pallid, insignificant.

Yet he had promised. He had given the story one week, he could not afford to expend more time on it. He must turn out the wordage that bought their bread and their cakes, their wine and their coffee, their roasts and their groceries, that paid for the servants.

While Cora copied the pages, he fled into the garden with Sponge at his heels. The tulips were blooming. In the park, he stood under trees that were as pink and white as little brides. It was good to be alive even at this price.

When *Blackwood's* rejected "The Clan of No Name," he raged. It was one of his favorite new stories.

"You must not let them upset you. Turn your anger into swords and cut them down in your next story. You can do it, Steve."

She had a new plan. She would handle the correspondence with Pinker and the solicitors; with Paul Reynolds, too, if he would permit it. "You are shy and I am not," she said. "We must have the money, and they can provide it."

"They've done as well as anyone can. Reynolds has the arrangement with *Harper's* for the 'Whilomville Stories.'"

"Pinker then. He'll do better, or he'll not have your work. There can be no good reason for English publishers not to pay the highest prices for Stephen Crane's work. They print rot and turn away clever and artistic stories." She became grim. "Pinker needs to be spurred. And I shall do it, Steve, while you write and write. I will handle the business affairs. I've managed many things, Steve!"

The last galled him, yet he had confidence in her and was impressed with her cunning.

"We could raise nearly four thousand pounds," she said, "one way and another, this year, if you put your mind to it."

"When shall I write them? There are only twenty-four hours in the day."

"It can be done if you delegate the business matters to *me*. We have already lost time."

"'Cruel as hawks the hours fly,'" he murmured.

She took his arm. "If that is settled, you may do nothing for a few days. We'll ride out on the countryside and enjoy the spring. We'll go over to Paris for a few days."

"But Pinker——"

"Damn Pinker!" she said sweetly. "Leave him to Cora!"

She was an excellent gadfly. He refused to endorse her letters to Pinker, they were so cold and terse. Yet her flat demands: "Please send to Oxted Bank £30." were answered sooner than his polite requests. When they were out of cash for the children, and had to draw on their own resources, she pressed Pinker to send, on account, a draft for Mrs. Burke's wages. She persuaded Stephen that they should legally adopt young Barry Frederic, and set the wheels in motion to arrange it. She contrived a further advance on *Active Service,* and wheedled the Lippincott man to obtain more money on *Wounds in the Rain,* the projected collection of the Cuban war stories. "Now to be quite frank," she wrote Pinker again, "Mr. Crane must have this week £50. He simply must have it." The money appeared.

"He's an ace," Stephen argued. "He's advanced money he's not collected.

"He knows that you are sending him everything you write. If it is painful to him now, he will benefit later. He understands that you can't work unless there is bread in the house."

Bread! It was cake she bought, wine and whiskey for the sideboard, ale for the pantry, and goodies for the little ones. The furnishings even in their living quarters were meager, so she scoured the neighborhood for couches and chairs, odd tables and lamps. The old pieces must be rubbed down, refinished, and waxed. More pillows must be made and filled, more coverlets and more tickings stuffed with feathers. She wanted linens for the sleeping rooms, damask and silver for the table, vases for flowers and cuttings, and rugs to cover the bare floors.

Heather was willing to serve as butler, but informed Cora that more servants must be hired. He recommended an excellent cook who, because she had worked for American families, might prepare dishes to American taste. Once hired, "Cook" made it clear that she was a cook only. She must have a scullery lass to peel potatoes, to scrub pots and pans, and to do the sundry kitchen chores. Chatters, her husband, would work in the yard. He would carry wood and coal, and, with old Mack, clean the fireplaces and draw the water from the well, but nothing more. Liza, the young, rosy-cheeked chambermaid, balked at cleaning the great hall used as a living room, so a general girl was hired. But windows must be cleaned by a window man; therefore, a villager was persuaded to come out every Friday morning.

The hard scrubbing was done by Peters, the aged charwoman, who was a Thursday person. Plastering and carpentry were the province of Davey Dwight, available only on Tuesdays. Samuels, the lad employed for the kitchen-garden, would tend no leaf outside of his domain, and brought in Lomax to weed in the big gardens and to shape the queer trees.

Ted wrote from Hartwood, congratulating Stephen on his "marriage." "Give our love to your wife," he said. He must have learned the news from Will, to whom Cora had written while Stephen was in Cuba. The rest of the letter was devoted to Ted's ice business and the horse Peanuts, whom he was boarding.

In June, a letter from Will, cleverly addressed to "My dear Cora," proposed that his daughter Helen, now eighteen, come to visit Brede Place. Distant cousins on the Peck side of the family were sailing for England; it was a "golden opportunity." Helen would stay a month or two, if they would have her. She was a fine, orderly, and well-behaved girl who would be no trouble and, since Stephen had always been her favorite uncle, might profit from the association.

Stephen was both amused and vexed. Will certainly had heard nothing of Cora's past. "He thinks we're living in great English splendor, at Woburn Abbey or Windsor Castle."

Yet he had slept many a night at Will's house and eaten many a dinner at Cornelia's table.

Cora professed that he was behaving ungratefully. "Isn't it time that I met a member of your family? We should be flattered that Will is willing to trust her to us."

"You don't know Will!" he groused. "If he's sending Helen away, he has his reasons. We can't afford to keep her for two months."

"Another cup of water in the broth!" Her eyes narrowed. "Unless you prefer that the girl be kept from me."

He glared as if her suspicion were beneath rebuttal.

"I'm pleased that the girl is coming," she went on. "I wish I had family to visit us. And it's time we made a social life. I don't want

England to think that you've secluded yourself because of the woman you've married."

"Cora!" He often wondered how she viewed herself, concluding that she had brushed the past under the carpet. The barbed remarks, which challenged him to refute them, testified that when she was alone with herself, perhaps when she escaped into the vacant chapel and sat in the dark, she took account of many things.

When he teased her about Roman Catholic leanings, she flared, "Does it matter how or where I say my prayers? God sees and hears all!" In an earlier age, she might easily, after her tragic experiences, have retired to a convent.

"It has never occurred to you to take me on your arm and drive over to Rye to call on Mr. James, or to ask the Conrads again, or the Hueffers. You talk to your characters or brood over them. To whom do I talk except to the children and the servants?"

Her flashes of resentment bewildered him. The routines that had made him a prisoner in his study had been established for their economic security. He had not intended to conceal her from England.

He invited the Conrads. He had to abandon his study the day before they arrived to permit a "good cleaning," and give up the two days following. However, he was pleased to sacrifice the time for the heart-to-heart talks with Joseph.

The award of fifty guineas by The Academy had made all the difference. Americans, though still cold, were buying more of Conrad's books. Old Blackwood had been increasingly thoughtful, never failing to meet Joseph's pleas for a new advance; he had paid only thirty pounds for *Youth,* but nearly one hundred for *Heart of Darkness.* Now Joseph was at work on *Lord Jim.*

Stephen advised him to consider an arrangement with James Pinker. "He'll talk for you, as he does for me, to editors and publishers, as we can't talk for ourselves. He's banker, counselor, and friend."

Conrad threw out his hands and shrugged. He was fearful of losing the good crutch he enjoyed with Meldrum and Blackwood. He alluded in passing to his collaboration with Hueffer, but his eloquence was muted as if he were wary of hurting Stephen's feelings.

He repeated praise of Stephen that Edward Garnett had voiced in London.

Crane, Garnett maintained, had a wonderful insight into, and a mastery of, the primary emotions; he also commanded an irony that derided the swelling emotions of self. It was the perfect fusion of these two forces of passion and irony that raised Crane's work, "at its finest," into the higher one of man's tragic conflict with the universe.

Stephen blushed. "I wish I could reach that level every time I sit down to write!"

They commiserated on the damn loneliness of the craft. "When I haven't been able to write," said Joseph, "I've felt like cutting my throat. I can't do anything. But I can be wretched and, by God, I am!" A man never knew whether he had succeeded until another voice sang his praises.

Stephen read aloud the second draft of *The Upturned Face*. It was about sixteen hundred words, lean and naked as a Rembrandt etching, this war tale of the burial of a dead officer. As simple and deadly, Stephen thought, as a clean bullet-hole through the lungs.

As Joseph listened, his heavy breathing filled the room.

"No one will buy that," Stephen said mournfully. They had often consoled each other, their words compounding hope and fear, disdain for the race of editors, dismay at the possibility of failure.

"Is it in the moonlight that they bury their friend?"

He could not remember. "Whenever death comes," Stephen answered.

It was one of his best, ghastly as a drawing by Goya, powerful as Ryder's painting, *Death on a Pale Horse*.

"You are the greatest of the boys!" Conrad said gruffly. The simple phrase tripped incongruously from his tongue.

CHAPTER 86

In Paris, they dined on shellfish in the Rue Ste. Anne. The next morning Stephen was so ill that he could not rise for breakfast.

Cora, alarmed, threatened to call a gendarme to arrest the proprietor of the café, his cook, and his kitchen-boy. "They have poisoned my husband! They have poisoned him!" she screamed. She was closer to hysteria than he had ever seen her.

He raised himself to the edge of the bed and clutched her wrists. "No, Cora, no!"

Her eyes were glazed with tears. "Steve, I couldn't live without you!"

The physician stated firmly that it was not ptomaine poisoning but a fever akin to malaria; perhaps the patient had brought it from England.

Stephen suggested Cuba. The doctor agreeably diagnosed it as a recurrence of a tropical ailment. His visit and an apothecary's remedy, which tasted like licorice-flavored rum, cost two pounds six.

After three days, the fever subsided as mysteriously as it had appeared. Crossing the Channel again, Stephen held Cora's hand and spoke softly to her, reassuringly.

They were in London in time to meet the boat upon which young Helen Crane was arriving.

His niece, a petite girl with a slender figure, came down the gangplank on the arm of a familiar-looking man. Helen had a strong profile, light blue eyes, and a winsome smile. "Uncle Steve!"

As Stephen shyly embraced her, the girl burst into tears.

"Steve!"

He turned to locate the voice. "Burt!" He was stunned. "You!"

The brothers hugged each other, clapped each other on the back, and, shaking hands, pumped each other up and down like pistons.

"Surprise, Steve!"

"God Almighty, Burt!" he vowed. "I'm glad to see you. Cora, my wife. Meet—this is Wilbur, my brother Burt."

Cora flashed him a brilliant smile. Burt, big, soft and easy-going, leaned over and soundly bussed her cheek.

"How's Mattie, Burt? And the children, are they well? What of Townley——"

Burt winced. "Whoa! Tell you everything later." He presented their companions on the voyage, Mr. and Mrs. Peck and their small daughter.

Stephen was eager for an hour alone with Burt. Why had Burt suddenly appeared in England? What of Townley? But Cora had taken charge. She wanted to take them sight-seeing. Helen and Burt and the Pecks must see London; the lovely day was ideal. Then they could all take the train for Brede Place.

That afternoon, on the Embankment, they met Mark and Mabel Barr, friends of Harold Frederic, and dark-haired "Snubby" Richie, Mabel's nineteen-year-old sister. Cora, delighted to introduce the family—"Stephen's favorite brother!" she said quickly—invited everyone to tea.

Mark Barr mentioned the next Henley Regatta. Cora clapped her hands. It would be wonderful to meet again at the Regatta on July 4th. "This is one day that I shall insist that my husband put all his manuscripts away and celebrate the holiday, even if we are so far from America!" They had acquired an equal share in a small boat with Joseph Conrad, the writer and former sea captain, and Stephen ought to attend this most famous of English boating events.

Burt was impressed. "Living it in style!" he murmured to his brother.

Stephen was appalled by Cora's exuberance. "We're overdrawn at the bank," he muttered. By the weekend, he must finish another story if Pinker was to send them a new advance and spare them further embarrassment.

In the shadow of Cleopatra's Needle, he unceremoniously pulled his brother aside. "How is Townley anyway? And why didn't you let us know that you were coming?"

463

Burt saddened. He was not the bearer of good tidings. "There was no time to write, Steve. After what happened to Townley——"

"What happened to Townley?" Stephen gasped.

"He went to pieces!" the other burst out. "Look here, Steve, this isn't anything to shout about. I guess you wouldn't want it to get out either, or to have your wife know."

Stephen gripped his arm. "Go on, Burt, go on!"

"Townley was the gay brother, wasn't he, when he was well and hearty?" Burt sighed. "When he began to slip—that damn drinking!—and his second wife left him, Mattie and I took him in. What else could we do? Although it was hard enough to feed my own family. With us, in Binghamton, he was out of sight. I think Will figured that out. You know he would. Occasionally Will sent a few dollars, so did George and Ted and Nellie, when they had any to spare."

Mostly, the others had sent advice. As long as Townley had been reasonably well behaved, Mattie had not minded his presence. When his conduct became increasingly bizarre, she began to complain.

"I couldn't blame her, but what could I do? No one else would give him a home!"

Stephen's face had become waxen.

"Oh, we had our times, Mattie and I, on account of him. She swore she'd leave me if I didn't get him out. I knew there was nothing that you could do, far away in England or Greece or Cuba, wherever you were. I wrote to you when he broke out and ran riot through the streets until the police caught him." He mopped his forehead. "He terrorized a lot of small boys. The big ones pelted him with mud and stones. He was a sight!"

"My God!" Stephen groaned. Poor Townley, poor Mattie, poor Burt!

"At first, he was good with the children, but I knew that we had to watch him, Steve. I'd seen such cases when I was in school. He has hardening of the arteries. The doctor said it has affected his brain. That, I guess, and those years of drinking, have wrecked him."

Little by little, the deterioration had become evident. Mattie had been terrified.

"I said that Townley would never hurt a child. Then, one day, some madness seized him. He picked up little Howard and tried to throw him down the stairs. A mercy that Mattie heard the child screaming and came running to stop Townley. Howard could have been killed!"

Stephen's eyes filled.

"That's why, Steve, we had to have him committed. He is in the State Hospital for the Insane. Last week, when I visited him, he was manacled."

Manacled! What if a fire broke out in the hospital? Stephen could see poor Townley struggling to release himself while the flames licked

464

at the floor and the walls, and crept toward his shackled limbs. Yet no one else would have suffered the disturbed man except Mattie and Burt. A pity that their happiness should have been disrupted by Townley's presence.

"Don't say anything to your wife," Burt repeated nervously, with a glance at the others. "Will said that I daren't write it. What if she, anyone, opened the letter and learned about it? Will thought it might be a blow for you in this society you're living in."

"Isn't there some hope? Get a new doctor!"

Burt shook his head. "No use. He'll be there until he dies. He can never get better. The brain is gone, Steve, the brain."

It occurred to Stephen that, in all these years, he had done nothing and Burt had carried the burden, Burt and Mattie. He would have to give Burt at least a hundred dollars toward some part of the cost that had been entailed, and do it without telling Cora.

He sadly remembered the tall, dashing Townley at Asbury Park. A pity that Brede was not closer to Binghamton. On these grounds, his brother could have roved freely. In its long history, Brede had probably harbored many madmen, beginning with the legendary ghost.

Manacled! He stared at Burt in awe.

"I'm sorry, Steve," his brother said. "We all know how much you loved him."

Helen tried on every gown in Cora's wardrobe. She was, of course, handsomer than poor Aggie had ever been, and had a lovely speaking voice. She sang well, and played the piano; her dearest ambition was to become a singer.

"Your Uncle Steve has known an operetta singer," Cora volunteered, with a flicker of malice. "Haven't you, Steve?"

He turned to Helen. "How long will your parents permit you to stay with us?"

The girl blushed. "They don't want me in Port Jervis, Uncle Steve. Papa doesn't."

When he and Cora were alone, he groaned, "I suspected that Will had his reasons for sending her to England."

Cora smugly revealed the contents of a private letter from Will. Helen was being wooed by a young man whom her father thought a ne'er-do-well.

"Poor Helen!" Now he understood why the girl seemed so unhappy.

"He must be a wonderful father to be so concerned for her welfare."

"My father, too, was concerned about his daughter's welfare. And my sister, Aggie, never married!"

"I had no real father to worry about me," she said jealously. "How would it have been for me if my father had lived? When my grandfather died, the first thing I did was to buy a long black velvet gown and a string of cheap pearls. I wouldn't criticize your brother Will, not I."

"If our 'family' becomes any larger, we'll be even deeper in debt than we are." Every discussion ended with his concern over funds. Money had no meaning for Cora until she was penniless, and even when penniless she would not retrench.

"After the holiday, you'll work better, Steve. And faster, too."

"And harder!" he added wryly. "Angel Child will manage."

"I will manage." She ran a silver-backed brush through her golden hair. "Money will come. That should be the least of our worries. Another year, with *Active Service* out and other books coming, you will see how foolish it was to have worried about money."

After three days at Brede Place, the Pecks were properly awed. They departed with an inscribed copy of *War is Kind* and the tenderest feelings for their young kinsman and his energetic wife. She had shocked them with her sandals and the Russian peasant costume she had got from Mrs. Pease, wife of the secretary of the Fabian Society, but they forgave her.

Burt adored his new sister-in-law. She was kind and effusive, which pleased him. He had thought that all English ladies were aloof and cold.

CHAPTER 87

The presence of Helen galvanized Cora to widen their social activities. She established Thursday as their day "at home" and received various of the neighbors, including Reverend Frewer, the Brede vicar. Writers and editors came down from London.

For the Regatta party she collected, in addition to Helen and "Snubby" Richie, the boisterous, redhaired George Lynch, a hailfellow correspondent whom Stephen had met in Cuba; A. E. W. Mason, a personable writer who had once been on the stage and now wrote light novels; and Karl Harriman, a young American from Michigan, who had called at Brede Place to pay his respects, and had lingered on at Cora's invitation.

They took a suite of rooms at The Angel by the riverside. The day of the Sixtieth Annual Regatta was uncommonly bright. They strolled in the sunshine over the arched stone bridge and toward Chiltern Hills, invited new acquaintances to tea, and adjured old ones to call at Brede: "We are at home on Thursdays." Cora, amused by the mock gallantry of George Lynch, who mimicked and swaggered and played practical jokes, bubbled over with gaiety.

Stephen heard a buzzing that the Marquis of Queensbury was passing by, and joined the curious. He had met Oscar Wilde, a gross, pathetic figure whose name was now forever linked with his Lordship's, wandering among café tables in Paris. Lord Queensbury, stocky and still athletic, moved like a determined ghost, his walk still springy, the underlip sagging, the eyes alive with a sick sullenness, as if he could not bear to be seen and yet must expose himself to flaunt his Pyrrhic triumph.

George Lynch said that all the prostitutes in England had rejoiced when Wilde had lost his case against Lord Queensbury.

That night, when the others had retired, Cora, primped and perfumed, was waiting for Stephen.

Her violet scent excited him; he loved her until she sobbed in blazing ecstasy. Renewed, he possessed her once more, exulting that his strength had returned.

"Steve, I've been so starved for you. It's like the old times, isn't it?"

They tangled like wicked children; he proved his mastery and she still clung to him. He peered into the darkness over her warm figure, and thought that he had never been so greedy for any woman.

Wearily, as his eyes shut, hypnagogic images advanced, mingled, faded, and shot into startling brightness. He heard taunting voices. Amy appeared and vanished, then Lillie Brewster, and finally, with a cryptic smile on her lips, Marie Widdicomb. He tossed feverishly and wished that he could plunge into the sea to cool himself. Instantly, the room was flooded with breakers that rushed and foamed and spilled. A pounding on the doors of memory made him taut. He was at Asbury Park, lying on the beach. High above, the sun, a glowing hole in the sky, became a wild, accusing eye.

She was shaking him, "Steve! Steve!"

The light was on.

"Bad dream," he mumbled.

In August, he was working doggedly. Each morning, he saw the dawn paling through the leaded windows and heard the birds twittering. He was driving himself from story to story and from article to article. He had settled into the life at Brede.

The Whilomville stories were moving easily. Robert Barr said that no one had ever touched "the innards of the actual boy" until Stephen Crane had written these stories. He was drawing on his childhood in Port Jervis, occasionally on Cora's experiences.

He had also launched a series of stories on the struggles of the settlers in the Wyoming Valley where the Pecks had lived and died.

Simultaneously, he was working on articles on the great battles of the world; with less enthusiasm, for these were recastings of the standard historical data that Kate Frederic gathered for him. However, Bunker Hill appealed to him, as did the Battle of New Orleans, the siege of Plevna, the storming of Burkersdorf Heights, and Napoleon at Solferino. He would have preferred to visit the European battlegrounds to study the terrains, and to read memoirs and contemporary accounts, but he dared not proceed so expensively; he must treat them as if they were newspaper assignments. Lippincott would publish the articles consecutively in their monthly magazine; next year, the battles would make another volume.

At any rate, he was satisfying Pinker, and Pinker, advancing the maximum less his commission, was providing for him and for Cora, for the children, the governess, Helen and "Snubby," Heather and old Mack and the motley brigade of servants, and for any guests who descended upon them.

Pinker sent money, always Pinker sent money. Reynolds did, too; there was never enough. Debts no longer upset him, any more than they worried Cora. When the pressure squeezed about his heart, he had to spend an extra hour in bed in the morning. Even on the warm summer nights, he slept in blankets.

The housekeeper complained that his pillow was sodden with perspiration and had to be aired every day. She called it "the poor man's fever."

Cora assured her that it was the creative fever of the artist. "Mr. Crane often thinks out his stories while he sleeps."

She was his sentinel. She marched him to the study each evening as dusk gathered and the lamps were lighted. To the tune of moths beating against the windows, toads and frogs chorusing, crickets chirping, sometimes the nightingale, he took up his pen. During the day, she typed his manuscripts; Helen offered to help, but Cora was unwilling to share the privilege. She posted the envelopes and banked the drafts; she kept the accounts and a daily journal.

Brede, those summer months, was enjoyable. Even in the heat of the day, the hall was cool, dampish but not unpleasant. A big log in the fireplace furnished warmth in the late evening. When the fog moved in, he had a shawl for his shoulders and wrapped his legs in the Mexican serape that Ted had sent on.

Under rainstorms, Brede was as sturdy as a sieve. Cora kept the servants trooping back and forth with tubs and buckets, for the rain seeped through assorted leaks.

There was also laughter at Brede Place. If "Snubby" Richie could not call again without Florence Bray, her school chum, then Florence, too, must be their guest. The Conrads must spend a weekend, Joseph and Jessie, Borys, and one of Jessie's sisters as a nursemaid for the child. Once Conrad brought Ford Hueffer. Tall, sensitive Lewis Hind, editor of the *Academy,* was another welcome guest. Cora, in favor of wooing editors, would have herded all Fleet Street and Bloomsbury to Brede.

Hind, who had launched H. G. Wells as a writer of fiction, suggested a call upon the author of *The Time Machine*. Cora was delighted. She had read not only this excellent fantasia, but also *The Invisible Man* and a number of the short stories. "He writes sensibly," she said.

Forthwith, they were off to Sandgate, where Bertie Wells and his wife occupied a house on a cliff. Cora's eyes shone tenderly as she whispered to Stephen that Wells had left his first wife for Amy Robbins, whom he called Jane, and had lived with her until he was free to marry again. Now they were blissfully wedded. "They're very happy," she assured him.

Wells, frail, with clear blue eyes and auburn mustaches, talked so vigorously and twinkled with so dry a humor that Stephen forgave him the piercing high voice and the unusually small hands. Wells ricocheted from subject to subject; he seemed to be informed on everything. When words failed him, as he sometimes pretended they did, Bertie seized a pencil and sketched his meaning. He was clever.

The Wellses had been to Italy, in Rome with George Gissing—"Do you know Gissing's *New Grub Street?*"—and then to Naples, Capri, and Pompeii.

Stephen admired Wells, although the Englishman was the reformer sort, like Hamlin Garland, with chatter of religion, politics, and economics.

Wells appraised *The Red Badge* as "original" and, in rapid-fire style, quoted liberally from the text as if to see whether the author would recognize his own prose. He lauded the mother's lament at the close of *Maggie*. He liked *The Open Boat* particularly, and quietly recited, "None of them knew the colour of the sky" and the rest of the opening paragraph.

"I like him," Stephen announced as they were driving home. He had been amazed that anyone should be familiar with so much of his work.

"I like them both, they're so very much in love," Cora sighed. "But he couldn't describe a sunset so you could see it."

Stephen smiled. "He could tell you how sunsets are made, and I can't do that."

From Jane, Cora had learned that Bertie was thirty-two, that he had a bad kidney, yet insisted on bicycling, that he had once been stricken with lung trouble and had suffered hemorrhages, but was certain that he had got over it.

Stephen wondered whether Bertie Wells had ever had a night sweat.

Her door was ajar. He knocked and thrust it open before she could call out.

For a moment, he held his breath. In a magnificent white ball gown, she was practicing curtseys before the pier mirror.

"Getting married, dear?"

She wheeled about, instantly a blazing fury. "That door was shut!"

"I knocked. Why the bridal outfit?"

"It is not a bridal outfit!" she snapped. "And I don't think that remark is in good taste at all, Stephen. It happens that I may be presented at Court. That is, I hope to be, as soon as Mrs. de Fries completes the arrangements. If she does, I shall only have to add a train to this gown."

She could not be serious. "You mean at the Palace?"

"Of course." She tossed her head. "Before Her Majesty the Queen."

A grin spread slowly over his face. It had been a possibility in Athens to meet the Queen of Greece. But in England?

"Do you find that so ridiculous?" she posed. In a flash, reading his reply, her eyes became cruel with resentment. "Do you?"

"Are you serious, Cora?"

"Why not?" She spat the words.

Astonishment had gripped him to this moment. Now the naked irony of the situation struck him. He uttered a howl of derisive laughter and collapsed on her bed.

"Don't you dare to laugh at me!" she shrieked, her cheeks livid. "Stephen Crane, don't you dare!" She stood over him, stamping her foot and clenching her fists.

He was gasping, trying to control himself. He pummeled the pillow and sought to conceal his face.

"Stephen!" She took his shoulders and, with a remarkable display of strength, shook him.

He sat up, still gurgling.

"I think you're horrid!" she shouted. "I'll never forgive you for this."

He looked into the pain-filled eyes, and regretted the laughter. She seemed totally crushed. "Cora, I'm sorry."

"You are positively hateful!" she grated. "How could you——"

"Darling, darling Cora, please forgive me." He wanted to take her into his arms. "I didn't mean to hurt you."

"Oh, but you did!" she snarled, and waved her hands wildly in his face. "You did. I know precisely what you were thinking, that I—— You have no right to laugh at me. I have never done anything to hurt you, never!"

"Forgive me, Cora. I had no right——"

"Indeed, you have no right. I am as much a lady, and more, as many a woman who has been to Court. There is no reason why Mrs. Stephen Crane, or even Mrs. Donald Stewart, should not be presented to the Queen of England!"

"I'm sorry," he repeated.

"Damn you!" she flung at him. She turned on her heel and, with the white gown swishing behind her, stormed from the room.

Only days of pleading and wooing brought her around. "I don't know what I should do without you, Cora," he confessed. That helped to soothe the wounded and outraged feelings.

Nothing came of her hopes. Mrs. de Fries informed her, with the American Embassy's unofficial regrets, that no divorced woman could be presented. The rules were inflexible. Nevertheless, Cora kept the beautiful white gown.

CHAPTER 88

They called upon Henry James in his beautiful Lamb House at Rye. James, the meticulous and shy, the large-headed stutterer with the carefully trimmed beard and mustaches, with far-seeing eyes and English manners, was not to be approached as lightly as Wells or Conrad.

He came out to greet them. Beaming, he clasped Stephen's hand, with only half his own, but eagerly as if he wished he might risk a full-palmed grip. He bowed to Cora. In the drawing room, he hovered over her, anxious that her tea should be right, ready to show her the walled garden and the hedges. His forehead shone like a moon when she exclaimed over a fine piece of furniture, an exquisite vase or a rare flower.

"He is deep and fine," Stephen thought. He resented Harold Frederic's condemnation of the older man. He found it difficult to read James, who wrote with criminal leisure, as if he had a century in which to complete every sentence. However, he was compelled to read him when James sent a manuscript and implored his opinion.

"His desperate struggle to talk in faultless prose!" Cora said impatiently. "How would such a man ever make love to a woman?"

"Hold on! Mr. James seems to like you."

"I don't think so."

"He does." James, when near Cora, behaved like an elderly uncle who remains fond of the niece of whom he had firmly disapproved when she was a child.

"He's heard things, Steve. He knows many people in London. He either despises or pities me."

"Perhaps covets?"

Her eyes narrowed. "Don't we always despise a little that which we covet?"

Her penetrating shrewdness was almost uncanny.

"It's you whom he adores, Steve. He is the 'Old Master,' but you are the young one. You may have a secret he may yet wrest from you."

"There is no secret," he returned soberly. "He writes leisurely because life, to him, is long. Time is his river. To me, it is a brook to leap over."

She gave him a frightened glance.

As often as he visited the house at Rye, there remained an awkwardness with James, who was twice his age, old enough to be his father. Nevertheless, goodness did radiate from James, and kindliness, too. He would walk about his study, for he claimed to think better on his feet, and invite Stephen to expound on his theories of writing. James worked like a watchmaker, with a loup glued to his eye, studying the tiny works, and somehow, from the minute gears and pawls, deriving a solemn concept of the awesome machinery of the Universe.

Sometimes, a personal flash illumined a point of tangent between their separate circles of existence. "When my dear sister Alice died"—James said absently, eyes lowered as if he were inspecting the tip of his beard—"she was dear to me, very dear——"

Stephen murmured, "My sister Aggie who died was closest to me."

The older man grew solemn. "You loved her."

"Very much."

Later, "And did your father, too, write?"

"My father and my uncles wrote of hellfire and sin."

James smiled. "Have we changed so much, except as to style and vehemence?" He said little of the America he had left behind him; he had closed that chapter.

"Have you ever dictated to the secretary at the typewriting machine?" James favored the method, composing aloud in his halting fashion and directing his words at a screen behind which a man tapped at the keys of the apparatus.

"I think too slowly. My brain is congealed."

James exploded, "No! No-o, don't say that, my boy." The derogation must have pleased him. The rest of the afternoon, with one hand comfortably in his pocket and the other gesturing, he was elaborately kind about his junior's work.

He displayed a handsome volume, *The Anglo-Saxon Review*, to which he had contributed a short story. The large periodical, called a quarterly and issued under the editorship of Lady Randolph Spencer Churchill, was bound in dark blue morocco and richly tooled in gold.

"Dear Lady Churchill——" he said. Her Ladyship was one of those wealthy American girls, one of the three Jerome sisters, who had married into the finer English families. "They paid me fifty pounds for the story. Not extraordinary, eh, but not paltry, either, I should say."

Lady Churchill, sister of Mrs. Frewen, had already invited Stephen to contribute an article, but he had assumed that he was to write it gratuitously. Cora had met Lady Churchill at the meetings of the Society of American Women in London.

"Fifty pounds!" James repeated, his face wreathed in a good-natured smile.

James, who often appeared at Brede Place, with his walking stick, gloves, and felt hat, was an easier man to be with away from the drawing room at Rye and his walled garden. At Brede he ambled about the grounds, sometimes with the Frederic children at his heels. He stayed to luncheon or to tea; frequently he brought acquaintances, and embarrassed Cora when she was not prepared to feed three or four extra guests.

When Reverend Frewer, pastor of Brede, enlisted Cora's aid for the bazaar in the rectory garden, she conscripted everyone's services. Old Mack was instructed to pot little plants that she might sell at her booth. Mrs. Burke, the governess, made nut fudge. Helen and "Snubby" puttered over marshmallow confections. George Lynch, who popped into Brede over weekends, was ordered to take photographs at sixpence a picture; he moaned that he lost a shilling every time he clicked his shutter.

Early on the morning of the bazaar, Cora persuaded Vernall, the cook, who had worked for the Richie family, to make twelve dozen raised doughnuts.

James, elegantly clad, with his special gold-headed cane in hand, appeared at the Crane booth. Cora took his hat, gloves, and cane, but he viewed the proceedings with such dismay that he was excused from selling goods.

He sampled the fudge, which he judged "excellent of its kind!" and also a doughnut. The latter brought unremitting praise. "Fit for the gods!"

"A very simple recipe," Cora assured him.

"A tuppence, please!" said Helen, with outstretched hand.

He passed a sixpence and, with a roguish twinkle, snatched at two more doughnuts. "Um-um, I say, Mrs. Crane, um-yum——"

"He says its yummy," interrupted George Lynch. He raised his camera to eye-level and snapped as the author's mouth was full.

James protested. "I shall, I vow, I do vow it, I shall look as if I had swallowed a w-wasp or a p-penny toy!"

When Brede villagers came to the booth, he recommended the doughnuts with a waving of his arms: "Fit-fit-fit for the gods!"

Cora, seeing the bald dome exposed to the blazing August sun, considerately fetched his hat. "You must, Mr. James. I feel responsible for you here."

He yielded like a small boy, not at all displeased at her attention in the presence of others. He attacked a fourth doughnut. "No more photographs!" he called amiably to Lynch.

"Another tuppence, Mr. James," Helen demanded.

He pretended that he had lost his purse, and tapped himself vigorously before he found a florin. He was amused at her efforts to make change in British currency.

He clung to them awhile, as if, being American, they were his anchor; then, as a titled lady sailed over, permitted himself, all smiles, to be borne off like the captive lion that he was.

In the accounting that evening, Cora discovered that she was short ten-and-six. She had dearly hoped to earn as much as five pounds for the Rectory's fund. The total receipts were only four pounds ten, and now ten-and-six was missing.

Stephen doubted that she knew how much they had taken in during the afternoon. She declared that she had watched every farthing.

"I'll make it up," she grumbled.

She questioned George Lynch, ready to suspect him of any prank. He rolled his eyes, and swore that he was innocent.

After supper, she methodically tallied her sales again. She demanded that the girls turn out their purses. The missing coins tumbled from Helen's pocketbook.

"Humph!" Cora snorted. "You!" She turned away in such disdain that the girl burst into weeping.

Stephen took Helen's side, but he retreated when Cora continued to scowl.

In his study, she walked the floor and stormed, "It is not the ten-and-six. For weeks, items have been missing. A brooch, my gold bracelet. I searched her things tonight. The girl has appropriated every trinket she could lay her hands on. I am shocked—shocked!"

"She would have returned them."

"Don't you defend her! She must learn to respect property rights. What will her father think when he hears this?"

"Don't tell him."

She stamped her foot. "You are incorrigible, Steve. We can't let her go on this way. Property rights are involved."

"You talk like Brother Will. Send for the constable."

"Steve!"

He was thinking that stealing a wife, or a husband, was not held larcenous, whereas taking ten-and-six became a criminal offense. "The girl's heart is broken. Her father has torn her away from a boy she cares for. I saw her post a letter——"

"And you allowed it?"

"I am not her guardian, only her uncle ten years her senior."

"I must tell Will. What will he think?"

"He'll convene the Supreme Court, or tell her to read *The Deerslayer* to improve her morals."

"No, he won't." She had a plan. Mabel Barr and her sister "Snubby" had attended the Rosemont School in Lausanne. Helen must go there to be taught her manners. She required "finishing."

He moaned, "Leave the girl in peace!"

Helen, somber, terrified he thought, stayed at his side. "Don't let anyone force you against your will," he counseled darkly; at her age, or younger, he had been running away from school. If her heart was set on the study of voice she must pursue that.

However, by end of summer, Cora had prevailed. Will "shook out the mattress," as Stephen put it, and provided fifty pounds for the first term. At Cora's suggestion, he sent his daughter a pound for pocket money. He also included bits of family news. He reported guardedly on Townley's incarceration, stating that their brother, "helpless and in need of constant care and attention," was still "living with Burt at Binghamton." Poor Townley was in Binghamton, all right, but not with Burt. *Manacled!*

Cora announced that they must all go to the Continent to take Helen to school. Stephen argued the costs. A long-planned novel on the Revolutionary War had misfired; he would do an Irish romance instead, a satire on the swashbuckling novels of Anthony Hope and that crowd. Stokes was demanding that he make his final choices of the Cuban war stories for "Wounds in the Rain." They were chronically short of funds.

Cora offered a compromise. They would take "Snubby" and Helen to Paris and, while she stayed with "Snubby" at the Hotel Louis le Grand, Stephen would go on with Helen to Lausanne.

At Folkestone, they stayed overnight with Bertie and Jane Wells. Wells again talked of George Gissing's tragedy. As a youth, the poor man had become infatuated with a streetwalker. After police trouble, friends had come to his rescue and sent him off to America. Utterly shaken, he had fled as far west as Chicago; then, still in terror, he had deliberately returned to England and married the woman. For Gissing, it had been expiation; for her, life in constant poverty had proved unendurable. She had fled from him and died in a public hospital. Still the wretched Gissing could not rid himself of her image. One Sunday afternoon, he accosted a servant girl in Regent's Park and, within days, married her. He lived now in misery, unhappy with his new wife and mired in a swamp of failure.

"Women either heal or kill," sighed Wells.

Stephen wondered what Wells could have heard in London to be forever discussing George Gissing. There seemed to be a Maggie, real or imagined, in the life of every creative man.

He stared into Wells' gray-blue eyes and listened to the voice that so often ended in squeaking laughter. Wells slaved like a tradesman, with regular hours and regular schedules, for the copy that he *must, must* produce as if it were so many crumpets. Wells confided that, in '95, he had earned eight hundred pounds, in '96 a thousand, in '97 enough to settle his parents in a little house. Last year, he had traveled for his health; this year, he would build a fine residence with lawns and summerhouses.

Stephen envied Bertie Wells the self-assurance, the brassy impudence.

When they left Paris, Helen observed that her Uncle Steve was despondent. As his depression soured to blackest melancholy, she cheered him with stories of the old acquaintances in Port Jervis.

He talked to Madame Eytel-Hubbe at the Rosemont-Dezaley School in Lausanne and turned over Will's money for the board and tuition. He gave Helen an extra five pounds as a gift, and, reluctantly, took the afternoon train back to Paris.

Cora was not ready to return to Brede Place. She was determined to go to the theater, and again to Versailles and to Fontainebleau. She must take "Snubby" to the top of the Eiffel Tower. She suggested Les Halles, where Stephen had once enjoyed a tripe stew and a certain sheepmilk cheese. She remembered a precious little family restaurant where the meats were cooked on spits on an open hearth.

He refused to accompany them. He shut himself in his room with his manuscripts. The cruel schedule and its demands! He was no Wells; he felt trapped. Would he ever be able to sit back for a week or two without chafing over money?

By midnight, he was suffering from vertigo and a ringing in his ears. When the dizziness passed, he became alarmed at the pounding in the top of his head. He broke out in a sweat. Once again, he would be ill in Paris.

The room was heaving. He gripped the table. The *Commodore* was sinking. He saw the tugboat going down, while his hands pulled at the oars in the open boat. Lights flashed as the dinghy climbed to the top of a crest. He rowed and dared not look up. A shadow fell across his face as if the Presence hovered.

With a shout, the waves broke and poured over him.

CHAPTER 89

September was witheringly hot, with a drought scorching the Sussex fields; even the nights rarely brought a cool breeze from the sea. When he opened the casement windows, large moths entered.

A tiny bat flew in. He did not try to dislodge it from the ceiling until dawn. As he stepped on a chair to strike it with a broom, he lost his balance and fell. The bat shot out through the window. His thump upon the floor brought Cora racing to his study.

He had sustained no injury, but now he had to reveal to Cora an ailment that he had wished to keep from her. He was harassed by a fistula that was not only embarrassing but extremely painful. The pressure had made riding in the saddle impossible and the long sessions at the writing table nearly unbearable.

"How could you try to conceal from me that you were suffering?" she chided him.

She drove him to Rye in the trap to consult Doctor Skinner, whom Henry James had recommended. The physician suggested hot compresses and a mild opiate to allay the pain. The swelling and tenderness would not subside until the abscess had drained. It might have to be incised.

For three weeks, Stephen could neither sit nor lie down comfortably. However, long before the abscess had healed completely, he was forcing himself to return to his work.

Grateful for even the partial relief, he speedily wrote a story in two days, and sent it on to Pinker. The following night, inspired again, he wrote a second story, revised it the next afternoon and evening, and once more dispatched the manuscript. Pinker would deposit a sum to their account at the Oxted Bank. He had advanced them more than two hundred pounds.

Cora recorded the titles, "Virtue in War" and "The Second Generation," while Stephen checked his list of assignments. The "War Memories" must be completed for the *Anglo-Saxon Review*. He must write another chapter on the Irish romance, to which Stokes was committed and in which serial rights could surely be sold in advance. *Active Service* was being serialized in the Buffalo *Courier*; the Irish romance might go to many American papers, possibly, also to *The Cosmopolitan*.

At Cora's footsteps, he arose. The post must have come.

"Steve!" She had opened the letter. "It would be far better if you didn't read this."

"Give it to me," he said coldly.

Pinker was rebelling. The agent declared that the constant demands were pinching him. Furthermore, he feared spoiling the market if too many Crane stories were dumped at one time. He advised that the battle articles be pursued instead.

The sheet rustled in Stephen's fingers. He should not have left the correspondence to Cora. Her imperious tone had roiled James Pinker; she had pressed him too hard.

"I'll write him again!" she fumed. "How dare he talk of spoiling the market? What a terrible, a fatal, thing to say to a writing man! He could sell a thousand short stories by Stephen Crane if only he had them. I think——"

He was not listening. What if Pinker were right and his mad production did spoil the market? He shuffled among his papers for the list of the stories and articles still unsold. What if Pinker were right? How many stories did the agent have on his ledger?

He began to perspire. He could not remember the last two, "The Second Generation" and—— He groped. Ah, "Virtue in War" was the second. The first was about a volunteer major, of the stripe of Theodore Roosevelt, and a private who—— His mind went blank. The major was shot and the private, who had thought his officer a stuffed shirt—— No, that was the second story, "Virtue in War."

He was perspiring heavily again. Could he have given the same story two separate titles? He could not recall the characters or dredge up the least trace of the second plot. Pinker would think him a blasted fool. "Look here, Crane! Now, you can't send me the same story under two different titles!"

He scanned the entries in his notebook. His eagerness to supply Pinker with literary collateral had caused the confusion. He must apologize; at least, he must inquire.

He got heavily to his feet. Cora was lying in that silly, theatrical bed with its posts and ruffles that stood upon a platform because the flooring had rotted. It suited her to have a regal bed in the big, otherwise empty chamber that had once been the Brede ballroom.

"The last two stories. Did you read them?"

"No. We put them in the post so hurriedly."

He stumbled back to his study. A piece of stupidity! Pinker would think that he was being guyed. Could it be—— How could he have forgotten, utterly erased, the plot of a story that he had written?

He struggled with a page of the Irish romance. He dropped his pen and stared at the flame in the lamp chimney. A moth had struck the hot glass and fallen to the table. He was himself like dry straw at the edge of a bonfire; a single spark and he would go up in flame, and *pouf!* vanish utterly.

He had been at these writing chores for eight months; he was stale. When it had seemed that war between the Boers and the British was inevitable, he had asked Pinker to see about the Transvaal, though the abscess was then severely painful. He had pleaded with Pinker to approach the *Westminster Gazette* or the *English Illustrated Magazine* to pay his way to South Africa.

He had assured Pinker that he was interested only in the men and how they met, or eluded, the Great Death. Hearst might send him. A month in Africa would supply him with enough articles to write himself free from debt.

Cora, fiercely against it, had conspired with Pinker to keep him at Brede Place. "Your health, Steve!" Damn his health, to be free again! Other newspapermen wandered footloose. Bass was in the Phillipines, Dick Davis wherever he pleased, while Stephen Crane was manacled to a wife, servants, a ruined manor-house, and another man's orphans.

He was back to the two stories. Still convinced that he had written only one, he was unnerved.

He had to badger Pinker before the man would reply. Blandly, Pinker wrote that, of course, there had been *two*. How could Crane have doubted it?

Cora scrutinized the wan features. "Of course, there were two different stories," she said, mystified.

He was shaken. Was it a portent of illness? "I had forgotten." He tried to jest. "Like the ghost of Brede Place. I thought I might have sawed one story into two." He pondered. "I should write about our ghost one day. Perhaps to amuse our friends at Christmastime."

"You've refused to write Christmas stories when Pinker could have got you a commission from Tillotson's Syndicate."

"It is the last year of the century," he countered with a crooked smile. "We'll usher it out gaily. Not with a story, but with a playlet. And we'll mock our ghost, too."

"I would not do that." A shadow passed over her face. "Leave the dead to their own."

He teased her as superstitious. In their early days in England, Cora had talked of friends in London who attended seances and traded tales of clairvoyance, hypnotism, and perturbations and disintegrations of personality. She was not a believer, but was morbidly fascinated. In Jacksonville, she had often consulted fortunetellers.

"If you could work on the Irish romance instead——"

"No." He put his arm about her. " 'The Ghost of Brede Place.' We'll assemble all the authors we know in a literary seance and hold hands by means of words."

She flounced out.

In the morning, he teased: "I heard a knocking and a rattling of chains last night."

She blanched. "Where?"

"From the room overhead."

"I dreamed last night that my father was in the room," she said mournfully. She had awakened because Sponge had sprung alert and barked madly, running about in circles and leaping at the walls.

"*Something* was present, Steve!" She had run wildly to "Snubby" 's chamber. Their young guest had slept on innocently, although it was her room that, tradition said, was haunted.

Contritely, he promised to abandon "The Ghost." She was susceptible, gullible where the supernatural was concerned; he had no wish to distress her further.

"You've set your heart on it." She was looking forward to a houseful of guests. Besides, they might also give a performance for the villagers.

It was for this occasion that she purchased a new guest-book. She would ask everyone who visited to inscribe his or her name.

He wrote solemnly on the first page: "God bless all here!"

He wrote to Conrad, Wells, James, Robert Barr, Edward Mason, Rider Haggard, George Gissing, H. B. Marriott-Watson, and Edwin Pugh, and proposed that they join him in the authorship of "The Ghost." He said that he had composed some "awful rubbish" which the players could speak to amuse the villagers at Christmastime. To associate themselves with "this crime," they might write as little as a word—"any word, *it, they, you*"—for a token contribution.

He concocted a silly plot about Friend Ghost in an empty room in Brede Place, and the tourists who came prying at two bob a head. Time: 1950. "When I shall reach fourscore years," he said with a wry grin, "and am a good solid ghost myself."

He named the characters after his own fictional creations, and borrowed from the others, too. Rufus Coleman from *Active Service*, and Doctor Moreau from Wells' *Island of Doctor Moreau*. From James's *Turn of the Screw*, he lifted Peter for the name of Doctor Moreau's son; Miranda from *Miranda of the Balcony* and *Heart of Miranda*, written independently by A. E. W. Mason and Marriott-Watson; Tony Drunn from Pugh's *Tony Drunn, Cockney Boy.*

After he had toyed with the script for an evening, he decided to turn it into a farce and to add music. He scrawled off several song titles. He enlisted the help of Mason and Wells for the writing of the lyrics, but he wrote most of the lines himself. He sang out the tunes, strummed them on a violin, and asked Jane Wells to vamp them on the piano.

Cora, meanwhile, had secured official permission to use the Brede schoolhouse for the performance. Neither Christmas Eve nor Christman Day was practical; the authorities reminded her that the day after was Boxing Day. So they fixed upon Thursday evening, December 28th. On Wednesday afternoon they would invite the children to a dress rehearsal.

Stephen was in so lively a mood that he was indifferent to the costs, which, doubtless, would be considerable. During the day he worked on his dialogue, reciting to Cora those lines that pleased him. In the early evening, he returned to the Irish romance, dutifully shaping chapter after chapter. Still excited about the play, he retired early to lie beside Cora in the big bed and talk over the scenes. She dwelt on her plans for the house party.

When he embraced her, she glowed, so seldom these days were his attentions voluntary. "You do love me, Steve?"

A new eroticism, sharp as a spear, had sprung alive in him. The possessiveness with which he seized her, after a long interval of deprivation, was tearfully welcomed.

She exulted, "Love me, love me, Steve!" She ran her fingers over his ribs. "How thin you are!" His arms were scrawny, his thighs lean. "But how strong in love, my beloved!"

He dreamed that he was pursuing a horse that had escaped from the stableyard. He was in a woods not far from the sea. He could hear the hooves clopping on the dry forest floor. Hands reached for him, and became clawing branches. He was chasing a riding-mare. He sped after her, shouting, but she galloped on, the golden mane streaming. He remembered that his purpose was to catch her and have her shod. He headed her off across a field, leaped upon her back, and clung to her mane. She turned into a woman of the night and struck her fists against his chest. "Steve, Steve, wake up!"

The invitations to the party went out. Several of the guests, told candidly that there was an insufficient supply at Brede, were asked to bring their own bedding. Cots were hired. The empty chambers must be cleaned, swept, rid of nests and cobwebs, and scrubbed and aired.

Extra servants were engaged. The village blacksmith was cajoled into hammering out two dozen iron sconces for candles to illumine the big hall and the spare bedrooms. Liquors, vegetables, meats, and groceries were ordered. Vernall, the cook, was promised an extra pound if she would bake scones and teacakes.

The play must be typed and the "sides" prepared for each participant. Mason, who was experienced in amateur theatricals, would take the role of the ghost. The rector's son would be Rufus Coleman. "Snubby," with her sister Mabel and one of the Bowen girls, would play the "Three Little Maids from Rye," one of the songs Stephen had written satirizing *The Mikado*. All the Bowens were assigned, the father to play Doctor Moreau, two of the other girls to play Suburbia and Miranda. "Snubby"'s friend, Florence Bray, would be the caretaker who recited the history of Brede. None of the authors, except Mason, would appear on stage. Jane Wells promised to play the piano.

Stephen grumbled that the piano alone would not produce enough volume for his songs. To please him, Cora assembled volunteer musicians from the village to make an orchestra of six instruments.

"We'll also give a ball for our guests," she announced. "It's so long since I've danced."

The Conrads sent regrets. Fountaine Hope, their good friend's son, who had mysteriously disappeared a few days ago, had been found dead, his body, stripped and beaten, in a ditch in the Essex marshes. The Hopes were crushed; Joseph and Jessie, who had known and loved the boy, were in mourning.

"I don't like it," Cora moaned.

She said that she had heard the rattling of chains and awful groans the very night that Fountaine had vanished.

"Our Brede ghost can't be summoned to the bar for every crime in England!"

"Fountaine was a child. You know the legend that children would be destroyed by the Ogre of Brede."

CHAPTER 90

The Wellses were the first to arrive, shortly after noon on Tuesday. They came from Sandgate in a cab heaped with bedding and blankets. They brought, also, sweets for the children, chocolates for Cora, and cigars and brandy for Stephen.

A light snow covered the ground. Old Mack, whom they had re-named "Tolstoy" because of his great beard, was stretching colored ropes spangled with tinsel over the entrance, while his troop of assistants fixed wreaths and candles over the doorways. A wagon appeared with the hired truckle beds. The traffic of servants crossing and recrossing the big hall astonished Stephen when he emerged from his study.

By the next morning, twenty guests had appeared. The fortunate couples had the private rooms. Cora moved in with Stephen; her bedroom had been converted into a dormitory for the men. Six women were grouped together in the next-largest chamber. Lewis Hind, grave as a preacher, drew the little room over the chapel; warned not to open the forbidden door, he promptly did so and nearly went headlong. "Lewis lacks hindsight!" Bertie Wells crowed.

Mason and Wells traded stories in shrill voices. The children, in new clothes and new shoes, slipped between the guests on the freshly-waxed floors, with the dogs sliding at their heels. Heather, as grim-faced as a brigadier, gruffly marched his people in to serve the cakes and ale. The log that had been dragged upon the huge hearth slowly took fire, sputtered, hissed, and shot tapers of blue and yellow flame. At dusk, the bitter wind that had arisen whistled through crevices in the casement frames, and the lighted candles in the sconces dripped shamelessly, bestowing globs of grease on the merrymakers.

Cora, in a red velvet gown, with the pearl necklace at her throat, moved about proudly. Stephen, remembering a similar gown, watched her circulating among the guests. "Miss Cora!" formed in his throat.

He interrupted the men, who had begun to spin yarns about their adventures, and delegated Wells and Marriott-Watson to direct the rehearsal.

In one corner, the three little maids were singing their song; in another, Mason was intoning the ghost's lines: "I am the ghost. . . . It is difficult to be a ghost here. . . . Tourists never give me a penny."

The next afternoon, with the weather balmy for December, the entire company traveled to Brede schoolhouse in two hired omnibuses to give the trial performance for the village children.

Cues were missed, and a number of lines proved awkwardly written. However, the ghost impressed the young auditors, and Holly, Buttercup, and Mistletoe, the three little maids, were roundly cheered. The musicians had not appeared, so Jane Wells accompanied the singers on the piano. Henry James, seated beside Cora, applauded heartily.

That night, after a late supper, the guests, who now numbered forty, filled Brede as it probably had not been filled in a half-century. Neighbors from as far as Hastings came to pay their respects and to marvel how Brede Place had changed. The musicians, having at last arrived, tuned up and played music for dancing. The couples paired off and the sounds of merriment floated through the old manor-house.

Stephen saw Cora, in the white gown tonight, waltzing gracefully with Lewis Hind, who was a head taller than she. Wells was bouncing up and down with the daughter of an embassy secretary, who had come in from London. Stephen led Jane Wells out upon the floor.

"I'm not skilled in this footwork."

She smiled, her eyes still following her ebullient husband.

Breakfast, served from eight in the morning until the last guest made his appearance at high noon, consisted of bacon and eggs, or ham, American sweet potatoes, which Cora had ordered from a greengrocer in London, and tea or coffee. Someone drolly asked for beer.

The afternoon was surprisingly warm but cloudy. At teatime, lightning flashed. A great clap of thunder pounded on the old roof and brought a sudden silence to Brede Place. "The Ghost!" someone said nervously.

Marriott-Watson and Edwin Pugh dashed out into the rain to find Sponge who, as usual, had wandered off and was soaking wet.

Thunder continued to crack overhead. Cora detailed three servants to place buckets under the roof leaks.

At seven o'clock, hailstones as large as peas rattled upon the windowpanes. The wind swooping down the chimney-pipes caused smoke to roll back from the fireplaces into the rooms. When it was time to leave for the grand performance, Heather organized a phalanx of umbrella-holders to shelter the players to the omnibuses.

Still the rain came down. The sky was riven by savage blue bolts.

A mile out of Brede Place, the first omnibus mired in the mud. The men had to get out and push. Immediately, the second omnibus, which had been compelled to halt, became stuck, and more pushing was necessary. Except for wet shoes, which in the instance of Cyril Frewer squeaked amusingly when he made his stage entrance, the players arrived, disgruntled but unharmed.

483

Despite the inclement weather, the assembly room was nearly filled. The play was delayed for half an hour to accommodate the late-comers.

Hawking and clearing of throats continued for a disturbing interval as the ghost entered from the wings. Then a hush fell.

Sylvia Bowen, whose part as Miranda had been fattened to allow for a castanet dance, a specialty in which she excelled, was applauded so vociferously that, at Stephen's signal, she repeated the dance.

As the third act ended, the audience applauded wildly. Rising, all sang, "For they are jolly good people," an adaptation in which Mr. James, too, shyly joined.

The festivities after the performance, as the company returned in the rain, struck Stephen as anticlimactic. He had wearied of amusing the guests. Jane and Bertie Wells organized the children for a game of witch-on-a-broomstick, and cantered up and down the halls, hooting and casting magic spells.

Stephen offered to teach the men to play poker. Few had any card-interest except in whist and cribbage, and they chattered too much as they played. In America, he told them, they would be shot for talking at poker.

The next morning, he was glad to see most of the guests taking their leave. Only the Wellses stayed on.

Robert Barr, whom he joshed for his resemblance to the bearded Prince of Wales, shook his hand warmly. "A great party! Come to us for New Year's?"

"Come back here again, Rob," he returned earnestly. "I'll need my days now to catch up with the work. Besides, this one rings in the new century. I want to spend it at Brede."

Barr insisted that it was not the new century coming. "The year Double Naught is the last of the old century. The new century opens with Naught One."

Stephen stared at him as if he had been cheated.

"What does it matter?" Barr slapped his shoulder. "We'll drink it in again, next year."

"Next year?"

"A man can end his century any day he pleases, can't he?"

Stephen was over-tired. It was past midnight when he dragged himself to his study.

Cora, in her nightgown, came to the threshold. "The rain has stopped. It will be a fair day tomorrow. Come to bed."

He lay beside her as if he had been felled. Every muscle in his body seemed to have knotted.

She leaned over to kiss him. "Sleep now, Steve."

Images marshaled before his eyelids. A door slammed. Suddenly he was overcome with the sensation of melting. Something had burst quietly in his chest. He licked his lips and tasted salt. "Cora!"

She raised the wick in the lamp, and uttered a shriek. His nightshirt, his pillow, and the sheets were bloodied. She stared at a pool that was becoming rounder and rounder.

She ran screaming into the hall.

Bertie Wells dressed hastily, took Heather's bicycle, and wheeled away into a misty foredawn on the muddy road to the village. The nearest doctor was in Rye.

As Cora wiped the stains from his mouth, Stephen opened his eyes. His chest had filled again, but he was warm and at peace.

He said slowly, "I'd like to see that new century." Then another bubble was rising, and he no longer cared.

CHAPTER 91

"I want to go home," he said weakly to Cora that second week in January. His eyes glittered metallically.

She sat beside his bed, the pad of writing paper on her lap ready for his dictation.

"Texas." Wistfully, "We'll settle in a shack in the sunshine and forget manor-houses." He licked at his dry, chapped lips. "Or Colorado, where there's fresh air without fog or mist."

"In a little while, Steve." She spoke as if he were a child to be soothed. Doctor Skinner had been positive that Stephen was tubercular. "As soon as there is enough to wipe out the debts to Pinker and the others."

"Pinker will carry us."

"The others will not. A whisper that you are planning to leave England, and they'll descend upon us with their writs and summonses." The bills for the holiday festivities were coming in. They had spent so much money!

Snow clung wetly to the window panes and robbed the room of daylight. She was at a loss for cheering news, except that Moreton Frewen had said they were not to worry about the rental on Brede Place. Doctor Skinner had advised that Stephen was not to work. But the Irish romance must be completed; so must the battle articles. He had promised Pinker.

"I want to go home," he repeated, and tried to smile. "I'd like to see old Ted in the coal and ice business!" For a moment, he was troubled again about Townley.

"In a little while, Steve. You've got to be well to travel."

"Ask Will for the passage money."

She was silent. Will had written that the Port Jervis bank had suffered embezzlement through a man he and Stephen had known

485

since the early days. The loss of funds had shaken the entire community.

"Have the servants been paid?" he asked suddenly. Tradesmen might wait; these people depended on their little wages.

They had been paid. The extra help had been sent away as soon as the guests had departed. She had insisted that Heather dismiss two of the maids, the coachman's helper, and one of the lads who had been at odd chores. She had written to Kate Frederic that, if Mr. Crane did not soon improve, the children must be withdrawn from Brede Place; it might be detrimental to their lungs to have them so close to a tubercular invalid. They had abandoned the plan to adopt Barry; a document had been requested showing proof of marriage of Cora and Stephen Crane.

She had been frantic at the hemorrhaging. Now she avoided mention of it. How stubborn and willful he had been to have run from her to exposure in Cuba!

Once their debts were paid she would take him on a long holiday, although the thought of Texas or Colorado chilled her; she would perish in those wastelands. He would be well again, surely, in the spring.

He took shallow breaths, careful to avoid straining those weak bellows that could spurt out his heart's blood. He owned a sound head, but no midriff; his body began to be useful somewhere in the region of his hips. Like the ghost of Brede, he was sawn in two.

As soon as his knees would support his poor weight, he got out of bed and hobbled to the writing table. He greeted the visitors like a wraith. To Conrad: "The boy, Joseph, how *is* he?" James, concerned, stammering, also appeared, and Ford Hueffer, who loomed over Stephen like a brontosaurus. One could see Hueffer mentally noting every labored breath of the invalid.

Wells came, cheerful as a robin. The *Manchester Guardian* had printed kind words about "The Ghost"; how the performance had come to its attention was a mystery. He chattered, threw out his hands, winked, and laughed. When it was time to leave, he bounced to his feet and said huskily, "Chaps like you and me, Crane, we can't die. We have to beat the game, don't we?"

Stephen tried short walks with Sponge for his companion. The dog, as if aware that the master was weak, stayed at his side and did not trot off.

He visited the horses. Poor things, he had not thrown a saddle over either Hengist or Horsa since the fistula had begun to torment him.

He was pleased that he had not become morose. Cora was apprehensive; it would be shocking if she were not. But one smash book would put him on top of the heap again. He should have made more of *The Red Badge* when it was the talk of England. He had lost the marvelous control with which he had written *The Red Badge*. Much of what he was sending to Pinker and to Reynolds was smooth and unruffled, blue clay perhaps, but with too few diamonds. Where was he failing? The loss of vitality had diluted the quality of his prose.

Once success threatened again—— Still, there was a trick to it. A man had to leap upon success and drag it off to bed. Kipling had done it, and the lesser fellows, Anthony Hope, even Marriott-Watson; Wells would do it.

Dictating to Cora was hard work. He had never been a talker of stories.

"If you tell me what you want in a chapter, give me the outline and tell me roughly, I'd try my hand," she proposed. "You could dictate it over again, of course, but it might save time."

His eyes became an angry blue.

She realized that she had gone too far.

He lay back in his chair and regarded the ceiling as if it were a lowered sky. The fault was his own. She had seen him driving through copy as if his only purpose was to satisfy Pinker. She knew nothing of his agony in shaping lines when a story flowed as slowly as molasses.

He had let the last two battle articles go from Cora's hands to the agent before he had approved of them. What would Pinker think?

Early the next morning, he was on his way. He gave Heather a message for Cora, who was still asleep. He had Pat drive him to Rye where he boarded the train for London.

"I'll take the last two articles I sent in," he said to Pinker.

The agent, a short round man with kindly turtle-green eyes behind rimless spectacles, gaped. "Not satisfied with them, eh?" Quietly, he reached for the heap of papers on his desk.

Stephen turned the pages. "I need a few days more to revise. They're not right, Pinker, not yet."

"You've been working too hard." The agent studied his haggard features. "You've recovered?"

"Fit as a fiddle." He gazed at Pinker's pasty skin. Beside this city man, he was confident that he must appear quite healthy.

"I don't know that Brede Place is the best place for you, Crane. The south of France might be kinder. For the cost of the servants at Brede, you could have more luxury and the sun all day."

"Next year," Stephen coughed. If it was sun he needed he should not have left Cuba. He tucked his manuscripts under his arm and went directly to the station.

"Where were you?" Cora demanded shrilly. "I've been terrified!"

"To London, to see Pinker." He waved the scripts. "I've not run away."

She blanched, but asked no further questions. She did not again offer to help with his writings.

CHAPTER 92

Heather shaved him, but he insisted on trimming his mustaches with his own hand. He emerged, as he always did after shaving, in a happier frame of mind. A soft spring rain was falling; a mist hung over the gardens and the park. He opened the windows and inhaled the damp air; the smell of the stirring earth was in it.

Cora had left for the St. Petersbourg Hotel in Paris. She was to meet Helen, who was leaving the school in Lausanne. The girl had been so unhappy in Switzerland that Will, reluctantly, had agreed to let her drop out. Will had authorized Cora to buy Helen a new wardrobe. Once more, a plea to Pinker, this time for an advance of travel funds. Always Pinker.

Birds were twittering. A gray fog filtered through the trees. He heard the padding of feet, and felt the cold nose at his hand. "Old Sponge!" He scratched behind the dog's ears. "Old Sponge!" The devotion of the animal touched him. "Best old doggie!"

He had completed twenty-five chapters in the Irish romance. The twenty-sixth lay on his table. The battle articles, straight journalism, were passable, but the novel plagued him. He was doing poorly with first-person narration. But Pinker wanted the finished manuscript, and Pinker was paying the piper.

Heather marched across the floor, and gravely shut the windows. With a reproving glance, he offered a fringed shawl for Mr. Crane's shoulders.

Stephen promised to come downstairs. He enjoyed staring into the big fireplace where a treetrunk, thick as a bear, was burning.

After the butler had left, Stephen shuffled aimlessly down the hall, halting before one door and another. At his knees, Sponge panted awhile, then padded away and looked back apprehensively from the head of the staircase. All the dogs were uneasy in the upper chambers.

Sponge uttered a growl and sped down the stairs.

Stephen turned quickly. Someone had been at his elbow.

There was no one. His heart pounded. Heather had gone below. The foolish legend of Brede!

He tried the doorknob before him. "Snubby" Richie had slept in this chamber and never been disturbed: a little cot, a small table with ewer and basin, a plain wardrobe, and an old chair.

He turned again, and a chill ran down his spine. In the gloom, someone was breathing hard. He placed his hand against the cold, dampish wall and edged toward the chair. He lifted the glass chim-

488

ney, struck a match, and ignited the wick. A long face peered from the glass surface. He smiled: his own.

The walls were alive with shadows that rose and fell like prancing hooves.

The breathing continued as if some sick animal were laboring for life. His father, dying, had struggled with such effort.

He stood up uncertainly. The shawl was being pulled from his shoulders! With a gasp, he tugged at the fringe.

A groan issued. But he was alert; the sound had scraped from his own throat. The stertorous breathing, too, had been his. It was all fear, made by man in the furnaces of his own mind and body to confound and destroy him.

A clanking stopped him. Unmistakably, chains! He wanted to snicker. A ghost after all? Again the clanking. It could be any metal, like a spear striking a shield.

Memories, vague, elusive, threatening nonetheless, clawed at his brow. Why had he entered this forbidden room?

"Come forth!" he beseeched silently, defying apparitions. Let the ghost of Brede loom like a genie out of Aladdin's lamp. No intelligent man could believe in such derangements.

Into his ears, the sea crashed furiously. He would be sick again. He reached for the chair and slumped. The surf boiled at his feet.

He tried to brace himself, but the sea was rising in his chest. He glanced about helplessly. The flame in the lamp was shooting up wildly, coating the glass with soot. The bubble filled and burst. No pain. A quiet gushing spilled warmly into his mouth and nose, and came forth in a red tide.

An hour later, Heather found him unconscious. Sponge, keening and scratching, had led him to the room.

From his bed, Stephen, as soon as he regained consciousness, forbade any word to Mrs. Crane. "I won't have her disturbed."

The butler promised, but "Cook" Vernall was not bound; she cabled Cora in Paris.

Twenty-four hours passed before she returned, bringing Helen with her on the night boat from Calais. She had telegraphed for help from Paris, and, by the time she appeared, he was under morphia again. He had suffered two massive hemorrhages.

Doctor J. T. MacLaglen, the lung specialist, who had been recommended by the American Embassy in London, came in on consultation with Doctor Skinner. They ordered two nurses to be in constant attendance.

"The notes for—the end," Stephen said calmly, resting between words, "for the end of—the romance—are there if—needed." His skin was the hue of alabaster; a round spot on each cheek was like the blush of a new peach. "If—needed," he repeated. "I did not want them—to call you."

"Steve!" she sobbed, at the shocking luster in his eyes.

He wanted to touch her, but could not lift his arm.

Doctor MacLaglen had been tersely professional. Night sweats, blood-streaked sputum—how long had Mr. Crane had these symptoms? The lung condition might have started during the exposure in the open boat, or in Greece. Undoubtedly, the shaking and the sweats, the yellowing of the skin that had been suspected to be yellow fever in Cuba, had been manifestations of tuberculosis. The high temperatures—— He should have heeded Doctor Trudeau. Two tablespoonfuls of brandy would pick up a man's spirit, but a cure was long and difficult.

Stephen had listened placidly when Doctor MacLaglen had implied that only one lung was bad. With rest and proper diet, many a patient lived to bury his physicians.

"My patients do well," the specialist said, with a sharp glance at the invalid, "*if* they obey my orders!"

Stephen looked sheepish.

"You must obey now," Cora pleaded. She was retaining the nurses night and day, at a cost of nearly five pounds a week and their meals. She had sent off new pleas to Will and to Pinker. "You must, Stephen. The next ten days you must surely obey."

He was dozing, drifting away. The doctor had said that the next ten days would tell.

When he awakened during the night, Cora was at his side. She stroked his hand.

"Texas then, Stevie, or Colorado. Anywhere you wish. As soon as you are well. I won't mind." The specialist's fee had been fifty pounds, including travel expenses to and from London. She had handed him a check on Brown & Shipley, but she was overdrawn; her letter to Pinker had begged for an immediate deposit to cover it. Perhaps Lippincott would advance more on the *Great Battles* volume. If they understood that it was a matter of saving Stephen Crane's life, they would surely comply.

"The notes——"

"I have them." She had considered it imperative to inform Pinker that the notes for the end of the Irish romance were available. Otherwise men, being men, would think of death, and shut their purses firmly. No one would lose—"except me!" she wailed as the penpoint sputtered. If Mr. Crane should die, the novel could be finished. Stephen was running away from her again, and this time, if he succeeded, she would never be able to bring him back.

Cora paced the big hall, whipping at her skirt with a riding-crop. The dogs lay on the floor eyeing her, Sponge sniffling and wheezing. She decided to rouse the coachman. He must ride into the village with a cable to Will. The illness, MacLaglen had affirmed, would be a long and costly one. If the American and British serial rights to the Irish romance could be sold—if only the manuscript were completed!—there would be plenty of funds. Lippincott's should be good for one hundred pounds when the last of the battle articles went in.

Although the hemorrhages did not recur and he took his nourishment obediently, Stephen's strength had left him. He was apathetic; time flowed past like the water of a river in which one bathes. The morning light pained his eyes.

Cora's features frequently swam into sharp focus. Her eyelids were red, the lines about her mouth set in fatigue. Sometimes, when her lips moved and he failed to catch the words, he resented her vitality. She had never suffered a cold or a fever, not even a blemish of the skin. She was spared even those bad days that were a curse to most women. When she slept, she lay curled like a cat, the soft breathing scarcely audible.

CHAPTER 93

Will wrote that he was alarmed and grieved, but unable to help; his bank account was depleted. A week later, he suggested that they leave the English climate and return to America. They would be welcome in Port Jervis.

Stephen winked broadly as she read the letter. Without funds, there was no way to leave England. But the doctor's "ten days" had passed, and he felt improved.

Doctor MacLaglen had counseled that he must not be moved under any circumstances. "Rest! Complete rest!" Doctor Skinner thought that he might, when better, go up to London for another consultation. Doctor Skinner, who knew the south of England intimately, further urged that they leave Brede for the seashore, perhaps for Bournemouth. Cora, torn between the advices of the medical men, discussed renting Brede Place as it stood, with servants, furniture, and horses. Moreton Frewen had agreed to the subletting.

"Did you call on Ceek Linson?" Stephen suddenly inquired.

She had not. She had intended to do so after Stephen had sent a message that he had heard Linson was in Paris. Then, within twenty-four hours, had come the terrible cable from Vernall.

"I would like to see Linson again," he said wistfully. To think of Ceek was to recall happier days, when fame had seemed out of reach and five cents' worth of potato salad had made a filling breakfast.

"We can have no guests until you're up and around," she reminded him. Sanford Bennett had come over from Paris, but she had asked James, Wells, Conrad, and several others to await word from her before they made the journey to Brede Place. Stephen must have rest and quiet.

Another letter from Will. Old Uncle Luther Peck had died, full of years and the classics. Will offered to send a book entitled *A Consumptive's Struggle for Life,* and recommended the use of a Dr. Howe's "breathing tube" to repair the disintegrating lungs. Stephen grinned sardonically.

One evening, the nurse informed Cora that the old fistula was swelling again. The patient was in severe pain. Cora fled to the musty chapel. She sank down on her knees and prayed.

Doctor Skinner was inclined now to favor a sea voyage. Doctor MacLaglen still insisted that the patient must not be moved at all.

The distraught Cora explained her dilemma to Stephen, who lay in his bed like a waxen doll. "Where can we go? Where should we go?"

"St. Helena," he offered. The Boer prisoners-of-war were interned there. He would interview them, as he had once interviewed the Spanish prisoners-of-war. "St. Helena." He would get his long sea voyage, with expenses paid by some newspaper.

They could go nowhere until the abscess drained. He lay on his stomach, and thought of the final battle article for Lippincott. He had been moved down the stairs to a room near the big hall from where he could be carried into the sunshine. But there was no sunshine, only mist and rain. Merrie England!

Ted wrote that Mame had given birth to twins, and one had been christened Stephen. So he had a namesake!

"I haven't a pound to send him!" he said mournfully. "At least a gold sovereign."

"He shares your name, and it's a good name. Ted and Mame know that you are ill."

He scrawled a brief letter of welcome to the infant: "You and I will struggle on with the name together and do as best as we may." He urged him to grow up to be as much as possible like his gentle, kindly, lovable father, and not to repeat the "vices and mistakes" of his uncle.

"What a letter to send to a baby!"

"If I could leave him something——" As their eyes met, he realized that he had failed to make a last will and testament to provide for her who could not show so much as a marriage license to prove that she was Mrs. Stephen Crane. There would be no widow's mite for Cora Crane.

"Send for Plant!"

Simply, "Thank you, Steve."

The solicitor came down from London the next day. He worked

without pause at Stephen's writing table until the will was drafted; evidently, Cora had consulted him before on this matter. A simple statement bequeathed all of Stephen's goods and properties to Cora and set aside a portion for his infant namesake. He appointed Will his American executor and Plant his English executor. That was all he required. Townley was a ward of the State of New York.

When the solicitor read the draft aloud, Stephen listened in astonishment to the tortured verbiage. The effect, Plant assured him, was that Cora would be provided for during her lifetime or her widowhood; if she married, the income would go half to his nephew Stephen, and half to Will and Ted in equal portions.

He scanned the language and was lost in the sea of legal repetitions and unpunctuated clauses.

"Does it protect Mrs. Crane?"

"Absolutely."

The solicitor added a codicil in which Cora was specifically given all "plate linen china glass books pictures prints wines liquors furniture and other household effects watches jewels trinkets personal ornaments and wearing apparel and any and all horses carriages harness saddlery and stable furniture plants and garden tools and implements." Also "all royalties during her life or until her remarriage."

"I don't care if she remarries. She may need the funds."

"It is the custom."

When the typed copy was returned, he insisted that Cora read it. She walked off with the document toward the window. When she returned, she repeated, white-faced, "Thank you, Steve."

He signed with a weak flourish. Dr. Skinner and Charlotte Gardiner, the day nurse, were the witnesses.

"Now you must sleep," Gardiner insisted. "Sleep!"

He was exhausted. But it was done. Cora would be saved from the machinations of anyone who discovered that she had no certificate of marriage to Stephen Crane. He had done all he could.

Heinemann's sent the page proofs of *Bowery Tales,* a reprint of *Maggie* and *George's Mother.* Mr. Howells' *Appreciation* of both novels had been included. He flicked the pages pridefully. Sometimes, he liked these two, his earliest works, best of all, excepting only *The Black Riders.*

It would be a fruitful year. The volume of *Whilomville Stories* would appear under the Harper imprint in August or September, and probably in the fall in London. *Wounds in the Rain* would be available in the bookstalls, from Stokes in New York, from Methuen in London, this year. An English edition of *The Monster* had been promised. So he would come before the public once more, as in '96, with a barrage of book offerings.

He tried to continue with the Irish romance, but his fingers were too weak to hold the pen.

A choking sensation brought on a fit of coughing. Helen rushed to bring the nurse, but the usual dosage, which Gardiner administered, failed to soothe him. Deep in his chest, a muscle seemed determined to pull on his rib cage, like a monk tolling a bell. He listened to the coughing as if it were issuing from another's body. Nearly a half hour passed before, from sheer exhaustion, the whooping diminished. He was spitting up blood-streaked plugs of mucus.

Cora's grim mouth and the pressed circles under her eyes telegraphed her own fatigue. He lay back, respiring with difficulty, and encouraged her to give an account of her activities. She said that she was now anxious to leave Brede Place, if the house could be rented and the creditors would look the other way while they decamped.

Henry James had suggested the cure at Davos in the Alps, where Stevenson had been invalided. Others urged the Falkenstein and the Reiboldsgrun Sanitoria. Still another recommended the Wehrwald at Baden. In England, there was the Royal National Sanitorium at Ventnor. A neighbor of the Peases, who was familiar with the Nordracht treatment in the Black Forest region, insisted that, while Nordrach-upon-Mendip had been opened in England, the original institution in Germany was to be preferred.

The Duchess of Manchester, whom Cora had met through the Frewens, was vehemently against Nordracht. The waiting list was long, the treatment of the patients "brutal." At Nordracht, they pushed food on the invalids and trusted to the heavy meals to cause the fever to abate and the tubercular process to subside.

Doctor MacLaglen was still adamant that Stephen was not to be moved; Doctor Skinner held that removal to a better climate was "not contra-indicated." Doctor Mitchell Bruce recommended Badenweiler. One urged a sea voyage, another a dry climate, a third, mountain air. She did not put it to Stephen; what weight could his opinion carry? His destiny lay in the doctors' hands, and "God's, Steve, God's!"

Another consultation the next day between the doctors resulted in an unanimous decision that the fistula should be incised. The following morning, Stephen helplessly submitted to the chloroform. The wound was left open to drain; dressings must be changed twice daily.

With their backs to the still groggy patient, the physicians conferred like coaches in the last inning of a game with the score against them.

A few days later, Cora was feverishly making preparations for a journey. He heard her driving off in the fly. If a decision had been taken, he was too weary to care; each time he coughed, the wound burst alive.

"The Black Forest," said Sister Gardiner. To some small inn in the Schwarzwald. They would leave within the week.

Cora was tense when she returned. Still in her driving habit, she reported the verdict of the physicians. The right lung was holding out, but he must leave this climate without delay. "Without delay!" she repeated, wringing her hands.

"The right lung," he thought drowsily, and clutched at his right side. Then his left lung had melted away. How could they know, since they could not see through the skin? Bertie Wells, who called himself "an expert in hemorrhages," had written that he bet "an even halo" that hemorrhages were not the way Stephen Crane would take "out of this terrestrial tumult." Wells might lose his bet.

He asked the night nurse, Sister Taylor, if she had ever had a consumptive patient with only one lung. She sniffed, "Many a one!" She plied him with a sickly-sweet concoction that reeked of vanilla; more brandy might have improved it.

In the afternoon, Cora, who had put on a tight black gown, swam into the room like a harbinger of sad tidings. She had made arrangements. He would be carried to Rye on an air bed, from Rye to Dover in an invalid carriage. She would take the nurses and Doctor Bruce. They would rest at the Lord Warden Hotel and then, in a deck cabin, cross the Channel to Calais. From Calais to the Black Forest in Germany.

"How much?"

"One hundred pounds."

"One—hundred pounds!" he coughed. "Is it—worth it?"

"Don't say that!" she pleaded. "I have asked the Royal General Literary Fund."

He snorted. The Fund might give assistance to English authors; he was an American. Certainly, if he went abroad they would not help him. He had urged Sanford Bennett to support Garnett's efforts to place Conrad on the Civil List. "He is poor and a gentleman and proud. His wife is not strong and they have a kid. . . . Please do me this last favor." Now Cora had appealed for his sake!

As he began to cough steadily once more, she impatiently left the room.

"Badenweiler," Gardiner was buzzing to Taylor. "In Germany."

So they were going to Badenweiler. Who had said that Badenweiler provided all the benefits of the Nordracht treatment but "without the brutality"? Yet where would Cora raise the hundred pounds?

Helen was pleading to accompany them, although her father urged her to return to the States. She so wanted to remain with her Uncle Steve and Auntie Cora that she offered to take the place of one of the nurses.

"What shall I do?" Cora asked distractedly. "Is it right to subject a young girl to such an ordeal?"

"Ordeal" offended him. He bridled that service to him might be thought distasteful. Then he subsided ruefully; tending the fistula had brought flashes of revulsion even to the faces of the professional nurses.

In the afternoon, a letter from Conrad apologized that he could offer no help. "I am a man without connections, without influence, and without means."

Stephen groaned. Why had Cora humbled herself and, at the same time, humiliated this good man who was so greatly in need himself?

The next morning, she was smiling. The mercurial Moreton Frewen had sent a check for one hundred pounds. He had promised also to call upon Mr. J. P. Morgan in London to propose regular and substantial help. Since Crane was an American, the financier might be generous.

"There are ancient Roman baths and the ruins of a castle in Badenweiler," Cora said quite cheerfully. "And return tickets are good for sixty days."

An urge to laugh seized him. Cora would never give up!

CHAPTER 94

The Lord Warden again, and Joseph at his bedside, the features pinched, the waist shrunken, the pea-jacket sagging. He had been plagued all spring with the gout and a recurrence of the debilitating Congo fever. How Joseph had aged! Although the leg still tortured him, he had dutifully made the trip from Pent Farm to Dover. "Old Pard, I could not let you leave England again without a shake of the hand."

While Stephen thought sadly on his friend's wasted appearance, Conrad, through eyes that suddenly glazed, stared incredulously at the emaciated figure on the bed. "Off to another battlefield, eh?"

"My last—war."

Joseph blurted out that he had completed *Lord Jim*, which had grown to one hundred thousand words, for *Blackwood's*.

"Finished?"

"All finished."

"We'll drink to it—when I come back."

Joseph's stick fell from his fist.

"Joseph!" Was he talking too loud? "I'm off to the—Black Forest."

Conrad plucked at his handkerchief and blew his nose. "You will be well, Old Pard." He hawked and cleared his throat. "You must for Cora's sake."

"Cora?" he asked dully, and coughed again, while Conrad stood erect, one hand in his pocket.

The little beard pointed at the sick man. Under the heavy brows, the troubled eyes wandered over Stephen's head and toward the windows.

"What are you thinking—Joseph?"

Conrad winced. He made empty gestures. "Bullets could not find you, Stephen, in Greece, in Cuba. You have nothing to fear in the Black Forest."

"I have nothing—to fear—in the Black Forest," he repeated. It was true. Death was not to be feared. Had he not sought it all his life? "How is—the boy?"

"Borys? Excellent, Stephen. He wanted to come to see you. Jessie sends her love."

"I—like him."

"Ah, he worships you."

"And—the dog?"

"He chases sheep and chickens. The farmer is angry."

Stephen chuckled, and shut his eyes. Who had lit the candles? Flames licked around the bed.

"Bless—the boy—for me."

Suddenly, Conrad reached for his hand on the blanket and squeezed it affectionately. "God keep you, Old Pard!" he said huskily, and limped away.

Robert Barr was in the room; it could not have been the same day. Barr, in profile, now resembled their dead friend, Harold Frederic.

"Cora is worried about the Irish romance. She said that you wanted me to finish it"—he crimsoned—"if you were delayed in this place Badenweiler."

Stephen gaped. Would Cora have made this request unless she suspected that he was dying? They owed Pinker so much! Calmly: "You can—do it." Must he dissemble even on his way to the Unknown? Yet Cora would be left destitute unless the work was completed. "The only—one, Rob."

"If you wish me to do it," Barr said awkwardly.

Laboriously, Stephen described his plans for the end of the novel. The hero was to seize the girl and barricade Brede Place against her father.

How could Barr follow what he was plotting without first reading the completed twenty-six chapters?

Barr nodded. "I can't write like Stephen Crane." He strove to sound modest. "Better hurry and get well, and do it yourself. I'll come over to Badenweiler in a few weeks. Wouldn't do me any harm. We'll take long walks, and talk it over."

The invalid said feebly, "I'll look forward—to it." He drolly winked one eye, and grinned.

"When you come to the hedge"—he was breathing with difficulty—"that we must all go over—it isn't bad. You feel—sleepy and—you don't care." He searched for the words. "Just a little dreamy—anxiety —curiosity—which world you're really in—that's all." His grin was a mockery of the once ironic smile.

He fell asleep wearing the smile. Cora, entering, was shocked. But he was still breathing shallowly.

She wrote to the Wellses that it was best that they should not journey to the Lord Warden. The visitors were draining his energies. Faithful Barr remained four days, to comfort her and further to discuss the Irish romance. But the lingering in Dover was depleting her travel funds. She asked Heather and the two nurses to take their meals at a cheap café. She went without her dinner.

She secured passport applications from the American consular agent in Dover. The party, after all, would consist of Stephen and herself, Helen, the two nurses, and Richard Heather, manservant.

His wrist was so weak that the document shifted under his hand, and he slowly scrawled his name, Stephen Crane, not on the line below the oath of allegiance but in the space where the consular agent should have attested. Mr. Prescott agreeably made a stroke to refer the crippled signature to the correct place.

"Mrs. Crane!" Sister Taylor called breathlessly that night. "He's been shouting and pleading. He doesn't want me. He's asking for Aggie."

Cora leaned over the invalid. He seemed so young, like a tired little boy.

He was moaning, "Aggie, don't leave me, Aggie!"

From the deck cabin, he watched the cliffs of Dover receding in the morning sun. Heather became seasick while the heights and the castle were still within sight, and did not come forth until they neared the quay. "The poor boy!" Sister Taylor said. Stephen thought she was alluding to Heather.

From Calais, they had a salon carriage on the express to Basel. He dozed fitfully, was fed and changed; he was shaken and rocked. Sponge clambered up beside him and, with his head on his paws, eyed the sick man until Cora ordered the dog down. Sponge snarled at her.

Sometimes, the locomotive whistling and the wheels clattering over the switches reminded Stephen of the train to Monticello scuttling through the Hills. He could not tell the day from the dusk.

As they were leaving the express in Basel, he suffered another coughing seizure. He was carried into the *Hotel Trois Rois.* Cora said the view over the Rhine was magnificent. He did not care; the journey had left him limp. He was eager to rest, only to rest, without the constant jogging and shaking.

She expected mail from Pinker; she hoped for an offer on the serial rights in the Irish romance. "I want this book dedicated to me. I do want it, Stephen."

He nodded wearily. He might never be well enough to finish the story; Robert Barr would do it. Grandly, Cora had proposed that Pinker should invite Rudyard Kipling to edit the script, but he had not seen Kipling since the New York days, though the writer lived less than ten miles from Brede.

"Simply 'To my wife,' Stephen."

"Write to Pinker."

"What else do I have to show the world that I was part of Stephen Crane?"

"Was!" The past tense was not lost on him. He was relieved when she went off with Helen to services in the hotel chapel. They would pray for him. They would pray for miracles; the thought gave him a flicker of amusement.

Only the proofs of *War Memories*, the article for Lady Randolph Churchill, arrived the next day. No other mail; no checks. Cora refused to be disheartened. On the morning of the third day, they crossed the river to the Badischer Bahnhof and boarded the train for Germany. Better news would be waiting at their destination.

They halted in Mulheim. The narrow-gauge railway afforded the cheapest transportation; the little coaches made the trip to Badenweiler in half an hour. However, Stephen begged to be allowed to rest again. He thought everyone was whispering.

Dismayed by his listlessness, Cora ordered Heather to secure two carriages, one spacious enough to accommodate the invalid in comfort. The hire was expensive, twelve marks for the entire group, but now she saw that she must proceed at a more leisurely pace.

"Only another hour," she pleaded. "We're nearly there."

His eyes shot open. The blue points of the pupils stabbed questioningly.

The slow journey, on an ascending road, consumed two and a half hours. He was dozing again.

He awakened as the carriage halted. The afternoon sun was bathing a prospect of villas in saffron light. The sky was sapphire blue, the hills jade green. "Port Jervis!"

"Villa Eberhardt," she said: Number 44 Luisenstrasse. "No more traveling, Stephen."

CHAPTER 95

The house, three stories high, was a half-timbered structure in the Swiss chalet style, surrounded by banks of flowers. Curtains fluttered from the windows.

"We're here, at last," Cora sighed. "And how lovely it is!" She inhaled the clear air. "And you're not to do anything, or try to do anything, until every bit of you has healed."

He cocked an eyebrow.

"Herr Eberhardt?" She addressed a handsome mustached figure who had bustled out, bare-headed, and was bowing deeply.

"*Gnadiges Frau! Willkommen.*"

Her first question, after mail, brought a discouraging reply. No mail, nothing.

Strong arms supported Stephen. He was carried up a dark staircase and into a large, cheerful room on the second floor.

While the nurses and Helen were inspecting the suite assigned to their party, a woman with rosy cheeks and a coronet of yellow hair bustled in. She put down a tray with two blue pitchers and several glasses. "*Milch?*" she asked. "*Wasser?*"

"Water." Shades of old Schneebuhr's Delicatessen! *Milch, Wasser?* He would ask for potato salad.

She studied him as keenly as if she intended to paint his portrait. "*Arme Junge!*" "Poor boy." She rattled on earnestly; he guessed that she was assuring him that Badenweiler and its magnificent waters and climate would improve his condition.

Within minutes, he had been placed between fresh sheets in a big, dark bed. His eyelids were drooping. Mama and Papa's tester-bed; he had been born in such a good, wide, comfortable bed. When he turned on his side, the familiar creaking startled him.

He felt it coming. The bubble burst silently. He did not stir as the blood poured down his chin. Nor did he call out. He waited patiently until Cora entered the room and gazed at him in frozen horror.

Doctor Fraenkel spoke an excellent English, precisely enunciated in the Teutonic way, studiedly perfect in its phrasing. "I have not had occasion to read your excellent *Red Badge of Courage*," he declared courteously during the examination. "Now I must do so at once."

Stephen was too weary to offer a copy. To Cora's annoyance, he had always given books away; he was too shy to let a compliment pass without making an effort to pay for it.

"Am I—going—out—this time, *Herr Doktor*?"

Doctor Fraenkel's face was long, with a fine brown spade-beard. "I would not say that, Mr. Crane," he returned smoothly. "Rest, good food, the excellent air, and, above all, no exertion. We have had some remarkable cures."

The blue eyes stared ironically. What else would any doctor say? Medicine valued truth too highly to employ it too often. One day, the world might discover that truth was the greatest therapy.

He sank his head on the pillow and eyed the snowy canopy. At birth, one must be careful not to injure the mother; at death, not to discommode the attending relatives; in between, not to offend wife, friends, parents, neighbors, and strangers. *Bitte!*

After another nap, he awoke in a pool of sweat. Sister Gardiner removed his gown and dried his body. She stripped the linens and placed dry sheets under him. In a fresh nightshirt, he relaxed and dozed again.

When he roused once more, he whispered, "Is there a storm?"

Cora shook her head.

He could hear a sighing in the trees. Or was it the sound of the sea. They were far from the sea or from any large body of water.

He was so tired. Since he had left Brede Place, his weariness had increased, although he had written nothing, dictated nothing, since Dover. Pinker would be vexed. Cora must be heavily overdrawn. How was she managing? She said that there had been no mail at all.

A huge bouquet of roses appeared in the doorway. "Flowers for Uncle Steve!" Helen beamed, her tiny figure almost concealed by her gift.

He brightened and, as she lowered the bouquet, inhaled gratefully of the sweet fragrance. Petals dropped upon his hands. "The—immortality of—roses."

Cora removed a single rose and placed the stem in his fingers. Sister Taylor fetched a vase. "I say that flowers are to be enjoyed by the living," she declared. At Cora's furious glance, she placed the vase on the table and departed.

"My mother—loved violets," Stephen said absently. The image and the scent of violets had shot across his mind.

"It is too late for violets, Uncle Steve."

"Too late——" He inhaled the fragrance of the roses thoughtfully. He began to cough steadily. The wound oozed again.

He was perplexed at an apparent inability to grasp firmly at any thought and to plow a new furrow with it. Memories blinked and were wiped out by stronger remembrances that, in turn, were pricked like soap bubbles and were gone. There had been a meaning in the heady scent of violets; already it had eluded him. About *The Third Violet* perhaps, and the women he had described. Lillie Brewster! Two months ago he had received a letter from Dotty, saying that Lillie had, at last, filed a divorce complaint against Harris Morrow. So, after ten years of marriage, Lillie would be free! What of the child? Jimmie would be seven. Had she dared to take this step five years ago there might have been hope for them together. He was filled with vague regrets.

"Are you comfortable, dear?" Cora's voice broke in.

He told her, haltingly, that he was; he reproached himself for the disloyal ruminations. She had ordered the trip to Badenweiler; any other woman would have abandoned hope and saved the money. If only she had not carried so many people with her and the dog Sponge! They would have trouble getting the dog back into England. It would take two years of hard work to pay everyone back.

Perhaps the authorities at Badenweiler would not permit him to leave until the bills were paid.

Between midnight and morning, Sister Annie Taylor always cat-napped. He had heard her; she sawed wood like a laborer. He had only to get out of bed quietly and to tiptoe down the stairs. He would stroll away in the shadows of the night. Mama would weep and be grieved, and strive to persuade him to return. She would send Townley after him.

He wondered whether any trains left Badenweiler at night. He would saddle Pudgy. They would dash off through the woods. He could hear the wind in his ears. He would give the roses to Mama.

The nurse was sponging his brow again. The bit cut into his mouth. It was only the basin; he rinsed mechanically.

"Steve!" Cora once more.

She would ask for the fifteenth time if he was comfortable. He grunted.

"What did you say?"

"Nothing."

"I heard you."

Weakly, "What—did I—say?"

"You said, 'Where's Papa?'"

He opened his eyes. "I did—not."

"Were you thinking of him, Steve?" The back of her cold hand went to his forehead.

He did not reply.

"We've never talked about us—if anything should happen."

Again, the eyes opened wide. You will be my widow, Cora.

"If either of us should go, we should try to communicate with the other."

"Spooks!" he said bluntly. "I'm sawed in half."

She prodded, "If I went first I'd watch over you. I'd try to get a message to you. If you—would you remember to try to come back to me?"

He was irritable. "Spooks!"

"Should I ask for a minister?"

He recoiled. The poor girl was so distraught that she thought he was dying. If he had said, "Where's Papa?" he had not meant to call for a minister. If God would not help him, what could he expect of one of the hired hands?

Again the bit was hard in his mouth. That damn basin! The wind had risen. There would be a storm.

"I love you so much, Steve. Don't leave me!"

"I said——" he began crossly.

A shutter opened to the color of the sky, and a light breeze chilled him. He tried to lift his head: where am I? Someone had forgotten to turn off a spigot; he was bleeding again. Frau Eberhardt would be angry about her sheets.

"Cora—take me—home."

"What is it, darling?"

Why was she whispering? "Take—me—home."

Her cheeks were tear-stained. "Yes, Steve."

"Don't—leave me—here. Not in Baden—ville."

An invisible hand slowly turned down the lamp.

She was pressing his forehead. "Hush, dear, I promise."

His feet were numb from the cold. His fingers were tingling.

"Are you in pain?"

He was facing a closed door, his hand reaching futilely for the knob. It was not a door at all, but the side of a dinghy. The sea was red. He heard faint voices from the shore. A lighthouse blinked.

A dog barked. "Quiet, Solomel!"

The sea was roaring. The dinghy rose on the waves, fell headlong into the troughs, jerked and plunged, shipping water. He was drenched from head to foot.

No man knows how to die. He is born by the grace and thrust of muscles not his own, and comes into the world squalling. Dying he never masters at all, though he live to be as old as Methusaleh. To pry him out of the living world, he must be dispossessed; if he lingers, those nearest and dearest become impatient.

He awakened in total darkness. The muslin curtains had been drawn. He was trapped in the forbidden bed. "Aggie!" he shouted in panic. "Aggie!"

Sister Taylor poked her head in.

He gazed at the curtains, his face bathed in sweat. "Open!"

Obediently, she pulled the curtains aside.

"Aggie, how——" It was a wonderful bed with bearpaw feet.

It seemed to him that he had become smaller. Or had he merely dreamed that he was full-grown? He was indeed small. He was not lying in the parents' bed at all, but in the walnut-spool cradle, lying there and being rocked.

The sensation was pleasant. He had a right to be in the forbidden room. He squirmed. Where was the doll Henry that used to lie here? Henry and the bobbins. *"Fire, Henry, dammit!"*

He strained to hear. His father was coughing. There was a "Gruff!" and Solomon emerged from under the bed and stood panting, the amber-brown eyes shining.

Hours must have passed. He was between midnight and dawn.

He smelled the sea, and felt the heat of the cruel Jersey sun. The sun must have made him sleepy; his cheeks were burning. A gull screeched.

Great, foam-lipped horses were riding four abreast over the waves. On their broad backs sat black riders, their heads hooded and eyes glittering and long cloaks flowing. He gaped at the flaring nostrils, the frothing mouths, and the flashing hooves. A vein distended in a ferocious muzzle, the swollen roundness of a great belly, the lifted tails.

A sharp wind stirred the lace curtains. They would soon vanish.

They were growing larger. With clang and clash of hoof and heel, they thrust forward, the hoods falling back, the cloaks lifting. His heart leaped. Now he would see them! At last, he would see them!

Light glittered from his father's spectacles; he was awed by the fine silky beard, and the piercing blue eyes. Beside him, astride a white horse, sat Aggie in a summery gown. He stared at Papa's young face. Aggie was smiling; she, too, had not aged a day.

The third rider trotted forward. *"Mama!"*

Her face was smooth, her hair was dark; had her hair grown in again? She, too, was smiling. She was so youthful in appearance that his heart gladdened.

At her side waited the fourth mount—riderless.

He glanced over his shoulder. The curtains swayed softly, and he saw the inert figure on the bed. How had Frau Eberhardt said it? *Arme Junge!* Poor boy. And he wondered who it could be.

"Come, Stevie!" Mama beckoned, and stretched out her hand.

A breaker, coming up stealthily, sluiced over him. He gasped and coughed as his mouth filled. Blindly, he caught at the bridle; expertly, he lifted himself upon the horse's back. He had not lost his strength at all.

504

A shout of warm triumph issued from his breast as the hooves struck at the waves and he was carried over the watery wastes.

Papa and Aggie rode on before him. He held his mother's soft hand and clutched at the mane and, exulting, lifted his head to the eternal sky.

Louis Zara, a native of New York, was educated in Chicago. To pay his way through college, he worked as a printer's devil. Since then, his creative activities have always centered around writing: in novels and short stories, for radio, television, and the stage, and as an advertising consultant. He is one of the few American authors who has earned his living as editor-in-chief of a publishing house.

Two of Mr. Zara's novels have won literary prizes: *This Land Is Ours,* the Foundation for Literature Award in 1940, and *Blessed Is The Land,* the Daroff Memorial Fiction Award in 1955. *Against This Rock,* which was published in 1946, has been translated into Spanish, Dutch, and Norwegian. His short stories have appeared in leading periodicals and anthologies.

Dark Rider, his tenth novel, was three years in the writing and, although fiction, is based on much hitherto unknown or concealed material on Stephen Crane's love affairs. Mr. Zara feels that his own experiences as both author and editor are particularly pertinent for his sympathetic portrayal in *Dark Rider* of Crane's struggles as a young writer.

When not at his writing or engaged in editorial activities, Mr. Zara manages to find time to ride a long list of hobbies, among which his favorites are ancient numismatics, astronomy, gemmology, and prowling the beach near his home with his wife and his collie.

THIS BOOK WAS SET IN CALEDONIA,

JANSON, AND POST MEDIAEVAL TYPES

BY HARRY SWEETMAN TYPESETTING CORPORATION.

IT WAS PRINTED AND BOUND AT

THE PRESS OF THE WORLD PUBLISHING COMPANY.

TYPOGRAPHY AND DESIGN ARE BY LARRY KAMP.

*"As long as he lived, he would
continue to pursue the horizon..."*

For the first time in fiction, here is sensi-
tively, blazingly revealed the life and
world of one of America's greatest writers, Stephen Crane. In this work, Louis
Zara's tenth novel, the story of Stephen
Crane becomes a stirring experience. The
truth itself holds all the ingredients of
drama—rebellion, fear, compulsion, passion, love, courage, tragedy—yet it remains for the master novelist, steeped in
years of "living" with his subject, to supply the reasons why—the dreams, the
thoughts, the *man* understood—and to
fashion a compelling story that will cap-
tivate the reader from beginning to end.
This Louis Zara has done.

When, at twenty-three, Stephen Crane
astounded the literary world with what is
still one of the great war stories of all
time, *The Red Badge of Courage,* some
wondered how one so young who had not
yet seen war could have written it. In the
same year a poignant book of verse, *The
Black Riders,* "poured from his heart in a
bloody stream."

In *Dark Rider* this climax of success in
the life of Stephen Crane comes with grip-
ping, hopeful suspense. For the story
begins much earlier, on the New Jersey
seashore, as a blond, blue-eyed boy sees in
the waves great, foam-lipped white horses
returning four abreast, their dark riders
astride. The youngest son of a Methodist
minister, Stephen grew up tortured by a
sense of his own sinfulness, which he
could never quite believe, and nurtured
by the love of his sister Aggie. He learned
early, too, of another kind of love, in
the soft, experienced arms of a married
woman. All that the man was to be is here
in the story of the young years.

After the death of his mother—the
Reverend Doctor Crane and the beloved

(continued on back flap)